THE AMERICAN ROMANTICS
1800-1860

THE VIKING PORTABLE LIBRARY

AMERICAN
LITERATURE
SURVEY

EDITED BY

Milton R. Stern
The University of Connecticut

AND

Seymour L. Gross
The University of Detroit

COLONIAL AND FEDERAL TO 1800
*General Introduction and Preface by
the Editors*

THE AMERICAN ROMANTICS · 1800–1860
Prefatory Essay by Van Wyck Brooks

NATION AND REGION · 1860–1900
Prefatory Essay by Howard Mumford Jones

THE TWENTIETH CENTURY
Prefatory Essay by Malcolm Cowley

THE
AMERICAN
ROMANTICS

1800-1860

REVISED AND EXPANDED

☆ ☆

WITH A PREFATORY ESSAY BY

Van Wyck Brooks

THE VIKING PRESS · NEW YORK

PS
507
S757
v.2

GENERAL
INTRODUCTION

In the spirit of his own time, Emerson insisted that every age must have its original relation to the universe. He reflected an older American belief that no age can hold a mortgage on any future time and that the world is for the living. Our Republic and our national literature share a democratic sense of time in which every age, besides shaping the world that exists, also remakes the past. Given the fact that history is never finally dead, all literary productions of the past can become meaningful in the human mind of the present. What, then, in our living moment, can we see of our identity in the total span of our literature?

One thing stands out clearly: American literature is a rebellious and iconoclastic body of art. The Puritan rebelled against the Anglican, the deist against the Puritan, the romantic against aspects of deism, the naturalist against aspects of romanticism, the symbolist against aspects of naturalism. In each case the rebellion was greeted with cries of outrage and prophecies of doom. It is true that almost any nation's literary history tells the same story: but besides this there is a deeper nay-saying that characterizes American literature and remains constant beneath the shifting faces of rebellion. On the surface it may seem strange that a nation in some ways tending toward a mass identity should produce a literature of which the underlying theme is revolutionary. But when one considers that the artist, with his keener sensibility and articulation, is most aware of tendencies in his society, including those he feels duty-bound to combat, and that the richest heritage of the Republic is its foundation in defense of freedom of the mind, then his rebelliousness becomes natural and inevitable. The American writer's "nay" is but a prelude to his resounding "yea!" uttered in behalf of new experience rather than hoarded conventions.

That constant and subterranean rebellion is a product of many forces which, to this day, make America a puzzle to observers. Our nation was founded in middle-class aspirations that were noble in many ways but still were capable of creating a business culture in which, as Edwin Arlington Robinson has it, "Your Dollar, Dove and Eagle make a Trinity that even you rate higher than you rate yourselves; it pays, it flatters, and it's new." On the other hand, those some aspirations demanded ideologies in which nothing is held to be greater than the integrity and freedom of the individual.

And still more contradictions. An extreme form of individualism, especially to be noted in the late nineteenth century, was a primitive, often savage, social and economic anarchy: each man for himself, but all with a common goal, which was the sack of a continent blessed with incredible resources that beckoned them ever westward. That same predatory impulse, however, was only one sequel to an image of America as the organic Great New West where the ultimate hungers of men's hearts could be satisfied, where the infinitude of human identity could be realized and personality could be fulfilled. Because the Republic faced away from the Old World, it was founded on a faith in experiment, newness, and youth. So founded, it could threaten to create a society in which age is a sin, human value is measured by personal appearance, and the teen-ager becomes the arbiter of popular taste. But this same naïve faith and innocence became something more than a mindless subject for the satire of a Sinclair Lewis: it also suggested an image of the American as a man free from stifling precedent who could break through old barriers in science, belief, and social institutions.

In short, the American writer began to see that there are really two Americas. One is the actual country that shares all the limitations of any human community in the Old World or the New; the other is the ideal America that, as Scott Fitzgerald told us, existed pure only as a wonderful and pathetically adolescent dream. One is a geographic location in the evolution of all human history; the other is a state of being that answers all human hopes. Whenever the ideal was put forward by mistaken patriotism as the real country, American writers protested—sometimes in full and bitter measure, as Mark

Twain, for one, has shown. And whenever the actual America threatened to destroy the ideal, American writers have again protested, with profound, poetic vigor, as Thoreau and Whitman have shown. It is because American culture is precariously and magnificently balanced in a bewildering variety of contradictions that the American writer has remained in a state of protest.

This is not to say that the present editors would return to the critical attitude of the 1930s, which regarded literature as a collection of social documents and interpreted every effort of artistic creation as an economic act. Rather, we think that there is a unifying identity in our cultural and intellectual production that is a deliberate dramatization of our total history. It is from this necessary and sensible orientation, as it seems to us, that we see the iconoclasm of the American writer as a major feature in our literature. What he expresses is a wholevoiced rejection of trammeling orthodoxies, conformities, hypocrisies, and delusions, wherever and whenever they are seen on the national landscape. Keeping that spirit in mind, we offer the following selections from American literature as a record of the continuing exploration that develops into and still speaks to our moment of time.

No student of American literature will feel that he has made a reasonably full perusal of the materials unless he has read complete Hawthorne's *The Scarlet Letter,* Thoreau's *Walden,* Melville's *Moby-Dick,* representative poems from Whitman's *Leaves of Grass,* and a novel or two each of James, Hemingway, and Faulkner. Those authors are most profitably read in full-length works, but before the reading revolution brought about by inexpensive paperback reprints, anthologists were forced to present them in more or less fragmented form. That is no longer necessary. The teacher today can include in his course, in addition to anthologized material, such representative works as those mentioned without feeling that his students are being asked to make an unreasonable expenditure for books.

In view of this change in the practical realities of courses in American literature, we have felt that it was both wise and necessary to omit from our anthology some of the authors who would, in any case, be read under separate cover. By deleting such material, we have been able to provide a wider selection than is usual from other authors, including Edward Taylor, Emily Dickinson, and Stephen Crane, who in many cases would not be read in separate editions. In this revised edition of *American Literature Survey,* we have added some representative works of Melville because it is impossible for students to buy an inexpensive reprint of *Moby-Dick* that also includes some of Melville's shorter fiction. We have added some basic poems by Whitman because in the majority of courses it is not feasible to read the entire *Leaves of Grass* in separate cover. And we have included some work by Henry James for the same reason we included Melville: none of the two or three James novels most commonly assigned is available in a volume that includes his shorter fiction and essays. Given the needs of courses in American literature, we feel that the present volumes maintain a proper balance of materials and meet the widest demands of common practice, flexibility, and usefulness.

As in the first edition of *American Literature Survey,* we have avoided excess editorial apparatus, in the belief that long historical interchapters, copious footnotes, and coercive critical judgments either duplicate or conflict with the teacher's work. The nature of interpretation and emphasis will vary from class to class, from teacher to teacher, and therefore we have been content to provide the student with a basic minimum of biographical, bibliographical, and textual information.

In general the selections are presented chronologically, though not where the logical placement of materials would make strict chronology a meaningless arrangement. In every case we have chosen texts that yield the highest combination of accuracy and readability, a principle which has led us to modernize the spelling and regularize the punctuation of the most reliable texts of some of the early writers. The dates placed after the works indicate publication; a second or third date indicates extensive revisions. In those instances where there has been a significant lapse of time between composition and publication, a "w." stands for date of writing, a "p." for date of publication.

Milton R. Stern
Seymour L. Gross

CONTENTS

General Introduction   v

Prefatory Essay by Van Wyck Brooks   xv

Washington Irving   1
   Rip Van Winkle, 3
   The Legend of Sleepy Hollow, 19

James Fenimore Cooper   49
   From *Notions of the Americans*, 52
     On American Literature
   From *Gleanings in Europe: England*, 55
     On the English and Americans
   From *The American Democrat*, 65
     An Aristocrat and a Democrat

William Cullen Bryant   68
   Thanatopsis, 70
   Inscription for the Entrance to a Wood, 72
   To a Waterfowl, 74
   The Yellow Violet, 75
   A Forest Hymn, 76
   To the Fringed Gentian, 79
   The Prairies, 79

Edgar Allan Poe   83
   Dreams, 86
   Romance, 87

Sonnet—To Science, 88

Song from *Al Aaraaf,* 88

A Dream Within a Dream, 90

To Helen, 91

Israfel, 92

The City in the Sea, 93

Lenore, 95

The Sleeper, 96

To One in Paradise, 97

Sonnet—Silence, 98

Dream-Land, 99

The Raven, 100

Ulalume, 105

The Bells, 108

Annabel Lee, 111

Eldorado, 112

Ligeia, 113

The Fall of the House of Usher, 128

The Purloined Letter, 147

The Cask of Amontillado, 165

Twice-Told Tales,
    by Nathaniel Hawthorne: A Review, 171

The Philosophy of Composition, 178

The Poetic Principle, 190

Ralph Waldo Emerson   **204**

Concord Hymn, 207

The Rhodora, 208

Each and All, 209

The Humble-Bee, 210

The Problem, 212

Woodnotes, 213

The Snow-Storm, 217

Compensation, 218

Grace, 219

Merops, 219

Fable, 219

Ode, 220

Give All to Love, 223

Hamatreya, 224

Uriel, 226

Days, 227

Brahma, 228

Terminus, 228

Nature, 229

    Introduction · I. Nature · II. Commodity ·
    III. Beauty · IV. Language · V. Discipline ·
    VI. Idealism · VII. Spirit · VIII. Prospects

The American Scholar, 267

Self-Reliance, 285

Experience, 309

From *Journals,* 331

    Self-Portraits · Language · Thoreau · Hawthorne

Henry David Thoreau   **342**

Nathaniel Hawthorne   **344**

Herman Melville   **347**

Bartleby, 351

Billy Budd, Sailor, 387

Walt Whitman   **467**

Song of Myself, 472

Crossing Brooklyn Ferry, 532

Out of the Cradle Endlessly Rocking, 539

Facing West from California's Shores, 545

When Lilacs Last in the Door-Yard Bloom'd, 546
Passage to India, 554

Henry Wadsworth Longfellow   565

A Psalm of Life, 567
Hymn to the Night, 569
The Arsenal at Springfield, 569
Seaweed, 571
Mezzo Cammin, 572
The Evening Star, 573
The Jewish Cemetery at Newport, 573
My Lost Youth, 575
Divina Commedia, 577
    I · II · III · IV · V · VI
Hawthorne, 580
Chaucer, 581
Milton, 581
Venice, 582
The Tide Rises, the Tide Falls, 582
The Cross of Snow, 583
Dedication from *Michael Angelo: A Fragment,* 583

John Greenleaf Whittier   584

Massachusetts to Virginia, 586
Skipper Ireson's Ride, 590
Snow-Bound, 592

Oliver Wendell Holmes   612

My Aunt, 614
The Last Leaf, 616
The Chambered Nautilus, 617
The Deacon's Masterpiece, 618
Dorothy Q., 621
From *The Autocrat of the Breakfast-Table,* 623

James Russell Lowell — 642

From *The Biglow Papers, Second Series*, 644
> The Courtin'

From *A Fable for Critics*, 647
> Emerson · Bryant · Whittier · Hawthorne · Poe · Irving · Holmes · Lowell

The Darkened Mind, 656
Auspex, 657
The Recall, 658
Verses, 658

Index — 660

Contents of Other Volumes — 664

PREFACE

By Van Wyck Brooks

☆ ☆

The period of the "American Romantics" corresponds almost exactly with the life and work of Washington Irving, who first ascended the Hudson River in 1800 and who died in 1859. On the Hudson, as a boy of seventeen, he heard from an Indian trader the later well-known legends of the river, and he died at a moment when Hawthorne and Emerson, Melville and Thoreau had published many of the writings for which they are famous. The arch-romantic Irving had not only written the American stories "Rip van Winkle" and "The Legend of Sleepy Hollow," giving his own country a color of tradition, but he had lived for seventeen years in England, Italy, Germany, and France as what Henry James was to call a "passionate pilgrim." He had signalized the change from the rationalistic eighteenth century, following Sir Walter Scott and the painter Turner in his love for the medieval and the picturesque, for the ancient manor-houses of England, the moldering castles of the Rhine, and the tales of bandits in the Italian mountains. He had lived in the Alhambra, the ruined old palace in Spain where roses and weeds grew wild on the terraces and gates, while beggars hovered in the grottoes and in holes in the walls, and he had written about the conquistadores who had sailed fabulous seas in quest of fountains of youth and golden temples. Then, after returning to America, where he wrote a life of Washington, he had found the picturesque in his *Tour on the Prairies,* when he had seen on the plains the perfect resemblance of a Moorish castle that might have had gloomy dungeons in its ruins.

As a type of the romantic epoch, Irving had much in common with Fenimore Cooper, Hawthorne, and particularly Poe, who shared his taste for the Gothic style in buildings and in atmosphere, though he had a profound feeling for the "glory that was Greece." At school in England, in a "misty" village, Poe lived in an old Gothic house with pointed windows, gates and ceilings of oak that left traces of shadowy glamour in some of his tales, and there he had almost certainly seen the Elgin Marbles that a friend of his foster father knew so well. In fact, John Galt had sailed with the marbles from Greece. With the black military cloak that Poe wore after he left West Point, he sometimes had the air of a Spanish brigand, and as a romantic, pre-eminently so, he shared, for the stories of Hoffmann and Tieck, the similar congenial feeling of Irving and Hawthorne. Poe's fine essay on Hawthorne's tales sufficiently revealed the traits these two authors had in common, remote as they were from the "toosey-woosey," Fenimore Cooper's phrase for the typically American raptures over ivied ruins. But toosey-woosey might have been, at times, applied to Longfellow in "Outre-Mer" and some of his earlier poems, expressing feelings that resembled Irving's in their love of the picturesque as well as of broken hearts and lovelorn maidens. Longfellow's vigor as a poet was revealed a little later in his sonnets, his translations of Dante, and his ballads of the Vikings.

Years before Longfellow, Fenimore Cooper had achieved universal fame and Audubon was well known as a draftsman and a writer, the "American woodsman," so called in England, where he also spent three years and found a fine engraver for his colored drawings. Audubon, with his wolfskin coat and his long flowing frontiersman's locks, represented fully the romance of the forest, which covered in his time most of the country, and, as he grew up near Philadelphia, he suggested the old French *voyageurs* in his daring and dash, sometimes dressing in dungarees, with a red handkerchief round his neck, rings in his ears, and a long mustache. He lived at a time when statesmen were actors, when real actors like Junius Brutus Booth played up and down the Western rivers, and when the American pupils of Benjamin West in London painted one another in

Highland dress and Spanish costume. Looking at times like a missionary priest, with the hair that flowed over his shoulders, Audubon had hunted once with Daniel Boone, and he lived for years in woodland cabins, or in Labrador, or on the Missouri River, or in Florida with the frigate pelicans and the sandhill cranes. Scott, with his scenes of Scottish mountains, romanticized for Audubon, if they had needed romanticizing, the forests of the West; for readers were so pleased with the Waverley novels, at this early nineteenth-century time, that they put them under their pillows to dream about. Years before even Audubon, William Bartram's *Travels* had described the Southern woods and mountains, leaving in the minds of Coleridge, Wordsworth, and the French Chateaubriand images that appeared in *Les Natchez*, "The Rime of the Ancient Mariner" and "Ruth."

The many-sided Cooper, who was a social critic too, and who was often called the American Scott, had all of Irving's love of the picturesque and found it, as Audubon found it, in the forest. Cooper's *Pathfinder*, as Balzac said, was the "school of study for literary landscape-painters," and "he would have uttered the last word of our art" if his painting of character had equaled his painting of nature. Natty Bumppo, the tall, gaunt hunter with his shirt of forest green and his foxskin cap and buckskin leggings, the most authentic character that Cooper ever drew, stood for the romantic belief in the natural man. This "myth," so called in later times, which Audubon embodied, this core of Crèvecœur's *Letters from an American Farmer*, was the core also of the Utopian hope of the Western American frontier and all the contemporary dreams of a wilderness Eden. Nearly two hundred communities were built on a faith in the American Adam, the best-known of these being Brook Farm, and even Bishop Berkeley had come to America looking for another golden age in the westering course of empire. William Blake had faith in it, and there were many Brook Farmers who saw the golden age just round the corner. This was the basis of Emerson's "self-reliance" and Thoreau's philosophy of Walden. Fenimore Cooper was well aware of all that was absurd in some of the phases of the romantic movement, and one of his characters was "Ione S.," the pen-name of Miss Phoebe Jones who wrote the poem addressed to her spirit-husband. This was the masculine essence, all soul and romance, whom she was to find in the regions of space and with whom she would finally soar to their native star. But no one had more than Cooper of the real romantic feeling; no one knew better the "pleasure in the pathless woods" or Byron's "rapture on the lonely shore."

The romantic movement, the romantic feeling characterized an expansive age, confident, with a belief in human nature, an age of exploration when Americans were bent on discovering the West, the Indians, the birds, the native fauna and flora. Bryant freed the country from the "faded fancies of an elder world" and gave his readers the bobolink and the fringed gentian. George Catlin lived on the Missouri River among the Sioux and Mandans there, John Lloyd Stephens uncovered the ruined Central American cities, Herman Melville voyaged among the Polynesian islands, and Whitman scanned with an affectionate eye the America of the present. The general confidence in man and the faith in his possibilities created the movement to liberate the slaves, a movement that was best expressed in the poems of Whittier and in the *Biglow Papers* of James Russell Lowell. The time of the American Romantics was a time of diastole when the chambers of the heart were filled with blood, when life was at high tide and literature came into being in almost every corner of the young republic.

THE AMERICAN ROMANTICS
1800-1860

WASHINGTON IRVING

(1783–1859)

America's first internationally acclaimed writer of fiction and polite letters was born in New York City, the son of a substantial and rather rigidly pious hardware merchant. The son turned out to be neither mercantile about his goals nor grim about his values. Given a random education because of his delicate health as a youth, Irving early developed an aristocratic dilettante's taste for the theater, for travel, for sophisticated company, and for light literature. His temperament remained the trademark of his existence in his conservative politics, in the generally easy qualities of his life, and in the good-natured, detached tolerance with which he genially infused his writing. The masters he loved were Addison, Fielding, Goldsmith, Hoffman, Scott, Sterne, Swift, and Tieck. Despite the fact that he consciously worked hard at writing, he always maintained the outward attitude that literature was the casual leisure amusement of a gentleman. Had he been born half a century earlier, he might well have been a mild and amusing Loyalist macaroni.

When he was nineteen he wrote the "Jonathan Oldstyle" papers for his brother Peter's *Morning Chronicle*. Then he traveled in Europe (1804–1806), where he became a friend of the famous American painter, Washington Allston. When he returned to New York, he became an attorney (to the surprise of his friends in the fashionable younger set), but his immediate work was not the practice of law so much as it was writing *Salmagundi* (1807–1808) with his brother, William, and a literary friend, James Kirke Paulding (1778–1860). In 1809 he moved yet closer to literature as a career with the delightful

"Knickerbocker" *History of New York,* which touched the reading public's funny-bone and heart. The following year he became a partner with his brothers in a hardware enterprise
which, in 1815, called him back to Europe for a business trip.
He stayed there for seventeen years. In 1818 the Irvings found
themselves bankrupt, and reflecting on his literary experience
(which had included the editorship of the *Analectic Magazine*
in Philadelphia), Washington Irving finally decided to turn to
writing for a living. He could afford to take the risk because he
had no family responsibilities: his fiancée, Matilda Hoffman,
had died in 1809, and he never married. Both American letters
and Irving profited from the choice of careers as the books
began to appear: *The Sketch Book* (1819–1820), *Bracebridge
Hall* (1822), *Tales of a Traveller* (1824), and, out of his experience as diplomatic attaché in Spain, *The Alhambra* (1832).
His acceptance by Europe's worlds of literature, state, and polite
society brought him fortune and, in America, reverent adulation.
Sensitive to European reaction yet insisting on cultural nationalism with the braggadocio of an adolescent, America was delighted to find in Irving a native product which proved that
America had arrived. On the high tide of his reputation he returned to Madrid as minister to Spain (1842–1845), and after
1845 settled at Sunnyside, his estate near Tarrytown, New
York.

He wrote books of biography and, in response to American
demands that he deal with native materials, books about the
West. Yet for all his nationalistic significance and his newness
in swinging American literature into the romantic nineteenth
century, Irving was in some significant ways not an exponent of
the spirit with which America thought itself identified. His
romanticism was a temperamental antipathy to change, a nostal-
gic love of the vanished past, rather than the rebellious heart's
desire for a New World freshness. Almost as though he were
writing out of a mechanically romantic predilection for strangeness, he treated the West as a setting for the bizarre and the
barbaric, not as a basic symbol of national identity.

In addition to the titles mentioned above, some of Irving's
works are: *A History of the Life and Voyages of Christopher
Columbus* (1828); *The Conquest of Granada* (1829); *Voyages
and Discoveries of the Companions of Columbus* (1831); *The
Crayon Miscellany,* which includes *A Tour on the Prairies*
(1835); *Astoria* (1836); *The Adventures of Captain Bonneville*
(1837); *The Life of Oliver Goldsmith* (1840); *The Life of*

George Washington, 5 vols. (1855–1859); and Wolfert's Roost (1855).

Editions and accounts of Irving and his work are to be found in the Author's Uniform Revised Edition of The Works of Washington Irving, 21 vols. (1860-1861), reissued in 1881 in 12 vols.; P. M. Irving, ed., The Life and Letters of Washington Irving, 4 vols. (1862–1864); C. D. Warner, Washington Irving (1890); G. S. Hellman, Washington Irving, Esquire (1925); S. T. Williams, The Life of Washington Irving, 2 vols. (1935); S. T. Williams and M. E. Edge, A Bibliography of the Writings of Washington Irving (1936); V. W. Brooks, The World of Washington Irving (1944); S. T. Williams, The Spanish Background of American Literature (1955); W. A. Reichart, Washington Irving and Germany (1957); T. Martin, "Rip, Ichabod, and the American Imagination," American Literature, XXXI (1959); E. Wagenknecht, Washington Irving: Moderation Displayed (1962); R. A. Bone, "Irving's Headless Hessian: Prosperity and the Inner Life," American Quarterly, XV (1963); L. Leary, Washington Irving (1963); M. J. Bruner, " 'The Legend of Sleepy Hollow': A Mythological Parody," College English, XXV (1964); J. Clendenning, "Irving and the Gothic Tradition," Bucknell Review, XII (1964); A. Guttman, "Washington Irving and the Conservative Imagination," American Literature, XXXVI (1964); and W. H. Hedges, Washington Irving, An American Study, 1802–1832 (1965).

Rip Van Winkle

A POSTHUMOUS WRITING
OF DIEDRICH KNICKERBOCKER

By Woden, God of Saxons,
From whence comes Wensday, that is Wodensday.
Truth is a thing that ever I will keep
Unto thylke day in which I creep into
My sepulchre—

—CARTWRIGHT

(The following Tale was found among the papers of the late Diedrich Knickerbocker, an old gentleman of New York, who was very curious in the Dutch history of the province, and the manners of the descendants from its primitive settlers. His historical researches, however, did not lie so much among books as among men; for the former are lamentably scanty on his favorite topics; whereas he found the old burghers, and still more their wives, rich in that legendary lore, so invaluable to true history. Whenever, therefore, he happened upon a genuine Dutch family, snugly shut up in its low-roofed farmhouse, under a spreading sycamore, he looked upon it as a little clasped volume of black-letter, and studied it with the zeal of a book-worm.

The result of all these researches was a history of the province during the reign of the Dutch governors, which he published some years since. There have been various opinions as to the literary character of his work, and, to tell the truth, it is not a whit better than it should be. Its chief merit is its scrupulous accuracy, which indeed was a little questioned on its first appearance, but has since been completely established; and it is now admitted into all historical collections, as a book of unquestionable authority.

The old gentleman died shortly after the publication of his work, and now that he is dead and gone, it cannot do much harm to his memory to say that his time might have been much better employed in weightier labors. He, however, was apt to ride his hobby his own way; and though it did now and then pick up the dust a little in the eyes of his neighbors, and grieve the spirit of some friends, for whom he felt the truest deference and affection; yet his errors and follies are remembered "more in sorrow than in anger," and it begins to be suspected, that he never intended to injure or offend. But however his memory may be appreciated by critics, it is still held dear by many folk, whose good opinion is well worth having; particularly by certain biscuit-bakers, who have gone so far as to imprint his likeness on their new-year cakes; and have thus given him a chance for immortality, almost equal to the being stamped on a Waterloo Medal, or a Queen Anne's Farthing.)

Whoever has made a voyage up the Hudson must remember the Kaatskill mountains. They are a dismembered branch of the great Appalachian family, and are seen away to the west of the river, swelling up to a noble height, and lording it over the surrounding country. Every change of season, every change of weather, indeed, every hour of the day, produces some change in the magical hues and shapes of these mountains, and they are regarded by all the good wives, far and near, as perfect barometers. When the weather is fair and settled, they are clothed in blue and purple, and print their bold outlines on the clear evening sky; but, sometimes, when the rest of the landscape is cloudless, they will gather a hood of gray vapors about their summits, which, in the last rays of the setting sun, will glow and light up like a crown of glory.

At the foot of these fairy mountains, the voyager may have described the light smoke curling up from a village, whose shingle-roofs gleam among the trees, just where the blue tints of the upland melt away into the fresh green of the nearer landscape. It is a little village, of great antiquity, having been founded by some of the Dutch colonists, in the early times of the province, just about the beginning of the government of the good Peter Stuyvesant (may he rest in peace!), and there were some of the houses of the original settlers standing within a few years, built of small yellow bricks brought from Holland, having latticed windows and gable fronts, surmounted with weathercocks.

In that same village, and in one of these very houses (which, to tell the precise truth, was sadly time-worn and weather-beaten), there lived many years since, while the country was yet a province of Great Britain, a simple good-natured fellow, of the name of Rip Van Winkle. He was a descendant of the Van Winkles who figured so gallantly in the chivalrous days of Peter Stuyvesant, and accompanied him to the siege of Fort Christina. He inherited, however, but little of the martial character of his ancestors. I have observed that he was a simple good-natured man; he was, moreover, a kind neighbor, and an obedient hen-pecked husband. Indeed, to the latter circumstance might be owing that meekness of spirit which gained him such universal popularity; for those men are most apt to be obsequious and conciliating abroad, who are under the discipline of shrews at home. Their tempers, doubtless, are rendered pliant and malleable in the fiery furnace of domestic tribulation; and a curtain lecture is worth all the sermons in the world for teaching the virtues of patience and long-suffering. A termagant wife may, therefore, in some respects, be considered a tolerable blessing; and if so, Rip Van Winkle was thrice blessed.

Certain it is, that he was a great favorite among all the good wives of the village, who, as usual, with the amiable sex, took his part in all family squabbles; and never failed, whenever they talked those matters over in their evening gossipings, to lay all the blame on Dame Van Winkle. The children of the village, too, would shout with joy whenever he approached. He assisted at their sports, made their playthings, taught them to fly kites and shoot marbles, and told them long stories of ghosts, witches, and Indians. Whenever he went dodging about the village, he was surrounded by a troop of them, hanging on his skirts, clambering on his back, and playing a thousand tricks on him with impunity; and not a dog would bark at him throughout the neighborhood.

The great error in Rip's composition was an insuperable aversion to all kinds of profitable labor. It could not be from the want of assiduity or perseverance; for he would sit on a wet rock, with a rod as long and heavy as a Tartar's lance, and fish all day without a murmur, even though he should not be encouraged by a single nibble. He would carry a fowling-piece on his shoulder for hours together, trudging through woods and swamps, and up hill and down dale, to shoot a few squirrels or wild pigeons. He would never refuse to assist a neighbor even in the roughest toil, and was a foremost man at all country frolics for husking Indian corn, or building stone-fences; the women of the village, too, used to employ him to run their errands, and to do such little odd jobs as their less obliging husbands would not do for them. In a word Rip was ready to attend to anybody's business but his own; but as to doing family duty, and keeping his farm in order, he found it impossible.

In fact, he declared it was of no use to work on his farm; it was the most pestilent little piece of ground in the whole country; everything about it went wrong, and would go wrong, in spite of him. His fences were continually falling to pieces; his cow would either go astray, or get among the cabbages; weeds were sure to grow quicker in his fields than anywhere else; the rain always made a point of setting in just as he had some outdoor work to do; so that though his patrimonial estate had dwindled away under his management, acre by acre, until there was little more left than a mere patch of Indian corn and potatoes, yet it was the worst conditioned farm in the neighborhood.

His children, too, were as ragged and wild as if they belonged to nobody. His son Rip, an urchin begotten in his own likeness, promised to inherit the habits, with the old clothes of his father. He was generally seen trooping like a colt at his mother's heels, equipped in a pair of his father's cast-off galligaskins [knee breeches], which he had much ado to hold up with one hand, as a fine lady does her train in bad weather.

Rip Van Winkle, however, was one of those happy mortals, of foolish, well-oiled dispositions, who take the world easy, eat white bread or brown, whichever can be got with least thought or trouble, and would rather starve on a penny than work for a pound. If left to himself, he would have whistled life away in perfect contentment; but his wife kept continually dinning in his ears about his idleness, his carelessness, and the ruin he was bringing on his family. Morning, noon, and night, her tongue was incessantly going, and every thing he said or did was sure to produce a torrent of household eloquence. Rip had but one way of replying to all lectures of the kind, and that, by frequent use, had grown into a habit. He shrugged his shoulders, shook his head, cast up his eyes, but said nothing. This, however, always provoked a fresh volley from his wife; so that he was fain to draw off his forces, and take to the outside of the house—the only side which, in truth, belongs to a henpecked husband.

Rip's sole domestic adherent was his dog Wolf, who was as much hen-pecked as his master; for Dame Van Winkle regarded them as companions in idleness, and even looked upon Wolf with an evil eye, as the cause of his master's going so often astray. True it is, in all points of spirit befitting an honorable dog, he was as courageous an animal as ever scoured the woods—but what courage can withstand the ever-during and all-besetting terrors of a woman's tongue? The moment Wolf entered the house his crest fell, his tail drooped to the ground, or curled between his legs, he sneaked about with a gallows air, casting many a sidelong glance at Dame Van Winkle, and at the least flourish of a broomstick or ladle, he would fly to the door with yelping precipitation.

Times grew worse and worse with Rip Van Winkle as years of matrimony rolled on; a tart temper never mellows with age, and a sharp tongue is the only edged tool that grows keener with constant use. For a long while he used to console himself, when driven from home, by frequenting a kind of perpetual club of the sages, philosophers, and other idle personages of the village; which held its sessions on a bench before a small inn, designated by a rubicund portrait of His Majesty George the Third. Here they used to sit in the shade through a long lazy summer's day, talking listlessly over village gossip, or telling endless sleepy stories about nothing. But it would have been worth any statesman's money to have heard the profound discussions that sometimes took place, when by chance an old newspaper fell into their hands from some passing traveller. How solemnly they would listen to the contents, as drawled out by Derrick Van Bummel, the schoolmaster, a dapper learned little man, who was not to be daunted by the most gigantic word in the dictionary; and how sagely they would deliberate upon public events some months after they had taken place.

The opinions of this junto were completely controlled by Nicholas Vedder, a patriarch of the village, and landlord of the inn, at the door of which he took his seat from morning till night, just moving sufficiently to avoid the sun and keep in the shade of a large tree; so that the neighbors could tell the hour by his movements as accurately as by a sun-dial. It is true he was rarely heard to speak, but smoked his pipe incessantly. His adherents, however (for every great man has his adherents), perfectly understood him, and knew how to gather his opinions. When any thing that was read or related displeased him, he was observed to smoke his pipe vehemently, and to send forth short, frequent and angry puffs; but when pleased, he would inhale the smoke slowly and tranquilly, and emit it in light and placid clouds; and sometimes, taking the pipe from his mouth, and letting the fragrant vapor curl about his nose, would gravely nod his head in token of perfect approbation.

From even this stronghold the unlucky Rip was at length routed by his termagant wife, who would suddenly break in upon the tranquillity of the assemblage and call the members all to naught; nor was that august personage, Nicholas Vedder himself, sacred from the daring tongue of this terrible virago, who charged him outright with encouraging her husband in habits of idleness.

Poor Rip was at last reduced almost to despair; and his only alternative, to escape from the labor of the farm and clamor of his wife, was to take gun in hand and stroll away into the woods. Here he would sometimes seat himself at the foot of a tree, and share the contents of his wallet with Wolf, with whom he sympathized as a fellow-sufferer in persecution. "Poor Wolf," he would say, "thy mistress leads thee a dog's life of it; but never mind, my lad, whilst I live thou shalt never want a friend to stand by thee!" Wolf would wag his tail, look wistfully in his master's face, and if dogs can feel pity I verily believe he reciprocated the sentiment with all his heart.

In a long ramble of the kind on a fine autumnal day, Rip had unconsciously scrambled to one of the highest parts of the Kaatskill mountains. He was after his favorite sport of squirrel shooting, and the still solitudes had echoed and re-echoed with the reports of his gun. Panting and fatigued, he threw himself, late in the afternoon, on a green knoll, covered with mountain herbage, that crowned the brow of a precipice. From an opening between the trees he could overlook all the lower country for many a mile of rich woodland. He saw at a distance the lordly Hudson, far, far below him, moving on its silent but majestic course, with the reflection of a purple cloud, or the sail of a lagging bark, here and there sleeping on its glassy bosom, and at last losing itself in the blue highlands.

On the other side he looked down into a deep mountain glen, wild, lonely, and shagged, the bottom filled with fragments from the impending cliffs, and scarcely lighted by the reflected rays of the setting sun. For some time Rip lay musing on this scene; evening was gradually advancing; the mountains began to throw their long blue shadows over the valleys; he saw that it would be dark long before he could reach the village, and he heaved a heavy sigh when he thought of encountering the terrors of Dame Van Winkle.

As he was about to descend, he heard a voice from a distance, hallooing, "Rip Van Winkle! Rip Van Winkle!" He looked round, but could see nothing but a crow winging its solitary flight across the mountain. He thought his fancy must have deceived him, and turned again to descend, when he heard the same cry through the still evening air; "Rip Van Winkle! Rip Van Winkle!"—at the same time Wolf bristled up his back, and giving a low growl, skulked to his master's side, looking fearfully down into the glen. Rip now felt a vague apprehension stealing over him; he looked anxiously in the same direction, and perceived a strange figure slowly toiling up the rocks, and bending under the weight of something he carried on his back. He was surprised to see any human being in this lonely and unfrequented place, but supposing it to be some one of the neighborhood in need of his assistance, he hastened down to yield it.

On nearer approach he was still more surprised at the singularity of the stranger's appearance. He was a short square-built old fellow, with thick bushy hair, and a grizzled beard. His dress was of the antique Dutch fashion—a cloth jerkin strapped round the waist—several pair of breeches, the outer one of ample volume, decorated with rows of buttons down the sides, and bunches at the knees. He bore on his shoulder a stout keg, that seemed full of liquor, and made signs for Rip to approach and assist him with the load. Though rather shy and distrustful of this new acquaintance, Rip complied with his usual alacrity; and mutually relieving one another, they clambered up a narrow gully, apparently the dry bed of a mountain torrent. As they ascended, Rip every now and then heard long rolling peals, like distant thunder, that seemed to issue out of a deep ravine, or rather cleft, between lofty rocks, toward which their rugged path conducted. He paused for an instant, but supposing it to be the muttering of one of those transient thunder-showers which often take place in mountain heights, he proceeded. Passing through the ravine, they came to a hollow, like a small amphitheatre, surrounded by perpendicular precipices, over the brinks of which impending trees shot their branches, so that you only caught glimpses of the azure sky and the bright evening cloud. During the whole time Rip and his companion had labored on in silence; for though the former marvelled greatly what could be the object of carrying a keg of liquor up this wild mountain, yet there was something strange and incomprehensible about the unknown, that inspired awe and checked familiarity.

On entering the amphitheatre, new objects of wonder presented themselves. On a level spot in the centre was a company of odd-looking personages playing at nine-pins. They were dressed in a quaint outlandish fashion; some wore short doublets, others jerkins, with long knives in their belts, and most of them had enormous breeches, of similar style with that of the guide's. Their visages, too, were peculiar: one had a large head, broad face, and small piggish eyes: the face of another seemed to consist entirely of nose, and was surmounted by a white sugar-loaf hat, set off with a little red cock's tail. They all had beards, of various shapes and colors. There was one who seemed to be the commander. He was a stout old gentleman, with a weather-beaten countenance; he wore a laced doublet, broad belt and hanger, high crowned hat and feather, red stockings, and high-heeled shoes, with roses in them. The whole group reminded Rip of the figures in an old Flemish painting, in the parlor of Dominie Van Shaick, the village parson, and which had been brought over from Holland at the time of the settlement.

What seemed particularly odd to Rip was, that though these folks were evidently amusing themselves, yet they maintained the gravest faces, the most mysterious silence, and were, withal, the most melancholy party of pleasure he had ever witnessed. Nothing interrupted the stillness of the scene but the noise of the balls, which, whenever they were rolled, echoed along the mountains like rumbling peals of thunder.

As Rip and his companion approached them, they suddenly desisted from their play, and stared at him with such fixed statue-like gaze, and such strange, uncouth, lacklustre countenances, that his heart turned within him, and his knees smote together. His companion now emptied the contents of the keg into large flagons, and made signs to him to wait upon the company. He obeyed with fear and trembling; they quaffed the liquor in profound silence, and then returned to their game.

By degrees Rip's awe and apprehension subsided. He even ventured, when no eye was fixed upon him, to taste the beverage, which he found had much of the flavor of excellent Hollands. He was naturally a thirsty soul, and was soon tempted to repeat the draught. One taste provoked another; and he reiterated his visits to the flagon so often that at length his senses were overpowered, his eyes swam in his head, his head gradually declined, and he fell into a deep sleep.

On waking, he found himself on the green knoll whence he had first seen the old man of the glen. He rubbed his eyes—it was a bright sunny morning. The birds were hopping and twittering among the bushes, and the eagle was wheeling aloft, and breasting the pure mountain breeze. "Surely," thought Rip, "I have not slept here all night." He recalled the occurrences before he fell asleep. The strange man with a keg of liquor—the mountain ravine—the wild retreat among the rocks—the wobegone party at ninepins—the flagon—"Oh! that flagon! that wicked flagon!"

thought Rip—"what excuse shall I make to Dame Van Winkle!"

He looked round for his gun, but in place of the clean well-oiled fowling-piece, he found an old firelock lying by him, the barrel incrusted with rust, the lock falling off, and the stock worm-eaten. He now suspected that the grave roysters of the mountain had put a trick upon him, and, having dosed him with liquor, had robbed him of his gun. Wolf, too, had disappeared, but he might have strayed away after a squirrel or partridge. He whistled after him and shouted his name, but all in vain; the echoes repeated his whistle and shout, but no dog was to be seen.

He determined to revisit the scene of the last evening's gambol, and if he met with any of the party, to demand his dog and gun. As he rose to walk, he found himself stiff in the joints, and wanting in his usual activity. "These mountain beds do not agree with me," thought Rip, "and if this frolic should lay me up with a fit of the rheumatism, I shall have a blessed time with Dame Van Winkle." With some difficulty he got down into the glen: he found the gully up which he and his companion had ascended the preceding evening; but to his astonishment a mountain stream was now foaming down it, leaping from rock to rock, and filling the glen with babbling murmurs. He, however, made shift to scramble up its sides, working his toilsome way through thickets of birch, sassafras, and witchhazel, and sometimes tripped up or entangled by the wild grapevines that twisted their coils or tendrils from tree to tree, and spread a kind of network in his path.

At length he reached to where the ravine had opened through the cliffs to the amphitheatre; but no traces of such opening remained. The rocks presented a high impenetrable wall over which the torrent came tumbling in a sheet of feathery foam, and fell into a broad deep basin, black from the shadows of the surrounding forest. Here, then, poor Rip was brought to a stand. He again called and whistled after his dog; he was only answered by the cawing of a flock of idle crows, sporting high in air about a dry tree that overhung a sunny precipice; and who, secure in their elevation, seemed to look down and scoff at the poor man's perplexities. What was to be done? the morning was passing away, and Rip felt famished for want of his breakfast. He grieved to give up his dog and gun; he dreaded to meet his wife; but it would not do to starve among the mountains. He shook his head, shouldered the rusty firelock, and, with a heart full of trouble and anxiety, turned his steps homeward.

As he approached the village he met a number of people, but none whom he knew, which somewhat surprised him, for he had thought himself acquainted with every one in the country round. Their dress, too, was of a different fashion from that to which he was accustomed. They all stared at him with equal marks of surprise, and whenever they cast their eyes upon him, invariably stroked their chins. The constant recurrence of this gesture induced Rip, involuntarily, to do the same, when, to his astonishment, he found his beard had grown a foot long!

He had now entered the skirts of the village. A troop of strange children ran at his heels, hooting after him, and pointing at his gray beard. The dogs, too, not one of which he recognized for an old acquaintance, barked at him as he passed. The very village was altered; it was larger and more populous. There were rows of houses which he had never seen before, and those which had been his familiar haunts had disappeared. Strange names were over the doors —strange faces at the windows—every thing was strange. His mind now misgave him; he began to doubt whether both he and the world around him were not bewitched. Surely this was his native village, which he had left but the day before. There stood the Kaatskill mountains—there ran the silver Hudson at a distance—there was every hill and dale precisely as it had always been—Rip was sorely perplexed—"That flagon last night," thought he, "has addled my poor head sadly!"

It was with some difficulty that he found the way to his own house, which he approached with silent awe, expecting every moment to hear the shrill voice of Dame Van Winkle. He found the house gone to decay—the roof fallen in, the windows shattered, and the doors off the hinges. A half-starved dog that looked like Wolf was skulking about it. Rip called him by name, but the cur snarled, showed his teeth, and passed on. This was an unkind cut indeed— "My very dog," sighed poor Rip, "has forgotten me!"

He entered the house, which, to tell the truth, Dame Van Winkle had always kept in neat order. It was empty, forlorn, and apparently abandoned. This desolateness overcame all his connubial fears—he called loudly for his wife and children—the lonely chambers rang for a moment with his voice, and then all again was silence.

He now hurried forth, and hastened to his old resort, the village inn—but it too was gone. A large rickety wooden building stood in its place, with great gaping windows, some of them broken and mended with old hats and petticoats, and over the door was painted, "The Union Hotel, by Jonathan Doolittle." Instead of the great tree that used to shelter the quiet little Dutch inn of yore, there now was reared a tall naked pole, with something on the top that looked like a red night-cap, and from it was fluttering a flag, on which was a singular assemblage of stars and stripes—all this was strange and incomprehensible. He recognized on the sign, however, the ruby face of King George, under which he had smoked so many a peaceful pipe; but even this was singularly metamorphosed. The red coat was changed for one of blue and buff, a sword was held in the hand instead of a sceptre, the head was decorated with a cocked hat, and underneath was painted in large characters, GENERAL WASHINGTON.

There was, as usual, a crowd of folk about the door, but none that Rip recollected. The very character of the people seemed changed. There was a busy, bustling, disputatious tone about it, instead of the accustomed phlegm and drowsy tranquillity. He looked in vain for the sage Nicholas Vedder, with his broad face, double chin, and fair long pipe, uttering clouds of tobacco-smoke instead of idle speeches; or Van Bummel, the schoolmaster, doling forth the contents of an ancient newspaper. In place of these, a lean, bilious-looking fellow, with his pockets full of handbills, was haranguing vehemently about rights of citizens—elections—members of congress—liberty—Bunker's Hill—heroes of seventy-six—and other words, which were a perfect Babylonish jargon to the bewildered Van Winkle.

The appearance of Rip, with his long grizzled beard, his rusty fowling-piece, his uncouth dress, and an army of women and children at his heels, soon attracted the attention of the tavern politicians. They crowded round him, eyeing him from head to foot with great curiosity. The orator bustled up to him, and, drawing him partly aside, inquired "on which side he voted?" Rip stared in vacant stupidity. Another short but busy little fellow pulled him by the arm, and, rising on tiptoe, inquired in his ear, "Whether he was Federal or Democrat?" Rip was equally at a loss to comprehend the question; when a knowing, self-important old gentleman, in a sharp cocked hat, made his way through the crowd, putting them to the right and left with his elbows as he passed, and planting himself before Van Winkle, with one arm akimbo, the other resting on his cane, his keen eyes and sharp hat penetrating, as it were, into his very soul, demanded in an austere tone, "what brought him to the election with a gun on his shoulder, and a mob at his heels, and whether he meant to breed a riot in the village?"—"Alas! gentlemen," cried Rip, somewhat dismayed, "I am a poor quiet man, a native of the place, and a loyal subject of the king, God bless him!"

Here a general shout burst from the by-standers—"A tory! a tory! a spy! a refugee! hustle him! away with him!" It was with great difficulty that the self-important man in the cocked hat restored order; and, having assumed a tenfold austerity of brow, demanded again of the unknown culprit, what he came there for, and whom he was seeking? The poor man humbly assured him that he meant no harm, but merely came there in search of some of his neighbors, who used to keep about the tavern.

"Well—who are they?—name them."

Rip bethought himself a moment, and inquired, "Where's Nicholas Vedder?"

There was a silence for a little while, when an old man replied, in a thin piping voice, "Nicholas Vedder! why, he is dead and gone these eighteen years! There was a wooden tombstone in the churchyard that used to tell all about him, but that's rotten and gone too."

"Where's Brom Dutcher?"

"Oh, he went off to the army in the beginning of the war; some say he was killed at the storming of Stony Point—others say he was drowned in a squall at the foot of Antony's Nose. I don't know—he never came back again."

"Where's Van Bummel, the schoolmaster?"

"He went off to the wars too, was a great militia general, and is now in congress."

Rip's heart died away at hearing of these sad changes in

his home and friends, and finding himself thus alone in the world. Every answer puzzled him too, by treating of such enormous lapses of time, and of matters which he could not understand: war—congress—Stony Point;—he had no courage to ask after any more friends, but cried out in despair, "Does nobody here know Rip Van Winkle?"

"Oh, Rip Van Winkle!" exclaimed two or three, "Oh, to be sure! that's Rip Van Winkle yonder, leaning against the tree."

Rip looked, and beheld a precise counterpart of himself, as he went up the mountain: apparently as lazy, and certainly as ragged. The poor fellow was now completely confounded. He doubted his own identity, and whether he was himself or another man. In the midst of his bewilderment, the man in the cocked hat demanded who he was, and what was his name?

"God knows," exclaimed he, at his wit's end; "I'm not myself—I'm somebody else—that's me yonder—no—that's somebody else got into my shoes—I was myself last night, but I fell asleep on the mountain, and they've changed my gun, and every thing's changed, and I'm changed, and I can't tell what's my name, or who I am!"

The by-standers began now to look at each other, nod, wink significantly, and tap their fingers against their foreheads. There was a whisper, also, about securing the gun, and keeping the old fellow from doing mischief, at the very suggestion of which the self-important man in the cocked hat retired with some precipitation. At this critical moment a fresh comely woman pressed through the throng to get a peep at the gray-bearded man. She had a chubby child in her arms, which, frightened at his looks, began to cry. "Hush, Rip," cried she, "hush, you little fool; the old man won't hurt you." The name of the child, the air of the mother, the tone of her voice, all awakened a train of recollections in his mind. "What is your name, my good woman?" asked he.

"Judith Gardenier."

"And your father's name?"

"Ah, poor man, Rip Van Winkle was his name, but it's twenty years since he went away from home with his gun, and never has been heard of since—his dog came home without him; but whether he shot himself, or was carried away by the Indians, nobody can tell. I was then but a little girl."

Rip had but one question more to ask; but he put it with a faltering voice:

"Where's your mother?"

"Oh, she too had died but a short time since; she broke a blood-vessel in a fit of passion at a New-England peddler."

There was a drop of comfort, at least, in this intelligence. The honest man could contain himself no longer. He caught his daughter and her child in his arms. "I am your father!" cried he—"Young Rip Van Winkle once—old Rip Van Winkle now!—Does nobody know poor Rip Van Winkle?"

All stood amazed, until an old woman, tottering out from among the crowd, put her hand to her brow, and peering under it in his face for a moment, exclaimed, "Sure enough! it is Rip Van Winkle—it is himself! Welcome home again, old neighbor—Why, where have you been these twenty long years?"

Rip's story was soon told, for the whole twenty years had been to him but as one night. The neighbors stared when they heard it; some were seen to wink at each other, and put their tongues in their cheeks: and the self-important man in the cocked hat, who, when the alarm was over, had returned to the field, screwed down the corners of his mouth, and shook his head—upon which there was a general shaking of the head throughout the assemblage.

It was determined, however, to take the opinion of old Peter Vanderdonk, who was seen slowly advancing up the road. He was a descendant of the historian of that name, who wrote one of the earliest accounts of the province. Peter was the most ancient inhabitant of the village, and well versed in all the wonderful events and traditions of the neighborhood. He recollected Rip at once, and corroborated his story in the most satisfactory manner. He assured the company that it was a fact, handed down from his ancestor the historian, that the Kaatskill mountains had always been haunted by strange beings. That it was affirmed that the great Hendrick Hudson, the first discoverer of the river and country, kept a kind of vigil there every twenty years, with his crew of the Half-moon; being permitted in this way to revisit the scenes of his enterprise, and keep a guardian eye upon the river, and the great city called by his name. That his father had once seen them in their old Dutch dresses playing at nine-pins in a hollow of the mountain; and that he himself had heard, one summer afternoon, the sound of their balls, like distant peals of thunder.

To make a long story short, the company broke up, and returned to the more important concerns of the election. Rip's daughter took him home to live with her; she had a snug, well-furnished house, and a stout cheery farmer for a husband, whom Rip recollected for one of the urchins that used to climb upon his back. As to Rip's son and heir, who was the ditto of himself, seen leaning against the tree, he was employed to work on the farm; but evinced an hereditary disposition to attend to any thing else but his business.

Rip now resumed his old walks and habits; he soon found many of his former cronies, though all rather the worse for the wear and tear of time; and preferred making friends among the rising generation, with whom he soon grew into great favor.

Having nothing to do at home, and being arrived at that happy age when a man can be idle with impunity, he took his place once more on the bench at the inn door, and was reverenced as one of the patriarchs of the village, and a chronicle of the old times "before the war." It was some time before he could get into the regular track of gossip, or could be made to comprehend the strange events that had taken place during his torpor. How that there had been a revolutionary war—that the country had thrown off the yoke of old England—and that, instead of being a subject of His Majesty George the Third, he was now a free citizen of the United States. Rip, in fact, was no politician; the changes of states and empires made but little impression on him; but there was one species of despotism under which he had long groaned, and that was—petticoat government. Happily that was at an end; he had got his neck out of the yoke of matrimony, and could go in and out whenever he pleased, without dreading the tyranny of Dame Van Winkle. Whenever her name was mentioned, however, he shook his head, shrugged his shoulders, and cast up his eyes; which might pass either for an expression of resignation to his fate, or joy at his deliverance.

He used to tell his story to every stranger that arrived

at Mr. Doolittle's hotel. He was observed, at first, to vary on some points every time he told it, which was, doubtless, owing to his having so recently awaked. It at last settled down precisely to the tale I have related, and not a man, woman, or child in the neighborhood, but knew it by heart. Some always pretended to doubt the reality of it, and insisted that Rip had been out of his head, and that this was one point on which he always remained flighty. The old Dutch inhabitants, however, almost universally gave it full credit. Even to this day they never hear a thunderstorm of a summer afternoon about the Kaatskill, but they say Hendrick Hudson and his crew are at their game of nine-pins; and it is a common wish of all hen-pecked husbands in the neighborhood, when life hangs heavy on their hands, that they might have a quieting draught out of Rip Van Winkle's flagon.

1819

The Legend of Sleepy Hollow

FOUND AMONG THE PAPERS
OF THE LATE DIEDRICH KNICKERBOCKER

A pleasing land of drowsy head it was,
Of dreams that wave before the half-shut eye,
And of gay castles in the clouds that pass,
For ever flushing round a summer sky.
—*Castle of Indolence*

In the bosom of one of those spacious coves which indent the eastern shore of the Hudson, at that broad expansion of the river denominated by the ancient Dutch navigators the Tappan Zee, and where they always prudently shortened sail, and implored the protection of St. Nicholas when they crossed, there lies a small market-town or rural port, which by some is called Greensburgh, but which is more generally and properly known by the name of Tarry Town. This name was given, we are told, in former days, by the good housewives of the adjacent country, from the inveterate propensity of their husbands to linger about the village tavern on market days. Be that as it may, I do not vouch for the fact, but merely advert to it, for the sake of being precise and authentic. Not far from this village, perhaps about two miles, there is a little valley, or rather lap of land, among high hills, which is one of the quietest places in the whole world. A small brook glides through it, with just murmur enough to lull one to repose; and the occasional whistle of a quail, or tapping of a woodpecker, is almost the only sound that ever breaks in upon the uniform tranquillity.

I recollect that, when a stripling, my first exploit in squirrel-shooting was in a grove of tall walnut-trees that shades one side of the valley. I had wandered into it at noon time, when all nature is peculiarly quiet, and was startled by the roar of my own gun, as it broke the Sabbath stillness around, and was prolonged and reverberated by the angry echoes. If ever I should wish for a retreat, whither I might steal from the world and its distractions, and dream quietly away the remnant of a troubled life, I know of none more promising than this little valley.

From the listless repose of the place, and the peculiar character of its inhabitants, who are descendants from the original Dutch settlers, this sequestered glen has long been known by the name of SLEEPY HOLLOW, and its rustic lads are called the Sleepy Hollow Boys throughout all the neighboring country. A drowsy, dreamy influence seems to hang over the land, and to pervade the very atmosphere. Some say that the place was bewitched by a high German doctor, during the early days of the settlement; others, that an old Indian chief, the prophet or wizard of his tribe, held his powwows there before the country was discovered by Master Hendrick Hudson. Certain it is, the place still continues under the sway of some witching power, that holds a spell over the minds of the good people, causing them to walk in a continual reverie. They are given to all kinds of marvellous beliefs; are subject to trances and visions; and frequently see strange sights, and hear music and voices in the air. The whole neighborhood abounds with local tales, haunted spots, and twilight superstitions; stars shoot and meteors glare oftener across the valley than in any other part of the country, and the nightmare, with her whole nine fold, seems to make it the favorite scene of her gambols.

The dominant spirit, however, that haunts this enchanted region, and seems to be commander-in-chief of all the powers of the air, is the apparition of a figure on horseback without a head. It is said by some to be the ghost of a Hessian trooper, whose head had been carried away by a cannon-ball, in some nameless battle during the revolutionary war; and who is ever and anon seen by the country folk, hurrying along in the gloom of night, as if on the wings of the wind. His haunts are not confined to the valley, but extend at times to the adjacent roads, and especially to the vicinity of a church at no great distance. Indeed, certain of the most authentic historians of those parts, who have been careful in collecting and collating the floating facts concerning this spectre, allege that the body of the trooper, having been buried in the church-yard, the ghost rides forth to the scene of battle in nightly quest of his head; and that the rushing speed with which he sometimes passes along the Hollow, like a midnight blast, is owing to his being belated, and in a hurry to get back to the church-yard before daybreak.

Such is the general purport of this legendary superstition, which has furnished materials for many a wild story in that region of shadows; and the spectre is known, at all the country firesides, by the name of the Headless Horseman of Sleepy Hollow.

It is remarkable that the visionary propensity I have mentioned is not confined to the native inhabitants of the valley, but is unconsciously imbibed by every one who resides there for a time. However wide awake they may have been before they entered that sleepy region, they are sure, in a little time, to inhale the witching influence of the air, and begin to grow imaginative—to dream dreams, and see apparitions.

I mention this peaceful spot with all possible laud; for it is in such little retired Dutch valleys, found here and there embosomed in the great State of New-York, that population, manners, and customs, remain fixed; while the great torrent of migration and improvement, which is making such incessant changes in other parts of this restless country, sweeps by them unobserved. They are like those little nooks of still water which border a rapid stream; where we may see the straw and bubble riding quietly at anchor, or slowly revolving in their mimic harbor, undisturbed by the rush of the passing current. Though many years have elapsed since I trod the drowsy shades of Sleepy

Hollow, yet I question whether I should not still find the same trees and the same families vegetating in its sheltered bosom.

In this by-place of nature, there abode, in a remote period of American history, that is to say, some thirty years since, a worthy wight of the name of Ichabod Crane; who sojourned, or, as he expressed it, "tarred," in Sleepy Hollow, for the purpose of instructing the children of the vicinity. He was a native of Connecticut; a State which supplies the Union with pioneers for the mind as well as for the forest, and sends forth yearly its legions of frontier woodsmen and country schoolmasters. The cognomen of Crane was not inapplicable to his person. He was tall, but exceedingly lank, with narrow shoulders, long arms and legs, hands that dangled a mile out of his sleeves, feet that might have served for shovels, and his whole frame most loosely hung together. His head was small, and flat at top, with huge ears, large green glassy eyes, and a long snipe nose, so that it looked like a weather-cock, perched upon his spindle neck, to tell which way the wind blew. To see him striding along the profile of a hill on a windy day, with his clothes bagging and fluttering about him, one might have mistaken him for the genius of famine descending upon the earth, or some scarecrow eloped from a cornfield.

His school-house was a low building of one large room, rudely constructed of logs; the windows partly glazed, and partly patched with leaves of old copy-books. It was most ingeniously secured at vacant hours, by a withe twisted in the handle of the door, and stakes set against the window shutters; so that, though a thief might get in with perfect ease, he would find some embarrassment in getting out; an idea most probably borrowed by the architect, Yost Van Houten, from the mystery of an eel-pot. The school-house stood in a rather lonely but pleasant situation, just at the foot of a woody hill, with a brook running close by, and a formidable birch tree growing at one end of it. From hence the low murmur of his pupils' voices, conning over their lessons, might be heard in a drowsy summer's day, like the hum of a bee-hive; interrupted now and then by the authoritative voice of the master, in the tone of menace or command; or, peradventure, by the appalling sound of the birch, as he urged some tardy loiterer along the flowery path of knowledge. Truth to say, he was a conscientious man, and ever bore in mind the golden maxim, "Spare the rod and spoil the child."—Ichabod Crane's scholars certainly were not spoiled.

I would not have it imagined, however, that he was one of those cruel potentates of the school, who joy in the smart of their subjects; on the contrary, he administered justice with discrimination rather than severity; taking the burthen off the backs of the weak, and laying it on those of the strong. Your mere puny stripling, that winced at the least flourish of the rod, was passed by with indulgence; but the claims of justice were satisfied by inflicting a double portion on some little, tough, wrong-headed, broad-skirted Dutch urchin, who sulked and swelled and grew dogged and sullen beneath the birch. All this he called "doing his duty by their parents"; and he never inflicted a chastisement without following it by the assurance, so consolatory to the smarting urchin, that "he would remember it, and thank him for it the longest day he had to live."

When school hours were over, he was even the companion and playmate of the larger boys; and on holiday afternoons would convoy some of the smaller ones home, who happened to have pretty sisters, or good housewives for mothers, noted for the comforts of the cupboard. Indeed it behooved him to keep on good terms with his pupils. The revenue arising from his school was small, and would have been scarcely sufficient to furnish him with daily bread, for he was a huge feeder, and though lank, had the dilating powers of an anaconda; but to help out his maintenance, he was, according to country custom in those parts, boarded and lodged at the houses of the farmers, whose children he instructed. With these he lived successively a week at a time; thus going the rounds of the neighborhood, with all his worldly effects tied up in a cotton handkerchief.

That all this might not be too onerous on the purses of his rustic patrons, who are apt to consider the costs of schooling a grievous burden, and schoolmasters as mere drones, he had various ways of rendering himself both useful and agreeable. He assisted the farmers occasionally in the lighter labors of their farms; helped to make hay; mended the fences; took the horses to water; drove the cows from pasture; and cut wood for the winter fire. He laid aside, too, all the dominant dignity and absolute sway with which he lorded it in his little empire, the school, and became wonderfully gentle and ingratiating. He found favor in the eyes of the mothers, by petting the children, particularly the youngest; and like the lion bold, which whilom so magnanimously the lamb did hold, he would sit with a child on one knee, and rock a cradle with his foot for whole hours together.

In addition to his other vocations, he was the singing-master of the neighborhood, and picked up many bright shillings by instructing the young folks in psalmody. It was a matter of no little vanity to him, on Sundays, to take his station in front of the church gallery, with a band of chosen singers; where, in his own mind, he completely carried away the palm from the parson. Certain it is, his voice resounded far above all the rest of the congregation; and there are peculiar quavers still to be heard in that church, and which may even be heard half a mile off, quite to the opposite side of the mill-pond, on a still Sunday morning, which are said to be legitimately descended from the nose of Ichabod Crane. Thus, by divers little make-shifts in that ingenious way which is commonly denominated "by hook and by crook," the worthy pedagogue got on tolerably enough, and was thought, by all who understood nothing of the labor of headwork, to have a wonderfully easy life of it.

The schoolmaster is generally a man of some importance in the female circle of a rural neighborhood; being considered a kind of idle gentlemanlike personage, of vastly superior taste and accomplishments to the rough country swains, and, indeed, inferior in learning only to the parson. His appearance, therefore, is apt to occasion some little stir at the tea-table of a farmhouse, and the addition of a supernumerary dish of cakes or sweetmeats, or peradventure, the parade of a silver tea-pot. Our man of letters, therefore, was peculiarly happy in the smiles of all the country damsels. How he would figure among them in the churchyard, between services on Sundays! gathering grapes for them from the wild vines that overrun the surrounding trees; reciting for their amusement all the epitaphs on the tombstones; or sauntering, with a whole bevy of them, along the banks of the adjacent mill-pond; while the more bashful country bumpkins hung sheepishly back, envying his superior elegance and address.

From his half itinerant life, also, he was a kind of travelling gazette, carrying the whole budget of local gossip from house to house; so that his appearance was always greeted with satisfaction. He was, moreover, esteemed by the women as a man of great erudition, for he had read several books quite through, and was a perfect master of Cotton Mather's history of New England Witchcraft, in which, by the way, he most firmly and potently believed.

He was, in fact, an odd mixture of small shrewdness and simple credulity. His appetite for the marvellous, and his powers of digesting it, were equally extraordinary; and both had been increased by his residence in this spellbound region. No tale was too gross or monstrous for his capacious swallow. It was often his delight, after his school was dismissed in the afternoon, to stretch himself on the rich bed of clover, bordering the little brook that whimpered by his school-house, and there con over old Mather's direful tales, until the gathering dusk of the evening made the printed page a mere mist before his eyes. Then, as he wended his way, by swamp and stream and awful woodland, to the farmhouse where he happened to be quartered, every sound of nature, at that witching hour, fluttered his excited imagination: the moan of the whip-poor-will from the hill-side; the boding cry of the tree-toad, that harbinger of storm; the dreary hooting of the screech-owl, or the sudden rustling in the thicket of birds frightened from their roost. The fire-flies, too, which sparkled most vividly in the darkest places, now and then startled him, as one of uncommon brightness would stream across his path; and if, by chance, a huge blockhead of a beetle came winging his blundering flight against him, the poor varlet was ready to give up the ghost, with the idea that he was struck with a witch's token. His only resource on such occasions, either to drown thought, or drive away evil spirits, was to sing psalm tunes;—and the good people of Sleepy Hollow, as they sat by their doors of an evening, were often filled with awe, at hearing his nasal melody, "in linked sweetness long drawn out," floating from the distant hill, or along the dusky road.

Another of his sources of fearful pleasure was, to pass long winter evenings with the old Dutch wives, as they sat spinning by the fire, with a row of apples roasting and spluttering along the hearth, and listen to their marvellous tales of ghosts and goblins, and haunted fields, and haunted brooks, and haunted bridges, and haunted houses, and particularly of the headless horseman, or galloping Hessian of the Hollow, as they sometimes called him. He would delight them equally by his anecdotes of witchcraft, and of the direful omens and portentous sights and sounds in the air, which prevailed in the earlier times of Connecticut; and would frighten them wofully with speculations upon comets and shooting stars; and with the alarming fact that the world did absolutely turn round, and that they were half the time topsy-turvy!

But if there was a pleasure in all this, while snugly cuddling in the chimney corner of a chamber that was all of a ruddy glow from the crackling wood fire, and where, of course, no spectre dared to show his face, it was dearly purchased by the terrors of his subsequent walk homewards. What fearful shapes and shadows beset his path amidst the dim and ghastly glare of a snowy night!—With what wistful look did he eye every trembling ray of light streaming across the waste fields from some distant window! —How often was he appalled by some shrub covered with snow, which, like a sheeted spectre, beset his very path!— How often did he shrink with curdling awe at the sound of his own steps on the frosty crust beneath his feet; and dread to look over his shoulder, lest he should behold some uncouth being tramping close behind him!—and how often was he thrown into complete dismay by some rushing blast, howling among the trees, in the idea that it was the Galloping Hessian on one of his nightly scourings!

All these, however, were mere terrors of the night, phantoms of the mind that walk in darkness; and though he had seen many spectres in his time, and been more than once beset by Satan in divers shapes, in his lonely perambulations, yet daylight put an end to all these evils; and he would have passed a pleasant life of it, in despite of the devil and all his works, if his path had not been crossed by a being that causes more perplexity to mortal man than ghosts, goblins, and the whole race of witches put together, and that was—a woman.

Among the musical disciples who assembled, one evening in each week, to receive his instructions in psalmody, was Katrina Van Tassel, the daughter and only child of a

substantial Dutch farmer. She was a blooming lass of fresh
eighteen; plump as a partridge; ripe and melting and rosy
cheeked as one of her father's peaches, and universally
famed, not merely for her beauty, but her vast expectations.
She was withal a little of a coquette, as might be perceived
even in her dress, which was a mixture of ancient and
modern fashions, as most suited to set off her charms. She
wore the ornaments of pure yellow gold, which her great-
great-grandmother had brought over from Saardam; the
tempting stomacher of the older time; and withal a provok-
ingly short petticoat, to display the prettiest foot and ankle
in the country round.

Ichabod Crane had a soft and foolish heart towards the
sex; and it is not to be wondered at, that so tempting a
morsel soon found favor in his eyes; more especially after
he had visited her in her paternal mansion. Old Baltus Van
Tassel was a perfect picture of a thriving, contented, liberal-
hearted farmer. He seldom, it is true, sent either his eyes
or his thoughts beyond the boundaries of his own farm;
but within those every thing was snug, happy, and well-
conditioned. He was satisfied with his wealth, but not
proud of it; and piqued himself upon the hearty abundance,
rather than the style in which he lived. His stronghold was
situated on the banks of the Hudson, in one of those green,
sheltered, fertile nooks, in which the Dutch farmers are so
fond of nestling. A great elm-tree spread its broad branches
over it; at the foot of which bubbled up a spring of the
softest and sweetest water, in a little well, formed of a barrel; and then stole sparkling away through the grass, to a
neighboring brook, that bubbled along among alders and
dwarf willows. Hard by the farmhouse was a vast barn,
that might have served for a church; every window and
crevice of which seemed bursting forth with the treasures
of the farm; the flail was busily resounding within it from
morning to night; swallows and martins skimmed twittering
about the eaves; and rows of pigeons, some with one eye
turned up, as if watching the weather, some with their
heads under their wings, or buried in their bosoms, and
others swelling, and cooing, and bowing about their dames,
were enjoying the sunshine on the roof. Sleek unwieldy
porkers were grunting in the repose and abundance of their
pens; whence sallied forth, now and then, troops of sucking
pigs, as if to snuff the air. A stately squadron of snowy

geese were riding in an adjoining pond, convoying whole
fleets of ducks; regiments of turkeys were gobbling through
the farmyard, and guinea fowls fretting about it, like ill-
tempered housewives, with their peevish discontented cry.
Before the barn door strutted the gallant cock, that pattern
of a husband, a warrior, and a fine gentleman clapping his
burnished wings, and crowing in the pride and gladness of
his heart—sometimes tearing up the earth with his feet, and
then generously calling his ever-hungry family of wives and
children to enjoy the rich morsel which he had discovered.

The pedagogue's mouth watered, as he looked upon this
sumptuous promise of luxurious winter fare. In his devour-
ing mind's eye, he pictured to himself every roasting-pig
running about with a pudding in his belly, and an apple in
his mouth; the pigeons were snugly put to bed in a comfortable pie, and tucked in with a coverlet of crust; the
geese were swimming in their own gravy; and the ducks
pairing cosily in dishes, like snug married couples, with a
decent competency of onion sauce. In the porkers he saw
carved out the future sleek side of bacon, and juicy relishing ham; not a turkey but he beheld daintily trussed up,
with its gizzard under its wing, and, peradventure, a necklace of savory sausages; and even bright chanticleer himself lay sprawling on his back, in a side-dish, with uplifted
claws, as if craving that quarter which his chivalrous spirit
disdained to ask while living.

As the enraptured Ichabod fancied all this, and as he
rolled his great green eyes over the fat meadowlands, the
rich fields of wheat, of rye, of buckwheat, and Indian corn,
and the orchards burthened with ruddy fruit, which surrounded the warm tenement of Van Tassel, his heart
yearned after the damsel who was to inherit these domains,
and his imagination expanded with the idea, how they
might be readily turned into cash, and the money invested
in immense tracts of wild land, and shingle palaces in the
wilderness. Nay, his busy fancy already realized his hopes,
and presented to him the blooming Katrina, with a whole
family of children, mounted on the top of a wagon loaded
with household trumpery, with pots and kettles dangling
beneath; and he beheld himself bestriding a pacing mare,
with a colt at her heels, setting out for Kentucky, Tennessee, or the Lord knows where.

When he entered the house the conquest of his heart was

complete. It was one of those spacious farmhouses, with high-ridged, but lowly-sloping roofs, built in the style handed down from the first Dutch settlers; the low projecting eaves forming a piazza along the front, capable of being closed up in bad weather. Under this were hung flails, harness, various utensils of husbandry, and nets for fishing in the neighboring river. Benches were built along the sides for summer use; and a great spinning-wheel at one end, and a churn at the other, showed the various uses to which this important porch might be devoted. From this piazza the wondering Ichabod entered the hall, which formed the centre of the mansion and the place of usual residence. Here, rows of resplendent pewter, ranged on a long dresser, dazzled his eyes. In one corner stood a huge bag of wool ready to be spun; in another a quantity of linsey-woolsey just from the loom; ears of Indian corn, and strings of dried apples and peaches, hung in gay festoons along the walls, mingled with the gaud of red peppers; and a door left ajar gave him a peep into the best parlor, where the claw-footed chairs, and dark mahogany tables, shone like mirrors; andirons, with their accompanying shovel and tongs, glistened from their covert of asparagus tops; mock-oranges and conch-shells decorated the mantel-piece; strings of various colored birds' eggs were suspended above it: a great ostrich egg was hung from the centre of the room, and a corner cupboard, knowingly left open, displayed immense treasures of old silver and well-mended china.

From the moment Ichabod laid his eyes upon these regions of delight, the peace of his mind was at an end, and his only study was how to gain the affections of the peerless daughter of Van Tassel. In this enterprise, however, he had more real difficulties than generally fell to the lot of a knight-errant of yore, who seldom had any thing but giants, enchanters, fiery dragons, and such like easily-conquered adversaries, to contend with; and had to make his way merely through gates of iron and brass, and walls of adamant, to the castle keep, where the lady of his heart was confined; all which he achieved as easily as a man would carve his way to the centre of a Christmas pie; and then the lady gave him her hand as a matter of course. Ichabod, on the contrary, had to win his way to the heart of a country coquette, beset with a labyrinth of whims and caprices, which were for ever presenting new difficulties and impediments; and he had to encounter a host of fearful adversaries of real flesh and blood, and numerous rustic admirers, who beset every portal to her heart; keeping a watchful and angry eye upon each other, but ready to fly out in the common cause against any new competitor.

Among these the most formidable was a burly, roaring, roystering blade, of the name of Abraham, or, according to the Dutch abbreviation, Brom Van Brunt, the hero of the country round, which rang with his feats of strength and hardihood. He was broad-shouldered and double-jointed, with short curly black hair, and a bluff, but not unpleasant countenance, having a mingled air of fun and arrogance. From his Herculean frame and great powers of limb, he had received the nickname of BROM BONES, by which he was universally known. He was famed for great knowledge and skill in horsemanship, being as dexterous on horseback as a Tartar. He was foremost at all races and cock-fights; and, with the ascendency which bodily strength acquires in rustic life, was the umpire in all disputes, setting his hat on one side, and giving his decisions with an air and tone admitting of no gainsay or appeal. He was always ready for either a fight or a frolic; but had more mischief than ill-will in his composition; and, with all his over-bearing roughness, there was a strong dash of waggish good humor at bottom. He had three or four boon companions, who regarded him as their model, and at the head of whom he scoured the country, attending every scene of feud or merriment for miles round. In cold weather he was distinguished by a fur cap, surmounted with a flaunting fox's tail; and when the folks at a country gathering descried this well-known crest at a distance, whisking about among a squad of hard riders, they always stood by for a squall. Sometimes his crew would be heard dashing along past the farmhouses at midnight, with whoop and halloo, like a troop of Don Cossacks; and the old dames, startled out of their sleep, would listen for a moment till the hurry-scurry had clattered by, and then exclaim, "Ay, there goes Brom Bones and his gang!" The neighbors looked upon him with a mixture of awe, admiration, and good will; and when any madcap prank, or rustic brawl, occurred in the vicinity, always shook their heads, and warranted Brom Bones was at the bottom of it.

This rantipole [reckless] hero had for some time singled

out the blooming Katrina for the object of his uncouth gallantries, and though his amorous toyings were something like the gentle caresses and endearments of a bear, yet it was whispered that she did not altogether discourage his hopes. Certain it is, his advances were signals for rival candidates to retire, who felt no inclination to cross a lion in his amours; insomuch, that when his horse was seen tied to Van Tassel's paling, on a Sunday night, a sure sign that his master was courting, or, as it is termed, "sparking," within, all other suitors passed by in despair, and carried the war into other quarters.

Such was the formidable rival with whom Ichabod Crane had to contend, and, considering all things, a stouter man than he would have shrunk from the competition, and a wiser man would have despaired. He had, however, a happy mixture of pliability and perseverance in his nature; he was in form and spirit like a supple-jack—yielding, but tough; though he bent, he never broke; and though he bowed beneath the slightest pressure, yet, the moment it was away— jerk! he was as erect, and carried his head as high as ever.

To have taken the field openly against his rival would have been madness; for he was not a man to be thwarted in his amours, any more than that stormy lover, Achilles. Ichabod, therefore, made his advances in a quiet and gently-insinuating manner. Under cover of his character of singing-master, he made frequent visits at the farmhouse; not that he had any thing to apprehend from the meddlesome interference of parents, which is so often a stumbling-block in the path of lovers. Balt Van Tassel was an easy indulgent soul; he loved his daughter better even than his pipe, and like a reasonable man and an excellent father, let her have her way in every thing. His notable little wife, too, had enough to do to attend to her housekeeping and manage her poultry; for, as she sagely observed, ducks and geese are foolish things, and must be looked after, but girls can take care of themselves. Thus while the busy dame bustled about the house, or plied her spinning-wheel at one end of the piazza, honest Balt would sit smoking his evening pipe at the other, watching the achievements of a little wooden warrior, who, armed with a sword in each hand, was most valiantly fighting the wind on the pinnacle of the barn. In the mean time, Ichabod would carry on his suit with the daughter by the side of the spring under the great elm, or sauntering along in the twilight, that hour so favorable to the lover's eloquence.

I profess not to know how women's hearts are wooed and won. To me they have always been matters of riddle and admiration. Some seem to have but one vulnerable point, or door of access; while others have a thousand avenues, and may be captured in a thousand different ways. It is a great triumph of skill to gain the former, but a still greater proof of generalship to maintain possession of the latter, for the man must battle for his fortress at every door and window. He who wins a thousand common hearts is therefore entitled to some renown; but he who keeps undisputed sway over the heart of a coquette, is indeed a hero. Certain it is, this was not the case with the redoubtable Brom Bones; and from the moment Ichabod Crane made his advances, the interests of the former evidently declined; his horse was no longer seen tied at the palings on Sunday nights, and a deadly feud gradually arose between him and the preceptor of Sleepy Hollow.

Brom, who had a degree of rough chivalry in his nature, would fain have carried matters to open warfare, and have settled their pretensions to the lady, according to the mode of those most concise and simple reasoners, the knights-errant of yore—by single combat; but Ichabod was too conscious of the superior might of his adversary to enter the lists against him: he had overheard a boast of Bones, that he would "double the schoolmaster up, and lay him on a shelf of his own school-house"; and he was too wary to give him an opportunity. There was something extremely provoking in this obstinately pacific system; it left Brom no alternative but to draw upon the funds of rustic waggery in his disposition, and to play off boorish practical jokes upon his rival: Ichabod became the object of whimsical persecution to Bones, and his gang of rough riders. They harried his hitherto peaceful domains; smoked out his singing school, by stopping up the chimney; broke into the school-house at night, in spite of its formidable fastenings of withe and window stakes, and turned every thing topsy-turvy: so that the poor schoolmaster began to think all the witches in the country held their meetings there. But what was still more annoying, Brom took all opportunities of turning him into ridicule in presence of his mistress, and had a scoundrel dog whom he taught to whine in the most ludicrous manner, and introduced as a rival of Ichabod's to instruct her in psalmody.

In this way matters went on for some time, without producing any material effect on the relative situation of the contending powers. On a fine autumnal afternoon, Ichabod, in pensive mood, sat enthroned on the lofty stool whence he usually watched all the concerns of his little literary realm. In his hand he swayed a ferule, that sceptre of despotic power; the birch of justice reposed on three nails, behind the throne, a constant terror to evil doers; while on the desk before him might be seen sundry contraband articles and prohibited weapons, detected upon the persons of idle urchins; such as half-munched apples, popguns, whirligigs, fly-cages, and whole legions of rampant little paper game-cocks. Apparently there had been some appalling act of justice recently inflicted, for his scholars were all busily intent upon their books, or slyly whispering behind them with one eye kept upon the master; and a kind of buzzing stillness reigned throughout the schoolroom. It was suddenly interrupted by the appearance of a negro, in towcloth jacket and trowsers, a round-crowned fragment of a hat, like the cap of Mercury, and mounted on the back of a ragged, wild, half-broken colt, which he managed with a rope by way of halter. He came clattering up to the school door with an invitation to Ichabod to attend a merry-making or "quilting frolic," to be held that evening at Mynheer Van Tassel's; and having delivered his message with that air of importance, and effort at fine language, which a negro is apt to display on petty embassies of the kind, he dashed over the brook, and was seen scampering away up the hollow, full of the importance and hurry of his mission.

All was now bustle and hubbub in the late quiet schoolroom. The scholars were hurried through their lessons, without stopping at trifles; those who were nimble skipped over half with impunity, and those who were tardy, had a smart application now and then in the rear, to quicken their speed, or help them over a tall word. Books were flung aside without being put away on the shelves, inkstands were overturned, benches thrown down, and the whole school was turned loose an hour before the usual time, bursting forth like a legion of young imps, yelping and racketing about the green, in joy at their early emancipation.

The gallant Ichabod now spent at least an extra half hour at his toilet, brushing and furbishing up his best, and indeed only suit of rusty black, and arranging his looks [sic] by a bit of broken looking-glass, that hung up in the schoolhouse. That he might make his appearance before his mistress in the true style of a cavalier, he borrowed a horse from the farmer with whom he was domiciliated, a choleric old Dutchman, of the name of Hans Van Ripper, and, thus gallantly mounted, issued forth, like a knight-errant in quest of adventures. But it is meet I should, in the true spirit of romantic story, give some account of the looks and equipments of my hero and his steed. The animal he bestrode was a broken-down plough-horse, that had outlived almost every thing but his viciousness. He was gaunt and shagged, with a ewe neck and a head like a hammer; his rusty mane and tail were tangled and knotted with burrs; one eye had lost its pupil, and was glaring and spectral; but the other had the gleam of a genuine devil in it. Still he must have had fire and mettle in his day, if we may judge from the name he bore of Gunpowder. He had, in fact, been a favorite steed of his master's, the choleric Van Ripper, who was a furious rider, and had infused, very probably, some of his own spirit into the animal; for, old and broken-down as he looked, there was more of the lurking devil in him than in any young filly in the country.

Ichabod was a suitable figure for such a steed. He rode with short stirrups, which brought his knees nearly up to the pommel of the saddle; his sharp elbows stuck out like grasshoppers'; he carried his whip perpendicularly in his hand, like a sceptre, and, as his horse jogged on, the motion of his arms was not unlike the flapping of a pair of wings. A small wool hat rested on the top of his nose, for so his scanty strip of forehead might be called; and the skirts of his black coat fluttered out almost to the horse's tail. Such was the appearance of Ichabod and his steed, as they shambled out of the gate of Hans Van Ripper, and it was altogether such an apparition as is seldom to be met with in broad daylight.

It was, as I have said, a fine autumnal day, the sky was clear and serene, and nature wore that rich and golden livery which we always associate with the idea of abundance. The forests had put on their sober brown and yellow, while some trees of the tenderer kind had been nipped by the frosts into brilliant dyes of orange, purple, and scarlet. Streaming files of wild ducks began to make their appearance high in the air; the bark of the squirrel might be heard from the groves of beech and hickory nuts, and the pensive whistle of the quail at intervals from the neighboring stubble-field.

The small birds were taking their farewell banquets. In the fulness of their revelry, they fluttered, chirping and frolicking, from bush to bush, and tree to tree, capricious from the very profusion and variety around them. There was the honest cock-robin, the favorite game of stripling sportsmen, with its loud querulous note; and the twittering blackbirds flying in sable clouds; and the golden-winged woodpecker, with his crimson crest, his broad black gorget, and splendid plumage; and the cedar bird, with its red-tipt wings and yellow-tipt tail, and its little monteiro cap of feathers; and the blue jay, that noisy coxcomb, in his gay light-blue coat and white underclothes; screaming and chattering, nodding and bobbing and bowing, and pretending to be on good terms with every songster of the grove.

As Ichabod jogged slowly on his way, his eye, ever open to every symptom of culinary abundance, ranged with delight over the treasures of jolly autumn. On all sides he beheld vast store of apples; some hanging in oppressive opulence on the trees; some gathered into baskets and barrels for the market; others heaped up in rich piles for the cider-press. Farther on he beheld great fields of Indian corn, with its golden ears peeping from their leafy coverts, and holding out the promise of cakes and hasty pudding; and the yellow pumpkins lying beneath them, turning up their fair round bellies to the sun, and giving ample prospects of the most luxurious of pies; and anon he passed the the fragrant buckwheat fields, breathing odor of the bee-hive, and as he beheld them, soft anticipations stole over his mind of dainty slapjacks, well buttered, and garnished with honey or treacle, by the delicate little dimpled hand of Katrina Van Tassel.

Thus feeding his mind with many sweet thoughts and "sugared suppositions," he journeyed along the sides of a range of hills which look out upon some of the goodliest scenes of the mighty Hudson. The sun gradually wheeled his broad disk down into the west. The wide bosom of the Tappan Zee lay motionless and glassy, excepting that here and there a gentle undulation waved and prolonged the blue shadow of the distant mountain. A few amber clouds floated in the sky, without a breath of air to move them. The horizon was of a fine golden tint, changing gradually into a pure apple green, and from that into the deep blue of the mid-heaven. A slanting ray lingered on the woody crests of the precipices that overhung some parts of the river, giving greater depth to the dark-gray and purple of their rocky sides. A sloop was loitering in the distance, dropping slowly down with the tide, her sail hanging uselessly against the mast; and as the reflection of the sky gleamed along the still water, it seemed as if the vessel was suspended in the air.

It was toward evening that Ichabod arrived at the castle of the Heer Van Tassel, which he found thronged with the pride and flower of the adjacent country. Old farmers, a spare leathern-faced race, in homespun coats and breeches, blue stockings, huge shoes, and magnificent pewter buckles. Their brisk withered little dames, in close crimped caps, longwaisted shortgowns, homespun petticoats, with scissors and pin-cushions, and gay calico pockets hanging on the outside. Buxom lasses, almost as antiquated as their mothers, excepting where a straw hat, a fine ribbon, or perhaps a white frock, gave symptoms of city innovation. The sons, in short square-skirted coats with rows of stupendous brass buttons, and their hair generally queued in the fashion of the times, especially if they could procure an eel-skin for the purpose, it being esteemed, throughout the country, as a potent nourisher and strengthener of the hair.

Brom Bones, however, was the hero of the scene, having come to the gathering on his favorite steed Daredevil, a creature, like himself, full of mettle and mischief, and which no one but himself could manage. He was, in fact, noted for preferring vicious animals, given to all kinds of tricks, which kept the rider in constant risk of his neck, for he held a tractable well-broken horse as unworthy of a lad of spirit.

Fain would I pause to dwell upon the world of charms that burst upon the enraptured gaze of my hero, as he entered the state parlor of Van Tassel's mansion. Not those of the bevy of buxom lasses, with their luxurious display of red and white; but the ample charms of a genuine Dutch country tea-table, in the sumptuous time of autumn. Such heaped-up platters of cakes of various and almost indescribable kinds, known only to experienced Dutch housewives! There was the doughty dough-nut, the tenderer oly koek, and the crisp and crumbling cruller; sweet cakes and short cakes, ginger cakes and honey cakes, and the whole family of cakes. And then there were apple pies and peach pies and pumpkin pies; besides slices of ham and smoked beef; and moreover delectable dishes of preserved plums, and peaches, and pears, and quinces; not to mention broiled shad and roasted chickens; together with bowls of milk and cream, all mingled higgledy-piggledy, pretty much as I have enumerated them, with the motherly tea-pot sending up its clouds of vapor from the midst—Heaven bless the mark! I want breath and time to discuss this banquet as it deserves, and am too eager to get on with my story. Happily, Ichabod Crane was not in so great a hurry as his historian, but did ample justice to every dainty.

He was a kind and thankful creature, whose heart dilated in proportion as his skin was filled with good cheer; and whose spirits rose with eating as some men's do with drink. He could not help, too, rolling his large eyes round him as he ate, and chuckling with the possibility that he might one day be lord of all this scene of almost unimaginable luxury and splendor. Then, he thought, how soon he'd turn his back upon the old school-house; snap his fingers in the face of Hans Van Ripper, and every other niggardly patron, and kick any itinerant pedagogue out of doors that should dare to call him comrade!

Old Baltus Van Tassel moved about among his guests with a face dilated with content and good humor, round and jolly as the harvest moon. His hospitable attentions were brief, but expressive, being confined to a shake of the hand, a slap on the shoulder, a loud laugh, and a pressing invitation to "fall to, and help themselves."

And now the sound of the music from the common room, or hall, summoned to the dance. The musician was an old grayheaded negro, who had been the itinerant orchestra of the neighborhood for more than half a century. His instrument was as old and battered as himself. The greater part of the time he scraped on two or three strings, accompanying every movement of the bow with a motion of the head; bowing almost to the ground, and stamping with his foot whenever a fresh couple were to start.

Ichabod prided himself upon his dancing as much as upon his vocal powers. Not a limb, not a fibre about him was idle; and to have seen his loosely hung frame in full motion, and clattering about the room, you would have thought Saint Vitus himself, that blessed patron of the dance, was figuring before you in person. He was the admiration of all the negroes; who, having gathered, of all ages and sizes, from the farm and the neighborhood, stood forming a pyramid of shining black faces at every door and window, gazing with delight at the scene, rolling their white eye-balls, and showing grinning rows of ivory from ear to ear. How could the flogger of urchins be otherwise than animated and joyous? the lady of his heart was his partner in the dance, and smiling graciously in reply to all his amorous oglings; while Brom Bones, sorely smitten with love and jealousy, sat brooding by himself in one corner.

When the dance was at an end, Ichabod was attracted to a knot of the sager folks, who, with old Van Tassel, sat smoking at one end of the piazza, gossiping over former times, and drawing out long stories about the war.

This neighborhood, at the time of which I am speaking, was one of those highly-favored places which abound with chronicle and great men. The British and American line had run near it during the war; it had, therefore, been the scene of marauding, and infested with refugees, cow-boys, and all kinds of border chivalry. Just sufficient time had elapsed to enable each story-teller to dress up his tale with a little becoming fiction, and, in the indistinctness of his recollection, to make himself the hero of every exploit.

There was the story of Doffue Martling, a large blue-bearded Dutchman, who had nearly taken a British frigate with an old iron nine-pounder from a mud breastwork, only that his gun burst at the sixth discharge. And there was an old gentleman who shall be nameless, being too rich a mynheer to be lightly mentioned, who, in the battle of Whiteplains, being an excellent master of defence, parried a musket ball with a small sword, insomuch that he absolutely felt it whiz round the blade, and glance off at the hilt: in proof of which, he was ready at any time to show the sword, with the hilt a little bent. There were several more that had been equally great in the field, not one of whom but was persuaded that he had a considerable hand in bringing the war to a happy termination.

But all these were nothing to the tales of ghosts and apparitions that succeeded. The neighborhood is rich in legendary treasures of the kind. Local tales and superstitions thrive best in these sheltered long-settled retreats; but are trampled under foot by the shifting throng that forms the population of most of our country places. Besides, there is no encouragement for ghosts in most of our villages, for they have scarcely had time to finish their first nap, and turn themselves in their graves, before their surviving friends have travelled away from the neighborhood; so that when they turn out at night to walk their rounds, they have no acquaintance left to call upon. This is perhaps the reason why we so seldom hear of ghosts except in our long-established Dutch communities.

The immediate cause, however, the prevalence of supernatural stories in these parts, was doubtless owing to the vicinity of Sleepy Hollow. There was a contagion in the very air that blew from that haunted region; it breathed forth an atmosphere of dreams and fancies infecting all the land. Several of the Sleepy Hollow people were present at Van Tassel's, and, as usual, were doling out their wild and wonderful legends. Many dismal tales were told about funeral trains, and mourning cries and wailings heard and seen about the great tree where the unfortunate Major André was taken, and which stood in the neighborhood. Some mention was made also of the woman in white, that haunted the dark glen at Raven Rock, and was often heard to shriek on winter nights before a storm, having perished there in the snow. The chief part of the stories, however, turned upon the favorite spectre of Sleepy Hollow, the headless horseman, who had been heard several times of late, patrolling the country; and, it was said, tethered his horse nightly among the graves in the churchyard.

The sequestered situation of this church seems always to have made it a favorite haunt of troubled spirits. It stands on a knoll, surrounded by locust-trees and lofty elms, from among which its decent whitewashed walls shine modestly forth, like Christian purity beaming through the shades of retirement. A gentle slope descends from it to a silver sheet of water, bordered by high trees, between which, peeps may be caught at the blue hills of the Hudson. To look upon its grass-grown yard, where the sunbeams seem to sleep so quietly, one would think that there at least the dead might rest in peace. On one side of the church extends a wide woody dell, along which raves a large brook among broken rocks and trunks of fallen trees. Over a deep black part of the stream, not far from the church, was formerly thrown a wooden bridge; the road that led to it, and the bridge itself, were thickly shaded by overhanging trees, which cast a gloom about it, even in the daytime; but occasioned a fearful darkness at night. This was one of the favorite haunts of the headless horseman; and the place where he was most frequently encountered. The tale was told of old Brouwer, a most heretical disbeliever in ghosts, how he met the horseman returning from his foray into Sleepy Hollow, and was obliged to get up behind him; how they galloped over bush and brake, over hill and swamp, until they reached the bridge; when the horseman suddenly turned into a skeleton, threw old Brouwer into the brook, and sprang away over the tree-tops with a clap of thunder.

This story was immediately matched by a thrice marvellous adventure of Brom Bones, who made light of the galloping Hessian as an arrant jockey [cheat]. He affirmed that, on returning one night from the neighboring village of Sing Sing, he had been overtaken by this midnight trooper; that he had offered to race with him for a bowl of punch, and should have won it too, for Daredevil beat the goblin-horse all hollow, but, just as they came to the church-bridge, the Hessian bolted, and vanished in a flash of fire.

All these tales, told in that drowsy undertone with which men talk in the dark, the countenances of the listeners only now and then receiving a casual gleam from the glare of a pipe, sank deep in the mind of Ichabod. He repaid them in kind with large extracts from his invaluable author, Cotton Mather, and added many marvellous events that had taken place in his native State of Connecticut, and fearful sights which he had seen in his nightly walks about Sleepy Hollow.

The revel now gradually broke up. The old farmers gathered together their families in their wagons, and were heard for some time rattling along the hollow roads, and over the distant hills. Some of the damsels mounted on pillions behind their favorite swains, and their light-hearted laughter, mingling with the clatter of hoofs, echoed along the silent woodlands, sounding fainter and fainter until they gradually died away—and the late scene of noise and frolic was all silent and deserted. Ichabod only lingered behind, according to the custom of country lovers, to have a tête-à-tête with the heiress, fully convinced that he was now on the high road to success. What passed at this interview I will not pretend to say, for in fact I do not know. Something, however, I fear me, must have gone wrong, for he certainly sallied forth, after no very great interval, with an air quite desolate and chop-fallen.—Oh these women! these women! Could that girl have been playing off any of her coquettish tricks?—Was her encouragement of the poor pedagogue all a mere sham to secure her conquest of his rival?— Heaven only knows, not I!—Let it suffice to say, Ichabod stole forth with the air of one who had been sacking a hen-roost, rather than a fair lady's heart. Without looking to the right or left to notice the scene of rural wealth, on which he had so often gloated, he went straight to the stable, and with several hearty cuffs and kicks, roused his steed most uncourteously from the comfortable quarters in which he was soundly sleeping, dreaming of mountains of corn and oats, and whole valleys of timothy and clover.

It was the very witching time of night that Ichabod, heavy-hearted and crest-fallen, pursued his travel homewards, along the sides of the lofty hills which rise above Tarry Town, and which he had traversed so cheerily in the afternoon. The hour was as dismal as himself. Far below him, the Tappan Zee spread its dusky and indistinct waste of waters, with here and there the tall mast of a sloop, riding quietly at anchor under the land. In the dead hush of midnight, he could even hear the barking of the watch dog from the opposite shore of the Hudson; but it was so vague and faint as only to give an idea of his distance from this faithful companion of man. Now and then, too, the long-drawn crowing of a cock, accidentally awakened, would sound far, far off, from some farmhouse away among the hills—but it was like a dreaming sound in his ear. No signs of life occurred near him, but occasionally the melancholy chirp of a cricket, or perhaps the guttural twang of a bull-frog, from a neighboring marsh, as if sleeping uncomfortably, and turning suddenly in his bed.

All the stories of ghosts and goblins that he had heard in the afternoon, now came crowding upon his recollection. The night grew darker and darker; the stars seemed to sink deeper in the sky, and driving clouds occasionally hid them from his sight. He had never felt so lonely and dismal. He was, moreover, approaching the very place where many of the scenes of the ghost stories had been laid. In the centre of the road stood an enormous tulip-tree, which towered like a giant above all the other trees of the neighborhood, and formed a kind of landmark. Its limbs were gnarled, and fantastic, large enough to form trunks for ordinary trees, twisting down almost to the earth, and rising again into the air. It was connected with the tragical story of the unfortunate André, who had been taken prisoner hard by; and was universally known by the name of Major André's tree. The common people regarded it with a mixture of respect and superstition, partly out of sympathy for the fate of its ill-starred namesake, and partly from the tales of strange sights and doleful lamentations told concerning it.

As Ichabod approached this fearful tree, he began to whistle: he thought his whistle was answered—it was but a blast sweeping sharply through the dry branches. As he approached a little nearer, he thought he saw something white, hanging in the midst of the tree—he paused and ceased whistling; but on looking more narrowly, perceived that it was a place where the tree had been scathed by lightning, and the white wood laid bare. Suddenly he heard a groan —his teeth chattered and his knees smote against the saddle: it was but the rubbing of one huge bough upon another, as they were swayed about by the breeze. He passed the tree in safety, but new perils lay before him.

About two hundred yards from the tree a small brook crossed the road, and ran into a marshy and thickly-wooded glen, known by the name of Wiley's swamp. A few rough logs, laid side by side, served for a bridge over this stream. On that side of the road where the brook entered the wood, a group of oaks and chestnuts, matted thick with wild grapevines, threw a cavernous gloom over it. To pass this bridge was the severest trial. It was at this identical spot that the unfortunate André was captured, and under the covert of those chestnuts and vines were the sturdy yeomen concealed who surprised him. This has ever since been considered a haunted stream, and fearful are the feelings of the schoolboy who has to pass it alone after dark.

As he approached the stream his heart began to thump; he summoned up, however, all his resolution, gave his horse half a score of kicks in the ribs, and attempted to dash briskly across the bridge; but instead of starting forward, the perverse old animal made a lateral movement, and ran broadside against the fence. Ichabod, whose fears increased with the delay, jerked the reins on the other side, and kicked lustily with the contrary foot: it was all in vain; his steed started, it is true, but it was only to plunge to the opposite side of the road into a thicket of brambles and alder bushes. The schoolmaster now bestowed both whip and heel upon the starveling ribs of old Gunpowder, who dashed forward, snuffling and snorting, but came to a stand just by the bridge, with a suddenness that had nearly sent his rider sprawling over his head. Just at this moment a plashy tramp by the side of the bridge caught the sensitive ear of Ichabod. In the dark shadow of the grove, on the margin of the brook, he beheld something huge, misshapen, black and towering. It stirred not, but seemed gathered up in the gloom, like some gigantic monster ready to spring upon the traveller.

The hair of the affrighted pedagogue rose upon his head with terror. What was to be done? To turn and fly was now too late; and besides, what chance was there of escaping ghost or goblin, if such it was, which could ride upon the wings of the wind? Summoning up, therefore, a show of courage, he demanded in stammering accents—"Who are you?" He received no reply. He repeated his demand in a still more agitated voice. Still there was no answer. Once more he cudgelled the sides of the inflexible Gunpowder, and, shutting his eyes, broke forth with involuntary fervor into a psalm tune. Just then the shadowy object of alarm put itself in motion, and, with a scramble and a bound, stood at once in the middle of the road. Though the night was dark and dismal, yet the form of the unknown might now in some degree be ascertained. He appeared to be a horseman of large dimensions, and mounted on a black horse of powerful frame. He made no offer of molestation or sociability, but kept aloof on one side of the road, jogging along on the blind side of old Gunpowder, who had now got over his fright and waywardness.

Ichabod, who had no relish for this strange midnight companion, and bethought himself of the adventure of Brom Bones with the Galloping Hessian, now quickened his steed, in hopes of leaving him behind. The stranger, however, quickened his horse to an equal pace. Ichabod pulled up, and fell into a walk, thinking to lag behind— the other did the same. His heart began to sink within him; he endeavored to resume his psalm tune, but his parched tongue clove to the roof of his mouth, and he could not utter a stave. There was something in the moody and dogged silence of this pertinacious companion, that was mysterious and appalling. It was soon fearfully accounted for. On mounting a rising ground, which brought the figure of his fellow-traveller in relief against the sky, gigantic in height, and muffled in a cloak, Ichabod was horror-struck, on perceiving that he was headless!—but his horror was still more increased, on observing that the head, which should have rested on his shoulders, was carried before him on the pommel of the saddle: his terror rose to desperation; he rained a shower of kicks and blows upon Gunpowder, hoping, by a sudden movement, to give his companion the slip—but the spectre started full jump with him. Away then they dashed, through thick and thin; stones flying, and sparks flashing at every bound. Ichabod's flimsy garments fluttered in the air, as he stretched his long lank body away over his horse's head, in the eagerness of his flight.

They had now reached the road which turns off to Sleepy Hollow; but Gunpowder, who seemed possessed with a demon, instead of keeping up it, made an opposite turn, and plunged headlong down hill to the left. This road leads through a sandy hollow, shaded by trees for about a quarter of a mile, where it crosses the bridge famous in goblin story, and just beyond swells the green knoll on which stands the whitewashed church.

As yet the panic of the steed had given his unskillful rider an apparent advantage in the chase; but just as he had got half way through the hollow, the girths of the saddle gave way, and he felt it slipping from under him. He seized it by the pommel, and endeavored to hold it firm, but in vain; and had just time to save himself by clasping old Gunpowder round the neck, when the saddle fell to the earth, and he heard it trampled under foot by his pursuer. For a moment the terror of Hans Van Ripper's wrath passed across his mind—for it was his Sunday saddle; but this was no time for petty fears; the goblin was hard on his haunches; and (unskillful rider that he was!) he had much ado to maintain his seat; sometimes slipping on one side, sometimes on another, and sometimes jolted on the high ridge of his horse's back-bone, with a violence that he verily feared would cleave him asunder.

An opening in the trees now cheered him with the hopes that the church bridge was at hand. The wavering reflection of a silver star in the bosom of the brook told him that he was not mistaken. He saw the walls of the church dimly glaring under the trees beyond. He recollected the place where Brom Bones's ghostly competitor had disappeared. "If I can but reach that bridge," thought Ichabod, "I am safe." Just then he heard the black steed panting and blowing close behind him; he even fancied that he felt his hot breath. Another convulsive kick in the ribs and old Gunpowder sprang upon the bridge; he thundered over the resounding planks; he gained the opposite side; and now Ichabod cast a look behind to see if his pursuer should vanish, according to rule, in a flash of fire and brimstone. Just then he saw the goblin rising in his stirrups, and in the very act of hurling his head at him. Ichabod endeavored to dodge the horrible missile, but too late. It encountered his cranium with a tremendous crash—he was tumbled headlong into the dust, and Gunpowder, the black steed, and the goblin rider, passed by like a whirlwind.

The next morning the old horse was found without his saddle, and with the bridle under his feet, soberly cropping the grass at his master's gate. Ichabod did not make his appearance at breakfast—dinner-hour came, but no Ichabod. The boys assembled at the school-house, and strolled idly about the banks of the brook; but no schoolmaster. Hans Van Ripper now began to feel some uneasiness about the fate of poor Ichabod, and his saddle. An inquiry was set on foot, and after diligent investigation they came upon his traces. In one part of the road leading to the church was found the saddle trampled in the dirt; the tracks of horses' hoofs deeply dented in the road, and evidently at furious speed, were traced to the bridge, beyond which, on the bank of a broad part of the brook, where the water ran deep and black, was found the hat of the unfortunate Ichabod, and close beside it a shattered pumpkin.

The brook was searched, but the body of the schoolmaster was not to be discovered. Hans Van Ripper, as executor of his estate, examined the bundle which contained all his worldly effects. They consisted of two shirts and a half; two stocks for the neck; a pair or two of worsted stockings; an old pair of corduroy small-clothes; a rusty razor; a book of psalm tunes, full of dogs' ears; and a broken pitch-pipe. As to the books and furniture of the schoolhouse, they belonged to the community, excepting Cotton Mather's History of Witchcraft, a New England Almanac, and a book of dreams and fortune-telling; in which last was a sheet of foolscap much scribbled and blotted in several fruitless attempts to make a copy of verses in honor of the heiress of Van Tassel. These magic books and the poetic scrawl were forthwith consigned to the flames by Hans Van Ripper; who from that time forward determined to send his children no more to school; observing, that he never knew any good come of this same reading and writing. Whatever money the schoolmaster possessed, and he had received his quarter's pay but a day or two before, he must have had about his person at the time of his disappearance.

The mysterious event caused much speculation at the church on the following Sunday. Knots of gazers and gossips were collected in the church yard, at the bridge, and at the spot where the hat and pumpkin had been found. The stories of Brouwer, of Bones, and a whole budget of others, were called to mind; and when they had diligently considered them all, and compared them with the symptoms of the present case, they shook their heads, and came to the conclusion that Ichabod had been carried off by the galloping Hessian. As he was a bachelor, and in nobody's debt, nobody troubled his head any more about him. The school was removed to a different quarter of the hollow, and another pedagogue reigned in his stead.

It is true, an old farmer, who had been down to New York on a visit several years after, and from whom this account of the ghostly adventure was received, brought home the intelligence that Ichabod Crane was still alive; that he had left the neighborhood, partly through fear of the goblin and Hans Van Ripper, and partly in mortification at having been suddenly dismissed by the heiress; that he had changed his quarters to a distant part of the country;

had kept school and studied law at the same time, had been admitted to the bar, turned politician, electioneered, written for the newspapers, and finally had been made a justice of the Ten Pound Court. Brom Bones too, who, shortly after his rival's disappearance, conducted the blooming Katrina in triumph to the altar, was observed to look exceedingly knowing whenever the story of Ichabod was related, and always burst into a hearty laugh at the mention of the pumpkin; which led some to suspect that he knew more about the matter than he chose to tell.

The old country wives, however, who are the best judges of these matters, maintain to this day that Ichabod was spirited away by supernatural means; and it is a favorite story often told about the neighborhood round the winter evening fire. The bridge became more than ever an object of superstitious awe, and that may be the reason why the road has been altered of late years, so as to approach the church by the border of the mill-pond. The school-house being deserted, soon fell to decay, and was reported to be haunted by the ghost of the unfortunate pedagogue; and the plough boy, loitering homeward of a still summer evening, has often fancied his voice at a distance, chanting a melancholy psalm tune among the tranquil solitudes of Sleepy Hollow.

Postscript, Found in the Handwriting of Mr. Knickerbocker

The preceding Tale is given, almost in the precise words in which I heard it related at a Corporation meeting of the ancient city of Manhattoes, at which were present many of its sagest and most illustrious burghers. The narrator was a pleasant, shabby, gentlemanly old fellow, in pepper-and-salt clothes, with a sadly humorous face; and one whom I strongly suspected of being poor,—he made such efforts to be entertaining. When his story was concluded, there was much laughter and approbation, particularly from two or three deputy aldermen, who had been asleep the greater part of the time. There was, however, one tall, dry-looking old gentleman, with beetling eyebrows, who maintained a grave and rather severe face throughout: now and then folding his arms, inclining his head, and looking down upon the floor, as if turning a doubt over in his mind. He was one of your wary men, who never laugh, but upon good grounds—when they have reason and the law on their side. When the mirth of the rest of the company had subsided, and silence was restored, he leaned one arm on the elbow of his chair, and sticking the other akimbo, demanded, with a slight, but exceedingly sage motion of the head, and contraction of the brow, what was the moral of the story, and what it went to prove?

The story-teller, who was just putting a glass of wine to his lips, as a refreshment after his toils, paused for a moment, looked at his inquirer with an air of infinite deference, and, lowering the glass slowly to the table, observed, that the story was intended most logically to prove:—

"That there is no situation in life but has its advantages and pleasures—providing we will but take a joke as we find it:

"That, therefore, he that runs races with goblin troopers is likely to have rough riding of it.

"Ergo, for a country schoolmaster to be refused the hand of a Dutch heiress, is a certain step to high preferment, in the state."

The cautious old gentleman knit his brows tenfold closer after this explanation, being sorely puzzled by the ratiocination of the syllogism; while, methought, the one in pepper-and-salt eyed him with something of a triumphant leer. At length he observed, that all this was very well, but still he thought the story a little on the extravagant—there were one or two points on which he had his doubts.

"Faith, sir," replied the story-teller, "as to that matter, I don't believe one-half of it myself."

D. K.
1820

JAMES FENIMORE COOPER

(1789–1851)

☆ ☆

James Fenimore Cooper was born in Burlington, New Jersey, to a family of strong Federalist, indeed antidemocratic, feeling. When the child was a year old, the family moved to its estate (now Cooperstown) of thousands of acres on the shores of Lake Otsego in New York State, where the father, Judge William Cooper, ruled his tenants like an old-time patroon. Cooperstown was the source of young Cooper's first-hand knowledge of both American frontier life and aristocratic prerogatives, conflicting attitudes which were to furnish the grown man with the materials for most of his writing.

Educated by an English tutor in Albany, New York, Cooper went on to Yale, from which he was expelled as a gentleman rowdy in 1806. He went to sea as a merchant sailor and from 1808 to 1811 was a United States Naval officer on Lake Ontario. Abandoning the nautical life, which was to provide him with heroes like Long Tom Coffin of *The Pilot* (1824), in 1811 he married Susan Augusta DeLancey of Mamaroneck, New York, daughter of a wealthy, landowning family of Tory sympathies. He settled down to the life of a country squire in Cooperstown and in his wife's native Westchester County, with no intention of writing. Tradition has it that at the age of thirty-one he became impatient with the latest English sentimental novel the family was reading and swore he could do as well himself. In answer to his wife's consequent challenge, he wrote *Precaution* (1820), one more in the popular legion of politely titillating and tediously moral tearjerkers. He followed that book in the next year with *The Spy,* which achieved great and sudden acclaim. A story of Westchester County during the Revolutionary War, it signaled the advent of American history into the realm of serious fiction and was hailed by the nation. Two years later Cooper moved to New York City and began producing his enormous list of titles, most famous of which were the "Leatherstocking Tales" (*The Pioneers,* 1823; *The Last of the Mohicans,* 1826; *The Prairie,* 1827; *The Pathfinder,* 1840; and *The Deerslayer,* 1841).

As American consul in Lyon, in 1826 he took his family to Europe for seven years, during which time, under the influence of Lafayette, the democratic persuasions his frontier experiences had given him were strengthened. As an ardent patriot he defended democracy and the New World in the face of European doubts and sneers, writing three historical novels in refutation of Sir Walter Scott's idealization of things medieval (*The Bravo,* 1831; *The Heidenmauer,* 1832; and *The Headsman,* 1833). Yet as an aristocrat he was not prepared for the triumph of frontier democracy he was to find in the Jacksonian era to which he returned. Emphasizing his belief in a Jeffersonian natural elite, he deplored a vulgar narrowness that would reduce democracy to smug mediocrity, aggressive conformity, and disrespect of property. Like the later Henry James, Cooper was able to utilize Europe and America as points of departure from which he could make criticisms of each. Although Cooper defended American democracy, his countrymen did not take kindly to the criticisms they found in such novels and essays as *Notions of the Americans* (1828); *A Letter to His Countrymen* (1834); *The American Democrat, Homeward Bound, Home as Found* (all in 1838); and the "Littlepage Manuscripts" (*Satanstoe,* 1845; *The Chainbearer,* 1845; and *The Redskins,* 1846). There was no tolerance for any hint that total egalitarianism might have pitfalls or that the New World was not the New Eden. The reviews became such slanderous personal attacks on Cooper, who popularly was assumed to be a Tory renegade (nothing could be further from the truth: with all of his strong Federalism, he was a staunch democrat), that Cooper spent much of the time after his return home in successful libel suits against his vilifiers. Indeed, although many scholars and critics claim that Cooper will be remembered as our first great novelist, it may well be that long after his frequently stilted style and dialogue, stock heroes and heroines, ridiculous situations, and pursuit-and-escape formulas have been forgotten, he will remain in our literary history as one of the most acute early critics of our republican identity.

In addition to the nineteen titles mentioned above, a few of Cooper's works are: *Lionel Lincoln* (1825); *The Red Rover* (1828); *The Wept of Wish-ton-Wish* (1829); *The Water-Witch* (1831); *Sketches of Switzerland* (two parts, both 1836); *Gleanings in Europe: France* (1837); *Gleanings in Europe: England* (1837); *Gleanings in Europe: Italy* (1838); *The History of the Navy of the United States* (1839); *The Wing-and-Wing* (1842); *Afloat and Ashore* (1844); *Lives of Distinguished American Naval Officers* (1846); and *The Crater* (1847).

Editions and accounts of Cooper and his works are to be found in T. R. Lounsbury, *James Fenimore Cooper* (1882); *The Works of James Fenimore Cooper*, 33 vols. (1895–1900); W. B. S. Clymer, *James Fenimore Cooper* (1900); E. E. Leisy, *The American Historical Novel* (1926); H. W. Boynton, *James Fenimore Cooper* (1931); R. E. Spiller, *Fenimore Cooper: Critic of His Times* (1931); R. E. Spiller and P. C. Blackburn, *A Descriptive Bibliography of the Writings of James Fenimore Cooper* (1934); M. Clavel, *Fenimore Cooper and His Critics* (1938); R. H. Pearce, "The Leatherstocking Tales Re-examined," *South Atlantic Quarterly*, XLVI (1947); J. Grossman, *James Fenimore Cooper* (1949); M. Bewley, "Revaluations: James Fenimore Cooper," *Scrutiny*, XIX (1952–1953); D. A. Ringe, "Cooper's Littlepage Novels: Change and Stability in American Society," *American Literature*, XXXII (1960); R. H. Zoellner, "Conceptual Ambivalence in Cooper's Leatherstocking," *American Literature*, XXXI (1960); D. A. Ringe, "Man and Nature in Cooper's *The Prairie*," *Nineteenth-Century Fiction*, XV (1961); R. H. Zoellner, "Fenimore Cooper: Alienated American," *American Quarterly*, XIII (1961); C. Boewe, "Cooper's Doctrine of Gifts," *Tennessee Studies in Literature*, VII (1962); D. A. Ringe, *James Fenimore Cooper* (1962); W. S. Walker, *James Fenimore Cooper: An Introduction and Interpretation* (1962); A. N. Kaul, *The American Vision: Actual and Ideal Society in Nineteenth-Century Fiction* (1963); D. W. Noble, "Cooper, Leatherstocking and the Death of the American Adam," *American Quarterly*, XVI (1964); T. Philbrick, "Cooper's *The Pioneers*: Origins and Structures," *PMLA*, LXXXIX (1964); J. F. Beard, ed., *The Letters and Journals of James Fenimore Cooper*—1800–1844—(1960–1964); K. S. House, *Cooper's Americans* (1965); K. S. House, "James Fenimore Cooper, *The Pioneers*," *The American Novel from James Fenimore Cooper to William Faulkner*, W. Stegner, ed. (1965); R. E. Spiller, *James Fenimore Cooper* (1965); W. S. Walker, ed., *Leatherstocking and the Critics* (1965); and F. Collins, "Cooper and the American Dream," *PMLA*, LXXI (1966).

FROM

Notions of the Americans

[On American Literature]

. . . The United States are the first nation that possessed institutions, and, of course, distinctive opinions of its own, that was ever dependent on a foreign people for its literature. Speaking the same language as the English, and long in the habit of importing their books from the mother country, the revolution effected no immediate change in the nature of their studies, or mental amusements. The works were reprinted, it is true, for the purposes of economy, but they still continued English. Had the latter nation used this powerful engine with tolerable address, I think they would have secured such an ally in this country as would have rendered their own decline not only more secure, but as illustrious as had been their rise. There are many theories entertained as to the effect produced in this country by the falsehoods and jealous calumnies which have been undeniably uttered in the mother country, by means of the press, concerning her republican descendant. It is my own opinion that, like all other ridiculous absurdities, they have defeated themselves, and that they are now more laughed at and derided, even here, than resented. By all that I can learn, twenty years ago, the Americans were, perhaps, far too much disposed to receive the opinions and to adopt the prejudices of their relatives; whereas, I think it is very apparent that they are now beginning to receive them with singular distrust. It is not worth our while to enter further into this subject, except as it has had, or is likely to have, an influence on the national literature.

It is quite obvious, that, so far as taste and forms alone are concerned, the literature of England and that of America must be fashioned after the same models. The authors, previously to the revolution, are common property, and it is quite idle to say that the American has not just as good a right to claim Milton, and Shakespeare, and all the old masters of the language, for his countrymen, as an Englishman. The Americans having continued to cultivate, and to cultivate extensively, an acquaintance with the writers of the mother country, since the separation, it is evident they must have kept pace with the trifling changes of the day. The only peculiarity that can, or ought to be expected in their literature, is that which is connected with the promulgation of their distinctive political opinions. They have not been remiss in this duty, as any one may see, who chooses to examine their books. . . .

The literature of the United States has, indeed, two powerful obstacles to conquer before (to use a mercantile expression) it can ever enter the markets of its own country on terms of perfect equality with that of England. Solitary and individual works of genius may, indeed, be occasionally brought to light, under the impulses of the high feeling which has conceived them; but, I fear, a good, wholesome, profitable and continued pecuniary support, is the applause that talent most craves. The fact, that an American publisher can get an English work without money, must for a few years longer (unless legislative protection shall be extended to their own authors), have a tendency to repress a national literature. No man will pay a writer for an epic, a tragedy, a sonnet, a history, or a romance, when he can get a work of equal merit for nothing. I have conversed with those who are conversant on the subject, and, I confess, I have been astonished at the information they imparted.

A capital American publisher has assured me that there are not a dozen writers in this country whose works he should feel confidence in publishing at all, while he reprints hundreds of English books without the least hesitation. This preference is by no means so much owing to any difference in merit, as to the fact that, when the price of the original author is to be added to the uniform hazard which accompanies all literary speculations, the risk becomes too great. The general taste of the reading world in this country is better than that of England. The fact is both proved and explained by the circumstances that thousands of works that are printed and read in the mother country, are not printed and read here. The publisher on this side of the Atlantic has the advantage of seeing the reviews of every book he wishes to reprint, and, what is of far more importance, he knows, with the exception of books that he is sure of selling, by means of a name, the decision of the English critics before he makes his choice. Nine times in ten, popularity, which is all he looks for, is a sufficient test of general merit. Thus, while you find every English work of character, or notoriety, on the shelves of an American book-store, you may ask in vain for most of the trash that is so greedily devoured in the circulating libraries of the mother country, and which would be just as eagerly devoured here, had not a better taste been treated by a compelled abstinence. That taste must now be overcome before such works could be sold at all.

When I say that books are not rejected here, from any want of talent in the writers, perhaps I ought to explain. I wish to express something a little different. Talent is sure of too many avenues to wealth and honors, in America, to seek, unnecessarily, an unknown and hazardous path. It is better paid in the ordinary pursuits of life, than it would be likely to be paid by an adventure in which an extraordinary and skilful, because practised, foreign competition is certain. Perhaps high talent does not often make the trial with the American bookseller; but it is precisely for the reason I have named.

The second obstacle against which American literature has to contend, is in the poverty of materials. There is scarcely an ore which contributes to the wealth of the author, that is found, here, in veins as rich as in Europe. There are no annals for the historian; no follies (beyond the most vulgar and commonplace) for the satirist; no manners for the dramatist; no obscure fictions for the writer of romance; no gross and hardy offences against decorum for the moralist; nor any of the rich artificial auxiliaries of poetry. The weakest hand can extract a spark from the flint, but it would baffle the strength of a giant to attempt kindling a flame with a pudding-stone. I very well know there are theorists who assume that the society and institutions of this country are, or ought to be, particularly favorable to novelties and variety. But the experience of one month, in these States, is sufficient to show any observant man the falsity of their position. The effect of a promiscuous assemblage anywhere, is to create a standard of deportment; and great liberty permits every one to aim at its attainment. I have never seen a nation so much alike in my life, as the people of the United States, and what is more, they are not only like each other, but they are remarkably like that which common sense tells them they ought to resemble. No doubt, traits of character that are a little peculiar, without, however, being either very poetical, or very rich, are to be found in remote districts; but they are rare, and not always happy exceptions. In short, it is not possible to conceive a state of society in which more of the attributes of plain good sense, or fewer of the artificial absurdities of life, are to be found, than here. There is no costume for the peasant (there is scarcely a peasant at all), no wig for the judge, no baton for the general, no diadem for the chief magistrate. The darkest ages of their history are illuminated by the light of truth; the utmost efforts of their chivalry are limited by the laws of God; and even the deeds of their sages and heroes are to be sung in a language that would differ but little from a version of the ten commandments. However useful and respectable all this may be in actual life, it indicates but one direction to the man of genius.

1828

FROM

Gleanings in Europe: England

[On the English and Americans]

It would be an occupation of interest, to note the changes, moral and physical, that time, climate, and different institutions, have produced between the people of England, and those of America.

Physically, I do not think the change as great as is usually imagined. Dress makes a sensible difference in appearance, and I find that the Americans, who have been under the hands of the English tailors, are not easily distinguished from the English themselves. The principal points of distinction strike me to be these. We are taller, and less fleshy; more disposed to stoop; have more prominent features, and faces less full; are less ruddy, and more tanned; have much smaller hands and feet, anti-democratical as it may be; and are more slouching in gait. The exceptions, of course, are numerous; but I think these distinctions may be deemed national. The American, who has become Europeanized by dress, however, is so very different a looking animal from what he is at home, that too much stress is not to be laid on them. Then the great extent of the United States is creating certain physical differences in our own population, that render all such comparisons liable to many qualifications.

As to stature and physical force, I see no reason to think that the animal has deteriorated in America. As between England and the Old Atlantic states, the difference is not striking, after one allows for the disparity in numbers, and the density of the population here, the eye always seeking exceptions; but I incline to believe that the south-west will turn the scale to our side. I believe it to be a fact, that the aborigines of that portion of the Union were larger than those of our section of the country.

There are obvious physical differences among the English themselves. One county is said to have an undue proportion of red heads, another to have men taller than the common, this again men that are shorter, and all to show traces of their remote origins. It is probable that some of these peculiarities have descended to ourselves, though they have become blended by the unusual admixture of the population.

Morally, we live under the influence of systems so completely the converse of each other, that it is matter of surprise so many points of resemblance still remain. The immediate tendency of the English system is, to create an extreme deference in all the subordinate classes for their superiors; while that of the American is to run into the opposite feeling. The effects of both these tendencies are certainly observable; though relatively, that of our own much less, I think, than that of England. It gives good models a rather better chance here, than they have with us.

In England, the disaffected to the government are among precisely those who most sustain government in America; and the disaffected in America (if so strong a word can properly be used, as applied to natives) are of a class whose interests it is to sustain government in England. These facts give very different aspects to the general features of society. Walking in Regent-street lately, I witnessed an attempt of the police to compel some hackney coachmen to quit their boxes, and go with them before the magistrate. A crowd of a thousand people collected immediately, and its feeling was decidedly against the ministers of the law; so much so, indeed, as to render it doubtful whether the coachmen, whose conduct had been flagrantly criminal, would not be rescued. Now, in America, I think the feeling of such a crowd, would have been just the other way. It would have taken an interest in supporting the authorities of the country, instead of an interest in opposing them. This was not the case of a mob, you will remember, in which passion puts down reason; but an ordinary occurrence of the exercise of the power of the police. Instances of this nature might be multiplied, to show that the mass of the two people act under the influence of feelings diametrically opposed to each other.

On the other hand, Englishmen of the higher classes are, with very few exceptions, and these exceptions are usually instances of mere party opposition, attached to their system, sensitive of the subject of its merits or defects, and ever ready to defend it when assailed. The American of the same class is accustomed to sneer at democracy, to cavil as its fruits, and to color and exaggerate its faults. Though this latter disposition may be, to a degree, accounted for by the facts, that all merit is comparative, and most of our people have not had the opportunities to compare; and that it is natural to resist most that which most annoys, although the substitution of any other for the actual system would produce even greater discontent; still, I think, the general tendency of aristocratical institutions on the one hand, and of democratical on the other, is to produce this broad difference in feeling, as between classes.

Both the Americans and the English are charged with being offensively boastful and arrogant as nations, and too much disposed to compare themselves advantageously with their neighbors. I have visited no country in which a similar disposition does not exist, and as communities are merely aggregations of men, I fancy that the disposition of a people to take this view of their own merits, is no more than carrying out the well known principle of individual vanity. The English and ourselves, however, well may, and probably do, differ from other nations in one circumstance connected with such a failing. The mass in both nations are better instructed, and are of more account than the mass in other countries, and their sentiments form more of a public opinion than elsewhere. When the bulk of a people are in a condition to make themselves heard, one is not to expect much refinement or delicacy, in the sentiments they utter. The English do not strike me as being a vainer nation than the French, although, in the way of ordinary intercourse, I believe that both they and we are more boastful.

The English are to be particularly distinguished from the Americans in the circumstance of their being a proud people. This is a useful and even an ennobling quality, when it is sustained by facts, though apt to render a people both uncomfortable and unpleasant, when the glory on which they pique themselves is passed away. We are almost entirely wanting in national pride, though abundantly supplied with an irritable vanity that might rise to pride, had we greater confidence in our facts. Most intelligent Englishmen are ready enough to admit the obvious faults of their climate, and even of their social condition; but it is an uncommon American that will concede anything material on such points, unless it can be made to bear on democracy. We have the sensitiveness of provincials, increased by the consciousness of having our spurs to earn, on all matters of glory and renown, and our jealousy extends even to the reputations of the cats and dogs. It is but an indifferent compliment to human nature to add, that the man who will join complacently, and I may say ignorantly, in the abuse of foreigners against the institutions of the country, and even against its people, always reserving a saving clause in favor of his own particular class, will take fire if an innuendo is hazarded against its beef, or a suggestion made that the four thousand feet of the Round Peak are not equal to the thirteen thousand feet of the Jung Frau. The English are tolerably free from this weakness, and travelling is daily increasing this species of liberality, at least. I presume that the insular situation of England, and our own distance from Europe, are equally the causes of these traits; though there may be said to be a "property qualification" in the very nature of man, that disposes him to view his own things with complacency, and those of his neighbors with disgust. Bishop Heber, in one of his letters to Lord Grenville, in speaking of the highest peaks of the Himalayas, throws into a parenthesis, "which I feel some exultation in saying, is completely within the limits of the British empire"; a sort of sentiment, of which I dare say, neither St. Chrysostom nor Polycarp was entirely free.

On the subject of sensibility to comments on their national habits and national characters, neither France nor England is by any means as philosophical or indifferent as one might suppose. As a rule, I believe all men are more easily enraged when their real faults are censured, than when their virtues are called in question; and if the defect happen to be unavoidable, or one for which they are not fairly responsible, the resentment is two-fold that which would attend a comment on a vice. The only difference I can discover between the English and ourselves in this particular, is easily to be traced to our greater provincialism, youth, and the consciousness that we are obliged to anticipate some of our renown. I should say that the English are *thin-skinned,* and the Americans *raw.* Both resent fair, frank, and manly comments with the same bad taste, resorting to calumny, blackguardism, and abuse, when wit and pleasantry would prove both more effective and wiser, and, perhaps, reformation wisest of all. I can only account for this peculiarity, by supposing that the institutions and political facts of the two countries have rendered vulgar-minded men of more account than is usually the case; and that their influence has created a species of public opinion which is less under the correction of taste, principles, and manners, than is the case in nations where the mass is more depressed. Of the fact itself, there can be no question.

In order to appreciate the effect of refinement on this nation, it will be necessary to recur to some of its statistical facts. England, including Wales, contains rather less than fifty-eight thousand square miles of territory; the state of New York, about forty-three thousand. On the former surface, there is a population of something like fifteen millions; on the latter, a population of less than two. One gives a proportion of about two hundred and sixty to the square mile, and the other a proportion of less than fifty. These premises, alone would show us the immense advantage that any given portion of surface in England must possess over the same extent of surface in America, in all those arts and improvements that depend on physical force. If there were ten men of education, and refinement, and fortune, in a county of New York, of one thousand square miles in extent, there ought to be more than fifty men of the same character and means, in an English county of equal territory. This is supposing that the real premises offer nothing more against us than the disproportion between numbers and surface; whereas, in fact, time, wealth, and an older civilization more than quadruple the odds. Even these do not make up the sum of the adverse elements. Though England has but fifteen millions of souls, the empire she controls has nearly ten times that population, and a very undue proportion of the results of so great a physical force center in this small spot.

The consideration of these truths suggest several useful heads of reflection. In the first place, they show us, if not the absolute impossibility, the great improbability, that the civilization, refinement, knowledge, wealth, and tastes of even the best portions of America can equal those of this country, and suggest the expediency of looking to other points for our sources of pride. I have said, that the two countries act under the influence of moral agencies that are almost the converse of each other. The condensation of improvement and cultivation is so great here, that even the base of society is affected by it, even to deportment; whereas, with us, these properties are so dispersed, as to render it difficult for those who are lucky enough to possess them, to keep what they have got, in face of the overshadowing influence of a lower school, instead of being able to impart them to society. Our standard, in nearly all things, as it is popular, is necessarily one of mediocrity; a highly respectable, and, circumstances considered, a singularly creditable one, but still a mediocrity; whereas, the condition of these people has enabled them to raise a standard which, however much it may be and is wanting in the better elements of a pure taste, has immensely the advantage of our own in most of the obvious blandishments of life. More than half of the peculiarities of America— peculiarities for which it is usual to seek a cause in the institutions, simply because they are so peculiar themselves —are to be traced to facts like these; or, in other words, to the disproportion between surface and numbers, the want of any other commercial towns, and our distance from the rest of the world.

Every condition of society has its own advantages, and its own disadvantages. To claim perfection for any one in particular, would be to deny the nature of man. Their comparative merits are to be decided, only, by the comparative gross results, and it is in this sense, that I contend for the superiority of our own. The utilitarian school, as it has been popularly construed, is not to my taste, either; for I believe there is great utility in the grace and elegance of life, and no one would feel more disposed to resist a system in which these essential properties are proscribed. That we are wanting in both, I am ready to allow; but I think the reason is to be found in facts entirely independent of the institutions, and that the time will come when the civilization of America will look down that of any other section of the world, if the country can pass that state of probation during which it is and will be exposed to the assaults of secret combinations to destroy it; and during which, moreover, it is, in an especial degree, liable to be affected by inherited opinions, and opinions that have been obtained under a system that has so many of the forms, while it has so few of the principles of our own, as easily to be confounded with it, by the ignorant and the un-reflecting.

We over-estimate the effects of intelligence as between ourselves and the English. The mass of information, here, probably exceeds that of America, though it is less equally distributed. In *general* knowledge of a practical nature, too, I think no people can compete with our own. But there is a species of information, that is both useful and refining, in which there are few European nations that do not surpass us. I allude, in particular, to most things that serve to embellish life. In addition to this superiority, the Europeans of the better classes very obviously possess over us an important advantage, in their intimate associations with each other, by which means they insensibly imbibe a great deal of current knowledge, of which the similar classes in America are nearly ignorant; or, which, if known at all, is only known through the medium of books. In the ex-hibition of this knowledge, which embraces all that belongs to what is commonly termed a knowledge of the world, the difference between the European and the American is the difference that is seen between the man who has passed all his days in good society, and the man who has got his knowledge of it from novels and plays.

In a correct estimate of their government, and in an acquaintance with its general action, the English are much our superiors, though we know most of details. This arises from the circumstances that the rights of an Englishman are little more than franchises, which require no very profound examination to be understood; while those of the

American depend on principles that demand study, and which are constantly exposed to the antagonist influence of opinions that have been formed under another system. It is true the English monarchy, as a monarchy and as it now exists, is a pure mystification; but the supremacy of parliament being admitted, there can arise no great difficulty on the score of interpretation. The American system, moreover, is complicated and double, and the only true Whig and Tory parties that can exist must have their origin in the circumstance. To these reasons may be added the general fact, that the educated Englishman reasons on his institutions like an Englishman only; while his American counterpart oftener reasons on the institutions of the republic like an Englishman, too, than like an American. A single fact will show you what I mean, although a hundred might be quoted. In England the government is composed, in theory, of three bases and one summit; in America, it is composed of one base and three summits. In one, there is supposed to be a balance in the powers of the state; and, as this is impossible in practice, it has resulted in a consolidated authority in its action; in the other, there is but one power, that of the entire people, and the balance is in the action of their agents. A very little reflection will show that the maxims of two such systems ought to be as different as the systems themselves.

The English are to be distinguished from the Americans by greater independence of personal habits. Not only the institutions, but the physical condition of our own country has a tendency to reduce us all to the same level of usages. The steam-boats, the overgrown taverns, the speculative character of the enterprises, and the consequent disposition to do all things in common, aid the tendency of the system in bringing about such a result. In England a man dines by himself, in a room filled with other hermits; he eats at his leisure, drinks his wine in silence, reads the paper by the hour; and, in all things, encourages his individuality and insists on his particular humors. The American is compelled to submit to a common rule; he eats when others eat, sleeps when others sleep, and he is lucky, indeed, if he can read a paper in a tavern without having a stranger looking over each shoulder. The Englishman would stare at a proposal that should invade his habits under the pretence of a common wish, while the American would be very apt to yield tacitly, though this common wish should be no more than an impudent assertion of some one who had contrived to effect his own purposes, under the popular plea. The Englishman is so much attached to his independence that he instinctively resists every effort to invade it, and nothing would be more likely to arouse him than to say the mass thinks differently from himself; whereas the American ever seems ready to resign his own opinion to that which is made to seem to be the opinion of the public. I say *seems* to be, for so manifest is the power of public opinion, that one of the commonest expedients of all American managers, is to create an impression that the public thinks in a particular way, in order to bring the common mind in subjection. One often renders himself ridiculous by a foolish obstinacy, and the other is as often contemptible by a weak compliance. A portion of what may be called the *community* of character and habits in America is doubtless owing to the rustic nature of its society, for one more easily maintains his independence in a capital than in a village, but I think the chief reasons are to be found in the practice of referring every thing to the common mind.

It is usual to ascribe the solitary and unsocial habits of English life to the natural dispositions of the people, but, I think, unjustly. The climate is made to bear the blame of no small portion of this peculiarity. Climate, probably, has an influence on us all, for we know that we are more elastic and more ready to be pleased in a clear bracing air, than in one that is close and *siroccoish,* but, on the whole I am led to think, the English owe their habits to their institutions, more than to any natural causes.

I know no subject, no feeling, nothing, on which an Englishman, as a rule, so completely loses sight of all the better points of his character, on which he is so uniformly bigoted and unjust, so ready to listen to misrepresentation and caricature, and so unwilling to receive truth—on which in short, he is so little himself in general, as on those connected with America.

As the result of this hasty and imperfect comparison, I am led to believe, that a national character somewhere between the two, would be preferable to either, as it is actually found. This may be saying no more than that man does not exist in a condition of perfection; but were the inequalities named, pared off from both people, an ingenious critic might still find faults of sufficient magnitude to preserve the identity with the human race, and qualities of sufficient elevation, to entitle both to be considered among the greatest and best nations of modern, if not of any other, times.

In most things that pertain to taste, the English have greatly the advantage of us, though *taste* is certainly not the strong side of English character. On this point, alone, one might write a book, but a very few remarks must now satisfy you. In nothing, however, is this superiority more apparent, than in their simplicity, and, particularly, in their simplicity of language. They call a spade, a spade. I very well know, that neither men nor women, in America, who are properly educated, and who are accustomed to its really better tone, differ much, if any, from the English in this particular; but, in this case, as in most others, in which *national* peculiarities are sought, the better tone of America is over-shadowed by its mediocrity. Although I deem the government of this country the very quintessence of hocus pocus, having scarcely a single practice that does not violate its theory, I believe that there is more honesty of public sentiment in England, than in America. The defect at home, I ascribe, in common with the majority of our national failings, to the greater activity, and greater *unresisted* force of ignorance and cupidity, there, than here. High qualities are nowhere collected in a sufficient phalanx to present a front to the enemy, in America.

The besetting, the degrading vice of America, is the moral cowardice by which men are led to truckle to what is called public opinion; though this opinion is as inconstant as the winds—though, in all cases that enlist the feelings of factions, there are *two* and sometimes twenty, each differing from all the others, and though, nine times in ten, these opinions are mere engines set in motion by the most corrupt and the least respectable portion of the community, for unworthy purposes. The English are a more respectable and constant nation than the Americans, as relates to this peculiarity; probably, because the condensed masses of intelligence and character enable the superior portion of the community to produce a greater impression on the inferior, by their collective force. In standing prejudices, they strike me as being worse than ourselves; but in passing impressions, greatly our superiors.

For the last I have endeavored to account, and I think the first may be ascribed to a system that is sustained by errors that it is not the interest of the more enlightened to remove, but which, instead of weakening in the ignorant, they rather encourage in themselves.

1837

FROM

The American Democrat

An Aristocrat and a Democrat

We live in an age when the words aristocrat and democrat are much used, without regard to the real significations. An aristocrat is one of a few who possess the political power of a country; a democrat, one of the many. The words are also properly applied to those who entertain notions favorable to aristocratical or democratical forms of government. Such persons are not necessarily either aristocrats or democrats in fact, but merely so in opinion. Thus a member of a democratical government may have an aristocratical bias, and vice versa.

To call a man who has the habits and opinions of a gentleman, an aristocrat from that fact alone, is an abuse of terms and betrays ignorance of the true principles of government, as well as of the world. It must be an equivocal freedom under which every one is not the master of his own innocent acts and associations; and he is a sneaking democrat indeed who will submit to be dictated to, in those habits over which neither law nor morality assumes a right of control.

Some men fancy that a democrat can only be one who seeks the level, social, mental and moral, of the majority, a rule that would at once exclude all men of refinement, education, and taste from the class. These persons are enemies of democracy, as they at once render it impracticable. They are usually great sticklers for their own associations and habits, too, though unable to comprehend any of a nature that are superior. They are, in truth, aristocrats in principle, though assuming a contrary pretension, the groundwork of all their feelings and arguments being self. Such is not the intention of liberty, whose aim is to leave every man to be the master of his own acts; denying hereditary honors, it is true, as unjust and unnecessary, but not denying the inevitable consequences of civilization.

The law of God is the only rule of conduct in this, as in other matters. Each man should do as he would be done by. Were the question put to the greatest advocate of indiscriminate association, whether he would submit to have his company and habits dictated to him, he would be one of the first to resist the tyranny; for they who are the most rigid in maintaining their own claims in such matters, are usually the loudest in decrying those whom they fancy to be better off than themselves. Indeed, it may be taken as a rule in social intercourse, that he who is the most apt to question the pretensions of others is the most conscious of the doubtful position he himself occupies; thus establishing the very claims he affects to deny, by letting his jealousy of it be seen. Manners, education, and refinement, are positive things, and they bring with them innocent tastes which are productive of high enjoyments; and it is as unjust to deny their possessors their indulgence as it would be to insist on the less fortunate's passing the time they would rather devote to athletic amusements, in listening to operas for which they have no relish, sung in a language they do not understand.

All that democracy means, is as equal a participation in rights as is practicable; and to pretend that social equality is a condition of popular institutions is to assume that the latter are destructive of civilization, for, as nothing is more self-evident than the impossibility of raising all men to the highest standard of tastes and refinement, the alternative would be to reduce the entire community to the lowest. The whole embarrassment on this point exists in the difficulty of making men comprehend qualities they do not themselves possess. We can all perceive the difference between ourselves and our inferiors, but when it comes to a question of the difference between us and our superiors, we fail to appreciate merits of which we have no proper conceptions. In face of this obvious difficulty, there is the safe and just governing rule, already mentioned, or that of permitting every one to be the undisturbed judge of his own habits and associations, so long as they are innocent and do not impair the rights of others to be equally judges for themselves. It follows, that social intercourse must regulate itself, independently of institutions, with the exception that the latter, while they withheld no natural, bestow no factitious advantages beyond those which are inseparable from the rights of property, and general civilization.

In a democracy, men are just as free to aim at the highest attainable places in society, as to attain the largest fortunes; and it would be clearly unworthy of all noble sentiment to say that the grovelling competition for money shall alone be free, while that which enlists all the liberal acquirements and elevated sentiments of the race, is denied the democrat. Such an avowal would be at once a declaration of the inferiority of the system, since nothing but ignorance and vulgarity could be its fruits.

The democratic gentleman must differ in many essential particulars from the aristocratical gentleman, though in their ordinary habits and tastes they are virtually identical. Their principles vary; and, to a slight degree, their deportment accordingly. The democrat, recognizing the right of all to participate in power, will be more liberal in his general sentiments, a quality of superiority in itself; but in conceding this much to his fellow man, he will proudly maintain his own independence of vulgar domination as indispensable to his personal habits. The same principles and manliness that would induce him to depose a royal despot would induce him to resist a vulgar tyrant.

There is no more capital, though more common error, than to suppose him an aristocrat who maintains his independence of habits; for democracy asserts the control of the majority, only in matters of law, and not in matters of custom. The very object of the institution is the utmost practicable personal liberty, and to affirm the contrary would be sacrificing the end to the means.

An aristocrat, therefore, is merely one who fortifies his exclusive privileges by positive institutions, and a democrat, one who is willing to admit of a free competition in all things. To say, however, that the last supposes this competition will lead to nothing is an assumption that means are employed without any reference to an end. He is the purest democrat who best maintains his rights, and no rights can be dearer to a man of cultivation than exemptions from unseasonable invasions on his time by the coarse minded and ignorant.

1838

WILLIAM CULLEN BRYANT

(1794–1878)

Bryant was born and reared in Cummington, a town snuggled into the natural beauty of the Berkshires and the conservative principles of western Massachusetts. The eighty-four years of his life spanned tremendous changes in the man and the nation, changes reflected in the style and themes of Bryant's poetry.

When Bryant was born, George Washington was in the second term of his administration. The Republic consisted of fifteen states and was largely an agrarian nation edging the Atlantic coast. When he died, Rutherford B. Hayes was President. The United States was an industrial nation of thirty-eight states, most of them west of the Alleghenies, and had just passed through the corruptions of the Grant administration and the Gilded Age.

Bryant was born into Puritan orthodoxies impressed upon him particularly by his Calvinistic grandfather; yet he became a Deist and, finally, a Unitarian. As a poet, he began with *The Embargo* (1808), in neoclassical heroic couplets that looked back to the influence of Addison, Pope, and Johnson; yet he became a romantic who wrote in blank verse and displayed the influence of Blair, Burns, Coleridge, Cowper, Gray, Thompson, Young, and—especially—Wordsworth. As a political thinker he was formed in the arch-Federalism of the household of his father, Dr. Peter Bryant. *The Embargo* espoused more than the literary conservatism of the thirteen-year-old William: it was a complete attack on Jefferson, Jeffersonianism, and Jefferson's foreign policies. Yet, twenty-one years later, when he became editor-in-chief of the New York *Evening Post*, his very position was a graphic indication of how far he and the nation had changed: Bryant used the *Evening Post*, founded by Alexander Hamilton, to espouse ideas that must have made Hamilton shudder in his grave. For Bryant championed free trade; the right of workingmen to form unions, bargain collectively, and strike; the destruction of debtor laws; the abolition of slavery; the Lincoln plan for reconstruction. He backed Andrew Jackson and the attack on the Bank of the United States; currency regulations that favored the have-nots; prison reforms. He broke party affiliations to endorse the Republicanism of Lincoln. As an editor, Bryant became a national figure in the traditions of native liberalism and elevated the *Evening Post* to a position of greatness in the history of American journalism. As America's first poet of high fame, Bryant shared a place in the contemporary literary trinity with Irving and Cooper. When opposition to his politics drove Cooper from his position of esteem, Bryant's *Evening Post* was the only New York newspaper that did not join in the attacks.

Bryant's approach to a poetic career was oblique. In 1809 he followed *The Embargo* with a second volume of juvenile poems. In 1810 he entered Williams College, but he had to withdraw after one year for lack of funds. So he read law. In 1815 he became a practicing lawyer in various western Massachusetts towns, particularly Great Barrington. In 1821 he married Fannie Fairchild; in that same year he published his first volume of *Poems*, the starting point from which American poetry came into its own. Bryant's father had sent William's poems to the influential *North American Review* in 1815, and among the manuscripts was the 1811 "Thanatopsis." R. H. Dana, Sr., and E. T. Channing were excitedly impressed, and hailed Bryant as the leading poetic genius of the nation. From 1816 until the publication of *Poems* the editorial board of the *Review* urged Bryant to turn his full attention to poetry.

A success as a writer, he moved to New York in 1825. Two years later he became an assistant editor of the *Evening Post* and editor-in-chief in 1829. Although he continued to produce many good poems, his poetic talent had come to its flowering in the New England nature experience gathered before 1825. His poetry in general is representative of America's literary emergence from the eighteenth century into the nineteenth. His public and poetic career made Bryant the contemporary dean of national poetry, rivaled in reputation in his later years only by Henry Wadsworth Longfellow.

Included in his bibliography are eight successive collections of *Poems* (1821, 1832, 1834, 1836, 1839, 1854, 1871, 1875); *The Fountain and Other Poems* (1842); *The White-Footed Deer and Other Poems* (1844); *Letters of a Traveller* (1850, Second Series, 1859); *A Discourse on . . . James Fenimore Cooper* (1852); *A Discourse on . . . Washington Irving* (1860); *Thirty Poems* (1864); *Letters from the East* (1869); and *The Flood of Years* (1878).

Editions and accounts of the man and his work are to be found in W. C. Bryant, ed., *The Poetical Works of William Cullen Bryant* (1876); G. W. Curtis, *The Life, Character, and Writings of William Cullen Bryant* (1879); P. Godwin, *A Biography of William Cullen Bryant*, 2 vols. (1883); P. Godwin, ed., *The Life and Works of William Cullen Bryant*, 6 vols. (1883–1884); J. Bigelow, *William Cullen Bryant* (1890); H. C. Sturges and R. H. Stoddard, eds., *The Poetical Works of William Cullen Bryant* (1903); W. A. Bradley, *William Cullen Bryant* (1905); N. Foerster, *Nature in American Literature* (1923); C. I. Glicksberg, "Bryant and the *United States Review*," *New England Quarterly*, VII (1934); G. W. Allen, *American Prosody* (1935); T. McDowell, "Bryant's Practice in Composition and Revision," *PMLA*, LII (1937); G. Arms, "William Cullen Bryant: A Respectable Station on Parnassus," *University of Kansas City Review*, XV (1949); H. H. Peckham, *Gothic Yankee* (1950); D. A. Ringe, "Bryant and Whitman: A Study in Artistic Affinities," *Boston University Studies in English*, II (1956); D. A. Ringe, "Bryant's Use of the American Past," *Papers of the Michigan Academy of Science, Arts and Letters*, LXI (1956); A. F. McLean, Jr., "Bryant's 'Thanatopsis': A Sermon in Stone," *American Literature*, XXXI (1960); C. Dahl, "Mound-Builders, Mormons, and William Cullen Bryant," *New England Quarterly*, XXXIV (1961); C. S. Curtiss, *Politics and a Belly-Full: Journalistic Career of William Cullen Bryant, Civil War Editor of the* New York Evening Post (1962); and A. F. McLean, Jr., *William Cullen Bryant* (1964).

Thanatopsis

To him who in the love of Nature holds
Communion with her visible forms, she speaks
A various language; for his gayer hours
She has a voice of gladness, and a smile
And eloquence of beauty, and she glides
Into his darker musings, with a mild
And healing sympathy, that steals away
Their sharpness, ere he is aware. When thoughts
Of the last bitter hour come like a blight
Over thy spirit, and sad images   10

Of the stern agony, and shroud, and pall,
And breathless darkness, and the narrow house,
Make thee to shudder, and grow sick at heart,—
Go forth, under the open sky, and list
To Nature's teachings, while from all around—
Earth and her waters, and the depths of air,—
Comes a still voice—

              Yet a few days, and thee
The all-beholding sun shall see no more
In all his course; nor yet in the cold ground,
Where thy pale form was laid, with many tears,   20
Nor in the embrace of ocean, shall exist
Thy image. Earth, that nourished thee, shall claim
Thy growth, to be resolved to earth again,
And, lost each human trace, surrendering up
Thine individual being, shalt thou go
To mix forever with the elements,
To be a brother to the insensible rock
And to the sluggish clod, which the rude swain
Turns with his share, and treads upon. The oak [share:
                              plowshare]
Shall send his roots abroad, and pierce thy mould.   30

    Yet not to thine eternal resting-place
Shalt thou retire alone, nor couldst thou wish
Couch more magnificent. Thou shalt lie down
With patriarchs of the infant world, with kings,
The powerful of the earth, the wise, the good,
Fair forms, and hoary seers of ages past,
All in one mighty sepulchre. The hills
Rock-ribbed and ancient as the sun, the vales
Stretching in pensive quietness between;
The venerable woods—rivers that move   40
In majesty, and the complaining brooks
That make the meadows green; and, poured round all,
Old Ocean's gray and melancholy waste,—
Are but the solemn decorations all
Of the great tomb of man. The golden sun,
The planets, all the infinite host of heaven,
Are shining on the sad abodes of death,
Through the still lapse of ages. All that tread
The globe are but a handful to the tribes
That slumber in its bosom.—Take the wings   50

Of morning, pierce the Barcan wilderness,
Or lose thyself in the continuous woods
Where rolls the Oregon, and hears no sound,
Save his own dashings—yet the dead are there:
And millions in those solitudes, since first
The flight of years began, have laid them down
In their last sleep—the dead reign there alone.
So shalt thou rest, and what if thou withdraw
In silence from the living, and no friend
Take note of thy departure? All that breathe   60
Will share thy destiny. The gay will laugh
When thou are gone, the solemn brood of care
Plod on, and each one as before will chase
His favorite phantom; yet all these shall leave
Their mirth and their employments, and shall come
And make their bed with thee. As the long train
Of ages glide away, the sons of men,
The youth in life's green spring, and he who goes
In the full strength of years, matron and maid,
The speechless babe, and the gray-headed man—   70
Shall one by one be gathered to thy side,
By those, who in their turn shall follow them.

So live, that when thy summons comes to join
The innumerable caravan, which moves
To that mysterious realm, where each shall take
His chamber in the silent halls of death,
Thou go not, like the quarry-slave at night,
Scourged to his dungeon, but, sustained and soothed
By an unfaltering trust, approach thy grave,
Like one who wraps the drapery of his couch   80
About him, and lies down to pleasant dreams.

w. 1811–1821
p. 1817, 1821

Inscription for the Entrance to a Wood

Stranger, if thou hast learned a truth which needs
No school of long experience, that the world
Is full of guilt and misery, and hast seen
Enough of all its sorrows, crimes, and cares
To tire thee of it, enter this wild wood

And view the haunts of Nature. The calm shade
Shall bring a kindred calm; and the sweet breeze,
That makes the green leaves dance, shall waft a balm
To thy sick heart. Thou wilt find nothing here
Of all that pained thee in the haunts of men   10
And made thee loathe thy life. The primal curse
Fell, it is true, upon the unsinning earth,
But not in vengeance. God hath yoked to guilt
Her pale tormentor, misery. Hence these shades
Are still the abodes of gladness: the thick roof
Of green and stirring branches is alive
And musical with birds, that sing and sport
In wantonness of spirit; while, below,
The squirrel, with raised paws and form erect,
Chirps merrily. Throngs of insects in the shade   20
Try their thin wings and dance in the warm beam
That waked them into life. Even the green trees
Partake the deep contentment; as they bend
To the soft winds, the sun from the blue sky
Looks in and sheds a blessing on the scene.
Scarce less the cleft-born wild-flower seems to enjoy
Existence than the wingèd plunderer
That sucks its sweets. The mossy rocks themselves,
And the old and ponderous trunks of prostrate trees
That lead from knoll to knoll a causey rude   30
Or bridge the sunken brook, and their dark roots,
With all their earth upon them, twisting high,
Breathe fixed tranquillity. The rivulet
Sends forth glad sounds, and, tripping o'er its bed
Of pebbly sands or leaping down the rocks,
Seems with continuous laughter to rejoice
In its own being. Softly tread the marge,
Lest from her midway perch thou scare the wren
That dips her bill in water. The cool wind,
That stirs the stream in play, shall come to thee,   40
Like one that loves thee nor will let thee pass
Ungreeted, and shall give its light embrace.

w. 1815
p. 1817

To a Waterfowl

Whither, 'midst falling dew,
While glow the heavens with the last steps of day,
Far, through their rosy depths, dost thou pursue
    Thy solitary way?

Vainly the fowler's eye
Might mark thy distant flight, to do thee wrong,
As, darkly seen against the crimson sky,
    Thy figure floats along.

Seek's thou the plashy brink
Of weedy lake, or marge of river wide,   10
Or where the rocking billows rise and sink
    On the chafed ocean side?

There is a Power, whose care
Teaches thy way along that pathless coast,—
The desert and illimitable air,
    Lone wandering, but not lost.

All day thy wings have fann'd,
At that far height, the cold thin atmosphere;
Yet stoop not, weary, to the welcome land,
    Though the dark night is near.   20

And soon that toil shall end,
Soon shalt thou find a summer home, and rest,
And scream among thy fellows; reeds shall bend,
    Soon, o'er thy sheltered nest.

Thou'rt gone, the abyss of heaven
Hath swallowed up thy form, yet, on my heart
Deeply hath sunk the lesson thou hast given,
    And shall not soon depart.

He, who, from zone to zone,
Guides through the boundless sky thy certain flight,   30

In the long way that I must trace alone,
    Will lead my steps aright.

w. 1815
p. 1818

The Yellow Violet

When beechen buds begin to swell,
    And woods the blue-bird's warble know,
The yellow violet's modest bell
    Peeps from the last year's leaves below.

Ere russet fields their green resume,
    Sweet flower, I love, in forest bare,
To meet thee, when thy faint perfume
    Alone is in the virgin air.

Of all her train, the hands of Spring
    First plant thee in the watery mould,   10
And I have seen thee blossoming
    Beside the snow-bank's edges cold.

Thy parent sun, who bade thee view
    Pale skies, and chilling moisture sip,
Has bathed thee in his own bright hue,
    And streaked with jet thy glowing lip.

Yet slight thy form, and low thy seat,
    And earthward bent thy gentle eye,
Unapt the passing view to meet
    When loftier flowers are flaunting nigh.   20

Oft, in the sunless April day,
    Thy early smile has stayed my walk;
But midst the gorgeous blooms of May,
    I passed thee on thy humble stalk.

So they, who climb to wealth, forget
    The friends in darker fortunes tried.
I copied them—but I regret
    That I should ape the ways of pride.

And when again the genial hour
   Awakes the painted tribes of light,   30
I'll not o'erlook the modest flower
   That made the woods of April bright.

w. 1814
p. 1821

A Forest Hymn

The groves were God's first temples. Ere man learned
To hew the shaft, and lay the architrave,
And spread the roof above them—ere he framed
The lofty vault, to gather and roll back
The sound of anthems; in the darkling wood,
Amid the cool and silence, he knelt down,
And offered to the Mightiest solemn thanks
And supplication. For his simple heart
Might not resist the sacred influence
Which, from the stilly twilight of the place,   10
And from the gray old trunks that high in heaven
Mingled their mossy boughs, and from the sound
Of the invisible breath that swayed at once
All their green tops, stole over him, and bowed
His spirit with the thought of boundless power
And inaccessible majesty. Ah, why
Should we, in the world's riper years, neglect
God's ancient sanctuaries, and adore
Only among the crowd, and under roofs
That our frail hands have raised? Let me, at least,   20
Here, in the shadow of this aged wood,
Offer one hymn—thrice happy, if it find
Acceptance in His ear.

                  Father, thy hand
Hath reared these venerable columns, thou
Didst weave this verdant roof. Thou didst look down
Upon the naked earth, and forthwith, rose
All these fair ranks of trees. They, in thy sun,
Budded, and shook their green leaves in thy breeze,
And shot toward heaven. The century-living crow
Whose birth was in their tops, grew old and died   30
Among their branches, till at last they stood,

As now they stand, massy and tall and dark,
Fit shrine for humble worshipper to hold
Communion with his Maker. These dim vaults,
These winding isles, of human pomp or pride
Report not; no fantastic carvings show
The boast of our vain race to change the form
Of thy fair works. But thou art here—thou fill'st
The solitude. Thou art in the soft winds,
That run along the summit of these trees   40
In music; thou art in the cooler breath,
That from the inmost darkness of the place,
Comes, scarcely felt; the barky trunks, the ground,
The fresh moist ground, are all instinct with thee.
Here is continual worship: Nature, here,
In the tranquillity that thou dost love,
Enjoys thy presence. Noiselessly around,
From perch to perch, the solitary bird
Passes; and yon clear spring, that midst its herbs
Wells softly forth and, wandering, steeps the roots   50
Of half the mighty forest, tells no tale
Of all the good it does. Thou hast not left
Thyself without a witness, in the shades,
Of thy perfections. Grandeur, strength, and grace
Are here to speak of thee. This mighty oak,
By whose immovable stem I stand and seem
Almost annihilated—not a prince,
In all that proud old world beyond the deep,
E'er wore his crown as loftily as he
Wears the green coronal of leaves with which   60
Thy hand has graced him. Nestled at his root
Is beauty such as blooms not in the glare
Of the broad sun: that delicate forest flower,
With scented breath and look so like a smile,
Seems, as it issues from the shapeless mould,
An emanation of the indwelling Life,
A visible token of the upholding Love,
That are the soul of this great universe.

My heart is awed within me when I think
Of the great miracle that still goes on,   70
In silence, round me—the perpetual work
Of thy creation, finished, yet renewed
Forever. Written on thy works I read

The lesson of thy own eternity:
Lo, all grow old and die; but see, again,
How on the faltering footsteps of decay
Youth presses, ever gay and beautiful youth
In all its beautiful forms. These lofty trees
Wave not less proudly that their ancestors
Moulder beneath them. Oh, there is not lost   80
One of earth's charms: upon her bosom yet,
After the flight of untold centuries,
The freshness of her far beginning lies
And yet shall lie. Life mocks the idle hate
Of his arch-enemy, Death; yea, seats himself
Upon the tyrant's throne, the sepulchre,
And of the triumphs of his ghastly foe
Makes his own nourishment; for he came forth
From thine own bosom, and shall have no end.

There have been holy men who hid themselves   90
Deep in the woody wilderness, and gave
Their lives to thought and prayer, till they outlived
The generation born with them, nor seemed
Less aged than the hoary trees and rocks
Around them; and there have been holy men
Who deemed it were not well to pass life thus.
But let me often to these solitudes
Retire, and in thy presence reassure
My feeble virtue. Here its enemies,
The passions, at thy plainer footsteps shrink   100
And tremble and are still. O God! when thou
Dost scare the world with tempests, set on fire
The heavens with falling thunderbolts, or fill
With all the waters of the firmament
The swift dark whirlwind that uproots the woods
And drowns the villages; when, at thy call,
Uprises the great deep and throws himself
Upon the continent and overwhelms
Its cities; who forgets not, at the sight
Of these tremendous tokens of thy power,   110
His pride, and lays his strifes and follies by?
Oh, from these sterner aspects of thy face
Spare me and mine, nor let us need the wrath
Of the mad unchained elements to teach
Who rules them. Be it ours to meditate

In these calm shades thy milder majesty,
And to the beautiful order of thy works
Learn to conform the order of our lives.

1825

To the Fringed Gentian

Thou blossom bright with autumn dew,
And colored with the heaven's own blue,
That openest when the quiet light
Succeeds the keen and frosty night—

Thou comest not when violets lean
O'er wandering brooks and springs unseen,
Or columbines, in purple dressed,
Nod o'er the ground-bird's hidden nest.

Thou waitest late and com'st alone,
When woods are bare and birds are flown,   10
And frosts and shortening days portend
The aged year is near his end.

Then doth thy sweet and quiet eye
Look through its fringes to the sky,
Blue—blue—as if that sky let fall
A flower from its cerulean wall.

I would that thus, when I shall see
The hour of death draw near to me,
Hope, blossoming within my heart,
May look to heaven as I depart.   20

w. 1829
p. 1832

The Prairies

These are the gardens of the Desert, these
The unshorn fields, boundless and beautiful,
For which the speech of England has no name—
The Prairies. I behold them for the first,
And my heart swells, while the dilated sight

Takes in the encircling vastness. Lo! they stretch
In airy undulations, far away,
As if the Ocean, in his gentlest swell,
Stood still, with all his rounded billows fixed,
And motionless forever. Motionless?—   10
No—they are all unchained again. The clouds
Sweep over with their shadows, and, beneath,
The surface rolls and fluctuates to the eye;
Dark hollows seem to glide along and chase
The sunny ridges. Breezes of the South!
Who toss the golden and the flame-like flowers,
And pass the prairie-hawk that, poised on high,
Flaps his broad wings, yet moves not—ye have played
Among the palms of Mexico and vines
Of Texas, and have crisped the limpid brooks   20
That from the fountains of Sonora glide
Into the calm Pacific—have ye fanned
A nobler or a lovelier scene than this?
Man hath no part in all this glorious work:
The hand that built the firmament hath heaved
And smoothed these verdant swells, and sown their slopes
With herbage, planted them with island-groves,
And hedged them round with forests. Fitting floor
For this magnificent temple of the sky—
With flowers whose glory and whose multitude   30
Rival the constellations! The great heavens
Seem to stoop down upon the scene in love,—
A nearer vault, and of a tenderer blue,
Than that which bends above our Eastern hills.

As o'er the verdant waste I guide my steed,
Among the high rank grass that sweeps his sides
The hollow beating of his footstep seems
A sacrilegious sound. I think of those
Upon whose rest he tramples. Are they here—
The dead of other days?—and did the dust   40
Of these fair solitudes once stir with life
And burn with passion? Let the mighty mounds
That overlook the rivers, or that rise
In the dim forest crowded with old oaks,
Answer. A race, that long has passed away,
Built them; a disciplined and populous race
Heaped, with long toil, the earth, while yet the Greek

Was hewing the Pentelicus to forms
Of symmetry, and rearing on its rock
The glittering Parthenon. These ample fields   50
Nourished their harvests, here their herds were fed,
When haply by their stalls the bison lowed,
And bowed his manèd shoulder to the yoke.
All day this desert murmured with their toils,
Till twilight blushed, and lovers walked, and wooed
In a forgotten language, and old tunes,
From instruments of unremembered form,
Gave the soft winds a voice. The red-man came—
The roaming hunter-tribes, warlike and fierce,
And the mound-builders vanished from the earth.   60
The solitude of centuries untold
Has settled where they dwelt. The prairie-wolf
Hunts in their meadows, and his fresh-dug den
Yawns by my path. The gopher mines the ground
Where stood their swarming cities. All is gone;
All—save the piles of earth that hold their bones,
The platforms where they worshipped unknown gods,
The barriers which they builded from the soil
To keep the foe at bay—till o'er the walls
The wild beleaguers broke, and, one by one,   70
The strongholds of the plain were forced, and heaped
With corpses. The brown vultures of the wood
Flocked to those vast uncovered sepulchres,
And sat, unscared and silent, at their feast.
Haply some solitary fugitive,
Lurking in marsh and forest, till the sense
Of desolation and of fear became
Bitterer than death, yielded himself to die.
Man's better nature triumphed then. Kind words
Welcomed and soothed him; the rude conquerors   80
Seated the captive with their chiefs; he chose
A bride among their maidens, and at length
Seemed to forget—yet ne'er forgot—the wife
Of his first love, and her sweet little ones,
Butchered, amid their shrieks, with all his race.

Thus change the forms of being. Thus arise
Races of living things, glorious in strength,
And perish, as the quickening breath of God
Fills them, or is withdrawn. The red-man, too,

Has left the blooming wilds he ranged so long,   90
And, nearer to the Rocky Mountains, sought
A wilder hunting-ground. The beaver builds
No longer by these streams, but far away,
On waters whose blue surface ne'er gave back
The white man's face—among Missouri's Springs,
And pools whose issues swell the Oregon—
He rears his little Venice. In these plains
The bison feeds no more. Twice twenty leagues
Beyond remotest smoke of hunter's camp,
Roams the majestic brute, in herds that shake   100
The earth with thundering steps—yet here I meet
His ancient footprints stamped beside the pool.

  Still this great solitude is quick with life.
Myriads of insects, gaudy as the flowers
They flutter over, gentle quadrupeds,
And birds, that scarce have learned the fear of man,
Are here, and sliding reptiles of the ground,
Startlingly beautiful. The graceful deer
Bounds to the wood at my approach. The bee,
A more adventurous colonist than man,   110
With whom he came across the eastern deep,
Fills the savannas with his murmurings,
And hides his sweets, as in the golden age,
Within the hollow oak. I listen long
To his domestic hum, and think I hear
The sound of that advancing multitude
Which soon shall fill these deserts. From the ground
Comes up the laugh of children, the soft voice
Of maidens, and the sweet and solemn hymn
Of Sabbath worshippers. The low of herds   120
Blends with the rustling of the heavy grain
Over the dark brown furrows. All at once
A fresher wind sweeps by, and breaks my dream,
And I am in the wilderness alone.

                                                   1833

EDGAR ALLAN POE

(1809–1849)

Poe's life is a fantastic study in insecurity, instability, frustration, and failure. He was born in Boston to David and Elizabeth Poe, traveling actors. When Edgar was one year old, his father disappeared; when he was two, his mother died in Richmond, Virginia. He was taken into the household (though never legally adopted) of John Allan, a wealthy Richmond tobacco merchant. Allan, an unfaithful husband, came to resent the attentions that his childless wife showered upon the boy. Allan's resentments, coupled with Poe's difficult nature, grew into constant antagonisms that served to feed Edgar's insecurities and yearnings. As an unadopted orphan dependent upon the will and favor of Allan, he was brought up with all the advantages of a rich young gentleman of Virginia but with none of the future expectation of a way of life to which he was so tantalizingly introduced.

From 1815 to 1820 he traveled in Europe with the Allans and attended the Stoke Newington school in England for three years. The possibilities opened by superior education only teased Poe's feelings of rejection, which became conscious by 1820, the year he was entered in the Richmond Academy. He was doomed never to find an emotionally secure acceptance by others. Once he found sympathy in Jane Stanard (the Helen of "To Helen"), the mother of a school chum, but she died in 1824. Once he found love in Sarah Elmira Royster, but opposition by her parents forced him to give her up and she married someone else. In February, 1826, Allan entered him in the University of Virginia, where Poe displayed high promise. In December, 1826, Allan withdrew him from the University for drinking and gambling debts. After a bitter quarrel, Poe left Allan's house, went to Boston, published *Tamerlane and Other Poems* (1827), and joined the army as Edgar A. Perry. Having reached the rank of sergeant-major (master sergeant), Poe resigned from the army in 1829, the year of Mrs. Allan's death, and published *Al Aaraaf, Tamerlane, and Other Poems.* Yearning for an identity as a poet, Poe was disappointed by the slight recognition won by both volumes—the disappointment was the story of his life. In 1830 he entered West Point with the support of Allan, with whom after Mrs. Allan's death, he had been temporarily reconciled. Not finding what he wished at West Point, he deliberately got himself dismissed for neglect of duty in 1831.

Turning to his relatives, Mrs. Maria Clemm and her daughter Virginia, he moved to their residence in Baltimore in 1831 and published a third volume of *Poems*: again, no acclaim. Forced to earn a living with his pen, he turned deliberately to the short story in order to emulate and satirize the popular tale of terror and cash in on its popularity. In 1832 he published five tales in the Philadelphia *Saturday Courier;* and when John Allan died in 1833, cutting him off from any expectations of financial help, Poe found himself committed to a career as a commercial writer. In that same year he won some of the small income he was to earn from literature (he suffered all the rest of his life from terrible and destructive poverty) with a $100 prize from the Baltimore *Saturday Visitor* for "Ms. Found in a Bottle." One of the judges, the writer John Pendleton Kennedy (1795–1870), obtained for Poe a job with the influential *Southern Literary Messenger.* As editor from 1835 to 1837, Poe began to write the biting attacks on second-rate literature that were to gain for him a wide reputation (but no money) as the leading critic and journalist of his day.

In 1836 he married his thirteen-year-old cousin, Virginia, and a year later he resigned from the *Messenger* because of insufficient pay and quarrels with the publishers. He moved to New York, where the hack work to which need forced him brought him no success, and then, in 1838, to Philadelphia. There he published *The Narrative of Arthur Gordon Pym* (1838; no recognition); worked on Burton's *Gentleman's Magazine* (1839); published *Tales of the Grotesque and Arabesque* (1840; no recognition); edited *Graham's Magazine* (1841–1842); worked on the *Saturday Museum* (1843); and won another $100 prize for "The Gold Bug" (1843), published in the Philadelphia

Dollar Newspaper. Unable to hold his position because of undependability—and, sometimes, drink, to which his failure and financial miseries occasionally drove him—he moved back to New York in 1844. There he worked on the New York *Evening Mirror* of the successful writer, N. P. Willis (1806–1867). His pitifully small wages rendered him incapable of helping Virginia in her losing battle with tuberculosis: there were times, indeed, when Poe did not have the money for firewood to keep her warm. Some measure of success came with the publication in 1845 of "The Raven," which won him wide popular acclaim—and no money. Finally he had the chance to publish his own magazine, *The Broadway Journal*, in 1845, but in two years it failed. When Virginia died in 1846, Poe went to pieces, entering a delirium of drink and delusive searches for female love and understanding. He did not even succeed in his suicide attempt of 1848.

Having discovered that his former sweetheart, Sarah Royster, was widowed and living in Richmond, he visited her to re-create old ties. On October 7, 1849, on his return from Richmond, he died rather mysteriously. Yet even then trouble did not desert his name. His literary executor, the Reverend Rufus Griswold, vented his dislike of the dead man in a series of distortions of Poe's character. The reverend gentleman turned out to be an excellent liar, whose combination of truths, half-truths, and lies created the famous image of Poe as a psychological and moral monster escaped from one of his own horror tales. It is not hard to see why Poe's work, culminating in *Eureka* (1848), attempted to create a transcendent world of unity and ultimate beauty which the poetic imagination could reach by destroying the hostile reality of the actual world, with its imperfect sympathies and its cold insufficiencies.

Some of Poe's works, in addition to those mentioned above, are *The Murders in the Rue Morgue and the Man that Was Used Up* (1843); *The Raven and other Poems* (1845); and *Tales* (1845).

Editions and accounts of the man and his works are to be found in E. C. Stedman and G. E. Woodberry, eds., *The Works of Edgar Allan Poe*, 10 vols. (1894–1895); G. E. Woodberry, *The Life of Edgar Allan Poe*, 2 vols. (1909); K. Campbell, *The Poems of Edgar Allan Poe* (1917); M. Alterton, *The Origins of Poe's Critical Theory* (1925); H. Allen, *Israfel*, 2 vols. (1926); J. W. Krutch, *Edgar Allan Poe* (1926); M. E. Phillips, *Edgar Allan Poe*, 2 vols. (1926); K. Campbell, *The Mind of Poe* (1933); J. W. Robertson, *A Bibliography of the Writings of Edgar A. Poe*, 2 vols. (1934); A. H. Quinn, *Edgar Allan Poe* (1941); T. S. Eliot, *From Poe to Valéry* (1948); J. Ostrom, ed.,

The Letters of Edgar Allan Poe, 2 vols. (1948) and two sup-
plements published in *American Literature*, XXIV (1952), and
XXIX (1957); N. B. Fagin, *The Histrionic Mr. Poe* (1949); M.
Bonaparte, *The Life and Works of Edgar Allan Poe* (1949);
H. Braddy, *Glorious Incense: The Fulfillment of Edgar Allan
Poe* (1953); A. Tate, *The Forlorn Demon* (1953); P. Miller,
The Raven and the Whale (1956); E. H. Davidson, *Poe: A
Critical Study* (1957); P. Quinn, *The French Face of Edgar
Allan Poe* (1957); H. Levin, *The Power of Blackness* (1958);
D. M. Rein, *Edgar A. Poe: The Inner Pattern* (1960); W. E.
Bezanson, "The Troubled Sleep of Arthur Gordon Pym," *Es-
says in Literary History Presented to J. Milton French*, R. Kirk
and C. F. Main, eds. (1961); V. Buranelli, *Edgar Allan Poe*
(1961); E. R. Marks, "Poe as Literary Theorist: A Reappraisal,"
American Literature, XXXIII (1961); W. Bittner, *Poe: A Biog-
raphy* (1962); S. L. Mooney, "Poe's Gothic Waste Land,"
Sewanee Review, LXX (1962); S. P. Moss, *Poe's Literary Bat-
tles: The Critic in Context of His Literary Milieu* (1963); I.
Porges, *Edgar Allan Poe* (1963); E. Wagenknecht, *Edgar Allan Poe: The Man Behind the Legend* (1963); E. Parks, *Edgar
Allan Poe as Literary Critic* (1964); R. L. Hough, ed., *Literary
Criticism of Edgar Allan Poe* (1965); G. Rans, *Edgar Allan Poe*
(1965); F. Stoval, ed., *Poems* (1965); E. Carlson, ed., *The
Recognition of Edgar Allan Poe* (1966); and T. Martin, "The
Imagination at Play: Edgar Allan Poe," *Kenyon Review*, XXVIII
(1966). *The Portable Poe* (1945), edited and with a critical and
biographical introduction by P. V. D. Stern, contains stories,
poems, criticism, and letters.

Dreams

Oh! that my life were a lasting dream!
My spirit not awak'ning till the beam
Of an Eternity should bring the morrow.
Yes! tho' that long dream were of hopeless sorrow,
'T were better than the cold reality
Of waking life, to him whose heart must be,
And hath been still, upon the lovely earth,
A chaos of deep passion, from his birth.
But should it be—that dream eternally
Continuing—as dreams have been to me   10
In my young boyhood—should it thus be giv'n,
'T were folly still to hope for higher Heav'n.
For I have revell'd, when the sun was bright
I' the summer sky, in dreams of living light
And loveliness,—have left my very heart
In climes of mine imagining, apart

From mine own home, with beings that have been
Of mine own thought—what more could I have seen?
'T was once—and only once—and the wild hour
From my remembrance shall not pass—some pow'r   20
Or spell had bound me—'t was the chilly wind
Came o'er me in the night, and left behind
Its image on my spirit—or the moon
Shone on my slumbers in her lofty noon
Too coldly—or the stars—howe'er it was,
That dream was as that night-wind—let it pass.

I *have been happy*, tho' but in a dream.
I have been happy—and I love the theme:
Dreams! in their vivid coloring of life,
As in that fleeting, shadowy, misty strife   30
Of semblance with reality which brings
To the delirious eye, more lovely things
Of Paradise and Love—and all our own!
Than young Hope in his sunniest hour hath known.   1827

Romance

Romance, who loves to nod and sing,
With drowsy head and folded wing,
Among the green leaves as they shake
Far down within some shadowy lake,
To me a painted paroquet
Hath been—a most familiar bird—
Taught me my alphabet to say,
To lisp my very earliest word,
While in the wild wood I did lie,
A child—with a most knowing eye.   10

Of late, eternal Condor years
So shake the very Heaven on high
With tumult as they thunder by,
I have no time for idle cares
Through gazing on the unquiet sky.
And when an hour with calmer wings
Its down upon my spirit flings—
That little time with lyre and rhyme
To while away—forbidden things!

My heart would feel to be a crime   20
Unless it trembled with the strings.   1829

Sonnet—To Science

Science! true daughter of Old Time thou art!
    Who alterest all things with thy peering eyes.
Why preyest thou thus upon the poet's heart,
    Vulture, whose wings are dull realities?
How should he love thee? or how deem thee wise?
    Who wouldst not leave him in his wandering
To seek for treasure in the jewelled skies,
    Albeit he soared with an undaunted wing.
Hast thou not dragged Diana from her car?
    And driven the Hamadryad from the wood   10
To seek a shelter in some happier star?
    Hast thou not torn the Naiad from her flood,
The Elfin from the green grass, and from me
The summer dream beneath the tamarind tree?   1829

Song from Al Aaraaf

" 'Neath blue-bell or streamer—
    Or tufted wild spray
That keeps from the dreamer
    The moonbeam away—
Bright beings! that ponder,
    With half closing eyes,
On the stars which your wonder
    Hath drawn from the skies,
Till they glance thro' the shade, and
    Come down to your brow   10
Like—eyes of the maiden
    Who calls on you now—
Arise! from your dreaming
    In violet bowers,
To duty beseeming
    These star-litten hours—
And shake from your tresses
    Encumber'd with dew
The breath of those kisses
    That cumber them too—   20

(O! how, without you, Love!
  Could angels be blest?)
Those kisses of true love
  That lull'd ye to rest!
Up!—shake from your wing
  Each hindering thing:
The dew of the night—
  It would weight down your flight;
And true love caresses—
  O! leave them apart: 30
They are light on the tresses,
  But lead on the heart.

"Ligeia! Ligeia!
  My beautiful one!
Whose harshest idea
  Will to melody run,
O! is it thy will
  On the breezes to toss?
Or, capriciously still,
  Like the lone Albatross,   40
Incumbent on night
  (As she on the air)
To keep watch with delight
  On the harmony there?

"Ligeia! wherever
  Thy image may be,
No magic shall sever
  Thy music from thee.
Thou hast bound many eyes
  In a dreamy sleep—   50
But the strains still arise
  Which *thy* vigilance keep:
The sound of the rain
  Which leaps down to the flower,
And dances again
  In the rhythm of the shower—
The murmur that springs
  From the growing of grass
Are the music of things—
  But are modell'd, alas!—   60

Away, then, my dearest,
  O! hie thee away
To springs that lie clearest
  Beneath the moon-ray—
To lone lake that smiles,
  In its dream of deep rest,
At the many star-isles
  That enjewel its breast—
Where wild flowers, creeping,
  Have mingled their shade,   70
On its margin is sleeping
  Full many a maid—
Some have left the cool glade, and
  Have slept with the bee—
Arouse them, my maiden,
  On moorland and lea—
Go! breathe on their slumber,
  All softly in ear,
The musical number
  They slumber'd to hear—   80
For what can awaken
  An angel so soon,
Whose sleep hath been taken
  Beneath the cold moon,
As the spell which no slumber
  Of witchery may test,
The rhythmical number
  Which lull'd him to rest?"

                           1829

A Dream Within a Dream

Take this kiss upon the brow!
And, in parting from you now,
Thus much let me avow—
You are not wrong, who deem
That my days have been a dream;
Yet if hope has flown away
In a night, or in a day,
In a vision, or in none,
Is it therefore the less *gone?*

All that we see or seem 10
Is but a dream within a dream.

I stand amid the roar
Of a surf-tormented shore,
And I hold within my hand
Grains of the golden sand—
How few! yet how they creep
Through my fingers to the deep,
While I weep—while I weep!
O God! can I not grasp
Them with a tighter clasp? 20
O God! can I not save
One from the pitiless wave?
Is *all* that we see or seem
But a dream within a dream?

1827, 1829, 1849

To Helen

Helen, thy beauty is to me
    Like those Nicéan barks of yore,
That gently, o'er a perfumed sea,
    The weary, way-worn wanderer bore
    To his own native shore.

On desperate seas long wont to roam,
    Thy hyacinth hair, thy classic face,
Thy Naiad airs have brought me home
    To the glory that was Greece,
And the grandeur that was Rome. 10

Lo! in yon brilliant window-niche
    How statue-like I see thee stand,
    The agate lamp within thy hand!
Ah, Psyche, from the regions which
    Are Holy Land!

1831

Israfel

*"And the angel Israfel, whose heart-strings are a lute,
and who has the sweetest voice of all God's creatures."*
                                                  —*Koran*

In Heaven a spirit doth dwell
    "Whose heart-strings are a lute";
None sing so wildly well
As the angel Israfel,
And the giddy stars (so legends tell),
Ceasing their hymns, attend the spell
    Of his voice, all mute.

Tottering above
    In her highest noon,
    The enamored moon   10
Blushes with love,
    While, to listen, the red levin
    (With the rapid Pleiads, even,
    Which were seven,)
    Pauses in Heaven.

And they say (the starry choir
    And the other listening things)
That Israfeli's fire
Is owing to that lyre
    By which he sits and sings—   20
The trembling living wire
    Of those unusual strings.

But the skies that angel trod,
    Where deep thoughts are a duty,
Where Love's grown-up God,
    Where the Houri glances are
Imbued with all the beauty
    Which we worship in a star.

Therefore, thou art not wrong,
    Israfeli, who despisest   30
An unimpassioned song;

To thee the laurels belong,
　　Best bard, because the wisest!
Merrily live, and long!

The ecstasies above
　　With thy burning measures suit—
Thy grief, thy joy, thy hate, thy love,
　　With the fervor of thy lute—
　　Well may the stars be mute!

Yes, Heaven is thine; but this　　　　　　　　　　40
　　Is a world of sweets and sours;
　　Our flowers are merely—flowers,
And the shadow of thy perfect bliss
　　Is the sunshine of ours.

If I could dwell
Where Israfel
　　Hath dwelt, and he where I,
He might not sing so wildly well
　　A mortal melody,
While a bolder note than this might swell　　　　50
　　From my lyre within the sky.

　　　　　　　　　　　　　　　　　　　　1831

The City in the Sea

Lo! Death has reared himself a throne
In a strange city lying alone
Far down within the dim West,
Where the good and the bad and the worst and the best
Have gone to their eternal rest.
There shrines and palaces and towers
(Time-eaten towers that tremble not!)
Resemble nothing that is ours.
Around, by lifting winds forgot,
Resignedly beneath the sky　　　　　　　　　　10
The melancholy waters lie.

No rays from the holy heaven come down
On the long night-time of that town;
But light from out the lurid sea

Streams up the turrets silently—
Gleams up the pinnacles far and free—
Up domes—up spires—up kingly halls—
Up fanes—up Babylon-like walls—
Up shadowy long-forgotten bowers
Of sculptured ivy and stone flowers—   20
Up many and many a marvellous shrine
Whose wreathèd friezes intertwine
The viol, the violet, and the vine.
Resignedly beneath the sky
The melancholy waters lie.
So blend the turrets and shadows there
That all seem pendulous in air,
While from a proud tower in the town
Death looks gigantically down.

There open fanes and gaping graves   30
Yawn level with the luminous waves;
But not the riches there that lie
In each idol's diamond eye—
Not the gaily-jewelled dead
Tempt the waters from their bed;
For no ripples curl, alas!
Along that wilderness of glass—
No swellings tell that winds may be
Upon some far-off happier sea—
No heavings hint that winds have been   40
On seas less hideously serene.

But lo, a stir is in the air!
The wave—there is a movement there!
As if the towers had thrust aside,
In slightly sinking, the dull tide—
As if their tops had feebly given
A void within the filmy Heaven.
The waves have now a redder glow—
The hours are breathing faint and low—
And when, amid no earthly moans,   50
Down, down that town shall settle hence,
Hell, rising from a thousand thrones,
Shall do it reverence.

1831

Lenore

Ah, broken is the golden bowl!—the spirit flown forever!
Let the bell toll!—a saintly soul floats on the Stygian
river:—
And, Guy De Vere, hast *thou* no tear?—weep now or never
more!
See! on yon drear and rigid bier low lies thy love, Lenore!
Come, let the burial rite be read—the funeral song be
sung!—
An anthem for the queenliest dead that ever died so
young—
A dirge for her the doubly dead in that she died so young.

"Wretches! ye loved her for her wealth, and ye hated her
for her pride;
And, when she fell in feeble health, ye blessed her—that
she died:—
How *shall* the ritual, then, be read—the requiem how be
sung   10
By you—by yours, the evil eye,—by yours, the slanderous
tongue
That did to death the innocence that died, and died so
young?"

Peccavimus; yet rave not thus! but let a Sabbath song [Pec-
cavimus: we have sinned]
Go up to God so solemnly the dead may feel no wrong!
The sweet Lenore hath gone before, with Hope that flew
beside,
Leaving thee wild for the dear child that should have been
thy bride—
For her, the fair and debonair, that now so lowly lies,
The life upon her yellow hair, but not within her eyes—
The life still there upon her hair, the death upon her eyes.

"Avaunt!—avaunt! to friends from fiends the indignant
ghost is riven—   20
From Hell unto a high estate within the utmost Heaven—

From moan and groan to a golden throne beside the King
　　of Heaven:—
Let *no* bell toll, then, lest her soul, amid its hallowed mirth,
Should catch the note as it doth float up from the damnèd
　　Earth!
And I—to-night my heart is light:—no dirge will I upraise,
But waft the angel on her flight with a Pæan of old days!"
　　　　　　　　　　　　　　　　　　　　　　　1831

The Sleeper

At midnight, in the month of June,
I stand beneath the mystic moon.
An opiate vapor, dewy, dim,
Exhales from out her golden rim,
And, softly dripping, drop by drop,
Upon the quiet mountain top,
Steals drowsily and musically
Into the universal valley.
The rosemary nods upon the grave;
The lily lolls upon the wave;　　　　　　　　　　　　　　10
Wrapping the fog about its breast,
The ruin moulders into rest;
Looking like Lethe, see! the lake
A conscious slumber seems to take,
And would not, for the world, awake.
All Beauty sleeps!—and lo! where lies
Irene, with her Destinies!

Oh, lady bright! can it be right—
This window open to the night?
The wanton airs, from the tree-top,　　　　　　　　　　20
Laughingly through the lattice drop—
The bodiless airs, a wizard rout,
Flit through thy chamber in and out,
And wave the curtain canopy
So fitfully—so fearfully—
Above the close and fringèd lid
'Neath which thy slumb'ring soul lies hid,
That, o'er the floor and down the wall,
Like ghosts the shadows rise and fall!

Oh, lady dear, hast thou no fear?   30
Why and what art thou dreaming here?
Sure thou art come o'er far-off seas,
A wonder to these garden trees!
Strange is thy pallor! strange thy dress!
Strange, above all, thy length of tress,
And this all solemn silentness!

The lady sleeps! Oh, may her sleep,
Which is enduring, so be deep!
Heaven have her in its sacred keep!
This chamber changed for one more holy,   40
This bed for one more melancholy,
I pray to God that she may lie
Forever with unopened eye,
While the pale sheeted ghosts go by!

My love, she sleeps! Oh, may her sleep,
As it is lasting, so be deep!
Soft may the worms about her creep!
Far in the forest, dim and old,
For her may some tall vault unfold—
Some vault that oft hath flung its black   50
And wingéd panels fluttering back,
Triumphant, o'er the crested palls,
Of her grand family funerals—

Some sepulchre, remote, alone,
Against whose portal she hath thrown,
In childhood, many an idle stone—
Some tomb from out whose sounding door
She ne'er shall force an echo more,
Thrilling to think, poor child of sin!
It was the dead who groaned within.   60

                                               1831

To One in Paradise

Thou wast that all to me, love,
  For which my soul did pine—
A green isle in the sea, love,
  A fountain and a shrine,

All wreathed with fairy fruits and flowers,
   And all the flowers were mine.

Ah, dream too bright to last!
   Ah, starry Hope! that didst arise
But to be overcast!
A voice from out the Future cries,   10
   "On! on!"—but o'er the Past
      (Dim gulf!) my spirit hovering lies
Mute, motionless, aghast!

For, alas! alas! with me
   The light of Life is o'er!
No more—no more—no more—
   (Such language holds the solemn sea
To the sands upon the shore)
   Shall bloom the thunder-blasted tree,
Or the stricken eagle soar!   20

And all my days are trances,
   And all my nightly dreams
Are where thy grey eye glances,
   And where thy footstep gleams—
In what ethereal dances,
   By what eternal streams.

                                                    1834

Sonnet—Silence

There are some qualities—some incorporate things,
   That have a double life, which thus is made
A type of that twin entity which springs
   From matter and light, evinced in solid and shade.
There is a two-fold *Silence*—sea and shore—
   Body and soul. One dwells in lonely places,
   Newly with grass o'ergrown; some solemn graces,
Some human memories and tearful lore,
Render him terrorless: his name's "No More."
He is the corporate Silence: dread him not!   10
   No power hath he of evil in himself;
But should some urgent fate (untimely lot!)
   Bring thee to meet his shadow (nameless elf,

That haunteth the lone regions where hath trod
Not foot of man), commend thyself to God!

1840

Dream-Land

By a route obscure and lonely,
Haunted by ill angels only,
Where an Eidolon, named NIGHT,
On a black throne reigns upright,
I have reached these lands but newly
From an ultimate dim Thule—
From a wild weird clime that lieth, sublime,
    Out of SPACE—out of TIME.

Bottomless vales and boundless floods,
And chasms, and caves, and Titan woods,   10
With forms that no man can discover
For the tears that drip all over;
Mountains toppling evermore
Into seas without a shore;
Seas that restlessly aspire,
Surging, unto skies of fire;
Lakes that endlessly outspread
Their lone waters—lone and dead,—
Their still waters—still and chilly
With the snows of the lolling lily.   20

By the lakes that thus outspread
Their lone waters, lone and dead,—
Their sad waters, sad and chilly
With the snows of the lolling lily,—

By the mountains—near the river
Murmuring lowly, murmuring ever,—
By the grey woods,—by the swamp
Where the toad and the newt encamp,—
By the dismal tarns and pools
    Where dwell the Ghouls,—   30
By each spot the most unholy—
In each nook most melancholy,—
There the traveller meets, aghast,

Sheeted Memories of the Past—
Shrouded forms that start and sigh
As they pass the wanderer by—
White-robed forms of friends long given,
In agony, to the Earth—and Heaven.

For the heart whose woes are legion
'Tis a peaceful, soothing region—   40
For the spirit that walks in shadow
'Tis—oh 'tis an Eldorado!
But the traveller, travelling through it,
May not—dare not openly view it;
Never its mysteries are exposed
To the weak human eye unclosed;
So wills its King, who hath forbid
The uplifting of the fringéd lid;
And thus the sad Soul that here passes
Beholds it but through darkened glasses.   50

By a route obscure and lonely,
Haunted by ill angels only,
Where an Eidolon, named NIGHT,
On a black throne reigns upright,
I have wandered home but newly
From this ultimate dim Thule.

                                        1844

The Raven

Once upon a midnight dreary, while I pondered, weak and
    weary,
Over many a quaint and curious volume of forgotten
    lore—
While I nodded, nearly napping, suddenly there came a
    tapping,
As of some one gently rapping, rapping at my chamber
    door.
" 'Tis some visitor," I muttered, "tapping at my chamber
    door—
    Only this and nothing more."

Ah, distinctly I remember it was in the bleak December;
And each separate dying ember wrought its ghost upon the
    floor.
Eagerly I wished the morrow;—vainly I had sought to
    borrow
From my books surcease of sorrow—sorrow for the lost
    Lenore—   10
For the rare and radiant maiden whom the angels name
    Lenore—
    Nameless *here* for evermore.

And the silken, sad, uncertain rustling of each purple cur-
    tain
Thrilled me—filled me with fantastic terrors never felt
    before;
So that now, to still the beating of my heart, I stood re-
    peating
" 'Tis some visitor entreating entrance at my chamber
    door—
Some late visitor entreating entrance at my chamber
    door;—
    This it is and nothing more."

Presently my soul grew stronger; hesitating then no longer,
"Sir," said I, "or Madam, truly your forgiveness I im-
    plore;   20
But the fact is I was napping, and so gently you came rap-
    ping,
And so faintly you came tapping, tapping at my chamber
    door,
That I scarce was sure I heard you"—here I opened wide
    the door;—
    Darkness there and nothing more.

Deep into that darkness peering, long I stood there wonder-
    ing, fearing,
Doubting, dreaming dreams no mortal ever dared to dream
    before;
But the silence was unbroken, and the stillness gave no
    token,
And the only word there spoken was the whispered word,
    "Lenore!"

This I whispered, and an echo murmured back the word
    "Lenore!"
  Merely this and nothing more.   30

Back into the chamber turning, all my soul within me burn-
    ing,
Soon again I heard a tapping somewhat louder than before.
"Surely," said I, "surely that is something at my window
    lattice;
Let me see, then, what thereat is, and this mystery ex-
    plore—
Let my heart be still a moment and this mystery explore;—
  'Tis the wind and nothing more!"

Open here I flung the shutter, when, with many a flirt and
    flutter
In there stepped a stately Raven of the saintly days of yore.
Not the least obeisance made he; not a minute stopped or
    stayed he;
But, with mien of lord or lady, perched above my chamber
    door—   40
Perched upon a bust of Pallas just above my chamber
    door—
  Perched, and sat, and nothing more.

Then this ebony bird beguiling my sad fancy into smiling,
By the grave and stern decorum of the countenance it
    wore,
"Though thy crest be shorn and shaven, thou," I said, "art
    sure no craven,
Ghastly grim and ancient Raven wandering from the
    Nightly shore—
Tell me what thy lordly name is on the Night's Plutonian
    shore!"
  Quoth the Raven, "Nevermore."

Much I marvelled this ungainly fowl to hear discourse so
    plainly,
Though its answer little meaning—little relevancy bore;   50
For we cannot help agreeing that no living human being
Ever yet was blessed with seeing bird above his chamber
    door—

Bird or beast upon the sculptured bust above his chamber
  door,
  With such name as "Nevermore."

But the Raven, sitting lonely on the placid bust, spoke only
That one word, as if his soul in that one word he did out-
  pour.
Nothing farther then he uttered—not a feather then he
  fluttered—
Till I scarcely more than muttered "Other friends have
  flown before—
On the morrow *he* will leave me, as my hopes have flown
  before."
  Then the bird said "Nevermore."   60

Startled at the stillness broken by reply so aptly spoken,
"Doubtless," said I, "what it utters is its only stock and
  store
Caught from some unhappy master whom unmerciful Dis-
  aster
Followed fast and followed faster till his songs one burden
  bore—
Till the dirges of his Hope that melancholy burden bore
  Of 'Never—nevermore.' "

But the Raven still beguiling all my fancy into smiling,
Straight I wheeled a cushioned seat in front of bird, and
  bust and door;
Then, upon the velvet sinking, I betook myself to linking
Fancy unto fancy, thinking what this ominous bird of
  yore—   70
What this grim, ungainly, ghastly, gaunt, and ominous bird
  of yore
  Meant in croaking "Nevermore."

This I sat engaged in guessing, but no syllable expressing
To the fowl whose fiery eyes now burned into my bosom's
  core;
This and more I sat divining, with my head at ease reclining
On the cushion's velvet lining that the lamplight gloated
  o'er,

But whose velvet violet lining with the lamplight gloating
o'er,
She shall press, ah, nevermore!

Then, methought, the air grew denser, perfumed from an
unseen censer
Swung by Seraphim whose foot-falls tinkled on the tufted
floor.   80
"Wretch," I cried, "thy God hath lent thee—by these angels
he hath sent thee
Respite—respite and nepenthe from thy memories of
Lenore;
Quaff, oh quaff this kind nepenthe and forget this lost
Lenore!"
Quoth the Raven "Nevermore."

"Prophet!" said I, "thing of evil! prophet still, if bird or
devil!—
Whether Tempter sent, or whether tempest tossed thee here
ashore,
Desolate yet all undaunted, on this desert land enchanted—
On this home by Horror haunted—tell me truly, I im-
plore—
Is there—*is* there balm in Gilead?—tell me—tell me, I im-
plore!"
Quoth the Raven "Nevermore."   90

"Prophet!" said I, "thing of evil!—prophet still, if bird or
devil!
By that Heaven that bends above us—by that God we both
adore—
Tell this soul with sorrow laden if, within the distant,
Aidenn,
It shall clasp a sainted maiden whom the angels name
Lenore—
Clasp a rare and radiant maiden whom the angels name
Lenore."
Quoth the Raven "Nevermore."

"Be that word our sign of parting, bird or fiend!" I shrieked,
upstarting—
"Get thee back into the tempest and the Night's Plutonian
shore!

Leave no black plume as a token of that lie thy soul hath
  spoken!
Leave my loneliness unbroken!—quit the bust above my
  door!   100
Take thy beak from out my heart, and take thy form from
  off my door!"
  Quoth the Raven "Nevermore."

And the Raven, never flitting, still is sitting, *still* is sitting
On the pallid bust of Pallas just above my chamber door;
And his eyes have all the seeming of a demon's that is
  dreaming,
And the lamp-light o'er him streaming throws his shadow
  on the floor;
And my soul from out that shadow that lies floating on the
  floor
  Shall be lifted—nevermore!

                                                          1845

Ulalume

The skies they were ashen and sober;
    The leaves they were crispèd and sere—
    The leaves they were withering and sere;
It was night in the lonesome October
    Of my most immemorial year;
It was hard by the dim lake of Auber,
    In the misty mid region of Weir—
It was down by the dank tarn of Auber,
    In the ghoul-haunted woodland of Weir.

Here once, through an alley Titanic,   10
    Of cypress, I roamed with my Soul—
    Of cypress, with Psyche, my Soul.
These were days when my heart was volcanic
    As the scoriac rivers that roll—
    As the lavas that restlessly roll
Their sulphurous currents down Yaanek
    In the ultimate climes of the pole—
That groan as they roll down Mount Yaanek
    In the realms of the boreal pole.

Our talk had been serious and sober,   20
     But our thoughts they were palsied and sere—
     Our memories were treacherous and sere—
For we knew not the month was October,
     And we marked not the night of the year—
     (Ah, night of all nights in the year!)
We noted not the dim lake of Auber—
     (Though once we have journeyed down here)—
Remembered not the dank tarn of Auber,
     Nor the ghoul-haunted woodland of Weir.

And now, as the night was senescent   30
     And star-dials pointed to morn—
     As the star-dials hinted of morn—
At the end of our path a liquescent
     And nebulous lustre was born,
Out of which a miraculous crescent
     Arose with a duplicate horn—
Astarte's bediamonded crescent
     Distinct with its duplicate horn.

And I said—"She is warmer than Dian:
     She rolls through an ether of sighs—   40
     She revels in a region of sighs:
She has seen that the tears are not dry on
     These cheeks, where the worm never dies,
And has come past the stars of the Lion
     To point us the path to the skies—
     To the Lethean peace of the skies—
Come up, in despite of the Lion,
     To shine on us with her bright eyes—
Come up through the lair of the Lion,
     With love in her luminous eyes."   50

But Psyche, uplifting her finger,
     Said—"Sadly this star I mistrust—
     Her pallor I strangely mistrust:—
Oh, hasten!—oh, let us not linger!
     Oh, fly!—let us fly!—for we must."
In terror she spoke, letting sink her
     Wings until they trailed in the dust—
In agony sobbed, letting sink her

Plumes till they trailed in the dust—
    Till they sorrowfully trailed in the dust.   60

I replied—"This is nothing but dreaming:
    Let us on by this tremulous light!
    Let us bathe in this crystalline light!
Its Sibyllic splendor is beaming
    With Hope and in Beauty to-night:—
See!—it flickers up the sky through the night!
Ah, we safely may trust to its gleaming,
    And be sure it will lead us aright—
We safely may trust to a gleaming
    That cannot but guide us aright,   70
    Since it flickers up to Heaven through the night."

Thus I pacified Psyche and kissed her,
    And tempted her out of her gloom—
    And conquered her scruples and gloom;
And we passed to the end of the vista,
    But were stopped by the door of a tomb—
    By the door of a legended tomb;
And I said—"What is written, sweet sister,
    On the door of this legended tomb?"
    She replied—"Ulalume—Ulalume—   80
    'Tis the vault of thy lost Ulalume!"

Then my heart it grew ashen and sober
    As the leaves that were crispèd and sere—
    As the leaves that were withering and sere,
And I cried—"It was surely October
    On *this* very night of last year
    That I journeyed—I journeyed down here—
    That I brought a dread burden down here—
    On this night of all nights in the year,
    Ah, what demon has tempted me here?   90
Well I know, now, this dim lake of Auber—
    This misty mid region of Weir—
Well I know, now, this dank tarn of Auber,
    This ghoul-haunted woodland of Weir."

Said we, then—the two, then: "Ah, can it
    Have been that the woodlandish ghouls—
    The pitiful, the merciful ghouls—

To bar up our way and to ban it
  From the secret that lies in these wolds—
  From the thing that lies hidden in these wolds—   100
Have drawn up the spectre of a planet
  From the limbo of lunary souls—
This sinfully scintillant planet
  From the Hell of the planetary souls?"

          1847

The Bells

1

  Hear the sledges with the bells—
    Silver bells!
What a world of merriment their melody foretells!
  How they tinkle, tinkle, tinkle,
    In the icy air of night!
  While the stars that oversprinkle
  All the heavens, seen to twinkle
    With a crystalline delight;
  Keeping time, time, time,
    In a sort of Runic rhyme   10
To the tintinnabulation that so musically wells
  From the bells, bells, bells, bells,
    Bells, bells, bells—
From the jingling and the tinkling of the bells.

2

  Hear the mellow wedding bells—
    Golden bells!
What a world of happiness their harmony foretells!
  Through the balmy air of night
  How they ring out their delight!—
    From the molten-golden notes,   20
      And all in tune,
    What a liquid ditty floats
  To the turtle-dove that listens, while she gloats
      On the moon!
    Oh, from out the sounding cells,
What a gush of euphony voluminously wells!
    How it swells!
    How it dwells

On the Future—how it tells
Of the rapture that impels   30
To the swinging and the ringing
Of the bells, bells, bells—
Of the bells, bells, bells, bells,
Bells, bells, bells—
To the rhyming and the chiming of the bells!

3

Hear the loud alarum bells—
Brazen bells!
What a tale of terror, now, their turbulency tells!
In the startled ear of night
How they scream out their affright!   40
Too much horrified to speak,
They can only shriek, shriek,
Out of tune,
In a clamorous appealing to the mercy of the fire,
In a mad expostulation with the deaf and frantic fire,
Leaping higher, higher, higher,
With a desperate desire,
And a resolute endeavor
Now—now to sit, or never,
By the side of the pale-faced moon.   50
Oh, the bells, bells, bells!
What a tale their terror tells
Of Despair!
How they clang, and clash, and roar!
What a horror they outpour
On the bosom of the palpitating air!
Yet the ear, it fully knows,
By the twanging
And the clanging,
How the danger ebbs and flows;   60
Yet the ear distinctly tells,
In the jangling
And wrangling,
How the danger sinks and swells,
By the sinking or the swelling in the anger of the bells—
Of the bells,—
Of the bells, bells, bells, bells,
Bells, bells, bells—
In the clamor and the clangor of the bells!

4

Hear the tolling of the bells—   70
          Iron bells!
What a world of solemn thought their monody compels!
     In the silence of the night,
     How we shiver with affright
At the melancholy menace of their tone!
     For every sound that floats
     From the rust within their throats
               Is a groan.
     And the people—ah, the people—
     They that dwell up in the steeple,   80
               All alone,
     And who tolling, tolling, tolling,
        In that muffled monotone,
     Feel a glory in so rolling
        On the human heart a stone—
     They are neither man nor woman—
     They are neither brute nor human—
               They are Ghouls:—
        And their king it is who tolls:—
        And he rolls, rolls, rolls,   90
               Rolls
          A paean from the bells!
     And his merry bosom swells
     With the paean of the bells!
     And he dances, and he yells;
     Keeping time, time, time,
     In a sort of Runic rhyme,
        To the paean of the bells—
               Of the bells:—
     Keeping time, time, time,   100
     In a sort of Runic rhyme
        To the throbbing of the bells—
        Of the bells, bells, bells—
        To the sobbing of the bells;
     Keeping time, time, time,
        As he knells, knells, knells
In a happy Runic rhyme,
        To the rolling of the bells—
        Of the bells, bells, bells:—
        To the tolling of the bells—   110

Of the bells, bells, bells, bells,
    Bells, bells, bells—
To the moanings and the groaning of the bells.

1849

Annabel Lee

It was many and many a year ago,
    In a kingdom by the sea,
That a maiden there lived whom you may know
    By the name of Annabel Lee;—
And this maiden she lived with no other thought
    Than to love and be loved by me.

She was a child and *I* was a child,
    In this kingdom by the sea,
But we loved with a love that was more than love—
    I and my Annabel Lee—   10
With a love that the wingéd seraphs of Heaven
    Coveted her and me.

And this was the reason that, long ago,
    In this kingdom by the sea,
A wind blew out of a cloud by night
    Chilling my Annabel Lee;
So that her highborn kinsmen came
    And bore her away from me,
To shut her up in a sepulchre
    In this kingdom by the sea.   20

The angels, not half so happy in Heaven,
    Went envying her and me:—
Yes! that was the reason (as all men know,
    In this kingdom by the sea)
That the wind came out of the cloud, chilling
    And killing my Annabel Lee.

But our love it was stronger by far than the love
    Of those who were older than we—
    Of many far wiser than we—
And neither the angels in Heaven above   30

Nor the demons down under the sea,
Can ever dissever my soul from the soul
   Of the beautiful Annabel Lee:—

For the moon never beams without bringing me dreams
   Of the beautiful Annabel Lee;
And the stars never rise but I see the bright eyes
   Of the beautiful Annabel Lee;
And so, all the night-tide, I lie down by the side
Of my darling, my darling, my life and my bride,
     In her sepulchre there by the sea—   40
     In her tomb by the side of the sea.

                      1849

Eldorado

   Gaily bedight
   A gallant knight,
In sunshine and in shadow,
   Had journeyed long,
   Singing a song,
In search of Eldorado.

   But he grew old—
   This knight so bold—
And o'er his heart a shadow
   Fell as he found   10
   No spot of ground
That looked like Eldorado.

   And, as his strength
   Failed him at length,
He met a pilgrim shadow—
   "Shadow," said he,
   "Where can it be—
This land of Eldorado?"

   "Over the Mountains
   Of the Moon,   20
Down the Valley of the Shadow.
   Ride, boldly ride,"

The shade replied,—
"If you seek for Eldorado."

1849

Ligeia

*And the will therein lieth, which dieth not. Who
knoweth the mysteries of the will, with its vigor? For God
is but a great will pervading all things by nature of its intentness. Man doth not yield himself to the angels, nor
unto death utterly, save only through the weakness of his
feeble will.*

—JOSEPH GLANVILL

I cannot, for my soul, remember how, when, or even
precisely where, I first became acquainted with the lady
Ligeia. Long years have since elapsed, and my memory is
feeble through much suffering. Or, perhaps, I cannot *now*
bring these points to mind, because, in truth, the character of my beloved, her rare learning, her singular yet placid
cast of beauty, and the thrilling and enthralling eloquence
of her low musical language, made their way into my heart
by pace so steadily and stealthily progressive that they
have been unnoticed and unknown. Yet I believe that I met
her first and most frequently in some large, old, decaying
city near the Rhine. Of her family—I have surely heard her
speak. That it is of a remotely ancient date cannot be
doubted. Ligeia! Ligeia! Buried in studies of a nature more
than all else adapted to deaden impressions of the outward
world, it is by that sweet word alone—by Ligeia—that I
bring before mine eyes in fancy the image of her who is no
more. And now, while I write, a recollection flashes upon
me that I have *never known* the paternal name of her who
was my friend and my betrothed, and who became the
partner of my studies, and finally the wife of my bosom.
Was it a playful charge on the part of my Ligeia? or was it
a test of my strength of affection, that I should institute no
inquiries upon this point? or was it rather a caprice of my
own—a wildly romantic offering on the shrine of the most
passionate devotion? I but indistinctly recall the fact itself
—what wonder that I have utterly forgotten the circumstances which originated or attended it? And, indeed, if
ever that spirit which is entitled *Romance*—if ever she, the

wan and the misty-winged Ashtophet of idolatrous Egypt, presided, as they tell, over marriages ill-omened, then most surely she presided over mine.

There is one dear topic, however, on which my memory fails me not. It is the *person* of Ligeia. In stature she was tall, somewhat slender, and, in her latter days, even emaciated. I would in vain attempt to portray the majesty, the quiet ease, of her demeanor, or the incomprehensible lightness and elasticity of her footfall. She came and departed as a shadow. I was never made aware of her entrance into my closed study, save by the dear music of her low sweet voice, as she placed her marble hand upon my shoulder. In beauty of face no maiden ever equalled her. It was the radiance of an opium-dream—an airy and spirit-lifting vision more wildly divine than the fantasies which hovered about the slumbering souls of the daughters of Delos. Yet her features were not of that regular mold which we have been falsely taught to worship in the classical labors of the heathen. "There is no exquisite beauty," says Bacon, Lord Verulam, speaking truly of all the forms and genera of beauty, "without some *strangeness* in the proportion." Yet, although I saw that the features of Ligeia were not of a classic regularity—although I perceived that her loveliness was indeed "exquisite," and felt that there was much of "strangeness" pervading it, yet I have tried in vain to detect the irregularity and to trace home my own perception of "the strange." I examined the contour of the lofty and pale forehead: it was faultless—how cold indeed that word when applied to a majesty so divine!—the skin rivalling the purest ivory, the commanding extent and repose, the gentle prominence of the regions above the temples; and then the ravenblack, the glossy, the luxuriant, and naturally-curling tresses, setting forth the full force of the Homeric epithet, "hyacinthine"! I looked at the delicate outlines of the nose—and nowhere but in the graceful medallions of the Hebrews had I beheld a similar perfection. There were the same luxurious smoothness of surface, the same scarcely perceptible tendency to the aquiline, the same harmoniously curved nostrils speaking the free spirit. I regarded the sweet mouth. Here was indeed the triumph of all things heavenly—the magnificent turn of the short upper lip—the soft, voluptuous slumber of the under—the dimples which sported, and the color which spoke—the teeth glancing back, with a brilliance almost startling, every ray of the holy light which fell upon them in her serene and placid, yet most exultingly radiant of all smiles. I scrutinized the formation of the chin: and here, too, I found the gentleness of breadth, the softness and the majesty, the fullness and the spirituality, of the Greek—the contour which the god Apollo revealed but in a dream to Cleomenes, the son of the Athenian. And then I peered into the large eyes of Ligeia.

For eyes we have no models in the remotely antique. It might have been, too, that in these eyes of my beloved lay the secret to which Lord Verulam alludes. They were, I must believe, far larger than the ordinary eyes of our own race. They were even fuller than the fullest of the gazelle eyes of the tribe of the valley of Nourjahad. Yet it was only at intervals—in moments of intense excitement—that this peculiarity became more than slightly noticeable in Ligeia. And at such moments was her beauty—in my heated fancy thus it appeared perhaps—the beauty of beings either above or apart from the earth, the beauty of the fabulous Houri of the Turk. The hue of the orbs was the most brilliant of black, and, far over them, hung jetty lashes of great length. The brows, slightly irregular in outline, had the same tint. The "strangeness," however, which I found in the eyes, was of a nature distinct from the formation, or the color, or the brilliancy of the features, and must, after all, be referred to the *expression*. Ah, word of no meaning! behind whose vast latitude of mere sound we intrench our ignorance of so much of the spiritual. The expression of the eyes of Ligeia! How for long hours have I pondered upon it! How have I, through the whole of a midsummer night, struggled to fathom it! What was it—that something more profound than the well of Democritus —which lay far within the pupils of my beloved? What *was* it? I was possessed with a passion to discover. Those eyes! those large, those shining, those divine orbs! they became to me twin stars of Leda, and I to them devoutest of astrologers.

There is no point, among the many incomprehensible anomalies of the science of mind, more thrillingly exciting than the fact—never, I believe, noticed in the schools— that in our endeavors to recall to memory something long forgotten, we often find ourselves *upon the very verge* of remembrance, without being able, in the end, to remember. And thus how frequently, in my intense scrutiny of Ligeia's eyes, have I felt approaching the full knowledge of their expression—felt it approaching, yet not quite be mine, and so at length entirely depart! And (strange, oh strangest mystery of all!) I found, in the commonest objects of the universe, a circle of analogies to that expression. I mean to say that, subsequently to the period when Ligeia's beauty passed into my spirit, there dwelling as in a shrine, I derived, from many existences in the material world, a sentiment such as I felt always aroused within me by her large and luminous orbs. Yet not the more could I define that sentiment, or analyze, or even steadily view it. I recognized it, let me repeat, sometimes in the survey of a rapidly growing vine—in the contemplation of a moth, a butterfly, a chrysalis, a stream of running water. I have felt it in the ocean; in the falling of a meteor. I have felt it in the glances of unusually aged people. And there are one or two stars in heaven (one especially, a star of the sixth magnitude, double and changeable, to be found near the large star in Lyra), in a telescopic scrutiny of which I have been made aware of the feeling. I have been filled with it by certain sounds from stringed instruments, and not unfrequently by passages from books. Among innumerable other instances, I well remember something in a volume of Joseph Glanvill, which (perhaps merely from its quaintness—who shall say?) never failed to inspire me with the sentiment: "And the will therein lieth, which dieth not. Who knoweth the mysteries of the will, with its vigor? For God is but a great will pervading all things by nature of its intentness. Man doth not yield him to the angels, nor unto death utterly, save only through the weakness of his feeble will."

Length of years and subsequent reflection have enabled me to trace, indeed, some remote connection between this passage in the English moralist and a portion of the character of Ligeia. An *intensity* in thought, action, or speech, was possibly, in her, a result, or at least an index, of that gigantic volition which, during our long intercourse, failed to give other and more immediate evidence of its existence. Of all the women whom I have ever known, she, the outwardly calm, the ever-placid Ligeia, was the most violently a prey to the tumultuous vultures of stern passion. And of such passion I could form no estimate, save by the miraculous expansion of those eyes which at once so delighted and appalled me—by the almost magical melody, modulation, distinctness, and placidity of her very low voice—and by the fierce energy (rendered doubly effective by contrast with her manner of utterance) of the wild words which she habitually uttered.

I have spoken of the learning of Ligeia: it was immense—such as I have never known in woman. In the classical tongues was she deeply proficient, and as far as my own acquaintance extended in regard to the modern dialects of Europe, I have never known her at fault. Indeed upon any theme of the most admired, because simply the most abstruse of the boasted erudition of the academy, have I *ever* found Ligeia at fault? How singularly, how thrillingly, this one point in the nature of my wife has forced itself, at this late period only, upon my attention! I said her knowledge was such as I have never known in woman—but where breathes the man who has traversed, and successfully, *all* the wide areas of moral, physical, and mathematical science? I saw not then what I now clearly perceive, that the acquisitions of Ligeia were gigantic, were astounding; yet I was sufficiently aware of her infinite supremacy to resign myself, with a child-like confidence, to her guidance through the chaotic world of metaphysical investigation at which I was most busily occupied during the earlier years of our marriage. With how vast a triumph, with how vivid a delight, with how much of all that is ethereal in hope, did I *feel*, as she bent over me in studies but little sought —but less known—that delicious vista by slow degrees expanding before me, down whose long, gorgeous, and all untrodden path, I might at length pass onward to the goal of a wisdom too divinely precious not to be forbidden!

How poignant, then, must have been the grief with which, after some years, I beheld my well-grounded expectations take wings to themselves and fly away! Without Ligeia I was but as a child groping benighted. Her presence, her readings alone, rendered vividly luminous the many mysteries of the transcendentalism in which we were immersed. Wanting the radiant lustre of her eyes, letters, lambent and golden, grew duller than Saturnian lead. And now those eyes shone less and less frequently upon the pages over which I pored. Ligeia grew ill. The wild eyes blazed with a too-too glorious effulgence; the pale fingers became of the transparent waxen hue of the grave; and the blue veins upon the lofty forehead swelled and sank impetuously with the tides of the most gentle emotion. I saw that she must die—and I struggled desperately in spirit with the grim Azrael. And the struggles of the passionate wife were, to my astonishment, even more energetic than my own. There had been much in her stern nature to impress me with the belief that, to her, death would have come without its terrors; but not so. Words are impotent to convey any just idea of the fierceness of resistance with which she wrestled with the Shadow. I groaned in anguish at the pitiable spectacle. I would have soothed—I would have reasoned; but, in the intensity of her wild desire for life—for life—*but* for life—solace and reason were alike the uttermost of folly. Yet not until the last instance, amid the most convulsive writhings of her fierce spirit, was shaken the external placidity of her demeanor. Her voice grew more gentle—grew more low—yet I would not wish to dwell upon the wild meaning of the quietly uttered words. My brain reeled as I hearkened, entranced, to a melody more than mortal—to assumptions and aspirations which mortality had never before known.

That she loved me I should not have doubted; and I might have been easily aware that, in a bosom such as hers, love would have reigned no ordinary passion. But in death only was I fully impressed with the strength of her affection. For long hours, detaining my hand, would she pour out before me the overflowing of a heart whose more than passionate devotion amounted to idolatry. How had I deserved to be so blessed by such confessions? How had I deserved to be so cursed with the removal of my beloved in the hour of her making them? But upon this subject I cannot bear to dilate. Let me say only, that in Ligeia's more than womanly abandonment to a love, alas! all unmerited, all unworthily bestowed, I at length recognized the principle of her longing, with so wildly earnest a desire, for the life which was now fleeing so rapidly away. It is this wild longing, it is this eager vehemence of desire for life—*but* for life, that I have no power to portray, no utterance capable of expressing.

At high noon of the night in which she departed, beckoning me peremptorily to her side, she bade me repeat, certain verses composed by herself not many days before. I obeyed her. They were these:

> Lo! 'tis a gala night
>   Within the lonesome latter years!
> An angel throng, bewinged, bedight
>   In veils, and drowned in tears,
> Sit in a theatre, to see
>   A play of hopes and fears,
> While the orchestra breathes fitfully
>   The music of the spheres.
>
> Mimes, in the form of God on high,
>   Mutter and mumble low,
> And hither and thither fly—
>   Mere puppets they, who come and go
> At bidding of vast formless things
>   That shift the scenery to and fro,
> Flapping from out their condor wings
>   Invisible Woe!
>
> That motley drama—oh, be sure
>   It shall not be forgot!
> With its Phantom chased for evermore,
>   By a crowd that seize it not,
> Through a circle that ever returneth in
>   To the self-same spot,
> And much of Madness, and more of Sin,
>   And Horror the soul of the plot.
>
> But see, amid the mimic rout
>   A crawling shape intrude!
> A blood-red thing that writhes from out
>   The scenic solitude!
> It writhes—it writhes! with mortal pangs
>   The mimes become its food,
> And seraphs sob at vermin fangs
>   In human gore imbued.
>
> Out—out are the lights—out all!
>   And over each quivering form
> The curtain, a funeral pall,

Comes down with the rush of a storm,
While the angels, all pallid and wan,
Uprising, unveiling, affirm
That the play is the tragedy, "Man,"
And its hero, the Conqueror Worm.

"O God!" half shrieked Ligeia, leaping to her feet and
extending her arms aloft with a spasmodic movement, as
I made an end of these lines—"O God! O Divine Father!
shall these things be undeviatingly so? shall this Conqueror
be not once conquered? Are we not part and parcel in
Thee? Who—who knoweth the mysteries of the will with
its vigor? 'Man doth not yield him to the angels, *nor unto
death utterly* save only through the weakness of his feeble
will.' "

And now, as if exhausted with emotion, she suffered her
white arms to fall, and returned solemnly to her bed of
death. And as she breathed her last sighs, there came
mingled with them a low murmur from her lips. I bent
to them my ear, and distinguished, again, the concluding
words of the passage in Glanvill: *"Man doth not yield him
to the angels, nor unto death utterly, save only through the
weakness of his feeble will."*

She died: and I, crushed into the very dust with sorrow,
could no longer endure the lonely desolation of my dwelling in the dim and decaying city by the Rhine. I had no
lack of what the world calls wealth. Ligeia had brought
me far more, very far more, than ordinarily falls to the lot
of mortals. After a few months, therefore, of weary and
aimless wandering, I purchased, and put in some repair, an
abbey, which I shall not name, in one of the wildest and
least frequented portions of fair England. The gloomy and
dreary grandeur of the building, the almost savage aspect
of the domain, the many melancholy and time-honored
memories connected with both, had much in unison with
the feelings of utter abandonment which had driven me
into that remote and unsocial region of the country. Yet
although the external abbey, with its verdant decay hanging about it, suffered but little alteration, I gave way with
a child-like perversity, and perchance with a faint hope of
alleviating my sorrows, to a display of more than regal
magnificence within. For such follies, even in childhood,

I had imbibed a taste, and now they came back to me as if in the dotage of grief. Alas, I feel how much even of incipient madness might have been discovered in the gorgeous and fantastic draperies, in the solemn carvings of Egypt, in the wild cornices and furniture, in the Bedlam patterns of the carpets of tufted gold! I had become a bounden slave in the trammels of opium, and my labors and my orders had taken a coloring from my dreams. But these absurdities I must not pause to detail. Let me speak only of that one chamber, ever accursed, whither, in a moment of mental alienation, I led from the altar as my bride—as the successor of the unforgotten Ligeia—the fair-haired and blue-eyed Lady Rowena Trevanion, of Tremaine.

There is no individual portion of the architecture and decoration of that bridal chamber which is not now visibly before me. Where were the souls of the haughty family of the bride, when through thirst of gold, they permitted to pass the threshold of an apartment *so* bedecked, a maiden and a daughter so beloved? I have said that I minutely remember the details of the chamber—yet I am sadly forgetful on topics of deep moment; and here there was no system, no keeping, in the fantastic display, to take hold upon the memory. The room lay in a high turret of the castellated abbey, was pentagonal in shape, and of capacious size. Occupying the whole southern face of the pentagon was the sole window—an immense sheet of unbroken glass from Venice—a single pane, and tinted of a leaden hue, so that the rays of either the sun or moon, passing through it, fell with a ghastly lustre on the objects within. Over the upper portion of this huge window extended the trellis-work of an aged vine, which clambered up the massy walls of the turret. The ceiling, of gloomy-looking oak, was excessively lofty, vaulted, and elaborately fretted with the wildest and most grotesque specimens of a semi-Gothic, semi-Druidical device. From out the most central recess of this melancholy vaulting depended, by a single chain of gold with long links, a huge censer of the same metal, Saracenic in pattern, and with many perforations so contrived that there writhed in and out of them, as if endued with a serpent vitality, a continual succession of parti-colored fires.

Some few ottomans and golden candelabra, of Eastern

figure, were in various stations about; and there was the couch, too—the bridal couch—of an Indian model, and low, and sculptured of solid ebony, with a pall-like canopy above. In each of the angles of the chamber stood on end a gigantic sarcophagus of black granite, from the tombs of the kings over against Luxor, with their aged lids full of immemorial sculpture. But in the draping of the apartment lay, alas! the chief fantasy of all. The lofty walls, gigantic in height, even unproportionably so, were hung from summit to foot, in vast folds, with a heavy and massive-looking tapestry—tapestry of a material which was found alike as a carpet on the floor, as a covering for the ottomans and the ebony bed, as a canopy for the bed, and as the gorgeous volutes of the curtains which partially shaded the window. The material was the richest cloth of gold. It was spotted all over, at irregular intervals, with arabesque figures, about a foot in diameter, and wrought upon the cloth in patterns of the most jetty black. But these figures partook of the true character of the arabesque only when regarded from a single point of view. By a contrivance now common, and indeed traceable to a very remote period of antiquity, they were made changeable in aspect. To one entering the room, they bore the appearance of simple monstrosities; but upon a farther advance, this appearance gradually departed; and, step by step, as the visitor moved his station in the chamber, he saw himself surrounded by an endless succession of the ghastly forms which belong to the superstition of the Norman, or arise in the guilty slumbers of the monk. The phantasmagoric effect was vastly heightened by the artificial introduction of a strong continual current of wind behind the draperies, giving a hideous and uneasy animation to the whole.

In halls such as these, in a bridal chamber such as this, I passed, with the Lady of Tremaine, the unhallowed hours of the first month of our marriage—passed them with but little disquietude. That my wife dreaded the fierce moodiness of my temper—that she shunned me, and loved me but little—I could not help perceiving; but it gave me rather pleasure than otherwise. I loathed her with a hatred belonging more to demon than to man. My memory flew back (oh, with what intensity of regret!) to Ligeia, the beloved, the august, the beautiful, the entombed. I revelled in recollections of her purity, of her wisdom, of her lofty, her ethereal nature, of her passionate, her idolatrous love. Now, then, did my spirit fully and freely burn with more than all the fires of her own. In the excitement of my opium dreams (for I was habitually fettered in the shackles of the drug), I would call aloud upon her name, during the silence of the night, or among the sheltered recesses of the glens by day, as if, through the wild eagerness, the solemn passion, the consuming ardor of my longing for the departed, I could restore her to the pathway she had abandoned—ah, *could* it be forever?—upon the earth.

About the commencement of the second month of the marriage, the Lady Rowena was attacked with sudden illness, from which her recovery was slow. The fever which consumed her rendered her nights uneasy; and in her perturbed state of half-slumber, she spoke of sounds, and of motions, in and about the chamber of the turret, which I concluded had no origin save in the distemper of her fancy, or perhaps in the phantasmagoric influences of the chamber itself. She became at length convalescent—finally, well. Yet but a brief period elapsed, ere a second more violent disorder again threw her upon a bed of suffering; and from this attack her frame, at all times feeble, never altogether recovered. Her illnesses were, after this epoch, of alarming character, and of more alarming recurrence, defying alike the knowledge and the great exertions of her physicians. With the increase of the chronic disease, which had thus apparently taken too sure hold upon her constitution to be eradicated by human means, I could not fail to observe a similar increase in the nervous irritation of her temperament, and in her excitability by trivial causes of fear. She spoke again, and now more frequently and pertinaciously, of the sounds—of the slight sounds—and of the unusual motions among the tapestries, to which she had formerly alluded.

One night, near the closing in of September, she pressed this distressing subject with more than usual emphasis upon my attention. She had just awakened from an unquiet slumber, and I had been watching, with feelings half of anxiety, half of vague terror, the workings of her emaciated countenance. I sat by the side of her ebony bed, upon one of the ottomans of India. She partly arose, and spoke, in an earnest low whisper, of sounds which she *then* heard, but which I could not hear—of motions which she *then* saw, but which I could not perceive. The wind was rushing hurriedly behind the tapestries, and I wished to show her (what, let me confess it, I could not *all* believe) that those almost inarticulate breathings, and those very gentle variations of the figures upon the wall, were but the natural effects of that customary rushing of the wind. But a deadly pallor, overspreading her face, had proved to me that my exertions to reassure her would be fruitless. She appeared to be fainting, and no attendants were within call. I remembered where was deposited a decanter of light wine which had been ordered by her physicians, and hastened across the chamber to procure it. But, as I stepped beneath the light of the censer, two circumstances of a startling nature attracted my attention. I had felt that some palpable although invisible object had passed lightly by my person; and I saw that there lay upon the golden carpet, in the very middle of the rich lustre thrown from the censer, a shadow—a faint, indefinite shadow of angelic aspect—such as might be fancied for the shadow of a shade. But I was wild with the excitement of an immoderate dose of opium, and heeded these things but little, nor spoke of them to Rowena. Having found the wine, I recrossed the chamber, and poured out a gobletful, which I held to the lips of the fainting lady. She had now partially recovered, however, and took the vessel herself, while I sank upon an ottoman near me, with my eyes fastened upon her person. It was then that I became distinctly aware of a gentle footfall upon the carpet, and near the couch; and in a second thereafter, as Rowena was in the act of raising the wine to her lips, I saw, or may have dreamed that I saw, fall within the goblet, as if from some invisible spring in the atmosphere of the room, three or four large drops of a brilliant and ruby-colored fluid. If this I saw—not so Rowena. She swallowed the wine unhesitatingly, and I forbore to speak to her of a circumstance which must after all, I considered, have been but the suggestion of a vivid imagination, rendered morbidly active by the terror of the lady, by the opium, and by the hour.

Yet I cannot conceal it from my own perception that, immediately subsequent to the fall of the ruby-drops, a rapid change for the worse took place in the disorder of my wife; so that, on the third subsequent night, the hands of her menials prepared her for the tomb, and on the fourth, I sat alone, with her shrouded body, in that fantastic chamber which had received her as my bride. Wild visions, opium-engendered, flitted shadow-like before me. I gazed with unquiet eye upon the sarcophagi in the angles of the room, upon the varying figures of the drapery, and upon the writhing of the particolored fires in the censer overhead. My eyes then fell, as I called to mind the circumstances of a former night, to the spot beneath the glare of the censer where I had seen the faint traces of the shadow. It was there, however, no longer; and breathing with greater freedom, I turned my glances to the pallid and rigid figure upon the bed. Then rushed upon me a thousand memories of Ligeia—and then came back upon my heart, with the turbulent violence of a flood, the whole of that unutterable woe with which I had regarded *her* thus enshrouded. The night waned; and still, with a bosom full of bitter thoughts of the one only and supremely beloved, I remained gazing upon the body of Rowena.

It might have been midnight, or perhaps earlier, or later, for I had taken no note of time, when a sob, low, gentle, but very distinct, startled me from my revery. I *felt* that it came from the bed of ebony—the bed of death. I listened in an agony of superstitious terror—but there was no repetition of the sound. I strained my vision to detect any motion in the corpse—but there was not the slightest perceptible. Yet I could not have been deceived. I *had* heard the noise, however faint, and my soul was awakened within me. I resolutely and perseveringly kept my attention riveted upon the body. Many minutes elapsed before any circumstance occurred tending to throw light upon the mystery. At length it became evident that a slight, a very feeble, and barely noticeable tinge of color had flushed up within the cheeks, and along the sunken small veins of the eyelids. Through a species of unutterable horror and awe, for which the language of mortality has no sufficiently energetic expression, I felt my heart cease to beat, my limbs grow rigid where I sat. Yet a sense of duty finally operated to restore my self-possession. I could no longer doubt that we had been precipitate in our preparations—that Rowena still lived. It was necessary that some immediate exertion be made; yet the turret was altogether apart from the portion of the abbey tenanted by the servants—there were none within call—I had no means of summoning them to my aid without leaving the room for many minutes—and this I could not venture to do. I therefore struggled alone in my endeavors to call back the spirit still hovering. In a short period it was certain, however, that a relapse had taken place; the color disappeared from both eyelid and cheek, leaving a wanness even more than that of marble; the lips became doubly shrivelled and pinched up in the ghastly expression of death; a repulsive clamminess and coldness overspread rapidly the surface of the body; and all the usual rigorous stiffness immediately supervened. I fell back with a shudder upon the couch from which I had been so startlingly aroused, and again gave myself up to passionate waking visions of Ligeia.

An hour thus elapsed, when (could it be possible?) I was a second time aware of some vague sound issuing from the region of the bed. I listened—in extremity of horror. The sound came again—it was a sigh. Rushing to the corpse, I saw—distinctly saw—a tremor upon the lips. In a minute afterwards they relaxed, disclosing a bright line of the pearly teeth. Amazement now struggled in my bosom with the profound awe which had hitherto reigned there alone. I felt that my vision grew dim, that my reason wandered; and it was only by a violent effort that I at length succeeded in nerving myself to the task which duty thus once more had pointed out. There was now a partial glow upon the forehead and upon the cheek and throat; a perceptible warmth pervaded the whole frame; there was even a slight pulsation at the heart. The lady *lived;* and with redoubled ardor I betook myself to the task of restoration. I chafed and bathed the temples and the hands, and used every exertion which experience, and no little medical reading, could suggest. But in vain. Suddenly, the color fled, the pulsation ceased, the lips resumed the expression of the dead, and, in an instant afterward, the whole body took upon itself the icy chilliness, the livid hue, the intense rigidity, the sunken outline, and all the loathsome peculiarities of that which has been, for many days, a tenant of the tomb.

And again I sunk into visions of Ligeia—and again (what marvel that I shudder while I write?) *again* there reached my ears a low sob from the region of the ebony bed. But why shall I minutely detail the unspeakable horrors of that night? Why shall I pause to relate how, time after time, until near the period of the gray dawn, this hideous drama of revivification was repeated; how each terrific relapse was only into a sterner and apparently more irredeemable death; how each agony wore the aspect of a struggle with some invisible foe; and how each struggle was succeeded by I know not what of wild change in the personal appearance of the corpse? Let me hurry to a conclusion.

The greater part of the fearful night had worn away, and she who had been dead, once again stirred—and now more vigorously than hitherto, although arousing from a dissolution more appalling in its utter helplessness than any. I had long ceased to struggle or to move, and remained sitting rigidly upon the ottoman, a helpless prey to a whirl of violent emotions, of which extreme awe was perhaps the least terrible, the least consuming. The corpse, I repeat, stirred, and now more vigorously than before. The hues of life flushed up with unwonted energy into the countenance—the limbs relaxed—and, say that the eyelids were yet pressed heavily together, and that the bandages and draperies of the grave still imparted their charnel character to the figure, I might have dreamed that Rowena had indeed shaken off, utterly, the fetters of Death. But if this idea was not, even then, altogether adopted, I could at least doubt no longer, when, arising from the bed, tottering, with feeble steps, with closed eyes, and with the manner of one bewildered in a dream, the thing that was enshrouded advanced bodily and palpably into the middle of the apartment.

I trembled not—I stirred not—for a crowd of unutterable fancies connected with the air, the stature, the demeanor of the figure, rushing hurriedly through my brain, had paralyzed—had chilled me into stone. I stirred not—but gazed upon the apparition. There was a mad disorder in my thoughts—a tumult unappeasable. Could it, indeed, be the *living* Rowena who confronted me? Could it indeed be Rowena *at all*—the fair-haired, the blue-eyed Lady

Rowena Trevanion of Tremaine? Why, *why* should I doubt it? The bandage lay heavily about the mouth—but then might it not be the mouth of the breathing Lady of Tremaine? And the cheeks—there were the roses as in her noon of life—yes, these might indeed be the fair cheeks of the living Lady of Tremaine. And the chin, with its dimples, as in health, might it not be hers? but *had she then grown taller since her malady?* What inexpressible madness seized me with that thought? One bound, and I had reached her feet! Shrinking from my touch, she let fall from her head the ghastly cerements which had confined it, and there streamed forth, into the rushing atmosphere of the chamber, huge masses of long and dishevelled hair; *it was blacker than the raven wings of the midnight!* And now slowly opened *the eyes* of the figure which stood before me. "Here then, at least," I shrieked aloud, "can I never—can I never be mistaken—these are the full, and the black, and the wild eyes—of my lost love—of the lady —of the LADY LIGEIA."

1838

The Fall of the House of Usher

Son cœur est un luth suspendu;
Sitôt qu'on le touche il résonne.

[*His heart is a suspended lute; as soon as it is touched, it resounds.*]

—DE BÉRANGER

During the whole of a dull, dark, and soundless day in the autumn of the year, when the clouds hung oppressively low in the heavens, I had been passing alone, on horseback, through a singularly dreary tract of country; and at length found myself, as the shades of the evening drew on, within view of the melancholy House of Usher. I know not how it was—but, with the first glimpse of the building, a sense of insufferable gloom pervaded my spirit. I say insufferable; for the feeling was unrelieved by any of that half-pleasurable, because poetic, sentiment with which the mind usually receives even the sternest natural images of the desolate or terrible. I looked upon the scene before me—upon the mere house, and the simple landscape features of the domain, upon the bleak walls, upon the vacant eye-like windows, upon a few rank sedges, and upon a few white trunks of decayed trees—with an utter depression of soul which I can compare to no earthly sensation more properly than to the after-dream of the reveller upon opium; the bitter lapse into everyday life, the hideous dropping off of the veil. There was an iciness, a sinking, a sickening of the heart, an unredeemed dreariness of thought which no goading of the imagination could torture into aught of the sublime. What was it—I paused to think—what was it that so unnerved me in the contemplation of the House of Usher? It was a mystery all insoluble; nor could I grapple with the shadowy fancies that crowded upon me as I pondered. I was forced to fall back upon the unsatisfactory conclusion, that while, beyond doubt, there *are* combinations of very simple natural objects which have the power of thus affecting us, still the analysis of this power lies among considerations beyond our depth. It was possible, I reflected, that a mere different arrangement of the particulars of the scene, of the details of the picture, would be sufficient to modify, or perhaps to annihilate, its capacity for sorrowful impression; and acting upon this idea, I reined my horse to the precipitous brink of a black and lurid tarn that lay in unruffled lustre by the dwelling, and gazed down—but with a shudder even more thrilling than before—upon the remodelled and inverted images of the gray sedge, and the ghastly tree-stems, and the vacant and eye-like windows.

Nevertheless, in this mansion of gloom I now proposed to myself a sojourn of some weeks. Its proprietor, Roderick Usher, had been one of my boon companions in boyhood; but many years had elapsed since our last meeting. A letter, however, had lately reached me in a distant part of the country—a letter from him—which in its wildly importunate nature had admitted of no other than a personal reply. The MS. gave evidence of nervous agitation. The writer spoke of acute bodily illness, of a mental disorder which oppressed him, and of an earnest desire to see me, as his best and indeed his only personal friend, with a view of attempting, by the cheerfulness of my society, some alleviation of his malady. It was the manner in which all this, and much more, was said—it was the apparent *heart* that went with his request—which allowed me no room for hesitation; and I accordingly obeyed forthwith what I still considered a very singular summons.

Although as boys we had been even intimate associates, yet I really knew little of my friend. His reserve had been always excessive and habitual. I was aware, however, that his very ancient family had been noted, time out of mind, for a peculiar sensibility of temperament, displaying itself, through long ages, in many works of exalted art, and manifested of late in repeated deeds of munificent yet unobtrusive charity, as well as in a passionate devotion to the intricacies, perhaps even more than to the orthodox and easily recognizable beauties, of musical science. I had learned, too, the very remarkable fact that the stem of the Usher race, all time-honored as it was, had put forth at no period any enduring branch; in other words, that the entire family lay in the direct line of descent, and had always, with very trifling and very temporary variation, so lain. It was this deficiency, I considered, while running over in thought the perfect keeping of the character of the premises with the accredited character of the people, and while speculating upon the possible influence which the one, in the long lapse of centuries, might have exercised upon the other—it was this deficiency, perhaps of collateral issue, and the consequent undeviating transmission from sire to son of the patrimony with the name, which had, at length, so identified the two as to merge the original title of the estate in the quaint and equivocal appellation of the "House of Usher"—an appellation which seemed to include, in the minds of the peasantry who used it, both the family and the family mansion.

I have said that the sole effect of my somewhat childish experiment, that of looking down within the tarn, had been to deepen the first singular impression. There can be no doubt that the consciousness of the rapid increase of my superstition—for why should I not so term it?—served mainly to accelerate the increase itself. Such, I have long known, is the paradoxical law of all sentiments having terror as a basis. And it might have been for this reason only, that, when I again uplifted my eyes to the house itself, from its image in the pool, there grew in my mind a strange fancy—a fancy so ridiculous, indeed, that I but mention it to show the vivid force of the sensations which oppressed me. I had so worked upon my imagination as really to believe that about the whole mansion and domain there hung an atmosphere peculiar to themselves and their immediate vicinity: an atmosphere which had no affinity with the air of heaven, but which had reeked up from the decayed trees, and the gray wall, and the silent tarn: a pestilent and mystic vapor, dull, sluggish, faintly discernible, and leaden-hued.

Shaking off from my spirit what *must* have been a dream, I scanned more narrowly the real aspect of the building. Its principal feature seemed to be that of an excessive antiquity. The discoloration of ages had been great. Minute fungi overspread the whole exterior, hanging in a fine tangled webwork from the eaves. Yet all this was apart from any extraordinary dilapidation. No portion of the masonry had fallen; and there appeared to be a wild inconsistency between its still perfect adaptation of parts and the crumbling condition of the individual stones. In this there was much that reminded me of the specious totality of old wood-work which has rotted for long years in some neglected vault, with no disturbance from the breath of the external air. Beyond this indication of extensive decay, however, the fabric gave little token of instability. Perhaps the eye of a scrutinizing observer might have discovered a barely perceptible fissure, which, extending from the roof of the building in front, made its way down the wall in a zigzag direction, until it became lost in the sullen waters of the tarn.

Noticing these things, I rode over a short causeway to the house. A servant in waiting took my horse, and I entered the Gothic archway of the hall. A valet, of stealthy step, thence conducted me, in silence, through many dark and intricate passages in my progress to the studio of his master. Much that I encountered on the way contributed, I know not how, to heighten the vague sentiments of which I have already spoken. While the objects around me— while the carvings of the ceilings, the sombre tapestries of the walls, the ebon blackness of the floors, and the phantasmagoric armorial trophies which rattled as I strode, were but matters to which, or to such as which, I had been accustomed from my infancy—while I hesitated not to acknowledge how familiar was all this—I still wondered to find how unfamiliar were the fancies which ordinary images were stirring up. On one of the staircases, I met the physician of the family. His countenance, I thought, wore a mingled expression of low cunning and perplexity. He accosted me with trepidation and passed on. The valet now threw open a door and ushered me into the presence of his master.

The room in which I found myself was very large and lofty. The windows were long, narrow, and pointed, and at so vast a distance from the black oaken floor as to be altogether inaccessible from within. Feeble gleams of encrimsoned light made their way through the trellised panes, and served to render sufficiently distinct the more prominent objects around; the eye, however, struggled in vain to reach the remoter angles of the chamber, or the recesses of the vaulted and fretted ceiling. Dark draperies hung upon the walls. The general furniture was profuse, comfortless, antique, and tattered. Many books and musical instruments lay scattered about, but failed to give any vitality to the scene. I felt that I breathed an atmosphere of sorrow. An air of stern, deep, and irredeemable gloom hung over and pervaded all.

Upon my entrance, Usher arose from a sofa on which he had been lying at full length, and greeted me with a vivacious warmth which had much in it, I at first thought, of an overdone cordiality—of the constrained effort of the *ennuyé* man of the world. A glance, however, at his countenance convinced me of his perfect sincerity. We sat down; and for some moments, while he spoke not, I gazed upon him with a feeling half of pity, half of awe. Surely man had never before so terribly altered, in so brief a period, as had Roderick Usher! It was with difficulty that I could bring myself to admit the identity of the wan being before me with the companion of my early boyhood. Yet the character of his face had been at all times remarkable. A cadaverousness of complexion; an eye large, liquid, and luminous beyond comparison; lips somewhat thin and very pallid, but of a surpassingly beautiful curve; a nose of a delicate Hebrew model, but with a breadth of nostril unusual in similar formations; a finely moulded chin, speaking, in its want of prominence, of a want of moral energy; hair of a more than web-like softness and tenuity; these features, with an inordinate expansion above the regions of the temple, made up altogether a countenance not easily to be forgotten. And now in the mere exaggeration of the prevailing character of these features, and of the expression they were wont to convey, lay so much of change that I doubted to whom I spoke. The now ghastly pallor of the skin, and the now miraculous lustre of the eye, above all things startled and even awed me. The silken hair, too, had been suffered to grow all unheeded, and as, in its wild gossamer texture, it floated rather than fell about the face, I could not, even with effort, connect its arabesque expression with any idea of simple humanity.

In the manner of my friend I was at once struck with an incoherence, an inconsistency; and I soon found this to arise from a series of feeble and futile struggles to overcome an habitual trepidancy, an excessive nervous agitation. For something of this nature I had indeed been prepared, no less by his letter than by reminiscences of certain boyish traits, and by conclusions deduced from his peculiar physical conformation and temperament. His action was alternately vivacious and sullen. His voice varied rapidly from a tremendous indecision (when the animal spirits seemed utterly in abeyance) to that species of energetic concision—that abrupt, weighty, unhurried, and hollow-sounding enunciation—that leaden, self-balanced and perfectly modulated guttural utterance—which may be observed in the lost drunkard, or the irreclaimable cater of opium, during the periods of his most intense excitement.

It was thus that he spoke of the object of my visit, of his earnest desire to see me, and of the solace he expected me to afford him. He entered, at some length, into what he conceived to be the nature of his malady. It was, he said, a constitutional and a family evil, and one for which he despaired to find a remedy—a mere nervous affection, he immediately added, which would undoubtedly soon pass off. It displayed itself in a host of unnatural sensations. Some of these, as he detailed them, interested and bewildered me; although, perhaps, the terms and the general manner of the narration had their weight. He suffered much from a morbid acuteness of the senses; the most insipid food was alone endurable; he could wear only garments of cerain texture; the odors of all flowers were oppressive; his eyes were tortured by even a faint light; and there were but peculiar sounds, and these from stringed instruments, which did not inspire him with horror.

To an anomalous species of terror I found him a bounden slave. "I shall perish," said he, "I *must* perish in this deplorable folly. Thus, thus, and not otherwise, shall I be lost. I dread the events of the future, not in themselves, but in their results. I shudder at the thought of any, even the most trivial, incident, which may operate upon this intolerable agitation of soul. I have, indeed, no abhorrence of danger, except in its absolute effect—in terror. In this unnerved—in this pitiable condition, I feel that the period will sooner or later arrive when I must abandon life and reason together, in some struggle with the grim phantasm, FEAR."

I learned moreover at intervals, and through broken and equivocal hints, another singular feature of his mental condition. He was enchained by certain superstitious impressions in regard to the dwelling which he tenanted, and whence, for many years, he had never ventured forth— in regard to an influence whose suppositious force was conveyed in terms too shadowy here to be restated—an influence which some peculiarities in the mere form and substance of his family mansion, had, by dint of long sufferance, he said, obtained over his spirit—an effect which the physique of the gray walls and turrets, and of the dim tarn into which they all looked down, had, at length, brought about upon the morale of his existence.

He admitted, however, although with hesitation, that much of the peculiar gloom which thus afflicted him could be traced to a more natural and far more palpable origin —to the severe and long-continued illness, indeed to the evidently approaching dissolution, of a tenderly beloved sister—his sole companion for long years, his last and only relative on earth. "Her decease," he said, with a bitterness which I can never forget, "would leave him (him the hopeless and the frail) the last of the ancient race of the Ushers." While he spoke the lady Madeline (for so was she called) passed slowly through a remote portion of the apartment, and, without having noticed my presence, disappeared. I regarded her with an utter astonishment not unmingled with dread, and yet I found it impossible to account for such feelings. A sensation of stupor oppressed me, as my eyes followed her retreating steps. When a door, at length, closed upon her, my glance sought instinctively and eagerly the countenance of the brother; but he had buried his face in his hands, and I could only perceive that a far more than ordinary wanness had overspread the emaciated fingers through which trickled many passionate tears.

The disease of the lady Madeline had long baffled the skill of her physicians. A settled apathy, a gradual wasting away of the person, and frequent although transient affections of a partially cataleptical character, were the unusual diagnoses. Hitherto she had steadily borne up against the pressure of her malady, and had not betaken herself finally to bed; but, on the closing in of the evening of my arrival at the house, she succumbed (as her brother told me at night with inexpressible agitation) to the prostrating power of the destroyer; and I learned that the glimpse I had obtained of her person would thus probably be the last I should obtain—that the lady, at least while living, would be seen by me no more.

For several days ensuing, her name was unmentioned by either Usher or myself; and during this period I was busied in earnest endeavors to alleviate the melancholy of my friend. We painted and read together; or I listened, as if in a dream, to the wild improvisations of his speaking guitar. And thus, as a closer and still closer intimacy admitted me more unreservedly into the recesses of his spirit, the more bitterly did I perceive the futility of all attempt at cheering a mind from which darkness, as if an inherent positive quality, poured forth upon all objects of the moral and physical universe, in one unceasing radiation of gloom.

I shall ever bear about me a memory of the many solemn hours I thus spent alone with the master of the House of Usher. Yet I should fail in any attempt to convey an idea of the exact character of the studies, or of the occupations, in which he involved me, or led me the way. An excited and highly distempered ideality threw a sulphureous lustre over all. His long improvised dirges will ring forever in my ears. Among other things, I hold painfully in mind a certain singular perversion and amplification of the wild air of the last waltz of Von Weber. From the

paintings over which his elaborate fancy brooded, and
which grew, touch by touch, into vaguenesses at which I
shuddered the more thrillingly because I shuddered knowing not why;—from these paintings (vivid as their images
now are before me) I would in vain endeavor to educe
more than a small portion which should lie within the
compass of merely written words. By the utter simplicity,
by the nakedness of his designs, he arrested and overawed
attention. If ever mortal painted an idea, that mortal was
Roderick Usher. For me at least, in the circumstances
then surrounding me, there arose, out of the pure abstrac-
tions which the hypochondriac contrived to throw upon
his canvas, an intensity of intolerable awe, no shadow of
which felt I ever yet in the contemplation of the certainly
glowing yet too concrete reveries of Fuseli.

One of the phantasmagoric conceptions of my friend,
partaking not so rigidly of the spirit of abstraction, may be
shadowed forth, although feebly, in words. A small picture
presented the interior of an immensely long and rectan-
gular vault or tunnel, with low walls, smooth, white, and
without interruption or device. Certain accessory points of
the design served well to convey the idea that this excava-
tion lay at an exceeding depth below the surface of the
earth. No outlet was observed in any portion of its vast
extent, and no torch or other artificial source of light was
discernible; yet a flood of intense rays rolled throughout,
and bathed the whole in a ghastly and inappropriate
splendor.

I have just spoken of that morbid condition of the audi-
tory nerve which rendered all music intolerable to the
sufferer, with the exception of certain effects of stringed
instruments. It was, perhaps, the narrow limits to which
he thus confined himself upon the guitar, which gave birth,
in great measure, to the fantastic character of his perform-
ances. But the fervid *facility* of his impromptus could not
be so accounted for. They must have been, and were, in the
notes, as well as in the words of his wild fantasias (for he
not unfrequently accompanied himself with rhymed verbal
improvisations), the result of that intense mental collected-
ness and concentration to which I have previously alluded
as observable only in particular moments of the highest
artificial excitement. The words of one of these rhapsodies
I have easily remembered. I was, perhaps, the more forcibly

impressed with it, as he gave it, because, in the under or mystic current of its meaning, I fancied that I perceived, and for the first time, a full consciousness, on the part of Usher, of the tottering of his lofty reason upon her throne. The verses, which were entitled "The Haunted Palace," ran very nearly, if not accurately, thus:

I

In the greenest of our valleys
    By good angels tenanted,
Once a fair and stately palace—
    Radiant palace—reared its head.
In the monarch Thought's dominion,
    It stood there!
Never seraph spread a pinion
    Over fabric half so fair!

II

Banners yellow, glorious, golden,
    On its roof did float and flow,
(This—all this—was in the olden
    Time long ago)
And every gentle air that dallied,
    In that sweet day,
Along the ramparts plumed and pallid,
    A wingèd odor went away.

III

Wanderers in that happy valley,
    Through two luminous windows, saw
Spirits moving musically
    To a lute's well-tunèd law,
Round about a throne where, sitting,
    Porphyrogene!
In state his glory well befitting,
    The ruler of the realm was seen.

IV

And all with pearl and ruby glowing
    Was the fair palace door,
Through which came flowing, flowing, flowing
    And sparkling evermore,

A troop of Echoes, whose sweet duty
　　Was but to sing,
In voices of surpassing beauty,
　　The wit and wisdom of their king.

V

But evil things, in robes of sorrow,
　　Assailed the monarch's high estate.
(Ah, let us mourn!—for never morrow
　　Shall dawn upon him, desolate!)
And round about his home the glory
　　That blushed and bloomed
Is but a dim-remembered story
　　Of the old time entombed.

VI

And travellers, now, within that valley,
　　Through the red-litten windows see
Vast forms that move fantastically
　　To a discordant melody;
While, like a ghastly rapid river,
　　Through the pale door
A hideous throng rush out forever,
　　And laugh—but smile no more.

I well remember that suggestions arising from this ballad led us into a train of thought, wherein there became manifest an opinion of Usher's which I mention not so much on account of its novelty (for other men* have thought thus), as on account of the pertinacity with which he maintained it. This opinion, in its general form, was that of the sentience of all vegetable things. But in his disordered fancy the idea had assumed a more daring character, and trespassed, under certain conditions, upon the kingdom of inorganization. I lack words to express the full extent, or the earnest *abandon* of his persuasion. The belief, however, was connected (as I have previously hinted) with the gray stones of the home of his forefathers. The conditions of the sentience had been here, he imagined, fulfilled in the method of collocation of these stones—in the order of their arrangement, as well as in that of the many fungi which

* Watson, Dr. Percival, Spallanzani, and especially the Bishop of Llandaff.—See *Chemical Essays,* vol. v. [Poe's note.]

overspread them, and of the decayed trees which stood around—above all, in the long undisturbed endurance of this arrangement, and in its reduplication in the still waters of the tarn. Its evidence—the evidence of the sentience—was to be seen, he said (and I here started as he spoke), in the gradual yet certain condensation of an atmosphere of their own about the waters and the walls. The result was discoverable, he added, in that silent, yet importunate and terrible influence which for centuries had moulded the destinies of his family, and which made *him* what I now saw him—what he was. Such opinions need no comment, and I will make none.

Our books—the books which, for years, had formed no small portion of the mental existence of the invalid—were, as might be supposed, in strict keeping with this character of phantasm. We pored together over such works as the *Ververt* and *Chartreuse* of Gresset; the *Belphegor* of Machiavelli; the *Heaven and Hell* of Swedenborg; the *Subterranean Voyage of Nicholas Klimm* by Holberg; the *Chiromancy* of Robert Flud, of Jean D'Indaginé, and of De la Chambre; the *Journey into the Blue Distance* of Tieck; and the *City of the Sun* of Campanella. One favorite volume was a small octavo edition of the *Directorium Inquisitorum* by the Dominican Eymeric de Gironne; and there were passages in Pomponius Mela, about the old African Satyrs and Ægipans, over which Usher would sit dreaming for hours. His chief delight, however, was found in the perusal of an exceedingly rare and curious book in quarto Gothic—the manual of a forgotten church—the *Vigilæ Mortuorum Secundum Chorum Ecclesiæ Maguntinæ*.

I could not help thinking of the wild ritual of this work, and of its probable influence upon the hypochondriac, when one evening, having informed me abruptly that the lady Madeline was no more, he stated his intention of preserving her corpse for a fortnight (previously to its final interment), in one of the numerous vaults within the main walls of the building. The worldly reason, however, assigned for this singular proceeding, was one which I did not feel at liberty to dispute. The brother had been led to his resolution (so he told me) by consideration of the unusual character of the malady of the deceased, of certain obtrusive and eager inquiries on the part of her medical men, and of the remote and exposed situation of the burial-ground of the family. I will not deny that when I called to mind the sinister countenance of the person whom I met upon the staircase, on the day of my arrival at the house, I had no desire to oppose what I regarded as at best but a harmless, and by no means an unnatural precaution.

At the request of Usher, I personally aided him in the arrangements for the temporary entombment. The body having been encoffined, we two alone bore it to its rest. The vault in which we placed it (and which had been so long unopened that our torches, half smothered in its oppressive atmosphere, gave us little opportunity for investigation) was small, damp, and entirely without means of admission for light; lying, at great depth, immediately beneath that portion of the building in which was my own sleeping apartment. It had been used, apparently, in remote feudal times, for the worst purposes of a donjon-keep, and in later days as a place of deposit for powder, or some other highly combustible substance, as a portion of its floor, and the whole interior of a long archway through which we reached it, were carefully sheathed with copper. The door, of massive iron, had been, also, similarly protected. Its immense weight caused an unusually sharp grating sound, as it moved upon its hinges.

Having deposited our mournful burden upon tressels within this region of horror, we partially turned aside the yet unscrewed lid of the coffin, and looked upon the face of the tenant. A striking similitude between the brother and sister now first arrested my attention; and Usher, divining, perhaps, my thoughts, murmured out some few words from which I learned that the deceased and himself had been twins, and that sympathies of a scarcely intelligible nature had always existed between them. Our glances, however, rested not long upon the dead—for we could not regard her unawed. The disease which had thus entombed the lady in the maturity of youth, had left, as usual in all maladies of a strictly cataleptical character, the mockery of a faint blush upon the bosom and the face, and that suspiciously lingering smile upon the lip which is so terrible in death. We replaced and screwed down the lid, and, having secured the door of iron, made our way, with toil, into the scarcely less gloomy apartments of the upper portion of the house.

And now, some days of bitter grief having elapsed, an observable change came over the features of the mental disorder of my friend. His ordinary manner had vanished. His ordinary occupations were neglected or forgotten. He roamed from chamber to chamber with hurried, unequal, and objectless step. The pallor of his countenance had assumed, if possible, a more ghastly hue—but the luminousness of his eye had utterly gone out. The once occasional huskiness of his tone was heard no more; and a tremulous quaver, as if of extreme terror, habitually characterized his utterance. There were times, indeed, when I thought his unceasingly agitated mind was laboring with some oppressive secret, to divulge which he struggled for the necessary courage. At times, again, I was obliged to resolve all into the mere inexplicable vagaries of madness, for I beheld him gazing upon vacancy for long hours, in an attitude of the profoundest attention, as if listening to some imaginary sound. It was no wonder that his condition terrified— that it infected me. I felt creeping upon me, by slow yet certain degrees, the wild influences of his own fantastic yet impressive superstitions.

It was, especially, upon retiring to bed late in the night of the seventh or eighth day after the placing of the lady Madeline within the donjon, that I experienced the full power of such feelings. Sleep came not near my couch, while the hours waned and waned away. I struggled to reason off the nervousness which had dominion over me. I endeavored to believe that much, if not all, of what I felt was due to the bewildering influence of the gloomy furniture of the room   of the dark and tattered draperies which, tortured into motion by the breath of a rising tempest, swayed fitfully to and fro upon the walls, and rustled uneasily about the decorations of the bed. But my efforts were fruitless. An irrepressible tremor gradually pervaded my frame; and at length there sat upon my very heart an incubus of utterly causeless alarm. Shaking this off with a gasp and a struggle, I uplifted myself upon the pillows, and, peering earnestly within the intense darkness of the chamber, hearkened—I know not why, except that an instinctive spirit prompted me—to certain low and indefinite sounds which came, through the pauses of the storm, at long intervals, I knew not whence. Overpowered by an intense sentiment of horror, unaccountable yet unendurable, I threw on my clothes with haste (for I felt that I should sleep no more during the night), and endeavored to arouse myself from the pitiable condition into which I had fallen, by pacing rapidly to and fro through the apartment.

I had taken but few turns in this manner, when a light step on an adjoining staircase arrested my attention. I presently recognized it as that of Usher. In an instant afterward he rapped with a gentle touch at my door, and entered, bearing a lamp. His countenance was, as usual, cadaverously wan—but, moreover, there was a species of mad hilarity in his eyes—an evidently restrained hysteria in his whole demeanor. His air appalled me—but anything was preferable to the solitude which I had so long endured, and I even welcomed his presence as a relief.

"And you have not seen it?" he said abruptly, after having stared about him for some moments in silence—"you have not then seen it?—but, stay! you shall." Thus speaking, and having carefully shaded his lamp, he hurried to one of the casements, and threw it freely open to the storm.

The impetuous fury of the entering gust nearly lifted us from our feet. It was, indeed, a tempestuous yet sternly beautiful night, and one wildly singular in its terror and its beauty. A whirlwind had apparently collected its force in our vicinity; for there were frequent and violent alterations in the direction of the wind; and the exceeding density of the clouds (which hung so low as to press upon the turrets of the house) did not prevent our perceiving the life-like velocity with which they flew careering from all points against each other, without passing away into the distance. I say that even their exceeding density did not prevent our perceiving this; yet we had no glimpse of the moon or stars, nor was there any flashing forth of the lightning. But the under surfaces of the huge masses of agitated vapor, as well as all terrestrial objects immediately around us, were glowing in the unnatural light of a faintly luminous and distinctly visible gaseous exhalation which hung about and enshrouded the mansion.

"You must not—you should not behold this!" said I, shudderingly, to Usher, as I led him with a gentle violence from the window to a seat. "These appearances, which bewilder you, are merely electrical phenomena not uncommon—or it may be that they have their ghastly origin in the rank miasma of the tarn. Let us close this casement; the air is chilling and dangerous to your frame. Here is one of your favorite romances. I will read, and you shall listen;—and so we will pass away this terrible night together."

The antique volume which I had taken up was the *Mad Trist* of Sir Launcelot Canning; but I had called it a favorite of Usher's more in sad jest than in earnest; for, in truth, there is little in its uncouth and unimaginative prolixity which could have had interest for the lofty and spiritual ideality of my friend. It was, however, the only book immediately at hand; and I indulged a vague hope that the excitement which now agitated the hypochondriac might find relief (for the history of mental disorder is full of similar anomalies) even in the extremeness of the folly which I should read. Could I have judged, indeed, by the wild overstrained air of vivacity with which he hearkened, or apparently hearkened, to the words of the tale, I might well have congratulated myself upon the success of my design.

I had arrived at that well-known portion of the story where Ethelred, the hero of the *Trist,* having sought in vain for peaceable admission into the dwelling of the hermit, proceeds to make good an entrance by force. Here, it will be remembered, the words of the narrative run thus:

And Ethelred, who was by nature of a doughty heart, and who was now mighty withal, on account of the powerfulness of the wine which he had drunken, waited no longer to hold parley with the hermit, who, in sooth, was of an obstinate and maliceful turn, but, feeling the rain upon his shoulders, and fearing the rising of the tempest, uplifted his mace outright, and with blows made quickly room in the plankings of the door for his gauntleted hand; and now pulling therewith sturdily, he so cracked, and ripped, and tore all asunder, that the noise of the dry and hollow-sounding wood alarmed and reverberated throughout the forest.

At the termination of this sentence I started, and for a moment paused; for it appeared to me (although I at once concluded that my excited fancy had deceived me)— It appeared to me that from some very remote portion of the mansion there came, indistinctly, to my ears, what might have been, in its exact similarity of character, the echo (but a stifled and dull one certainly) of the very cracking and ripping sound which Sir Launcelot had so particularly described. It was, beyond doubt, the coincidence alone which had arrested my attention; for, amid the rattling of the sashes of the casements, and the ordinary commingled noises of the still increasing storm, the sound, in itself, had nothing, surely, which should have interested or disturbed me. I continued the story:

But the good champion Ethelred, now entering within the door, was sore enraged and amazed to perceive no signal of the maliceful hermit; but, in the stead thereof, a dragon of a scaly and prodigious demeanor, and of a fiery tongue, which sate in guard before a palace of gold, with a floor of silver; and upon the wall there hung a shield of shining brass with this legend enwritten—

Who entereth herein, a conqueror hath bin;
Who slayeth the dragon, the shield he shall win.

And Ethelred uplifted his mace, and struck upon the head of the dragon, which fell before him, and gave up his pesty breath, with a shriek so horrid and harsh, and withal so piercing, that Ethelred had fain to close his ears with his hands against the dreadful noise of it, the like whereof was never before heard.

Here again I paused abruptly, and now with a feeling of wild amazement; for there could be no doubt whatever that, in this instance, I did actually hear (although from what direction it proceeded I found it impossible to say) a low and apparently distant, but harsh, protracted, and most unusual screaming or grating sound—the exact counterpart of what my fancy had already conjured up for the dragon's unnatural shriek as described by the romancer.

Oppressed, as I certainly was, upon the occurrence of this second and most extraordinary coincidence, by a thousand conflicting sensations, in which wonder and extreme terror were predominant, I still retained sufficient presence of mind to avoid exciting, by any observation, the sensitive nervousness of my companion. I was by no means certain that he had noticed the sounds in question; although, assuredly, a strange alteration had during the last few minutes taken place in his demeanor. From a position fronting my own, he had gradually brought round his chair, so as to sit with his face to the door of the chamber; and thus I could but partially perceive his features, although I saw that his lips trembled as if he were murmuring inaudibly. His head had dropped upon his breast—yet I knew that he was not asleep, from the wide and rigid opening of the eye as I caught a glance of it in profile. The motion of his body, too, was at variance with this idea—for he rocked from side to side with a gentle yet constant and uniform sway. Having rapidly taken notice of all this, I resumed the narrative of Sir Launcelot, which thus proceeded:

And now, the champion, having escaped from the terrible fury of the dragon, bethinking himself of the brazen shield, and of the breaking up of the enchantment which was upon it, removed the carcass from out of the way before him, and approached valorously over the silver pavement of the castle to where the shield was upon the wall; which in sooth tarried not for his full coming; but fell down at his feet upon the silver floor, with a mighty great and terrible ringing sound.

No sooner had these syllables passed my lips, than—as if a shield of brass had indeed, at the moment, fallen heavily upon a floor of silver—I became aware of a distinct, hollow, metallic and clangorous yet apparently muffled reverberation. Completely unnerved, I leaped to my feet; but the measured rocking movement of Usher was undisturbed. I rushed to the chair in which he sat. His eyes were bent fixedly before him, and throughout his whole countenance there reigned a stony rigidity. But as I placed my hand upon his shoulder, there came a strong shudder over his whole person; a sickly smile quivered about his lips; and I saw that he spoke in a low, hurried, and gibbering murmur, as if unconscious of my presence. Bending closely over him, I at length drank in the hideous import of his words.

"Not hear it?—yes, I hear it, and *have* heard it. Long—long—long—many minutes, many hours, many days, have I heard it—yet I dared not—oh, pity me, miserable wretch that I am!—I dared not—I *dared* not speak! *We have put her living in the tomb!* Said I not that my senses were acute? I *now* tell you that I heard her first feeble movements in the hollow coffin. I heard them—many, many days ago—yet I dared not—*I dared not speak!* And now—to-night—Ethelred—ha! ha!—the breaking of the hermit's door, and the death-cry of the dragon, and the clangor of the shield!—say, rather, the rending of her coffin, and the grating of the iron hinges of her prison, and her struggles within the coppered archway of the vault! Oh, whither shall I fly? Will she not be here anon? Is he not hurrying to upbraid me for my haste? Have I not heard her footstep on the stair? Do I not distinguish that heavy and horrible beating of her heart? Madman!"—here he sprang furiously to his feet, and shrieked out his syllables, as if in the effort he were giving up his soul—*"Madman! I tell you that she now stands without the door!"*

As if in the superhuman energy of his utterance there had been found the potency of a spell, the huge antique panels to which the speaker pointed threw slowly back, upon the instant, their ponderous and ebony jaws. It was the work of the rushing gust—but then without those doors there *did* stand the lofty and enshrouded figure of the lady Madeline of Usher. There was blood upon her white robes, and the evidence of some bitter struggle upon every portion of her emaciated frame. For a moment she remained trembling and reeling to and fro upon the threshold—then, with a low moaning cry, fell heavily inward upon the person of her brother, and, in her violent and now final death agonies, bore him to the floor a corpse, and a victim to the terrors he had anticipated.

From that chamber, and from that mansion, I fled aghast. The storm was still abroad in all its wrath as I found myself crossing the old causeway. Suddenly there shot along the path a wild light, and I turned to see whence a gleam so unusual could have issued; for the vast house and its shadows were alone behind me. The radiance was that of the full, setting, and blood-red moon, which now shone vividly through that once barely discernible fissure, of which I have before spoken as extending from the roof of the building, in a zigzag direction, to the base. While I gazed, this fissure rapidly widened—there came a fierce breath of the whirlwind—the entire orb of the satellite burst at once upon my sight—my brain reeled as I saw the mighty walls rushing asunder—there was a long tumultuous shouting sound like the voice of a thousand waters—and the deep and dank tarn at my feet closed sullenly and silently over the fragments of the *"House of Usher."*

1839

The Purloined Letter

Nil sapientiae odiosius acumine nimio.
[*Nothing is more odious to good sense than too much cleverness.*]

—SENECA

At Paris, just after dark one gusty evening in the autumn of 18——, I was enjoying the twofold luxury of meditation and a meerschaum, in company with my friend C. Auguste Dupin, in his little back library, or bookcloset, *au troisième, No. 33, Rue Dunôt, Faubourg St. Germain.* For one hour at least we had maintained a profound silence; while each, to any casual observer, might have seemed intently and exclusively occupied with the curling eddies of smoke that oppressed the atmosphere of the chamber. For myself, however, I was mentally discussing certain topics which had formed matter for conversation between us at an earlier period of the evening; I mean the affair of the Rue Morgue, and the mystery attending the murder of Marie Rogêt. I looked upon it, therefore, as something of a coincidence, when the door of our apartment was thrown open and admitted our old acquaintance, Monsieur G——, the Prefect of the Parisian police.

We gave him a hearty welcome; for there was nearly half as much of the entertaining as of the contemptible about the man, and we had not seen him for several years. We had been sitting in the dark, and Dupin now arose for the purpose of lighting a lamp, but sat down again, without doing so, upon G——'s saying that he had called to consult us, or rather to ask the opinion of my friend, about some official business which had occasioned a great deal of trouble.

"If it is any point requiring reflection," observed Dupin, as he forebore to enkindle the wick, "we shall examine it to better purpose in the dark."

"That is another of your odd notions," said the Prefect,

who had a fashion of calling every thing "odd" that was beyond his comprehension, and thus lived amid an absolute legion of "oddities."

"Very true," said Dupin, as he supplied his visitor with a pipe, and rolled towards him a comfortable chair.

"And what is the difficulty now?" I asked. "Nothing more in the assassination way, I hope?"

"Oh no; nothing of that nature. The fact is, the business is *very* simple indeed, and I make no doubt that we can manage it sufficiently well ourselves; but then I thought Dupin would like to hear the details of it, because it is so excessively *odd*."

"Simple and odd," said Dupin.

"Why, yes; and not exactly that, either. The fact is, we have all been a good deal puzzled because the affair *is* so simple, and yet baffles us altogether."

"Perhaps it is the very simplicity of the thing which puts you at fault," said my friend.

"What nonsense you *do* talk!" replied the Prefect, laughing heartily.

"Perhaps the mystery is a little *too* plain," said Dupin.

"Oh, good heavens! who ever heard of such an idea?"

"A little *too* self-evident."

"Ha! ha! ha!—ha! ha! ha!—ho! ho! ho!"—roared our visitor, profoundly amused, "oh, Dupin, you will be the death of me yet!"

"And what, after all, *is* the matter on hand?" I asked.

"Why, I will tell you," replied the Prefect, as he gave a long, steady, and contemplative puff, and settled himself in his chair. "I will tell you in a few words; but, before I begin, let me caution you that this is an affair demanding the greatest secrecy, and that I should most probably lose the position I now hold, were it known that I confided it to any one."

"Proceed," said I.

"Or not," said Dupin.

"Well, then; I have received personal information, from a very high quarter, that a certain document of the last importance has been purloined from the royal apartments. The individual who purloined it is known; this beyond a doubt; he was seen to take it. It is known, also, that it still remains in his possession."

"How is this known?" asked Dupin.

"It is clearly inferred," replied the Prefect, "from the nature of the document, and from the non-appearance of certain results which would at once arise from its passing *out* of the robber's possession;—that is to say, from his employing it as he must design in the end to employ it."

"Be a little more explicit," I said.

"Well, I may venture so far as to say that the paper gives its holder a certain power in a certain quarter where such power is immensely valuable." The Prefect was fond of the cant of diplomacy.

"Still I do not quite understand," said Dupin.

"No? Well; the disclosure of the document to a third person who shall be nameless would bring in question the honor of a personage of most exalted station; and this fact gives the holder of the document an ascendancy over the illustrious personage whose honor and peace are so jeopardized."

"But this ascendancy," I interposed, "would depend upon the robber's knowledge of the loser's knowledge of the robber. Who would dare—"

"The thief," said G——, "is the Minister D——, who dares all things, those unbecoming as well as those becoming a man. The method of the theft was not less ingenious than bold. The document in question—a letter, to be frank —had been received by the personage robbed while alone in the royal *boudoir*. During its perusal she was suddenly interrupted by the entrance of the other exalted personage from whom especially it was her wish to conceal it. After a hurried and vain endeavor to thrust it in a drawer, she was forced to place it, open as it was, upon a table. The address, however, was uppermost, and, the contents thus unexposed, the letter escaped notice. At this juncture enters the Minister D——. His lynx eye immediately perceives the paper, recognizes the handwriting of the address, observes the confusion of the personage addressed, and fathoms her secret. After some business transactions, hurried through in his ordinary manner, he produces a letter somewhat similar to the one in question, opens it, pretends to read it, and then places it in close juxtaposition to the other. Again he converses, for some fifteen minutes, upon the public affairs. At length, in taking leave, he takes also from the table the letter to which he had no claim. Its rightful owner saw, but, of course, dared not call attention to the act, in the presence of the third personage who stood at her elbow. The Minister decamped; leaving his own letter—one of no importance—upon the table."

"Here, then," said Dupin to me, "you have precisely what you demand to make the ascendancy complete—the robber's knowledge of the loser's knowledge of the robber."

"Yes," replied the Prefect; "and the power thus attained has, for some months past, been wielded, for political purposes, to a very dangerous extent. The personage robbed is more thoroughly convinced, every day, of the necessity of reclaiming her letter. But this, of course, cannot be done openly. In fine, driven to despair, she has committed the matter to me."

"Than whom," said Dupin, amid a perfect whirlwind of smoke, "no more sagacious agent could, I suppose, be desired, or even imagined."

"You flatter me," replied the Prefect; "but it is possible that some such opinion may have been entertained."

"It is clear," said I, "as you observe, that the letter is still in possession of the Minister; since it is this possession, and not any employment of the letter, which bestows the power. With the employment the power departs."

"True," said G——; "and upon this conviction I proceeded. My first care was to make thorough search of the Minister's hotel; and here my chief embarrassment lay in the necessity of searching without his knowledge. Beyond all things, I have been warned of the danger which would result from giving him reason to suspect our design."

"But," said I, "you are quite *au fait* in these investigations. The Parisian police have done this thing often before."

"Oh yes; and for this reason I did not despair. The habits of the Minister gave me, too, a great advantage. He is frequently absent from home all night. His servants are by no means numerous. They sleep at a distance from their master's apartment, and, being chiefly Neapolitans, are readily made drunk. I have keys, as you know, with which I can open any chamber or cabinet in Paris. For three months a night has not passed, during the greater part of which I have not been engaged, personally, in ransacking the D—— Hôtel. My honor is interested, and, to mention a great secret, the reward is enormous. So I did not abandon the search until I had become fully satisfied

that the thief is a more astute man than myself. I fancy
that I have investigated every nook and corner of the
premises in which it is possible that the paper can be
concealed."

"But is it not possible," I suggested, "that although the
letter may be in the possession of the Minister, as it unquestionably is, he may have concealed it elsewhere than upon
his own premises?"

"This is barely possible," said Dupin. "The present
peculiar condition of affairs at court, and especially of
those intrigues in which D—— is known to be involved,
would render the instant availability of the document—its
susceptibility of being produced at a moment's notice—a
point of nearly equal importance with its possession."

"It's susceptibility of being produced?" said I.

"That is to say, of being *destroyed*," said Dupin.

"True," I observed; "the paper is clearly then upon the
premises. As for its being upon the person of the Minister,
we may consider that as out of the question."

"Entirely," said the Prefect. "He has been twice waylaid,
as if by footpads, and his person rigorously searched under
my own inspection."

"You might have spared yourself this trouble," said
Dupin. "D——, I presume, is not altogether a fool, and,
if not, must have anticipated these waylayings, as a matter
of course."

"Not *altogether* a fool," said G——, "but then he's a
poet, which I take to be only one remove from a fool."

"True," said Dupin, after a long and thoughtful whiff
from his meerschaum, "although I have been guilty of
certain doggerel myself."

"Suppose you detail," said I, "the particulars of your
search."

"Why the fact is, we took our time, and we searched
every where. I have had long experience in these affairs.
I took the entire building, room by room; devoting the
nights of a whole week to each. We examined, first, the
furniture of each apartment. We opened every possible
drawer; and I presume you know that, to a properly trained
police agent, such a thing as a *secret* drawer is impossible.
Any man is a dolt who permits a 'secret' drawer to escape
him in a search of this kind. The thing is *so* plain. There
is a certain amount of bulk—a space—to be accounted

for in every cabinet. Then we have accurate rules. The fiftieth part of a line could not escape us. After the cabinets we took the chairs. The cushions we probed with the fine long needles you have seen me employ. From the tables we removed the tops."

"Why so?"

"Sometimes the top of a table, or other similarly arranged piece of furniture, is removed by the person wishing to conceal an article; then the leg is excavated, the article deposited within the cavity, and the top replaced. The bottoms and tops of bed-posts are employed in the same way."

"But could not the cavity be detected by sounding?" I asked.

"By no means, if, when the article is deposited, a sufficient wadding of cotton be placed around it. Besides, in our case, we were obliged to proceed without noise."

"But you could not have removed—you could not have taken to pieces *all* articles of furniture in which it would have been possible to make a deposit in the manner you mention. A letter may be compressed into a thin spiral roll, not differing much in shape or bulk from a large knitting-needle, and in this form it might be inserted into the rung of a chair, for example. You did not take to pieces all the chairs?"

"Certainly not; but we did better—we examined the rungs of every chair in the hotel, and, indeed, the jointings of every description of furniture, by the aid of a most powerful microscope. Had there been any traces of recent disturbance we should not have failed to detect it instantly. A single grain of gimlet-dust, for example, would have been as obvious as an apple. Any disorder in the glueing—any unusual gaping in the joints—would have sufficed to insure detection."

"I presume you looked to the mirrors, between the boards and the plates, and you probed the beds and the bed-clothes, as well as the curtains and carpets."

"That of course; and when we had absolutely completed every particle of the furniture in this way, then we examined the house itself. We divided its entire surface into compartments, which we numbered, so that none might be missed; then we scrutinized each individual square inch throughout the premises, including the two houses immediately adjoining, with the microscope, as before."

"The two houses adjoining!" I exclaimed; "you must have had a great deal of trouble."

"We had; but the reward offered is prodigious."

"You include the *grounds* about the houses?"

"All the grounds are paved with brick. They gave us comparatively little trouble. We examined the moss between the bricks, and found it undisturbed."

"You looked among D——'s papers, of course, and into the books of the library?"

"Certainly; we opened every package and parcel; we not only opened every book, but we turned over every leaf in each volume, not contenting ourselves with a mere shake, according to the fashion of some of our police officers. We also measured the thickness of every book-*cover*, with the most accurate admeasurement, and applied to each the most jealous scrutiny of the microscope. Had any of the bindings been recently meddled with, it would have been utterly impossible that the fact should have escaped observation. Some five or six volumes, just from the hands of the binder, we carefully probed, longitudinally, with the needles."

"You explored the floors beneath the carpets?"

"Beyond doubt. We removed every carpet, and examined the boards with the microscope."

"And the paper on the walls?"

"Yes."

"You looked into the cellars?"

"We did."

"Then," I said, "you have been making a miscalculation, and the letter is *not* upon the premises, as you suppose."

"I fear you are right there," said the Prefect. "And now, Dupin, what would you advise me to do?"

"To make a thorough re-search of the premises."

"That is absolutely needless," replied G——. "I am not more sure that I breathe than I am that the letter is not at the Hôtel."

"I have no better advice to give you," said Dupin. "You have, of course, an accurate description of the letter?"

"Oh yes!"—And here the Prefect, producing a memorandum-book, proceeded to read aloud a minute account of the internal, and especially of the external appearance of the missing document. Soon after finishing the perusal of this description, he took his departure, more entirely depressed in spirits than I had ever known the good gentleman before.

In about a month afterwards he paid us another visit, and found us occupied very nearly as before. He took a pipe and a chair and entered into some ordinary conversation. At length I said,—

"Well, but G——, what of the purloined letter? I presume you have at last made up your mind that there is no such thing as overreaching the Minister?"

"Confound him, say I—yes; I made the re-examination, however, as Dupin suggested—but it was all labor lost, as I knew it would be."

"How much was the reward offered, did you say?" asked Dupin.

"Why, a very great deal—a *very* liberal reward—I don't like to say how much, precisely; but one thing I *will* say, that I wouldn't mind giving my individual check for fifty thousand francs to any one who could obtain me that letter. The fact is, it is becoming of more and more importance every day; and the reward has been lately doubled. If it were trebled, however, I could do no more than I have done."

"Why, yes," said Dupin, drawlingly, between the whiffs of his meerschaum, "I really—think, G——, you have not exerted yourself—to the utmost in this matter. You might —do a little more, I think, eh?"

"How?—in what way?"

"Why—puff, puff—you might—puff, puff—employ counsel in the matter, eh?—puff, puff, puff. Do you remember the story they tell of Abernethy?"

"No; hang Abernethy!"

"To be sure! hang him and welcome. But, once upon a time, a certain rich miser conceived the design of sponging upon this Abernethy for a medical opinion. Getting up, for this purpose, an ordinary conversation in a private company, he insinuated his case to his physician, as that of an imaginary individual.

" 'We will suppose,' said the miser, 'that his symptoms are such and such; now, doctor, what would *you* have directed him to take?' "

" 'Take!' said Abernethy, 'why, take *advice,* to be sure.' "

"But," said the Prefect, a little discomposed, "*I am perfectly* willing to take advice, and to pay for it. I would *really* give fifty thousand francs to any one who would aid me in the matter."

"In that case," replied Dupin, opening a drawer, and producing a check-book, "you may as well fill me up a check for the amount mentioned. When you have signed it, I will hand you the letter."

I was astounded. The Prefect appeared absolutely thunder-stricken. For some minutes he remained speechless and motionless, looking incredulously at my friend with open mouth, and eyes that seemed starting from their sockets; then, apparently recovering himself in some measure, he seized a pen, and after several pauses and vacant stares, finally filled up and signed a check for fifty thousand francs, and handed it across the table to Dupin. The latter examined it carefully and deposited it in his pocket-book; then, unlocking an *escritoire,* took thence a letter and gave it to the Prefect. This functionary grasped it in a perfect agony of joy, opened it with a trembling hand, cast a rapid glance at its contents, and then, scrambling and struggling to the door, rushed at length unceremoniously from the room and from the house, without having uttered a syllable since Dupin had requested him to fill up the check.

When he had gone, my friend entered into some explanations.

"The Parisian police," he said, "are exceedingly able in their way. They are persevering, ingenious, cunning, and thoroughly versed in the knowledge which their duties seem chiefly to demand. Thus, when G—— detailed to us his mode of searching the premises at the Hôtel D——, I felt entire confidence in his having made a satisfactory investigation—so far as his labors extended."

"So far as his labors extended?" said I.

"Yes," said Dupin. "The measures adopted were not only the best of their kind, but carried out to absolute perfection. Had the letter been deposited with the range of their search, these fellows would, beyond a question, have found it."

I merely laughed—but he seemed quite serious in all that he said.

"The measures, then," he continued, "were good in their kind, and well executed; their defect lay in their being inapplicable to the case, and to the man. A certain set of highly ingenious resources are, with the Prefect, a sort of Procrustean bed, to which he forcibly adapts his designs. But he perpetually errs by being too deep or too shallow, for the matter in hand; and many a schoolboy is a better reasoner than he. I knew one about eight years of age, whose success at guessing in the game of 'even and odd' attracted universal admiration. This game is simple, and is played with marbles. One player holds in his hand a number of these toys, and demands of another whether that number is even or odd. If the guess is right, the guesser wins one; if wrong, he loses one. The boy to whom I allude won all the marbles of the school. Of course he had some principle of guessing; and this lay in mere observation and admeasurement of the astuteness of his opponents. For example, an arrant simpleton is his opponent, and, holding up his closed hand, asks, 'are they even or odd?' Our schoolboy replies, 'odd,' and loses; but upon the second trial he wins, for he then says to himself, 'the simpleton had them even upon the first trial, and his amount of cunning is just sufficient to make him have them odd upon the second; I will therefore guess odd';—he guesses odd, and wins. Now, with a simpleton a degree above the first, he would have reasoned thus: 'This fellow finds that in the first instance I guessed odd, and, in the second, he will propose to himself upon the first impulse, a simple variation from even to odd, as did the first simpleton; but then a second thought will suggest that this is too simple a variation, and finally he will decide upon putting it even as before. I will therefore guess even';—he guesses even, and wins. Now this mode of reasoning in the schoolboy, whom his fellows termed 'lucky,'—what, in its last analysis, is it?"

"It is merely," I said, "an identification of the reasoner's intellect with that of his opponent."

"It is," said Dupin; "and, upon inquiring of the boy by what means he effected the *thorough* identification in which his success consisted, I received answer as follows: 'When I wish to find out how wise, or how stupid, or how good, or how wicked is any one, or what are his thoughts at the moment, I fashion the expression of my face, as accurately as possible, in accordance with the expression of his, and then wait to see what thoughts or sentiments arise in my mind or heart, as if to match or correspond with the expression.' This response of the schoolboy lies at the bottom of all the spurious profundity which has been attributed to Rochefoucauld, to La Bougive, to Machiavelli, and to Campanella."

"And the identification," I said, "of the reasoner's intellect with that of his opponent, depends, if I understand you aright, upon the accuracy with which the opponent's intellect is admeasured."

"For its practical value it depends upon this," replied Dupin; "and the Prefect and his cohort fail so frequently, first, by default of this identification, and, secondly, by ill-admeasurement, or rather through non-admeasurement of the intellect with which they are engaged. They consider only their *own* ideas of ingenuity; and, in searching for anything hidden, advert only to the modes in which *they* would have hidden it. They are right in this much—that their own ingenuity is a faithful representative of that of *the mass;* but when the cunning of the individual felon is diverse in character from their own, the felon foils them, of course. This always happens when it is above their own, and very usually when it is below. They have no variation of principle in their investigations; at best, when urged by some unusual emergency—by some extraordinary reward —they extend or exaggerate their old modes of *practice,* without touching their principles. What, for example, in this case of D——, has been done to vary the principle of action? What is all this boring, and probing, and sounding, and scrutinizing with the microscope, and dividing the surface of the building into registered square inches—what is it all but an exaggeration *of the application* of the one principle or set of principles of search, which are based upon the one set of notions regarding human ingenuity, to which the Prefect, in the long routine of his duty, has been accustomed? Do you not see he has taken it for granted that *all* men proceed to conceal a letter—not exactly in a gimlet-hole bored in a chair-leg—but, at least, in *some* out-of-the-way hole or corner suggested by the same tenor of thought which would urge a man to secrete a letter in a gimlet-hole bored in a chair-leg? And do you not see also, that such *recherchés* nooks for concealment are adopted only for ordinary occasions, and would be adopted only by ordinary intellects; for, in all cases of concealment, a disposal of the article concealed—a disposal of it in this *recherché* manner —is, in the very first instance, presumable and presumed;

and thus its discovery depends, not at all upon the acumen, but altogether upon the mere care, patience, and determination of the seekers; and where the case is of importance— or, what amounts to the same thing in the policial eyes, when the reward is of magnitude,—the qualities in question have *never* been known to fail? You will now understand what I meant in suggesting that, had the purloined letter been hidden any where within the limits of the Prefect's examination—in other words, had the principle of its concealment been comprehended within the principles of the Prefect—its discovery would have been a matter altogether beyond question. This functionary, however, has been thoroughly mystified; and the remote source of his defeat lies in the supposition that the Minister is a fool, because he has acquired renown as a poet. All fools are poets; this the Prefect *feels;* and he is merely guilty of a *non distributio medii* [undistributed middle] in thence inferring that all poets are fools."

"But is this really the poet?" I asked. "There are two brothers, I know; and both have attained reputation in letters. The Minister I believe has written learnedly on the Differential Calculus. He is a mathematician, and no poet."

"You are mistaken; I know him well; he is both. As poet *and* mathematician, he would reason well; as mere mathematician, he could not have reasoned at all, and thus would have been at the mercy of the Prefect."

"You surprise me," I said, "by these opinions, which have been contradicted by the voice of the world. You do not mean to set at naught the well-digested idea of centuries. The mathematical reason has long been regarded as *the* reason *par excellence.*"

" '*Il y a à parier,*' " replied Dupin, quoting from Chamfort, " " '*que toute idée publique, toute convention reçue, est une sottise, car elle a convenu au plus grand nombre.*' [I'll bet that every popular idea, every set convention, is an idiocy, because it has suited the majority.] The mathematicians, I grant you, have done their best to promulgate the popular error to which you allude, and which is none the less an error for its promulgation as truth. With an art worthy a better cause, for example, they have insinuated the term 'analysis' into application to algebra. The French are the originators of this particular deception; but if a term is of any importance—if words derive any value from applicability—then 'analysis' conveys 'algebra' about as much as, in Latin, *'ambitus'* implies 'ambition,' *'religio'* 'religion,' or *'homines honesti'* a set of *honorable* men."

"You have a quarrel on hand, I see," said I, "with some of the algebraists of Paris; but proceed."

"I dispute the availability, and thus the value, of that reason which is cultivated in any especial form other than the abstractly logical. I dispute, in particular, the reason educed by mathematical study. The mathematics are the science of form and quantity; mathematical reasoning is merely logic applied to observation upon form and quantity. The great error lies in supposing that even the truths of what is called *pure* algebra, are abstract or general truths. And this error is so egregious that I am confounded at the universality with which it has been received. Mathematical axioms are *not* axioms of general truth. What is true of *relation*—of form and quantity—is often grossly false in regard to morals, for example. In this latter science it is very usually *un*true that the aggregated parts are equal to the whole. In chemistry also the axiom fails. In the consideration of motive it fails; for two motives, each of a given value, have not, necessarily, a value when united, equal to the sum of their values apart. There are numerous other mathematical truths which are only truths within the limits of *relation*. But the mathematician argues, from his *finite truths,* through habit, as if they were of an absolutely general applicability —as the world indeed imagines them to be. Bryant, in his very learned 'Mythology,' mentions an analogous source of error, when he says that 'although the Pagan fables are not believed, yet we forget ourselves continually, and make inferences from them as existing realities.' With the algebraists, however, who are Pagans themselves, the 'Pagan fables' *are* believed, and the inferences are made, not so much through lapse of memory, as through an unaccountable addling of the brains. In short, I never yet encountered the mere mathematician who could be trusted out of equal roots, or one who did not clandestinely hold it as a point of his faith that $x^2 + px$ was absolutely and unconditionally equal to q. Say to one of these gentlemen, by way of experiment, if you please, that you believe occasions may occur where $x^2 + px$ is *not* altogether equal to q, and, having made him understand what you mean, get out of his reach as speedily as convenient, for, beyond doubt, he will endeavor to knock you down.

"I mean to say," continued Dupin, while I merely laughed at his last observations, "that if the Minister had been no more than a mathematician, the Prefect would have been under no necessity of giving me this check. I knew him, however, as both mathematician and poet, and my measures were adapted to his capacity, with reference to the circumstances by which he was surrounded. I knew him as a courtier, too, and as a bold *intriguant.* Such a man, I considered, could not fail to be aware of the ordinary policial modes of action. He could not have failed to anticipate—and events have proved that he did not fail to anticipate—the waylayings to which he was subjected. He must have foreseen, I reflected, the secret investigations of his premises. His frequent absences from home at night, which were hailed by the Prefect as certain aids to his success, I regarded only as *ruses,* to afford opportunity for thorough search to the police, and thus the sooner to impress them with the conviction to which G——, in fact, did finally arrive—the conviction that the letter was not upon the premises. I felt, also, that the whole train of thought, which I was at some pains in detailing to you just now, concerning the invariable principal of policial action in searches for articles concealed—I felt that this whole train of thought would necessarily pass through the mind of the Minister. It would imperatively lead him to despise all the ordinary *nooks* of concealment. *He* could not, I reflected, be so weak as not to see that the most intricate and remote recess of his hotel would be as open as his commonest closets to the eyes, to the probes, to the gimlets, and to the microscopes of the Prefect. I saw, in fine, that he would be driven, as a matter of course, to *simplicity,* if not deliberately induced to it as a matter of choice. You will remember, perhaps, how desperately the Prefect laughed when I suggested, upon our first interview, that it was just possible this mystery troubled him so much on account of its being so *very* self-evident."

"Yes," said I, "I remember his merriment well. I really thought he would have fallen into convulsions."

"The material world," continued Dupin, "abounds with the very strict analogies to the immaterial; and thus some color of truth has been given to the rhetorical dogma, that metaphor, or simile, may be made to strengthen an argument, as well as to embellish a description. The principle of the *vis inertiæ* [force of inertia], for example, seems to be identical in physics and metaphysics. It is not more true in the former, that a large body is with more difficulty set in motion than a smaller one, and that its subsequent *momentum* is commensurate with this difficulty, than it is, in the latter, that intellects of the vaster capacity, while more forcible, more constant, and more eventful in their movements than those of inferior grade, are yet the less readily moved, and more embarrassed and full of hesitation in the first few steps of their progress. Again: have you ever noticed which of the street signs, over the shop doors, are the most attractive of attention?"

"I have never given the matter a thought," I said.

"There is a game of puzzles," he resumed, "which is played upon a map. One party playing requires another to find a given word—the name of town, river, state or empire—any word, in short, upon the motley and perplexed surface of the chart. A novice in the game generally seeks to embarrass his opponents by giving them the most minutely lettered names; but the adept selects such words as stretch, in large characters, from one end of the chart to the other. These, like the over-largely lettered signs and placards of the street, escape observation by dint of being excessively obvious; and here the physical oversight is precisely analogous with the moral inapprehension by which the intellect suffers to pass unnoticed those considerations which are too obtrusively and too palpably self-evident. But this is a point, it appears, somewhat above or beneath the understanding of the Prefect. He never once thought it probable, or possible, that the Minister had deposited the letter immediately beneath the nose of the whole world, by way of best preventing any portion of that world from perceiving it.

"But the more I reflected upon the daring, dashing, and discriminating ingenuity of D——; upon the fact that the document must always have been *at hand,* if he intended to use it to good purpose; and upon the decisive evidence, obtained by the Prefect, that it was not hidden within the limits of that dignitary's ordinary search—the more satisfied I became that, to conceal this letter, the Minister had resorted to the comprehensive and sagacious expedient of not attempting to conceal it at all.

"Full of these ideas, I prepared myself with a pair of green spectacles, and called one fine morning, quite by accident, at the Ministerial hotel. I found G—— at home, yawning, lounging, and dawdling, as usual, and pretending to be in the last extremity of *ennui*. He is, perhaps, the most really energetic human being now alive—but that is only when nobody sees him.

"To be even with him, I complained of my weak eyes, and lamented the necessity of the spectacles, under cover of which I cautiously and thoroughly surveyed the apartment, while seemingly intent only upon the conversation of my host.

"I paid especial attention to a large writing-table near which he sat, and upon which lay confusedly some miscellaneous letters and other papers, with one or two musical instruments and a few books. Here, however, after a long and very deliberate scrutiny, I saw nothing to excite particular suspicion.

"At length my eyes, in going the circuit of the room, fell upon a trumpery filigree card-rack of pasteboard, that hung dangling by a dirty blue ribbon, from a little brass knob just beneath the middle of the mantel-piece. In this rack, which had three or four compartments, were five or six visiting cards and a solitary letter. This last was much soiled and crumpled. It was torn nearly in two, across the middle —as if a design, in the first instance, to tear it entirely up as worthless, had been altered, or stayed, in the second. It had a large black seal, bearing the D—— cipher *very* conspicuously, and was addressed, in a diminutive female hand, to D——, the Minister, himself. It was thrust carelessly, and even, as it seemed, contemptuously, into one of the upper divisions of the rack.

"No sooner had I glanced at this letter, than I concluded it to be that of which I was in search. To be sure, it was, to all appearance, radically different from the one of which the Prefect had read us so minute a description. Here the seal was large and black, with the D—— cipher; there it was small and red, with the ducal arms of the S—— family. Here, the address, to the Minister, was diminutive and feminine; there the superscription, to a certain royal personage, was markedly bold and decided; the size alone formed a point of correspondence. But, then, the *radical-ness* of these differences, which was excessive; the dirt; the soiled and torn condition of the paper, so inconsistent with the *true* methodical habits of D——, and so suggestive of a design to delude the beholder into an idea of the worthlessness of the document;—these things, together with the hyperobtrusive situation of this document, full in the view of every visitor, and thus exactly in accordance with the conclusions to which I had previously arrived; these things, I say, were strongly corroborative of suspicion, in one who came with the intention to suspect.

"I protracted my visit as long as possible, and, while I maintained a most animated discussion with the Minister, on a topic which I knew well had never failed to interest and excite him, I kept my attention really riveted upon the letter. In this examination, I committed to memory its external appearance and arrangement in the rack; and also fell, at length, upon a discovery which set at rest whatever trivial doubt I might have entertained. In scrutinizing the edges of the paper, I observed them to be more *chafed* than seemed necessary. They presented the *broken* appearance which is manifested when a stiff paper, having been once folded and pressed with a folder, is refolded in a reversed direction, in the same creases or edges which had formed the original fold. This discovery was sufficient. It was clear to me that the letter had been turned, as a glove, inside out, re-directed, and resealed. I bade the Minister good morning, and took my departure at once, leaving a gold snuff-box upon the table.

"The next morning I called for the snuff-box, when we resumed, quite eagerly, the conversation of the preceding day. While thus engaged, however, a loud report, as if of a pistol, was heard immediately beneath the windows of the hotel, and was succeeded by a series of fearful screams, and the shoutings of a mob. D—— rushed to a casement, threw it open, and looked out. In the meantime, I stepped to the card-rack, took the letter, and put it in my pocket, and re-placed it by a *fac-simile* (so far as regards externals), which I had carefully prepared at my lodgings; imitating the D—— cipher, very readily, by means of a seal formed of bread.

"The disturbance in the street had been occasioned by the frantic behavior of a man with a musket. He had fired it among a crowd of women and children. It proved, however, to have been without ball, and the fellow was suffered to go his way as a lunatic or a drunkard. When he had gone, D—— came from the window, whither I had followed him immediately upon securing the object in view. Soon afterwards I bade him farewell. The pretended lunatic was a man in my own pay."

"But what purpose had you," I asked, "in replacing the letter by a *fac-simile?* Would it not have been better, at the first visit, to have seized it openly, and departed?"

"D——," replied Dupin, "is a desperate man, and a man of nerve. His hotel, too, is not without attendants devoted to his interests. Had I made the wild attempt you suggest, I might never have left the Ministerial presence alive. The good people of Paris might have heard of me no more. But I had an object apart from these considerations. You know my political prepossessions. In this matter, I act as a partisan of the lady concerned. For eighteen months the Minister has had her in his power. She has now him in hers—since, being unaware that the letter is not in his possession, he will proceed with his exactions as if it was. Thus will he inevitably commit himself, at once, to his political destruction. His downfall, too, will not be more precipitate than awkward. It is all very well to talk about the *facilis descensus Averni* [facile descent to Hades]; but in all kinds of climbing, as Catalani said of singing, it is far more easy to get up than to come down. In the present instance I have no sympathy—at least no pity—for him who descends. He is that *monstrum horrendum* [horrendous monster], an unprincipled man of genius. I confess, however, that I should like very well to know the precise character of his thoughts, when, being defied by her whom the Prefect terms 'a certain personage,' he is reduced to opening the letter which I left for him in the card-rack."

"How? did you put any thing particular in it?"

"Why—it did not seem altogether right to leave the interior blank—that would have been insulting. D——, at Vienna once, did me an evil turn, which I told him, quite good-humoredly, that I should remember. So, as I knew he would feel some curiosity in regard to the identity of the person who had outwitted him, I thought it a pity not to give him a clue. He is well acquainted with my MS., and I just copied into the middle of the blank sheet the words—

"—*Un dessein si funeste,
S'il n'est digne d'Atrée, est digne de Thyeste.*

[A plan so deadly is worthy of Thyestes, if not of Atreus.] They are to be found in Crébillon's 'Atrée.' "

1845

The Cask of Amontillado

The thousand injuries of Fortunato I had borne as I best could, but when he ventured upon insult I vowed revenge. You, who so well know the nature of my soul, will not suppose, however, that I gave utterance to a threat. *At length* I would be avenged; this was a point definitely settled— but the very definitiveness with which it was resolved precluded the idea of risk. I must not only punish but punish with impunity. A wrong is unredressed when retribution overtakes its redresser. It is equally unredressed when the avenger fails to make himself felt as such to him who has done the wrong.

It must be understood that neither by word nor deed had I given Fortunato cause to doubt my good will. I continued, as was my wont, to smile in his face, and he did not perceive that my smile *now* was at the thought of his immolation.

He had a weak point—this Fortunato—although in other regards he was a man to be respected and even feared. He prided himself on his connoisseurship in wine. Few Italians have the true virtuoso spirit. For the most part their enthusiasm is adopted to suit the time and opportunity, to practise imposture upon the British and Austrian *millionaires*. In painting and gemmary, Fortunato, like his countrymen, was a quack, but in the matter of old wines he was sincere. In this respect I did not differ from him materially; —I was skilful in the Italian vintages myself, and bought largely whenever I could.

It was about dusk, one evening during the supreme madness of the carnival season, that I encountered my friend. He accosted me with excessive warmth, for he had been drinking much. The man wore motley. He had on a tight-fitting parti-striped dress, and his head was surmounted by the conical cap and bells. I was so pleased to see him that I thought I should never have done wringing his hand.

I said to him—"My dear Fortunato, you are luckily met. How remarkably well you are looking today. But I have received a pipe [a cask of 126 gals.] of what passes for Amontillado, and I have my doubts."

"How?" said he. "Amontillado? A pipe? Impossible! And in the middle of the carnival!"

"I have my doubts," I replied; "and I was silly enough to pay the full Amontillado price without consulting you in the matter. You were not to be found, and I was fearful of losing a bargain."

"Amontillado!"

"I have my doubts."

"Amontillado!"

"And I must satisfy them."

"Amontillado!"

"As you are engaged, I am on my way to Luchresi. If any one has a critical turn it is he. He will tell me——"

"Luchresi cannot tell Amontillado from Sherry."

"And yet some fools will have it that his taste is a match for your own."

"Come, let us go."

"Whither?"

"To your vaults."

"My friend, no; I will not impose upon your good nature. I perceive you have an engagement. Luchresi——"

"I have no engagement;—come."

"My friend, no. It is not the engagement, but the severe cold with which I perceive you are afflicted. The vaults are insufferably damp. They are encrusted with nitre."

"Let us go, nevertheless. The cold is merely nothing. Amontillado! You have been imposed upon. And as for Luchresi, he cannot distinguish Sherry from Amontillado."

Thus speaking, Fortunato possessed himself of my arm; and putting on a mask of black silk and drawing a *roquelaire* closely about my person, I suffered him to hurry me to my palazzo.

There were no attendants at home; they had absconded to make merry in honor of the time. I had told them that I should not return until the morning, and had given them explicit orders not to stir from the house. These orders were sufficient, I well knew, to insure their immediate disappearance, one and all, as soon as my back was turned.

I took from their sconces two flambeaux, and giving one to Fortunato, bowed him through several suites of rooms to the archway that led into the vaults. I passed down a long and winding staircase, requesting him to be cautious as he followed. We came at length to the foot of the descent, and stood together upon the damp ground of the catacombs of the Montresors.

The gait of my friend was unsteady, and the bells upon his cap jingled as he strode.

"The pipe," he said.

"It is farther on," I said; "but observe the white webwork which gleams from these cavern walls."

He turned towards me, and looked into my eyes with two filmy orbs that distilled the rheum of intoxication.

"Nitre?" he asked, at length.

"Nitre," I replied. "How long have you had that cough?"

"Ugh! ugh! ugh!—ugh! ugh! ugh!—ugh! ugh! ugh!—ugh! ugh! ugh!—ugh! ugh! ugh!"

My poor friend found it impossible to reply for many minutes.

"It is nothing," he said, at last.

"Come," I said, with decision, "we will go back; your health is precious. You are rich, respected, admired, beloved; you are happy, as once I was. You are a man to be missed. For me it is no matter. We will go back; you will be ill, and I cannot be responsible. Besides, there is Luchresi——"

"Enough," he said; "the cough is a mere nothing; it will not kill me. I shall not die of a cough."

"True—true," I replied; "and, indeed, I had no intention of alarming you unnecessarily—but you should use all proper caution. A draught of this Medoc will defend us from the damps."

Here I knocked off the neck of a bottle which I drew from a long row of its fellows that lay upon the mould.

"Drink," I said, presenting him the wine.

He raised it to his lips with a leer. He paused and nodded to me familiarly, while his bells jingled.

"I drink," he said, "to the buried that repose around us."

"And I to your long life."

He again took my arm, and we proceeded.

"These vaults," he said, "are extensive."

"The Montresors," I replied, "were a great and numerous family."

"I forget your arms."

"A huge human foot d'or, in a field azure; the foot crushes a serpent rampant whose fangs are imbedded in the heel."

"And the motto?"

"*Nemo me impune lacessit.*" ["No one can injure me with impunity."]

"Good!" he said.

The wine sparkled in his eyes and the bells jingled. My own fancy grew warm with the Medoc. We had passed through long walls of piled skeletons, with casks and puncheons intermingling, into the inmost recesses of the catacombs. I paused again, and this time I made bold to seize Fortunato by an arm above the elbow.

"The nitre!" I said: "see, it increases. It hangs like moss upon the vaults. We are below the river's bed. The drops of moisture trickle among the bones. Come, we will go back ere it is too late. Your cough——"

"It is nothing," he said; "let us go on. But first, another draught of the Medoc."

I broke and reached him a flagon of De Grâve. He emptied it at a breath. His eyes flashed with a fierce light. He laughed and threw the bottle upwards with a gesticulation I did not understand.

I looked at him in surprise. He repeated the movement —a grotesque one.

"You do not comprehend?" he said.

"Not I," I replied.

"Then you are not of the brotherhood."

"How?"

"You are not of the masons."

"Yes, yes," I said; "yes, yes."

"You? Impossible! A mason?"

"A mason," I replied.

"A sign," he said, "a sign."

"It is this," I answered, producing from beneath the folds of my *roquelaire* a trowel.

"You jest," he exclaimed, recoiling a few paces. "But let us proceed to the Amontillado."

"Be it so," I said, replacing the tool beneath the cloak and again offering him my arm. He leaned upon it heavily. We continued our route in search of the Amontillado. We passed through a range of low arches, descended, passed on, and descending again, arrived at a deep crypt, in which the foulness of the air caused our flambeaux rather to glow than flame.

At the most remote end of the crypt there appeared another less spacious. Its walls had been lined with human remains, piled to the vault overhead, in the fashion of the great catacombs of Paris. Three sides of this interior crypt were still ornamented in this manner. From the fourth side the bones had been thrown down, and lay promiscuously upon the earth, forming at one point a mound of some size. Within the wall thus exposed by the displacing of the bones, we perceived a still interior crypt or recess, in depth about four feet, in width three, in height six or seven. It seemed to have been constructed for no especial use within itself, but formed merely the interval between two of the colossal supports of the roof of the catacombs, and was backed by one of their circumscribing walls of solid granite.

It was in vain that Fortunato, uplifting his dull torch, endeavored to pry into the depth of the recess. Its termination the feeble light did not enable us to see.

"Proceed," I said; "herein is the Amontillado. As for Luchresi—"

"He is an ignoramus," interrupted my friend, as he stepped unsteadily forward, while I followed immediately at his heels. In an instant he had reached the extremity of the niche, and finding his progress arrested by the rock, stood stupidly bewildered. A moment more and I had fettered him to the granite. In its surface were two iron staples, distant from each other about two feet, horizontally. From one of these depended a short chain, from the other a padlock. Throwing the links about his waist, it was but the work of a few seconds to secure it. He was too much astounded to resist. Withdrawing the key I stepped back from the recess.

"Pass your hand," I said, "over the wall; you cannot help feeling the nitre. Indeed, it is *very* damp. Once more let me *implore* you to return. No? Then I must positively leave you. But I must first render you all the little attentions in my power."

"The Amontillado!" ejaculated my friend, not yet recovered from his astonishment.

"True," I replied; "the Amontillado."

As I said these words I busied myself among the pile of bones of which I have before spoken. Throwing them aside, I soon uncovered a quantity of building stone and mortar. With these materials and with the aid of my trowel, I began vigorously to wall up the entrance of the niche.

I had scarcely laid the first tier of the masonry when I discovered that the intoxication of Fortunato had in a great measure worn off. The earliest indication I had of this was a low moaning cry of a drunken man. There was then a long and obstinate silence. I laid the second tier, and the third, and the fourth; and then I heard the furious vibrations of the chain. The noise lasted for several minutes, during which, that I might hearken to it with the more satisfaction, I ceased my labors and sat down upon the bones. When at last the clanking subsided, I resumed the trowel, and finished without interruption the fifth, the sixth, and the seventh tier. The wall was now nearly upon a level with my breast. I again paused, and holding the flambeaux over the mason-work, threw a few feeble rays upon the figure within.

A succession of loud and shrill screams, bursting suddenly from the throat of the chained form, seemed to thrust me violently back. For a brief moment I hesitated, I trembled. Unsheathing my rapier, I began to grope with it about the recess; but the thought of an instant reassured me. I placed my hand upon the solid fabric of the catacombs, and felt satisfied. I reapproached the wall; I replied to the yells of him who clamored. I re-echoed, I aided, I surpassed them in volume and in strength. I did this, and the clamorer grew still.

It was now midnight, and my task was drawing to a close. I had completed the eighth, the ninth and the tenth tier. I had finished a portion of the last and the eleventh; there remained but a single stone to be fitted and plastered in. I struggled with its weight; I placed it partially in its destined position. But now there came from out the niche a low laugh that erected the hairs upon my head. It was succeeded by a sad voice, which I had difficulty in recognizing as that of the noble Fortunato. The voice said—

"Ha! ha! ha!—he! he! he!—a very good joke, indeed—an excellent jest. We will have many a rich laugh about it at the palazzo—he! he! he!—over our wine—he! he! he!"

"The Amontillado!" I said.

"He! he! he!—he! he! he!—yes, the Amontillado. But is it not getting late? Will not they be awaiting us at the palazzo, the Lady Fortunato and the rest? Let us be gone."

"Yes," I said, "let us be gone."

"For the love of God, Montresor!"

"Yes," I said, "for the love of God!"

But to these words I hearkened in vain for a reply. I grew impatient. I called aloud—

"Fortunato!"

No answer. I called again—

"Fortunato!"

No answer still. I thrust a torch through the remaining aperture and let it fall within. There came forth in return only a jingling of the bells. My heart grew sick; it was the dampness of the catacombs that made it so. I hastened to make an end of my labor. I forced the last stone into its position; I plastered it up. Against the new masonry I re-erected the old rampart of bones. For the half of a century no mortal has disturbed them. *In pace requiescat!* [Rest in peace!]

1846

Twice-Told Tales, by Nathaniel Hawthorne: A Review

We said a few hurried words about Mr. Hawthorne in our last number, with the design of speaking more fully in the present. We are still, however, pressed for room, and must necessarily discuss his volumes more briefly and more at random than their high merits deserve.

The book professes to be a collection of tales, yet is, in two respects, misnamed. These pieces are now in their third republication, and, of course, are thrice-told. Moreover, they are by no means *all* tales, either in the ordinary or in the legitimate understanding of the term. Many of them are pure essays; for example, "Sights from a Steeple," "Sunday at Home," "Little Annie's Ramble," "A Rill from the Town Pump," "The Toll-Gatherer's Day," "The Haunted Mind," "The Sister Years," "Snow-Flakes," "Night Sketches," and "Foot-Prints on the Sea-Shore." We mention these matters chiefly on account of their discrepancy with that marked precision and finish by which the body of the work is distinguished.

Of the essays just named, we must be content to speak in brief. They are each and all beautiful, without being characterized by the polish and adaptation so visible in the tales proper. A painter would at once note their leading or predominant feature, and style it *repose*. There is no attempt at effect. All is quiet, thoughtful, subdued. Yet this repose may exist simultaneously with high originality of thought; and Mr. Hawthorne has demonstrated the fact. At every turn we meet with novel combinations; yet these combinations never surpass the limits of the quiet. We are soothed as we read; and withal is a calm astonishment that ideas so apparently obvious have never occurred or been presented to us before. Herein our author differs materially from Lamb or Hunt or Hazlitt—who, with vivid originality of manner and expression, have less of the true novelty of thought than is generally supposed, and whose originality, at best, has an uneasy and meretricious quaintness, replete with startling effects unfounded in nature, and inducing trains of reflection which lead to no satisfactory result. The Essays of Hawthorne have much of the character of Irving, with more of originality, and less of finish; while, compared with the Spectator, they have a vast superiority at all points. The Spectator, Mr. Irving, and Mr. Hawthorne have in common that tranquil and subdued manner which we have chosen to denominate *repose;* but, in the case of the two former, this repose is attained rather by the absence of novel combination, or of originality, than otherwise, and consists chiefly in the calm, quiet, unostentatious expression of commonplace thoughts, in an unambitious, unadulterated Saxon. In them, by strong effort, we are made to conceive the absence of all. In the essays before us the absence of effort is too obvious to be mistaken, and a strong under-current of *suggestion* runs continuously beneath the upper stream of the tranquil thesis. In short, these effusions of Mr. Hawthorne are the product of a truly imaginative intellect, restrained, and in some measure repressed, by fastidiousness of taste, by constitutional melancholy, and by indolence.

But it is of his tales that we desire principally to speak. The tale proper, in our opinion, affords unquestionably the fairest field for the exercise of the loftiest talent, which can be afforded by the wide domains of mere prose. Were we bidden to say how the highest genius could be most advantageously employed for the best display of its own powers, we should answer, without hesitation—in the composition of a rhymed poem, not to exceed in length what might be perused in an hour. Within this limit alone can the highest order of true poetry exist. We need only here say, upon this topic, that, in almost all classes of composition, the unity of effect or impression is a point of the greatest importance. It is clear, moreover, that this unity cannot be thoroughly preserved in productions whose perusal cannot be completed at one sitting. We may continue the reading of a prose composition, from the very nature of prose itself, much longer than we can persevere, to any good purpose, in the perusal of a poem. This latter, if truly fulfilling the demands of the poetic sentiment, induces an exaltation of the soul which cannot be long sustained. All high excitements are necessarily transient. Thus a long poem is a paradox. And, without unity of impression, the deepest effects cannot be brought about. Epics were the offspring of an imperfect sense of Art, and their reign is no more. A poem *too* brief may produce a vivid, but never an intense or enduring impression. Without a certain continuity of effort—without a certain duration or repetition of purpose—the soul is never deeply moved. There must be the dropping of the water upon the rock. De Béranger has wrought brilliant things—pungent and spirit-stirring—but, like all immassive bodies, they lack *momentum,* and thus fail to satisfy the Poetic Sentiment. They sparkle and excite, but, from want of continuity, fail deeply to impress. Extreme brevity will degenerate into epigrammatism; but the sin of extreme length is even more unpardonable. *In medio tutissimus ibis* [The middle course is the safest to steer].

Were we called upon, however, to designate that class of composition which, next to such a poem as we have suggested, should best fulfil the demands of high genius—should offer it the most advantageous field of exertion—we should unhesitatingly speak of the prose tale, as Mr.

Hawthorne has here exemplified it. We allude to the short prose narrative, requiring from a half-hour to one or two hours in its perusal. The ordinary novel is objectionable, from its length, for reasons already stated in substance. As it cannot be read at one sitting, it deprives itself, of course, of the immense force derivable from *totality*. Worldly interests intervening during the pauses of perusal, modify, annul, or counteract, in a greater or less degree, the impressions of the book. But simple cessation in reading would, of itself, be sufficient to destroy the true unity. In the brief tale, however, the author is enabled to carry out the fulness of his intention, be it what it may. During the hour of perusal the soul of the reader is at the writer's control. There are no external or extrinsic influences— resulting from weariness or interruption.

A skilful literary artist has constructed a tale. If wise, he has not fashioned his thoughts to accommodate his incidents; but having conceived, with deliberate care, a certain unique or single *effect* to be wrought out, he then invents such incidents—he then combines such events as may best aid him in establishing this preconceived effect. If his very initial sentence tend not to the outbringing of this effect, then he has failed in his first step. In the whole composition there should be no word written, of which the tendency, direct or indirect, is not to the one pre-established design. And by such means, with such care and skill, a picture is at length painted which leaves in the mind of him who contemplates it with a kindred art, a sense of the fullest satisfaction. The idea of the tale has been presented unblemished, because undisturbed; and this is an end unattainable by the novel. Undue brevity is just as exceptionable here as in the poem; but undue length is yet more to be avoided.

We have said that the tale has a point of superiority even over the poem. In fact, while the *rhythm* of this latter is an essential aid in the development of the poem's highest idea—the idea of the Beautiful—the artificialities of this rhythm are an inseparable bar to the development of all points of thought or expression which have their basis in *Truth*. But Truth is often, and in very great degree, the aim of the tale. Some of the finest tales are tales of ratiocination. Thus the field of this species of composition, if not in so elevated a region on the mountain of Mind, is a table-land of far vaster extent than the domain of the mere poem. Its products are never so rich, but infinitely more numerous, and more appreciable by the mass of mankind. The writer of the prose tale, in short, may bring to his theme a vast variety of modes or inflections of thought and expression—(the ratiocinative, for example, the sarcastic, or the humorous) which are not only antagonistical to the nature of the poem, but absolutely forbidden by one of its most peculiar and indispensable adjuncts; we allude, of course, to rhythm. It may be added here, *par parenthèse,* that the author who aims at the purely beautiful in a prose tale is laboring at a great disadvantage. For Beauty can be better treated in the poem. Not so with terror, or passion, or horror, or a multitude of such other points. And here it will be seen how full of prejudice are the usual animadversions against those *tales of effect,* many fine examples of which were found in the earlier numbers of *Blackwood.* The impressions produced were wrought in a legitimate sphere of action, and constituted a legitimate although sometimes an exaggerated interest. They were relished by every man of genius: although there were found many men of genius who condemned them without just ground. The true critic will but demand that the design intended be accomplished, to the fullest extent, by the means most advantageously applicable.

We have very few American tales of real merit—we may say, indeed, none, with the exception of *The Tales of a Traveller* of Washington Irving, and these *Twice-Told Tales* of Mr. Hawthorne. Some of the pieces of Mr. John Neal abound in vigor and originality; but, in general, his compositions of this class are excessively diffuse, extravagant, and indicative of an imperfect sentiment of Art. Articles at random are, now and then, met with in our periodicals which might be advantageously compared with the best effusions of the British Magazines; but, upon the whole, we are far behind our progenitors in this department of literature.

Of Mr. Hawthorne's tales we should say, emphatically, that they belong to the highest region of Art—an Art subservient to genius of a very lofty order. We had supposed, with good reason for so supposing, that he had been thrust into his present position by one of the impudent *cliques* which beset our literature, and whose pretensions it is our full purpose to expose at the earliest opportunity; but we have been most agreeably mistaken. We know of few compositions which the critic can more honestly commend than these *Twice-Told Tales*. As Americans, we feel proud of the book.

Mr. Hawthorne's distinctive trait is invention, creation, imagination, originality—a trait which, in the literature of fiction, is positively worth all the rest. But the nature of the originality, so far as regards its manifestation in letters, is but imperfectly understood. The inventive or original mind as frequently displays itself in novelty of *tone* as in novelty of matter. Mr. Hawthorne is original at *all* points.

It would be a matter of some difficulty to designate the best of these tales; we repeat that, without exception, they are beautiful. "Wakefield" is remarkable for the skill with which an old idea—a well-known incident—is worked up or discussed. A man of whims conceives the purpose of quitting his wife and residing *incognito,* for twenty years, in her immediate neighborhood. Something of this kind actually happened in London. The force of Mr. Hawthorne's tale lies in the analysis of the motives which must or might have impelled the husband to such folly, in the first instance, with the possible causes of his perseverance. Upon this thesis a sketch of singular power has been constructed.

"The Wedding Knell" is full of the boldest imagination —an imagination fully controlled by taste. The most captious critic could find no flaw in this production.

"The Minister's Black Veil" is a masterly composition, of which the sole defect is that to the rabble its exquisite skill will be *caviare*. The *obvious* meaning of this article will be found to smother its insinuated one. The *moral* put into the mouth of the dying minister will be supposed to convey the *true* import of the narrative; and that a crime of dark dye (having reference to the "young lady") has been committed, is a point which only minds congenial with that of the author will perceive.

"Mr. Higginbotham's Catastrophe" is vividly original, and managed most dexterously.

"Dr. Heidegger's Experiment" is exceedingly well imagined, and executed with surpassing ability. The artist breathes in every line of it.

"The White Old Maid" is objectionable even more than the "Minister's Black Veil," on the score of its mysticism. Even with the thoughtful and analytic, there will be much trouble in penetrating its entire import.

"The Hollow of the Three Hills" we would quote in full had we space;—not as evincing higher talent than any of the other pieces, but as affording an excellent example of the author's peculiar ability. The subject is commonplace. A witch subjects the Distant and the Past to the view of a mourner. It has been the fashion to describe, in such cases, a mirror in which the images of the absent appear; or a cloud of smoke is made to arise, and thence the figures are gradually unfolded. Mr. Hawthorne has wonderfully heightened his effect by making the car, in place of the eye, the medium by which the fantasy is conveyed. The head of the mourner is enveloped in the cloak of the witch, and within its magic folds there arise sounds which have an all-sufficient intelligence. Throughout this article also, the artist is conspicuous—not more in positive than in negative merits. Not only is all done that should be done, but (what perhaps is an end with more difficulty attained) there is nothing done which should not be. Every word *tells,* and there is not a word which does *not* tell.

In "Howe's Masquerade" we observe something which resembles plagiarism—but which *may be* a very flattering coincidence of thought. We quote the passage in question. . . .

The idea here is, that the figure in the cloak is the phantom or reduplication of Sir William Howe; but in an article called "William Wilson," one of the *Tales of the Grotesque and Arabesque,* we have not only the same idea, but the same idea similarly presented in several respects. We quote two paragraphs, which our readers may compare with what has been already given. We have italicized, above, the immediate particulars of resemblance. . . .

Here it will be observed that, not only are the two general conceptions identical, but there are various *points* of similarity. In each case the figure seen is the wraith or duplication of the beholder. In each case the scene is a masquerade. In each case the figure is cloaked. In each, there is a quarrel—that is to say, angry words pass between the parties. In each the beholder is enraged. In each the cloak and sword fall upon the floor. The "villain, un-muffle yourself," of Mr. H. is precisely paralleled by a passage at page 56 of "William Wilson."

In the way of objection we have scarcely a word to say of these tales. There is, perhaps, a somewhat too general or prevalent *tone*—a tone of melancholy and mysticism. The subjects are insufficiently varied. There is not so much of *versatility* evinced as we might well be warranted in expecting from the high powers of Mr. Hawthorne. But beyond these trivial exceptions we have really none to make. The style is purity itself. Force abounds. High imagination gleams from every page. Mr. Hawthorne is a man of the truest genius. We only regret that the limits of our Magazine will not permit us to pay him that full tribute of commendation, which, under other circumstances, we should be so eager to pay.

1842

The Philosophy of Composition

Charles Dickens, in a note now lying before me, alluding to an examination I once made of the mechanism of *Barnaby Rudge,* says—"By the way, are you aware that Godwin wrote his *Caleb Williams* backwards? He first involved his hero in a web of difficulties, forming the second volume, and then, for the first, cast about him for some mode of accounting for what had been done."

I cannot think this the *precise* mode of procedure on the part of Godwin—and indeed what he himself acknowledges, is not altogether in accordance with Mr. Dickens' idea—but the author of *Caleb Williams* was too good an artist not to perceive the advantage derivable from at least a somewhat similar process. Nothing is more clear than that every plot, worth the name, must be elaborated to its *dénouement* before anything be attempted with the pen. It is only with the *dénouement* constantly in view that we can give a plot its indispensable air of consequence, or causation, by making the incidents, and especially the tone at all points, tend to the development of the intention.

There is a radical error, I think, in the usual mode of constructing a story. Either history affords a thesis—or one is suggested by an incident of the day—or, at best, the author sets himself to work in the combination of striking events to form merely the basis of his narrative—designing, generally, to fill in with description, dialogue, or autorial comment, whatever crevices of fact, or action, may, from page to page, render themselves apparent.

I prefer commencing with the consideration of an *effect*. Keeping originality *always* in view—for he is false to himself who ventures to dispense with so obvious and so easily attainable a source of interest—I say to myself, in the first place, "Of the innumerable effects, or impressions, of which the heart, the intellect, or (more generally) the soul is susceptible, what one shall I, on the present occasion, select?" Having chosen a novel, first, and secondly, a vivid effect, I consider whether it can be best wrought by incident or tone—whether by ordinary incidents and peculiar tone, or the converse, or by peculiarity both of incident and tone—afterward looking about me (or rather within) for such combinations of event, or tone, as shall best aid me in the construction of the effect.

I have often thought how interesting a magazine paper might be written by any author who would—that is to say who could—detail, step by step, the processes by which any one of his compositions attained its ultimate point of completion. Why such a paper has never been given to the world, I am much at a loss to say—but, perhaps, the autorial vanity has had more to do with the omission than any one other cause. Most writers—poets in especial—prefer having it understood that they compose by a species of fine frenzy—an ecstatic intuition—and would positively shudder at letting the public take a peep behind the scenes, at the elaborate and vacillating crudities of thought—at the true purposes seized only at the last moment—at the innumerable glimpses of idea that arrived not at the maturity of full view—at the fully matured fancies discarded in despair as unmanageable—at the cautious selections and rejections—at the painful erasures and interpolations—in a word, at the wheels and pinions—the tackle for scene-shifting—the step-ladders and demon-traps—the cock's feathers, the red paint and the black patches, which, in ninety-nine cases out of the hundred, constitute the properties of the literary *histrio*.

I am aware, on the other hand, that the case is by no means common, in which an author is at all in condition to retrace the steps by which his conclusions have been attained. In general, suggestions, having arisen pell-mell, are pursued and forgotten in a similar manner.

For my own part, I have neither sympathy with the repugnance alluded to, nor, at any time the least difficulty in recalling to mind the progressive steps of any of my compositions; and, since the interest of an analysis, or reconstruction, such as I have considered a *desideratum*, is quite independent of any real or fancied interest in the thing analyzed, it will not be regarded as a breach of decorum on my part to show the *modus operandi* by which some one of my own works was put together. I select "The Raven," as most generally known. It is my design to render it manifest that no one point in its composition is referable either to accident or intuition—that the work proceeded, step by step, to its completion with the precision and rigid consequence of a mathematical problem.

Let us dismiss, as irrelevant to the poem, *per se,* the circumstance—or say the necessity—which, in the first place, gave rise to the intention of composing *a* poem that should suit at once the popular and the critical taste.

We commence, then, with this intention.

The initial consideration was that of extent. If any literary work is too long to be read at one sitting, we must be content to dispense with the immensely important effect derivable from unity of impression—for, if two sittings be required, the affairs of the world interfere, and everything like totality is at once destroyed. But since, *ceteris paribus,* no poet can afford to dispense with *anything* that may advance his design, it but remains to be seen whether there is, in extent, any advantage to counterbalance the loss of unity which attends it. Here I say no, at once. What we term a long poem is, in fact, merely a succession of brief ones—that is to say, of brief poetical effects. It is needless to demonstrate that a poem is such, only inasmuch as it intensely excites, by elevating, the soul; and all intense excitements are, through a psychal necessity, brief. For this reason, at least one half of the *Paradise Lost* is essentially prose—a succession of poetical excitements interspersed, *inevitably,* with corresponding depressions—the whole being deprived, through the extremeness of its length, of the vastly important artistic element, totality, or unity, of effect.

It appears evident, then, that there is a distinct limit, as regards length, to all works of literary art—the limit of a single sitting—and that, although in certain classes of prose composition, such as *Robinson Crusoe* (demanding no unity), this limit may be advantageously overpassed, it can never properly be overpassed in a poem. Within this limit, the extent of a poem may be made to bear mathematical relation to its merit—in other words, to the excitement or elevation—again in other words, to the degree of the true poetical effect which it is capable of inducing; for it is clear that the brevity must be in direct ratio of the intensity of the intended effect:—this, with one proviso—that a certain degree of duration is absolutely requisite for the production of any effect at all.

Holding in view these considerations, as well as that degree of excitement which I deemed not above the popular, while not below the critical, taste, I reached at once what I conceived the proper *length* for my intended poem —a length of about one hundred lines. It is, in fact, a hundred and eight.

My next thought concerned the choice of an impression, or effect, to be conveyed: and here I may as well observe that, throughout the construction, I kept steadily in view the design of tendering the work *universally* appreciable. I should be carried too far out of my immediate topic were I to demonstrate a point upon which I have repeatedly insisted, and which, with the poetical, stands not in the slightest need of demonstration—the point, I mean, that Beauty is the sole legitimate province of the poem. A few words, however, in elucidation of my real meaning, which some of my friends have evinced a disposition to misrepresent. That pleasure which is at once the most intense, the most elevating, and the most pure, is, I believe, found in the contemplation of the beautiful. When, indeed, men speak of Beauty, they mean, precisely, not a quality, as is supposed, but an effect—they refer, in short, just to that intense and pure elevation of *soul*—*not* of intellect, or of heart—upon which I have commented, and which is experienced in consequence of contemplating "the beautiful." Now I designate Beauty as the province of the poem, merely because it is an obvious rule of Art that effects should be made to spring from direct causes—that objects should be attained through means best adapted for their attainment—no one as yet having been weak enough to deny that the peculiar elevation alluded to is *most readily* attained in the poem. Now the object Truth, or the satisfaction of the intellect, and the object Passion, or the excitement of the heart, are, although attainable, to a certain extent, in poetry, far more readily attainable in prose. Truth, in fact, demands a precision, and Passion a *homeliness* (the truly passionate will comprehend me) which are absolutely antagonistic to that Beauty which, I maintain, is the excitement, or pleasurable elevation, of the soul. It by no means follows from any thing here said, that passion, or even truth, may not be introduced, and even profitably introduced, into a poem—for they may serve in elucidation, or aid the general effect, as do discords in music, by contrast—but the true artist will always contrive, first, to tone them into proper subservience to the predominant aim, and, secondly, to enveil them, as far as possible, in that Beauty which is the atmosphere and the essence of the poem.

Regarding, then, Beauty as my province, my next question referred to the *tone* of its highest manifestation—and all experience has shown that this tone is one of *sadness.* Beauty of whatever kind, in its supreme development, invariably excites the sensitive soul to tears. Melancholy is thus the most legitimate of all the poetical tones.

The length, the province, and the tone, being thus determined, I betook myself to ordinary induction, with the view of obtaining some artistic piquancy which might serve me as a key-note in the construction of the poem— some pivot upon which the whole structure might turn. In carefully thinking over all the usual artistic effects— or more properly *points,* in the theatrical sense—I did not fail to perceive immediately that no one had been so universally employed as that of the *refrain.* The universality of its employment sufficed to assure me of its intrinsic value, and spared me the necessity of submitting it to analysis. I considered it, however, with regard to its susceptibility of improvement, and soon saw it to be in a primitive condition. As commonly used, the *refrain,* or burden, not only is limited to lyric verse, but depends for its impression upon the force of monotone—both in sound and thought. The pleasure is deduced solely from the sense of identity—of repetition. I resolved to diversify, and so

heighten, the effect, by adhering, in general, to the monotone of sound, while I continually varied that of thought:
that is to say, I determined to produce continuously novel
effects, by the variation *of the application* of the *refrain*—
the *refrain* itself remaining, for the most part, unvaried.

These points being settled, I next bethought me of the
nature of my *refrain*. Since its application was to be repeatedly varied, it was clear that the *refrain* itself must be
brief, for there would have been an insurmountable difficulty in frequent variations of application in any sentence
of length. In proportion to the brevity of the sentence,
would, of course, be the facility of the variation. This led
me at once to a single word as the best *refrain*.

The question now arose as to the *character* of the word.
Having made up my mind to a *refrain,* the division of the
poem into stanzas was, of course, a corollary: the *refrain*
forming the close of each stanza. That such a close, to
have force, must be sonorous and susceptible of protracted
emphasis, admitted no doubt: and these considerations
inevitably led me to the long *o* as the most sonorous vowel,
in connection with *r* as the most producible consonant.

The sound of the *refrain* being thus determined, it
became necessary to select a word embodying this sound,
and at the same time in the fullest possible keeping with
that melancholy which I had predetermined as the tone of
the poem. In such a search it would have been absolutely
impossible to overlook the word "Nevermore." In fact, it
was the very first which presented itself.

The next *desideratum* was a pretext for the continuous
use of the one word "nevermore." In observing the difficulty which I at once found in inventing a sufficiently
plausible reason for its continuous repetition, I did not
fail to perceive that this difficulty arose solely from the
pre-assumption that the word was to be so continuously
or monotonously spoken by a *human* being—I did not fail
to perceive, in short, that the difficulty lay in the recon-
ciliation of this monotony with the exercise of reason on
the part of the creature repeating the word. Here, then,
immediately arose the idea of a *non*-reasoning creature
capable of speech; and, very naturally, a parrot, in the first
instance, suggested itself, but was superseded forthwith by
a Raven, as equally capable of speech, and infinitely more
in keeping with the intended *tone*.

I had now gone so far as the conception of a Raven—the bird of ill omen—monotonously repeating the one word, "Nevermore," at the conclusion of each stanza, in a poem of melancholy tone, and in length about one hundred lines. Now, never losing sight of the object *supremeness,* or perfection, at all points, I asked myself—"Of all melancholy topics, what, according to the *universal* understanding of mankind, is the *most* melancholy?" Death—was the obvious reply. "And when," I said, "is this most melancholy of topics most poetical?" From what I have already explained at some length, the answer, here also, is obvious—"When it most closely allies itself to *Beauty:* the death, then, of a beautiful woman is, unquestionably, the most poetical topic in the world—and equally is it beyond doubt that the lips best suited for such topic are those of a bereaved lover."

I had now to combine the two ideas, of a lover lamenting his deceased mistress and a Raven continuously repeating the word "Nevermore."—I had to combine these, bearing in mind my design of varying, at every turn, the *application* of the word repeated; but the only intelligible mode of such combination is that of imagining the Raven employing the word in answer to the queries of the lover. And here it was that I saw at once the opportunity afforded for the effect on which I had been depending—that is to say, the effect of the *variation of application.* I saw that I could make the first query propounded by the lover—the first query to which the Raven should reply "Nevermore"—that I could make this first query a commonplace one—the second less so—the third still less, and so on—until at length the lover, startled from his original *nonchalance* by the melancholy character of the word itself—by its frequent repetition—and by a consideration of the ominous reputation of the fowl that uttered it—is at length excited to superstition, and wildly propounds queries of a far different character—queries whose solution he has passionately at heart—propounds them half in superstition and half in that species of despair which delights in self-torture—propounds them not altogether because he believes in the prophetic or demoniac character of the bird (which, reason assures him, is merely repeating a lesson learned by rote) but because he experiences a frenzied pleasure in so modeling his questions as to receive from the *expected* "Never-

more" the most delicious because the most intolerable of
sorrow. Perceiving the opportunity thus afforded me—or,
more strictly, thus forced upon me in the progress of the
construction—I first established in mind the climax, or concluding query—that query to which "Nevermore" should
be in the last place an answer—that in reply to which this
word "Nevermore" should involve the utmost conceivable
amount of sorrow and despair.

Here then the poem may be said to have its beginning
—at the end, where all works of art should begin—for it
was here, at this point of my preconsiderations, that I first
put pen to paper in the composition of the stanza:

"Prophet," said I, "thing of evil! prophet still if bird
    or devil!
By that heaven that bends above us—by what God we
    both adore,
Tell this soul with sorrow laden, if within the distant
    Aidenn,
It shall clasp a sainted maiden whom the angels name
    Lenore—
Clasp a rare and radiant maiden whom the angels name
    Lenore."
Quoth the Raven "Nevermore."

I composed this stanza, at this point, first that, by establishing the climax, I might the better vary and graduate, as
regards seriousness and importance, the preceding queries
of the lover—and, secondly, that I might definitely settle
the rhythm, the metre, and the length and general arrangement of the stanza—as well as graduate the stanzas which
were to precede, so that none of them might surpass this
in rhythmical effect. Had I been able, in the subsequent
composition, to construct more vigorous stanzas, I should,
without scruple, have purposely enfeebled them, so as not
to interfere with the climacteric effect.

And here I may as well say a few words of the versification. My first object (as usual) was originality. The extent
to which this has been neglected, in versification, is one of
the most unaccountable things in the world. Admitting that
there is little possibility of variety in mere *rhythm,* it is
still clear that the possible varieties of metre and stanza
are absolutely infinite—and yet, *for centuries, no man, in*

verse, has ever done, or ever seemed to think of doing, an original thing. The fact is, that originality (unless in minds of very unusual force) is by no means a matter, as some suppose, of impulse or intuition. In general, to be found, it must be elaborately sought, and although a positive merit of the highest class, demands in its attainment less of invention than negation.

Of course, I pretend to no originality in either the rhythm or metre of the "Raven." The former is trochaic—the latter is octameter acatalectic, alternating with heptameter catalectic repeated in the *refrain* of the fifth verse, and terminating with tetrameter catalectic. Less pedantically— the feet employed throughout (trochees) consist of a long syllable followed by a short: the first line of the stanza consists of eight of these feet—the second of seven and a half (in effect two-thirds)—the third of eight—the fourth of seven and a half—the fifth the same—the sixth three and a half. Now, each of these lines, taken individually, has been employed before, and what originality the "Raven" has, is in their *combination into stanza; nothing even re-* motely approaching this combination has ever been attempted. The effect of this originality of combination is aided by other unusual, and some altogether novel effects, arising from an extension of the application of the principles of rhyme and alliteration.

The next point to be considered was the mode of bringing together the lover and the Raven—and the first branch of this consideration was the *locale*. For this the most natural suggestion might seem to be a forest, or the fields —but it has always appeared to be that a close *circumscription of space* is absolutely necessary to the effect of insulated incident:—it has the force of a frame to a picture. It has an indisputable moral power in keeping concentrated the attention, and, of course, must not be confounded with mere unity of place.

I determined, then, to place the lover in his chamber— in a chamber rendered sacred to him by memories of her who had frequented it. The room is represented as richly furnished—this is mere pursuance of the ideas I have already explained on the subject of Beauty, as the sole true poetical thesis.

The *locale* being thus determined, I had now to introduce

the bird—and the thought of introducing him through the window, was inevitable. The idea of making the lover suppose, in the first instance, that the flapping of the wings of the bird against the shutter, is a "tapping" at the door, originated in a wish to increase, by prolonging, the reader's curiosity, and in a desire to admit the incidental effect arising from the lover's throwing open the door, finding all dark, and thence adopting the half-fancy that it was the spirit of his mistress that knocked.

I made the night tempestuous, first, to account for the Raven's seeking admission, and secondly, for the effect of contrast with the (physical) serenity within the chamber.

I made the bird alight on the bust of Pallas, also for the effect of contrast between the marble and the plumage —it being understood that the bust was absolutely *suggested* by the bird—the bust of *Pallas* being chosen, first, as most in keeping with the scholarship of the lover, and, secondly, for the sonorousness of the word, Pallas, itself.

About the middle of the poem, also, I have availed myself of the force of contrast, with a view of deepening the ultimate impression. For example, an air of the fantastic—approaching as nearly to the ludicrous as was admissible—is given to the Raven's entrance. He comes in "with many a flirt and flutter."

Not the *least obeisance made he*—not a moment stopped
    or stayed he,
But with mien of lord or lady, perched above my chamber
    door.

In the two stanzas which follow, the design is more obviously carried out:—

Then this ebony bird beguiling my sad fancy into smiling
By the *grave and stern decorum of the countenance it wore,*
"Though thy *crest be shorn and shaven* thou," I said, "art
    sure no craven,
Ghastly grim and ancient Raven wandering from the
    nightly shore—
Tell me what thy lordly name is on the Night's Plutonian
    shore?"
    Quoth the Raven "Nevermore."

Much I marvelled *this ungainly fowl* to hear discourse so
   plainly
Though its answer little meaning—little relevancy bore;
For we cannot help agreeing that no living human being
*Ever yet was blessed with seeing bird above his chamber
   door—*
*Bird or beast upon the sculptured bust above his chamber
   door,*
   With such name as "Nevermore."

The effect of the *dénouement* being thus provided for, I
immediately drop the fantastic for a tone of the most
profound seriousness:—this tone commencing in the stanza
directly following the one last quoted, with the line,

But the Raven, sitting lonely on that placid bust, spoke
   only, etc.

From this epoch the lover no longer jests—no longer
sees anything even of the fantastic in the Raven's demeanor.
He speaks of him as a "grim, ungainly, ghastly, gaunt, and
ominous bird of yore," and feels the "fiery eyes" burning
into his "bosom's core." This revolution of thought, or
fancy, on the lover's part, is intended to induce a similar
one on the part of the reader—to bring the mind into a
proper frame for the *dénouement*—which is now brought
about as rapidly and as *directly* as possible.

With the *dénouement* proper—with the Raven's reply,
"Nevermore," to the lover's final demand if he shall meet
his mistress in another world—the poem, in its obvious
phase, that of a simple narrative, may be said to have its
completion. So far, everything is within the limits of the
accountable—of the real. A raven, having learned by rote
the single word "Nevermore," and having escaped from
the custody of its owner, is driven at midnight, through the
violence of a storm, to seek admission at a window from
which a light still gleams—the chamber-window of a student, occupied half in poring over a volume, half in dreaming of a beloved mistress deceased. The casement being
thrown open at the fluttering of the bird's wings, the bird
itself perches on the most convenient seat out of the immediate reach of the student, who, amused by the incident
and the oddity of the visitor's demeanor, demands of it, in

jest and without looking for a reply, its name. The raven addressed, answers with its customary word, "Nevermore" —a word which finds immediate echo in the melancholy heart of the student, who, giving utterance aloud to certain thoughts suggested by the occasion, is again startled by the fowl's repetition of "Nevermore." The student now guesses the state of the case, but is impelled, as I have before explained, by the human thirst for self-torture, and in part by superstition, to propound such queries to the bird as will bring him, the lover, the most of the luxury of sorrow, through the anticipated answer "Nevermore." With the indulgence, to the extreme, of this self-torture, the narration, in what I have termed its first or obvious phase, has a natural termination, and so far there has been no overstepping of the limits of the real.

But in subjects so handled, however skilfully, or with however vivid an array of incident, there is always a certain hardness or nakedness, which repels the artistical eye. Two things are invariably required—first, some amount of complexity, or more properly, adaptation; and, secondly, some amount of suggestiveness—some undercurrent, however indefinite, of meaning. It is this latter, in especial, which imparts to a work of art so much of that *richness* (to borrow from colloquy a forcible term) which we are too fond of confounding with *the ideal*. It is the *excess* of the suggested meaning—it is the rendering this the upper instead of the undercurrent of the theme—which turns into prose (and that of the very flattest kind) the so called poetry of the so called transcendentalists.

Holding these opinions, I added the two concluding stanzas of the poem—their suggestiveness being thus made to pervade all the narrative which has preceded them. The undercurrent of meaning is rendered first apparent in the lines—

"Take thy beak from out *my heart,* and take thy form from
off my door!"
Quoth the Raven "Nevermore!"

It will be observed the words, "from out my heart," involve the first metaphorical expression in the poem. They, with the answer, "Nevermore," dispose the mind to seek a moral in all that has been previously narrated. The

reader begins now to regard the Raven as emblematical—
but it is not until the very last line of the very last stanza,
that the intention of making him emblematical of *Mournful and Never-ending Remembrance* is permitted distinctly
to be seen:

And the Raven, never flitting, still is sitting, still is sitting,
On the pallid bust of Pallas, just above my chamber door;
And his eyes have all the seeming of a demon's that is
    dreaming,
And the lamplight o'er him streaming throws his shadow on
    the floor;
And my soul *from out that shadow* that lies floating on the
    floor
    Shall be lifted—nevermore.

                       1846

The Poetic Principle

In speaking of the Poetic Principle, I have no design to
be either thorough or profound. While discussing, very
much at random, the essentiality of what we call Poetry,
my principal purpose will be to cite for consideration some
few of those minor English or American poems which best
suit my own taste, or which, upon my own fancy, have left
the most definite impression. By "minor poems" I mean, of
course, poems of little length. And here, in the beginning,
permit me to say a few words in regard to a somewhat
peculiar principle, which, whether rightfully or wrongfully,
has always had its influence in my own critical estimate of
the poem. I hold that a long poem does not exist. I maintain that the phrase, "a long poem," is simply a flat contradiction in terms.

I need scarcely observe that a poem deserves its title only
inasmuch as it excites, by elevating the soul. The value
of the poem is in the ratio of this elevating excitement. But
all excitements are, through a psychal necessity, transient.
That degree of excitement which would entitle a poem to
be so called at all, cannot be sustained throughout a composition of any great length. After the lapse of half an
hour, at the very utmost, it flags—fails—a revulsion ensues

—and then the poem is, in effect, and in fact, no longer such.

There are, no doubt, many who have found difficulty in reconciling the critical dictum that the "Paradise Lost" is to be devoutly admired throughout, with the absolute impossibility of maintaining for it, during perusal, the amount of enthusiasm which that critical dictum would demand. This great work, in fact, is to be regarded as poetical only when, losing sight of that vital requisite in all works of Art, Unity, we view it merely as a series of minor poems. If, to preserve its Unity—its totality of effect or impression—we read it (as would be necessary) at a single sitting, the result is but a constant alternation of excitement and depression. After a passage of what we feel to be true poetry, there follows, inevitably, a passage of platitude which no critical pre-judgment can force us to admire; but if, upon completing the work, we read it again, omitting the first book—that is to say, commencing with the second—we shall be surprised at now finding that admirable which we before condemned—that damnable which we had previously so much admired. It follows from all this that the ultimate, aggregate, or absolute effect of even the best epic under the sun, is a nullity: and this is precisely the fact.

In regard to the Iliad, we have, if not positive proof, at least very good reason, for believing it intended as a series of lyrics; but, granting the epic intention, I can say only that the work is based in an imperfect sense of Art. The modern epic is, of the supposititious ancient model, but an inconsiderate and blindfold imitation. But the day of these artistic anomalies is over. If, at any time, any very long poem were popular in reality, which I doubt, it is at least clear that no very long poem will ever be popular again.

That the extent of a poetical work is, *ceteris paribus* [other things being equal], the measure of its merit, seems undoubtedly, when we thus state it, a proposition sufficiently absurd—yet we are indebted for it to the Quarterly Reviews. Surely there can be nothing in mere size, abstractly considered—there can be nothing in mere bulk, so far as a volume is concerned, which has so continuously elicited admiration from these saturnine pamphlets! A mountain, to be sure, by the mere sentiment of physical magnitude which it conveys, does impress us with a sense of the sublime—but no man is impressed after *this* fashion by the material grandeur of even "The Columbiad." Even the Quarterlies have not instructed us to be so impressed by it. As yet, they have not insisted on our estimating Lamartine by the cubic foot, or Pollok by the pound—but what else are we to infer from their continued prating about "sustained effort"? If, by "sustained effort," any little gentleman has accomplished an epic, let us frankly commend him for the effort—if this indeed be a thing commendable—but let us forbear praising the epic on the effort's account. It is to be hoped that common sense, in the time to come, will prefer deciding upon a work of Art, rather by the impression it makes—by the effect it produces—than by the time it took to impress the effect, or by the amount of "sustained effort" which had been found necessary in effecting the impression. The fact is, that perseverance is one thing and genius quite another—nor can all the Quarterlies in Christendom confound them. By-and-by, this proposition, with many which I have just been urging, will be received as self-evident. In the meantime, by being generally condemned as falsities, they will not be essentially damaged as truths.

On the other hand, it is clear that a poem may be improperly brief. Undue brevity degenerates into mere epigrammatism. A very short poem, while now and then producing a brilliant or vivid, never produces a profound or enduring effect. There must be the steady pressing down of the stamp upon the wax. De Béranger has wrought innumerable things, pungent and spirit-stirring; but in general they have been too imponderous to stamp themselves deeply into the public attention, and thus, as so many feathers of fancy, have been blown aloft only to be whistled down the wind.

A remarkable instance of the effect of undue brevity in depressing a poem—in keeping it out of the popular view—is afforded by the following exquisite little Serenade:

> I arise from dreams of thee
>   In the first sweet sleep of night,
> When the winds are breathing low,
>   And the stars are shining bright;
> I arise from dreams of thee,
>   And a spirit in my feet

> Has led me—who knows how?—
>   To thy chamber-window, sweet!
>
> The wandering airs, they faint
>   On the dark, the silent stream—
> The champak odors fail
>   Like sweet thoughts in a dream;
> The nightingale's complaint,
>   It dies upon her heart,
> As I must die on thine,
>   O, beloved as thou art!
>
> O, lift me from the grass!
>   I die, I faint, I fail!
> Let thy love in kisses rain
>   On my lips and eyelids pale.
> My cheek is cold and white, alas!
>   My heart beats loud and fast:
> Oh! press it close to thine again,
>   Where it will break at last!

Very few perhaps are familiar with these lines—yet no less a poet than Shelley is their author. Their warm, yet delicate and ethereal imagination will be appreciated by all—but by none so thoroughly as by him who has himself arisen from sweet dreams of one beloved, to bathe in the aromatic air of a southern midsummer night.

One of the finest poems by Willis—the very best in my opinion which he has ever written—has, no doubt, through this same defect of undue brevity, been kept back from its proper position, not less in the critical than in the popular view.

> The shadows lay along Broadway,
>   'Twas near the twilight-tide—
> And slowly there a lady fair
>   Was walking in her pride.
> Alone walk'd she; but, viewlessly,
>   Walk'd spirits at her side.
>
> Peace charm'd the street beneath her feet,
>   And Honour charm'd the air;
> And all astir looked kind on her,
>   And call'd her good and fair—

For all God ever gave to her
  She kept with chary care.

She kept with care her beauties rare
  From lovers warm and true—
For her heart was cold to all but gold,
  And the rich came not to woo—
But honour'd well are charms to sell,
  If priests the selling do.

Now walking there was one more fair—
  A slight girl, lily-pale;
And she had unseen company
  To make the spirit quail—
'Twixt Want and Scorn she walk'd forlorn,
  And nothing could avail.

No mercy now can clear her brow
  For this world's peace to pray;
For, as love's wild prayer dissolved in air,
  Her woman's heart gave way!—
But the sin forgiven by Christ in Heaven
  By man is cursed alway!

In this composition we find it difficult to recognize the Willis who has written so many mere "verses of society." The lines are not only richly ideal, but full of energy; while they breathe an earnestness—an evident sincerity of sentiment—for which we look in vain throughout all the other works of this author.

While the epic mania—while the idea that, to merit in poetry, prolixity is indispensable—has for some years past been gradually dying out of the public mind by mere dint of its own absurdity—we find it succeeded by a heresy too palpably false to be long tolerated, but one which, in the brief period it has already endured, may be said to have accomplished more in the corruption of our Poetical Literature than all its other enemies combined. I allude to the heresy of The Didactic. It has been assumed, tacitly and avowedly, directly and indirectly, that the ultimate object of all Poetry is Truth. Every poem, it is said, should inculcate a moral; and by this moral is the poetical merit of the work to be adjudged. We Americans especially have patronized this happy idea; and we Bostonians, very especially, have developed it in full. We have taken it into our heads that to write a poem simply for the poem's sake, and to acknowledge such to have been our design, would be to confess ourselves radically wanting in the true Poetic dignity and force:—but the simple fact is, that would we but permit ourselves to look into our own souls, we should immediately there discover that under the sun there neither exists nor can exist any work more thoroughly dignified— more supremely noble than this very poem—this poem *per se*, this poem which is a poem and nothing more—this poem written solely for the poem's sake.

With as deep a reverence for the True as ever inspired the bosom of man, I would nevertheless limit, in some measure, its modes of inculcation. I would limit to enforce them. I would not enfeeble them by dissipation. The demands of Truth are severe. She has no sympathy with the myrtles. All *that* which is so indispensable in Song is precisely all that with which she has nothing whatever to do. It is but making her a flaunting paradox to wreathe her in gems and flowers. In enforcing a truth, we need severity rather than efflorescence of language. We must be simple, precise, terse. We must be cool, calm, unimpassioned. In a word, we must be in that mood which, as nearly as possible, is the exact converse of the poetical. *He* must be blind indeed who does not perceive the radical and chasmal differences between the truthful and the poetical modes of inculcation. He must be theory-mad beyond redemption who, in spite of these differences, shall still persist in attempting to reconcile the obstinate oils and waters of Poetry and Truth.

Dividing the world of mind into its three most immediately obvious distinctions, we have the Pure Intellect, Taste, and the Moral Sense. I place Taste in the middle, because it is just this position which, in the mind, it occupies. It holds intimate relations with either extreme; but from the Moral Sense is separated by so faint a difference that Aristotle has not hesitated to place some of its operations among the virtues themselves. Nevertheless, we find the offices of the trio marked with a sufficient distinction. Just as the Intellect concerns itself with Truth, so Taste informs us of the Beautiful while the Moral Sense is regardful of Duty. Of this latter, while Conscience teaches the obligation, and Reason the expediency, Taste contents herself with displaying the charms:—waging war upon Vice solely on the ground of her deformity, her disproportion, her animosity to the fitting, to the appropriate, to the harmonious, in a word, to Beauty.

An immortal instinct, deep within the spirit of man, is thus plainly a sense of the Beautiful. This it is which administers to his delight in the manifold forms, and sounds, and odors, and sentiments, amid which he exists. And just as the lily is repeated in the lake, or the eyes of Amaryllis in the mirror, so is the mere oral or written repetition of these forms, and sounds, and colors, and odors, and sentiments, a duplicate source of delight. But this mere repetition is not poetry. He who shall simply sing, with however glowing enthusiasm, or with however vivid a truth of description, of the sights, and sounds, and odors, and colors, and sentiments, which greet him in common with all mankind—he, I say, has yet failed to prove his divine title. There is still a something in the distance which he has been unable to attain. We have still a thirst unquenchable, to allay which he has not shown us the crystal springs. This thirst belongs to the immortality of Man. It is at once a consequence and an indication of his perennial existence. It is the desire of the moth for the star. It is no mere appreciation of the Beauty before us—but a wild effort to reach the Beauty above. Inspired by an ecstatic prescience of the glories beyond the grave, we struggle by multiform combinations among the things and thoughts of Time, to attain a portion of that Loveliness whose very elements, perhaps, appertain to eternity alone. And thus when by Poetry—or when by Music, the most entrancing of the Poetic moods—we find ourselves melted into tears—we weep then—not as the Abbate Gravina supposes—through excess of pleasure, but through a certain, petulant, impatient sorrow at our inability to grasp now, wholly, here on earth, at once and forever, those divine and rapturous joys, of which through the poem or through the music, we attain to but brief and indeterminate glimpses.

The struggle to apprehend the supernal Loveliness—this struggle, on the part of souls fittingly constituted—has given to the world all that which it (the world) has ever been enabled at once to understand and to feel as poetic.

The Poetic Sentiment, of course, may develop itself in various modes—in Painting, in Sculpture, in Architecture, in the Dance—very especially in Music—and very peculiarly, and with a wide field, in the composition of the Landscape Garden. Our present theme, however, has regard only to its manifestation in words. And here let me speak briefly on the topic of rhythm. Contenting myself with the certainty that Music, in its various modes of metre, rhythm, and rhyme, is of so vast a moment in Poetry as never to be wisely rejected—is so vitally important an adjunct that he is simply silly who declines its assistance, I will not now pause to maintain its absolute essentiality. It is in Music, perhaps, that the soul most nearly attains the great end for which, when inspired by the Poetic Sentiment, it struggles—the creation of supernal Beauty. It may be, indeed, that here this sublime end is, now and then, attained in fact. We are often made to feel, with a shivering delight, that from an earthly harp are stricken notes which cannot have been unfamiliar to the angels. And thus there can be little doubt that in the union of Poetry with Music in its popular sense, we shall find the widest field for the Poetic development. The old Bards and Minnesingers had advantages which we do not possess—and Thomas Moore, singing his own songs, was, in the most legitimate manner, perfecting them as poems.

To recapitulate, then:—I would define, in brief, the Poetry of Words as The Rhythmical Creation of Beauty. Its sole arbiter is Taste. With the Intellect or with the Conscience, it has only collateral relations. Unless incidentally, it has no concern whatever either with Duty or with Truth.

A few words, however, in explanation. That pleasure which is at once the most pure, the most elevating, and the most intense, is derived, I maintain, from the contemplation of the Beautiful. In the contemplation of Beauty we alone find it possible to attain that pleasurable elevation, or excitement, of the soul, which we recognize as the Poetic Sentiment, and which is so easily distinguished from Truth, which is the satisfaction of the Reason, or from Passion, which is the excitement of the heart. I make Beauty, therefore—using the word as inclusive of the sublime—I make Beauty the province of the poem, simply because it is an obvious rule of Art that effects should be made to spring as directly as possible from their causes:—no one as yet having been weak enough to deny that the peculiar elevation in question is at least most readily attainable in the poem. It by no means follows, however, that the incitements of Passion, or the precepts of Duty, or even the lessons of Truth, may not be introduced into a poem, and with advantage; for they may subserve, incidentally, in various ways, the general purposes of the work:—but the true artist will always contrive to tone them down in proper subjection to that Beauty which is the atmosphere and the real essence of the poem.

I cannot better introduce the few poems which I shall present for your consideration, than by the citation of the Proem to Mr. Longfellow's "Waif":

> The day is done, and the darkness
>   Falls from the wings of Night,
> As a feather is wafted downward
>   From an eagle in his flight.
>
> I see the lights of the village
>   Gleam through the rain and the mist,
> And a feeling of sadness comes o'er me,
>   That my soul cannot resist;
>
> A feeling of sadness and longing,
>   That is not akin to pain,
> And resembles sorrow only
>   As the mist resembles the rain.
>
> Come, read to me some poem,
>   Some simple and heartfelt lay,
> That shall soothe this restless feeling,
>   And banish the thoughts of day.
>
> Not from the grand old masters,
>   Not from the bards sublime,
> Whose distant footsteps echo
>   Through the corridors of Time.
>
> For, like strains of martial music,
>   Their mighty thoughts suggest
> Life's endless toil and endeavor;
>   And to-night I long for rest.
>
> Read from some humbler poet,
>   Whose songs gushed from his heart,
> As showers from the clouds of summer,
>   Or tears from the eyelids start;

Who through long days of labor,
    And nights devoid of ease,
Still heard in his soul the music
    Of wonderful melodies.

Such songs have power to quiet
    The restless pulse of care,
And come like the benediction
    That follows after prayer.

Then read from the treasured volume
    The poem of thy choice,
And lend to the rhyme of the poet
    The beauty of thy voice.

And the night shall be filled with music,
    And the cares, that infest the day,
Shall fold their tents, like the Arabs,
    And as silently steal away.

With no great range of imagination, these lines have been justly admired for their delicacy of expression. Some of the images are very effective. Nothing can be better than

————The bards sublime,
Whose distant footsteps echo
Down the corridors of Time.

The idea of the last quatrain is also very effective. The poem, on the whole, however, is chiefly to be admired for the graceful *insouciance* of its metre, so well in accordance with the character of the sentiments, and especially for the *ease* of the general manner. This "ease" or naturalness, in a literary style, it has long been the fashion to regard as ease in appearance alone—as a point of really difficult attainment. But not so:—a natural manner is difficult only to him who should never meddle with it—to the unnatural. It is but the result of writing with the understanding, or with the instinct, that the *tone,* in composition, should always be that which the mass of mankind would adopt—and must perpetually vary, of course, with the occasion. The author who, after the fashion of "The North American Review," should be, upon all occasions, merely "quiet," must necessarily upon many occasions be simply silly, or stupid; and has no more right to be considered "easy" or "natural" than a Cockney exquisite, or than the sleeping Beauty in the wax-works.

Among the minor poems of Bryant, none has so much impressed me as the one which he entitles "June." I quote only a portion of it:

> There, through the long, long summer hours,
>   The golden light should lie,
> And thick young herbs and groups of flowers
>   Stand in their beauty by.
> The oriole should build and tell
> His love-tale, close beside my cell;
>   The idle butterfly
> Should rest him there, and there be heard
> The housewife-bee and humming bird.
>
> And what, if cheerful shouts, at noon
>   Come, from the village sent,
> Or songs of maids, beneath the moon,
>   With fairy laughter blent?
> And what if, in the evening light,
> Betrothed lovers walk in sight
>   Of my low monument?
> I would the lovely scene around
> Might know no sadder sight nor sound.
>
> I know, I know I should not see
>   The season's glorious show,
> Nor would its brightness shine for me,
>   Nor its wild music flow;
> But if, around my place of sleep,
> The friends I love should come to weep,
>   They might not haste to go.
> Soft airs, and song, and light, and bloom
> Should keep them lingering by my tomb.
>
> These to their soften'd hearts should bear
>   The thought of what has been,
> And speak of one who cannot share
>   The gladness of the scene;
> Whose part in all the pomp that fills
> The circuit of the summer hills,
>   Is—that his grave is green;

> And deeply would their hearts rejoice
> To hear again his living voice.

The rhythmical flow, here, is even voluptuous—nothing could be more melodious. The poem has always affected me in a remarkable manner. The intense melancholy which seems to well up, perforce, to the surface of all the poet's cheerful sayings about his grave, we find thrilling us to the soul—while there is the truest poetic elevation in the thrill. The impression left is one of a pleasurable sadness. And if, in the remaining compositions which I shall introduce to you, there be more or less of a similar tone always apparent, let me remind you that (how or why we know not) this certain taint of sadness is inseparably connected with all the higher manifestations of true Beauty. . . .

From Alfred Tennyson—although in perfect sincerity I regard him as the noblest poet that ever lived—I have left myself time to cite only a very brief specimen. I call him, and think him the noblest of poets—not because the impressions he produces are, at all times, the most profound —not because the poetical excitement which he induces is, at all times, the most intense—but because it is, at all times, the most ethereal—in other words, the most elevating and most pure. No poet is so little of the earth, earthy. What I am about to read is from his last long poem, "The Princess":

> Tears, idle tears, I know not what they mean,
> Tears from the depth of some divine despair
> Rise in the heart, and gather to the eyes,
> In looking on the happy Autumn-fields,
> And thinking of the days that are no more.
>
> Fresh as the first beam glittering on a sail,
> That brings our friends up from the underworld,
> Sad as the last which reddens over one
> That sinks with all we love below the verge;
> So sad, so fresh, the days that are no more.
>
> Ah, sad and strange as in dark summer dawns
> The earliest pipe of half-awaken'd birds
> To dying ears, when unto dying eyes
> The casement slowly grows a glimmering square;
> So sad, so strange, the days that are no more.

Dear as remember'd kisses after death,
And sweet as those by hopeless fancy feign'd
On lips that are for others; deep as love,
Deep as first love, and wild with all regret;
O Death in Life, the days that are no more.

Thus, although in a very cursory and imperfect manner, I have endeavored to convey to you my conception of the Poetic Principle. It has been my purpose to suggest that, while this Principle itself is strictly and simply the Human Aspiration for Supernal Beauty, the manifestation of the Principle is always found in an elevating excitement of the Soul—quite independent of that passion which is the intoxication of the Heart—or of that Truth which is the satisfaction of the Reason. For in regard to Passion, alas! its tendency is to degrade, rather than to elevate the Soul. Love, on the contrary—Love—the true, the divine Eros—the Uranian, as distinguished from the Dionaean Venus—is unquestionably the purest and truest of all poetical themes. And in regard to Truth—if, to be sure, through the attainment of a truth, we are led to perceive a harmony where none was apparent before, we experience, at once, the true poetical effect—but this effect is referable to the harmony alone, and not in the least degree to the truth which merely served to render the harmony manifest.

We shall reach, however, more immediately a distinct conception of what the true Poetry is, by mere reference to a few of the simple elements which induce in the Poet himself the true poetical effect. He recognizes the ambrosia which nourishes his soul, in the bright orbs that shine in Heaven—in the volutes of the flower—in the clustering of low shrubberies—in the waving of the grain-fields—in the slanting of tall, Eastern trees—in the blue distance of mountains—in the grouping of clouds—in the twinkling of half-hidden brooks—in the gleaming of silver rivers—in the repose of sequestered lakes—in the star-mirroring depths of lonely wells. He perceives it in the songs of birds—in the harp of Aeolus—in the sighing of the night-wind—in the repining voice of the forest—in the surf that complains to the shore—in the fresh breath of the woods—in the scent of the violet—in the voluptuous perfume of the hyacinth—in the suggestive odor that comes to him, at eventide, from far-distant, undiscovered islands, over dim oceans, illimitable and unexplored. He owns it in all noble thoughts—in all unworldly motives—in all holy impulses—in all chivalrous, generous, and self-sacrificing deeds. He feels it in the beauty of woman—in the grace of her step —in the lustre of her eye—in the melody of her voice—in her soft laughter—in her sigh—in the harmony of the rustling of her robes. He deeply feels it in her winning endearments—in her burning enthusiasms—in her gentle charities—in her meek and devotional endurances—but above all—ah, far above all—he kneels to it—he worships it in the faith, in the purity, in the strength, in the altogether divine majesty—of her *love*.

Let me conclude by the recitation of yet another brief poem—one very different in character from any that I have before quoted. It is by Motherwell, and is called "The Song of the Cavalier." With our modern and altogether rational ideas of the absurdity and impiety of warfare, we are not precisely in that frame of mind best adapted to sympathize with the sentiments, and thus to appreciate the real excellence of the poem. To do this fully we must identify ourselves in fancy with the soul of the old cavalier.

> Then mounte! then mounte, brave gallants, all,
>   And don your helmes amaine:
> Deathe's couriers, Fame and Honour, call
>   Us to the field againe.
> No shrewish teares shall fill our eye
>   When the sword-hilt's in our hand,—
> Heart-whole we'll part, and no whit sighe
>   For the fayrest of the land;
> Let piping swaine, and craven wight,
>   Thus weepe and puling crye,
> Our business is like men to fight,
>   And hero-like to die!

1850

RALPH WALDO EMERSON

(1803–1882)

Emerson was born in Boston, the descendant of a long line of ministers. His father, pastor of the First Church, died in 1811, leaving the mother to bring up the five sons in financial difficulty. In 1814 the family moved to Concord, where Emerson's extremely able mother and his aunt, Mary Moody Emerson, reared the children with an eye to the education and vocation that characterized their ancestry.

Emerson was sent to Boston Latin School, from which he graduated to Harvard College in 1817. The man who was to demonstrate the most seminal mind of his time showed no early promise, graduating from Harvard in 1821 as thirtieth in a class of fifty-nine. In order to save money for attending Harvard Divinity School and to help pay for the education of his brothers, he taught—uncomfortably—from 1821 to 1825 in the school for girls established by his older brother, William. Waldo entered the Divinity School in 1825 and was licensed for the ministry in 1826, but ill health sent him southward to recuperate. Family circumstances and the state of his health as well as financial necessities further delayed his career, but in 1829 he became the associate pastor to Henry Ware in the Second Church of Boston. In that same year he married Ellen Tucker, who died in 1831.

Slowly the young Emerson had been carrying forward within himself a questioning search for the certitudes with which man might establish a direct, intuitional, and infinite relation with the process of life itself. Slowly, without at first recognizing his apostasy, he began to repudiate the restricting forms of Christianity generally and the "pale negations" of Unitarianism in particular. He made his first outward announcement of the distance he had traveled from the early teachings of Aunt Mary and the more sophisticated doctrines of his Harvard mentors when in 1831 he resigned his pastorate. The surface issue was the administration of the Lord's Supper; what was really at stake was his growing belief in the potential ability of the individual to transcend church forms by piercing the symbolic veil of nature in order to merge with the Oversoul and domesticate its laws in his own character and life.

Searching and still rudderless, he went to Europe in 1832; there he talked with Landor, Wordsworth, Coleridge, and Carlyle, and became more closely acquainted with the philosophies of German idealism. He returned in 1833, settled in Concord in 1834, married Lydia Jackson in 1835, and in 1836 published *Nature*. The argument of this little book represented the result of his inner questioning, particularly since his voyage to Europe. It was the strongest motivating statement of American Transcendentalism and remains as the most instructive brief expression of high romantic and, indeed, American expectation.

In order to supplement the income left him from the estate of Ellen Tucker, Emerson became a frequent speaker in the Lyceums. After "The American Scholar," his Phi Beta Kappa address in 1837, and the Divinity School Address of 1838 (which provoked a storm of abuse from orthodox ministers), he became one of the most famous and sought-after speakers in the nation. With the publication of *Essays, First Series* in 1841 and *Essays, Second Series* in 1844, his position as the leading figure of the "newness" was consolidated. He remains to this day a directing force in the school of American thought opposed to a materialism that is divorced from the uses of life and from the necessities of healthy human personality. From 1842 to 1844 he edited *The Dial* (1840–1844), the "official" outlet for the Transcendentalists, including Emerson himself, Thoreau, Theodore Parker, and Margaret Fuller. In 1847 he published *Poems* and returned to Europe, where he delivered the lectures that were later published as *Representative Men* (1850) and where he absorbed the materials that were to become *English Traits* (1856).

Beginning in 1850, with his renunciation of Webster's stand on the Fugitive Slave Law, Emerson lost some of his belief in the possibility of total freedom for the individual and became increasingly concerned with history and politics. Although the later Emerson found that he painfully had to make place for historical experience in his epistemology, he remained true to his idealistic belief in the infinite role of man. "Experience" is one result of Emerson's wrestling with the problem of man's ultimate being and his historical limitations.

By the 1860's Emerson began to accept his diminished powers ("Terminus" was written in 1866). The onslaught of age and increasing weakness had become noticeable before 1872, when he made an unsuccessful journey of recuperation to Europe. He lived on in Concord as the respected and revered visible symbol of his thought until his death in 1882.

In his vigorous life he had traveled widely throughout the Republic, declaiming from countless lecterns the energy of his ideas which, in theories of poetry, history, science, being, and knowing, unified into an organic purpose the spiritual meaning of America. By now Emerson is no longer considered either the cool and bloodless sage of Concord or the easily optimistic Yankee who denied the existence of evil. While there is partial truth in both identifications of the man, recent scholarship, from a vantage point in time, has reconstructed a thinker whose restorative message of liberation will speak to the human condition as long as there exists the human mind, whose primacy he championed.

Among the titles of Emerson's works, besides those mentioned above, are *The Method of Nature* (1841); *Man the Reformer* (1842); *Orations, Lectures and Addresses* (1844); *The Conduct of Life* (1860); *May-Day and Other Pieces* (1867); *Society and Solitude* (1870); and *Selected Poems* (1876).

Editions and accounts of the man and his work are to be found in G. W. Cooke, *Ralph Waldo Emerson* (1881); A. B. Alcott, *Ralph Waldo Emerson* (1882); M. D. Conway, *Emerson at Home and Abroad* (1882); A. Ireland, *Ralph Waldo Emerson* (1882); O. W. Holmes, *Ralph Waldo Emerson* (1884); F. B. Sanborn, ed., *The Genius and Character of Emerson* (1885); J. E. Cabot, *A Memoir of Ralph Waldo Emerson*, 2 vols. (1887); E. W. Emerson, *Emerson in Concord* (1889); C. J. Woodbury, *Talks with Ralph Waldo Emerson* (1890); J. J. Chapman, *Emerson and Other Essays* (1898); E. W. Emerson, ed., *The Complete Works of Ralph Waldo Emerson*, 12 vols. (1903–1904), the Centenary Edition; F. B. Sanborn, *The Personality of Emerson* (1903); G. E. Woodberry, *Ralph Waldo Emerson* (1907); H. C. Goddard, *Studies in New England Transcendentalism* (1908); E. W. Emerson and W. E. Forbes, eds., *The Journals of Ralph Waldo Emerson*, 10 vols. (1909–1914); C. Bigelow, ed., *Uncollected Writings . . . by Ralph Waldo Emer-*

son (1912); O. W. Firkins, *Ralph Waldo Emerson* (1915); H. D. Gray, *Emerson* (1917); P. Russell, *Emerson* (1929); F. I. Carpenter, *Emerson and Asia* (1930); B. Perry, *Emerson Today* (1931); V. W. Brooks, *The Life of Emerson* (1932); A. E. Christy, *The Orient in American Transcendentalism* (1932); R. L. Rusk, ed., *The Letters of Ralph Waldo Emerson,* 6 vols. (1939); F. O. Matthiessen, *The American Renaissance* (1941); F. W. Connor, *Cosmic Optimism* (1949); R. L. Rusk, *The Life of Ralph Waldo Emerson* (1949); H. M. Jones, *The Iron String* (1950); D. Aaron, *Men of Good Hope* (1951); V. C. Hopkins, *Spires of Form* (1951); S. Paul, *Emerson's Angle of Vision* (1952); F. I. Carpenter, *Emerson Handbook* (1953); C. Feidelson, Jr., *Symbolism and American Literature* (1953); S. Whicher, *Freedom and Fate* (1953); C. R. Metzger, *Emerson and Greenough* (1954); J. R. Reaver, *Emerson as Mythmaker* (1954); R. W. B. Lewis, *The American Adam* (1955); N. Arvin "The House of Pain: Emerson and The Tragic Sense," *Hudson Review,* XII (1959). P. L. Nicoloff, *Emerson on Race and History: An Examination of English Traits* (1961); K. W. Cameron, *A Commentary on Emerson's Early Lectures (1833–1836), with an Index-Concordance* (1962); M. R. Konvitz and S. E. Whicher, eds., *Emerson: A Collection of Critical Essays* (1962); K. W. Cameron, ed., *Transcendental Climate: New Resources for the Study of Emerson, Thoreau, and Their Contemporaries,* 3 vols. (1963); J. Bishop, *Emerson on the Soul* (1964); J. R. Bryer and R. A. Rees, *A Checklist of Emerson Criticism, 1951–1961* (1964); J. Miles, *Ralph Waldo Emerson* (1964); J. Slater, ed., *The Correspondence of Emerson and Carlyle* (1964); S. E. Whicher, R. E. Spiller, and W. E. Williams, eds., *The Early Lectures of Ralph Waldo Emerson,* 2 vols. (1964); L. Baritz, *City on a Hill: History of Ideas and Myths in America* (1965); J. Cawelti, *Apostles of the Self-Made Man* (1965); M. M. Sealts, et al., eds., *The Journals and Miscellaneous Notebooks of Ralph Waldo Emerson (1819–1838),* 6 vols. (1961–1966); J. Porte, *Emerson and Thoreau: Transcendalists in Conflict* (1966); and W. M. Wynkoop, *Three Children of the Universe: Emerson's View of Shakespeare, Bacon and Milton* (1966). *The Portable Emerson* (1946), selected and with an introduction and notes by M. Van Doren, contains essays, poems, selections from the *Journals,* and letters.

Concord Hymn

Sung at the Completion of the Battle Monument,
July 4, 1837

By the rude bridge that arched the flood,
   Their flag to April's breeze unfurled,
Here once the embattled farmers stood
   And fired the shot heard round the world.

The foe long since in silence slept;
　　Alike the conqueror silent sleeps;
And Time the ruined bridge has swept
　　Down the dark stream which seaward creeps.

On this green bank, by this soft stream,
　　We set today a votive stone;
That memory may their deed redeem,
　　When, like our sires, our sons are gone.

Spirit, that made those heroes dare
　　To die, and leave their children free,
Bid Time and Nature gently spare
　　The shaft we raise to them and thee.

1837

The Rhodora:

On Being Asked, Whence Is the Flower?

In May, when sea-winds pierced our solitudes,
I found the fresh Rhodora in the woods,
Spreading its leafless blooms in a damp nook,
To please the desert and the sluggish brook.
The purple petals, fallen in the pool,
Made the black water with their beauty gay;
Here might the red-bird come his plumes to cool,
And court the flower that cheapens his array.
Rhodora! if the sages ask thee why
This charm is wasted on the earth and sky,　　　　　10
Tell them, dear, that if eyes were made for seeing,
Then Beauty is its own excuse for being:
Why thou wert there, O rival of the rose!
I never thought to ask, I never knew;
But, in my simple ignorance, suppose
The self-same Power that brought me there brought you.

w. 1834
p. 1839

Each and All

Little thinks, in the field, yon red-cloaked clown
Of thee from the hill-top looking down;
The heifer that lows in the upland farm,
Far-heard, lows not thine ear to charm;
The sexton, tolling his bell at noon,
Deems not that great Napoleon
Stops his horse, and lists with delight,
Whilst his files sweep round yon Alpine height;
Nor knowest thou what argument
Thy life to thy neighbor's creed has lent.   10
All are needed by each one;
Nothing is fair or good alone.
I thought the sparrow's note from heaven,
Singing at dawn on the alder bough;
I brought him home, in his nest, at even;
He sings the song, but it cheers not now,
For I did not bring home the river and sky;—
He sang to my ear,—they sang to my eye.
The delicate shells lay on the shore;
The bubbles of the latest wave   20
Fresh pearls to their enamel gave,
And the bellowing of the savage sea
Greeted their safe escape to me.
I wiped away the weeds and foam,
I fetched my sea-born treasures home;
But the poor, unsightly, noisome things
Had left their beauty on the shore
With the sun and the sand and the wild uproar.
The lover watched his graceful maid,
As 'mid the virgin train she strayed,   30
Nor knew her beauty's best attire
Was woven still by the snow-white choir.
At last she came to his hermitage,
Like the bird from the woodlands to the cage;—
The gay enchantment was undone,
A gentle wife, but fairy none.
Then I said, "I covet truth;
Beauty is unripe childhood's cheat;
I leave it behind with the games of youth":—
As I spoke, beneath my feet   40

The ground-pine curled its pretty wreath,
Running over the club-moss burrs;
I inhaled the violet's breath;
Around me stood the oaks and firs;
Pine-cones and acorns lay on the ground;
Over me soared the eternal sky,
Full of light and of deity;
Again I saw, again I heard,
The rolling river, the morning bird;—
Beauty through my senses stole;
I yielded myself to the perfect whole.   50

w. c1834
p. 1839

The Humble-Bee

Burly, dozing humble-bee,
Where thou art is clime for me.
Let them sail for Porto Rique,
Far-off heats through seas to seek;
I will follow thee alone,
Thou animated torrid-zone!
Zigzag steerer, desert cheerer,
Let me chase thy waving lines;
Keep me nearer, me thy hearer,
Singing over shrubs and vines.   10

Insect lover of the sun,
Joy of thy dominion!
Sailor of the atmosphere;
Swimmer through the waves of air;
Voyager of light and noon;
Epicurean of June;
Wait, I prithee, till I come
Within earshot of thy hum,—
All without is martyrdom.

When the south wind, in May days,   20
With a net of shining haze
Silvers the horizon wall,
And with softness touching all,

Tints the human countenance
With a color of romance,
And infusing subtle heats,
Turns the sod to violets,
Thou, in sunny solitudes,
Rover of the underwoods,
The green silence dost displace   30
With thy mellow, breezy bass.

Hot midsummer's petted crone,
Sweet to me thy drowsy tone
Tells of countless sunny hours,
Long days, and solid banks of flowers;
Of gulfs of sweetness without bound
In Indian wildernesses found;
Of Syrian peace, immortal leisure,
Firmest cheer, and bird-like pleasure.

Aught unsavory or unclean   40
Hath my insect never seen;
But violets and bilberry bells,
Maple-sap and daffodels,
Grass with green flag half-mast high,
Succory to match the sky,
Columbine with horn of honey,
Scented fern, and agrimony,
Clover, catchfly, adder's-tongue
And brier-roses, dwelt among;
All beside was unknown waste,
All was picture as he passed.   50

Wiser far than human seer,
Yellow-breeched philosopher!
Seeing only what is fair,
Sipping only what is sweet,
Thou dost mock at fate and care,
Leave the chaff, and take the wheat.
When the fierce northwestern blast
Cools sea and land so far and fast,
Thou already slumberest deep;   60
Woe and want thou canst outsleep;
Want and woe, which torture us,
Thy sleep makes ridiculous.

1839

The Problem

I like a church; I like a cowl;
I love a prophet of the soul;
And on my heart monastic aisles
Fall like sweet strains, or pensive smiles;
Yet not for all his faith can see
Would I that cowlèd churchman be.

Why should the vest on him allure,
Which I could not on me endure?

Not from a vain or shallow thought
His awful Jove young Phidias brought;   10
Never from lips of cunning fell
The thrilling Delphic oracle;
Out from the heart of nature rolled
The burdens of the Bible old;
The litanies of nations came,
Like the volcano's tongue of flame,
Up from the burning core below,—
The canticles of love and woe:
The hand that rounded Peter's dome
And groined the aisles of Christian Rome   20
Wrought in a sad sincerity:
Himself from God he could not free;
He builded better than he knew;—
The conscious stone to beauty grew.

Know'st thou what wove yon woodbird's nest
Of leaves, and feathers from her breast?
Or how the fish outbuilt her shell,
Painting with morn her annual cell?
Or how the sacred pine-tree adds
To her old leaves new myriads?   30
Such and so grew these holy piles,
Whilst love and terror laid the tiles.
Earth proudly wears the Parthenon,
As the best gem upon her zone,
And Morning opes with haste her lids
To gaze upon the Pyramids;
O'er England's abbeys bends the sky,
As on its friends, with kindred eye;
For out of Thought's interior sphere

These wonders rose to upper air;   40
And Nature gladly gave them place,
Adopted them into her race,
And granted them an equal date
With Andes and with Ararat.
These temples grew as grows the grass;
Art might obey, but not surpass.
The passive Master lent his hand
To the vast soul that o'er him planned;
And the same power that reared the shrine
Bestrode the tribes that knelt within.   50
Ever the fiery Pentecost
Girds with one flame the countless host,
Trances the heart through chanting choirs,
And through the priest the mind inspires.
The word unto the prophet spoken
Was writ on tables yet unbroken;
The word by seers or sibyls told,
In groves of oak, or fanes of gold,
Still floats upon the morning wind,
Still whispers to the willing mind.   60
One accent of the Holy Ghost
The heedless world hath never lost.
I know what say the fathers wise,—
The Book itself before me lies,
Old *Chrysostom,* best Augustine,
And he who blent both in his line,
The younger *Golden Lips* or mines,
Taylor, the Shakespeare of divines.
His words are music in my ear,
I see this cowlèd portrait dear;   70
And yet, for all his faith could see,
I would not the good bishop be.   1840

Woodnotes, I

1

When the pine tosses its cones
To the song of its waterfall tones,
Who speeds to the woodland walks?
To birds and trees who talks?
Cæsar of his leafy Rome,
There the poet is at home.
He goes to the river-side,—

Not hook nor line hath he;
He stands in the meadows wide,—
Nor gun nor scythe to see.   10
Sure some god his eye enchants:
What he knows nobody wants.
In the wood he travels glad,
Without better fortune had,
Melancholy without bad.
Knowledge this man prizes best
Seems fantastic to the rest:
Pondering shadows, colors, clouds,
Grass-buds and caterpillar-shrouds,
Boughs on which the wild bees settle,   20
Tints that spot the violet's petal,
Why Nature loves the number five,
And why the star-form she repeats:
Lover of all things alive,
Wonderer at all he meets,
Wonderer chiefly at himself,
Who can tell him what he is?
Or how meet in human elf
Coming and past eternities?

2

And such I knew, a forest seer,   30
A minstrel of the natural year,
Foreteller of the vernal ides,
Wise harbinger of spheres and tides,
A lover true, who knew by heart
Each joy the mountain dales impart;
It seemed that Nature could not raise
A plant in any secret place,
In quaking bog, on snowy hill,
Beneath the grass that shades the rill,
Under the snow, between the rocks,   40
In damp fields known to bird and fox,
But he would come in the very hour
It opened in its virgin bower,
As if a sunbeam showed the place,
And tell its long-descended race.
It seemed as if the breezes brought him,
It seemed as if the sparrows taught him;
As if by secret sight he knew
Where, in far fields, the orchis grew.

Many haps fall in the field 50
Seldom seen by wishful eyes,
But all her shows did Nature yield,
To please and win this pilgrim wise.
He saw the partridge drum in the woods;
He heard the woodcock's evening hymn;
He found the tawny thrushes' broods;
And the shy hawk did wait for him;
What others did at distance hear,
And guessed within the thicket's gloom,
Was shown to this philosopher, 60
And at his bidding seemed to come.

3

In unploughed Maine he sought the lumberers' gang
Where from a hundred lakes young rivers sprang;
He trode the unplanted forest floor, whereon
The all-seeing sun for ages hath not shone;
Where feeds the moose, and walks the surly bear,
And up the tall mast runs the woodpecker.
He saw beneath dim aisles, in odorous beds,
The slight Linnæa hang its twin-born heads,
And blessed the monument of the man of flowers, 70
Which breathes his sweet fame through the northern bowers.
He heard, when in the grove, at intervals,
With sudden roar the aged pine-tree falls,—
One crash, the death-hymn of the perfect tree,
Declares the close of its green century.
Low lies the plant to whose creation went
Sweet influence from every element;
Whose living towers the years conspired to build,
Whose giddy top the morning loved to gild.
Through these green tents, by eldest Nature dressed, 80
He roamed, content alike with man and beast.
Where darkness found him he lay glad at night;
There the red morning touched him with its light.
Three moons his great heart him a hermit made,
So long he roved at will the boundless shade.
The timid it concerns to ask their way,
And fear what foe in caves and swamps can stray,
To make no step until the event is known,
And ills to come as evils past bemoan.
Not so the wise; no coward watch he keeps 90
To spy what danger on his pathway creeps;

Go where he will, the wise man is at home,
His hearth the earth,—his hall the azure dome;
Where his clear spirit leads him, there's his road
By God's own light illumined and foreshadowed.

4

'Twas one of the charmèd days
When the genius of God doth flow;
The wind may alter twenty ways,
A tempest cannot blow;
It may blow north, it still is warm;   100
Or south, it still is clear;
Or east, it smells like a clover-farm;
Or west, no thunder fear.
The musing peasant, lowly great,
Beside the forest water sate;
The rope-like pine-roots crosswise grown
Composed the network of his throne;
The wide lake, edged with sand and grass,
Was burnished to a floor of glass,
Painted with shadows green and proud   110
Of the tree and of the cloud.
He was the heart of all the scene;
On him the sun looked more serene;
To hill and cloud his face was known,—
It seemed the likeness of their own;
They knew by secret sympathy
The public child of earth and sky.
"You ask," he said, "what guide
Me through trackless thickets led,
Through thick-stemmed woodlands rough and wide,   120
I found the water's bed.
The watercourses were my guide;
I travelled grateful by their side,
Or through their channel dry;
They led me through the thick damp,
Through brake and fern, the beavers' camp,
Through beds of granite cut my road,
And their resistless friendship showed.
The falling waters led me,
The foodful waters fed me,   130
And brought me to the lowest land,
Unerring to the ocean sand.

The moss upon the forest bark
Was pole-star when the night was dark;
The purple berries in the wood
Supplied me necessary food;
For Nature ever faithful is
To such as trust her faithfulness.
When the forest shall mislead me,
When the night and morning lie,   140
When sea and land refuse to feed me,
'Twill be time enough to die;
Then will yet my mother yield
A pillow in her greenest field,
Nor the June flowers scorn to cover
The clay of their departed lover."

                                                    1840

The Snow-Storm

Announced by all the trumpets of the sky,
Arrives the snow, and, driving o'er the fields,
Seems nowhere to alight: the whited air
Hides hills and woods, the river, and the heaven,
And veils the farm-house at the garden's end.
The sled and traveller stopped, the courier's feet
Delayed, all friends shut out, the housemates sit
Around the radiant fireplace, enclosed
In a tumultuous privacy of storm.

    Come see the north wind's masonry.   10
Out of an unseen quarry evermore
Furnished with tile, the fierce artificer
Curves his white bastions with projected roof
Round every windward stake, or tree, or door.
Speeding the myriad-handed, his wild work
So fanciful, so savage, nought cares he
For number or proportion. Mockingly,
On coop or kennel he hangs Parian wreaths;
A swan-like form invests the hidden thorn;
Fills up the farmer's lane from wall to wall,   20
Maugre the farmer's sighs; and at the gate
                              [Maugre: in spite of]
A tapering turret overtops the work.

And when his hours are numbered, and the world
Is all his own, retiring, as he were not,
Leaves, when the sun appears, astonished Art
To mimic in slow structures, stone by stone,
Built in an age, the mad wind's night-work,
The frolic architecture of the snow.

1841

Compensation

I

The wings of Time are black and white,
Pied with morning and with night.
Mountain tall and ocean deep
Trembling balance duly keep.
In changing moon and tidal wave
Glows the feud of Want and Have.
Gauge of more and less through space,
Electric star or pencil plays,
The lonely Earth amid the balls
That hurry through the eternal halls,   10
A makeweight flying to the void,
Supplemental asteroid,
Or compensatory spark,
Shoots across the neutral Dark.

II

Man's the elm, and Wealth the vine;
Stanch and strong the tendrils twine:
Though the frail ringlets thee deceive,
None from its stock that vine can reave.
Fear not, then, thou child infirm,
There's no god dare wrong a worm;   20
Laurel crowns cleave to deserts,
And power to him who power exerts.
Hast not thy share? On wingéd feet,
Lo! it rushes thee to meet;
And all that Nature made thy own,
Floating in air or pent in stone,
Will rive the hills and swim the sea,
And, like thy shadow, follow thee.

1841

Grace

How much, preventing God! how much I owe
To the defenses thou hast round me set:
Example, custom, fear, occasion slow,—
These scornèd bondmen were my parapet.
I dare not peep over this parapet,
To gauge with glance the roaring gulf below,
The depths of sin to which I had descended,
Had not these me against myself defended.

1842

Merops

What care I, so they stand the same,—
    Things of the heavenly mind,—
How long the power to give them name
    Tarries yet behind?

Thus far today your favors reach,
    O fair, appeasing presences!
Ye taught my lips a single speech,
    And a thousand silences.

Space grants beyond his fated road
    No inch to the god of day;   10
And copious language still bestowed
    One word, no more, to say.

1846

Fable

The mountain and the squirrel
Had a quarrel,
And the former called the latter "Little Prig";
Bun replied,
"You are doubtless very big;
But all sorts of things and weather
Must be taken in together,

To make up a year
And a sphere.
And I think it no disgrace   10
To occupy my place.
If I'm not so large as you,
You are not so small as I,
And not half so spry.
I'll not deny you make
A very pretty squirrel track;
Talents differ; all is well and wisely put;
If I cannot carry forests on my back,
Neither can you crack a nut."

                                                              1846

Ode

Inscribed to W. H. Channing

Though loath to grieve
The evil time's sole patriot,
I cannot leave
My honied thought
For the priest's cant,
Or statesman's rant.

If I refuse
My study for their politique,
Which at the best is trick,
The angry Muse   10
Puts confusion in my brain.

But who is he that prates
Of the culture of mankind,
Of better arts and life?
Go, blindworm, go,
Behold the famous States
Harrying Mexico
With rifle and with knife!

Or who, with accent bolder,
Dare praise the freedom-loving mountaineer?   20
I found by thee, O rushing Contoocook!

And in thy valleys, Agiochook!
The jackals of the negro-holder.

The God who made New Hampshire
Taunted the lofty land
With little men;
Small bat and wren
House in the oak:
If earth-fire cleave
The upheaved land, and bury the folk,   30
The southern crocodile would grieve.
Virtue palters; Right is hence;
Freedom praised, but hid;
Funeral eloquence
Rattles the coffin-lid.

What boots thy zeal,
O glowing friend,
That would indignant rend
The northland from the south?
Wherefore? to what good end?   40
Boston Bay and Bunker Hill
Would serve things still;
Things are of the snake.

The horseman serves the horse,
The neatherd serves the neat, [neat: cattle]
The merchant serves the purse,
The eater serves his meat;
'Tis the day of the chattel,
Web to weave, and corn to grind;
Things are in the saddle,   50
And ride mankind.

There are two laws discrete,
Not reconciled—
Law for man, and law for thing;
The last builds town and fleet,
But it runs wild,
And doth the man unking.

'Tis fit the forest fall,
The steep be graded,

The mountain tunnelled,
The sand shaded,
The orchard planted,
The glebe tilled,
The prairie granted,
The steamer built.

Let man serve law for man;
Live for friendship, live for love,
For truth's and harmony's behoof;
The state may follow how it can,
As Olympus follows Jove.

Yet do not I implore
The wrinkled shopman to my sounding woods,
Nor bid the unwilling senator
Ask votes of thrushes in the solitudes.
Every one to his chosen work;
Foolish hands may mix and mar;
Wise and sure the issues are.
Round they roll till dark is light,
Sex to sex, and even to odd;
The over-god
Who marries Right to Might,
Who peoples, unpeoples,
He who exterminates
Races by stronger races,
Black by white faces,
Knows to bring honey
Out of the lion;
Grafts gentlest scion
On pirate and Turk.

The Cossack eats Poland,
Like stolen fruit;
Her last noble is ruined,
Her last poet mute:
Straight, into double band
The victors divide;
Half for freedom strike and stand;
The astonished Muse finds thousands at her side.

1847

Give All to Love

Give all to love;
Obey thy heart;
Friends, kindred, days,
Estate, good-fame,
Plans, credit and the Muse,—
Nothing refuse.

'Tis a brave master;
Let it have scope:
Follow it utterly,
Hope beyond hope: 10
High and more high
It dives into noon,
With wing unspent,
Untold intent;
But it is a god,
Knows its own path
And the outlets of the sky.

It was never for the mean;
It requireth courage stout.
Souls above doubt,   20
Valor unbending,
It will reward,—
They shall return
More than they were,
And ever ascending.

Leave all for love;
Yet, hear me, yet,
One word more thy heart behoved,
One pulse more of firm endeavor,—
Keep thee today,
Tomorrow, forever,
Free as an Arab
Of thy beloved.

Cling with life to the maid;
But when the surprise,
First vague shadow of surmise

Flits across her bosom young,
Of a joy apart from thee,
Free be she, fancy-free;
Nor thou detain her vesture's hem,   40
Nor the palest rose she flung
From her summer diadem.

Though thou loved her as thyself,
As a self of purer clay,
Though her parting dims the day,
Stealing grace from all alive;
Heartily know,
When half-gods go,
The gods arrive.

                                                            1847

Hamatreya

Bulkeley, Hunt, Willard, Hosmer, Meriam, Flint,
Possessed the land which rendered to their toil
Hay, corn, roots, hemp, flax, apples, wool and wood.
Each of these landlords walked amidst his farm,
Saying, " 'Tis mine, my children's and my name's.
How sweet the west wind sounds in my own trees!
How graceful climb those shadows on my hill!
I fancy these pure waters and the flags
Know me, as does my dog: we sympathize;
And, I affirm, my actions smack of the soil."   10

Where are these men? Asleep beneath their grounds:
And strangers, fond as they, their furrows plough.
                                         [fond: foolish]
Earth laughs in flowers, to see her boastful boys
Earth-proud, proud of the earth which is not theirs;
Who steer the plough, but cannot steer their feet
Clear of the grave.
They added ridge to valley, brook to pond,
And sighed for all that bounded their domain;
"This suits me for a pasture; that's my park;
We must have clay, lime, gravel, granite-ledge,   20
And misty lowland, where to go for peat.

The land is well,—lies fairly to the south.
'Tis good, when you have crossed the sea and back,
To find the sitfast acres where you left them."
Ah! the hot owner sees not Death, who adds
Him to his land, a lump of mould the more.
Hear what the Earth says:

EARTH-SONG

"Mine and yours;
Mine, not yours.
Earth endures;   30
Stars abide—
Shine down in the old sea;
Old are the shores;
But where are old men?
I who have seen much,
Such have I never seen.

"The lawyer's deed
Ran sure,
In tail, [In tail: entail]
To them, and to their heirs   40
Who shall succeed,
Without fail,
Forevermore.

"Here is the land,
Shaggy with wood,
With its old valley,
Mound and flood.
But the heritors?—
Fled like the flood's foam.
The lawyer, and the laws,   50
And the kingdom,
Clean swept herefrom.

"They called me theirs,
Who so controlled me;
Yet every one
Wished to stay, and is gone,
How am I theirs,
If they cannot hold me,
But I hold them?"

When I heard the Earth-song   60
I was no longer brave;
My avarice cooled
Like lust in the chill of the grave.

1847

Uriel

It fell in the ancient periods
   Which the brooding soul surveys,
Or ever the wild Time coined itself
   Into calendar months and days.

This was the lapse of Uriel,
Which in Paradise befell.
Once, among the Pleiads walking,
Seyd overheard the young gods talking;
And the treason, too long pent,
To his ears was evident.   10
The young deities discussed
Laws of form, and metre just,
Orb, quintessence, and sunbeams,
What subsisteth, and what seems.
One, with low tones that decide,
And doubt and reverend use defied,
With a look that solved the sphere,
And stirred the devils everywhere,
Gave his sentiment divine
Against the being of a line.   20
"Line in nature is not found;
Unit and universe are round;
In vain produced, all rays return;
Evil will bless, and ice will burn."
As Uriel spoke with piercing eye,
A shudder ran around the sky;
The stern old war-gods shook their heads,
The seraphs frowned from myrtle-beds;
Seemed to the holy festival
The rash word boded ill to all;   30
The balance-beam of Fate was bent;
The bounds of good and ill were rent;

Strong Hades could not keep his own,
But all slid to confusion.

A sad self-knowledge, withering, fell
On the beauty of Uriel;
In heaven once eminent, the god
Withdrew, that hour, into his cloud;
Whether doomed to long gyration
In the sea of generation,   40
Or by knowledge grown too bright
To hit the nerve of feebler sight.
Straightway, a forgetting wind
Stole over the celestial kind,
And their lips the secret kept,
If in ashes the fire-seed slept.
But now and then, truth-speaking things
Shamed the angels' veiling wings;
And, shrilling from the solar course,
Or from fruit of chemic force,   50
Procession of a soul in matter,
Or the speeding change of water,
Or out of the good of evil born,
Came Uriel's voice of cherub scorn,
And a blush tinged the upper sky,
And the gods shook, they knew not why.

1847

Days

Daughters of Time, the hypocritic Days,
Muffled and dumb like barefoot dervishes,
And marching single in an endless file,
Bring diadems and fagots in their hands.
To each they offer gifts after his will,
Bread, kingdoms, stars, and sky that holds them all.
I, in my pleached garden, watched the pomp,
Forgot my morning wishes, hastily
Took a few herbs and apples, and the Day
Turned and departed silent. I, too late,   10
Under her solemn fillet saw the scorn.

w. c1851
p. 1857

Brahma

If the red slayer think he slays,
   Or if the slain think he is slain,
They know not well the subtle ways
   I keep, and pass, and turn again.

Far or forgot to me is near;
   Shadow and sunlight are the same;
The vanished gods to me appear;
   And one to me are shame and fame.

They reckon ill who leave me out;
   When me they fly, I am the wings;   10
I am the doubter and the doubt,
   And I the hymn the Brahmin sings.

The strong gods pine for my abode,
   And pine in vain the sacred Seven,
              [Seven: highest saints of Hindu faith]
But thou, meek lover of the good!
   Find me, and turn thy back on heaven.

                        1857

Terminus

It is time to be old
To take in sail:
The god of bounds,
          [bounds: Terminus was god of boundaries]
Came to me in his fatal rounds
And said: "No more!
No farther spread
Thy broad ambitious branches and thy root.
Fancy departs: no more invent;
Contract thy firmament
To compass of a tent.   10
There's not enough for this and that,
Make thy option which of two;
Economize the failing river,

Not the less revere the Giver;
Leave the many and hold the few.
Timely wise, accept the terms,
Soften the fall with wary foot;
Still plan and smile,
And, fault of novel germs, [fault: in the lack]
Mature the unfallen fruit.   20
Curse, if thou wilt, thy sires,
Bad husbands of their fires,
Who, when they gave thee breath,
Failed to bequeath
The needful sinew stark as once,
The Baresark marrow to thy bones,
But left a legacy of ebbing veins,
Inconstant heat and nerveless reins;
Amid the Muses left thee deaf and dumb,
Amid the gladiators halt and numb."   30

As the bird trims her to the gale,
I trim myself to the storm of time;
I man the rudder, reef the sail,
Obey the voice at eve obeyed at prime:
"Lowly faithful, banish fear,
Right onward drive unharmed;
The port, well worth the cruise, is near,
And every wave is charmed."

w. 1860
p. 1867

Nature

Introduction

Our age is retrospective. It builds the sepulchres of the
fathers. It writes biographies, histories, and criticism. The
foregoing generations beheld God and nature face to face;
we, through their eyes. Why should not we also enjoy an
original relation to the universe? Why should not we have
a poetry and philosophy of insight and not of tradition, and
a religion by revelation to us, and not the history of theirs?
Embosomed for a season in nature, whose floods of life

stream around and through us, and invite us, by the powers they supply, to action proportioned to nature, why should we grope among the dry bones of the past, or put the living generation into masquerade out of its faded wardrobe? The sun shines to-day also. There is more wool and flax in the fields. There are new lands, new men, new thoughts. Let us demand our own works and laws and worship.

Undoubtedly we have no questions to ask which are unanswerable. We must trust the perfection of the creation so far as to believe that whatever curiosity the order of things has awakened in our minds, the order of things can satisfy. Every man's condition is a solution in hieroglyphic to those inquiries he would put. He acts it as life, before he apprehends it as truth. In like manner, nature is already, in its forms and tendencies, describing its own design. Let us interrogate the great apparition that shines so peacefully around us. Let us inquire, to what end is nature?

All science has one aim, namely, to find a theory of nature. We have theories of races and of functions, but scarcely yet a remote approach to an idea of creation. We are now so far from the road to truth, that religious teachers dispute and hate each other, and speculative men are esteemed unsound and frivolous. But to a sound judgment, the most abstract truth is the most practical. Whenever a true theory appears, it will be its own evidence. Its test is, that it will explain all phenomena. Now many are thought not only unexplained but inexplicable; as language, sleep, madness, dreams, beasts, sex.

Philosophically considered, the universe is composed of Nature and the Soul. Strictly speaking, therefore, all that is separate from us, all which Philosophy distinguishes as the NOT ME, that is, both nature and art, all other men and my own body, must be ranked under this name, NATURE. In enumerating the values of nature and casting up their sum, I shall use the word in both senses;—in its common and in its philosophical import. In inquiries so general as our present one, the inaccuracy is not material; no confusion of thought will occur. *Nature,* in the common sense, refers to essences unchanged by man; space, the air, the river, the leaf. *Art* is applied to the mixture of his will with the same things, as in a house, a canal, a statue, a picture. But his operations taken together are so insignificant, a little chipping, baking, patching, and washing, that in an impression so grand as that of the world on the human mind, they do not vary the result.

I. Nature

To go into solitude, a man needs to retire as much from his chamber as from society. I am not solitary whilst I read and write, though nobody is with me. But if a man would be alone, let him look at the stars. The rays that come from those heavenly worlds will separate between him and what he touches. One might think the atmosphere was made transparent with this design, to give man, in the heavenly bodies, the perpetual presence of the sublime. Seen in the streets of cities, how great they are! If the stars should appear one night in a thousand years, how would men believe and adore; and preserve for many generations the remembrance of the city of God which had been shown! But every night come out these envoys of beauty, and light the universe with their admonishing smile.

The stars awaken a certain reverence, because though always present, they are inaccessible; but all natural objects make a kindred impression, when the mind is open to their influence. Nature never wears a mean appearance. Neither does the wisest man extort her secret, and lose his curiosity by finding out all her perfection. Nature never became a toy to a wise spirit. The flowers, the animals, the mountains, reflected the wisdom of his best hour, as much as they had delighted the simplicity of his childhood.

When we speak of nature in this manner, we have a distinct but most poetical sense in the mind. We mean the integrity of impression made by manifold natural objects. It is this which distinguishes the stick of timber of the wood-cutter, from the tree of the poet. The charming landscape which I saw this morning is indubitably made up of some twenty or thirty farms. Miller owns this field, Locke that, and Manning the woodland beyond. But none of them owns the landscape. There is a property in the horizon which no man has but he whose eye can integrate all the parts, that is, the poet. This is the best part of these men's farms, yet to this their warranty-deeds give no title.

To speak truly, few adult persons can see nature. Most

persons do not see the sun. At least they have a very superficial seeing. The sun illuminates only the eye of the man, but shines into the eye and the heart of the child. The lover of nature is he whose inward and outward senses are still truly adjusted to each other; who has retained the spirit of infancy even into the era of manhood. His intercourse with heaven and earth becomes part of his daily food. In the presence of nature a wild delight runs through the man, in spite of real sorrows. Nature says,—he is my creature, and maugre all his impertinent griefs, he shall be glad with me. Not the sun or the summer alone, but every hour and season yields its tribute of delight; for every hour and change corresponds to and authorizes a different state of the mind, from breathless noon to grimmest midnight. Nature is a setting that fits equally well a comic or a mourning piece. In good health, the air is a cordial of incredible virtue. Crossing a bare common, in snow puddles, at twilight, under a clouded sky, without having in my thoughts any occurrence of special good fortune, I have enjoyed a perfect exhilaration. I am glad to the brink of fear. In the woods, too, a man casts off his years, as the snake his slough, and at what period soever of life, is always a child. In the woods is perpetual youth. Within these plantations of God, a decorum and sanctity reign, a perennial festival is dressed, and the guest sees not how he should tire of them in a thousand years. In the woods, we return to reason and faith. There I feel that nothing can befall me in life,—no disgrace, no calamity (leaving me my eyes), which nature cannot repair. Standing on the bare ground,—my head bathed by the blithe air, and uplifted into infinite space,—all mean egotism vanishes. I become a transparent eye-ball; I am nothing; I see all; the currents of the Universal Being circulate through me. I am part or parcel of God. The name of the nearest friend sounds then foreign and accidental: to be brothers, to be acquaintances, master or servant, is then a trifle and a disturbance. I am the lover of uncontained and immortal beauty. In the wilderness, I find something more dear and connate than in streets or villages. In the tranquil landscape, and especially in the distant line of the horizon, man beholds somewhat as beautiful as his own nature.

The greatest delight which the fields and woods minister is the suggestion of an occult relation between man and the vegetable. I am not alone and unacknowledged. They nod to me, and I to them. The waving of the boughs in the storm is new to me and old. It takes me by surprise, and yet is not unknown. Its effect is like that of a higher thought or a better emotion coming over me, when I deemed I was thinking justly or doing right.

Yet it is certain that the power to produce this delight does not reside in nature, but in man, or in a harmony of both. It is necessary to use these pleasures with great temperance. For nature is not always tricked in holiday attire, but the same scene which yesterday breathed perfume and glittered as for the frolic of the nymphs, is overspread with melancholy to-day. Nature always wears the colors of the spirit. To a man laboring under calamity, the heat of his own fire hath sadness in it. Then there is a kind of contempt of the landscape felt by him who has just lost by death a dear friend. The sky is less grand as it shuts down over less worth in the population.

II. Commodity

Whoever considers the final cause of the world will discern a multitude of uses that enter as parts into that result. They all admit of being thrown into one of the following classes: Commodity; Beauty; Language; and Discipline.

Under the general name of commodity, I rank all those advantages which our senses owe to nature. This, of course, is a benefit which is temporary and mediate, not ultimate, like its service to the soul. Yet although low, it is perfect in its kind, and is the only use of nature which all men apprehend. The misery of man appears like childish petulance, when we explore the steady and prodigal provision that has been made for his support and delight on this green ball which floats him through the heavens. What angels invented these splendid ornaments, these rich conveniences, this ocean of air above, this ocean of water beneath, this firmament of earth between? this zodiac of lights, this tent of dropping clouds, this striped coat of climates, this fourfold year? Beasts, fire, water, stones, and corn serve him. The field is at once his floor, his workyard, his play-ground, his garden.

More servants wait on man
Than he'll take notice of.

Nature, in its ministry to man, is not only the material, but is also the process and the result. All the parts incessantly work into each other's hands for the profit of man. The wind sows the seed; the sun evaporates the sea; the wind blows the vapor to the field; the ice, on the other side of the planet, condenses rain on this; the rain feeds the plant; the plant feeds the animal; and thus the endless circulations of the divine charity nourish man.

The useful arts are reproductions or new combinations by the wit of man, of the same natural benefactors. He no longer waits for favoring gales, but by means of steam, he realizes the fable of Æolus's bag, and carries the two and thirty winds in the boiler of his boat. To diminish friction, he paves the road with iron bars, and, mounting a coach with a ship-load of men, animals, and merchandise behind him, he darts through the country, from town to town, like an eagle or a swallow through the air. By the aggregate of these aids, how is the face of the world changed, from the era of Noah to that of Napoleon! The private poor man hath cities, ships, canals, bridges, built for him. He goes to the post-office, and the human race run on his errands; to the book-shop, and the human race read and write of all that happens, for him; to the court-house, and nations repair his wrongs. He sets his house upon the road, and the human race go forth every morning, and shovel out the snow, and cut a path for him.

But there is no need of specifying particulars in this class of uses. The catalogue is endless, and the examples so obvious, that I shall leave them to the reader's reflection, with the general remark, that this mercenary benefit is one which has respect to a farther good. A man is fed, not that he may be fed, but that he may work.

III. Beauty

A nobler want of man is served by nature, namely, the love of Beauty.

The ancient Greeks called the world κόσμος, beauty. Such is the constitution of all things, or such the plastic power of the human eye, that the primary forms, as the sky, the mountain, the tree, the animal, give us a delight *in and for themselves;* a pleasure arising from outline, color, motion, and grouping. This seems partly owing to the eye itself. The eye is the best of artists. By the mutual action of its structure and of the laws of light, perspective is produced, which integrates every mass of objects, of what character soever, into a well colored and shaded globe, so that where the particular objects are mean and unaffecting, the landscape which they compose is round and symmetrical. And as the eye is the best composer, so light is the first of painters. There is no object so foul that intense light will not make beautiful. And the stimulus it affords to the sense, and a sort of infinitude which it hath, like space and time, make all matter gay. Even the corpse has its own beauty. But besides this general grace diffused over nature, almost all the individual forms are agreeable to the eye, as is proved by our endless imitations of some of them, as the acorn, the grape, the pine-cone, the wheat-ear, the egg, the wings and forms of most birds, the lion's claw, the serpent, the butterfly, seashells, flames, clouds, buds, leaves, and the forms of many trees, as the palm.

For better consideration, we may distribute the aspects of Beauty in a threefold manner.

1. First, the simple perception of natural forms is a delight. The influence of the forms and actions in nature is so needful to man, that, in its lowest functions, it seems to lie on the confines of commodity and beauty. To the body and mind which have been cramped by noxious work or company, nature is medicinal and restores their tone. The tradesman, the attorney comes out of the din and craft of the street and sees the sky and the woods, and is a man again. In their eternal calm, he finds himself. The health of the eye seems to demand a horizon. We are never tired, so long as we can see far enough.

But in other hours, Nature satisfies by its loveliness, and without any mixture of corporeal benefit. I see the spectacle of morning from the hill-top over against my house, from day-break to sun-rise, with emotions which an angel might share. The long slender bars of cloud float like fishes in the sea of crimson light. From the earth, as a shore, I look out into that silent sea. I seem to partake its rapid transformations; the active enchantment reaches my dust, and I dilate and conspire with the morning wind. How does Nature deify us with a few and cheap elements! Give me health and a day, and I will make the pomp of emperors ridiculous. The dawn is my Assyria; the sunset and moon-rise my Paphos, and unimaginable realms of faerie; broad noon shall be my England of the senses and the understanding; the night shall be my Germany of mystic philosophy and dreams.

Not less excellent, except for our less susceptibility in the afternoon, was the charm, last evening, of a January sunset. The western clouds divided and subdivided themselves into pink flakes modulated with tints of unspeakable softness, and the air had so much life and sweetness that it was a pain to come within doors. What was it that nature would say? Was there no meaning in the live repose of the valley behind the mill, and which Homer or Shakespeare could not reform for me in words? The leafless trees become spires of flame in the sunset, with the blue east for their background, and the stars of the dead calices of flowers, and every withered stem and stubble rimed with frost, contribute something to the mute music.

The inhabitants of cities suppose that the country landscape is pleasant only half the year. I please myself with the graces of the winter scenery, and believe that we are as much touched by it as by the genial influences of summer. To the attentive eye, each moment of the year has its own beauty, and in the same field, it beholds, every hour, a picture which was never seen before, and which shall never be seen again. The heavens change every moment, and reflect their glory or gloom on the plains beneath. The state of the crop in the surrounding farms alters the expression of the earth from week to week. The succession of native plants in the pastures and roadsides, which makes the silent clock by which time tells the summer hours, will make even the divisions of the day sensible to a keen observer. The tribes of birds and insects, like the plants punctual to their time, follow each other, and the year has room for all. By water-courses, the variety is greater. In July, the blue pontederia or pickerel-weed blooms in large beds in the shallow parts of our pleasant river, and swarms with yellow butterflies in continual motion. Art cannot rival this pomp of purple and gold. Indeed the river is a perpetual gala, and boasts each month a new ornament.

But this beauty of Nature which is seen and felt as beauty, is the least part. The shows of day, the dewy morning, the rainbow, mountains, orchards in blossom, stars, moonlight, shadows in still water, and the like, if too eagerly hunted, become shows merely, and mock us with their unreality. Go out of the house to see the moon, and 'tis mere tinsel; it will not please as when its light shines upon your necessary journey. The beauty that shimmers in the yellow afternoons of October, who ever could clutch it? Go forth to find it, and it is gone; 'tis only a mirage as you look from the windows of diligence.

2. The presence of a higher, namely, of the spiritual element is essential to its perfection. The high and divine beauty which can be loved without effeminacy, is that which is found in combination with the human will. Beauty is the mark God sets upon virtue. Every natural action is graceful. Every heroic act is also decent, and causes the place and the bystanders to shine. We are taught by great actions that the universe is the property of every individual in it. Every rational creature has all nature for his dowry and estate. It is his, if he will. He may divest himself of it; he may creep into a corner, and abdicate his kingdom, as most men do, but he is entitled to the world by his constitution. In proportion to the energy of his thought and will, he takes up the world into himself. "All those things for which men plough, build, or sail, obey virtue," said Sallust. "The winds and waves," said Gibbon, "are always on the side of the ablest navigators." So are the sun and moon and all the stars of heaven. When a noble act is done,—perchance in a scene of great natural beauty; when Leonidas and his three hundred martyrs consume one day in dying, and the sun and moon come each and look at them once in the steep defile of Thermopylæ; when Arnold Winkelried, in the high Alps, under the shadow of the avalanche, gathers in his side a sheaf of Austrian spears to break the line for his comrades; are not these heroes entitled to add the beauty of the scene to the beauty of the deed? When the bark of Columbus nears the shore of America;— before it, the beach lined with savages, fleeing out of all their huts of cane; the sea behind; and the purple mountains of the Indian Archipelago around, can we separate the man from the living picture? Does not the New World

clothe his form with her palm-groves and savannahs as
fit drapery? Ever does natural beauty steal in like air, and
envelope great actions. When Sir Harry Vane was dragged
up the Tower-hill, sitting on a sled, to suffer death as the
champion of the English laws, one of the multitude cried
out to him, "You never sate on so glorious a seat!" Charles
II, to intimidate the citizens of London, caused the patriot
Lord Russell to be drawn in an open coach through the
principal streets of the city on his way to the scaffold.
"But," his biographer says, "the multitude imagined they
saw liberty and virtue sitting by his side." In private places,
among sordid objects, an act of truth or heroism seems at
once to draw to itself the sky as its temple, the sun as its
candle. Nature stretches out her arms to embrace man,
only let his thoughts be of equal greatness. Willingly does
she follow his steps with the rose and the violet, and bend
her lines of grandeur and grace to the decoration of her
darling child. Only let his thoughts be of equal scope, and
the frame will suit the picture. A virtuous man is in
unison with her works, and makes the central figure of the
visible sphere. Homer, Pindar, Socrates, Phocion, associate
themselves fitly in our memory with the geography and
climate of Greece. The visible heavens and earth sympathize with Jesus. And in common life whosoever has seen
a person of powerful character and happy genius, will have
remarked how easily he took all things along with him,—
the persons, the opinions, and the day, and nature became
ancillary to a man.

3. There is still another aspect under which the beauty
of the world may be viewed, namely, as it becomes an
object of the intellect. Beside the relation of things to virtue,
they have a relation to thought. The intellect searches out
the absolute order of things as they stand in the mind of
God, and without the colors of affection. The intellectual
and the active powers seem to succeed each other, and the
exclusive activity of the one generates the exclusive activity
of the other. There is something unfriendly in each to the
other, but they are like the alternate periods of feeding
and working in animals; each prepares and will be followed
by the other. Therefore does beauty, which, in relation to
actions, as we have seen, comes unsought, and comes
because it is unsought, remain for the apprehension and

pursuit of the intellect; and then again, in its turn, of the active power. Nothing divine dies. All good is eternally reproductive. The beauty of nature reforms itself in the mind, and not for barren comtemplation, but for new creation.

All men are in some degree impressed by the face of the world; some men even to delight. This love of beauty is Taste. Others have the same love in such excess, that, not content with admiring, they seek to embody it in new forms. The creation of beauty is Art.

The production of a work of art throws a light upon the mystery of humanity. A work of art is an abstract or epitome of the world. It is the result or expression of nature, in miniature. For although the works of nature are innumerable and all different, the result or the expression of them all is similar and single. Nature is a sea of forms radically alike and even unique. A leaf, a sunbeam, a landscape, the ocean, make an analogous impression on the mind. What is common to them all,—that perfectness and harmony, is beauty. The standard of beauty is the entire circuit of natural forms,—the totality of nature; which the Italians expressed by defining beauty "il più nell' uno" [many made one]. Nothing is quite beautiful alone; nothing but is beautiful in the whole. A single object is only so far beautiful as it suggests this universal grace. The poet, the painter, the sculptor, the musician, the architect, seek each to concentrate this radiance of the world on one point, and each in his several work to satisfy the love of beauty which stimulates him to produce. Thus is Art a nature passed through the alembic of man. Thus in art does Nature work through the will of a man filled with the beauty of her first works.

The world thus exists to the soul to satisfy the desire of beauty. This element I call an ultimate end. No reason can be asked or given why the soul seeks beauty. Beauty, in its largest and profoundest sense, is one expression for the universe. God is the all-fair. Truth, and goodness, and beauty, are but different faces of the same All. But beauty in nature is not ultimate. It is the herald of inward and eternal beauty, and is not alone a solid and satisfactory good. It must stand as a part, and not as yet the last or highest expression of the final cause of Nature.

IV. Language

Language is a third use which Nature subserves to man. Nature is the vehicle of thought, and in a simple, double, and threefold degree.

1. Words are signs of natural facts.
2. Particular natural facts are symbols of particular spiritual facts.
3. Nature is the symbol of spirit.

1. Words are signs of natural facts. The use of natural history is to give us aid in supernatural history; the use of the outer creation, to give us language for the beings and changes of the inward creation. Every word which is used to express a moral or intellectual fact, if traced to its root, is found to be borrowed from some material appearance. *Right* means *straight; wrong* means *twisted. Spirit* primarily means *wind; transgression,* the crossing of a *line; supercilious,* the *raising of the eyebrow.* We say the *heart* to express emotion, the *head* to denote thought; and *thought* and *emotion* are words borrowed from sensible things, and now appropriated to spiritual nature. Most of the process by which this transformation is made, is hidden from us in the remote time when language was framed; but the same tendency may be daily observed in children. Children and savages use only nouns or names of things, which they convert into verbs, and apply to analogous mental acts.

2. But this origin of all words that convey a spiritual import,—so conspicuous a fact in this history of language, —is our least debt to nature. It is not words only that are emblematic; it is things which are emblematic. Every natural fact is a symbol of some spiritual fact. Every appearance in nature corresponds to some state of the mind, and that state of the mind can only be described by presenting that natural appearance as its picture. An enraged man is a lion, a cunning man is a fox, a firm man is a rock, a learned man is a torch. A lamb is innocence; a snake is subtle spite; flowers express to us the delicate affections. Light and darkness are our familiar expression for knowledge and ignorance; and heat for love. Visible

distance behind and before us, is respectively our image of memory and hope. Who looks upon a river in a meditative hour and is not reminded of the flux of all things? Throw a stone into the stream, and the circles that propagate themselves are the beautiful type of all influence. Man is conscious of a universal soul within or behind his individual life, wherein, as in a firmament, the natures of Justice, Truth, Love, Freedom, arise and shine. The universal soul he calls Reason: it is not mine, or thine, or his, but we are its; we are its property and men. And the blue sky in which the private earth is buried, the sky with its eternal calm, and full of everlasting orbs, is the type of Reason. That which intellectually considered we call Reason, considered in relation to nature, we call Spirit. Spirit is the Creator. Spirit hath life in itself. And man in all ages and countries embodies it in his language as the FATHER.

It is easily seen that there is nothing lucky or capricious in these analogies, but that they are constant, and pervade nature. These are not the dreams of a few poets, here and there, but man is an analogist, and studies relations in all objects. He is placed in the center of beings, and a ray of relation passes from every other being to him. And neither can man be understood without these objects, nor these objects without man. All the facts in natural history taken by themselves, have no value, but are barren, like a single sex. But marry it to human history, and it is full of life. Whole floras, all Linnæus' and Buffon's volumes, are dry catalogues of facts; but the most trivial of these facts, the habit of a plant, the organs, or work, or noise of an insect, applied to the illustration of a fact in intellectual philosophy, or in any way associated to human nature, affects us in the most lively and agreeable manner. The seed of a plant,— to what affecting analogies in the nature of man is that little fruit made use of, in all discourse, up to the voice of Paul, who calls the human corpse a seed,—"It is sown a natural body; it is raised a spiritual body." The motion of the earth round its axis and round the sun makes the day and the year. These are certain amounts of brute light and heat. But is there no intent of an analogy between man's life and the seasons? And do the seasons gain no grandeur or pathos from that analogy? The instincts of the ant are very unimportant considered as the ant's; but the moment a ray of relation is seen to extend from it to man, and the little drudge is seen to be a monitor, a little body with a mighty heart, then all its habits, even that said to be recently observed, that it never sleeps, become sublime.

Because of this radical correspondence between visible things and human thoughts, savages, who have only what is necessary, converse in figures. As we go back in history, language becomes more picturesque, until its infancy, when it is all poetry; or all spiritual facts are represented by natural symbols. The same symbols are found to make the original elements of all languages. It has moreover been observed, that the idioms of all languages approach each other in passages of the greatest eloquence and power. And as this is the first language, so is it the last. This immediate dependence of language upon nature, this conversion of an outward phenomenon into a type of somewhat inhuman life, never loses its power to affect us. It is this which gives that piquancy to the conversation of a strong-natured farmer or backwoodsman, which all men relish.

A man's power to connect his thought with its proper symbol, and so to utter it, depends on the simplicity of his character, that is, upon his love of truth and his desire to communicate it without loss. The corruption of man is followed by the corruption of language. When simplicity of character and the sovereignty of ideas is broken up by the prevalence of secondary desires,—the desire of riches, of pleasure, of power, and of praise,—and duplicity and falsehood take place of simplicity and truth, the power over nature as an interpreter of the will is in a degree lost; new imagery ceases to be created, and old words are perverted to stand for things which are not; a paper currency is employed, when there is no bullion in the vaults. In due time the fraud is manifest, and words lose all power to stimulate the understanding or the affections. Hundreds of writers may be found in every long-civilized nation who for a short time believe and make others believe that they see and utter truths, who do not of themselves clothe one thought in its natural garment, but who feed unconsciously on the language created by the primary writers of the country, those, namely, who hold primarily on nature.

But wise men pierce this rotten diction and fasten words again to visible things; so that picturesque language is at once a commanding certificate that he who employs it is a man in alliance with truth and God. The moment our discourse rises above the ground line of familiar facts and is inflamed with passion or exalted by thought, it clothes itself in images. A man conversing in earnest, if he watch his intellectual processes, will find that a material image more or less luminous arises in his mind, contemporaneous with every thought, which furnishes the vestment of the thought. Hence, good writing and brilliant discourse are perpetual allegories. This imagery is spontaneous. It is the blending of experience with the present action of the mind. It is proper creation. It is the working of the Original Cause through the instruments he has already made.

These facts may suggest the advantage which the country-life possesses, for a powerful mind, over the artificial and curtailed life of cities. We know more from nature than we can at will communicate. Its light flows into the mind evermore, and we forget its presence. The poet, the orator, bred in the woods, whose senses have been nourished by their fair and appeasing changes, year after year, without design and without heed,—shall not lose their lesson altogether, in the roar of cities or the broil of politics. Long hereafter, amidst agitation and terror in national council,—in the hour of revolution,—these solemn images shall reappear in their morning lustre, as fit symbols and words of the thoughts which the passing events shall awaken. At the call of a noble sentiment, again the woods wave, the pines murmur, the river rolls and shines, and the cattle low upon the mountains, as he saw and heard them in his infancy. And with these forms, the spells of persuasion, the keys of power are put into his hands.

3. We are thus assisted by natural objects in the expression of particular meanings. But how great a language to convey such pepper-corn informations! Did it need such noble races of creatures, this profusion of forms, this host of orbs in heaven, to furnish man with the dictionary and grammar of his municipal speech? Whilst we use this grand cipher to expedite the affairs of our pot and kettle, we feel that we have not yet put it to its use, neither are able. We are like travellers using the cinders of a volcano to roast their eggs. Whilst we see that it always stands ready to clothe what we would say, we cannot avoid the question whether the characters are not significant of themselves. Have mountains, and waves, and skies, no significance but

what we consciously give them when we employ them as emblems of our thoughts? The world is emblematic. Parts of speech are metaphors, because the whole of nature is a metaphor of the human mind. The laws of moral nature answer to those of matter as face to face in a glass. "The visible world and the relation of its parts, is the dial plate of the invisible." The axioms of physics translate the laws of ethics. Thus, "the whole is greater than its part"; "reaction is equal to action"; "the smallest weight may be made to lift the greatest, the difference of weight being compensated by time"; and many the like propositions, which have an ethical as well as physical sense. These propositions have a much more extensive and universal sense when applied to human life, than when confined to technical use.

In like manner, the memorable words of history and the proverbs of nations consist usually of a natural fact, selected as a picture or parable of a moral truth. Thus: A rolling stone gathers no moss; A bird in the hand is worth two in the bush; A cripple in the right way will beat a racer in the wrong; Make hay while the sun shines; 'Tis hard to carry a full cup even; Vinegar is the son of wine; The last ounce broke the camel's back; Long-lived trees make roots first;—and the like. In their primary sense these are trivial facts, but we repeat them for the value of their analogical import. What is true of proverbs, is true of all fables, parables, and allegories.

This relation between the mind and matter is not fancied by some poet, but stands in the will of God, and so is free to be known by all men. It appears to men, or it does not appear. When in fortunate hours we ponder this miracle, the wise man doubts if at all other times he is not blind and deaf;

> Can these things be,
> And overcome us like a summer's cloud,
> Without our special wonder?

for the universe becomes transparent, and the light of higher laws than its own shines through it. It is the standing problem which has exercised the wonder and the study of every fine genius since the world began; from the era of the Egyptians and the Brahmins to that of Pythagoras, of Plato, of Bacon, of Leibnitz, of Swedenborg. There sits the

Sphinx at the roadside, and from age to age, as each prophet comes by, he tries his fortune at reading her riddle. There seems to be a necessity in spirit to manifest itself in material forms; and day and night, river and storm, beast and bird, acid and alkali, pre-exist in necessary Ideas in the mind of God, and are what they are by virtue of preceding affections in the world of spirit. A fact is the end or last issue of spirit. The visible creation is the terminus or the circumference of the invisible world. "Material objects," said a French philosopher, "are necessarily kinds of *scoriæ* [slag] of the substantial thoughts of the Creator, which must always preserve an exact relation to their first origin; in other words, visible nature must have a spiritual and moral side."

This doctrine is abstruse, and though the images of "garment," "scoriæ," "mirror," etc., may stimulate the fancy, we must summon the aid of subtler and more vital expositors to make it plain. "Every scripture is to be interpreted by the same spirit which gave it forth,"—is the fundamental law of criticism. A life in harmony with Nature, the love of truth and of virtue, will purge the eyes to understand her text. By degrees we may come to know the primitive sense of the permanent objects of nature, so that the world shall be to us an open book, and every form significant of its hidden life and final cause.

A new interest surprises us, whilst, under the view now suggested, we contemplate the fearful extent and multitude of objects; since "every object rightly seen, unlocks a new faculty of the soul." That which was unconscious truth, becomes, when interpreted and defined in an object, a part of the domain of knowledge,—a new weapon in the magazine of power.

V. Discipline

In view of the significance of nature, we arrive at once at a new fact, that nature is a discipline. This use of the world includes the preceding uses, as parts of itself.

Space, time, society, labor, climate, food, locomotion, the animals, the mechanical forces, give us sincerest lessons, day by day, whose meaning is unlimited. They educate both the Understanding and the Reason. Every property of matter is a school for the understanding,—its solidity or resistance, its inertia, its extension, its figure, its divisibility. The understanding adds, divides, combines, measures, and finds nutriment and room for its activity in this worthy scene. Meantime, Reason transfers all these lessons into its own world of thought, by perceiving the analogy that marries Matter and Mind.

1. Nature is a discipline of the understanding in intellectual truths. Our dealing with sensible objects is a constant exercise in the necessary lessons of difference, of likeness, of order, of being and seeming, of progressive arrangement; of ascent from particular to general; of combination to one end of manifold forces. Proportioned to the importance of the organ to be formed, is the extreme care with which its tuition is provided,—a care pretermitted in no single case. What tedious training, day after day, year after year, never ending, to form the common sense; what continual reproduction of annoyances, inconveniences, dilemmas; what rejoicing over us of little men; what disputing of prices, what reckonings of interest,—and all to form the Hand of the mind;—to instruct us that "good thoughts are no better than good dreams, unless they be executed!"

The same good office is performed by Property and its filial systems of debt and credit. Debt, grinding debt, whose iron face the widow, the orphan, and the sons of genius fear and hate;—debt, which consumes so much time, which so cripples and disheartens a great spirit with cares that seem so base, is a preceptor whose lessons cannot be forgone, and is needed most by those who suffer from it most. Moreover, property, which has been well compared to snow,—"if it fall level today, it will be blown into drifts tomorrow,"—is the surface action of internal machinery, like the index on the face of a clock. Whilst now it is the gymnastics of the understanding, it is hiving, in the foresight of the spirit, experience in profounder laws.

The whole character and fortune of the individual are affected by the least inequalities in the culture of the understanding; for example, in the perception of differences. Therefore is Space, and therefore Time, that man may know that things are not huddled and lumped, but sundered and individual. A bell and a plough have each their use, and neither can do the office of the other. Water is good to drink, coal to burn, wool to wear; but wool cannot be drunk, nor water spun, nor coal eaten. The wise man shows his wisdom in separation, in gradation, and his scale of creatures and of merits is as wide as nature. The foolish have no range in their scale, but suppose every man is as every other man. What is not good they call the worst, and what is not hateful, they call the best.

In like manner, what good heed Nature forms in us! She pardons no mistakes. Her yea is yea, and her nay, nay.

The first steps in Agriculture, Astronomy, Zoölogy (those first steps which the farmer, the hunter, and the sailor take), teach that Nature's dice are always loaded; that in her heaps and rubbish are concealed sure and useful results.

How calmly and genially the mind apprehends one after another the laws of physics! What noble emotions dilate the mortal as he enters into the councils of the creation, and feels by knowledge the privilege to BE! His insight refines him. The beauty of nature shines in his own breast. Man is greater that he can see this, and the universe less, because Time and Space relations vanish as laws are known.

Here again we are impressed and even daunted by the immense Universe to be explored. "What we know is a point to what we do not know." Open any recent journal of science, and weigh the problems suggested concerning Light, Heat, Electricity, Magnetism, Physiology, Geology, and judge whether the interest of natural science is likely to be soon exhausted.

Passing by many particulars of the discipline of nature, we must not omit to specify two.

The exercise of the Will, or the lesson of power, is taught in every event. From the child's successive possession of his several senses up to the hour when he saith, "Thy will be done!" he is learning the secret that he can reduce under his will, not only particular events but great classes, nay, the whole series of events, and so conform all facts to his character. Nature is thoroughly mediate. It is made to serve. It receives the dominion of man as meekly as the ass on which the Saviour rode. It offers all its kingdoms to man as the raw material which he may mould into what is useful. Man is never weary of working it up. He forges the subtile and delicate air into wise and melodious words, and gives them wing as angels of persuasion and command.

One after another his victorious thought comes up with and reduces all things, until the world becomes at last only a realized will,—the double of the man.

2. Sensible objects conform to the premonitions of Reason and reflect the conscience. All things are moral; and in their boundless changes have an unceasing reference to spiritual nature. Therefore is nature glorious with form, color, and motion—that every globe in the remotest heaven, every chemical change from the rudest crystal up to the laws of life, every change of vegetation from the first principle of growth in the eye of a leaf, to the tropical forest and antediluvian coal-mine, every animal function from the sponge up to Hercules, shall hint or thunder to man the laws of right and wrong, and echo the Ten Commandments. Therefore is Nature ever the ally of Religion—lends all her pomp and riches to the religious sentiment. Prophet and priest, David, Isaiah, Jesus, have drawn deeply from this source. This ethical character so penetrates the bone and marrow of nature, as to seem the end for which it was made. Whatever private purpose is answered by any member or part, this is its public and universal function, and is never omitted. Nothing in nature is exhausted in its first use. When a thing has served an end to the uttermost, it is wholly new for an ulterior service. In God, every end is converted into a new means. Thus the use of commodity, regarded by itself, is mean and squalid. But it is to the mind an education in the doctrine of Use, namely, that a thing is good only so far as it serves; that a conspiring of parts and efforts to the production of an end is essential to any being. The first and gross manifestation of this truth is our inevitable and hated training in values and wants, in corn and meat.

It has already been illustrated, that every natural process is a version of a moral sentence. The moral law lies at the center of nature and radiates to the circumference. It is the pith and marrow of every substance, every relation, and every process. All things with which we deal, preach to us. What is a farm but a mute gospel? The chaff and the wheat, weeds and plants, blight, rain, insects, sun,—it is a sacred emblem from the first furrow of spring to the last stack which the snow of winter overtakes in the fields. But the sailor, the shepherd, the miner, the merchant, in their several resorts, have each an experience precisely parallel, and leading to the same conclusion: because all organizations are radically alike. Nor can it be doubted that this moral sentiment which thus scents the air, grows in the grain, and impregnates the waters of the world, is caught by man and sinks into his soul. The moral influence of nature upon every individual is that amount of truth which it illustrates to him. Who can estimate this? Who can guess how much firmness the sea-beaten rock has taught the fisherman? how much tranquillity has been reflected to man from the azure sky, over whose unspotted deeps the winds forever-more drive flocks of stormy clouds, and leave no wrinkle or stain? how much industry and providence and affection we have caught from the pantomime of brutes? What a searching preacher of self-command is the varying phenomenon of Health!

Herein is especially apprehended the unity of Nature,— the unity in variety,—which meets us everywhere. All the endless variety of things make an identical impression. Xenophanes complained in his old age that, look where he would, all things hastened back to Unity. He was weary of seeing the same entity in the tedious variety of forms. The fable of Proteus has a cordial truth. A leaf, a drop, a crystal, a moment of time, is related to the whole, and partakes of the perfection of the whole. Each particle is a microcosm, and faithfully renders the likeness of the world.

Not only resemblances exist in things whose analogy is obvious, as when we detect the type of the human hand in the flipper of the fossil saurus, but also in objects wherein there is great superficial unlikeness. Thus architecture is called "frozen music," by De Staël and Goethe. Vitruvius thought an architect should be a musician. "A Gothic church," said Coleridge, "is a petrified religion." Michael Angelo maintained that, to an architect, a knowledge of anatomy is essential. In Haydn's oratorios, the notes present to the imagination not only motions, as of the snake, the stag, and the elephant, but colors also; as the green grass. The law of harmonic sounds reappears in the harmonic colors. The granite is differenced in its laws only by the more or less of heat from the river that wears it away. The river, as it flows, resembles the air that flows over it; the air resembles the light which traverses it with more subtle currents; the light resembles the heat which rides with it through Space. Each creature is only a modification of the other; the likeness in them is more than the difference, and their radical law is one and the same. A rule of one art, or a law of one organization, holds true throughout nature. So intimate is this Unity, that, it is easily seen, it lies under the undermost garment of nature, and betrays its source in Universal Spirit. For it pervades Thought also. Every universal truth which we express in words, implies or supposes every other truth. *Omne verum vero consonat* [Every truth harmonizes with every other]. It is like a great circle on a sphere, comprising all possible circles; which, however, may be drawn and comprise it in like manner. Every such truth is the absolute Ens [Being] seen from one side. But it has innumerable sides.

The central Unity is still more conspicuous in actions. Words are finite organs of the infinite mind. They cannot cover the dimensions of what is in truth. They break, chop and impoverish it. An action is the perfection and publication of thought. A right action seems to fill the eye, and to be related to all nature. "The wise man, in doing one thing, does all; or, in the one thing he does rightly, he sees the likeness of all which is done rightly."

Words and actions are not the attributes of brute nature. They introduce us to the human form, of which all other organizations appear to be degradations. When this appears among so many that surround it, the spirit prefers it to all others. It says, "From such as this have I drawn joy and knowledge; in such as this have I found and beheld myself; I will speak to it; it can speak again; it can yield me thought already formed and alive." In fact, the eye,—the mind,—is always accompanied by these forms, male and female; and these are incomparably the richest informations of the power and order that lie at the heart of things. Unfortunately every one of them bears the marks as of some injury; is marred and superficially defective. Nevertheless, far different from the deaf and dumb nature around them, these all rest like fountain-pipes on the unfathomed sea of thought and virtue whereto they alone, of all organizations, are the entrances.

It were a pleasant inquiry to follow into detail their ministry to our education, but where would it stop? We are associated in adolescent and adult life with some friends, who, like skies and waters, are coextensive with our idea;

who, answering each to a certain affection of the soul,
satisfy our desire on that side; whom we lack power to put
at such focal distance from us, that we can mend or even
analyze them. We cannot choose but love them. When
much intercourse with a friend has supplied us with a
standard of excellence, and has increased our respect for
the resources of God who thus sends a real person to outgo
our idea; when he has, moreover, become an object of
thought, and, whilst his character retains all its unconscious
effect, is converted in the mind into solid and sweet wisdom,—it is a sign to us that his office is closing, and he is
commonly withdrawn from our sight in a short time.

VI. Idealism

Thus is the unspeakable but intelligible and practicable
meaning of the world conveyed to man, the immortal
pupil, in every object of sense. To this one end of Discipline, all parts of nature conspire.

A noble doubt perpetually suggests itself,—whether this
end be not the Final Cause of the Universe; and whether
nature outwardly exists. It is a sufficient account of that
Appearance we call the World, that God will teach a
human mind, and so makes it the receiver of a certain
number of congruent sensations, which we call sun and
moon, man and woman, house and trade. In my utter
impotence to test the authenticity of the report of my
senses, to know whether the impressions they make on me
correspond with outlying objects, what difference does it
make, whether Orion is up there in heaven, or some god
paints the image in the firmament of the soul? The relations
of parts and the end of the whole remaining the same,
what is the difference, whether land and sea interact, and
worlds revolve and intermingle without number or end,—
deep yawning under deep, and galaxy balancing galaxy,
throughout absolute space,—or whether, without relations
of time and space, the same appearances are inscribed in
the constant faith of man? Whether nature enjoy a substantial existence without, or is only in the apocalypse of
the mind, it is alike useful and alike venerable to me. Be
it what it may, it is ideal to me so long as I cannot try the
accuracy of my senses.

The frivolous make themselves merry with the Ideal

theory, as if its consequences were burlesque; as if it affected the stability of nature. It surely does not. God never jests with us, and will not compromise the end of nature by permitting any inconsequence in its procession. Any distrust of the permanence of laws would paralyze the faculties of man. Their permanence is sacredly respected, and his faith therein is perfect. The wheels and springs of man are all set to the hypothesis of the permanence of nature. We are not built like a ship to be tossed, but like a house to stand. It is a natural consequence of this structure, that so long as the active powers predominate over the reflective, we resist with indignation any hint that nature is more short-lived or mutable than spirit. The broker, the wheelwright, the carpenter, the tollman, are much displeased at the intimation.

But whilst we acquiesce entirely in the permanence of natural laws, the question of the absolute existence of nature still remains open. It is the uniform effect of culture on the human mind, not to shake our faith in the stability of particular phenomena, as of heat, water, azote; but to lead us to regard nature as phenomenon, not a substance; to attribute necessary existence to spirit; to esteem nature as an accident and an effect.

To the senses and the unrenewed understanding, belongs a sort of instinctive belief in the absolute existence of nature. In their view man and nature are indissolubly joined. Things are ultimates, and they never look beyond their sphere. The presence of Reason mars this faith. The first effort of thought tends to relax this despotism of the senses which binds us to nature as if we were a part of it, and shows us nature aloof, and, as it were, afloat. Until this higher agency intervened, the animal eye sees, with wonderful accuracy, sharp outlines and colored surfaces. When the eye of Reason opens, to outline and surface are at once added grace and expression. These proceed from imagination and affection, and abate somewhat of the angular distinctness of objects. If the Reason be stimulated to more earnest vision, outlines and surfaces become transparent, and are no longer seen; causes and spirits are seen through them. The best moments of life are these delicious awakenings of the higher powers, and the reverential withdrawing of nature before its God.

Let us proceed to indicate the effects of culture.

1. Our first institution in the Ideal philosophy is a hint from Nature herself.

Nature is made to conspire with spirit to emancipate us. Certain mechanical changes, a small alteration in our local position, apprizes us of a dualism. We are strangely affected by seeing the shore from a moving ship, from a balloon, or through the tints of an unusual sky. The least change in our point of view gives the whole world a pictorial air. A man who seldom rides, needs only to get into a coach and traverse his own town, to turn the street into a puppet-show. The men, the women,—talking, running, bartering, fighting,—the earnest mechanic, the lounger, the beggar, the boys, the dogs, are unrealized at once, or, at least, wholly detached from all relation to the observer, and seen as apparent, not substantial beings. What new thoughts are suggested by seeing a face of country quite familiar, in the rapid movement of the railroad car! Nay, the most wonted objects (make a very slight change in the point of vision) please us most. In a camera obscura, the butcher's cart, and the figure of one of our own family amuse us. So a portrait of a well-known face gratifies us. Turn the eyes upside down, by looking at the landscape through your legs, and how agreeable is the picture, though you have seen it any time these twenty years!

In these cases, by mechanical means, is suggested the difference between the observer and the spectacle,—between man and nature. Hence arises a pleasure mixed with awe; I may say, a low degree of the sublime is felt, from the fact, probably, that man is hereby apprized that whilst the world is a spectacle, something in himself is stable.

2. In a higher manner the poet communicates the same pleasure. By a few strokes he delineates—as on air—the sun, the mountain, the camp, the city, the hero, the maiden, not different from what we know them, but only lifted from the ground and afloat before the eye. He unfixes the land and the sea, makes them revolve around the axis of his primary thought, and disposes them anew. Possessed himself by a heroic passion, he uses matter as symbols of it. The sensual man conforms thoughts to things; the poet conforms things to his thoughts. The one esteems nature as rooted and fast; the other, as fluid, and impresses his being thereon. To him, the refractory world is ductile and flexible; he invests dust and stones with humanity, and makes them

the words of the Reason. The Imagination may be defined to be the use which the Reason makes of the material world. Shakespeare possesses the power of subordinating nature for the purposes of expression, beyond all poets. His imperial muse tosses the creation like a bauble from hand to hand, and uses it to embody any caprice of thought that is uppermost in his mind. The remotest spaces of nature are visited, and the farthest sundered things are brought together, by a subtile spiritual connection. We are made aware that magnitude of material things is relative, and all objects shrink and expand to serve the passion of the poet. Thus in his sonnets, the lays of birds, the scents and dyes of flowers he finds to be the *shadow* of his beloved; time, which keeps her from him, is his *chest;* the suspicion she has awakened, is her *ornament:*

> The ornament of beauty is Suspect,
> A crow which flies in heaven's sweetest air.

His passion is not the fruit of chance; it swells, as he speaks, to a city, or a state:

> No, it was builded far from accident;
> It suffers not in smiling pomp, nor falls
> Under the brow of thralling discontent;
> It fears not policy, that heretic,
> That works on leases of short numbered hours,
> But all alone stands hugely politic.

In the strength of his constancy, the Pyramids seem to him recent and transitory. The freshness of youth and love dazzles him with its resemblance to morning:

> Take those lips away
> Which so sweetly were forsworn;
> And those eyes,—the break of day,
> Lights that do mislead the morn.

The wild beauty of his hyperbole, I may say in passing, it would not be easy to match in literature.

This transfiguration which all material objects undergo through the passion of the poet,—this power which he exerts to dwarf the great, to magnify the small,—might be illustrated by a thousand examples from his plays. I have before me the Tempest, and will cite only these few lines:

> ARIEL. The strong based promontory
> Have I made shake, and by the spurs plucked up
> The pine and cedar.

Prospero calls for music to soothe the frantic Alonzo, and his companions:

> A solemn air, and the best comforter
> To an unsettled fancy, cure thy brains
> Now useless, boiled within thy skull.

Again:

> The charm dissolves apace,
> And, as the morning steals upon the night,
> Melting the darkness, so their rising senses
> Begin to chase the ignorant fumes that mantle
> Their clearer reason.
> Their understanding
> Begins to swell: and the approaching tide
> Will shortly fill the reasonable shores
> That now lie foul and muddy.

The perception of real affinities between events (that is to say, of *ideal* affinities, for those only are real) enables the poet thus to make free with the most imposing forms and phenomena of the world, and to assert the predominance of the soul.

3. Whilst thus the poet animates nature with his own thoughts, he differs from the philosopher only herein, that the one proposes Beauty as his main end; the other Truth. But the philosopher, not less than the poet, postpones the apparent order and relations of things to the empire of thought. "The problem of philosophy," according to Plato, "is, for all that exists conditionally, to find a ground unconditioned and absolute." It proceeds on the faith that a law determines all phenomena, which being known, the phenomena can be predicted. That law, when in the mind, is an idea. Its beauty is infinite. The true philosopher and the true poet are one, and a beauty, which is truth, and a truth, which is beauty, is the aim of both. Is not the charm

of one of Plato's or Aristotle's definitions strictly like that of the Antigone of Sophocles? It is, in both cases, that a spiritual life has been imparted to nature; that the solid seeming block of matter has been pervaded and dissolved by a thought; that this feeble human being has penetrated the vast masses of nature with an informing soul, and recognized itself in their harmony, that is, seized the law. In physics, when this is attained, the memory disburthens itself of its cumbrous catalogues of particulars, and carries centuries of observation in a single formula.

Thus even in physics, the material is degraded before the spiritual. The astronomer, the geometer, rely on their irrefragable analysis, and disdain the results of observation. The sublime remark of Euler on his law of arches, "This will be found contrary to all experience, yet is true," had already transferred nature into the mind, and left matter like an outcast corpse.

4. Intellectual science has been observed to beget invariably a doubt of the existence of matter. Turgot said, "He that has never doubted the existence of matter, may be assured he has no aptitude for metaphysical inquiries." It fastens the attention upon immortal necessary uncreated natures, that is, upon Ideas; and in their presence we feel that the outward circumstance is a dream and a shade. Whilst we wait in this Olympus of gods, we think of nature as an appendix to the soul. We ascend into their region, and know that these are the thoughts of the Supreme Being. "These are they who were set up from everlasting, from the beginning, or ever the earth was. When he prepared the heavens, they were there; when he established the clouds above, when he strengthened the fountains of the deep. Then they were by him, as one brought up with him. Of them took he counsel."

Their influence is proportionate. As objects of science they are accessible to few men. Yet all men are capable of being raised by piety or by passion, into their region. And no man touches these divine natures, without becoming, in some degree, himself divine. Like a new soul, they renew the body. We become physically nimble and lightsome; we tread on air; life is no longer irksome, and we think it will never be so. No man fears age or misfortune or death in their serene company, for he is transported out of the district of change. Whilst we behold unveiled the nature of

Justice and Truth, we learn the difference between the absolute and the conditional or relative. We apprehend the absolute. As it were, for the first time, *we exist*. We become immortal, for we learn that time and space are relations of matter; that with a perception of truth or a virtuous will they have no affinity.

5. Finally, religion and ethics, which may be fitly called the practice of ideas, or the introduction of ideas into life, have an analogous effect with all lower culture, in degrading nature and suggesting its dependence on spirit. Ethics and religion differ herein; that the one is the system of human duties commencing from man; the other, from God. Religion includes the personality of God; Ethics does not. They are one to our present design. They both put nature under foot. The first and last lesson of religion is, "The things that are seen, are temporal; the things that are unseen, are eternal." It puts an affront upon nature. It does that for the unschooled, which philosophy does for Berkeley and Viasa. The uniform language that may be heard in the churches of the most ignorant sects is,—"Contemn the unsubstantial shows of the world; they are vanities, dreams, shadows, unrealities; seek the realities of religion." The devotee flouts nature. Some theosophists have arrived at a certain hostility and indignation towards matter, as the Manichean and Plotinus. They distrusted in themselves any looking back to these flesh-pots of Egypt. Plotinus was ashamed of his body. In short, they might all say of matter, which Michael Angelo said of external beauty, "It is the frail and weary weed, in which God dresses the soul which he has called into time."

It appears that motion, poetry, physical and intellectual science, and religion, all tend to affect our convictions of the reality of the external world. But I own there is something ungrateful in expanding too curiously the particulars of the general proposition, that all culture tends to imbue us with idealism. I have no hostility to nature, but a child's love to it. I expand and live in the warm day like corn and melons. Let us speak her fair. I do not wish to fling stones at my beautiful mother, nor soil my gentle nest. I only wish to indicate the true position of nature in regard to man, wherein to establish man all right education tends; as the ground which to attain is the object of human life, that is, of man's connection with nature. Culture inverts the

vulgar views of nature, and brings the mind to call that
apparent which it uses to call real, and that real which
it uses to call visionary. Children, it is true, believe in the
external world. The belief that it appears only, is an after-
thought, but with culture this faith will as surely arise on
the mind as did the first.

The advantage of the ideal theory over the popular faith
is this, that it presents the world in precisely that view
which is most desirable to the mind. It is, in fact, the view
which Reason, both speculative and practical, that is,
philosophy and virtue, take. For seen in the light of
thought, the world always is phenomenal; and virtue subordinates it to the mind. Idealism sees the world in God.
It beholds the whole circle of persons and things, of
actions and events, of country and religion, not as painfully accumulated, atom after atom, act after act, in an
aged creeping Past, but as one vast picture which God
paints on the instant eternity for the contemplation of the
soul. Therefore the soul holds itself off from a too trivial
and microscopic study of a universal tablet. It respects the
end too much to immerse itself in the means. It sees something more important in Christianity than the scandals of
ecclesiastical history or the niceties of criticism; and, very
incurious concerning persons or miracles, and not at all
disturbed by chasms of historical evidence, it accepts from
God the phenomenon, as it finds it, as the pure and awful
form of religion in the world. It is not hot and passionate
at the appearance of what it calls its own good or bad
fortune, at the union or opposition of other persons. No
man is its enemy. It accepts whatsoever befalls, as part of
its lesson. It is a watcher more than a doer, and it is a
doer, only that it may the better watch.

VII. Spirit

It is essential to a true theory of nature and of man, that
it should contain somewhat progressive. Uses that are
exhausted or that may be, and facts that end in the statement, cannot be all that is true of this brave lodging
wherein man is harbored, and wherein all his faculties
find appropriate and endless exercise. And all the uses of
nature admit of being summed in one, which yields the
activity of man an infinite scope. Through all its kingdoms,

to the suburbs and outskirts of things, it is faithful to the cause whence it had its origin. It always speaks of Spirit. It suggests the absolute. It is a perpetual effect. It is a great shadow pointing always to the sun behind us.

The aspect of Nature is devout. Like the figure of Jesus, she stands with bended head, and hands folded upon the breast. The happiest man is he who learns from nature the lesson of worship.

Of that ineffable essence which we call Spirit, he that thinks most, will say least. We can foresee God in the coarse, and, as it were, distant phenomena of matter; but when we try to define and describe himself, both language and thought desert us, and we are as helpless as fools and savages. That essence refuses to be recorded in propositions, but when man has worshipped him intellectually, the noblest ministry of nature is to stand as the apparition of God. It is the organ through which the universal spirit speaks to the individual, and strives to lead back the individual to it.

When we consider Spirit, we see that the views already presented do not include the whole circumference of man. We must add some related thoughts.

Three problems are put by nature to the mind: What is matter? Whence is it? and Whereto? The first of these questions only, the ideal theory answers. Idealism saith: matter is a phenomenon, not a substance. Idealism acquaints us with the total disparity between the evidence of our own being and the evidence of the world's being. The one is perfect; the other, incapable of any assurance; the mind is a part of the nature of things; the world is a divine dream, from which we may presently awake to the glories and certainties of day. Idealism is a hypothesis to account for nature by other principles than those of carpentry and chemistry. Yet, if it only deny the existence of matter, it does not satisfy the demands of the spirit. It leaves God out of me. It leaves me in the splendid labyrinth of my perceptions, to wander without end. Then the heart resists it, because it balks the affections in denying substantive being to men and women. Nature is so pervaded with human life that there is something of humanity in all and in every particular. But this theory makes nature foreign to me, and does not account for that consanguinity which we acknowledge to it.

Let it stand then, in the present state of our knowledge, merely as a useful introductory hypothesis, serving to apprise us of the eternal distinction between the soul and the world.

But when, following the invisible steps of thought, we come to inquire, Whence is matter? and Whereto? many truths arise to us out of the recesses of consciousness. We learn that the highest is present to the soul of man; that the dread universal essence, which is not wisdom, or love, or beauty, or power, but all in one, and each entirely, is that for which all things exist, and that by which they are; that spirit creates; that behind nature, throughout nature, spirit is present; one and not compound it does not act upon us from without, that is, in space and time, but spiritually, or through ourselves: therefore, that spirit, that is, the Supreme Being, does not build up nature around us but puts it forth through us, as the life of the tree puts forth new branches and leaves through the pores of the old. As a plant upon the earth, so a man rests upon the bosom of God; he is nourished by unfailing fountains, and draws at his need inexhaustible power. Who can set bounds to the possibilities of man? Once inhale the upper air, being admitted to behold the absolute natures of justice and truth, and we learn that man has access to the entire mind of the Creator, is himself the creator in the finite. This view, which admonishes me where the sources of wisdom and power lie, and points to virtue as to

The golden key
Which opes the palace of eternity,

carries upon its face the highest certificate of truth, because it animates me to create my own world through the purification of the soul.

The world proceeds from the same spirit as the body of man. It is a remoter and inferior incarnation of God, a projection of God in the unconscious. But it differs from the body in one important respect. It is not, like that, now subjected to the human will. Its serene order is inviolable by us. It is, therefore, to us, the present expositor of the divine mind. It is a fixed point whereby we may measure our departure. As we degenerate, the contrast between us and our house is more evident. We are as much strangers in nature as we are aliens from God. We do not understand the notes of birds. The fox and the deer run away from us; the bear and tiger rend us. We do not know the uses of more than a few plants, as corn and the apple, the potato and the vine. Is not the landscape, every glimpse of which hath a grandeur, a face of him? Yet this may show us what discord is between man and nature, for you cannot freely admire a noble landscape if laborers are digging in the field hard by. The poet finds something ridiculous in his delight until he is out of the sight of men.

VIII. Prospects

In inquiries respecting the laws of the world and the frame of things, the highest reason is always the truest. That which seems faintly possible, it is so refined, is often faint and dim because it is deepest seated in the mind among the eternal verities. Empirical science is apt to cloud the sight, and by the very knowledge of functions and processes to bereave the student of the manly contemplation of the whole. The savant becomes unpoetic. But the best read naturalist who lends an entire and devout attention to truth, will see that there remains much to learn of his relation to the world, and that it is not to be learned by any addition or subtraction or other comparison of known quantities, but is arrived at by untaught sallies of the spirit, by a continual self-recovery, and by entire humility. He will perceive that there are far more excellent qualities in the student than preciseness and infallibility; that a guess is often more fruitful than an indisputable affirmation, and that a dream may let us deeper into the secret of nature than a hundred concerted experiments.

For the problems to be solved are precisely those which the physiologist and the naturalist omit to state. It is not so pertinent to man to know all the individuals of the animal kingdom, as it is to know whence and whereto is this tyrannizing unity in his constitution, which evermore separates and classifies things, endeavoring to reduce the most diverse to one form. When I behold a rich landscape, it is less to my purpose to recite correctly the order and superposition of the strata, than to know why all thought of multitude is lost in a tranquil sense of unity. I cannot greatly honor minuteness in details, so long as there is no hint to explain

the relation between things and thoughts; no ray upon the
metaphysics of conchology, of botany, of the arts, to show
the relation of the forms of flowers, shells, animals, architecture, to the mind, and build science upon ideas. In a
cabinet of natural history, we become sensible of a certain
occult recognition and sympathy in regard to the most un-
wieldly and eccentric forms of beast, fish, and insect. The
American who has been confined, in his own country, to
the sight of buildings designed after foreign models, is surprised on entering York Minster or St. Peter's at Rome, by
the feeling that these structures are imitations also,—faint
copies of an invisible archetype. Nor has science sufficient
humanity, so long as the naturalist overlooks that wonderful congruity which subsists between man and the world;
of which he is lord, not because he is the most subtile inhabitant, but because he is its head and heart, and finds
something of himself in every great and small thing, in
every mountain stratum, in every new law of color, fact
of astronomy, or atmospheric influence which observation
or analysis lays open. A perception of this mystery inspires
the muse of George Herbert, the beautiful psalmist of the
seventeenth century. The following lines are part of his
little poem on Man.

> Man is all symmetry,
> Full of proportions, one limb to another,
> And to all the world besides.
> Each part may call the farthest, brother;
> For head with foot hath private amity,
> And both with moons and tides.
>
> Nothing hath got so far
> But man hath caught and kept it as his prey;
> His eyes dismount the highest star:
> He is in little all the sphere.
> Herbs gladly cure our flesh, because that they
> Find their acquaintance there.
>
> For us, the winds do blow,
> The earth doth rest, heaven move, and fountains flow.
> Nothing we see, but means our good,
> As our delight, or as our treasure;

The whole is either our cupboard of food,
  Or cabinet of pleasure.

  The stars have us to bed:
Night draws the curtain; which the sun withdraws.
  Music and light attend our head.
  All things unto our flesh are kind,
In their descent and being; to our mind,
  In their ascent and cause.

  More servants wait on man
Than he'll take notice of. In every path,
  He treads down that which doth befriend him
  When sickness makes him pale and wan.
Oh mighty love! Man is one world, and hath
  Another to attend him.

The perception of this class of truths makes the attraction which draws men to science, but the end is lost sight of in attention to the means. In view of this half-sight of science, we accept the sentence of Plato, that "poetry comes nearer to vital truth than history." Every surmise and vaticination of the mind is entitled to a certain respect, and we learn to prefer imperfect theories, and sentences which contain glimpses of truth, to digested systems which have no one valuable suggestion. A wise writer will feel that the ends of study and composition are best answered by announcing undiscovered regions of thought, and so communicating, through hope, new activity to the torpid spirit.

I shall therefore conclude this essay with some traditions of man and nature, which a certain poet sang to me; and which, as they have always been in the world, and perhaps reappear to every bard, may be both history and prophecy.

"The foundations of man are not in matter, but in spirit. But the element of spirit is eternity. To it, therefore, the longest series of events, the oldest chronologies are young and recent. In the cycle of the universal man, from whom the known individuals proceed, centuries are points, and all history is but the epoch of one degradation.

"We distrust and deny inwardly our sympathy with nature. We own and disown our relation to it, by turns. We are like Nebuchadnezzar, dethroned, bereft of reason, and eating grass like an ox. But who can set limits to the remedial force of spirit?

"A man is a god in ruins. When men are innocent, life shall be longer, and shall pass into the immortal as gently as we awake from dreams. Now, the world would be insane and rabid, if these disorganizations should last for hundreds of years. It is kept in check by death and infancy. Infancy is the perpetual Messiah, which comes into the arms of fallen men, and pleads with them to return to paradise.

"Man is the dwarf of himself. Once he was permeated and dissolved by spirit. He filled nature with his overflowing currents. Out from him sprang the sun and moon; from man the sun, from woman the moon. The laws of his mind, the periods of his actions externized themselves into day and night, into the year and the seasons. But, having made for himself this huge shell, his waters retired; he no longer fills the veins and veinlets; he is shrunk to a drop. He sees that the structure still fits him, but fits him colossally. Say, rather, once it fitted him, now it corresponds to him from far and on high. He adores timidly his own work. Now is man the follower of the sun, and woman the follower of the moon. Yet sometimes he starts in his slumber, and wonders at himself and his house, and muses strangely at the resemblance betwixt him and it. He perceives that if his law is still paramount, if still he have elemental power, if his word is sterling yet in nature, it is not conscious power, it is not inferior, but superior to his will. It is instinct." Thus my Orphic poet sang.

At present, man applies to nature but half his force. He works on the world with his understanding alone. He lives in it and masters it by a penny-wisdom; and he that works most in it is but a half-man, and whilst his arms are strong and his digestion good, his mind is imbruted, and he is a selfish savage. His relation to nature, his power over it, is through the understanding, as by manure; the economic use of fire, wind, water, and the mariner's needle; steam, coal, chemical agriculture; the repairs of the human body by the dentist and the surgeon. This is such a resumption of power as if a banished king should buy his territories inch by inch, instead of vaulting at once into his throne. Meantime, in the thick darkness, there are not wanting gleams of a better light,—occasional examples of the action of man upon nature with his entire force,—with reason as well as understanding. Such examples are: the traditions of miracles in the earliest antiquity of all nations; the history of Jesus Christ; the achievements of a principle, as religious and political revolutions, and in the abolition of the slave-trade; the miracles of enthusiasm, as those reported of Swedenborg, Hohenlohe, and the Shakers; many obscure and yet contested facts, now arranged under the name of Animal Magnetism; prayer; eloquence; self healing; and the wisdom of children. These are examples of Reason's momentary grasp of the sceptre; the exertions of a power which exists not in time or space, but an instantaneous instreaming causing power. The difference between the actual and the ideal force of man is happily figured by the schoolmen, in saying that the knowledge of man is an evening knowledge, *vespertina cognitio,* but that of God is a morning knowledge, *matutina cognitio.*

The problem of restoring to the world original and eternal beauty is solved by the redemption of the soul. The ruin or the blank that we see when we look at nature, is in our own eye. The axis of vision is not coincident with the axis of things, and so they appear not transparent but opaque. The reason why the world lacks unity, and lies broken and in heaps, is because man is disunited with himself. He cannot be a naturalist until he satisfies all the demands of the spirit. Love is as much its demand as perception. Indeed, neither can be perfect without the other. In the uttermost meaning of the words, thought is devout, and devotion is thought. Deep calls unto deep. But in actual life, the marriage is not celebrated. There are innocent men who worship God after the tradition of their fathers, but their sense of duty has not yet extended to the use of all their faculties. And there are patient naturalists, but they freeze their subject under the wintry light of the understanding. Is not prayer also a study of truth,—a sally of the soul into the unfound infinite? No man ever prayed heartily without learning something. But when a faithful thinker, resolute to detach every object from personal relations and see it in the light of thought, shall, at the same time, kindle science with the fire of the holiest affections, then will God go forth anew into the creation.

It will not need, when the mind is prepared for study, to search for objects. The invariable mark of wisdom is to see the miraculous in the common. What is a day? What is a year? What is summer? What is woman? What is a child? What is sleep? To our blindness, these things seem unaffecting. We make fables to hide the baldness of the fact and conform it, as we say, to the higher law of the mind. But when the fact is seen under the light of an idea, the gaudy fable fades and shrivels. We behold the real higher law. To the wise, therefore, a fact is true poetry, and the most beautiful of fables. These wonders are brought to our own door. You also are a man. Man and woman and their social life, poverty, labor, sleep, fear, fortune, are known to you. Learn that none of these things is superficial, but that each phenomenon has its roots in the faculties and affections of the mind. Whilst the abstract question occupies your intellect, nature brings it in the concrete to be solved by your hands. It were a wise inquiry for the closet, to compare, point by point, especially at remarkable crises in life, our daily history with the rise and progress of ideas in the mind.

So shall we come to look at the world with new eyes. It shall answer the endless inquiry of the intellect,—What is truth? and of the affections,—What is good? by yielding itself passive to the educated Will. Then shall come to pass what my poet said: "Nature is not fixed but fluid. Spirit alters, moulds, makes it. The immobility or bruteness of nature is the absence of spirit; to pure spirit it is fluid, it is volatile, it is obedient. Every spirit builds itself a house and beyond its house a world and beyond its world a heaven. Know then that the world exists for you. For you is the phenomenon perfect. What we are, that only can we see. All that Adam had, all that Cæsar could, you have and can do. Adam called his house, heaven and earth; Cæsar called his house, Rome; you perhaps call yours, a cobbler's trade; a hundred acres of ploughed land; or a scholar's garret. Yet line for line and point for point your dominion is as great as theirs, though without fine names. Build therefore your own world. As fast as you conform your life to the pure idea in your mind, that will unfold its great proportions. A correspondent revolution in things will attend the influx of the spirit. So fast will disagreeable appearances, swine, spiders, snakes, pests, madhouses, prisons, enemies, vanish; they are temporary and shall be no more seen. The sordor and filths of nature, the sun shall dry up and the wind exhale. As when the summer comes from the south, the snow-banks melt and the face of the earth becomes green before it, so shall the advancing spirit create its ornaments along its path, and carry with it the beauty it visits and the song which enchants it; it shall draw beautiful faces, warm hearts, wise discourse, and heroic acts, around its way, until evil is no more seen. The kingdom of man over nature, which cometh not with observation,—a dominion such as now is beyond his dream of God,—he shall enter without more wonder than the blind man feels who is gradually restored to perfect sight."

1836

The American Scholar

I greet you on the recommencement of our literary year. Our anniversary is one of hope, and, perhaps, not enough of labor. We do not meet for games of strength or skill, for the recitation of histories, tragedies, and odes, like the ancient Greeks; for parliaments of love and poesy, like the Troubadours; nor for the advancement of science, like our contemporaries in the British and European capitals. Thus far, our holiday has been simply a friendly sign of the survival of the love of letters amongst a people too busy to give to letters any more. As such it is precious as the sign of an indestructible instinct. Perhaps the time is already come when it ought to be, and will be, something else; when the sluggard intellect of this continent will look from under its iron lids and fill the postponed expectation of the world with something better than the exertions of mechanical skill. Our day of dependence, our long apprenticeship to the learning of other lands, draws to a close. The millions that around us are rushing into life, cannot always be fed on the sere remains of foreign harvests. Events, actions arise, that must be sung, that will sing themselves. Who can doubt that poetry will revive and lead in a new age, as the star in the constellation Harp, which now flames in our zenith, astronomers announce, shall one day be the pole-star for a thousand years?

In this hope I accept the topic which not only usage but the nature of our association seem to prescribe to this day, —the AMERICAN SCHOLAR. Year by year we come up hither to read one more chapter of his biography. Let us inquire what light new days and events have thrown on his character and his hopes.

It is one of those fables which out of an unknown antiquity convey an unlooked-for wisdom, that the gods, in the beginning, divided Man into men, that he might be more helpful to himself; just as the hand was divided into fingers, the better to answer its end.

The old fable covers a doctrine ever new and sublime; that there is One man,—present to all particular men only partially, or through one faculty; and that you must take the whole society to find the whole man. Man is not a farmer, or a professor, or an engineer, but he is all. Man is priest, and scholar, and statesman, and producer, and soldier. In the *divided* or social state these functions are parcelled out to individuals, each of whom aims to do his stint of the joint work, whilst each other performs his. The fable implies that the individual, to possess himself, must sometimes return from his own labor to embrace all the other laborers. But, unfortunately, this original unit, this fountain of power, has been so distributed to multitudes, has been so minutely subdivided and peddled out, that it is spilled into drops, and cannot be gathered. The state of society is one in which the members have suffered amputation from the trunk, and strut about so many walking monsters,—a good finger, a neck, a stomach, an elbow, but never a man.

Man is thus metamorphosed into a thing, into many things. The planter, who is Man sent out into the field to gather food, is seldom cheered by an idea of the true dignity of his ministry. He sees his bushel and his cart, and nothing beyond, and sinks into the farmer, instead of Man on the farm. The tradesman scarcely ever gives an ideal worth to his work, but is ridden by the routine of his craft, and the soul is subject to dollars. The priest becomes a form; the attorney a statute-book; the mechanic a machine; the sailor a rope of the ship.

In this distribution of functions the scholar is the delegated intellect. In the right state he is *Man Thinking*. In the degenerate state, when the victim of society, he tends to become a mere thinker, or still worse, the parrot of other men's thinking.

In this view of him, as Man Thinking, the theory of his office is contained. Him Nature solicits with all her placid, all her monitory pictures; him the past instructs; him the future invites. Is not indeed every man a student, and do not all things exist for the student's behoof? And, finally is not the true scholar the only true master? But the old oracle said, "All things have two handles: beware of the wrong one." In life, too often, the scholar errs with mankind and forfeits his privilege. Let us see him in his school, and consider him in reference to the main influences he receives.

I. The first in time and the first in importance of the influences upon the mind is that of nature. Every day, the sun; and, after the sunset, night and her stars. Ever the winds blow; ever the grass grows. Every day, men and women, conversing, beholding and beholden. The scholar is he of all men whom this spectacle most engages. He must settle its value in his mind. What is nature to him? There is never a beginning, there is never an end, to the inexplicable continuity of this web of God, but always circular power returning into itself. Therein it resembles his own spirit, whose beginning, whose ending, he never can find,—so entire, so boundless. Far too as her splendors shine, system on system shooting like rays, upward, downward, without center, without circumference,—in the mass and in the particle. Nature hastens to render account of herself to the mind. Classification begins. To the young mind every thing is individual, stands by itself. By and by, it finds how to join two things and see in them one nature; then three, then three thousand; and so, tyrannized over by its own unifying instinct, it goes on tying things together, diminishing anomalies, discovering roots running under ground whereby contrary and remote things cohere and flower out from one stem. It presently learns that since the dawn of history there has been a constant accumulation and classifying of facts. But what is classification but the perceiving that these objects are not chaotic, and are not foreign, but have a law which is also a law of the human mind? The astronomer discovers that geometry, a pure abstraction of the human mind, is the measure of planetary motion. The chemist finds proportions and intelligible method throughout matter; and science is nothing but the finding of analogy, identity, in the most remote parts. The ambitious soul sits down before each refractory fact; one after another reduces all strange constitutions, all new powers, to their class and their law, and goes on forever to animate the last fibre of organization, the outskirts of nature, by insight.

Thus to him, to this school-boy under the bending dome of day, is suggested that he and it proceed from one root; one is leaf and one is flower; relation, sympathy, stirring in every vein. And what is that root? Is not that the soul of his soul? A thought too bold; a dream too wild. Yet when this spiritual light shall have revealed the law of more earthly natures,—when he has learned to worship the soul, and to see that the natural philosophy that now is, is only the first gropings of its gigantic hand, he shall look forward to an ever expanding knowledge as to a becoming creator. He shall see that nature is the opposite of the soul, answering to it part for part. One is seal and one is print. Its beauty is the beauty of his own mind. Its laws are the laws of his own mind. Nature then becomes to him the measure of his attainments. So much of nature as he is ignorant of, so much of his own mind does he not yet possess. And, in fine, the ancient precept, "Know thyself," and the modern precept, "Study nature," become at last one maxim.

II. The next great influence into the spirit of the scholar is the mind of the Past,—in whatever form, whether of literature, of art, of institutions, that mind is inscribed. Books are the best type of the influence of the past, and perhaps we shall get at the truth,—learn the amount of this influence more conveniently,—by considering their value alone.

The theory of books is noble. The scholar of the first age received into him the world around; brooded thereon; gave it the new arrangement of his own mind, and uttered it again. It came into him life; it went out from him truth. It came to him short-lived actions; it went out from him immortal thoughts. It came to him business; it went from him poetry. It was a dead fact; now, it is quick thought. It can stand, and it can go. It now endures, it now flies, it now inspires. Precisely in proportion to the depth of mind from which it issued, so high does it soar, so long does it sing.

Or, I might say, it depends on how far the process had gone, of transmuting life into truth. In proportion to the completeness of the distillation, so will the purity and imperishableness of the product be. But none is quite perfect.

As no air-pump can by any means make a perfect vacuum, so neither can any artist entirely exclude the conventional, the local, the perishable from his book, or write a book of pure thought, that shall be as efficient, in all respects, to a remote posterity, as to contemporaries, or rather to the second age. Each age, it is found, must write its own books; or rather, each generation for the next succeeding. The books of an older period will not fit this.

Yet hence arises a grave mischief. The sacredness which attaches to the act of creation, the act of thought, is transferred to the record. The poet chanting was felt to be a divine man: henceforth the chant is divine also. The writer was a just and wise spirit: henceforward it is settled the book is perfect; as love of the hero corrupts into worship of his statue. Instantly the book becomes noxious: the guide is a tyrant. The sluggish and perverted mind of the multitude, slow to open to the incursions of Reason, having once so opened, having once received this book, stands upon it, and makes an outcry if it is disparaged. Colleges are built on it. Books are written on it by thinkers, not by Man Thinking; by men of talent, that is, who start wrong, who set out from accepted dogmas, not from their own sight of principles. Meek young men grow up in libraries, believing it their duty to accept the views which Cicero, which Locke, which Bacon, have given; forgetful that Cicero, Locke, and Bacon were only young men in libraries when they wrote these books.

Hence, instead of Man Thinking, we have the bookworm. Hence the book-learned class, who value books, as such; not as related to nature and the human constitution, but as making a sort of Third Estate with the world and the soul. Hence the restorers of readings, the emendators, the bibliomaniacs of all degrees.

Books are the best of things, well used; abused, among the worst. What is the right use? What is the one end which all means go to effect? They are for nothing but to inspire. I had better never see a book than to be warped by its attraction clean out of my own orbit, and made a satellite instead of a system. The one thing in the world, of value, is the active soul. This every man is entitled to; this every man contains within him, although in almost all men obstructed, and as yet unborn. The soul active sees absolute truth and utters truth, or creates. In this action it is genius; not the privilege of here and there a favorite, but the sound estate of every man. In its essence, it is progressive. The book, the college, the school of art, the institution of any kind, stop with some past utterance of genius. This is good, say they,—let us hold by this. They pin me down. They look backward and not forward. But genius looks forward: the eyes of man are set in his forehead, not in his hind-head: man hopes: genius creates. Whatever talents may be, if the man create not, the pure efflux of the Deity is not his; —cinders and smoke there may be, but not yet flame. There are creative manners, there are creative actions, and creative words; manners, actions, words, that is, indicative of no custom or authority, but springing spontaneous from the mind's own sense of good and fair.

On the other part, instead of being its own seer, let it receive from another mind its truth, though it were in torrents of light, without periods of solitude, inquest, and self-recovery, and a fatal disservice is done. Genius is always sufficiently the enemy of genius by over-influence. The literature of every nation bears me witness. The English dramatic poets have Shakespearized now for two hundred years.

Undoubtedly there is a right way of reading, so it be sternly subordinated. Man Thinking must not be subdued by his instruments. Books are for the scholar's idle times. When he can read God directly, the hour is too precious to be wasted in other men's transcripts of their readings. But when the intervals of darkness come, as come they must,— when the sun is hid and the stars withdraw their shining,— we repair to the lamps which were kindled by their ray, to guide our steps to the East again, where the dawn is. We hear, that we may speak. The Arabian proverb says, "A fig tree, looking on a fig tree, becometh fruitful."

It is remarkable, the character of the pleasure we derive from the best books. They impress us with the conviction that one nature wrote and the same reads. We read the verses of one of the great English poets, of Chaucer, of Marvell, of Dryden, with the most modern joy,—with a pleasure, I mean, which is in great part caused by the abstraction of all *time* from their verses. There is some awe mixed with the joy of our surprise, when this poet, who lived in some past world, two or three hundred years ago, says that which lies close to my own soul, that which I also had well-nigh thought and said. But for the evidence thence afforded to the philosophical doctrine of the identity of all minds, we should suppose some preëstablished harmony, some foresight of souls that were to be, and some preparation of stores for their future wants, like the fact observed in insects, who lay up food before death for the young grub they shall never see.

I would not be hurried by any love of system, by any exaggeration of instincts, to underrate the Book. We all know, that as the human body can be nourished on any food, though it were boiled grass and the broth of shoes, so the human mind can be fed by any knowledge. And great and heroic men have existed who had almost no other information than by the printed page. I only would say that it needs a strong head to bear that diet. One must be an inventor to read well. As the proverb says, "He that would bring home the wealth of the Indies, must carry out the wealth of the Indies." There is then creative reading as well as creative writing. When the mind is braced by labor and invention, the page of whatever book we read becomes luminous with manifold allusion. Every sentence is doubly significant, and the sense of our author is as broad as the world. We then see, what is always true, that as the seer's hour of vision is short and rare among heavy days and months, so is its record, perchance the least part of his volume. The discerning will read, in his Plato or Shakespeare, only that least part,—only the authentic utterances of the oracle;—all the rest he rejects, were it never so many times Plato's and Shakespeare's.

Of course there is a portion of reading quite indispensable to a wise man. History and exact science he must learn by laborious reading. Colleges, in like manner, have their indispensable office,—to teach elements. But they can only highly serve us when they aim not to drill, but to create; when they gather from far every ray of various genius to their hospitable halls, and by the concentrated fires, set the hearts of their youth on flame. Thought and knowledge are natures in which apparatus and pretension avail nothing. Gowns and pecuniary foundations, though of towns of gold, can never countervail the least sentence or syllable of wit. Forget this, and our American colleges will recede in their public importance, whilst they grow richer every year.

III. There goes in the world a notion that the scholar should be a recluse, a valetudinarian,—as unfit for any handiwork or public labor as a pen-knife for an axe. The so-called "practical men" sneer at speculative men, as if, because they speculate or *see,* they could do nothing. I have heard it said that the clergy,—who are always, more universally than any other class, the scholars of their day, —are addressed as women; that the rough, spontaneous conversation of men they do not hear, but only a mincing and diluted speech. They are often virtually disfranchised; and indeed there are advocates for their celibacy. As far as this is true of the studious classes, it is not just and wise. Action is with the scholar subordinate, but it is essential. Without it he is not yet man. Without it thought can never ripen into truth. Whilst the world hangs before the eye as a cloud of beauty, we cannot even see its beauty. Inaction is cowardice, but there can be no scholar without the heroic mind. The preamble of thought, the transition through which it passes from the unconscious to the conscious, is action. Only so much do I know, as I have lived. Instantly we know whose words are loaded with life, and whose not.

The world,—this shadow of the soul, or *other me,*— lies wide around. Its attractions are the keys which unlock my thoughts and make me acquainted with myself. I run eagerly into this resounding tumult. I grasp the hands of those next me, and take my place in the ring to suffer and to work, taught by an instinct that so shall the dumb abyss be vocal with speech. I pierce its order; I dissipate its fear; I dispose of it within the circuit of my expanding life. So much only of life as I know by experience, so much of the wilderness have I vanquished and planted, or so far have I extended my being, my dominion. I do not see how any man can afford, for the sake of his nerves and his nap, to spare any action in which he can partake. It is pearls and rubies to his discourse. Drudgery, calamity, exasperation, want, are instructors in eloquence and wisdom. The true scholar grudges every opportunity of action past by, as a loss of power. It is the raw material out of which the intellect moulds her splendid products. A strange process too, this by which experience is converted into thought, as a mulberry leaf is converted into satin. The manufacture goes forward at all hours.

The actions and events of our childhood and youth are now matters of calmest observation. They lie like fair pictures in the air. Not so with our recent actions,—with the business which we now have in hand. On this we are quite unable to speculate. Our affections as yet circulate through it. We no more feel or know it than we feel the feet, or the hand, or the brain of our body. The new deed is yet a part of life,—remains for a time immersed in our unconscious life. In some contemplative hour it detaches itself from the life like a ripe fruit, to become a thought of the mind. Instantly it is raised, transfigured; the corruptible has put on incorruption. Henceforth it is an object of beauty, however base its origin and neighborhood. Observe too the impossibility of ante-dating this act. In its grub state, it cannot fly, it cannot shine, it is a dull grub. But suddenly, without observation, the selfsame thing unfurls beautiful wings, and is an angel of wisdom. So is there no fact, no event, in our private history, which shall not, sooner or later, lose its adhesive, inert form, and astonish us by soaring from our body into the empyrean. Cradle and infancy, school and playground, the fear of boys, and dogs, and ferules, the love of little maids and berries, and many another fact that once filled the whole sky, are gone already; friend and relative, profession and party, town and country, nation and world, must also soar and sing.

Of course, he who has put forth his total strength in fit actions has the richest return of wisdom. I will not shut myself out of this globe of action, and transplant an oak into a flower-pot, there to hunger and pine; nor trust the revenue of some single faculty, and exhaust one vein of thought, much like those Savoyards, who, getting their livelihood by carving shepherds, shepherdesses, and smoking Dutchmen, for all Europe, went out one day to the mountain to find stock, and discovered that they had whittled up the last of their pine-trees. Authors we have, in numbers, who have written out their vein, and who, moved by a commendable prudence, sail for Greece or Palestine, follow the trapper into the prairie, or ramble round Algiers, to replenish their merchantable stock.

If it were only for a vocabulary, the scholar would be covetous of action. Life is our dictionary. Years are well spent in country labors; in town; in the insight into trades and manufactures; in frank intercourse with many men and women; in science; in art; to the one end of mastering in all their facts a language by which to illustrate and embody our perceptions. I learn immediately from any speaker how much he has already lived, through the poverty or the splendor of his speech. Life lies behind us as the quarry from whence we get tiles and copestones for the masonry of today. This is the way to learn grammar. Colleges and books only copy the language which the field and the work-yard made.

But the final value of action, like that of books, and better than books, is that it is a resource. That great principle of Undulation in nature, that shows itself in the inspiring and expiring of the breath; in desire and satiety; in the ebb and flow of the sea; in day and night; in heat and cold; and, as yet more deeply ingrained in every atom and every fluid, is known to us under the name of Polarity, —these "fits of easy transmission and reflection," as Newton called them, are the law of nature because they are the law of spirit.

The mind now thinks, now acts, and each fit reproduces the other. When the artist has exhausted his materials, when the fancy no longer paints, when thoughts are no longer apprehended and books are a weariness,—he has always the resource *to live*. Character is higher than intellect. Thinking is the function. Living is the functionary. The stream retreats to its source. A great soul will be strong to live, as well as strong to think. Does he lack organ or medium to impart his truth? He can still fall back on this elemental force of living them. This is a total act. Thinking is a partial act. Let the grandeur of justice shine in his affairs. Let the beauty of affection cheer his lowly roof. Those "far from fame," who dwell and act with him, will feel the force of his constitution in the doings and passages of the day better than it can be measured by any public and designed display. Time shall teach him that the scholar loses no hour which the man lives. Herein he unfolds the sacred germ of his instinct, screened from influence. What is lost in seemliness is gained in strength. Not out of those on whom systems of education have exhausted their culture, comes the helpful giant to destroy the old or to build the new, but out of unhandselled savage nature; out of terrible Druids and Berserkers come at last Alfred and Shakespeare.

I hear therefore with joy whatever is beginning to be said of the dignity and necessity of labor to every citizen. There is virtue yet in the hoe and the spade, for learned as well as for unlearned hands. And labor is everywhere welcome; always we are invited to work; only be this limitation observed, that a man shall not for the sake of wider activity sacrifice any opinion to the popular judgments and modes of action.

I have now spoken of the education of the scholar by nature, by books, and by action. It remains to say somewhat of his duties.

They are such as become Man Thinking. They may all be comprised in self-trust. The office of the scholar is to cheer, to raise, and to guide men by showing them facts amidst appearances. He plies the slow, unhonored, and unpaid task of observation. Flamsteed and Herschel, in their glazed observatories, may catalogue the stars with the praise of all men, and the results being splendid and useful, honor is sure. But he, in his private observatory, cataloguing obscure and nebulous stars of the human mind, which as yet no man has thought of as such,—watching days and months sometimes for a few facts; correcting still his old records;—must relinquish display and immediate fame. In the long period of his preparation he must betray often an ignorance and shiftlessness in popular arts, incurring the disdain of the able who shoulder him aside. Long he must stammer in his speech; often forego the living for the dead. Worse yet, he must accept—how often!—poverty and solitude. For the ease and pleasure of treading the old road, accepting the fashions, the education, the religion of society, he takes the cross of making his own, and, of course, the self-accusation, the faint heart, the frequent uncertainty and loss of time, which are the nettles and tangling vines in the way of the self-relying and self-directed; and the state of virtual hostility in which he seems to stand to society, and especially to educated society. For all this loss and scorn, what offset? He is to find consolation in exercising the highest functions of human nature. He is one who raises himself from private considerations and breathes and lives on public and illustrious thoughts. He is the world's eye. He is the world's heart. He is to resist the vulgar prosperity that retrogrades ever to barbarism, by preserving and communicating heroic sentiments, noble biographies, melodious verse, and the conclusions of history. Whatsoever oracles the human heart, in all emergencies, in all solemn hours, has uttered as its commentary on the world of actions,—these he shall receive and impart. And whatsoever new verdict Reason from her inviolable seat pronounces on the passing men and events of today,—this he shall hear and promulgate.

These being his functions, it becomes him to feel all confidence in himself, and to defer never to the popular cry. He and he only knows the world. The world of any moment is the merest appearance. Some great decorum, some fetish of a government, some ephemeral trade, or war, or man, is cried up by half mankind and cried down by the other half, as if all depended on this particular up or down. The odds are that the whole question is not worth the poorest thought which the scholar has lost in listening to the controversy. Let him not quit his belief that a popgun is a popgun, though the ancient and honorable of the earth affirm it to be the crack of doom. In silence, in steadiness, in severe abstraction, let him hold by himself; add observation to observation, patient of neglect, patient of reproach, and bide his own time,— happy enough if he can satisfy himself alone that this day he has seen something truly. Success treads on every right step. For the instinct is sure, that prompts him to tell his brother what he thinks. He then learns that in going down into the secrets of his own mind he has descended into the secrets of all minds. He learns that he who has mastered any law in his private thoughts, is master to that extent of all men whose language he speaks, and of all into whose language his own can be translated. The poet, in utter solitude remembering his spontaneous thoughts and recording them, is found to have recorded that which men in crowded cities find true for them also. The orator distrusts at first the fitness of his frank confessions, his want of knowledge of the persons he addresses, until he finds that he is the complement of his hearers;—that they drink his words because he fulfils for them their own nature; the deeper he dives into his privatest, secretest presentiment, to his wonder he finds this is the most acceptable, most public, and universally true. The people delight in it; the better part of every man feels, This is my music; this myself.

In self-trust all the virtues are comprehended. Free should the scholar be,—free and brave. Free even to the definition of freedom, "without any hindrance that does not arise out of his own constitution." Brave; for fear is a thing which a scholar by his very function puts behind him. Fear always springs from ignorance. It is a shame to him if his tranquility, amid dangerous times, arise from the presumption that like children and women his is a protected class; or if he seek a temporary peace by the diversion of his thoughts from politics or vexed questions, hiding his head like an ostrich in the flowering bushes, peeping into microscopes, and turning rhymes, as a boy whistles to keep his courage up. So is the danger a danger still; so is the fear worse. Manlike let him turn and face it. Let him look into its eye and search its nature, inspect its origin,—see the whelping of this lion,—which lies no great way back; he will then find in himself a perfect comprehension of its nature and extent; he will have made his hands meet on the other side, and can henceforth defy it and pass on superior. The world is his who can see through its pretension. What deafness, what stone-blind custom, what overgrown error you behold is there only by sufferance,- -by your sufferance. See it to be a lie, and you have already dealt it its mortal blow.

Yes, we are the cowed,—we the trustless. It is a mischievous notion that we are come late into nature; that the world was finished a long time ago. As the world was plastic and fluid in the hands of God, so it is ever to so much of his attributes as we bring to it. To ignorance and sin, it is flint. They adapt themselves to it as they may; but in proportion as a man has any thing in him divine, the firmament flows before him and takes his signet and form. Not he is great who can alter matter, but he who can alter my state of mind. They are the kings of the world who give the color of their present thought to all nature and all art, and persuade men by the cheerful serenity of their carrying the matter, that this thing which they do is the apple which the ages have desired to pluck, now at last ripe, and inviting nations to the harvest. The great man makes the great thing. Wherever Macdonald sits, there is the head of the table. Linnæus makes botany the most alluring of studies, and wins it from the farmer and the herb-woman; Davy, chemistry; and Cuvier, fossils. The day is always his who works in it with serenity and great aims. The unstable estimates of men crowd to him whose mind is filled with a truth, as the heaped waves of the Atlantic follow the moon.

For this self-trust, the reason is deeper than can be fathomed,—darker than can be enlightened. I might not carry with me the feeling of my audience in stating my own belief. But I have already shown the ground of my hope, in adverting to the doctrine that man is one. I believe man has been wronged; he has wronged himself. He has almost lost the light that can lead him back to his prerogatives. Men are become of no account. Men in history, men in the world of to-day, are bugs, are spawn, and are called "the mass" and "the herd." In a century, in a millennium, one or two men; that is to say, one or two approximations to the right state of every man. All the rest behold in the hero or the poet their own green and crude being,—ripened; yes, and are content to be less, so *that* may attain to its full stature. What a testimony, full of grandeur, full of pity, is borne to the demands of his own nature, by the poor clansman, the poor partisan, who rejoices in the glory of his chief. The poor and the low find some amends to their immense moral capacity, for their acquiescence in a political and social inferiority. They are content to be brushed like flies from the path of a great person, so that justice shall be done by him to that common nature which it is the dearest desire of all to see enlarged and glorified. They sun themselves in the great man's light, and feel it to be their own element. They cast the dignity of man from their downtrod selves upon the shoulders of a hero, and will perish to add one drop of blood to make that great heart beat, those giant sinews combat and conquer. He lives for us, and we live in him.

Men such as they are, very naturally seek money or power; and power because it is as good as money,—the "spoils," so called, "of office." And why not? for they aspire to the highest, and this, in their sleep-walking, they dream is highest. Wake them and they shall quit the false good and leap to the true, and leave governments to clerks and desks. This revolution is to be wrought by the gradual domestication of the idea of Culture. The main enterprise of the world for splendor, for extent, is the upbuilding of a man. Here are the materials strewn along the ground. The private life of one man shall be a more illustrious monarchy, more formidable to its enemy, more sweet and serene in its influence to its friend, than any kingdom in history. For a man, rightly viewed, comprehendeth the particular natures of all men. Each philosopher, each bard, each actor has only done for me, as by a delegate, what one day I can do for myself. The books which once we valued more than the apple of the eye, we have quite exhausted. What is that but saying that we have come up with the point of view which the universal mind took through the eyes of one scribe; we have been that man, and have passed on. First, one, then another, we drain all cisterns, and waxing greater by all these supplies, we crave a better and more abundant food. The man has never lived that can feed us ever. The human mind cannot be enshrined in a person who shall set a barrier on any one side to this unbounded, unboundable empire. It is one central fire, which, flaming now out of the lips of Etna, lightens the capes of Sicily, and now out of the throat of Vesuvius, illuminates the towers and vineyards of Naples. It is one light which beams out of a thousand stars. It is one soul which animates all men.

But I have dwelt perhaps tediously upon this abstraction of the Scholar. I ought not to delay longer to add what I have to say of nearer reference to the time and to this country.

Historically, there is thought to be a difference in the ideas which predominate over successive epochs, and there are data for marking the genius of the Classic, of the Romantic, and now of the Reflective or Philosophical age. With the views I have intimated of the oneness or the identity of the mind through all individuals, I do not much dwell on these differences. In fact, I believe each individual passes through all three. The boy is a Greek; the youth, romantic; the adult, reflective. I deny not, however, that a revolution in the leading idea may be distinctly enough traced.

Our age is bewailed as the age of Introversion. Must that needs be evil? We, it seems, are critical; we are embarrassed with second thoughts; we cannot enjoy any thing for hankering to know whereof the pleasure consists; we are lined with eyes; we see with our feet; the time is infected with Hamlet's unhappiness,

Sicklied o'er with the pale cast of thought.

It is so bad then? Sight is the last thing to be pitied. Would we be blind? Do we fear lest we should outsee nature and God, and drink truth dry? I look upon the discontent of the literary class as a mere announcement of the fact that they find themselves not in the state of mind of their fathers, and regret the coming state as untried; as a boy dreads the water before he has learned that he can swim. If there is any period one would desire to be born in, is it not the age of Revolution; when the old and the new stand side by side and admit of being compared; when the energies of all men are searched by fear and by hope; when the historic glories of the old can be compensated by the rich possibilities of the new era? This time, like all times, is a very good one, if we but know what to do with it.

I read with some joy of the auspicious signs of the coming days, as they glimmer already through poetry and art, through philosophy and science, through church and state.

One of these signs is the fact that the same movement which effected the elevation of what was called the lowest class in the state, assumed in literature a very marked and as benign an aspect. Instead of the sublime and beautiful, the near, the low, the common, was explored and poetized. That which had been negligently trodden under foot by those who were harnessing and provisioning themselves for long journeys into far countries, is suddenly found to be richer than all foreign parts. The literature of the poor, the feelings of the child, the philosophy of the street, the meaning of household life, are the topics of the time. It is a great stride. It is a sign—is it not?—of new vigor when the extremities are made active, when currents of warm life run into the hands and the feet. I ask not for the great, the remote, the romantic; what is doing in Italy or Arabia; what is Greek art, or Provençal minstrelsy; I embrace the common, I explore and sit at the feet of the familiar, the low. Give me insight into to-day, and you may have the antique and future worlds. What would we really know the meaning of? The meal in the firkin; the milk in the pan; the ballad in the street; the news of the boat; the glance of the eye; the form and the gait of the body;—show me the ultimate reason of these matters; show me the sublime presence of the highest spiritual cause lurking, as always it does lurk, in these suburbs and extremities of nature; let me see every trifle bristling with the polarity that ranges it instantly on an eternal law; and the shop, the plough, and the ledger referred to the like cause by which light undulates and poets sing;—and the world lies no longer a dull miscellany and lumber-room, but has form and order; there is no trifle, there is no puzzle, but one design unites and animates the farthest pinnacle and the lowest trench.

This idea has inspired the genius of Goldsmith, Burns, Cowper, and, in a newer time, of Goethe, Wordsworth, and Carlyle. This idea they have differently followed and with various success. In contrast with their writing, the style of Pope, of Johnson, of Gibbon, looks cold and pedantic. This writing is blood-warm. Man is surprised to find that things near are not less beautiful and wondrous than things remote. The near explains the far. The drop is a small ocean. A man is related to all nature. This perception of the worth of the vulgar is fruitful in discoveries. Goethe, in this very thing the most modern of the moderns, has shown us as none ever did, the genius of the ancients.

There is one man of genius who has done much for this philosophy of life, whose literary value has never yet been rightly estimated;—I mean Emanuel Swedenborg. The most imaginative of men, yet writing with the precision of a mathematician, he endeavored to engraft a purely philosophical Ethics on the popular Christianity of his time. Such an attempt of course must have difficulty which no genius could surmount. But he saw and showed the connection between nature and the affections of the soul. He pierced the emblematic or spiritual character of the visible, audible, tangible world. Especially did his shade-loving muse hover over and interpret the lower parts of nature; he showed the mysterious bond that allies moral evil to the foul material forms, and has given in epical parables a theory of insanity, of beasts, of unclean and fearful things.

Another sign of our times, also marked by an analogous political movement, is the new importance given to the single person. Every thing that tends to insulate the individual, —to surround him with barriers of natural respect, so that each man shall feel the world is his, and man shall treat with man as a sovereign state with a sovereign state,—tends to true union as well as greatness. "I learned," said the melancholy Pestalozzi, "that no man in God's wide earth is either willing or able to help any other man." Help must come from the bosom alone. The scholar is that man who must take up into himself all the ability of the time, all the contributions of the past, all the hopes of the future. He must be an university of knowledges. If there be one lesson more than another which should pierce his ear, it is, The world is nothing, the man is all; in yourself is the law of all nature, and you know not yet how a globule of sap ascends; in yourself slumbers the whole of Reason; it is for you to know all; it is for you to dare all. Mr. President and Gentlemen, this confidence in the unsearched might of man belongs, by all motives, by all prophecy, by all preparation, to the American Scholar. We have listened too long to the courtly muses of Europe. The spirit of the American freeman is already suspected to be timid, imitative, tame. Public and private avarice make the air we breathe thick and fat. The scholar is decent, indolent, complaisant. See already the tragic consequence. The mind of this country, taught to aim at low objects, eats upon itself. There is no work for any but the decorous and the complaisant. Young men of the fairest promise, who begin life upon our shores, inflated by the mountain winds, shined upon by all the stars of God, find the earth below not in unison with these, but are hindered from action by the disgust which the principles on which business is managed inspire, and turn drudges, or die of disgust, some of them suicides. What is the remedy? They did not yet see, and thousands of young men as hopeful now crowding to the barriers for the career do not yet see, that if the single man plant himself indomitably on his instincts, and there abide, the huge world will come round to him. Patience,—patience; with the shades of all the good and great for company; and for solace the perspective of your own infinite life; and for work the study and the communication of principles, the making those instincts prevalent, the conversion of the world. Is it not the chief disgrace in the world, not to be an unit;—not to be reckoned one character;—not to yield that peculiar fruit which each man was created to bear, but to be reckoned in the gross, in the hundred, or the thousand, of the party, the section, to which we belong; and our opinion predicted geographically, as the north, or the south? Not so, brothers and friends,—please God, ours shall not be so. We will walk on our own feet; we will work with our own hands; we will speak our own minds. The study of letters shall be no longer a name for pity, for doubt, and for sensual indulgence. The dread of man and the love of man shall be a wall of defence and a wreath of joy around all. A nation of men will for the first time exist, because each believes himself inspired by the Divine Soul which also inspires all men.

1837

Self-Reliance

"Ne te quaesiveris extra."
[*"Seek not yourself outside yourself."*]

"Man is his own star; and the soul that can
Render an honest and a perfect man,
Commands all light, all influence, all fate;
Nothing to him falls early or too late.
Our acts our angels are, or good or ill,
Our fatal shadows that walk by us still."
                    Epilogue to Beaumont and Fletcher's
                    Honest Man's Fortune

Cast the bantling on the rocks,
Suckle him with the she-wolf's teat,
Wintered with the hawk and fox,
Power and speed be hands and feet.

I read the other day some verses written by an eminent painter which were original and not conventional. The soul always hears an admonition in such lines, let the subject be what it may. The sentiment they instil is of more value than any thought they may contain. To believe your own thought, to believe that what is true for you in your private heart is true for all men—that is genius. Speak your latent conviction, and it shall be the universal sense; for the inmost in due time becomes the outmost, and our first thought is rendered back to us by the trumpets of the Last Judgment. Familiar as the voice of the mind is to each, the highest merit we ascribe to Moses, Plato, and Milton is that they set at naught books and traditions, and spoke not what men, but what *they* thought. A man should learn to detect and watch that gleam of light which flashes across his mind from within, more than the lustre of the firmament of bards and sages. Yet he dismisses without notice his thought, because it is his. In every work of genius we recognize our own rejected thoughts; they come back to us with a certain alienated majesty. Great works of art have no more affecting lesson for us than this. They teach us to abide by our spontaneous impression with good-humored inflexibility then most when the whole cry of voices is on the other side. Else tomorrow a stranger will say with masterly good sense precisely what we have thought and felt all the time, and we shall be forced to take with shame our own opinion from another.

There is a time in every man's education when he arrives at the conviction that envy is ignorance; that imitation is suicide; that he must take himself for better for worse as his portion; that though the wide universe is full of good, no kernel of nourishing corn can come to him but through his toil bestowed on that plot of ground which is given to him to till. The power which resides in him is new in nature, and none but he knows what that is which he can do, nor does he know until he has tried. Not for nothing one face, one character, one fact, makes much impression on him, and another none. This sculpture in the memory is not without pre-established harmony. The eye was placed where one ray should fall, that it might testify of that particular ray. We but half express ourselves, and are ashamed of that divine idea which each of us represents. It may be safely trusted as proportionate and of good issues, so it be faithfully imparted, but God will not have his work made manifest by cowards. A man is relieved and gay when he has put his heart into his work and done his best; but what he has said or done otherwise shall give him no peace. It is a deliverance which does not deliver. In the attempt his genius deserts him; no muse befriends; no invention, no hope.

Trust thyself: every heart vibrates to that iron string. Accept the place the divine providence has found for you, the society of your contemporaries, the connection of events. Great men have always done so, and confided themselves childlike to tue genius of their age, betraying their perception that the absolutely trustworthy was seated at their heart, working through their hands, predominating in all their being. And we are now men, and must accept in the highest mind the same transcendent destiny; and not minors and invalids in a protected corner, not cowards fleeing before a revolution, but guides, redeemers, and benefactors, obeying the Almighty effort and advancing on Chaos and the Dark.

What pretty oracles nature yields us on this text in the face and behavior of children, babes, and even brutes! That divided and rebel mind, that distrust of a sentiment because our arithmetic has computed the strength and means opposed to our purpose, these have not. Their mind being whole, their eye is as yet unconquered, and when we look in their faces we are disconcerted. Infancy conforms to nobody; all conform to it; so that one babe commonly makes four or five out of the adults who prattle and play to it. So God has armed youth and puberty and manhood no less with its own piquancy and charm, and made it enviable and gracious and its claims not to be put by, if it will stand by itself. Do not think the youth has no force, because he cannot speak to you and me. Hark! in the next room his voice is sufficiently clear and emphatic. It seems he knows how to speak to his contemporaries. Bashful or bold then, he will know how to make us seniors very unnecessary.

The nonchalance of boys who are sure of a dinner, and would disdain as much as a lord to do or say aught to conciliate one, is the healthy attitude of human nature. A boy is in the parlor what the pit is in the playhouse; independent, irresponsible, looking out from his corner on such people and facts as pass by, he tries and sentences them on their merits, in the swift, summary way of boys, as good, bad, interesting, silly, eloquent, troublesome. He cumbers himself never about consequences, about interests; he gives an independent, genuine verdict. You must court him; he does not court you. But the man is as it were clapped into jail by his consciousness. As soon as he has once acted or spoken with *éclat* he is a committed person, watched by the sympathy or the hatred of hundreds, whose affections must now enter into his account. There is no Lethe for this. Ah, that he could pass again into his neutrality! Who can thus avoid all pledges and, having observed, observe again from the same unaffected, unbiased, unbribable, unaffrighted innocence, must always be formidable. He would utter opinions on all passing affairs, which being seen to be not private but necessary, would sink like darts into the ear of men and put them in fear.

These are the voices which we hear in solitude, but they grow faint and inaudible as we enter into the world. Society everywhere is in conspiracy against the manhood of every one of its members. Society is a joint-stock company, in which the members agree, for the better securing of his bread to each shareholder, to surrender the liberty and culture of the eater. The virtue in most request is conformity. Self-reliance is its aversion. It loves not realities and creators, but names and customs.

Whoso would be a man, must be a nonconformist. He who would gather immortal palms must not be hindered by the name of goodness, but must explore if it be goodness. Nothing is at last sacred but the integrity of your own mind. Absolve you to yourself, and you shall have the suffrage of the world. I remember an answer which when quite young I was prompted to make to a valued adviser who was wont to importune me with the dear old doctrines of the church. On my saying, "What have I to do with the sacredness of traditions, if I live wholly from within?" my friend suggested, "But these impulses may be from below, not from above." I replied, "They do not seem to me to be such; but if I am the Devil's child, I will live then from the Devil." No law can be sacred to me but that of my nature. Good and bad are but names very readily transferable to that or this; the only right is what is after my constitution; the only wrong what is against it. A man is to carry himself in the presence of all opposition as if every thing were titular and ephemeral but he. I am ashamed to think how easily we capitulate to badges and names, to large societies and dead institutions. Every decent and well spoken individual affects and sways me more than is right. I ought to go upright and vital, and speak the rude truth in all ways. If malice and vanity wear the coat of philanthropy, shall that pass? If an angry bigot assumes this bountiful cause of Abolition, and comes to me with his last news from Barbadoes, why should I not say to him, "Go love thy infant; love thy wood-chopper; be good-natured and modest; have that grace; and never varnish your hard, uncharitable ambition with this incredible tenderness for black folk a thousand miles off. Thy love afar is spite at home." Rough and graceless would be such greeting, but truth is handsomer than the affectation of love. Your goodness must have some edge to it—else it is none. The doctrine of hatred must be preached, as the counteraction of the doctrine of love, when that pules and whines. I shun father and mother and wife and brother when my genius calls me. I would write on the lintels of the door-post, *Whim*. I hope it is somewhat better than whim at last, but we cannot spend the day in explanation. Expect me not to show cause why I seek or why I exclude company. Then again, do not tell me, as a good man did today, of my obligation to put all poor men in good situations. Are they *my* poor? I tell thee, thou foolish philanthropist, that I grudge the dollar, the dime, the cent I give to such men as do not belong to me and to whom I do not belong. There is a class of persons to whom by all spiritual affinity I am bought and sold; for them I will go to prison if need be; but your miscellaneous popular charities, the education at college of fools, the building of meetinghouses to the vain end to which many now stand, alms to sots, and the thousand-fold Relief Societies—though I confess with shame I sometimes succumb and give the dollar, it is a wicked dollar, which by and by I shall have the manhood to withhold.

Virtues are, in the popular estimate, rather the exception than the rule. There is the man *and* his virtues. Men do what is called a good action, as some piece of courage or charity, much as they would pay a fine in expiation of daily non-appearance on parade. Their works are done as

an apology or extenuation of their living in the world—
as invalids and the insane pay a high board. Their virtues
are penances. I do not wish to expiate, but to live. My
life is for itself and not for a spectacle. I much prefer that
it should be of a lower strain, so it be genuine and equal,
than that it should be glittering and unsteady. I wish it to
be sound and sweet, and not to need diet and bleeding. I
ask primary evidence that you are a man, and refuse this
appeal from the man to his actions. I know that for myself it makes no difference whether I do or forbear those
actions which are reckoned excellent. I cannot consent to
pay for a privilege where I have intrinsic right. Few and
mean as my gifts may be, I actually am, and do not need
for my own assurance or the assurance of my fellows any
secondary testimony.

What I must do is all that concerns me, not what the
people think. This rule, equally arduous in actual and in
intellectual life, may serve for the whole distinction between greatness and meanness. It is the harder because you
will always find those who think they know what is your
duty better than you know it. It is easy in the world to
live after the world's opinion; it is easy in solitude to live
after our own; but the great man is he who in the midst
of the crowd keeps with perfect sweetness the independence
of solitude.

The objection to conforming to usages that have become dead to you is that it scatters your force. It loses
your time and blurs the impression of your character. If
you maintain a dead church, contribute to a dead Bible-
society, vote with a great party either for the government
or against it, spread your table like base housekeepers—
under all these screens I have difficulty to detect the precise man you are: and of course so much force is withdrawn from your proper life. But do your work, and I
shall know you. Do your work, and you shall reinforce
yourself. A man must consider what a blind-man's-buff
is this game of conformity. If I know your sect I anticipate your argument. I hear a preacher announce for his
text and topic the expediency of one of the institutions of
his church. Do I know beforehand that not possibly can
he say a new and spontaneous word? Do I not know that
with all this ostentation of examining the grounds of the
institution he will do no such thing? Do I not know that

he is pledged to himself not to look but at one side, the permitted side, not as a man, but as a parish minister? He is a retained attorney, and these airs of the bench are the emptiest affectation. Well, most men have bound their eyes with one or another handkerchief, and attached themselves to some one of these communities of opinion. This conformity makes them not false in a few particulars, authors of a few lies, but false in all particulars. Their every truth is not quite true. Their two is not the real two, their four not the real four; so that every word they say chagrins us and we know not where to begin to set them right. Meantime nature is not slow to equip us in the prison-uniform of the party to which we adhere. We come to wear one cut of face and figure, and acquire by degrees the gentlest asinine expression. There is a mortifying experience in particular, which does not fail to wreak itself also in the general history; I mean "the foolish face of praise," the forced smile which we put on in company where we do not feel at ease, in answer to conversation which does not interest us. The muscles, not spontaneously moved but moved by a low usurping wilfulness, grow tight about the outline of the face, with the most disagreeable sensation.

For nonconformity the world whips you with its displeasure. And therefore a man must know how to estimate a sour face. The by-standers look askance on him in the public street or in the friend's parlor. If this aversion had its origin in contempt and resistance like his own he might well go home with a sad countenance; but the sour faces of the multitude, like their sweet faces, have no deep cause, but are put on and off as the wind blows and a newspaper directs. Yet is the discontent of the multitude more formidable than that of the senate and the college. It is easy enough for a firm man who knows the world to brook the rage of the cultivated classes. Their rage is decorous and prudent, for they are timid, as being very vulnerable themselves. But when to their feminine rage the indignation of the people is added, when the ignorant and the poor are aroused, when the unintelligent brute force that lies at the bottom of society is made to growl and mow, it needs the habit of magnanimity and religion to treat it godlike as a trifle of no concernment.

The other terror that scares us from self-trust is our

consistency; a reverence for our past act or word because the eyes of others have no other data for computing our orbit than our past acts, and we are loth to disappoint them.

But why should you keep your head over your shoulder? Why drag about this corpse of your memory, lest you contradict somewhat you have stated in this or that public place? Suppose you should contradict yourself; what then? It seems to be a rule of wisdom never to rely on your memory alone, scarcely even in acts of pure memory, but to bring the past for judgment into the thousand-eyed present, and live ever in a new day. In your metaphysics you have denied personality to the Deity, yet when the devout motions of the soul come, yield to them heart and life, though they should clothe God with shape and color. Leave your theory, as Joseph his coat in the hand of the harlot, and flee.

A foolish consistency is the hobgoblin of little minds, adored by little statesmen and philosophers and divines. With consistency a great soul has simply nothing to do. He may as well concern himself with his shadow on the wall. Speak what you think now in hard words and tomorrow speak what tomorrow thinks in hard words again, though it contradict every thing you said today.—"Ah, so you shall be sure to be misunderstood."—Is it so bad then to be misunderstood? Pythagoras was misunderstood, and Socrates, and Jesus, and Luther, and Copernicus, and Galileo, and Newton, and every pure and wise spirit that ever took flesh. To be great is to be misunderstood.

I suppose no man can violate his nature. All the sallies of his will are rounded in by the law of his being, as the inequalities of Andes and Himmaleh are insignificant in the curve of the sphere. Nor does it matter how you gauge and try him. A character is like an acrostic or Alexandrian stanza;—read it forward, backward, or across, it still spells the same thing. In this pleasing contrite wood-life which God allows me, let me record day by day my honest thought without prospect or retrospect, and, I cannot doubt, it will be found symmetrical, though I mean it not and see it not. My book should smell of pines and re-sound with the hum of insects. The swallow over my window should interweave that thread or straw he carries in his bill into my web also. We pass for what we are. Character teaches above our wills. Men imagine that they communicate their virtue or vice only by overt actions, and do not see that virtue or vice emit a breath every moment.

There will be an agreement in whatever variety of actions, so they be each honest and natural in their hour. For of one will, the actions will be harmonious, however unlike they seem. These varieties lost sight of at a little distance, at a little height of thought one tendency unites them all. The voyage of the best ship is a zigzag line of a hundred tacks. See the line from a sufficient distance and it straightens itself to the average tendency. Your genuine action will explain itself and will explain your other genuine actions. Your conformity explains nothing. Act singly, and what you have already done singly will justify you now. Greatness appeals to the future. If I can be firm enough today to do right and scorn eyes, I must have done so much right before as to defend me now. Be it how it will, do right now. Always scorn appearances and you always may. The force of character is cumulative. All the foregone days of virtue work their health into this. What makes the majesty of the heroes of the senate and the field, which so fills the imagination? The consciousness of a train of great days and victories behind. They shed a united light on the advancing actor. He is attended as by a visible escort of angels. That is it which throws thunder into Chatham's voice, and dignity into Washington's port, and America into Adams' eye. Honor is venerable to us because it is no ephemera. It is always ancient virtue. We worship it today because it is not of today. We love it and pay it homage because it is not a trap for our love and homage, but is self-dependent, self-derived, and therefore of an old immaculate pedigree, even if shown in a young person.

I hope in these days we have heard the last of conformity and consistency. Let the words be gazetted and ridiculous henceforward. Instead of the gong for dinner, let us hear a whistle from the Spartan fife. Let us never bow and apologize more. A great man is coming to eat at my house. I do not wish to please him; I wish that he should wish to please me. I will stand here for humanity, and though I would make it kind, I would make it true. Let us affront and reprimand the smooth mediocrity and squalid contentment of the times, and hurl in the face of custom and trade and office, the fact which is the upshot of all history, that there is a great responsible Thinker and Actor working wherever a man works; that a true man belongs to no other time or place, but is the center of things. Where he is, there is nature. He measures you and all men and all events. Ordinarily, everybody in society reminds us of somewhat else, or of some other person. Character, reality, reminds you of nothing else; it takes place of the whole creation. The man must be so much that he must make all circumstances indifferent. Every true man is a cause, a country, and an age; requires infinite spaces and numbers and time fully to accomplish his design; and posterity seem to follow his steps as a train of clients. A man Caesar is born, and for ages after we have a Roman Empire. Christ is born, and millions of minds so grow and cleave to his genius that he is confounded with virtue and the possible of man. An institution is the lengthened shadow of one man; as, Monachism, of the Hermit Antony; the Reformation, of Luther; Quakerism, of Fox; Methodism, of Wesley; Abolition, of Clarkson. Scipio, Milton called "the height of Rome"; and all history resolves itself very easily into the biography of a few stout and earnest persons.

Let a man then know his worth, and keep things under his feet. Let him not peep or steal, or skulk up and down with the air of a charity-boy, a bastard, or an interloper in the world which exists for him. But the man in the street, finding no worth in himself which corresponds to the force which built a tower or sculptured a marble god, feels poor when he looks on these. To him a palace, a statue, or a costly book have an alien and forbidding air, much like a gay equipage, and seem to say like that, "Who are you, Sir?" Yet they all are his, suitors for his notice, petitioners to his faculties that they will come out and take possession. The picture waits for my verdict; it is not to command me, but I am to settle its claims to praise. That popular fable of the sot who was picked up dead-drunk in the street, carried to the duke's house, washed and dressed and laid in the duke's bed, and, on his waking, treated with all obsequious ceremony like the duke, and assured that he had been insane, owes its popularity to the fact that it symbolizes so well the state of man, who is in the world a sort of sot, but now and then wakes up, exercises his reason and finds himself a true prince.

Our reading is mendicant and sycophantic. In history our imagination plays us false. Kingdom and lordship, power and estate, are a gaudier vocabulary than private John and Edward in a small house and common day's work; but the things of life are the same to both; the sum total of both is the same. Why all this deference to Alfred and Scanderbeg and Gustavus? Suppose they were virtuous; did they wear out virtue? As great a stake depends on your private act today as followed their public and renowned steps. When private men shall act with original views, the lustre will be transferred from the actions of kings to those of gentlemen.

The world has been instructed by its kings, who have so magnetized the eyes of nations. It has been taught by this colossal symbol the mutual reverence that is due from man to man. The joyful loyalty with which men have everywhere suffered the king, the noble, or the great proprietor to walk among them by a law of his own, make his own scale of men and things and reverse theirs, pay for benefits not with money but with honor, and represent the law in his person, was the hieroglyphic by which they obscurely signified their consciousness of their own right and comeliness, the right of every man.

The magnetism which all original action exerts is explained when we inquire the reason of self-trust. Who is the Trustee? What is the aboriginal Self, on which a universal reliance may be grounded? What is the nature and power of that science-baffling star, without parallax, without calculable elements, which shoots a ray of beauty even into trivial and impure actions, if the least mark of independence appear? The inquiry leads us to that source, at once the essence of genius, of virtue, and of life, which we call Spontaneity or Instinct. We denote this primary wisdom as Intuition, whilst all later teachings are tuitions. In that deep force, the last fact behind which analysis cannot go, all things find their common origin. For the sense of being which in calm hours rises, we know not how, in the soul, is not diverse from things, from space, from light, from time, from man, but one with them and proceeds obviously from the same source whence their life and being also proceed. We first share the life by which things exist and afterwards see them as appearances in nature and forget that we have shared their cause. Here is the fountain of action and of thought. Here are the lungs of that inspiration which giveth man wisdom and which cannot be denied without impiety and atheism. We lie in the lap of immense intelligence, which makes us receivers of its truth and organs of its activity. When we discern justice, when we discern truth, we do nothing of ourselves, but allow a passage to its beams. If we ask whence this comes, if we seek to pry into the soul that causes, all philosophy is at fault. Its presence or its absence is all we can affirm. Every man discriminates between the voluntary acts of his mind and his involuntary perceptions, and knows that to his involuntary perceptions a perfect faith is due. He may err in the expression of them, but he knows that these things are so, like day and night, not to be disputed. My wilful actions and acquisitions are but roving; the idlest reverie, the faintest native emotion, command my curiosity and respect. Thoughtless people contradict as readily the statement of perceptions as of opinions, or rather much more readily; for they do not distinguish between perception and notion. They fancy that I choose to see this or that thing. But perception is not whimsical, but fatal. If I see a trait, my children will see it after me, and in course of time all mankind,—although it may chance that no one has seen it before me. For my perception of it is as much a fact as the sun.

The relations of the soul to the divine spirit are so pure that it is profane to seek to interpose helps. It must be that when God speaketh he should communicate, not one thing, but all things; should fill the world with his voice; should scatter forth light, nature, time, souls, from the center of the present thought; and new date and new create the whole. Whenever a mind is simple and receives a divine wisdom, old things pass away—means, teachers, texts, temples fall; it lives now, and absorbs past and future into the present hour. All things are made sacred by relation to it—one as much as another. All things are dissolved to their center by their cause, and in the universal miracle petty and particular miracles disappear. If therefore a man claims to know and speak of God and carries you backward to the phraseology of some old moldered nation in another country, in another world, believe him not. Is the acorn better than the oak which is its fulness and completion? Is the parent better than the child into whom he has cast his ripened being? Whence then this worship of the past? The centuries are conspirators against the sanity and authority of the soul. Time and space are but physiological colors which the eye makes, but the soul is light: where it is, is day; where it was, is night; and history is an impertinence and an injury if it be any thing more than a cheerful apologue or parable of my being and becoming.

Man is timid and apologetic; he is no longer upright; he dares not say "I think," "I am," but quotes some saint or sage. He is ashamed before the blade of grass or the blowing rose. These roses under my window make no reference to former roses or to better ones; they are for what they are; they exist with God today. There is no time to them. There is simply the rose; it is perfect in every moment of its existence. Before a leaf-bud has burst, its whole life acts; in the full-blown flower there is no more; in the leafless root there is no less. Its nature is satisfied and it satisfies nature in all moments alike. But man postpones or remembers; he does not live in the present, but with reverted eye laments the past, or, heedless of the riches that surround him, stands on tiptoe to foresee the future. He cannot be happy and strong until he too lives with nature in the present, above time.

This should be plain enough. Yet see what strong intellects dare not yet hear God himself unless he speak the phraseology of I know not what David, or Jeremiah, or Paul. We shall not always set so great a price on a few texts, on a few lives. We are like children who repeat by rote the sentences of grandames and tutors, and, as they grow older, of the men of talents and character they chance to see—painfully recollecting the exact words they spoke; afterwards, when they come into the point of view which those had who uttered these sayings, they understand them and are willing to let the words go; for at any time they can use words as good when occasion comes. If we live truly, we shall see truly. It is as easy for the strong man to be strong, as it is for the weak to be weak. When we have new perception, we shall gladly disburden the memory of its hoarded treasures as old rubbish. When a man lives with God, his voice shall be as sweet as the murmur of the brook and the rustle of the corn.

And now at last the highest truth on this subject remains unsaid; probably cannot be said; for all that we say is the far-off remembering of the intuition. That thought by what I can now nearest approach to say it, is this. When good is near you, when you have life in yourself, it is not by any known or accustomed way; you shall not discern the footprints of any other; you shall not see the face of man; you shall not hear any name—the way, the thought, the good, shall be wholly strange and new. It shall exclude example and experience. You take the way from man, not to man. All persons that ever existed are its forgotten ministers. Fear and hope are alike beneath it. There is somewhat low even in hope. In the hour of vision there is nothing that can be called gratitude, nor properly joy. The soul raised over passion beholds identity and eternal causation, perceives the self-existence of Truth and Right, and calms itself with knowing that all things go well. Vast spaces of nature, the Atlantic Ocean, the South Sea; long intervals of time, years, centuries, are of no account. This which I think and feel underlay every former state of life and circumstances, as it does underlie my present, and what is called life and what is called death.

Life only avails, not the having lived. Power ceases in the instant of repose; it resides in the moment of transition from a past to a new state, in the shooting of the gulf, in the darting to an aim. This one fact the world hates: that the soul *becomes;* for that forever degrades the past, turns all riches to poverty, all reputation to a shame, confounds the saint with the rogue, shoves Jesus and Judas equally aside. Why then do we prate of self-reliance? Inasmuch as the soul is present there will be power not confident but agent. To talk of reliance is a poor external way of speaking. Speak rather of that which relies because it works and is. Who has more obedience than I masters me, though he should not raise his finger. Round him I must revolve by the gravitation of spirits. We fancy it rhetoric when we speak of eminent virtue. We do not yet see that virtue is Height, and that a man or a company of men, plastic and permeable to principles, by the law of nature must overpower and ride all cities, nations, kings, rich men, poets, who are not.

This is the ultimate fact which we so quickly reach on this, as on every topic, the resolution of all into the ever-blessed ONE. Self-existence is the attribute of the Supreme Cause, and it constitutes the measure of good by the degree in which it enters into all lower forms. All things real are so by so much virtue as they contain. Commerce, husbandry, hunting, whaling, war, eloquence, personal weight, are somewhat, and engage my respect as examples of its presence and impure action. I see the same law working in nature for conservation and growth. Power is, in nature, the essential measure of right. Nature suffers nothing to remain in her kingdoms which cannot help itself. The genesis and maturation of a planet, its poise and orbit, the bended tree recovering itself from the strong wind, the vital resources of every animal and vegetable, are demonstrations of the self-sufficing and therefore self-relying soul.

Thus all concentrates: let us not rove; let us sit at home with the cause. Let us stun and astonish the intruding rabble of men and books and institutions by a simple declaration of the divine fact. Bid the invaders take the shoes from off their feet, for God is here within. Let our simplicity judge them, and our docility to our own law demonstrate the poverty of nature and fortune beside our native riches.

But now we are a mob. Man does not stand in awe of man, nor is his genius admonished to stay at home, to put itself in communication with the internal ocean, but it goes abroad to beg a cup of water of the urns of other men. We must go alone. I like the silent church before the service begins, better than any preaching. How far off, how cool, how chaste the persons look, begirt each one with a precinct or sanctuary! So let us always sit. Why should we assume the faults of our friend, or wife, or father, or child, because they sit around our hearth, or are said to have the same blood? All men have my blood and I all men's. Not for that will I adopt their petulance or folly, even to the extent of being ashamed of it. But your isolation must not be mechanical, but spiritual—that is, must be elevation. At times the whole world seems to be in conspiracy to importune you with emphatic trifles. Friend, client, child, sickness, fear, want, charity, all knock at once at thy closet door and say, "Come out unto us." But keep thy state; come not into their confusion. The power men possess to annoy me I give them by a weak curiosity. No man can come near me but through my act. "What we love that we have, but by desire we bereave ourselves of the love."

If we cannot at once rise to the sanctities of obedience and faith, let us at least resist our temptations; let us enter into the state of war and wake Thor and Woden, courage and constancy, in our Saxon breasts. This is to be done in our smooth times by speaking the truth. Check this lying hospitality and lying affection. Live no longer to the expectation of these deceived and deceiving people with whom we converse. Say to them, "O father, O mother, O wife, O brother, O friend, I have lived with you after appearances hitherto. Henceforward I am the truth's. Be it known unto you that henceforward I obey no law less than the eternal law. I will have no covenants but proximities. I shall endeavor to nourish my parents, to support my family, to be the chaste husband of one wife—but these relations I must fill after a new and unprecedented way. I appeal from your customs. I must be myself. I cannot break myself any longer for you, or you. If you can love' me for what I am, we shall be the happier. If you cannot, I will still seek to deserve that you should. I will not hide my tastes or aversions. I will so trust that what is deep is holy, that I will do strongly before the sun and moon whatever inly rejoices me and the heart appoints. If you are noble, I will love you; if you are not, I will not hurt you and myself by hypocritical attentions. If you are true, but not in the same truth with me, cleave to your companions; I will seek my own. I do this not selfishly but humbly and truly. It is alike your interest, and mine, and all men's, however long we have dwelt in lies, to live in truth. Does this sound harsh today? You will soon love what is dictated by your nature as well as mine, and if we follow the truth it will bring us out safe at last."—But so may you give these friends pain. Yes, but I cannot sell my liberty and my power, to save their sensibility. Besides, all persons have their moments of reason, when they look out into the region of absolute truth; then will they justify me and do the same thing.

The populace think that your rejection of popular standards is a rejection of all standard, and mere antinomianism; and the bold sensualist will use the name of philosophy to gild his crimes. But the law of consciousness abides.

There are two confessionals, in one or the other of which we must be shriven. You may fulfil your round of duties by clearing yourself in the *direct*, or in the *reflex* way. Consider whether you have satisfied your relations to father, mother, cousin, neighbor, town, cat and dog— whether any of these can upbraid you. But I may also neglect this reflex standard and absolve me to myself. I have my own stern claims and perfect circle. It denies the name of duty to many offices that are called duties. But if I can discharge its debts it enables me to dispense with the popular code. If any one imagines that this law is lax, let him keep its commandment one day.

And truly it demands something godlike in him who has cast off the common motives of humanity and has ventured to trust himself for a taskmaster. High be his heart, faithful his will, clear his sight, that he may in good earnest be doctrine, society, law, to himself, that a simple purpose may be to him as strong as iron necessity is to others!

If any man consider the present aspects of what is called by distinction *society,* he will see the need of these ethics. The sinew and heart of man seem to be drawn out, and we are become timorous, desponding whimperers. We are afraid of truth, afraid of fortune, afraid of death, and afraid of each other. Our age yields no great and perfect persons. We want men and women who shall renovate life and our social state, but we see that most natures are insolvent, cannot satisfy their own wants, have an ambition out of all proportion to their practical force and do lean and beg day and night continually. Our housekeeping is mendicant, our arts, our occupations, our marriages, our religion we have not chosen, but society has chosen for us. We are parlor soldiers. We shun the rugged battle of fate, where strength is born.

If our young men miscarry in their first enterprises they lose all heart. If the young merchant fails, men say he is *ruined.* If the finest genius studies at one of our colleges and is not installed in an office within one year afterwards in the cities or suburbs of Boston or New York, it seems to his friends and to himself that he is right in being disheartened and in complaining the rest of his life. A sturdy lad from New Hampshire or Vermont, who in turn tries all the professions, who *teams it, farms it, peddles,* keeps a school, preaches, edits a newspaper, goes to Congress, buys a township, and so forth, in successive years, and always like a cat falls on his feet, is worth a hundred of these city dolls. He walks abreast with his days and feels no shame in not "studying a profession," for he does not postpone his life, but lives already. He has not one chance, but a hundred chances. Let a Stoic open the resources of man and tell men they are not leaning willows, but can and must detach themselves; that with the exercise of self-trust, new powers shall appear; that a man is the word made flesh, born to shed healing to the nations; that he should be ashamed of our compassion, and that the moment he acts from himself, tossing the laws, the books, idolatries and customs out of the window, we pity him no more but thank and revere him—and that teacher shall restore the life of man to splendor and make his name dear to all history.

It is easy to see that a greater self-reliance must work a revolution in all the offices and relations of men; in their religion; in their education; in their pursuits; their modes of living; their association; in their property; in their speculative views.

1. In what prayers do men allow themselves! That which they call a holy office is not so much as brave and manly. Prayer looks abroad and asks for some foreign addition to come through some foreign virtue, and loses itself in endless mazes of natural and supernatural, and mediatorial and miraculous. Prayer that craves a particular commodity, anything less than all good, is vicious. Prayer is the contemplation of the facts of life from the highest point of view. It is the soliloquy of a beholding and jubilant soul. It is the spirit of God pronouncing his works good. But prayer as a means to effect a private end is meanness and theft. It supposes dualism and not unity in nature and consciousness. As soon as the man is at one with God, he will not beg. He will then see prayer in all action. The prayer of the farmer kneeling in his field to weed it, the prayer of the rower kneeling with the stroke of his oar, are true prayers heard throughout nature, though for cheap ends. Caratach, in Fletcher's "Bonduca," when admonished to inquire the mind of the god Audate, replies:

His hidden meaning lies in our endeavors;
Our valors are our best gods.

Another sort of false prayers are our regrets. Discontent is the want of self-reliance: it is infirmity of will. Regret calamities if you can thereby help the sufferer; if not, attend your own work and already the evil begins to be repaired. Our sympathy is just as base. We come to them who weep foolishly and sit down and cry for company, instead of imparting to them truth and health in rough electric shocks, putting them once more in communication with their own reason. The secret of fortune is joy in our hands. Welcome evermore to gods and men is the self-helping man. For him all doors are flung wide; him all tongues greet, all honors crown, all eyes follow with desire. Our love goes out to him and embraces him because he did not need it. We solicitously and apologetically caress and celebrate him because he held on his way and scorned our disapprobation. The gods love him because men hated him. "To the persevering mortal," said Zoroaster, "the blessed Immortals are swift."

As men's prayers are a disease of the will, so are their creeds a disease of the intellect. They say with those foolish Israelites, "Let not God speak to us, lest we die. Speak thou, speak any man with us, and we will obey." Everywhere I am hindered of meeting God in my brother, because he has shut his own temple doors and recites fables merely of his brother's, or his brother's brother's God. Every new mind is a new classification. If it prove a mind of uncommon activity and power, a Locke, a Lavoisier, a Hutton, a Bentham, a Fourier, it imposes its classification on other men, and lo! a new system. In proportion to the depth of the thought, and so to the number of the objects it touches and brings within reach of the pupil, is his complacency. But chiefly is this apparent in creeds and churches, which are also classifications of some powerful mind acting on the elemental thought of duty and man's relation to the Highest. Such is Calvinism, Quakerism, Swedenborgism. The pupil takes the same delight in subordinating every thing to the new terminology as a girl who has just learned botany in seeing a new earth and new seasons thereby. It will happen for a time that the pupil will find his intellectual power has grown by the study of his master's mind. But in all unbalanced minds the classification is idolized, passes for the end and not for a speedily exhaustible means, so that the walls of the system blend to their eye in the remote horizon with the walls of the universe; the luminaries of heaven seem to them hung on the arch their master built. They cannot imagine how you aliens have any right to see—how you can see; "It must be somehow that you stole the light from us." They do not yet perceive that light, unsystematic, indomitable, will break into any cabin, even into theirs. Let them chirp awhile and call it their own. If they are honest and do well, presently their neat new pinfold will be too strait and low, will crack, will lean, will rot and vanish, and the immortal light, all young and joyful, million-orbed, million-colored, will beam over the universe as on the first morning.

2. It is for want of self-culture that the superstition of Traveling, whose idols are Italy, England, Egypt, retains its fascination for all educated Americans. They who made England, Italy, or Greece venerable in the imagination, did so by sticking fast where they were, like an axis of the earth. In manly hours we feel that duty is our place. The soul is no traveler; the wise man stays at home, and when his necessities, his duties, on any occasion call him from his house, or into foreign lands, he is at home still and shall make men sensible by the expression of his countenance that he goes, the missionary of wisdom and virtue, and visits cities and men like a sovereign and not like an interloper or a valet.

I have no churlish objection to the circumnavigation of the globe for the purposes of art, of study, and benevolence, so that the man is first domesticated, or does not go abroad with the hope of finding somewhat greater than he knows. He who travels to be amused, or to get somewhat which he does not carry, travels away from himself, and grows old even in youth among old things. In Thebes, in Palmyra, his will and mind have become old and dilapidated as they. He carries ruins to ruins.

Traveling is a fool's paradise. Our first journeys discover to us the indifference of places. At home I dream that at Naples, at Rome, I can be intoxicated with beauty and lose my sadness. I pack my trunk, embrace my friends, embark on the sea, and at last wake up in Naples, and there beside me is the stern fact, the sad self, unrelenting, identical, that I fled from. I seek the Vatican and the palaces. I affect to be intoxicated with sights and suggestions, but I am not intoxicated. My giant goes with me wherever I go.

3. But the rage of traveling is a symptom of a deeper unsoundness affecting the whole intellectual action. The intellect is vagabond, and our system of education fosters restlessness. Our minds travel when our bodies are forced to stay at home. We imitate; and what is imitation but the traveling of the mind? Our houses are built with foreign taste; our shelves are garnished with foreign ornaments; our opinions, our tastes, our faculties, lean, and follow the Past and the Distant. The soul created the arts wherever they have flourished. It was in his own mind that the artist sought his model. It was an application of his own thought to the thing to be done and the conditions to be observed. And why need we copy the Doric or the Gothic model? Beauty, convenience, grandeur of thought, and quaint expression are as near to us as to any, and if the American artist will study with hope and love the precise thing to be done by him, considering the climate, the soil, the length of the day, the wants of the people, the habit and form of the government, he will create a house in which all these will find themselves fitted, and taste and sentiment will be satisfied also.

Insist on yourself; never imitate. Your own gift you can present every moment with the cumulative force of a whole life's cultivation; but of the adopted talent of another you have only an extemporaneous half possession. That which each can do best, none but his Maker can teach him. No man yet knows what it is, nor can, till that person has exhibited it. Where is the master who could have taught Shakespeare? Where is the master who could have instructed Franklin, or Washington, or Bacon, or Newton? Every great man is a unique. The Scipionism of Scipio is precisely that part he could not borrow. Shakespeare will never be made by the study of Shakespeare. Do that which is assigned you, and you cannot hope too much or dare too much. There is at this moment for you an utterance brave and grand as that of the colossal chisel of

Phidias, or trowel of the Egyptians, or the pen of Moses or Dante, but different from all these. Not possibly will the soul, all rich, all eloquent, with thousand-cloven tongue, deign to repeat itself; but if you can hear what these patriarchs say, surely you can reply to them in the same pitch of voice; for the ear and the tongue are two organs of one nature. Abide in the simple and noble regions of thy life, obey thy heart, and thou shalt reproduce the Foreworld again.

4. As our Religion, our Education, our Art look abroad, so does our spirit of society. All men plume themselves on the improvement of society, and no man improves.

Society never advances. It recedes as fast on one side as it gains on the other. It undergoes continual changes; it is barbarous, it is civilized, it is christianized, it is rich, it is scientific; but this change is not amelioration. For every thing that is given something is taken. Society acquires new arts and loses old instincts. What a contrast between the well-clad, reading, writing, thinking American, with a watch, a pencil, and a bill of exchange in his pocket, and the naked New Zealander, whose property is a club, a spear, a mat, and an undivided twentieth of a shed to sleep under! But compare the health of the two men and you shall see that the white man has lost his aboriginal strength. If the traveler tell us truly, strike the savage with a broad-axe and in a day or two the flesh shall unite and heal as if you struck the blow into soft pitch, and the same blow shall send the white to his grave.

The civilized man has built a coach, but has lost the use of his feet. He is supported on crutches, but lacks so much support of muscle. He has a fine Geneva watch, but he fails of the skill to tell the hour by the sun. A Greenwich nautical almanac he has, and so being sure of the information when he wants it, the man in the street does not know a star in the sky. The solstice he does not observe; the equinox he knows as little; and the whole bright calendar of the year is without a dial in his mind. His notebooks impair his memory; his libraries overload his wit; the insurance-office increases the number of accidents; and it may be a question whether machinery does not encumber; whether we have not lost by refinement some energy, by a Christianity entrenched in establishments and forms some vigor of wild virtue. For every Stoic was a Stoic; but in Christendom where is the Christian?

There is no more deviation in the moral standard than in the standard of height or bulk. No greater men are now than ever were. A singular equality may be observed between the great men of the first and of the last ages; nor can all the science, art, religion, and philosophy of the nineteenth century avail to educate greater men than Plutarch's heroes, three or four and twenty centuries ago. Not in time is the race progressive. Phocion, Socrates, Anaxagoras, Diogenes are great men, but they leave no class. He who is really of their class will not be called by their name, but will be his own man, and in his turn the founder of a sect. The arts and inventions of each period are only its costume and do not invigorate men. The harm of the improved machinery may compensate its good. Hudson and Behring accomplished so much in their fishing boats as to astonish Parry and Franklin, whose equipment exhausted the resources of science and art. Galileo, with an opera-glass, discovered a more splendid series of celestial phenomena than any one since. Columbus found the New World in an undecked boat. It is curious to see the periodical disuse and perishing of means and machinery which were introduced with loud laudation a few years or centuries before. The great genius returns to essential man. We reckoned the improvements of the art of war among the triumphs of science, and yet Napoleon conquered Europe by the bivouac, which consisted of falling back on naked valor and disencumbering it of all aids. The Emperor held it impossible to make a perfect army, says Las Cases, "without abolishing our arms, magazines, commissaries and carriages, until, in imitation of the Roman custom, the soldier should receive his supply of corn, grind it in his hand-mill and bake his bread himself."

Society is a wave. The wave moves onward, but the water of which it is composed does not. The same particle does not rise from the valley to the ridge. Its unity is only phenomenal. The persons who make up a nation today, next year die, and their experience dies with them.

And so the reliance on Property, including the reliance on governments which protect it, is the want of self-reliance. Men have looked away from themselves and at things so long that they have come to esteem the religious, learned, and civil institutions as guards of property, and they deprecate assaults on these, because they feel them to be assaults on property. They measure their esteem of each other by what each has, and not by what each is. But a cultivated man becomes ashamed of his property, out of new respect for his nature. Especially he hates what he has if he sees that it is accidental—came to him by inheritance, or gift, or crime; then he feels that it is not having; it does not belong to him, has no root in him, and merely lies there because no revolution or no robber takes it away. But that which a man is, does always by necessity acquire; and what the man acquires, is living property, which does not wait the beck of rulers, or mobs, or revolutions, or fire, or storm, or bankruptcies, but perpetually renews itself wherever the man breathes. "Thy lot or portion of life," said the Caliph Ali, "is seeking after thee; therefore be at rest from seeking after it." Our dependence on these foreign goods leads us to our slavish respect for numbers. The political parties meet in numerous conventions; the greater the concourse and with each new uproar of announcement, The delegation from Essex! The Democrats from New Hampshire! The Whigs of Maine! the young patriot feels himself stronger than before by a new thousand of eyes and arms. In like manner the reformers summon conventions and vote and resolve in multitude. Not so, O friends! will the God deign to enter and inhabit you, but by a method precisely the reverse. It is only as a man puts off all foreign support and stands alone that I see him to be strong and to prevail. He is weaker by every recruit to his banner. Is not a man better than a town? Ask nothing of men, and, in the endless mutation, thou only firm column must presently appear the upholder of all that surrounds thee. He who knows that power is inborn, that he is weak because he has looked for good out of him and elsewhere, and, so perceiving, throws himself unhesitatingly on his thought, instantly rights himself, stands in the erect position, commands his limbs, works miracles; just as a man who stands on his feet is stronger than a man who stands on his head.

So use all that is called Fortune. Most men gamble with her, and gain all, and lose all, as her wheel rolls.

But do thou leave as unlawful these winnings, and deal with Cause and Effect, the chancellors of God. In the Will work and acquire, and thou hast chained the wheel of Chance, and shall sit hereafter out of fear from her rotations. A political victory, a rise of rents, the recovery of your sick or the return of your absent friend, or some other favorable event raises your spirits, and you think good days are preparing for you. Do not believe it. Nothing can bring you peace but yourself. Nothing can bring you peace but the triumph of principles.

1841

Experience

The lords of life, the lords of life—
I saw them pass,
In their own guise,
Like and unlike,
Portly and grim,
Use and Surprise,
Surface and Dream,
Succession swift, and spectral Wrong,
Temperament without a tongue,
And the inventor of the game
Omnipresent without name;
Some to see, some to be guessed,
They marched from east to west:
Little man, least of all,
Among the legs of his guardians tall,
Walked about with puzzled look:
Him by the hand dear Nature took;
Dearest Nature, strong and kind,
Whispered, "Darling, never mind!
To-morrow they will wear another face,
The founder thou! these are thy race!"

Where do we find ourselves? In a series of which we do not know the extremes, and believe that it has none. We wake and find ourselves on a stair; there are stairs below us, which we seem to have ascended; there are stairs above us, many a one, which go upward and out of sight. But the Genius which according to the old belief stands at the door by which we enter, and gives us the lethe to drink, that we may tell no tales, mixed the cup too strongly, and we cannot shake off the lethargy now at noonday. Sleep lingers all our lifetime about our eyes, as night hovers all day in the boughs of the fir-tree. All things swim and glitter. Our life is not so much threatened as our perception. Ghostlike we glide through nature, and should not know our place again. Did our birth fall in some fit of indigence and frugality in nature, that she was so sparing of her fire and so liberal of her earth that it appears to us that we lack the affirmative principle, and though we have health and reason, yet we have no superfluity of spirit for new creation? We have enough to live and bring the year about, but not an ounce to impart or to invest. Ah that our Genius were a little more of a genius! We are like millers on the lower levels of a stream, when the factories above them have exhausted the water. We too fancy that the upper people must have raised their dams.

If any of us knew what we were doing, or where we are going, then when we think we best know! We do not know to-day whether we are busy or idle. In times when we thought ourselves indolent, we have afterwards discovered that much was accomplished and much was begun in us. All our days are so unprofitable while they pass, that 't is wonderful where or when we ever got anything of this which we call wisdom, poetry, virtue. We never got it on any dated calendar day. Some heavenly days must have been intercalated somewhere, like those that Hermes won with dice of the Moon, that Osiris might be born. It is said all martyrdoms looked mean when they were suffered. Every ship is a romantic object, except that we sail in. Embark, and the romance quits our vessel and hangs on every other sail in the horizon. Our life looks trivial, and we shun to record it. Men seem to have learned of the horizon the art of perpetual retreating and reference. "Yonder uplands are rich pasturage, and my neighbor has fertile meadow, but my field," says the querulous farmer, "only holds the world together." I quote another man's saying; unluckily that other withdraws himself in the same way, and quotes me. 'T is the trick of nature thus to degrade to-day; a good deal of buzz, and somewhere a result slipped magically in. Every roof is agreeable to the eye until it is lifted; then we find tragedy and moaning women and hard-eyed husbands and deluges of lethe, and the men ask, "What's the news?" as if the old were so bad. How many individuals can we count in society? how many actions? how many opinions? So much of our time is preparation, so much is routine, and so much retrospect, that the pith of each man's genius contracts itself to a very few hours. The history of literature—take the net result of Tiraboschi, Warton, or Schlegel—is a sum of very few ideas and of very few original tales; all the rest being variation of these. So in this great society wide lying around us, a critical analysis would find very few spontaneous actions. It is almost all custom and gross sense. There are even few opinions, and these seem organic in the speakers, and do not disturb the universal necessity.

What opium is instilled into all disaster! It shows formid-able as we approach it, but there is at last no rough rasping friction, but the most slippery sliding surfaces; we fall soft on a thought; *Ate Dea* [i.e., disaster] is gentle—

> Over men's heads walking aloft,
> With tender feet treading so soft.

People grieve and bemoan themselves, but it is not half so bad with them as they say. There are moods in which we court suffering, in the hope that here at least we shall find reality, sharp peaks and edges of truth. But it turns out to be scene-painting and counterfeit. The only thing grief has taught me is to know how shallow it is. That, like all the rest, plays about the surface, and never introduces me into the reality, for contact with which we would even pay the costly price of sons and lovers. Was it Boscovich who found out that bodies never come in contact? Well, souls never touch their objects. An innavigable sea washes with silent waves between us and the things we aim at and converse with. Grief too will make us idealists. In the death of my son, now more than two years ago, I seem to have lost a beautiful estate—no more. I cannot get it nearer to me. If to-morrow I should be informed of the bankruptcy of my principal debtors, the loss of my property would be a great inconvenience to me, perhaps, for many years; but it would leave me as it found me—neither better nor worse. So is it with this calamity; it does not touch me; something which I fancied was a part of me, which could not be torn away without tearing me nor enlarged without enriching me, falls off from me and leaves no scar. It was caducous. I grieve that grief can teach me nothing, nor carry me one step into real nature. The Indian who was laid under a curse that the wind should not blow on him, nor water flow to him, nor fire burn him, is a type of us all. The dearest events are summer-rain, and we the Para coats that shed every drop. Nothing is left us now but death. We look to that with a grim satisfaction, saying, There at least is reality that will not dodge us.

I take this evanescence and lubricity of all objects, which lets them slip through our fingers then when we clutch hardest, to be the most unhandsome part of our condition. Nature does not like to be observed, and likes that we should be her fools and playmates. We may have the sphere for our cricket-ball, but not a berry for our philosophy. Direct strokes she never gave us power to make; all our blows glance, all our hits are accidents. Our relations to each other are oblique and casual.

Dream delivers us to dream, and there is no end to illusion. Life is a train of moods like a string of beads, and as we pass through them they prove to be many-colored lenses which paint the world their own hue, and each shows only what lies in its focus. From the mountain you see the mountain. We animate what we can, and we see only what we animate. Nature and books belong to the eyes that see them. It depends on the mood of the man whether he shall see the sunset or the fine poem. There are always sunsets, and there is always genius; but only a few hours so serene that we can relish nature or criticism. The more or less depends on structure or temperament. Temperament is the iron wire on which the beads are strung. Of what use is fortune or talent to a cold and defective nature? Who cares what sensibility or discrimination a man has at some time shown, if he falls asleep in his chair? or if he laugh and giggle? or if he apologize? or is infected with egotism? or thinks of his dollar? or cannot go by food? or has gotten a child in his boyhood? Of what use is genius, if the organ is too convex or too concave and cannot find a focal distance within the actual horizon of human life? Of what use, if the brain is too cold or too hot, and the man does not care enough for results to stimulate him to experiment, and hold him up in it? or if the web is too finely woven, too irritable by pleasure and pain, so that life stagnates from too much reception without due outlet? Of what use to make heroic vows of amendment, if the same old law-breaker is to keep them? What cheer can the religious sentiment yield, when that is suspected to be secretly dependent on the seasons of the year and the state of the blood? I knew a witty physician who found the creed in the biliary duct, and used to affirm that if there was disease in the liver, the man became a Calvinist, and if that organ was sound, he became a Unitarian. Very mortifying is the reluctant experience that some unfriendly excess or imbecility neutralizes the promise of genius. We see young men who owe us a new world, so readily and lavishly they promise, but they never acquit the debt; they die young and dodge the account; or if they live they lose themselves in the crowd.

Temperament also enters fully into the system of illusions and shuts us in a prison of glass which we cannot see. There is an optical illusion about every person we meet. In truth they are all creatures of given temperament, which will appear in a given character, whose boundaries they will never pass; but we look at them, they seem alive, and we presume there is impulse in them. In the moment it seems impulse; in the year, in the lifetime, it turns out to be a certain uniform tune which the revolving barrel of the music-box must play. Men resist the conclusion in the morning, but adopt it as the evening wears on, that temper prevails over everything of time, place, and condition, and is inconsumable in the flames of religion. Some modifications the moral sentiment avails to impose, but the individual texture holds its dominion, if not to bias the moral judgments, yet to fix the measure of activity and of enjoyment.

I thus express the law as it is read from the platform of ordinary life, but must not leave it without noticing the capital exception. For temperament is a power which no man willingly hears any one praise but himself. On the platform of physics we cannot resist the contracting influ-

ences of so-called science. Temperament puts all divinity
to rout. I know the mental proclivity of physicians. I hear
the chuckle of the phrenologists. Theoretic kidnappers and
slave-drivers, they esteem each man the victim of another,
who winds him round his finger by knowing the law of his
being; and, by such cheap signboards as the color of his
beard or the slope of his occiput, reads the inventory of his
fortunes and character. The grossest ignorance does not
disgust like this impudent knowingness. The physicians say
they are not materialists; but they are—Spirit is matter
reduced to an extreme thinness: O *so* thin! But the definition of *spiritual* should be, *that which is its own evidence.*
What notions do they attach to love! what to religion!
One would not willingly pronounce these words in their
hearing, and give them the occasion to profane them.
I saw a gracious gentleman who adapts his conversation
to the form of the head of the man he talks with! I had
fancied that the value of life lay in its inscrutable possibilities; in the fact that I never know, in addressing myself to
a new individual, what may befall me. I carry the keys
of my castle in my hand, ready to throw them at the feet
of my lord, whenever and in what disguise soever he shall
appear. I know he is in the neighborhood, hidden among
vagabonds. Shall I preclude my future by taking a high
seat and kindly adapting my conversation to the shape of
heads? When I come to that, the doctors shall buy me
for a cent. "But sir, medical history; the report to the
Institute; the proven facts!" I distrust the facts and the
inferences. Temperament is the veto or limitation-power
in the constitution, very justly applied to restrain an opposite excess in the constitution, but absurdly offered as a bar
to original equity. When virtue is in presence, all sub-ordi-
nate powers sleep. On its own level, or in view of nature,
temperament is final. I see not, if one be once caught in
this trap of so-called sciences, any escape for the man from
the links of the chain of physical necessity. Given such an
embryo, such a history must follow. On this platform one
lives in a sty of sensualism, and would soon come to
suicide. But it is impossible that the creative power should
exclude itself. Into every intelligence there is a door which
is never closed, through which the creator passes. The
intellect, seeker of absolute truth, or the heart, lover of

absolute good, intervenes for our succor, and at one
whisper of these high powers we awake from ineffectual
struggles with this nightmare. We hurl it into its own hell,
and cannot again contract ourselves to so base a state.

The secret of the illusoriness is in the necessity of a
succession of moods or objects. Gladly we would anchor,
but the anchorage is quicksand. This onward trick of nature
is too strong for us: *Pero si muove* [still it moves]. When
at night I look at the moon and stars, I seem stationary,
and they to hurry. Our love of the real draws us to permanence, but health of body consists in circulation, and
sanity of mind in variety or facility of association. We
need change of objects. Dedication to one thought is
quickly odious. We house with the insane, and must humor
them; then conversation dies out. Once I took such delight
in Montaigne that I thought I should not need any other
book; before that, in Shakespeare; then in Plutarch; then
in Plotinus; at one time in Bacon; afterwards in Goethe;
even in Bettine; but now I turn the pages of either of
them languidly, whilst I still cherish their genius. So with
pictures; each will bear an emphasis of attention once,
which it cannot retain, though we fain would continue to
be pleased in that manner. How strongly I have felt of
pictures that when you have seen one well, you must take
your leave of it; you shall never see it again. I have had
good lessons from pictures which I have since seen without
emotion or remark. A deduction must be made from the
opinion which even the wise express on a new book or
occurrence. Their opinion gives me tidings of their mood,
and some vague guess at the new fact, but is nowise to be
trusted as the lasting relation between that intellect and
that thing. The child asks, "Mamma, why don't I like the
story as well as when you told it me yesterday?" Alas!
child, it is even so with the oldest cherubim of knowledge.
But will it answer thy question to say, Because thou wert
born to a whole and this story is a particular? The reason
of the pain this discovery causes us (and we make it late
in respect to works of art and intellect) is the plaint of
tragedy which murmurs from it in regard to persons, to
friendship and love.

That immobility and absence of elasticity which we find

in the arts, we find with more pain in the artist. There is no power of expansion in men. Our friends early appear to us as representatives of certain ideas which they never pass or exceed. They stand on the brink of the ocean of thought and power, but they never take the single step that would bring them there. A man is like a bit of Labrador spar, which has no lustre as you turn it in your hand until you come to a particular angle; then it shows deep and beautiful colors. There is no adaptation or universal applicability in men, but each has his special talent, and the mastery of successful men consists in adroitly keeping themselves where and when that turn shall be oftenest to be practised. We do what we must, and call it by the best names we can, and would fain have the praise of having intended the result which ensues. I cannot recall any form of man who is not superfluous sometimes. But is not this pitiful? Life is not worth the taking, to do tricks in.

Of course it needs the whole society to give the symmetry we seek. The parti-colored wheel must revolve very fast to appear white. Something is earned too by conversing with so much folly and defect. In fine, whoever loses, we are always of the gaining party. Divinity is behind our failures and follies also. The plays of children are nonsense, but very educative nonsense. So it is with the largest and solemnest things, with commerce, government, church, marriage, and so with the history of every man's bread, and the ways by which he is to come by it. Like a bird which alights nowhere, but hops perpetually from bough to bough, is the Power which abides in no man and in no woman, but for a moment speaks from this one, and for another moment from that one.

But what help from these fineries or pedantries? What help from thought? Life is not dialectics. We, I think, in these times, have had lessons enough of the futility of criticism. Our young people have thought and written much on labor and reform, and for all that they have written, neither the world nor themselves have got on a step. Intellectual tasting of life will not supersede muscular activity. If a man should consider the nicety of the passage of a piece of bread down his throat, he would starve. At Education Farm the noblest theory of life sat on the noblest figures of young men and maidens, quite powerless and melancholy. It would not rake or pitch a ton of hay; it would not rub down a horse; and the men and maidens it left pale and hungry. A political orator wittily compared our party promises to western roads, which opened stately enough, with planted trees on either side to tempt the traveller, but soon became narrow and narrower and ended in a squirrel-track and ran up a tree. So does culture with us; it ends in headache. Unspeakably sad and barren does life look to those who a few months ago were dazzled with the splendor of the promise of the times. "There is now no longer any right course of action nor any self-devotion left among the Iranis." Objections and criticism we have had our fill of. There are objections to every course of life and action, and the practical wisdom infers an indifferency, from the omnipresence of objection. The whole frame of things preaches indifferency. Do not craze yourself with thinking, but go about your business anywhere. Life is not intellectual or critical, but sturdy. Its chief good is for well-mixed people who can enjoy what they find, without question. Nature hates peeping, and our mothers speak her very sense when they say, "Children, eat your victuals, and say no more of it." To fill the hour —that is happiness; to fill the hour and leave no crevice for a repentance or an approval. We live amid surfaces, and the true art of life is to skate well on them. Under the oldest mouldiest conventions a man of native force prospers just as well as in the newest world, and that by skill of handling and treatment. He can take hold anywhere. Life itself is a mixture of power and form, and will not bear the least excess of either. To finish the moment, to find the journey's end in every step of the road, to live the greatest number of good hours, is wisdom. It is not the part of men, but of fanatics, or of mathematicians if you will, to say that, the shortness of life considered, it is not worth caring whether for so short a duration we were sprawling in want or sitting high. Since our office is with moments, let us husband them. Five minutes of to-day are worth as much to me as five minutes in the next millennium. Let us be poised, and wise, and our own, to-day. Let us treat the men and women well; treat them as if they were real; perhaps they are. Men live in their fancy, like drunkards whose hands are too soft and tremulous for successful labor. It is a tempest of fancies, and the only ballast I know is a respect to the present hour. Without any shadow of doubt, amidst this vertigo of shows and politics, I settle myself ever the firmer in the creed that we should not postpone and refer and wish, but do broad justice where we are, by whomsoever we deal with, accepting our actual companions and circumstances, however humble or odious, as the mystic officials to whom the universe has delegated its whole pleasure for us. If these are mean and malignant, their contentment, which is the last victory of justice, is a more satisfying echo to the heart than the voice of poets and the casual sympathy of admirable persons. I think that however a thoughtful man may suffer from the defects and absurdities of his company, he cannot without affectation deny to any set of men and women a sensibility to extraordinary merit. The coarse and frivolous have an instinct of superiority, if they have not a sympathy, and honor it in their blind capricious way with sincere homage.

The fine young people despise life, but in me, and in such as with me are free from dyspepsia, and to whom a day is a sound and solid good, it is a great excess of politeness to look scornful and to cry for company. I am grown by sympathy a little eager and sentimental, but leave me alone and I should relish every hour and what it brought me, the potluck of the day, as heartily as the oldest gossip in the bar-room. I am thankful for small mercies. I compared notes with one of my friends who expects everything of the universe and is disappointed when anything is less than the best, and I found that I begin at the other extreme, expecting nothing, and am always full of thanks for moderate goods. I accept the clangor and jangle of contrary tendencies. I find my account in sots and bores also. They give a reality to the circumjacent picture which such a vanishing meteorous appearance can ill spare. In the morning I awake and find the old world, wife, babes and mother, Concord and Boston, the dear old spiritual world and even the dear old devil not far off. If we will take the good we find, asking no questions, we shall have heaping measures. The great gifts are not got by analysis. Everything good is on the highway. The middle region of our being is the temperate zone. We may climb into the thin and cold realm of pure geometry and lifeless science, or sink into that of sensation. Between these extremes is the equator of life, of thought, of spirit, of poetry—a narrow belt. Moreover, in popular experience everything good is on the highway. A collector peeps into all the picture-shops of Europe for a landscape of Poussin, a crayon-sketch of Salvator; but the Transfiguration, the Last Judgment, the Communion of Saint Jerome, and what are as transcendent as these, are on the walls of the Vatican, the Uffizi, or the Louvre, where every footman may see them; to say nothing of Nature's pictures in every street, of sunsets and sunrises every day, and the sculpture of the human body never absent. A collector recently bought at public auction, in London, for one hundred and fifty-seven guineas, an autograph of Shakespeare; but for nothing a school-boy can read *Hamlet* and can detect secrets of highest concernment yet unpublished therein. I think I will never read any but the commonest books—the Bible, Homer, Dante, Shakespeare, and Milton. Then we are impatient of so public a life and planet, and run hither and thither for nooks and secrets. The imagination delights in the woodcraft of Indians, trappers, and bee-hunters. We fancy that we are strangers, and not so intimately domesticated in the planet as the wild man and the wild beast and bird. But the exclusion reaches them also; reaches the climbing, flying, gliding, feathered and four-footed man. Fox and woodchuck, hawk and snipe and bittern, when nearly seen, have no more root in the deep world than man, and are just such superficial tenants of the globe. Then the new molecular philosophy shows astronomical interspaces betwixt atom and atom, shows that the world is all outside; it has no inside.

The mid-world is best. Nature, as we know her, is no saint. The lights of the church, the ascetics, Gentoos and corn-eaters, she does not distinguish by any favor. She comes eating and drinking and sinning. Her darlings, the great, the strong, the beautiful, are not children of our law; do not come out of the Sunday School, nor weigh their food, nor punctually keep the commandments. If we will be strong with her strength we must not harbor such disconsolate consciences, borrowed too from the consciences of other nations. We must set up the strong present tense against all the rumors of wrath, past or to come. So many things are unsettled which it is of the first importance to settle; and, pending their settlement, we will do as we do. Whilst the debate goes forward on the equity of commerce, and will not be closed for a century or two, New and Old England may keep shop. Law of copyright and international copyright is to be discussed, and in the interim we will sell our books for the most we can. Expediency of literature, reason of literature, lawfulness of writing down a thought, is questioned; much is to say on both sides, and, while the fight waxes hot, thou, dearest scholar, stick to thy foolish task, add a line every hour, and between whiles add a line. Right to hold land, right of property, is disputed, and the conventions convene, and before the vote is taken, dig away in your garden, and spend your earnings as a waif or godsend to all serene and beautiful purposes. Life itself is a bubble and a scepticism, and a sleep within a sleep. Grant it, and as much more as they will—but thou, God's darling! heed thy private dream; thou wilt not be missed in the scorning and scepticism; there are enough of them; stay there in thy closet and toil until the rest are agreed what to do about it. Thy sickness, they say, and thy puny habit require that thou do this or avoid that, but know that thy life is a flitting state, a tent for a night, and do thou, sick or well, finish that stint. Thou art sick, but shalt not be worse, and the universe, which holds thee dear, shall be the better.

Human life is made up of the two elements, power and form, and the proportion must be invariably kept if we would have it sweet and sound. Each of these elements in excess makes a mischief as hurtful as its defect. Everything runs to excess; every good quality is noxious if unmixed, and, to carry the danger to the edge of ruin, nature causes each man's peculiarity to superabound. Here, among the forms, we adduce the scholars as examples of this treachery. They are nature's victims of expression. You who see the artist, the orator, the poet, too near, and find their life no more excellent than that of mechanics or farmers, and themselves victims of partiality, very hollow and haggard, and pronounce them failures, not heroes, but quacks— conclude very reasonably that these arts are not for man, but are disease. Yet nature will not bear you out. Irresistible nature made men such, and makes legions more of such, every day. You love the boy reading in a book, gazing at a drawing or a cast; yet what are these millions who read and behold, but incipient writers and sculptors? Add a little more of that quality which now reads and sees, and they will seize the pen and chisel. And if one remembers how innocently he began to be an artist, he perceives that nature joined with his enemy. A man is a golden impossibility. The line he must walk is a hair's breadth. The wise through excess of wisdom is made a fool.

How easily, if fate would suffer it, we might keep forever these beautiful limits, and adjust ourselves, once for all, to the perfect calculation of the kingdom of known cause and effect. In the street and in the newspapers, life appears so plain a business that manly resolution and adherence to the multiplication-table through all weathers will insure success. But ah! presently comes a day, or is it only a half-hour, with its angel-whispering—which discomfits the conclusions of nations and of years! To-morrow again every thing looks real and angular, the habitual standards are reinstated, common-sense is as rare as genius—is the basis of genius, and experience is hands and feet to every enterprise; and yet, he who should do his business on this understanding would be quickly bankrupt. Power keeps quite another road than the turnpikes of choice and will; namely the subterranean and invisible tunnels and channels of life. It is ridiculous that we are diplomatists, and doctors, and considerate people; there are no dupes like these. Life is a series of surprises, and would not be worth taking or keeping if it were not. God delights to isolate us every day, and hide from us the past and the future. We would look about us, but with grand politeness he draws down before us an impenetrable screen of purest sky, and another behind us of purest sky. "You will not remember," he seems to say, "and you will not expect." All good conversation, manners and action come from a spontaneity which forgets usages and makes the moment great. Nature hates calculators; her methods are saltatory and impulsive. Man lives by pulses; our organic movements are such; and the chemical and ethereal agents are undulatory and alternate; and the mind goes antagonizing on, and never prospers but by fits. We thrive by casualties. Our chief experiences have been casual. The most attractive class of people are those who are powerful obliquely and not by the direct stroke; men

of genius, but not yet accredited; one gets the cheer of their
light without paying too great a tax. Theirs is the beauty
of the bird or the morning light, and not of art. In the
thought of genius there is always a surprise; and the moral
sentiment is well called "the newness," for it is never
other; as new to the oldest intelligence as to the young
child; "the kingdom that cometh without observation." In
like manner, for practical success, there must not be too
much design. A man will not be observed in doing that
which he can do best. There is a certain magic about his
properest action which stupefies your powers of observation, so that though it is done before you, you wist not
of it. The art of life has a pudency, and will not be exposed.
Every man is an impossibility until he is born; every thing
impossible until we see a success. The ardors of piety
agree at last with the coldest scepticism—that nothing is of
us or our works—that all is of God. Nature will not spare
us the smallest leaf of laurel. All writing comes by the
grace of God, and all doing and having. I would gladly be
moral and keep due metes and bounds, which I dearly
love, and allow the most to the will of man; but I have set
my heart on honesty in this chapter, and I can see nothing
at last, in success or failure, than more or less of vital
force supplied from the Eternal. The results of life are
uncalculated and uncalculable. The years teach much
which the days never know. The persons who compose
our company converse, and come and go, and design and
execute many things, and somewhat comes of it all, but an
unlooked-for result. The individual is always mistaken.
He designed many things, and drew in other persons as
coadjutors, quarrelled with some or all, blundered much,
and something is done; all are a little advanced, but the
individual is always mistaken. It turns out somewhat new
and very unlike what he promised himself.

The ancients, struck with this irreducibleness of the
elements of human life to calculation, exalted Chance into
a divinity; but that is to stay too long at the spark, which
glitters truly at one point, but the universe is warm with
the latency of the same fire. The miracle of life which
will not be expounded but will remain a miracle, introduces
a new element. In the growth of the embryo, Sir Everard

Home I think noticed that the evolution was not from one central point, but coactive from three or more points. Life has no memory. That which proceeds in succession might be remembered, but that which is coexistent, or ejaculated from a deeper cause, as yet far from being conscious, knows not its own tendency. So is it with us, now sceptical or without unity, because immersed in forms and effects all seeming to be of equal yet hostile value, and now religious, whilst in the reception of spiritual law. Bear with these distractions, with this coetaneous growth of the parts; they will one day be *members,* and obey one will. On that one will, on that secret cause, they nail our attention and hope. Life is hereby melted into an expectation or a religion. Underneath the inharmonious and trivial particulars, is a musical perfection; the Ideal journeying always with us, the heaven without rent or seam. Do but observe the mode of our illumination. When I converse with a profound mind, or if at any time being alone I have good thoughts, I do not at once arrive at satisfactions, as when, being thirsty, I drink water; or go to the fire, being cold; no! but I am at first apprised of my vicinity to a new and excellent region of life. By persisting to read or to think, this region gives further sign of itself, as it were in flashes of light, in sudden discoveries of its profound beauty and repose, as if the clouds that covered it parted at intervals and showed the approaching traveller the inland mountains, with the tranquil eternal meadows spread at their base, whereon flocks graze and shepherds pipe and dance. But every insight from this realm of thought is felt as initial, and promises a sequel. I do not make it; I arrive there, and behold what was there already. I make! O no! I clap my hands in infantine joy and amazement before the first opening to me of this august magnificence, old with the love and homage of innumerable ages, young with the life of life, the sunbright Mecca of the desert. And what a future it opens! I feel a new heart beating with the love of the new beauty. I am ready to die out of nature and be born again into this new yet unapproachable America I have found in the West:

Since neither now nor yesterday began
These thoughts, which have been ever, nor yet can
A man be found who their first entrance knew.

If I have described life as a flux of moods, I must now add that there is that in us which changes not and which ranks all sensations and states of mind. The consciousness in each man is a sliding scale, which identifies him now with the First Cause, and now with the flesh of his body; life above life, in infinite degrees. The sentiment from which it sprung determines the dignity of any deed, and the question ever is, not what you have done or forborne, but at whose command you have done or forborne it.

Fortune, Minerva, Muse, Holy Ghost—these are quaint names, too narrow to cover this unbounded substance. The baffled intellect must still kneel before this cause, which refuses to be named—ineffable cause, which every fine genius has essayed to represent by some emphatic symbol, as, Thales by water, Anaximenes by air, Anaxagoras by (Νοῦς) thought, Zoroaster by fire, Jesus and the moderns by love; and the metaphor of each has become a national religion. The Chinese Mencius has not been the least successful in his generalization. "I fully understand language," he said, "and nourish well my vast-flowing vigor." "I beg to ask what you call vast-flowing vigor?" said his companion. "The explanation," replied Mencius, "is difficult. This vigor is supremely great, and in the highest degree unbending. Nourish it correctly and do it no injury, and it will fill up the vacancy between heaven and earth. This vigor accords with and assists justice and reason, and leaves no hunger." In our more correct writing we give to this generalization the name of Being, and thereby confess that we have arrived as far as we can go. Suffice it for the joy of the universe that we have not arrived at a wall, but at interminable oceans. Our life seems not present so much as prospective; not for the affairs on which it is wasted, but as a hint of this vast-flowing vigor. Most of life seems to be mere advertisement of faculty; information is given us not to sell ourselves cheap; that we are very great. So, in particulars, our greatness is always in a tendency or direction, not in an action. It is for us to believe in the rule, not in the exception. The noble are thus known from the ignoble. So in accepting the leading of the sentiments, it is not what we believe concerning the immortality of the soul or the like, but *the universal impulse to believe,* that is the material circumstance and is the principal fact in the history of the globe. Shall we describe this cause as that which works directly? The spirit is not helpless or needful of mediate organs. It has plentiful powers and direct effects. I am explained without explaining, I am felt without acting, and where I am not. Therefore all just persons are satisfied with their own praise. They refuse to explain themselves, and are content that new actions should do them that office. They believe that we communicate without speech and above speech, and that no right action of ours is quite unaffecting to our friends, at whatever distance; for the influence of action is not to be measured by miles. Why should I fret myself because a circumstance has occurred which hinders my presence where I was expected? If I am not at the meeting, my presence where I am should be as useful to the commonwealth of friendship and wisdom, as would be my presence in that place. I exert the same quality of power in all places. Thus journeys the mighty Ideal before us; it never was known to fall into the rear. No man ever came to an experience which was satiating, but his good is tidings of a better. Onward and onward! In liberated moments we know that a new picture of life and duty is already possible; the elements already exist in many minds around you of a doctrine of life which shall transcend any written record we have. The new statement will comprise the scepticisms as well as the faiths of society, and out of unbeliefs a creed shall be formed. For scepticisms are not gratuitous or lawless, but are limitations of the affirmative statement, and the new philosophy must take them in and make affirmations outside of them, just as much as it must include the oldest beliefs.

It is very unhappy, but too late to be helped, the discovery we have made that we exist. That discovery is called the Fall of Man. Ever afterwards we suspect our instruments. We have learned that we do not see directly, but mediately, and that we have no means of correcting these colored and distorting lenses which we are, or of computing the amount of their errors. Perhaps these subjectlenses have a creative power; perhaps there are no objects. Once we lived in what we saw; now, the rapaciousness of this new power, which threatens to absorb all things, engages us. Nature, art, persons, letters, religions, objects, successively tumble in, and God is but one of its ideas. Nature and literature are subjective phenomena; every evil and every good thing is a shadow which we cast. The street is full of humiliations to the proud. As the fop contrived to dress his bailiffs in his livery and make them wait on his guests at table, so the chagrins which the bad heart gives off as bubbles, at once take form as ladies and gentlemen in the street, shopmen or barkeepers in hotels, and threaten or insult whatever is threatenable and insultable in us. 'T is the same with our idolatries. People forget that it is the eye which makes the horizon, and the rounding mind's eye which makes this or that man a type or representative of humanity, with the name of hero or saint. Jesus, the "providential man," is a good man on whom many people are agreed that these optical laws shall take effect. By love on one part and by forbearance to press objection on the other part, it is for a time settled that we will look at him in the centre of the horizon, and ascribe to him the properties that will attach to any man so seen. But the longest love or aversion has a speedy term. The great and crescive self, rooted in absolute nature, supplants all relative existence and ruins the kingdom of mortal friendship and love. Marriage (in what is called the spiritual world) is impossible, because of the inequality between every subject and every object. The subject is the receiver of Godhead, and at every comparison must feel his being enhanced by that cryptic might. Though not in energy, yet by presence, this magazine of substance cannot be otherwise than felt; nor can any force of intellect attribute to the object the proper deity which sleeps or wakes forever in every subject. Never can love make consciousness and ascription equal in force. There will be the same gulf between every me and thee as between the original and the picture. The universe is the bride of the soul. All private sympathy is partial. Two human beings are like globes, which can touch only in a point, and whilst they remain in contact all other points of each of the spheres are inert; their turn must also come, and the longer a particular union lasts the more energy of appetency the parts not in union acquire.

Life will be imaged, but cannot be divided nor doubled. Any invasion of its unity would be chaos. The soul is not twin-born but the only begotten, and though revealing itself as child in time, child in appearance, is of a fatal and universal power, admitting no co-life. Every day, every act betrays the ill-concealed deity. We believe in ourselves as we do not believe in others. We permit all things to ourselves, and that which we call sin in others is experiment for us. It is an instance of our faith in ourselves that men never speak of crime as lightly as they think; or every man thinks a latitude safe for himself which is nowise to be indulged to another. The act looks very differently on the inside and on the outside; in its quality and in its consequences. Murder in the murderer is no such ruinous thought as poets and romancers will have it; it does not unsettle him or fright him from his ordinary notice of trifles; it is an act quite easy to be contemplated; but in its sequel it turns out to be a horrible jangle and confounding of all relations. Especially the crimes that spring from love seem right and fair from the actor's point of view, but when acted are found destructive of society. No man at last believes that he can be lost, or that the crime in him is as black as in the felon. Because the intellect qualifies in our own case the moral judgments. For there is no crime to the intellect. That is antinomian or hypernomian, and judges law as well as fact. "It is worse than a crime, it is a blunder," said Napoleon, speaking the language of the intellect. To it, the world is a problem in mathematics or the science of quantity, and it leaves out praise and blame and all weak emotions. All stealing is comparative. If you come to absolutes, pray who does not steal? Saints are sad, because they behold sin (even when they speculate) from the point of view of the conscience, and not of the intellect; a confusion of thought. Sin, seen from the thought, is a diminution, or *less;* seen from the conscience or will, it is pravity or *bad.* The intellect names it shade, absence of light, and no essence. The conscience must feel it as essence, essential evil. This it is not; it has an objective existence, but no subjective.

Thus inevitably does the universe wear our color, and every object fall successively into the subject itself. The subject exists, the subject enlarges; all things sooner or later fall into place. As I am, so I see; use what language we will, we can never say anything but what we are; Hermes, Cadmus, Columbus, Newton, Bonaparte, are the mind's ministers. Instead of feeling a poverty when we encounter a great man, let us treat the newcomer like a travelling geologist who passes through our estate and shows us good slate, or limestone, or anthracite, in our brush pasture. The partial action of each strong mind in one direction is a telescope for the objects on which it is pointed. But every other part of knowledge is to be pushed to the same extravagance, ere the soul attains her due sphericity. Do you see that kitten chasing so prettily her own tail? If you could look with her eyes you might see her surrounded with hundreds of figures performing complex dramas, with tragic and comic issues, long conversations, many characters, many ups and downs of fate—and meantime it is only puss and her tail. How long before our masquerade will end its noise of tambourines, laughter and shouting, and we shall find it was a solitary performance? A subject and an object—it takes so much to make the galvanic circuit complete, but magnitude adds nothing. What imports it whether it is Kepler and the sphere, Columbus and America, a reader and his book, or puss with her tail?

It is true that all the muses and love and religion hate these developments, and will find a way to punish the chemist who publishes in the parlor the secrets of the laboratory. And we cannot say too little of our constitutional necessity of seeing things under private aspects, or saturated with our humors. And yet is the God the native of these bleak rocks. That need makes in morals the capital virtue of self-trust. We must hold hard to this poverty, however scandalous, and by more vigorous self-recoveries, after the sallies of action, possess our axis more firmly. The life of truth is cold and so far mournful; but it is not the slave of tears, contritions and perturbations. It does not attempt another's work, nor adopt another's facts. It is a main lesson of wisdom to know your own from another's. I have learned that I cannot dispose of other people's facts; but I possess such a key to my own as persuades me, against all their denials, that they also have a key to theirs. A sympathetic person is placed in the dilemma of a swimmer among drowning men, who all catch at him, and if he give so much as a leg or a finger they will drown him. They wish to be saved from the mischiefs of their vices, but not from their vices. Charity would be wasted on this poor waiting on the symptoms. A wise and hardy physician will say, *Come out of that,* as the first condition of advice.

In this our talking America we are ruined by our good

nature and listening on all sides. This compliance takes away the power of being greatly useful. A man should not be able to look other than directly and forthright. A pre-occupied attention is the only answer to the importunate frivolity of other people; an attention, and to an aim which makes their wants frivolous. This is a divine answer, and leaves no appeal and no hard thoughts. In Flaxman's drawing of the Eumenides of Aeschylus, Orestes supplicates Apollo, whilst the Furies sleep on the threshold. The face of the god expresses a shade of regret and compassion, but is calm with the conviction of the irreconcilableness of the two spheres. He is born into other politics, into the eternal and beautiful. The man at his feet asks for his interest in turmoils of the earth, into which his nature cannot enter. And the Eumenides there lying express pictorially this disparity. The god is surcharged with his divine destiny.

Illusion, Temperament, Succession, Surface, Surprise, Reality, Subjectiveness—these are threads on the loom of time, these are the lords of life. I dare not assume to give their order, but I name them as I find them in my way. I know better than to claim any completeness for my picture. I am a fragment, and this is a fragment of me. I can very confidently announce one or another law, which throws itself into relief and form, but I am too young yet by some ages to compile a code. I gossip for my hour concerning the eternal politics. I have seen many fair pictures not in vain. A wonderful time I have lived in. I am not the novice I was fourteen, nor yet seven years ago. Let who will ask, Where is the fruit? I find a private fruit sufficient. This is a fruit—that I should not ask for a rash effect from meditations, counsels and the hiving of truths. I should feel it pitiful to demand a result on this town and county, an overt effect on the instant month and year. The effect is deep and secular as the cause. It works on periods in which mortal lifetime is lost. All I know is reception; I am and I have: but I do not get, and when I have fancied I had gotten anything, I found I did not. I worship with wonder the great Fortune. My reception has been so large, that I am not annoyed by receiving this or that superabundantly. I say to the Genius, if he will pardon the proverb, *In for a mill, in for a million.* When I receive a new gift, I do not macerate my body to make the account square, for if I should die I could not make the account square. The benefit overran the merit the first day, and has overrun the merit ever since. The merit itself, so-called, I reckon part of the receiving.

Also that hankering after an overt or practical effect seems to me an apostasy. In good earnest I am willing to spare this most unnecessary deal of doing. Life wears to me a visionary face. Hardest roughest action is visionary also. It is but a choice between soft and turbulent dreams. People disparage knowing and the intellectual life, and urge doing. I am very content with knowing, if only I could know. That is an august entertainment, and would suffice me a great while. To know a little would be worth the expense of this world. I hear always the law of Adrastia, "that every soul which had acquired any truth, should be safe from harm until another period."

I know that the world I converse with in the city and in the farms, is not the world I *think*. I observe that difference, and shall observe it. One day I shall know the value and law of this discrepance. But I have not found that much was gained by manipular attempts to realize the world of thought. Many eager persons successively make an experiment in this way, and make themselves ridiculous. They acquire democratic manners, they foam at the mouth, they hate and deny. Worse, I observe that in the history of mankind there is never a solitary example of success—taking their own tests of success. I say this polemically, or in reply to the inquiry, Why not realize your world? But far be from me the despair which prejudges the law by a paltry empiricism; since there never was a right endeavor but it succeeded. Patience and patience, we shall win at the last. We must be very suspicious of the deceptions of the element of time. It takes a good deal of time to eat or to sleep, or to earn a hundred dollars, and a very little time to entertain a hope and an insight which becomes the light of our life. We dress our garden, eat our dinners, discuss the household with our wives, and these things make no impression, are forgotten next week; but, in the solitude to which every man is always returning, he has a sanity and revelations which in his passage into new worlds he will carry with him. Never mind the ridicule, never mind the defeat; up again, old heart?—it seems to say—there is victory yet for all justice; and the true romance which the world exists to realize will be the transformation of genius into practical power.

1844

FROM

Journals

[Self-Portraits]

April 18, 1824. Myself.— . . . I am beginning my professional studies. In a month I shall be legally a man. And I deliberately dedicate my time, my talents, and my hopes to the Church. . . .

I cannot dissemble that my abilities are below my ambition. . . . I have, or had, a strong imagination, and consequently a keen relish for the beauties of poetry. The exercise which the practice of composition gives to this faculty is the cause of my immoderate fondness for writing, which has swelled these pages to a voluminous extent. My reasoning faculty is proportionably weak, nor can I ever hope to write a Butler's Analogy or an Essay of Hume. Nor is it strange that with this confession I should choose theology, which is from everlasting to everlasting "debateable ground." For, the highest species of reasoning upon divine subjects is rather the fruit of a sort of moral imagination, than of the "Reasoning Machines." . . . I may add that the preaching most in vogue at the present day depends chiefly on imagination for its success, and asks those accomplishments which I believe are most within my grasp. I have set down little which can gratify my vanity, and I must further say that every comparison of myself with my mates that six or seven, perhaps sixteen or seventeen, years have made, has convinced me that there exists a signal defect of character which neutralizes in great part the just influence my talents ought to have. Whether that defect be in the *address,* in the fault of good forms—which, Queen Isabella said, were like perpetual letters-commendatory—or deeper seated in an absence of common *sympathies,* or even in a levity of the understanding, I cannot tell. But its bitter fruits are a sore uneasiness in the company of most men and women, a frigid fear of offending and jealousy of disrespect, an inability to lead and an unwillingness to follow the current conversation, which contrive to make me second with all those among whom chiefly I wish to be first. . . .

But in Divinity I hope to thrive. I inherit from my sire a formality of manner and speech, but I derive from him, or his patriotic parent, a passionate love for the strains of eloquence. I burn after the *"aliquid immensum infinitumque"* [something without limits and bounds] which Cicero desired. What we ardently love we learn to imitate. My understanding venerates and my heart loves that cause which is dear to God and man—the laws of morals, the Revelations which sanction, and the blood of martyrs and triumphant suffering of the saints which seal them. In my better hours, I am the believer (if not the dupe) of brilliant promises, and can respect myself as the possessor of those powers which command the reason and passions of the multitude. . . . My trust is that my profession shall be my regeneration of mind, manners, inward and outward estate; or rather my starting-point, for I have hoped to put on eloquence as a robe, and by goodness and zeal and the awfulness of Virtue to press and prevail over the false judgments, the rebel passions and corrupt habits of men. . . .

Cambridge, September 28, 1826. I was born cold. My bodily habit is cold. I shiver in and out; don't heat to the good purposes called enthusiasm a quarter so quick and kindly as my neighbours.

Boston, January 10, 1832. It is the best part of the man, I sometimes think, that revolts most against his being a minister. His good revolts from official goodness. If he never spoke or acted but with the full consent of his understanding, if the whole man acted always, how powerful would be every act and every word. Well then, or ill then, how much power he sacrifices by conforming himself to say and do in other folks' time instead of in his own! The difficulty is that we do not make a world of our own, but fall into institutions already made, and have to accommodate ourselves to them to be useful at all, and this accommodation is, I say, a loss of so much integrity and, of course, of so much power.

Boston, June 2, 1832. I have sometimes thought that,

in order to be a good minister, it was necessary to leave the ministry. The profession is antiquated. In an altered age, we worship in the dead forms of our forefathers. Were not a Socratic paganism better than an effete, superannuated Christianity?

Paris, July 13, 1833. . . . The universe is a more amazing puzzle than ever, as you glance along this bewildering series of animated forms—the hazy butterflies, the carved shells, the birds, beasts, fishes, insects, snakes, and the unheaving principle of life everywhere incipient, in the very rock aping organized forms. Not a form so grotesque, so savage, nor so beautiful but is an expression of some property inherent in man the observer—an occult relation between the very scorpions and man. I feel the centipede in me—cayman, carp, eagle, and fox. I am moved by strange sympathies; I say continually "I will be a naturalist."

September 6, 1833. Fair; fine wind; still in the Channel, off the coast of Ireland, but not in sight of land. This morning 37 sail in sight.

I like my book about Nature, and wish I knew where and how I ought to live. God will show me. I am glad to be on my way home, yet not so glad as others, and my way to the bottom I could find perchance with less regret, for I think it would not hurt me—that is, the ducking or drowning.

July 30, 1835. You affirm that the moral development contains all the intellectual, and that Jesus was the perfect man. I bow in reverence unfeigned before that benign man. I know more, hope more, am more, because he has lived. But, if you tell me that in your opinion he has fulfilled all the conditions of man's existence, carried out to the utmost, at least by implication, all man's powers, I suspend my assent. I do not see in him cheerfulness: I do not see in him the love of natural science: I see in him no kindness for art; I see in him nothing of Socrates, of Laplace, of Shakespeare. The perfect man should remind us of all great men. Do you ask me if I would rather resemble Jesus than any other man? If I should say Yes, I should suspect myself of superstition.

May 21, 1837. I see a good in such emphatic and universal calamity as the times bring, that they dissatisfy me with society. Under common burdens we say there is much virtue in the world, and what evil coexists is inevitable. I am not aroused to say, "I have sinned; I am in the gall of bitterness, and bond of iniquity"; but when these full measures come, it then stands confessed—society has played out its last stake; it is check-mated. Young men have no hope. Adults stand like day-laborers idle in the streets. None calleth us to labor. The old wear no crown of warm life on their gray hairs. The present generation is bankrupt of principles and hope, as of property. I see man is not what man should be. He is the treadle of a wheel. He is a tassel at the apron-string of society. He is a money-chest. He is the servant of his belly. This is the causal bankruptcy, this the cruel oppression, that the ideal should serve the actual; that the head should serve the feet. Then first, I am forced to inquire if the Ideal might not also be tried. Is it to be taken for granted that it is impracticable? Behold the boasted world has come to nothing. Prudence itself is at her wits' end. Pride, and Thrift, and Expediency, who jeered and chirped and were so well pleased with themselves, and made merry with the dream, as they termed it, of Philosophy and Love—behold they are all flat, and here is the Soul erect and unconquered still. What answer is it now to say, It has always been so? I acknowledge that, as far back as I can see the widening procession of humanity, the marchers are lame and blind and deaf; but to the soul that whole past is but one finite series in its infinite scope. Deteriorating ever and now desperate. Let me begin anew. Let me teach the finite to know its master. Let me ascend above my fate and work down upon my world.

March 4, 1838. Last night a remembering and remembering talk with Lidian. I went back to the first smile of Ellen [Emerson's first wife, who died in 1831] on the door-stone at Concord. I went back to all that delicious relation to feel, as ever, how many shades, how much reproach. Strange is it that I can go back to no part of youth, no past relation, without shrinking and shrinking. Not Ellen, not Edward, not Charles [Emerson's dead brothers]. Infinite compunctions embitter each of those dear names, and all who surrounded them. Ah! could I have felt in the presence of the first, as now I feel, my own power and hope, and so have offered her in every word and look the heart of a man humble and wise, but resolved to be true and perfect with God, and not, as I fear it seemed, the uneasy, uncentered joy of one who received in her a good—a lovely good—out of all proportion to his deserts, I might haply have made her days longer and certainly sweeter, and at least have recalled her seraph smile without a pang. I console myself with the thought that if Ellen, if Edward, if Charles, could have read my entire heart, they should have seen nothing but rectitude of purpose and generosity conquering the superficial coldness and prudence. But I ask now, Why was not I made like all these beatified mates of mine, *superficially* generous and noble, as well as *internally* so? They never needed to shrink at any remembrance—and I at so many sad passages that look to me now as if I [had] been blind and mad. Well, O God, I will try and learn from this sad memory to be brave and circumspect and true henceforth and weave now a web that will not shrink. This is the thorn in the flesh.

June 23, 1838. I hate goodies. I hate goodness that preaches. Goodness that preaches undoes itself. A little electricity of virtue lurks here and there in kitchens and among the obscure, chiefly women, that flashes out occasional light and makes the existence of the thing still credible. But one had as lief curse and swear as be guilty of this odious religion that watches the beef and watches the cider in the pitcher at table, that shuts the mouth hard at any remark it cannot twist nor wrench into a sermon, and preaches as long as itself and its hearer is awake. Goodies make us very bad. . . . We will almost sin to spite them. Better indulge yourself, feed fat, drink liquors, than go straitlaced for such cattle as these.

November 3, 1838. I told Jones Very [a poet friend] that I had never suffered, that I could scarce bring myself to feel a concern for the safety and life of my nearest friends that would satisfy them; that I saw clearly that if my wife, my child, my mother, should be taken from me, I should still remain whole, with the same capacity of cheap enjoyment from all things. I should not grieve enough, although I love them. But could I make them feel what I feel—the boundless resources of the soul, remaining entire when particular threads of relation are snapped—I should then dismiss forever the little remains of uneasiness I have in regard to them.

January 28, 1842. Yesterday night, at fifteen minutes after eight, my little Waldo ended his life. [Emerson's son died in his sixth year.]

January 30, 1842. . . . The boy had his full swing in this world; never, I think, did a child enjoy more; he had been thoroughly respected by his parents and those around him, and not interfered with; and he had been the most fortunate in respect to the influences near him, for his Aunt Elizabeth had adopted him from his infancy and treated him ever with that plain and wise love which belongs to her and, as she boasted, had never given him sugarplums. So he was won to her, and always signalized her arrival as a visit to him, and left playmates, playthings, and all to go to her. Then Mary Russell had been his friend and teacher for two summers, with true love and wisdom. Then Henry Thoreau had been one of the family for the last year, and charmed Waldo by the variety of toys, whistles, boats, popguns, and all kinds of instruments which he could make and mend; and possessed his love and respect by the gentle firmness with which he always treated him. Margaret Fuller and Caroline Sturgis had also marked the boy and caressed and conversed with him whenever they were here. Meantime every day his grandmother gave him his reading-lesson and had by patience taught him to read and spell; by patience and by love, for she loved him dearly. . . .

The morning of Friday, I woke at three o'clock, and every cock in every barnyard was shrilling with the most unnecessary noise. The sun went up the morning sky with all his light, but the landscape was dishonored by this loss. For this boy, in whose remembrance I have both slept and awaked so oft, decorated for me the morning star, the evening cloud. . . . A boy of early wisdom, of a grave and even majestic deportment, of a perfect gentleness.

Every tramper that ever tramped is abroad, but the little feet are still.

He gave up his little innocent breath like a bird.

Sorrow makes us all children again—destroys all differences of intellect. The wisest knows nothing.

March 20, 1842. I comprehend nothing of this fact but its bitterness. Explanations have I none, consolation none that rises out of the fact itself; only diversion; only oblivion of this and pursuit of new objects.

May 21, 1843. Man sheds grief as his skin sheds rain. A preoccupied mind an immense protection. There is a great concession on all hands to the ideal decorum in grief, as well as joy, but few hearts are broken.

April, 1859. I have been writing and speaking what were once called novelties, for twenty-five or thirty years, and have not now one disciple. Why? Not that what I said was not true; not that it has not found intelligent receivers; but because it did not go from any wish in me to bring men to me, but to themselves. I delight in driving them from me. What could I do, if they came to me?— they would interrupt and encumber me. This is my boast that I have no school follower. I should account it a measure of the impurity of insight, if it did not create independence. . . .

I have now for more than a year, I believe, ceased to write in my Journal, in which I formerly wrote almost daily. I see few intellectual persons, and even those to no purpose, and sometimes believe that I have no new thoughts, and that my life is quite at an end. But the magnet that lies in my drawer, for years, may believe it has no magnetism, and, on touching it with steel, it knows the old virtue; and, this morning, came by a man with knowledge and interests like mine, in his head, and suddenly I had thoughts again.

June, 1861. Advantages of old age. I reached the other day the end of my fifty-seventh year, and am easier in my mind than hitherto. I could never give much reality to evil and pain. But now when my wife says perhaps this tumor on your shoulder is a cancer, I say, What if it is.

June, 1864. Within, I do not find wrinkles and used heart, but unspent youth.

June, 1874. Egypt. Mrs. Helen Bell, it seems, was asked, "What do you think the Sphinx said to Mr. Emerson?" "Why," replied Mrs. Bell, "the Sphinx probably said to him, 'You're another.' "

[Language]

June 27, 1839. Rhyme.—Rhyme; not tinkling rhyme, but grand Pindaric strokes, as firm as the tread of a horse. Rhyme that vindicates itself as an art, the stroke of the bell of a cathedral. Rhyme which knocks at prose and dull-

ness with the stroke of a cannon ball. Rhyme which builds
out into Chaos and old night a splendid architecture to
bridge the impassable, and call aloud on all the children
of morning that the Creation is recommencing. I wish to
write such rhymes as shall not suggest a restraint, but con-
trariwise the wildest freedom.

June 24, 1840. The language of the street is always
strong. What can describe the folly and emptiness of
scolding like the word *jawing?* I feel too the force of the
double negative, though clean contrary to our grammar
rules. And I confess to some pleasure from the stinging
rhetoric of a rattling oath in the mouth of truckmen and
teamsters. How laconic and brisk it is by the side of a
page of the *North American Review.* Cut these words and
they would bleed; they are vascular and alive; they walk
and run. Moreover they who speak them have this ele-
gancy, that they do not trip in their speech. It is a shower
of bullets, whilst Cambridge men and Yale men correct
themselves and begin again at every half sentence. . . .

[Thoreau]

October, 1841. . . . I told Henry Thoreau that his
freedom is in the form, but he does not disclose new matter. I am very familiar with all his thoughts—they are my
own quite originally drest. But if the question be, what
new ideas has he thrown into circulation, he has not yet
told what that is which he was created to say. I said to
him what I often feel, I only know three persons who
seem to me fully to see this law of reciprocity or compensation—himself, Alcott, and myself: and 'tis odd that
we should all be neighbors, for in the wide land or the
wide earth I do not know another who seems to have it
as deeply and originally as these three Gothamites.

July, 1846. The State is a poor, good beast who means
the best: it means friendly. A poor cow who does well by
you—do not grudge it its hay. [Thoreau went to jail rather
than pay his poll-tax.] It cannot eat bread, as you can; let
it have without grudge a little grass for its four stomachs.
It will not stint to yield you milk from its teat. You, who
are a man walking cleanly on two feet, will not pick a
quarrel with a poor cow. Take this handful of clover and
welcome. But if you go to hook me when I walk in the
fields, then, poor cow, I will cut your throat.

Don't run amuck against the world. Have a good case to try the question on. It is the part of a fanatic to fight out a revolution on the shape of a hat or surplice, on paedo-baptism, or altar-rails, or fish on Friday. As long as the state means you well, do not refuse your pistareen. You have a tottering cause: ninety parts of the pistareen it will spend for what you think also good: ten parts for mischief. You cannot fight heartily for a fraction. But wait until you have a good difference to join issue upon. Thus Socrates was told he should not teach. "Please God, but I will." And he could die well for that. And Jesus had a cause. You will get one by and by. But now I have no sympathy. . . .

Alcott thought he could find as good a ground for quarrel in the state tax as Socrates did in the edict of the Judges. Then I say, Be consistent, and never more put an apple or a kernel of corn into your mouth. Would you feed the devil? Say boldly, "There is a sword sharp enough to cut sheer between flesh and spirit, and I will use it, and not any longer belong to this double-faced, equivocating, mixed, Jesuitical universe."

The Abolitionists should resist, because they are literalists; they know exactly what they object to, and there is a government possible which will content them. Remove a few specified grievances, and this present commonwealth will suit them. They are the new Puritans, and as easily satisfied. But you, nothing will content. No government short of a monarchy consisting of one king and one subject, will appease you. Your objection, then, to the State of Massachusetts is deceptive. Your true quarrel is with the state of Man.

In the particular, it is worth considering that refusing payment of the state tax does not reach the evil so nearly as many other methods within your reach. The state tax does not pay the Mexican War. Your coat, your sugar, your Latin and French and German book, your watch does. Yet these you do not stick at buying.

But really a scholar has too humble an opinion of the population, of their possibilities, of their future, to be entitled to go to war with them, as with equals.

The prison is one step to suicide.

He knows that nothing they can do will ever please him. Why should he poorly pound on some one string of discord, when all is jangle?

June, 1863. In reading Henry Thoreau's journal [Thoreau died in 1862], I am very sensible of the vigor of his constitution. That oaken strength which I noted whenever he walked, or worked, or surveyed wood-lots, the same unhesitating hand with which a field-laborer accosts a piece of work, which I should shun as a waste of strength, Henry shows in his literary task. He has muscle, and ventures on and performs feats which I am forced to decline. In reading him, I find the same thought, the same spirit that is in me, but he takes a step beyond, and illustrates by excellent images that which I should have conveyed in a sleepy generality. 'Tis as if I went into a gymnasium, and saw youths leap, climb, and swing with a force unapproachable—though their feats are only continuations of my initial grapplings and jumps.

[Hawthorne]

September, 1842. Nathaniel Hawthorne's reputation as a writer is a very pleasing fact, because his writing is not good for anything, and this is a tribute to the man.

May, 1846. Hawthorne invites his readers too much into his study, opens the process before them. As if the confectioner should say to his customers, "Now, let us make the cake."

May 24, 1864. Yesterday, May 23, we buried Hawthorne in Sleepy Hollow, in a pomp of sunshine and verdure, and gentle winds. James Freeman Clarke read the service in the church and at the grave. Longfellow, Lowell, Holmes, Agassiz, Hoar, Dwight, Whipple, Norton, Alcott, Hillard, Fields, Judge Thomas, and I attended the hearse as pallbearers. Franklin Pierce was with the family. The church was copiously decorated with white flowers delicately arranged. The corpse was unwillingly shown—only a few moments to this company of his friends. But it was noble and serene in its aspect—nothing amiss —a calm and powerful head. A large company filled the church and the grounds of the cemetery. All was so bright and quiet that pain or mourning was hardly suggested, and Holmes said to me that it looked like a happy meeting.

Clarke in the church said that Hawthorne had done more justice than any other to the shades of life, shown a sympathy with the crime in our nature, and, like Jesus, was the friend of sinners.

I thought there was a tragic element in the event, that might be more fully rendered—in the painful solitude of the man, which, I suppose, could not longer be endured, and he died of it.

I have found in his death a surprise and disappointment. I thought him a greater man than any of his works betray, that there was still a great deal of work in him, and that he might one day show a purer power. Moreover, I have felt sure of him in his neighborhood, and in his necessities of sympathy and intelligence—that I could well wait his time, his unwillingness and caprice—and might one day conquer a friendship. It would have been a happiness, doubtless to both of us, to have come into habits of unreserved intercourse. It was easy to talk with him—there were no barriers—only, he said so little, that I talked too much, and stopped only because, as he gave no indications, I feared to exceed. He showed no egotism or self-assertion, rather a humility, and, at one time, a fear that he had written himself out. One day, when I found him on the top of his hill, in the woods, he paced back the path to his house, and said, "This path is the only remembrance of me that will remain." Now it appears that I waited too long. . . .

HENRY DAVID THOREAU

(1817–1862)

Editions of the work of Henry David Thoreau are: H. G. O. Blake, ed., *The Writings of Henry David Thoreau*, 10 vols. (1894), the Riverside Edition; The Cambridge Edition, 11 vols. (1894, 1932); The Manuscript Edition, 20 vols. (1906); and *The Writings of Henry David Thoreau*, 20 vols. (1906), the standard (Walden) edition. Thoreau's published works include *A Week on the Concord and Merrimac Rivers* (1849); *Walden, or Life in the Woods* (1854); *Excursions* (1863); *The Maine Woods (1864); Cape Cod* (1865); *Letters to Various Persons* (1865); *A Yankee in Canada, with Antislavery and Reform Papers* (1866); *Early Spring in Massachusetts* (1881); *Summer* (1884); *Winter* (1888); *Autumn* (1892); *Miscellanies* (1894); *Familiar Letters of Henry David Thoreau* (1894); *Poems of Nature* (1895); *The Service* (1902); *Sir Walter Raleigh* (1905); *The Moon* (1927); *The Transmigration of the Seven Brahmans: A Translation* (1932); F. H. Allen, ed., *The Journals of Henry David Thoreau*, 14 vols. (1949); H. Hardin and C. Bode, eds., *The Correspondence of Henry David Thoreau* (1958); and P. Miller, ed., *Consciousness in Concord: The Text of Thoreau's Hitherto Lost Journal (1840–1841)* (1958); see also J. L. Shanley (1957) below.

THE VIKING PORTABLE THOREAU, edited by Carl Bode, contains *Walden*, complete, and full selections from *The Maine Woods, A Week on the Concord and Merrimac Rivers, A Yankee in Canada,* and *Cape Cod.* The essay is further represented by *The Natural History of Massachusetts,* "A Winter Walk," "Civil Disobedience," "Walking," and "Life without Principle." There are eighteen poems, selections from the *Journals,* seven letters, and a Thoreau chronology, biography, and bibliography.

Studies of the man and his work are to be found in H. S. Salt, *The Life of Henry David Thoreau* (1890); N. Foerster, *Nature in American Literature* (1923); L. Bazalgette, *Henry Thoreau, Bachelor of Nature,* transl. V. W. Brooks (1924); B. Atkinson, *Henry Thoreau, The Cosmic Yankee* (1927); O.

Shepard, ed., *The Heart of Thoreau's Journals* (1927); A. E. Christy, *The Orient in American Transcendentalism* (1933); B. V. Crawford, ed., *Henry David Thoreau: Representative Selections* (1934); H. S. Canby, *Thoreau* (1939); R. L. Cook, *The Concord Saunterer* (1940); C. C. Walcutt, "Thoreau in the Twentieth Century," *South Atlantic Quarterly*, XXXIX (1940); F. O. Matthiessen, *American Renaissance* (1941); C. Bode, ed., *Collected Poems of Henry Thoreau* (1943); G. F. Whicher, *Walden Revisited* (1945); J. W. Krutch, *Henry David Thoreau* (1948); R. F. Stowell, *A Thoreau Gazetteer* (1948); R. L. Cook, *Passage to Walden* (1949); H. Elau, "Wayside Challenger— Some Remarks on the Politics of Henry David Thoreau," *Antioch Review*, IX (1949); L. Kleinfeld, *Henry David Thoreau Chronology* (1950); E. Seybold, *Thoreau: The Quest and the Classics* (1951); W. M. Condry, *Thoreau* (1954); W. Harding, ed., *Thoreau: A Century of Criticism* (1954); E. B. White, "Walden—1954," *Yale Review*, XLIV (1954); R. W. B. Lewis, *The American Adam* (1955); H. B. Hough, *Thoreau of Walden* (1956); L. Leary, "Henry David Thoreau," in F. Stovall, ed., *Eight American Authors: A Review of Research and Criticism* (1956); J. L. Shanley, *The Making of Walden, with the Text of the First Version* (1957); S. Paul, *The Shores of America: Thoreau's Inward Exploration* (1958); L. Stoller, *After Walden: Thoreau's Changing View of Economic Man* (1958); C. Bode, *The Young Rebel in American Literature* (1959); W. Harding, *A Thoreau Handbook* (1959); W. Harding, *Thoreau: Man of Concord* (1960); L. Lane Jr., "On the Organic Structure of Walden," *College English*, XXI (1960); J. S. Sherwin and R. C. Reynolds, *A Word Index to Walden* (1960); L. Lane, Jr., ed., *Approaches to Walden* (1961); C. R. Metzger, *Thoreau and Whitman: A Study of Their Esthetics* (1961); A. Derleth, *Concord Rebel: A Life of Henry D. Thoreau* (1962); M. Meltzer and W. Harding, *A Thoreau Profile* (1962); S. Paul, ed., *Thoreau: A Collection of Critical Essays* (1962); E. W. Teale, ed., *The Thoughts of Thoreau* (1962); M. Meltzer, ed., *Thoreau: People, Principles, and Politics* (1963); E. J. Rose, "The Wit and Wisdom of Thoreau's 'Higher Laws'," *Queens Quarterly*, LXIX (1963); R. N. Weaver, "Two Types of American Individualism," *Modern Age*, VII (1963); C. Bode, ed., *Collected Poems* (1964); W. Harding, ed., *The Thoreau Centennial* (1964); P. O. Williams, "The Concept of Inspiration in Thoreau's Poetry," *PMLA*, LXXIX (1964); C. Bode, *The Half-World of American Culture* (1965); J. A. Christie, *Thoreau as World Traveler* (1965); W. Harding, *The Days of Henry David Thoreau, A Biography* (1965); D. M. Greene, *The Frail Duration: A Key to Symbolic Structure in Walden* (1966); and A. B. Hovey, *The Hidden Thoreau* (1966).

NATHANIEL HAWTHORNE

(1804–1864)

Editions of the works of Nathaniel Hawthorne are G. P. Lathrop, ed., *The Complete Works of Nathaniel Hawthorne*, 12 vols. (1883), the standard (Riverside) edition; *The Complete Writings of Nathaniel Hawthorne*, 22 vols. (1900), The Autograph Edition. There is no complete edition of the collected writings of Hawthorne; editions of his letters and of the French and Italian notebooks are under way. Hawthorne's published works include *Fanshawe* (1828); *Peter Parley's Universal History* (1837); *Twice-Told Tales* (1837); *Grandfather's Chair* (1841); *Famous Old People* (1841); *Liberty Tree* (1841); *Biographical Stories for Children* (1842); *Mosses from an Old Manse* (1846); *The Scarlet Letter* (1850); *True Stories from History and Biography* (1851); *The House of the Seven Gables* (1851); *A Wonder-book for Girls and Boys* (1852); *The Snow Image* (1852); *The Blithedale Romance* (1852); *Life of Franklin Pierce* (1852); *Tanglewood Tales* (1853); *The Marble Faun* (1860); *Our Old Home* (1863); *Septimius Felton* (1872); *The Dolliver Romance* (1876); *Doctor Grimshawe's Secret* (1883; edited definitively, E. H. Davidson, 1954); *The Ancestral Footstep*, in *The Complete Works* (1883); *The Ghost of Doctor Harris* (1900); *The Love Letters of Nathaniel Hawthorne* (1907); *Letters of Hawthorne to William D. Ticknor*, 2 vols. (1910); N. Arvin, ed., *The Heart of Hawthorne's Journals* (1929); R. Stewart, ed., *The American Notebooks of Nathaniel Hawthorne* (1932); A. Warren, ed., *Nathaniel Hawthorne* (1934); R. Stewart, ed., *The English Notebooks of Nathaniel Hawthorne* (1941); and A. Turner, ed., *Hawthorne as Editor* (1941).

THE VIKING PORTABLE HAWTHORNE, edited by Malcolm Cowley, contains *The Scarlet Letter* and selections from *The House of Seven Gables*, *The Marble Faun*, and *The Dolliver Romance* as examples of Hawthorne's novels. In addition, there are selections from the American Notebooks, the English Notebooks, and the French and Italian Notebooks, plus eleven letters and a bibliography. The tales presented are "An Old Woman's Tale," "My Kinsman, Major Molineux," "The Gray Champion," "Young Goodman Brown," "The Golden Touch," "Feathertop," "Wakefield," "Egotism; or, the Bosom Serpent," "The Birthmark," "Earth's Holocaust," "The Artist of the Beautiful," and "Ethan Brand." The volume also includes Hawthorne's Preface to *Twice-Told Tales*.

Studies of the man and his work are to be found in G. P. Lathrop, *A Study of Hawthorne* (1876); Henry James, *Hawthorne* (1879); A. Trollope, "The Genius of Nathaniel Hawthorne," *North American Review*, CXXIX (1879); J. Hawthorne, *Nathaniel Hawthorne and His Wife*, 2 vols. (1885); M. D. Conway, *Life of Nathaniel Hawthorne* (1890); H. Bridge, *Personal Recollections of Nathaniel Hawthorne* (1893); R. H. Lathrop, *Memories of Hawthorne* (1897); G. E. Woodberry, *Nathaniel Hawthorne* (1902); J. Hawthorne, *Hawthorne and His Circle* (1903); P. E. More, *Shelburne Essays: First Series* (1904); F. B. Sanborn, *Hawthorne and His Friends* (1908); H. A. Clarke, *Hawthorne's Country* (1910); C. Ticknor, *Hawthorne and His Publisher* (1913); S. P. Sherman, *Americans* (1922); N. Arvin, *Hawthorne* (1929); V. W. Brooks, *The Flowering of New England* (1936); Y. Winters, *Maule's Curse* (1938); B. Faust, *Hawthorne's Contemporaneous Reputation* (1940); A. M. Jackson, *Nathaniel Hawthorne: A Modest Man* (1940); F. O. Matthiessen, *American Renaissance* (1941); P. Rahv, "The Dark Lady of Salem," *Partisan Review*, VIII (1941); V. Astrov, "Hawthorne and Dostoevski as Explorers of the Human Conscience," *New England Quarterly*, XV (1942); L. Hall, *Hawthorne: Critic of Society* (1944); L. Schubert, *Hawthorne the Artist* (1944); N. F. Adkins, "The Early Projected Works of Nathaniel Hawthorne," *Papers of the Bibliographical Society of America*, XXXIX (1945); J. Lundblad, *Nathaniel Hawthorne and the Tradition of Gothic Romance* (1946); J. Lundblad, *Nathaniel Hawthorne and European Literary Tradition* (1947); R. Cantwell, *Nathaniel Hawthorne: The American Years* (1948); M. Cowley, "Hawthorne in the Looking Glass," *Sewanee Review*, LVI (1948); B. Mills, "Hawthorne and Puritanism," *New England Quarterly*, XXI (1948); R. H. Pearce, "Hawthorne and the Twilight of Romance," *Yale Review*, XXXVII (1948); R. Stewart, *Nathaniel Hawthorne* (1948); A. Warren, *Rage for Order* (1948); E. Davidson, *Hawthorne's Last Phase* (1949); M. Kesselring, *Hawthorne's Reading* (1949); M. Van Doren, *Nathaniel Hawthorne* (1949); Q. D. Leavis, "Hawthorne as Poet," *Sewanee Review*, LIX (1951); V. Loggins, *The Hawthornes: The Story of Seven Generations of an American Family* (1951); M. Bewley, *The Complex Fate* (1952); R. H. Fogle, *Hawthorne's Fiction* (1952); C. Feidelson, Jr., *Symbolism and American Literature* (1953); L. Howard, "Hawthorne's Fiction," *Nineteenth-Century Fiction*, VII (1953); W. B. Stein, *Hawthorne's Faust* (1953); R. W. B. Lewis, *The American Adam* (1955); J. E. Miller, Jr., "Hawthorne and Melville: The Unpardonable Sin," *PMLA*, LXX (1955); A. Reid, *The Yellow Ruff & The Scarlet Letter* (1955); R. Von Abele, *The Death of* the Artist: A Study of Hawthorne's Disintegration (1955); H. H. Waggoner, Hawthorne, A Critical Study (1955); W. Blair, "Nathaniel Hawthorne," in F. Stovall, ed., Eight American Authors: A Review of Research and Criticism, (1956); H. Fairbanks, "Sin, Free Will, and 'Pessimism' in Hawthorne," PMLA, LXXI (1956); L. Marx, "The Machine in the Garden," New England Quarterly, XXIX (1956); R. P. Adams, "Hawthorne's Provincial Tales," New England Quarterly, XXX (1957); R. Chase, The American Novel and Its Tradition (1957); R. Male, Jr., Hawthorne's Tragic Vision (1957); E. Fussell, "Hawthorne, James, and 'The Common Doom,' " American Quarterly, X (1958); H. Levin, The Power of Blackness: Hawthorne, Poe, Melville (1958); H. McPherson, "Hawthorne's Mythology: A Mirror for Puritans," University of Toronto Quarterly, XXVII (1959); S. Gross, ed., A "Scarlet Letter" Handbook (1960); E. Wagenknecht, Nathaniel Hawthorne (1961); H. H. Clark, "Hawthorne's Literary and Aesthetic Doctrines as Embodied in His Tales," Transactions of the Wisconsin Academy of Sciences, Arts, and Letters, L (1961); D. G. Hoffman, Form and Fable in American Fiction (1961); B. R. McElderry, Jr., "The Transcendental Hawthorne," Midwest Quarterly, II (1961); C. F. Strauch, ed., "Symposium on Nathaniel Hawthorne," Emerson Society Quarterly, No. 25 (1961); A. Turner, Nathaniel Hawthorne (1961); M. Bell, Hawthorne's View of the Artist (1962); H. H. Hoeltje, Inward Sky: The Mind and Art of Nathaniel Hawthorne (1962); G. Monteiro, "Hawthorne, James, and the Destructive Self," Texas Studies in Language and Literature, IV (1962); E. Sandeen, "The Scarlet Letter as a Love Story," PMLA, LXXVII (1962); J. K. Folsom, Man's Accidents and God's Purposes: Multiplicity in Hawthorne's Fiction (1963); A. N. Kaul, The American Vision: Actual and Ideal Society in Nineteenth-Century Fiction (1963); Essex Institute Historical Collections, C, iv (Special Hawthorne Issue) (1964); R. H. Pearce, ed., Hawthorne Centenary Essays (1964); H. Fairbanks, The Lasting Loneliness of Nathaniel Hawthorne (1965); E. Fussell, Frontier: American Literature and the American West (1965); T. Martin, Nathaniel Hawthorne (1965); A. Warren, "The Scarlet Letter: A Literary Exercise in Moral Theology," Southern Review, I (1965); F. C. Crews, The Sins of the Fathers: Hawthorne's Psychological Themes (1966); and R. J. Jacobson, Hawthorne's Conception of the Creative Process (1966).

HERMAN MELVILLE

(1819–1891)

Perhaps Herman Melville first went to sea with some of the
feelings he assigned to Ishmael: "whenever it is a damp,
drizzly November in my soul . . . I quietly take to the ship."
Doubtless the young Melville did not have Ishmael's psychological and metaphysical "hypos," but he went to sea to
escape poverty, country schoolteaching, engineering studies,
and job-hunting. After financial, physical, and moral exhaus-
tion, Melville's father died in 1832, leaving the family dependent upon the largesse of the Gansevoorts, the wealthy patroon
family of Herman's mother. To ease the family's burdens,
Melville shipped as a green hand on the *St. Lawrence* bound
for Liverpool and was entered on the crew-list as "Norman
Melville." This misnomer presaged a life of uneven literary
fame; indeed, when he died one obituary called him "Herman
Melvin."

As long as he wrote what the public was prepared for,
Melville had his share of luck in the marketplace. *Typee*
(1846) and *Omoo* (1847), his first two books, were based on
his wanderings in the South Seas and were greeted by popularity and a measure of financial success. However, with the
appearance in 1849 of his third book, *Mardi*, which was his
first attempt in the metaphysics of oceanic speculations rather
than in the romance of glimpses into the exotic, his critics
turned hostile ("*Robinson Crusoe* run mad," one writer termed
it). Although this novel (like the later *Pierre*) is a tortured
and often tedious book, most of the critics objected not so
much to Melville's overwrought intensity as they did to the

pretensions of a pleasant travel writer indulging himself in philosophical rambles. His next two books, *Redburn* (1849) and *White-Jacket* (1850), based respectively on his first sea voyage and his experiences in the navy, were "done for money." "Dollars damn me," he later complained, and considered these books "botches" because he could neither keep attempts at profundity out of his travel narratives nor be content merely to be a purveyor of entertaining travelogues.

With his sixth book, the monumental *Moby-Dick*, he lost both his audience and most of what was left of favorable critical reaction; *Pierre*, in 1852, put him in a literary graveyard. The critics gave him up as crazy, and he was soon forgotten except as that entertaining figure, occasionally recalled, who, in *Typee*, "had lived among cannibals." The Herman Melville whom we hail today as one of the foremost geniuses of our imaginative literature might just as well have been "Norman Melville" or "Herman Melvin" for all his own time cared.

However, a small cult of readers kept the memory of Melville's books alive in a small way, and in the 1920s, largely through the efforts of Raymond M. Weaver, Melville re-entered the national literary consciousness. The huge tide of "rediscovery" came in the 1940s—and it has never ebbed. Although Melville worked as an obscure U. S. Customs inspector for nineteen years, writing no fiction from *The Confidence-Man* (1857) until he began *Billy Budd* in the late 1880s, and died in literary oblivion, his work, like the great whale of the depths, has boiled up into "white water" to the inexhaustible delight and fascination of readers throughout the world. Melville, as Camus recognized, is the most philosophical of American novelists; and the record of his search for ultimate value is one of the most gripping accounts of the human mind ever penned—bewildered, bewildering, and beautiful. As Hawthorne put it in his notebook, "Melville as he always does began to reason of Providence and Futurity, and of everything that lies beyond human ken. . . . It is strange how he persists . . . in wandering to and fro over these deserts. . . . He can neither believe nor feel comfortable in unbelief. And he is too honest and courageous not to try to do one or the other . . . he has a very high and noble nature and is better worth immortality than most of us."

In addition to the titles mentioned above, Melville's works include *Israel Potter* (1855); *The Piazza Tales* (1856); *Battle-*

Pieces (1866); *Clarel* (1876); *John Marr and Other Sailors* (1888); *Timoleon* (1891); *Poems* (1924); R. W. Weaver, ed., *Journal up the Straits* (1935), re-edited by H. C. Horsford as *Journal of a Visit to Europe and the Levant* (1955); E. M. Metcalf, ed., *Journal of a Visit to London and the Continent, 1849–1850* (1948); E. M. Metcalf, ed., *Herman Melville: Cycle and Epicycle* (1935); and M. R. Davis and W. H. Gilman, eds., *The Letters of Herman Melville* (1960). An edition of Melville's complete writings is now in progress. *The Portable Melville* is edited by Jay Leyda.

Studies of the man and his work are to be found in R. M. Weaver, *Herman Melville: Mariner and Mystic* (1921); L. Mumford, *Herman Melville* (1929, 1962); H. S. Canby, *Classic Americans* (1931); L. S. Mansfield, *Herman Melville: Author and New Yorker, 1844–1851* (1938); W. Thorpe, ed., *Herman Melville: Representative Selections* (1938); Y. Winters, *Maule's Curse* (1938); C. R. Anderson, *Melville in the South Seas* (1939); J. Simon, *Herman Melville, Marin, Métaphysicien et Poète* (1939); R. P. Blackmur, *The Expense of Greatness* (1940); R. E. Watters, "Melville's Metaphysics of Evil," *University of Toronto Quarterly*, IX (1940); F. O. Matthiessen, *American Renaissance* (1941); W. Braswell, *Melville's Religious Thought* (1943); W. E. Sedgwick, *Herman Melville: The Tragedy of Mind* (1944); H. P. Vincent, ed., *Collected Poems of Herman Melville* (1945); R. E. Watters, "Melville's 'Isolatoes,'" *PMLA*, LX (1945); H. Hayford, "Hawthorne, Melville, and the Sea," *New England Quarterly*, XIX (1946); R. P. Warren, "Melville the Poet," *Kenyon Review*, VIII (1946); C. Olson, *Call Me Ishmael* (1947); R. W. Short, "Melville as Symbolist," *University of Kansas City Review*, XV (1948); N. Arvin, "Melville's Shorter Poems," *Partisan Review*, XVI (1949); R. Chase, *Herman Melville* (1949); G. Stone, *Melville* (1949); W. Weber, "Some Characteristic Symbols in Melville's Works," *English Studies*, XXX (1949); N. Wright, *Melville's Use of the Bible* (1949); H. Vincent, *The Trying-Out of Moby Dick* (1949); N. Arvin, *Herman Melville* (1950); W. H. Auden, *The Enchaféd Flood* (1950); P. Frédérix, *Herman Melville* (1950); D. G. Hoffman, "Melville in the American Grain," *Southern Folklore Quarterly*, XIV (1950); T. Hillway, *Melville and the Whale* (1950); A. Kazin, "On Melville as Scripture," *Partisan Review*, XVII (1950); M. O. Percival, *A Reading of Moby-Dick* (1950); Philip Rahv, "Melville and His Critics," *Partisan Review*, XVII (1950); M. Sealts, *Melville's Reading* (1950); W. H. Gilman, *Melville's Early Life and Redburn (1951)*; L. Howard, *Herman Melville* (1951); J. Leyda, *The Melville Log*, 2 vols. (1951); R. Mason, *The Spirit Above the Dust: A Study of Herman Melville* (1951); H. A.

Murray, "In Nomine Diaboli," *New England Quarterly,* XXIV (1951); M. R. Davis, *Melville's Mardi: A Chartless Voyage* (1952); *Princeton University Library Chronicle,* XIII (Winter, 1952), a Melville issue; R. Stewart, "Melville and Hawthorne," *South Atlantic Quarterly,* LI (1952); L. Thompson, *Melville's Quarrel with God* (1952); F. I. Carpenter, "Melville: The World in a Man-of-War," *University of Kansas City Review,* XIX (1953); C. Feidelson, Jr., *Symbolism and American Literature* (1953); C. G. Hoffman, "The Shorter Fiction of Herman Melville," *South Atlantic Quarterly,* LII (1953); S. E. Hyman, "Melville the Scrivener," *New Mexico Quarterly,* XXIII (1953); C. L. R. James, *Mariners, Renegades, and Castaways* (1953); T. Hillway and L. S. Mansfield, eds., *Moby-Dick, Centennial Essays* (1953); P. Miller, "Melville and Transcendentalism," *Virginia Quarterly Review,* XXIX (1953); *American Literature,* XXV (Jan., 1954), a Melville issue; R. W. B. Lewis, *The American Adam* (1955); J. E. Miller, Jr., "Hawthorne and Melville," *PMLA,* LXX (1955); W. V. O'Connor, "Melville on the Nature of Hope," *University of Kansas City Review,* XXII (1955); E. H. Rosenberry, *Melville and the Comic Spirit* (1955); J. Baird, *Ishmael* (1956); P. Miller, *The Raven and the Whale* (1956); S. T. Williams, "Herman Melville," in F. Stovall, ed., *Eight American Authors: A Review of Research and Criticism* (1956); M. Sealts, *Melville as Lecturer* (1957); M. R. Stern, *The Fine Hammered Steel of Herman Melville* (1957); H. Levin, *The Power of Blackness: Hawthorne, Poe, Melville* (1958); M. R. Stern, "Some Techniques of Melville's Perception," *PMLA,* LXXIII (1958); J. E. Miller, Jr., "Melville's Quest in Life and Art," *South Atlantic Quarterly,* LVIII (1959); M. Bowen, *The Long Encounter: Self and Experience in the Writings of Herman Melville* (1960); R. H. Fogle, *Melville's Shorter Tales* (1960); M. R. Stern, ed., *Discussions of Moby-Dick* (1960); J. J. Mayoux, *Melville* (1960); H. W. Hetherington, *Melville and the Reviewers* (1961); W. E. Bezanson, ed., *Clarel: A Poem and Pilgrimage in the Holy Land* (1961); D. M. Finkelstein, *Melville's Orienda* (1961); R. H. Fogle, "The Themes of Melville's Later Poetry," *Tennessee Studies in English,* XI (1961); D. G. Hoffman, *Form and Fable in American Fiction* (1961); S. Kaplan, ed., *Battle-Pieces and Aspects of the War* (1961); R. Schulman, "The Serious Functions of Melville's Phallic Jokes," *American Literature,* XXXIII (1961); W. T. Stafford, ed., *Melville's Billy Budd and the Critics* (1961); W. Berthoff, *The Example of Melville* (1962); H. C. Brashers, "Ishmael's Tattoos," *Sewanee Review,* LXX (1962); R. Chase, ed., *Melville: A Collection of Critical Essays* (1962); *Herman Melville Special Number, Modern Fiction Studies,* VIII (1962); A. R. Humphreys, *Herman Melville* (1962); J. E. Miller, Jr., *A Reader's Guide to Herman Melville* (1962); J. Stanonik, *Moby Dick, The Myth and the Symbol: A Study in Folklore and Literature* (1962); H. Hayford and M. Sealts, eds., *Billy Budd, Sailor* (1962); W. Chase, *Narrative of the Most Extraordinary and Distressing Shipwreck of the Whaleship Essex. Supplementary Accounts of Survivors and Herman Melville's Notes* (1963); H. B. Franklin,

The Wake of the Gods: Melville's Mythology (1963); T. Hill-way, *Herman Melville* (1963); A. N. Kaul, *The American Vision: Actual and Ideal Society in Nineteenth-Century Fiction* (1963); J. Bernstein, *Pacifism and Rebellion in the Writings of Herman Melville* (1964); L. Baritz, *City on a Hill: A History of Ideas and Myths in America* (1964); P. Brodtkorb, Jr., *Ishmael's White World: A Phenomenological Reading of Moby Dick* (1965); S. L. Gross, ed., *A Benito Cereno Handbook* (1965); and H. P. Vincent, ed., *A Symposium: Bartleby the Scrivener* (1966).

Bartleby

I am a rather elderly man. The nature of my avocations, for the last thirty years, has brought me into more than ordinary contact with what would seem an interesting and somewhat singular set of men, of whom, as yet, nothing, that I know of, has ever been written—I mean, the law-copyists, or scriveners. I have known very many of them, professionally and privately, and, if I pleased, could re-late divers histories, at which good-natured gentlemen might smile, and sentimental souls might weep. But I waive the biographies of all other scriveners, for a few passages in the life of Bartleby, who was a scrivener, the strangest I ever saw, or heard of. While, of other law-copyists, I might write the complete life, of Bartleby nothing of that sort can be done. I believe that no materials exist, for a full and satisfactory biography of this man. It is an ir-reparable loss to literature. Bartleby was one of those beings of whom nothing is ascertainable, except from the original sources, and, in his case, those are very small. What my own astonished eyes saw of Bartleby, *that* is all I know of him, except, indeed, one vague report, which will appear in the sequel.

Ere introducing the scrivener, as he first appeared to me, it is fit I make some mention of myself, my *employés,* my business, my chambers, and general surroundings; be-cause some such description is indispensable to an adequate understanding of the chief character about to be presented. Imprimis: I am a man who, from his youth upwards, has been filled with a profound conviction that the easiest way of life is the best. Hence, though I belong to a profession proverbially energetic and nervous, even to turbulence, at times, yet nothing of that sort have I ever suffered to in-vade my peace. I am one of those unambitious lawyers who never address a jury, or in any way draw down public applause; but, in the cool tranquillity of a snug retreat, do a snug business among rich men's bonds, and mortgages, and title-deeds. All who know me, consider me an eminently *safe* man. The late John Jacob Astor, a personage little given to poetic enthusiasm, had no hesitation in pronouncing my first grand point to be prudence; my next, method. I do not speak it in vanity, but simply record the fact, that I was not unemployed in my profession by the late John Jacob Astor; a name which, I admit, I love to repeat; for it hath a rounded and orbicular sound to it, and rings like unto bullion. I will freely add, that I was not insensible to the late John Jacob Astor's good opinion.

Some time prior to the period at which this little history begins, my avocations had been largely increased. The good old office, now extinct in the State of New York, of a Master in Chancery, had been conferred upon me. It was not a very arduous office, but very pleasantly remunerative. I seldom lose my temper; much more seldom indulge in dangerous indignation at wrongs and outrages; but I must be permitted to be rash here and declare, that I consider the sudden and violent abrogation of the office of Master in Chancery, by the new Constitution, as a —— premature act; inasmuch as I had counted upon a life-lease of the profits, whereas I only received those of a few short years. But this is by the way.

My chambers were up stairs at No. — Wall Street. At one end, they looked upon the white wall of the interior of a spacious sky-light shaft, penetrating the building from top to bottom.

This view might have been considered rather tame than otherwise, deficient in what landscape painters call "life." But, if so, the view from the other end of my chambers offered, at least, a contrast, if nothing more. In that direction, my windows commanded an unobstructed view of a lofty brick wall, black by age and everlasting shade; which wall required no spy-glass to bring out its lurking beauties, but, for the benefit of all near-sighted spectators, was pushed up to within ten feet of my window-panes. Owing to the great height of the surrounding buildings, and my chambers being on the second floor, the interval between this wall and mine not a little resembled a huge square cistern.

At the period just preceding the advent of Bartleby, I

had two persons as copyists in my employment, and a promising lad as an office-boy. First, Turkey; second, Nippers; third, Ginger Nut. These may seem names the like of which are not usually found in the Directory. In truth, they were nicknames, mutually conferred upon each other by my three clerks, and were deemed expressive of their respective persons or characters. Turkey was a short, pursy Englishman, of about my own age—that is, somewhere not far from sixty. In the morning, one might say, his face was of a fine florid hue, but after twelve o'clock, meridian —his dinner hour—it blazed like a grate full of Christmas coals; and continued blazing—but, as it were, with a gradual wane—till six o'clock, P.M., or thereabouts; after which, I saw no more of the proprietor of the face, which, gaining its meridian with the sun, seemed to set with it, to rise, culminate, and decline the following day, with the like regularity and undiminished glory. There are many singular coincidences I have known in the course of my life, not the least among which was the fact, that, exactly when Turkey displayed his fullest beams from his red and radiant countenance, just then, too, at that critical moment, began the daily period when I considered his business capacities as seriously disturbed for the remainder of the twenty-four hours. Not that he was absolutely idle, or averse to business then; far from it. The difficulty was, he was apt to be altogether too energetic. There was a strange, inflamed, flurried, flighty recklessness of activity about him. He would be incautious in dipping his pen into his inkstand. All his blots upon my documents were dropped there after twelve o'clock, meridian. Indeed, not only would he be reckless, and sadly given to making blots in the afternoon, but, some days, he went further, and was rather noisy. At such times, too, his face flamed with augmented blazonry, as if cannel coal had been heaped on anthracite. He made an unpleasant racket with his chair; spilled his sand-box; in mending his pens, impatiently split them all to pieces, and threw them on the floor in a sudden passion; stood up, and leaned over his table, boxing his papers about in a most indecorous manner, very sad to behold in an elderly man like him. Nevertheless, as he was in many ways a most valuable person to me, and all the time before twelve o'clock, meridian, was the quickest, steadiest creature, too, accomplishing a great deal of work in a style not easily to be matched—for these reasons, I was willing to overlook his eccentricities, though, indeed, occasionally, I remonstrated with him. I did this very gently, however, because, though the civilest, nay, the blandest and most reverential of men in the morning, yet, in the afternoon, he was disposed, upon provocation, to be slightly rash with his tongue—in fact, insolent. Now, valuing his morning services as I did, and resolved not to lose them—yet, at the same time, made uncomfortable by his inflamed ways after twelve o'clock—and being a man of peace, unwilling by my admonitions to call forth unseemly retorts from him, I took upon me, one Saturday noon (he was always worse on Saturdays) to hint to him, very kindly, that, perhaps, now that he was growing old, it might be well to abridge his labors; in short, he need not come to my chambers after twelve o'clock, but, dinner over, had best go home to his lodgings, and rest himself till tea-time. But no; he insisted upon his afternoon devotions. His countenance became intolerably fervid, as he oratorically assured me—gesticulating with a long ruler at the other end of the room—that if his services in the morning were useful, how indispensable, then, in the afternoon?

"With submission, sir," said Turkey, on this occasion, "I consider myself your right-hand man. In the morning I but marshal and deploy my columns; but in the afternoon I put myself at their head, and gallantly charge the foe, thus"—and he made a violent thrust with the ruler.

"But the blots, Turkey," intimated I.

"True; but, with submission, sir, behold these hairs! I am getting old. Surely, sir, a blot or two of a warm afternoon is not to be severely urged against gray hairs. Old age—even if it blot the page—is honorable. With submission, sir, we *both* are getting old."

This appeal to my fellow-feeling was hardly to be resisted. At all events, I saw that go he would not. So, I made up my mind to let him stay, resolving, nevertheless, to see to it that, during the afternoon, he had to do with my less important papers.

Nippers, the second on my list, was a whiskered, sallow, and, upon the whole, rather piratical-looking young man, of about five-and-twenty. I always deemed him the victim of two evil powers—ambition and indigestion. The ambition was evinced by a certain impatience of the duties of a mere copyist, an unwarrantable usurpation of strictly professional affairs, such as the original drawing up of legal documents. The indigestion seemed betokened in an occasional nervous testiness and grinning irritability, causing the teeth to audibly grind together over mistakes committed in copying; unnecessary maledictions, hissed, rather than spoken, in the heat of business; and especially by a continual discontent with the height of the table where he worked. Though of a very ingenious mechanical turn, Nippers could never get this table to suit him. He put chips under it, blocks of various sorts, bits of pasteboard, and at last went so far as to attempt an exquisite adjustment, by final pieces of folded blotting-paper. But no invention would answer. If, for the sake of easing his back, he brought the table-lid at a sharp angle well up towards his chin, and wrote there like a man using the steep roof of a Dutch house for his desk, then he declared that it stopped the circulation in his arms. If now he lowered the table to his waistbands, and stooped over it in writing, then there was a sore aching in his back. In short, the truth of the matter was, Nippers knew not what he wanted. Or, if he wanted anything, it was to be rid of a scrivener's table altogether. Among the manifestations of his diseased ambition was a fondness he had for receiving visits from certain ambiguous-looking fellows in seedy coats, whom he called his clients. Indeed, I was aware that not only was he, at times, considerable of a ward-politician, but he occasionally did a little business at the Justices' courts, and was not unknown on the steps of the Tombs. I have good reason to believe, however, that one individual who called upon him at my chambers, and who, with a grand air, he insisted was his client, was no other than a dun, and the alleged title-deed, a bill. But, with all his failings, and the annoyances he caused me, Nippers, like his compatriot Turkey, was a very useful man to me; wrote a neat, swift hand; and, when he chose, was not deficient in a gentlemanly sort of deportment. Added to this, he always dressed in a gentlemanly sort of way; and so, incidentally, reflected credit upon my chambers. Whereas, with respect to Turkey, I had much ado to keep him from being a reproach to me. His clothes were apt to look oily, and smell of eating-houses. He wore his pantaloons very loose and baggy in summer. His coats were execrable; his hat not to be handled. But while the hat was a thing of indifference to me, inasmuch as his natural civility and deference, as a dependent Englishman, always led him to doff it the moment he entered the room, yet his coat was another matter. Concerning his coats, I reasoned with him; but with no effect. The truth was, I suppose, that a man with so small an income could not afford to sport such a lustrous face and a lustrous coat at one and the same time. As Nippers once observed, Turkey's money went chiefly for red ink. One winter day, I presented Turkey with a highly respectable-looking coat of my own —a padded gray coat, of a most comfortable warmth, and which buttoned straight up from the knee to the neck. I thought Turkey would appreciate the favor, and abate his rashness and obstreperousness of afternoons. But no; I verily believe that buttoning himself up in so downy and blanket-like a coat had a pernicious effect upon him— upon the same principle that too much oats are bad for horses. In fact, precisely as a rash, restive horse is said to feel his oats, so Turkey felt his coat. It made him insolent. He was a man whom prosperity harmed.

Though, concerning the self-indulgent habits of Turkey, I had my own private surmises, yet, touching Nippers, I was well persuaded that, whatever might be his faults in other respects, he was, at least, a temperate young man. But, indeed, nature herself seemed to have been his vintner, and, at his birth, charged him so thoroughly with an irritable, brandy-like disposition, that all subsequent potations were needless. When I consider how, amid the stillness of my chambers, Nippers would sometimes impatiently rise from his seat, and stooping over his table, spread his arms wide apart, seize the whole desk, and move it, and jerk it, with a grim, grinding motion on the floor, as if the table were a perverse voluntary agent, intent on thwarting and vexing him, I plainly perceive that, for Nippers, brandy-and-water were altogether superfluous.

It was fortunate for me that, owing to its peculiar cause —indigestion—the irritability and consequent nervousness of Nippers were mainly observable in the morning, while in the afternoon he was comparatively mild. So that, Turkey's paroxysms only coming on about twelve o'clock, I never had to do with their eccentricities at one time. Their fits relieved each other, like guards. When Nippers's was on, Turkey's was off; and *vice versa*. This was a good natural arrangement, under the circumstances.

Ginger Nut, the third on my list, was a lad, some

twelve years old. His father was a carman, ambitious of seeing his son on the bench instead of a cart, before he died. So he sent him to my office, as student at law, errand-boy, cleaner and sweeper, at the rate of one dollar a week. He had a little desk to himself, but he did not use it much. Upon inspection, the drawer exhibited a great array of the shells of various sorts of nuts. Indeed, to this quick-witted youth, the whole noble science of the law was contained in a nutshell. Not the least among the employments of Ginger Nut, as well as one which he discharged with the most alacrity, was his duty as cake and apple purveyor for Turkey and Nippers. Copying law-papers being proverbially a dry, husky sort of business, my two scriveners were fain to moisten their mouths very often with Spitzenbergs, to be had at the numerous stalls nigh the Custom House and Post Office. Also, they sent Ginger Nut very frequently for that peculiar cake—small, flat, round, and very spicy—after which he had been named by them. Of a cold morning, when business was but dull, Turkey would gobble up scores of these cakes, as if they were mere wafers—indeed, they sell them at the rate of six or eight for a penny—the scrape of his pen blending with the crunching of the crisp particles in his mouth. Of all the fiery afternoon blunders and flurried rashnesses of Turkey, was his once moistening a ginger-cake between his lips, and clapping it on to a mortgage, for a seal. I came within an ace of dismissing him then. But he mollified me by making an oriental bow, and saying—

"With submission, sir, it was generous of me to find you in stationery on my own account."

Now my original business—that of a conveyancer and title hunter, and drawer-up of recondite documents of all sorts—was considerably increased by receiving the Master's office. There was now great work for scriveners. Not only must I push the clerks already with me, but I must have additional help.

In answer to my advertisement, a motionless young man one morning stood upon my office threshold, the door being open, for it was summer. I can see that figure now—pallidly neat, pitiably respectable, incurably forlorn! It was Bartleby.

After a few words touching his qualifications, I engaged him, glad to have among my corps of copyists a man of so singularly sedate an aspect, which I thought might operate beneficially upon the flighty temper of Turkey, and the fiery one of Nippers.

I should have stated before that ground-glass folding-doors divided my premises into two parts, one of which was occupied by my scriveners, the other by myself. According to my humor, I threw open these doors, or closed them. I resolved to assign Bartleby a corner by the folding-doors, but on my side of them, so as to have this quiet man within easy call, in case any trifling thing was to be done. I placed his desk close up to a small side-window in that part of the room, a window which originally had afforded a lateral view of certain grimy backyards and bricks, but which, owing to subsequent erections, commanded at present no view at all, though it gave some light. Within three feet of the panes was a wall, and the light came down from far above, between two lofty buildings, as from a very small opening in a dome. Still further to a satisfactory arrangement, I procured a high green folding screen, which might entirely isolate Bartleby from my sight, though not remove him from my voice. And thus, in a manner, privacy and society were conjoined.

At first, Bartleby did an extraordinary quantity of writing. As if long famishing for something to copy, he seemed to gorge himself on my documents. There was no pause for digestion. He ran a day and night line, copying by sunlight and by candle-light. I should have been quite delighted with his application, had he been cheerfully industrious. But he wrote on silently, palely, mechanically.

It is, of course, an indispensable part of a scrivener's business to verify the accuracy of his copy, word by word. Where there are two or more scriveners in an office, they assist each other in this examination, one reading from the copy, the other holding the original. It is a very dull, wearisome, and lethargic affair. I can readily imagine that, to some sanguine temperaments, it would be altogether intolerable. For example, I cannot credit that the mettlesome poet, Byron, would have contentedly sat down with Bartleby to examine a law document of, say, five hundred pages, closely written in a crimpy hand.

Now and then, in the haste of business, it had been my habit to assist in comparing some brief document myself, calling Turkey or Nippers for this purpose. One object I had, in placing Bartleby so handy to me behind the screen, was, to avail myself of his services on such trivial occasions. It was on the third day, I think, of his being with me, and before any necessity had arisen for having his own writing examined, that, being much hurried to complete a small affair I had in hand, I abruptly called to Bartleby. In my haste and natural expectancy of instant compliance, I sat with my head bent over the original on my desk, and my right hand sideways, and somewhat nervously extended with the copy, so that, immediately upon emerging from his retreat, Bartleby might snatch it and proceed to business without the least delay.

In this very attitude did I sit when I called to him, rapidly stating what it was I wanted him to do—namely, to examine a small paper with me. Imagine my surprise, nay, my consternation, when, without moving from his privacy, Bartleby, in a singularly mild, firm voice, replied, "I would prefer not to."

I sat awhile in perfect silence, rallying my stunned faculties. Immediately it occurred to me that my ears had deceived me, or Bartleby had entirely misunderstood my meaning. I repeated my request in the clearest tone I could assume; but in quite as clear a one came the previous reply, "I would prefer not to."

"Prefer not to," echoed I, rising in high excitement, and crossing the room with a stride. "What do you mean? Are you moon-struck? I want you to help me compare this sheet here—take it," and I thrust it towards him.

"I would prefer not to," said he.

I looked at him steadfastly. His face was leanly composed; his gray eye dimly calm. Not a wrinkle of agitation rippled him. Had there been the least uneasiness, anger, impatience or impertinence in his manner; in other words, had there been anything ordinarily human about him, doubtless I should have violently dismissed him from the premises. But as it was, I should have as soon thought of turning my pale plaster-of-paris bust of Cicero out of doors. I stood gazing at him awhile, as he went on with his own writing, and then reseated myself at my desk. This is very strange, thought I. What had one best do? But my business hurried me. I concluded to forget the matter for the present, reserving it for my future leisure. So, calling Nippers from the other room, the paper was speedily examined.

A few days after this, Bartleby concluded four lengthy

documents, being quadruplicates of a week's testimony taken before me in my High Court of Chancery. It became necessary to examine them. It was an important suit, and great accuracy was imperative. Having all things arranged, I called Turkey, Nippers, and Ginger Nut, from the next room, meaning to place the four copies in the hands of my four clerks, while I should read from the original. Accordingly, Turkey, Nippers, and Ginger Nut had taken their seats in a row, each with his document in his hand, when I called to Bartleby to join this interesting group.

"Bartleby! quick, I am waiting."

I heard a slow scrape of his chair legs on the uncarpeted floor, and soon he appeared standing at the entrance of his hermitage.

"What is wanted?" said he, mildly.

"The copies, the copies," said I, hurriedly. "We are going to examine them. There"—and I held towards him the fourth quadruplicate.

"I would prefer not to," he said, and gently disappeared behind the screen.

For a few moments I was turned into a pillar of salt, standing at the head of my seated column of clerks. Recovering myself, I advanced towards the screen, and demanded the reason for such extraordinary conduct.

"*Why* do you refuse?"

"I would prefer not to."

With any other man I should have flown outright into a dreadful passion, scorned all further words, and thrust him ignominiously from my presence. But there was something about Bartleby that not only strangely disarmed me, but, in a wonderful manner, touched and disconcerted me. I began to reason with him.

"These are your own copies we are about to examine. It is labor saving to you, because one examination will answer for your four papers. It is common usage. Every copyist is bound to help examine his copy. Is it not so? Will you not speak? Answer!"

"I prefer not to," he replied in a flute-like tone. It seemed to me that, while I had been addressing him, he carefully revolved every statement that I made; fully comprehended the meaning; could not gainsay the irresistible conclusion; but, at the same time, some paramount consideration prevailed with him to reply as he did.

"You are decided, then, not to comply with my request—

a request made according to common usage and common sense?"

He briefly gave me to understand, that on that point my judgment was sound. Yes: his decision was irreversible.

It is not seldom the case that, when a man is brow-beaten in some unprecedented and violently unreasonable way, he begins to stagger in his own plainest faith. He begins, as it were, vaguely to surmise that, wonderful as it may be, all the justice and all the reason is on the other side. Accordingly, if any disinterested persons are present, he turns to them for some reinforcement for his own faltering mind.

"Turkey," said I, "what do you think of this? Am I not right?"

"With submission, sir," said Turkey, in his blandest tone, "I think that you are."

"Nippers," said I, "what do *you* think of it?"

"I think I should kick him out of the office."

(The reader of nice perceptions will here perceive that, it being morning, Turkey's answer is couched in polite and tranquil terms, but Nippers replies in ill-tempered ones. Or, to repeat a previous sentence, Nippers's ugly mood was on duty, and Turkey's off.)

"Ginger Nut," said I, willing to enlist the smallest suffrage in my behalf, "what do *you* think of it?"

"I think, sir, he's a little *luny*," replied Ginger Nut, with a grin.

"You hear what they say," said I, turning towards the screen, "come forth and do your duty."

But he vouchsafed no reply. I pondered a moment in sore perplexity. But once more business hurried me. I determined again to postpone the consideration of this dilemma to my future leisure. With a little trouble we made out to examine the papers without Bartleby, though at every page or two Turkey deferentially dropped his opinion, that this proceeding was quite out of the common; while Nippers, twitching in his chair with a dyspeptic nervousness, ground out, between his set teeth, occasional hissing maledictions against the stubborn oaf behind the screen. And for his (Nippers's) part, this was the first and the last time he would do another man's business without pay.

Meanwhile Bartleby sat in his hermitage, oblivious to everything but his own peculiar business there.

Some days passed, the scrivener being employed upon another lengthy work. His late remarkable conduct led me to regard his ways narrowly. I observed that he never went to dinner; indeed, that he never went anywhere. As yet I had never, of my personal knowledge, known him to be outside of my office. He was a perpetual sentry in the corner. At about eleven o'clock though, in the morning, I noticed that Ginger Nut would advance toward the opening in Bartleby's screen, as if silently beckoned thither by a gesture invisible to me where I sat. The boy would then leave the office, jingling a few pence, and reappear with a handful of ginger-nuts, which he delivered in the hermitage, receiving two of the cakes for his trouble.

He lives, then, on ginger-nuts, thought I; never eats a dinner, properly speaking; he must be a vegetarian, then, but no; he never eats even vegetables, he eats nothing but ginger-nuts. My mind then ran on in reveries concerning the probable effects upon the human constitution of living entirely on ginger-nuts. Ginger-nuts are so called, because they contain ginger as one of their peculiar constituents, and the final flavoring one. Now, what was ginger? A hot, spicy thing. Was Bartleby hot and spicy? Not at all. Ginger, then, had no effect upon Bartleby. Probably he preferred it should have none.

Nothing so aggravates an earnest person as a passive resistance. If the individual so resisted be of a not inhumane temper, and the resisting one perfectly harmless in his passivity, then, in the better moods of the former, he will endeavor charitably to construe to his imagination what proves impossible to be solved by his judgment. Even so, for the most part, I regarded Bartleby and his ways. Poor fellow! thought I, he means no mischief; it is plain he intends no insolence; his aspect sufficiently evinces that his eccentricities are involuntary. He is useful to me. I can get along with him. If I turn him away, the chances are he will fall in with some less indulgent employer, and then he will be rudely treated, and perhaps driven forth miserably to starve. Yes. Here I can cheaply purchase a delicious self-approval. To befriend Bartleby, to humor him in his strange wilfulness, will cost me little or nothing, while I lay up in my soul what will eventually prove a sweet morsel for my conscience. But this mood was not invariable with me. The passiveness of Bartleby sometimes irritated me. I felt strangely goaded on to encounter him in new opposition—to elicit some angry spark from him answerable to my own. But, indeed, I might as well have essayed to strike fire with my knuckles against a bit of Windsor soap. But one afternoon the evil impulse in me mastered me, and the following little scene ensued:

"Bartleby," said I, "when those papers are all copied, I will compare them with you."

"I would prefer not to."

"How? Surely you do not mean to persist in that mulish vagary?"

No answer.

I threw open the folding-doors near by, and, turning upon Turkey and Nippers, exclaimed:

"Bartleby a second time says, he won't examine his papers. What do you think of it, Turkey?"

It was afternoon, be it remembered. Turkey sat glowing like a brass boiler; his bald head steaming; his hands reeling among his blotted papers.

"Think of it?" roared Turkey. "I think I'll just step behind his screen, and black his eyes for him!"

So saying, Turkey rose to his feet and threw his arms into a pugilistic position. He was hurrying away to make good his promise, when I detained him, alarmed at the effect of incautiously rousing Turkey's combativeness after dinner.

"Sit down, Turkey," said I, "and hear what Nippers has to say. What do you think of it, Nippers? Would I not be justified in immediately dismissing Bartleby?"

"Excuse me, that is for you to decide, sir. I think his conduct quite unusual, and, indeed, unjust, as regards Turkey and myself. But it may only be a passing whim."

"Ah," exclaimed I, "you have strangely changed your mind, then—you speak very gently of him now."

"All beer," cried Turkey; "gentleness is effects of beer —Nippers and I dined together to-day. You see how gentle *I* am, sir. Shall I go and black his eyes?"

"You refer to Bartleby, I suppose. No, not to-day, Turkey," I replied; "pray, put up your fists."

I closed the doors, and again advanced towards Bartleby. I felt additional incentives tempting me to my fate. I burned to be rebelled against again. I remembered that Bartleby never left the office.

"Bartleby," said I, "Ginger Nut is away; just step

around to the Post Office, won't you?" (it was but a three minutes' walk) "and see if there is anything for me."

"I would prefer not to."

"You *will* not?"

"I *prefer* not."

I staggered to my desk, and sat there in a deep study. My blind inveteracy returned. Was there any other thing in which I could procure myself to be ignominiously repulsed by this lean, penniless wight?—my hired clerk? What added thing is there, perfectly reasonable, that he will be sure to refuse to do?

"Bartleby!"

No answer.

"Bartleby," in a louder tone.

No answer.

"Bartleby," I roared.

Like a very ghost, agreeably to the laws of magical invocation, at the third summons, he appeared at the entrance of his hermitage.

"Go to the next room, and tell Nippers to come to me."

"I prefer not to," he respectfully and slowly said, and mildly disappeared.

"Very good, Bartleby," said I, in a quiet sort of serenely severe self-possessed tone, intimating the unalterable purpose of some terrible retribution very close at hand. At the moment I half intended something of the kind. But upon the whole, as it was drawing towards my dinner-hour, I thought it best to put on my hat and walk home for the day, suffering much from perplexity and distress of mind.

Shall I acknowledge it? The conclusion of this whole business was, that it soon became a fixed fact of my chambers, that a pale young scrivener, by the name of Bartleby, had a desk there; that he copied for me at the usual rate of four cents a folio (one hundred words); but he was permanently exempt from examining the work done by him, that duty being transferred to Turkey and Nippers, out of compliment, doubtless, to their superior acuteness; moreover, said Bartleby was never, on any account, to be dispatched on the most trivial errand of any sort; and that even if entreated to take upon him such a matter, it was generally understood that he would "prefer not to"— in other words, that he would refuse point-blank.

As days passed on, I became considerably reconciled

to Bartleby. His steadiness, his freedom from all dissipation, his incessant industry (except when he chose to throw himself into a standing revery behind his screen), his great stillness, his unalterableness of demeanor under all circumstances, made him a valuable acquisition. One prime thing was this—*he was always there*—first in the morning, continually through the day, and the last at night. I had a singular confidence in his honesty. I felt my most precious papers perfectly safe in his hands. Sometimes, to be sure, I could not, for the very soul of me, avoid falling into sudden spasmodic passions with him. For it was exceeding difficult to bear in mind all the time those strange peculiarities, privileges, and unheard-of exemptions, forming the tacit stipulations on Bartleby's part under which he remained in my office. Now and then, in the eagerness of dispatching pressing business, I would inadvertently summon Bartleby, in a short, rapid tone, to put his finger, say, on the incipient tie of a bit of red tape with which I was about compressing some papers. Of course, from behind the screen the usual answer, "I prefer not to," was sure to come; and then, how could a human creature, with the common infirmities of our nature, refrain from bitterly exclaiming upon such perverseness —such unreasonableness? However, every added repulse of this sort which I received only tended to lessen the probability of my repeating the inadvertence.

Here it must be said, that, according to the custom of most legal gentlemen occupying chambers in densely populated law buildings, there were several keys to my door. One was kept by a woman residing in the attic, which person weekly scrubbed and daily swept and dusted my apartments. Another was kept by Turkey for convenience sake. The third I sometimes carried in my own pocket. The fourth I knew not who had.

Now, one Sunday morning I happened to go to Trinity Church, to hear a celebrated preacher, and finding myself rather early on the ground I thought I would walk round to my chambers for a while. Luckily I had my key with me; but upon applying it to the lock, I found it resisted by something inserted from the inside. Quite surprised, I called out; when to my consternation a key was turned from within; and thrusting his lean visage at me, and holding the door ajar, the apparition of Bartleby appeared, in his shirt-sleeves, and otherwise in a strangely tattered deshabille, saying quietly that he was sorry, but he was deeply engaged just then, and—preferred not admitting me at present. In a brief word or two, he moreover added, that perhaps I had better walk round the block two or three times, and by that time he would probably have concluded his affairs.

Now, the utterly unsurmised appearance of Bartleby, tenanting my law-chambers of a Sunday morning, with his cadaverously gentlemanly *nonchalance,* yet withal firm and self-possessed, had such a strange effect upon me, that incontinently I slunk away from my own door, and did as desired. But not without sundry twinges of impotent rebellion against the mild effrontery of this unaccountable scrivener. Indeed, it was his wonderful mildness chiefly, which not only disarmed me, but unmanned me, as it were. For I consider that one, for the time, is a sort of unmanned when he tranquilly permits his hired clerk to dictate to him, and order him away from his own premises. Furthermore, I was full of uneasiness as to what Bartleby could possibly be doing in my office in his shirtsleeves, and in an otherwise dismantled condition of a Sunday morning. Was anything amiss going on? Nay, that was out of the question. It was not to be thought of for a moment that Bartleby was an immoral person. But what could he be doing there?—copying? Nay again, whatever might be his eccentricities, Bartleby was an eminently decorous person. He would be the last man to sit down to his desk in any state approaching to nudity. Besides, it was Sunday; and there was something about Bartleby that forbade the supposition that he would by any secular occupation violate the proprieties of the day.

Nevertheless, my mind was not pacified; and full of a restless curiosity, at last I returned to the door. Without hindrance I inserted my key, opened it, and entered. Bartleby was not to be seen. I looked round anxiously, peeped behind his screen; but it was very plain that he was gone. Upon more closely examining the place, I surmised that for an indefinite period Bartleby must have ate, dressed, and slept in my office, and that too without plate, mirror, or bed. The cushioned seat of a rickety old sofa in one corner bore the faint impress of a lean, reclining form. Rolled away under his desk, I found a blanket; under the empty grate, a blacking box and brush; on a chair, a tin basin, with soap and a ragged towel; in a newspaper a few crumbs of ginger-nuts and a morsel of cheese. Yes, thought I, it is evident enough that Bartleby has been making his home here, keeping bachelor's hall all by himself. Immediately then the thought came sweeping across me, what miserable friendlessness and loneliness are here revealed! His poverty is great; but his solitude, how horrible! Think of it. Of a Sunday, Wall Street is deserted as Petra; and every night of every day it is an emptiness. This building, too, which of week-days hums with industry and life, at nightfall echoes with sheer vacancy, and all through Sunday is forlorn. And here Bartleby makes his home; sole spectator of a solitude which he has seen all populous—a sort of innocent and transformed Marius brooding among the ruins of Carthage!

For the first time in my life a feeling of overpowering stinging melancholy seized me. Before, I had never experienced aught but a not unpleasing sadness. The bond of a common humanity now drew me irresistibly to gloom. A fraternal melancholy! For both I and Bartleby were sons of Adam. I remembered the bright silks and sparkling faces I had seen that day, in gala trim, swan-like sailing down the Mississippi of Broadway; and I contrasted them with the pallid copyist, and thought to myself, Ah, happiness courts the light, so we deem the world is gay; but misery hides aloof, so we deem that misery there is none. These sad fancyings—chimeras, doubtless, of a sick and silly brain—led on to other and more special thoughts, concerning the eccentricities of Bartleby. Presentiments of strange discoveries hovered round me. The scrivener's pale form appeared to me laid out, among uncaring strangers, in its shivering winding-sheet.

Suddenly I was attracted by Bartleby's closed desk, the key in open sight left in the lock.

I mean no mischief, seek the gratification of no heartless curiosity, thought I; besides, the desk is mine, and its contents, too, so I will make bold to look within. Everything was methodically arranged, the papers smoothly placed. The pigeon-holes were deep, and removing the files of documents, I groped into their recesses. Presently I felt something there, and dragged it out. It was an old bandanna handkerchief, heavy and knotted. I opened it, and saw it was a savings bank.

I now recalled all the quiet mysteries which I had noted in the man. I remembered that he never spoke but to answer; that, though at intervals he had considerable time to himself, yet I had never seen him reading—no, not even a newspaper; that for long periods he would stand looking out, at his pale window behind the screen, upon the dead brick wall; I was quite sure he never visited any refectory or eating-house; while his pale face clearly indicated that he never drank beer like Turkey, or tea and coffee even, like other men; that he never went anywhere in particular that I could learn; never went out for a walk, unless, indeed, that was the case at present; that he had declined telling who he was, or whence he came, or whether he had any relatives in the world; that though so thin and pale, he never complained of ill-health. And more than all, I remembered a certain unconscious air of pallid—how shall I call it?—of pallid haughtiness, say, or rather an austere reserve about him, which had positively awed me into my tame compliance with his eccentricities, when I had feared to ask him to do the slightest incidental thing for me, even though I might know, from his long-continued motionlessness, that behind his screen he must be standing in one of those dead-wall reveries of his.

Revolving all these things, and coupling them with the recently discovered fact, that he made my office his constant abiding place and home, and not forgetful of his morbid moodiness; revolving all these things, a prudential feeling began to steal over me. My first emotions had been those of pure melancholy and sincerest pity; but just in proportion as the forlornness of Bartleby grew and grew to my imagination, did that same melancholy merge into fear, that pity into repulsion. So true it is, and so terrible, too, that up to a certain point the thought or sight of misery enlists our best affections; but, in certain special cases, beyond that point it does not. They err who would assert that invariably this is owing to the inherent selfishness of the human heart. It rather proceeds from a certain hopelessness of remedying excessive and organic ill. To a sensitive being, pity is not seldom pain. And when at last it is perceived that such pity cannot lead to effectual succor, common sense bids the soul be rid of it. What I saw that morning persuaded me that the scrivener was the victim of innate and incurable disorder. I might give alms to his body; but his body did not pain him; it was his soul that suffered, and his soul I could not reach.

I did not accomplish the purpose of going to Trinity

Church that morning. Somehow, the things I had seen disqualified me for the time from church-going. I walked homeward, thinking what I would do with Bartleby. Finally, I resolved upon this—I would put certain calm questions to him the next morning, touching his history, etc., and if he declined to answer them openly and unreservedly (and I supposed he would prefer not), then to give him a twenty-dollar bill over and above whatever I might owe him, and tell him his services were no longer required; but that if in any other way I could assist him, I would be happy to do so, especially if he desired to return to his native place, wherever that might be, I would willingly help to defray the expenses. Moreover, if, after reaching home, he found himself at any time in want of aid, a letter from him would be sure of a reply.

The next morning came.

"Bartleby," said I, gently calling to him behind his screen.

No reply.

"Bartleby," said I, in a still gentler tone, "come here; I am not going to ask you to do anything you would prefer not to do—I simply wish to speak to you."

Upon this he noiselessly slid into view.

"Will you tell me, Bartleby, where you were born?"

"I would prefer not to."

"Will you tell me *anything* about yourself?"

"I would prefer not to."

"But what reasonable objection can you have to speak to me? I feel friendly towards you."

He did not look at me while I spoke, but kept his glance fixed upon my bust of Cicero, which, as I then sat, was directly behind me, some six inches, above my head.

"What is your answer, Bartleby?" said I, after waiting a considerable time for a reply, during which his countenance remained immovable, only there was the faintest conceivable tremor of the white attenuated mouth.

"At present I prefer to give no answer," he said, and retired into his hermitage.

It was rather weak in me I confess, but his manner, on this occasion, nettled me. Not only did there seem to lurk in it a certain calm disdain, but his perverseness seemed ungrateful, considering the undeniable good usage and indulgence he had received from me.

Again I sat ruminating what I should do. Mortified as

I was at his behavior, and resolved as I had been to dismiss him when I entered my office, nevertheless I strangely felt something superstitious knocking at my heart, and forbidding me to carry out my purpose, and denouncing me for a villain if I dared to breathe one bitter word against this forlornest of mankind. At last, familiarly drawing my chair behind his screen, I sat down and said: "Bartleby, never mind, then, about revealing your history; but let me entreat you, as a friend, to comply as far as may be with the usages of this office. Say now, you will help to examine papers to-morrow or next day: in short, say now, that in a day or two you will begin to be a little reasonable:—say so, Bartleby."

"At present I would prefer not to be a little reasonable," was his mildly cadaverous reply.

Just then the folding-doors opened, and Nippers approached. He seemed suffering from an unusually bad night's rest, induced by severer indigestion than common. He overheard those final words of Bartleby.

"*Prefer not,* eh?" gritted Nippers—"I'd *prefer* him, if I were you, sir," addressing me—"I'd *prefer* him; I'd give him preferences, the stubborn mule! What is it, sir, pray, that he *prefers* not to do now?"

Bartleby moved not a limb.

"Mr. Nippers," said I, "I'd prefer that you would withdraw for the present."

Somehow, of late, I had got into the way of involuntarily using this word "prefer" upon all sorts of not exactly suitable occasions. And I trembled to think that my contact with the scrivener had already and seriously affected me in a mental way. And what further and deeper aberration might it not yet produce? This apprehension had not been without efficacy in determining me to summary measures.

As Nippers, looking very sour and sulky, was departing, Turkey blandly and deferentially approached.

"With submission, sir," said he, "yesterday I was thinking about Bartleby here, and I think that if he would but prefer to take a quart of good ale every day, it would do much towards mending him, and enabling him to assist in examining his papers."

"So you have got the word, too," said I, slightly excited.

"With submission, what word, sir?" asked Turkey, respectfully crowding himself into the contracted space behind the screen, and by so doing, making me jostle the scrivener. "What word, sir?"

"I would prefer to be left alone here," said Bartleby, as if offended at being mobbed in his privacy.

"*That's* the word, Turkey," said I—"*that's* it."

"Oh, *prefer?* oh yes—queer word. I never use it myself. But, sir, as I was saying, if he would but prefer—"

"Turkey," interrupted I, "you will please withdraw."

"Oh certainly, sir, if you prefer that I should."

As he opened the folding-door to retire, Nippers at his desk caught a glimpse of me, and asked whether I would prefer to have a certain paper copied on blue paper or white. He did not in the least roguishly accent the word "prefer." It was plain that it involuntarily rolled from his tongue. I thought to myself, surely I must get rid of a demented man, who already has in some degree turned the tongues, if not the heads, of myself and clerks. But I thought it prudent not to break the dismission at once.

The next day I noticed that Bartleby did nothing but stand at his window in his dead-wall revery. Upon asking him why he did not write, he said that he had decided upon doing no more writing.

"Why, how now? what next?" exclaimed I, "do no more writing?"

"No more."

"And what is the reason?"

"Do you not see the reason for yourself?" he indifferently replied.

I looked steadfastly at him, and perceived that his eyes looked dull and glazed. Instantly it occurred to me, that his unexampled diligence in copying by his dim window for the first few weeks of his stay with me might have temporarily impaired his vision.

I was touched. I said something in condolence with him. I hinted that of course he did wisely in abstaining from writing for a while; and urged him to embrace that opportunity of taking wholesome exercise in the open air. This, however, he did not do. A few days after this, my other clerks being absent, and being in a great hurry to dispatch certain letters by the mail, I thought that, having nothing else earthly to do, Bartleby would surely be less inflexible than usual, and carry these letters to the post-office. But he blankly declined. So, much to my inconvenience, I went myself.

Still added days went by. Whether Bartleby's eyes improved or not, I could not say. To all appearance, I thought they did. But when I asked him if they did, he vouchsafed no answer. At all events, he would do no copying. At last, in reply to my urgings, he informed me that he had permanently given up copying.

"What!" exclaimed I; "suppose your eyes should get entirely well—better than ever before—would you not copy then?"

"I have given up copying," he answered, and slid aside.

He remained as ever, a fixture in my chamber. Nay—if that were possible—he became still more of a fixture than before. What was to be done? He would do nothing in the office; why should he stay there? In plain fact, he had now become a millstone to me, not only useless as a necklace, but afflictive to bear. Yet I was sorry for him. I speak less than truth when I say that, on his own account, he occasioned me uneasiness. If he would but have named a single relative or friend, I would instantly have written, and urged their taking the poor fellow away to some convenient retreat. But he seemed alone, absolutely alone in the universe. A bit of wreck in the mid-Atlantic. At length, necessities connected with my business tyrannized over all other considerations. Decently as I could, I told Bartleby that in six days' time he must unconditionally leave the office. I warned him to take measures, in the interval, for procuring some other abode. I offered to assist him in this endeavor, if he himself would but take the first step towards a removal. "And when you finally quit me, Bartleby," added I, "I shall see that you go not away entirely unprovided. Six days from this hour, remember."

At the expiration of that period, I peeped behind the screen, and lo! Bartleby was there.

I buttoned up my coat, balanced myself; advanced slowly towards him, touched his shoulder, and said, "The time has come; you must quit this place; I am sorry for you; here is money; but you must go."

"I would prefer not," he replied, with his back still towards me.

"You *must*."

He remained silent.

Now I had an unbounded confidence in this man's common honesty. He had frequently restored to me sixpences and shillings carelessly dropped upon the floor, for I am apt to be very reckless in such shirt-button affairs. The proceeding, then, which followed will not be deemed extraordinary.

"Bartleby," said I, "I owe you twelve dollars on account; here are thirty-two; the odd twenty are yours—Will you take it?" and I handed the bills towards him.

But he made no motion.

"I will leave them here, then," putting them under a weight on the table. Then taking my hat and cane and going to the door, I tranquilly turned and added—"After you have removed your things from these offices, Bartleby, you will of course lock the door—since every one is now gone for the day but you—and if you please, slip your key underneath the mat, so that I may have it in the morning. I shall not see you again; so good-bye to you. If, hereafter, in your new place of abode, I can be of any service to you, do not fail to advise me by letter. Good-bye, Bartleby, and fare you well."

But he answered not a word; like the last column of some ruined temple, he remained standing mute and solitary in the middle of the otherwise deserted room.

As I walked home in a pensive mood, my vanity got the better of my pity. I could not but highly plume myself on my masterly management in getting rid of Bartleby. Masterly I call it, and such it must appear to any dispassionate thinker. The beauty of my procedure seemed to consist in its perfect quietness. There was no vulgar bullying, no bravado of any sort, no choleric hectoring, and striding to and fro across the apartment, jerking out vehement commands for Bartleby to bundle himself off with his beggarly traps. Nothing of the kind. Without loudly bidding Bartleby depart—as an inferior genius might have done—I *assumed* the ground that depart he must; and upon that assumption built all I had to say. The more I thought over my procedure, the more I was charmed with it. Nevertheless, next morning, upon awakening, I had my doubts—I had somehow slept off the fumes of vanity. One of the coolest and wisest hours a man has, is just after he awakes in the morning. My procedure seemed as sagacious as ever—but only in theory. How it would prove in practice—there was the rub. It was truly a beautiful thought to have assumed Bartleby's departure; but, after all, that assumption was simply my own, and none of Bartleby's. The great point was, not whether I had assumed that he would quit me, but whether he would prefer so to do. He was more a man of preferences than assumptions.

After breakfast, I walked down town, arguing the probabilities *pro* and *con*. One moment I thought it would prove a miserable failure, and Bartleby would be found all alive at my office as usual; the next moment it seemed certain that I should find his chair empty. And so I kept veering about. At the corner of Broadway and Canal Street, I saw quite an excited group of people standing in earnest conversation.

"I'll take odds he doesn't," said a voice as I passed.

"Doesn't go?—done!" said I, "put up your money."

I was instinctively putting my hand in my pocket to produce my own, when I remembered that this was an election day. The words I had overheard bore no reference to Bartleby, but to the success or non-success of some candidate for the mayoralty. In my intent frame of mind, I had, as it were, imagined that all Broadway shared in my excitement, and were debating the same question with me. I passed on, very thankful that the uproar of the street screened my momentary absent-mindedness.

As I had intended, I was earlier than usual at my office door. I stood listening for a moment. All was still. He must be gone. I tried the knob. The door was locked. Yes, my procedure had worked to a charm; he indeed must be vanished. Yet a certain melancholy mixed with this: I was almost sorry for my brilliant success. I was fumbling under the door mat for the key, which Bartleby was to have left there for me, when accidentally my knee knocked against a panel, producing a summoning sound, and in response a voice came to me from within —"Not yet; I am occupied."

It was Bartleby.

I was thunderstruck. For an instant I stood like the man who, pipe in mouth, was killed one cloudless afternoon long ago in Virginia, by summer lightning; at his own warm open window he was killed, and remained leaning out there upon the dreamy afternoon, till some one touched him, when he fell.

"Not gone!" I murmured at last. But again obeying that wondrous ascendancy which the inscrutable scrivener had over me, and from which ascendancy, for all my chafing, I could not completely escape, I slowly went down stairs and out into the street, and while walking round the block, considered what I should next do in this unheard-of perplexity. Turn the man out by an actual thrusting I could not; to drive him away by calling him hard names would not do; calling in the police was an unpleasant idea; and yet, permit him to enjoy his cadaverous triumph over me—this, too, I could not think of. What was to be done? or, if nothing could be done, was there anything further that I could *assume* in the matter? Yes, as before I had prospectively assumed that Bartleby would depart, so now I might retrospectively assume that departed he was. In the legitimate carrying out of this assumption, I might enter my office in a great hurry, and pretending not to see Bartleby at all, walk straight against him as if he were air. Such a proceeding would in a singular degree have the appearance of a home-thrust. It was hardly possible that Bartleby could withstand such an application of the doctrine of assumptions. But upon second thoughts the success of the plan seemed rather dubious. I resolved to argue the matter over with him again.

"Bartleby," said I, entering the office, with a quietly severe expression, "I am seriously displeased. I am pained, Bartleby. I had thought better of you. I had imagined you of such a gentlemanly organization, that in any delicate dilemma a slight hint would suffice—in short, an assumption. But it appears I am deceived. Why," I added, unaffectedly starting, "you have not even touched that money yet," pointing to it, just where I had left it the evening previous.

He answered nothing.

"Will you, or will you not, quit me?" I now demanded in a sudden passion, advancing close to him.

"I would prefer *not* to quit you," he replied, gently emphasizing the *not*.

"What earthly right have you to stay here? Do you pay any rent? Do you pay my taxes? Or is this property yours?"

He answered nothing.

"Are you ready to go on and write now? Are your eyes recovered? Could you copy a small paper for me this morning? or help examine a few lines? or step round to the post-office? In a word, will you do anything at all, to give a coloring to your refusal to depart the premises?"

He silently retired into his hermitage.

I was now in such a state of nervous resentment that I

thought it but prudent to check myself at present from further demonstrations. Bartleby and I were alone. I remembered the tragedy of the unfortunate Adams and the still more unfortunate Colt in the solitary office of the latter; and how poor Colt, being dreadfully incensed by Adams, and imprudently permitting himself to get wildly excited, was at unawares hurried into his fatal act—an act which certainly no man could possibly deplore more than the actor himself. Often it had occurred to me in my ponderings upon the subject that had that altercation taken place in the public street, or at a private residence, it would not have terminated as it did. It was the circumstance of being alone in a solitary office, up stairs, of a building entirely unhallowed by humanizing domestic associations —an uncarpeted office, doubtless, of a dusty, haggard sort of appearance—this it must have been, which greatly helped to enhance the irritable desperation of the hapless Colt.

But when this old Adam of resentment rose in me and tempted me concerning Bartleby, I grappled him and threw him. How? Why, simply by recalling the divine injunction: "A new commandment give I unto you, that ye love one another." Yes, this it was that saved me. Aside from higher considerations, charity often operates as a vastly wise and prudent principle—a great safeguard to its possessor. Men have committed murder for jealousy's sake, and anger's sake, and hatred's sake, and selfishness' sake, and spiritual pride's sake; but no man, that ever I heard of, ever committed a diabolical murder for sweet charity's sake. Mere self-interest, then, if no better motive can be enlisted, should, especially with high-tempered men, prompt all beings to charity and philanthropy. At any rate, upon the occasion in question, I strove to drown my exasperated feelings towards the scrivener by benevolently construing his conduct. Poor fellow, poor fellow! thought I, he don't mean anything; and besides, he has seen hard times, and ought to be indulged.

I endeavored, also, immediately to occupy myself, and at the same time to comfort my despondency. I tried to fancy, that in the course of the morning, at such time as might prove agreeable to him, Bartleby, of his own free accord, would emerge from his hermitage and take up some decided line of march in the direction of the door. But no. Half-past twelve o'clock came; Turkey began to glow in the face, overturn his inkstand, and become generally obstreperous; Nippers abated down into quietude and courtesy; Ginger Nut munched his noon apple; and Bartleby remained standing at his window in one of his profoundest dead-wall reveries. Will it be credited? Ought I to acknowledge it? That afternoon I left the office without saying one further word to him.

Some days now passed, during which, at leisure intervals I looked a little into "Edwards on the Will," and "Priestley on Necessity." Under the circumstances, those books induced a salutary feeling. Gradually I slid into the persuasion that these troubles of mine, touching the scrivener, had been all predestinated from eternity, and Bartleby was billeted upon me for some mysterious purpose of an all-wise Providence, which it was not for a mere mortal like me to fathom. Yes, Bartleby, stay there behind your screen, thought I; I shall persecute you no more; you are harmless and noiseless as any of these old chairs; in short, I never feel so private as when I know you are here. At last I see it, I feel it; I penetrate to the predestinated purpose of my life. I am content. Others may have loftier parts to enact; but my mission in this world, Bartleby, is to furnish you with office-room for such period as you may see fit to remain.

I believe that this wise and blessed frame of mind would have continued with me, had it not been for the unsolicited and uncharitable remarks obtruded upon me by my professional friends who visited the rooms. But thus it often is, that the constant friction of illiberal minds wears out at last the best resolves of the more generous. Though to be sure, when I reflected upon it, it was not strange that people entering my office should be struck by the peculiar aspect of the unaccountable Bartleby, and so be tempted to throw out some sinister observations concerning him. Sometimes an attorney, having business with me, and calling at my office, and finding no one but the scrivener there, would undertake to obtain some sort of precise information from him touching my whereabouts; but without heeding his idle talk, Bartleby would remain standing immovable in the middle of the room. So after contemplating him in that position for a time, the attorney would depart, no wiser than he came.

Also, when a reference was going on, and the room full of lawyers and witnesses, and business driving fast,

some deeply occupied legal gentleman present, seeing
Bartleby wholly unemployed, would request him to run
round to his (the legal gentleman's) office and fetch some
papers for him. Thereupon, Bartleby would tranquilly
decline, and yet remain idle as before. Then the lawyer
would give a great stare, and turn to me. And what
could I say? At last I was made aware that all through the
circle of my professional acquaintance, a whisper of
wonder was running round, having reference to the strange
creature I kept at my office. This worried me very much.
And as the idea came upon me of his possibly turning out
a long-lived man, and keep occupying my chambers, and
denying my authority; and perplexing my visitors; and
scandalizing my professional reputation; and casting a
general gloom over the premises; keeping soul and body
together to the last upon his savings (for doubtless he spent
but half a dime a day), and in the end perhaps outlive
me, and claim possession of my office by right of his perpetual occupancy: as all these dark anticipations crowded
upon me more and more, and my friends continually intruded their relentless remarks upon the apparition in
my room; a great change was wrought in me. I resolved to
gather all my faculties together, and forever rid me of
this intolerable incubus.

Ere revolving any complicated project, however, adapted
to this end, I first simply suggested to Bartleby the pro-
priety of his permanent departure. In a calm and serious
tone, I commended the idea to his careful and mature consideration. But, having taken three days to meditate upon
it, he apprised me, that his original determination remained
the same; in short, that he still preferred to abide with me.

What shall I do? I now said to myself, buttoning up my
coat to the last button. What shall I do? what ought I to
do? what does conscience say I *should* do with this man,
or, rather, ghost. Rid myself of him, I must; go, he shall.
But how? You will not thrust him, the poor, pale, passive
mortal—you will not thrust such a helpless creature out
of your door? you will not dishonor yourself by such
cruelty? No, I will not, I cannot do that. Rather would I
let him live and die here, and then mason up his remains
in the wall. What, then, will you do? For all your coaxing,
he will not budge. Bribes he leaves under your own paper-

weight on your table; in short, it is quite plain that he prefers to cling to you.

Then something severe, something unusual, must be done. What! surely you will not have him collared by a constable, and commit his innocent pallor to the common jail? And upon what ground could you procure such a thing to be done?—a vagrant, is he? What! he a vagrant, a wanderer, who refuses to budge? It is because he will *not* be a vagrant, then, that you seek to count him *as* a vagrant. That is too absurd. No visible means of support: there I have him. Wrong again: for indubitably he *does* support himself, and that is the only unanswerable proof that any man can show of his possessing the means so to do. No more, then. Since he will not quit me, I must quit him. I will change my offices; I will move elsewhere, and give him fair notice, that if I find him on my new premises I will then proceed against him as a common trespasser.

Acting accordingly, next day I thus addressed him: "I find these chambers too far from the City Hall; the air is unwholesome. In a word, I propose to remove my offices next week, and shall no longer require your services. I tell you this now, in order that you may seek another place."

He made no reply, and nothing more was said.

On the appointed day I engaged carts and men, proceeded to my chambers, and, having but little furniture, everything was removed in a few hours. Throughout, the scrivener remained standing behind the screen, which I directed to be removed the last thing. It was withdrawn; and, being folded up like a huge folio, left him the motionless occupant of a naked room. I stood in the entry watching him a moment, while something from within me upbraided me.

I re-entered, with my hand in my pocket—and—and my heart in my mouth.

"Good-bye, Bartleby; I am going—good-bye, and God some way bless you; and take that," slipping something in his hand. But it dropped upon the floor, and then—strange to say—I tore myself from him whom I had so longed to be rid of.

Established in my new quarters, for a day or two I

kept the door locked, and started at every footfall in the passages. When I returned to my rooms, after any little absence, I would pause at the threshold for an instant, and attentively listen, ere applying my key. But these fears were needless. Bartleby never came nigh me.

I thought all was going well, when a perturbed-looking stranger visited me, inquiring whether I was the person who had recently occupied rooms at No. — Wall Street.

Full of forebodings, I replied that I was.

"Then, sir," said the stranger, who proved a lawyer, "you are responsible for the man you left there. He refuses to do any copying; he refuses to do anything; he says he prefers not to; and he refuses to quit the premises."

"I am very sorry, sir," said I, with assumed tranquillity, but an inward tremor, "but, really, the man you allude to is nothing to me—he is no relation or apprentice of mine, that you should hold me responsible for him."

"In mercy's name, who is he?"

"I certainly cannot inform you. I know nothing about him. Formerly I employed him as a copyist; but he has done nothing for me now for some time past."

"I shall settle him, then—good morning, sir."

Several days passed, and I heard nothing more; and, though I often felt a charitable prompting to call at the place and see poor Bartleby, yet a certain squeamishness, of I know not what, withheld me.

All is over with him, by this time, thought I, at last, when, through another week, no further intelligence reached me. But, coming to my room the day after, I found several persons waiting at my door in a high state of nervous excitement.

"That's the man—here he comes," cried the foremost one, whom I recognized as the lawyer who had previously called upon me alone.

"You must take him away, sir, at once," cried a portly person among them, advancing upon me, and whom I knew to be the landlord of No. — Wall Street. "These gentlemen, my tenants, cannot stand it any longer; Mr. B——," pointing to the lawyer, "has turned him out of his room, and he now persists in haunting the building generally, sitting upon the banisters of the stairs by day, and sleeping in the entry by night. Everybody is concerned; clients are leaving the offices; some fears are entertained of a mob; something you must do, and that without delay."

Aghast at this torrent, I fell back before it, and would fain have locked myself in my new quarters. In vain I persisted that Bartleby was nothing to me—no more than to any one else. In vain—I was the last person known to have anything to do with him, and they held me to the terrible account. Fearful, then, of being exposed in the papers (as one person present obscurely threatened), I considered the matter, and, at length, said, that if the lawyer would give me a confidential interview with the scrivener, in his (the lawyer's) own room, I would, that afternoon, strive my best to rid them of the nuisance they complained of.

Going up stairs to my old haunt, there was Bartleby silently sitting upon the banister at the landing.

"What are you doing here, Bartleby?" said I.

"Sitting upon the banister," he mildly replied.

I motioned him into the lawyer's room, who then left us.

"Bartleby," said I, "are you aware that you are the cause of great tribulation to me, by persisting in occupying the entry after being dismissed from the office?"

No answer.

"Now one of two things must take place. Either you must do something, or something must be done to you. Now what sort of business would you like to engage in? Would you like to re-engage in copying for some one?"

"No; I would prefer not to make any change."

"Would you like a clerkship in a dry-goods store?"

"There is too much confinement about that. No, I would not like a clerkship; but I am not particular."

"Too much confinement," I cried, "why, you keep yourself confined all the time!"

"I would prefer not to take a clerkship," he rejoined, as if to settle that little item at once.

"How would a bar-tender's business suit you? There is no trying of the eye-sight in that."

"I would not like it at all; though, as I said before, I am not particular."

His unwonted wordiness inspirited me. I returned to the charge.

"Well, then, would you like to travel through the country collecting bills for the merchants? That would improve your health."

"No, I would prefer to be doing something else."

"How, then, would going as a companion to Europe, to entertain some young gentleman with your conversation—how would that suit you?"

"Not at all. It does not strike me that there is anything definite about that. I like to be stationary. But I am not particular."

"Stationary you shall be, then," I cried, now losing all patience, and, for the first time in all my exasperating connection with him, fairly flying into a passion. "If you do not go away from these premises before night, I shall feel bound—indeed, I *am* bound—to—to—to quit the premises myself!" I rather absurdly concluded, knowing not with what possible threat to try to frighten his immobility into compliance. Despairing of all further efforts, I was precipitately leaving him, when a final thought occurred to me—one which had not been wholly unindulged before.

"Bartleby," said I, in the kindest tone I could assume under such exciting circumstances, "will you go home with me now—not to my office, but my dwelling—and remain there till we can conclude upon some convenient arrangement for you at our leisure? Come, let us start now, right away."

"No: at present I would prefer not to make any change at all."

I answered nothing; but, effectually dodging every one by the suddenness and rapidity of my flight, rushed from the building, ran up Wall Street towards Broadway, and, jumping into the first omnibus, was soon removed from pursuit. As soon as tranquillity returned, I distinctly perceived that I had now done all that I possibly could, both in respect to the demands of the landlord and his tenants, and with regard to my own desire and sense of duty, to benefit Bartleby, and shield him from rude persecution. I now strove to be entirely care-free and quiescent; and my conscience justified me in the attempt; though, indeed, it was not so successful as I could have wished. So fearful was I of being again hunted out by the incensed landlord and his exasperated tenants, that, surrendering my business to Nippers for a few days, I drove about the upper part of the town and through the suburbs, in my rockaway; crossed over to Jersey City and Hoboken, and paid fugitive visits to Manhattanville and Astoria. In fact, I almost lived in my rockaway for the time.

When again I entered my office, lo, a note from the landlord lay upon the desk. I opened it with trembling hands. It informed me that the writer had sent to the police, and had Bartleby removed to the Tombs as a vagrant. Moreover, since I knew more about him than any one else, he wished me to appear at that place, and make a suitable statement of the facts. These tidings had a conflicting effect upon me. At first I was indignant; but at last, almost approved. The landlord's energetic, summary disposition, had led him to adopt a procedure which I do not think I would have decided upon myself; and yet, as a last resort, under such peculiar circumstances, it seemed the only plan.

As I afterwards learned, the poor scrivener, when told that he must be conducted to the Tombs, offered not the slightest obstacle, but, in his pale, unmoving way, silently acquiesced.

Some of the compassionate and curious by-standers joined the party; and headed by one of the constables arm-in-arm with Bartleby, the silent procession filed its way through all the noise, and heat, and joy of the roaring thoroughfares at noon.

The same day I received the note, I went to the Tombs, or, to speak more properly, the Halls of Justice. Seeking the right officer, I stated the purpose of my call, and was informed that the individual I described was, indeed, within. I then assured the functionary that Bartleby was a perfectly honest man, and greatly to be compassionated, however unaccountably eccentric. I narrated all I knew, and closed by suggesting the idea of letting him remain in as indulgent confinement as possible, till something less harsh might be done—though, indeed, I hardly knew what. At all events, if nothing else could be decided upon, the alms-house must receive him. I then begged to have an interview.

Being under no disgraceful charge, and quite serene and harmless in all his ways, they had permitted him freely to wander about the prison, and, especially, in the inclosed grass-platted yards thereof. And so I found him there, standing all alone in the quietest of the yards, his face towards a high wall, while all around, from the narrow slits of the jail windows, I though I saw peering out upon him the eyes of murderers and thieves.

"Bartleby!"

"I know you," he said, without looking round—"and I want nothing to say to you."

"It was not I that brought you here, Bartleby," said I, keenly pained at his implied suspicion. "And to you, this should not be so vile a place. Nothing reproachful attaches to you by being here. And see, it is not so sad a place as one might think. Look, there is the sky, and here is the grass."

"I know where I am," he replied, but would say nothing more, and so I left him.

As I entered the corridor again, a broad meat-like man, in an apron, accosted me, and, jerking his thumb over his shoulder, said—"Is that your friend?"

"Yes."

"Does he want to starve? If he does, let him live on the prison fare, that's all."

"Who are you?" asked I, not knowing what to make of such an unofficially speaking person in such a place.

"I am the grub-man. Such gentlemen as have friends here, hire me to provide them with something good to eat."

"Is this so?" said I, turning to the turnkey.

He said it was.

"Well, then," said I, slipping some silver into the grub-man's hands (for so they called him), "I want you to give particular attention to my friend there; let him have the best dinner you can get. And you must be as polite to him as possible."

"Introduce me, will you?" said the grub-man, looking at me with an expression which seemed to say he was all impatience for an opportunity to give a specimen of his breeding.

Thinking it would prove of benefit to the scrivener, I acquiesced; and, asking the grub-man his name, went up with him to Bartleby.

"Bartleby, this is a friend; you will find him very useful to you."

"Your sarvant, sir, your sarvant," said the grub-man, making a low salutation behind his apron. "Hope you find it pleasant here, sir; nice grounds—cool apartments—hope you'll stay with us some time—try to make it agreeable. What will you have for dinner to-day?"

"I prefer not to dine to-day," said Bartleby, turning away.

"It would disagree with me; I am unused to dinners." So saying, he slowly moved to the other side of the inclosure, and took up a position fronting the dead-wall.

"How's this?" said the grub-man, addressing me with a stare of astonishment. "He's odd, ain't he?"

"I think he is a little deranged," said I, sadly.

"Deranged? deranged is it? Well, now, upon my word, I thought that friend of yourn was a gentleman forger; they are always pale and genteel-like, them forgers. I can't help pity 'em—can't help it, sir. Did you know Monroe Edwards?" he added, touchingly, and paused. Then, laying his hand piteously on my shoulder, sighed, "he died of consumption at Sing-Sing. So you weren't acquainted with Monroe?"

"No, I was never socially acquainted with any forgers. But I cannot stop longer. Look to my friend yonder. You will not lose by it. I will see you again."

Some few days after this, I again obtained admission to the Tombs, and went through the corridors in quest of Bartleby; but without finding him.

"I saw him coming from his cell not long ago," said a turnkey, "may be he's gone to loiter in the yards."

So I went in that direction.

"Are you looking for the silent man?" said another turnkey, passing me. "Yonder he lies—sleeping in the yard there. 'Tis not twenty minutes since I saw him lie down."

The yard was entirely quiet. It was not accessible to the common prisoners. The surrounding walls, of amazing thickness, kept off all sounds behind them. The Egyptian character of the masonry weighed upon me with its gloom. But a soft imprisoned turf grew under foot. The heart of the eternal pyramids, it seemed, wherein, by some strange magic, through the clefts, grass-seed, dropped by birds, had sprung.

Strangely huddled at the base of the wall, his knees drawn up, and lying on his side, his head touching the cold stones, I saw the wasted Bartleby. But nothing stirred. I paused; then went close up to him; stooped over, and saw that his dim eyes were open; otherwise he seemed profoundly sleeping. Something prompted me to touch him. I felt his hand, when a tingling shiver ran up my arm and down my spine to my feet.

The round face of the grub-man peered upon me now. "His dinner is ready. Won't he dine to-day, either? Or does he live without dining?"

"Lives without dining," said I, and closed the eyes.

"Eh!—He's asleep, ain't he?"

"With kings and counselors," murmured I.

There would seem little need for proceeding further in this history. Imagination will readily supply the meager recital of poor Bartleby's interment. But, ere parting with the reader, let me say, that if this little narrative has sufficiently interested him, to awaken curiosity as to who Bartleby was, and what manner of life he led prior to the present narrator's making his acquaintance, I can only reply, that in such curiosity I fully share, but am wholly unable to gratify it. Yet here I hardly know whether I should divulge one little item of rumor, which came to my ear a few months after the scrivener's decease. Upon what basis it rested, I could never ascertain; and hence, how true it is I cannot now tell. But, inasmuch as this vague report has not been without a certain suggestive interest to me, however sad, it may prove the same with some others; and so I will briefly mention it. The report was this: that Bartleby had been a subordinate clerk in the Dead Letter Office at Washington, from which he had been suddenly removed by a change in the administration. When I think over this rumor, hardly can I express the emotions which seize me. Dead letters! does it not sound like dead men? Conceive a man by nature and misfortune prone to a pallid hopelessness, can any business seem more fitted to heighten it than that of continually handling these dead letters, and assorting them for the flames? For by the cart-load they are annually burned. Sometimes from out the folded paper the pale clerk takes a ring—the finger it was meant for, perhaps, moulders in the grave; a bank-note sent in swiftest charity—he whom it would relieve, nor eats nor hungers any more; pardon for those who died despairing; hope for those who died unhoping; good tidings for those who died stifled by unrelieved calamities. On errands of life, these letters speed to death.

Ah, Bartleby! Ah, humanity!

1853

Billy Budd
Sailor

(An inside narrative)*

Dedicated to
Jack Chase, Englishman

wherever that great heart may now be, here on earth
or harboured in paradise. Captain of the maintop in
the year 1843 in the U.S. Frigate United States.

[1]

In the time before steamships, or then more frequently than now, a stroller along the docks of any considerable sea-port would occasionally have his attention arrested by a group of bronzed mariners, man-of-war's men or merchant-sailors in holiday attire ashore on liberty. In certain instances they would flank, or, like a body-guard quite surround some superior figure of their own class, moving along with them like Aldebaran among the lesser lights of his constellation. That signal object was the "Handsome Sailor" of the less prosaic time alike of the military and merchant navies. With no perceptible trace of the vainglorious about him, rather with the off-hand unaffectedness of natural regality, he seemed to accept the spontaneous homage of his shipmates. A somewhat remarkable instance recurs to me. In Liverpool, now half a century ago, I saw under the shadow of the great dingy street-wall of Prince's Dock (an obstruction long since removed) a common sailor, so intensely black that he must needs have been a native African of the unadulterate blood of Ham. A symmetric figure much above the average height. The two ends of a gay silk handkerchief thrown loose about

---

* *Billy Budd*, incomplete when Melville died, has had an intricate history. Raymond M. Weaver was shown the manuscript by Melville's granddaughter, Elizabeth Melville Metcalf; Weaver's faulty transcription of the manuscript was in part corrected by F. Barron Freeman in 1948. Freeman's edition was in turn partly corrected by Elizabeth Treeman in 1952. Milton Stern collated the Freeman-Treeman text with the original manuscript and made a few further changes in 1958. In 1962, Harrison Hayford and Merton M. Sealts, Jr., published their exhaustive study of the manuscripts. The present text places in brackets some debatable sections left out by Hayford and Sealts.

the neck danced upon the displayed ebony of his chest; in his ears were big hoops of gold, and a Scotch Highland bonnet with a tartan band set off his shapely head.

It was a hot noon in July; and his face, lustrous with perspiration, beamed with barbaric good humor. In jovial sallies right and left, his white teeth flashing into view, he rollicked along, the centre of a company of his shipmates. These were made up of such an assortment of tribes and complexions as would have well fitted them to be marched up by Anacharsis Cloots before the bar of the first French Assembly as Representatives of the Human Race. At each spontaneous tribute rendered by the wayfarers to this black pagod of a fellow—the tribute of a pause and stare, and less frequent an exclamation,—the motley retinue showed that they took that sort of pride in the evoker of it which the Assyrian priests doubtless showed for their grand sculptured Bull when the faithful prostrated themselves.

To return.

If in some cases a bit of a nautical Murat in setting forth his person ashore, the handsome sailor of the period in question evinced nothing of the dandified Billy-be-Damn, an amusing character all but extinct now, but occasionally to be encountered, and in a form yet more amusing than the original, at the tiller of the boats on the tempestuous Erie Canal or, more likely, vaporing in the groggeries along the tow-path. Invariably a proficient in his perilous calling, he was also more or less of a mighty boxer or wrestler. It was strength and beauty. Tales of his prowess were recited. Ashore he was the champion; afloat the spokesman; on every suitable occasion always foremost. Close-reefing top-sails in a gale, there he was, astride the weather yard-arm-end, foot in the Flemish horse as "stirrup," both hands tugging at the "earring" as at a bridle, in very much the attitude of young Alexander curbing the fiery Bucephalus. A superb figure, tossed up as by the horns of Taurus against the thunderous sky, cheerily hallooing to the strenuous file along the spar.

The moral nature was seldom out of keeping with the physical make. Indeed, except as toned by the former, the comeliness and power, always attractive in masculine conjunction, hardly could have drawn the sort of honest homage the Handsome Sailor in some examples received from his less gifted associates.

Such a cynosure, at least in aspect, and something such too in nature, though with important variations made apparent as the story proceeds, was welkin-eyed Billy Budd, or Baby Budd, as more familiarly under circumstances hereafter to be given he at last came to be called, aged twenty-one, a foretopman of the British fleet toward the close of the last decade of the eighteenth century. It was not very long prior to the time of the narration that follows that he had entered the King's Service, having been impressed on the Narrow Seas from a homeward-bound English merchantman into a seventy-four outward-bound, H.M.S. *Bellipotent*;* which ship, as was not unusual in those hurried days, having been obliged to put to sea short of her proper complement of men. Plump upon Billy at first sight in the gangway the boarding officer Lieutenant Ratcliffe pounced, even before the merchantman's crew was formally mustered on the quarter-deck for his deliberate inspection. And him only he elected. For whether it was because the other men when ranged before him showed to ill advantage after Billy, or whether he had some scruples in view of the merchantman being rather short-handed, however it might be, the officer contented himself with his first spontaneous choice. To the surprise of the ship's company, though much to the Lieutenant's satisfaction, Billy made no demur. But, indeed, any demur would have been as idle as the protest of a goldfinch popped into a cage.

Noting this uncomplaining acquiescence, all but cheerful one might say, the shipmates turned a surprised glance of silent reproach at the sailor. The shipmaster was one of those worthy mortals found in every vocation, even the humbler ones—the sort of person whom everybody agrees in calling "a respectable man." And—nor so strange to report as it may appear to be—though a ploughman of the troubled waters, life-long contending with the intractable elements, there was nothing this honest soul at heart loved better than simple peace and quiet. For the rest, he was fifty or thereabouts, a little inclined to corpulence, a prepossessing face, unwhiskered, and of an agreeable color— a rather full face, humanely intelligent in expression. On

---

* Melville changed the name of the ship in only a few chapters of the manuscript before he died. The ship appears as the *Indomitable* in most of the manuscript and was so named in all editions of Billy Budd before 1962.

a fair day with a fair wind and all going well, a certain musical chime in his voice seemed to be the veritable unobstructed outcome of the innermost man. He had much prudence, much conscientiousness, and there were occasions when these virtues were the cause of overmuch disquietude in him. On a passage, so long as his craft was in any proximity to land, no sleep for Captain Graveling. He took to heart those serious responsibilities not so heavily borne by some shipmasters.

Now while Billy Budd was down in the forecastle getting his kit together, the *Bellipotent*'s lieutenant, burly and bluff, nowise disconcerted by Captain Graveling's omitting to proffer the customary hospitalities on an occasion so unwelcome to him, an omission simply caused by preoccupation of thought, unceremoniously invited himself into the cabin, and also to a flask from the spirit-locker, a receptacle which his experienced eye instantly discovered. In fact he was one of those sea-dogs in whom all the hardship and peril of naval life in the great prolonged wars of his time never impaired the natural instinct for sensuous enjoyment. His duty he always faithfully did; but duty is sometimes a dry obligation, and he was for irrigating its aridity, whensoever possible, with a fertilizing decoction of strong waters. For the cabin's proprietor there was nothing left but to play the part of the enforced host with whatever grace and alacrity were practicable. As necessary adjuncts to the flask, he silently placed tumbler and water-jug before the irrepressible guest. But excusing himself from partaking just then, he dismally watched the unembarrassed officer deliberately diluting his grog a little, then tossing it off in three swallows, pushing the empty tumbler away, yet not so far as to be beyond easy reach, at the same time settling himself in his seat and smacking his lips with high satisfaction, looking straight at the host.

These proceedings over, the Master broke the silence; and there lurked a rueful reproach in the tone of his voice; "Lieutenant, you are going to take my best man from me, the jewel of 'em."

"Yes, I know" rejoined the other, immediately drawing back the tumbler preliminary to a replenishing; "Yes, I know. Sorry."

"Beg pardon, but you don't understand, Lieutenant. See here now. Before I shipped that young fellow, my forecastle was a rat-pit of quarrels. It was black times, I tell you, aboard the *'Rights'* here. I was worried to that degree my pipe had no comfort for me. But Billy came; and it was like a Catholic priest striking peace in an Irish shindy. Not that he preached to them or said or did anything in particular; but a virtue went out of him, sugaring the sour ones. They took to him like hornets to treacle; all but the bluffer of the gang, the big shaggy chap with the fire-red whiskers. He indeed out of envy, perhaps, of the newcomer, and thinking such a 'sweet and pleasant fellow,' as he mockingly designated him to the others, could hardly have the spirit of a game-cock, must needs bestir himself in trying to get up an ugly row with him. Billy forebore with him and reasoned with him in a pleasant way—he is something like myself, lieutenant, to whom aught like a quarrel is hateful—but nothing served. So, in the second dog-watch one day the Red Whiskers in presence of the others, under pretence of showing Billy just whence a sirloin steak was cut—for the fellow had once been a butcher—insultingly gave him a dig under the ribs. Quick as lightning Billy let fly his arm. I dare say he never meant to do quite as much as he did, but anyhow he gave the burly fool a terrible drubbing. It took about half a minute, I should think. And, lord bless you, the lubber was astonished at the celerity. And will you believe it, Lieutenant, the Red Whiskers now really loves Billy—loves him, or is the biggest hypocrite that ever I heard of. But they all love him. Some of 'em do his washing, darn his old trousers for him; the carpenter is at odd times making a pretty little chest of drawers for him. Anybody will do anything for Billy Budd; and it's the happy family here. But now, Lieutenant, if that young fellow goes—I know how it will be aboard the *'Rights.'* Not again very soon shall I, coming up from dinner, lean over the capstan smoking a quiet pipe—no, not very soon again, I think. Ay, Lieutenant, you are going to take away the jewel of 'em; you are going to take away my peacemaker!" And with that the good soul had really some ado in checking a rising sob.

"Well," said the officer who had listened with amused interest to all this, and now waxing merry with his tipple; "Well, blessed are the peacemakers especially the fighting peacemakers! And such are the seventy-four beauties some of which you see poking their noses out of the port-holes of yonder war-ship lying-to for me," pointing thro' the cabin window at the *Bellipotent*. "But courage! don't look so downhearted, man. Why, I pledge you in advance the royal approbation. Rest assured that His Majesty will be delighted to know that in a time when his hard tack is not sought for by sailors with such avidity as should be; a time also when some shipmasters privily resent the borrowing from them a tar or two for the service; His Majesty, I say, will be delighted to learn that *one* shipmaster at least cheer-fully surrenders to the King, the flower of his flock, a sailor who with equal loyalty makes no dissent.—But where's my beauty? Ah," looking through the cabin's open door, "here he comes; and, by Jove—lugging along his chest—Apollo with his portmanteau!—My man," stepping out to him, "you can't take that big box aboard a warship. The boxes there are mostly shot-boxes. Put your duds in a bag, lad. Boot and saddle for the cavalryman, bag and hammock for the man-of-war's man."

The transfer from chest to bag was made. And, after seeing his man into the cutter and then following him down, the lieutenant pushed off from the *Rights-of-Man*. That was the merchant-ship's name; tho' by her master and crew abbreviated in sailor fashion into *The Rights*. The hard-headed Dundee owner was a staunch admirer of Thomas Paine whose book in rejoinder to Burke's arraign-ment of the French Revolution had then been published for some time and had gone everywhere. In christening his vessel after the title of Paine's volume, the man of Dundee was something like his contemporary shipowner, Stephen Girard of Philadelphia, whose sympathies, alike with his native land and its liberal philosophers, he evinced by naming his ships after Voltaire, Diderot, and so forth.

But now, when the boat swept under the merchant-man's stern, and officer and oarsmen were noting—some bitterly and others with a grin,—the name emblazoned there; just then it was that the new recruit jumped up from the bow where the coxswain had directed him to sit, and waving his hat to his silent shipmates sorrowfully looking over at him from the taffrail, bade the lads a genial good-bye. Then, making a salutation as to the ship herself, "And good-bye to you too, old *Rights of Man*."

"Down, Sir!" roared the lieutenant; instantly assuming

all the rigor of his rank, though with difficulty repressing a smile.

To be sure, Billy's action was a terrible breach of naval decorum. But in that decorum he had never been instructed; in consideration of which the lieutenant would hardly have been so energetic in reproof but for the concluding farewell to the ship. This he rather took as meant to convey a covert sally on the new recruit's part, a sly slur at impressment in general, and that of himself in especial. And yet, more likely, if satire it was in effect, it was hardly so by intention, for Billy tho' happily endowed with the gayety of high health, youth, and a free heart, was yet by no means of a satirical turn. The will to it and the sinister dexterity were alike wanting. To deal in double meanings and insinuations of any sort was quite foreign to his nature.

As to his enforced enlistment, that he seemed to take pretty much as he was wont to take any vicissitude of weather. Like the animals, though no philosopher, he was, without knowing it, practically a fatalist. And, it may be, that he rather liked this adventurous turn in his affairs, which promised an opening into novel scenes and martial excitements.

Aboard the *Bellipotent* our merchant-sailor was forthwith rated as an able-seaman and assigned to the starboard watch of the fore-top. He was soon at home in the service, not at all disliked for his unpretentious good looks and a sort of genial happy-go-lucky air. No merrier man in his mess: in marked contrast to certain other individuals included like himself among the impressed portion of the ship's company; for these when not actively employed were sometimes, and more particularly in the last dog-watch when the drawing near of twilight induced revery, apt to fall into a saddish mood which in some partook of sullenness. But they were not so young as our foretopman, and no few of them must have known a hearth of some sort; others may have had wives and children left, too probably, in uncertain circumstances, and hardly any but must have had acknowledged kith and kin, while for Billy, as will shortly be seen, his entire family was practically invested in himself.

[2]

Though our new-made foretopman was well received in the top and on the gun-decks, hardly here was he that cynosure he had previously been among those minor ship's companies of the merchant marine, with which companies only had he hitherto consorted.

He was young; and despite his all but fully developed frame, in aspect looked even younger than he really was, owing to a lingering adolescent expression in the as yet smooth face, all but feminine in purity of natural complexion, but where, thanks to his seagoing, the lily was quite suppressed and the rose had some ado visibly to flush through the tan.

To one essentially such a novice in the complexities of factitious life, the abrupt transition from his former and simpler sphere to the ampler and more knowing world of a great warship; this might well have abashed him had there been any conceit or vanity in his composition. Among her miscellaneous multitude, the *Bellipotent* mustered several individuals who, however inferior in grade, were of no common natural stamp, sailors more signally susceptive of that air which continuous martial discipline and repeated presence in battle can in some degree impart even to the average man. As the *handsome sailor,* Billy Budd's position aboard the seventy-four was something analogous to that of a rustic beauty transplanted from the provinces and brought into competition with the highborn dames of the court. But this change of circumstances he scarce noted. As little did he observe that something about him provoked an ambiguous smile in one or two harder faces among the bluejackets. Nor less unaware was he of the peculiar favorable effect his person and demeanor had upon the more intelligent gentlemen of the quarter-deck. Nor could this well have been otherwise. Cast in a mould peculiar to the finest physical examples of those Englishmen in whom the Saxon strain would seem not at all to partake of any Norman or other admixture, he showed in face that humane look of reposeful good nature which the Greek sculptor in some instances gave to his heroic strong man, Hercules. But this again was subtly modified by another and pervasive quality. The ear, small and shapely, the arch of the foot, the curve in mouth and nostril, even the indurated hand dyed to the orange-tawny of the toucan's bill, a hand telling alike of the halyards and tar-bucket; but, above all, something in the mobile expression, and every chance attitude and movement, something suggestive of a mother eminently favored by Love and the Graces; all this strangely indicated a lineage in direct contradiction to his lot. The mysteriousness here, became less mysterious through a matter-of-fact elicited when Billy, at the capstan, was being formally mustered into the service. Asked by the officer, a small brisk little gentleman, as it chanced among other questions, his place of birth, he replied, "Please, Sir, I don't know."

"Don't know where you were born?—Who was your father?"

"God knows, Sir."

Struck by the straightforward simplicity of these replies, the officer next asked, "Do you know anything about your beginning?"

"No, Sir. But I have heard that I was found in a pretty silk-lined basket hanging one morning from the knocker of a good man's door in Bristol."

"*Found* say you? Well," throwing back his head and looking up and down the new recruit; "Well, it turns out to have been a pretty good find. Hope they'll find some more like you, my man; the fleet sadly needs them."

Yes, Billy Budd was a foundling, a presumable by-blow, and, evidently, no ignoble one. Noble descent was as evident in him as in a blood horse.

For the rest, with little or no sharpness of faculty or any trace of the wisdom of the serpent, nor yet quite a dove, he possessed that kind and degree of intelligence going along with the unconventional rectitude of a sound human creature, one to whom not yet has been proffered the questionable apple of knowledge. He was illiterate; he could not read, but he could sing, and like the illiterate nightingale was sometimes the composer of his own song.

Of self-consciousness he seemed to have little or none, or about as much as we may reasonably impute to a dog of Saint Bernard's breed.

Habitually living with the elements and knowing little more of the land than as a beach, or, rather, that portion of the terraqueous globe providentially set apart for dance-houses, doxies and tapsters, in short what sailors call a "fiddlers'-green," his simple nature remained unsophisticated by those moral obliquities which are not in every case incompatible with that manufacturable thing known as respectability. But are sailors, frequenters of "fiddlers'-greens," without vices? No; but less often than with landsmen do their vices, so called, partake of crookedness of heart, seeming less to proceed from viciousness than exuberance of vitality after long constraint; frank manifestations in accordance with natural law. By his original constitution aided by the cooperating influences of his lot, Billy in many respects was little more than a sort of upright barbarian, much such perhaps as Adam presumably might have been ere the urbane Serpent wriggled himself into his company.

And here be it submitted that apparently going to corroborate the doctrine of man's fall, a doctrine now popularly ignored, it is observable that where certain virtues pristine and unadulterate peculiarly characterize anybody in the external uniform of civilization, they will upon scrutiny seem not to be derived from custom or convention, but rather to be out of keeping with these, as if indeed exceptionally transmitted from a period prior to Cain's city and citified man. The character marked by such qualities has to an unvitiated taste an untampered-with flavor like that of berries, while the man thoroughly civilized, even in a fair specimen of the breed, has to the same moral palate a questionable smack as of a compounded wine. To any stray inheritor of these primitive qualities found, like Caspar Hauser, wandering dazed in any Christian capital of our time, the good-natured poet's famous invocation, near two thousand years ago, of the good rustic out of his latitude in the Rome of the Cesars, still appropriately holds:—

> "Honest and poor, faithful in word and thought
> What has thee, Fabian, to the city brought."

Though our Handsome Sailor had as much of masculine beauty as one can expect anywhere to see; nevertheless, like the beautiful woman in one of Hawthorne's minor tales, there was just one thing amiss in him. No visible blemish indeed, as with the lady; no, but an occasional liability to a vocal defect. Though in the hour of elemental uproar or peril, he was everything that a sailor should be, yet under sudden provocation of strong heart-feeling, his voice otherwise singularly musical, as if expressive of the harmony within, was apt to develop an organic hesitancy, in fact more or less of a stutter or even worse. In this particular Billy was a striking instance that the arch interferer, the envious marplot of Eden, still has more or less to do with every human consignment to this planet of earth. In every case, one way or another he is sure to slip in his little card, as much as to remind us—I too have a hand here.

The avowal of such an imperfection in the Handsome Sailor should be evidence not alone that he is not presented as a conventional hero, but also that the story in which he is the main figure is no romance.

[3]

At the time of Billy Budd's arbitrary enlistment into the *Bellipotent* that ship was on her way to join the Mediterranean fleet. No long time elapsed before the junction was effected. As one of that fleet the seventy-four participated in its movements, tho' at times on account of her superior sailing qualities, in the absence of frigates, despatched on separate duty as a scout and at times on less temporary service. But with all this the story has little concernment, restricted as it is to the inner life of one particular ship and the career of an individual sailor.

It was the summer of 1797. In the April of that year had occurred the commotion at Spithead followed in May by a second and yet more serious outbreak in the fleet at the Nore. The latter is known, and without exaggeration in the epithet, as the Great Mutiny. It was indeed a demonstration more menacing to England than the contemporary manifestoes and conquering and proselyting armies of the French Directory.

To the British Empire the Nore Mutiny was what a strike in the fire-brigade would be to London threatened by general arson. In a crisis when the kingdom might well have anticipated the famous signal that some years later published along the naval line of battle what it was that upon occasion England expected of Englishmen; *that* was the time when at the mast-heads of the three-deckers and seventy-fours moored in her own roadstead—a fleet, the right arm of a Power then all but the sole free conservative one of the Old World, the blue-jackets, to be numbered by thousands, ran up with huzzas the British colors with

the union and cross wiped out; by that cancellation transmuting the flag of founded law and freedom defined, into
the enemy's red meteor of unbridled and unbounded revolt.
Reasonable discontent growing out of practical grievances
in the fleet had been ignited into irrational combustion, as
by live cinders blown across the Channel from France in
flames.

The event converted into irony for a time those spirited
strains of Dibdin—as a song-writer no mean auxiliary to
the English Government at the European conjuncture—
strains celebrating, among other things, the patriotic devotion of the British tar:

> *"And as for my life, 'tis the King's!"*

Such an episode in the Island's grand naval story her
naval historians naturally abridge; one of them (G. P. R.
James) candidly acknowledging that fain would he pass it
over did not "impartiality forbid fastidiousness." And yet
his mention is less a narration than a reference, having to
do hardly at all with details. Nor are these readily to be
found in the libraries. Like some other events in every age
befalling states everywhere, including America, the Great
Mutiny was of such character that national pride along
with views of policy would fain shade it off into the historical background. Such events can not be ignored, but
there is a considerate way of historically treating them. If
a well-constituted individual refrains from blazoning aught
amiss or calamitous in his family, a nation in the like
circumstance may without reproach be equally discreet.

Though after parleyings between Government and the
ring-leaders, and concessions by the former as to some glaring abuses, the first uprising—that at Spithead—with difficulty was put down, or matters for the time pacified; yet
at the Nore the unforeseen renewal of insurrection on a
yet larger scale, and emphasized in the conferences that
ensued by demands deemed by the authorities not only in-
admissible but aggressively insolent, indicated—if the Red
Flag did not sufficiently do so—what was the spirit animat-
ing the men. Final suppression, however, there was; but
only made possible perhaps by the unswerving loyalty of
the marine corps and a voluntary resumption of loyalty
among influential sections of the crews.

To some extent the Nore Mutiny may be regarded as

analogous to the distempering irruption of contagious fever in a frame constitutionally sound, and which anon throws it off.

At all events, of these thousands of mutineers were some of the tars who not so very long afterwards—whether wholly prompted thereto by patriotism, or pugnacious instinct, or by both,—helped to win a coronet for Nelson at the Nile, and the naval crown of crowns for him at Trafalgar. To the mutineers those battles, and especially Trafalgar, were a plenary absolution and a grand one. For all that goes to make up scenic naval display, heroic magnificence in arms, those battles, especially Trafalgar, stand unmatched in human annals.

[4]
Concerning "The greatest sailor since our world began."—Tennyson

In this matter of writing, resolve as one may to keep to the main road, some by-paths have an enticement not readily to be withstood. I am going to err into such a by-path. If the reader will keep me company I shall be glad. At the least we can promise ourselves that pleasure which is wickedly said to be in sinning, for a literary sin the divergence will be.

Very likely it is no new remark that the inventions of our time have at last brought about a change in sea-warfare in degree corresponding to the revolution in all warfare effected by the original introduction from China into Europe of gunpowder. The first European fire-arm, a clumsy contrivance, was, as is well known, scouted by no few of the knights as a base implement, good enough peradventure for weavers too craven to stand up crossing steel with steel in frank fight. But as ashore knightly valor, tho' shorn of its blazonry, did not cease with the knights, neither on the seas, though nowadays in encounters there a certain kind of displayed gallantry be fallen out of date as hardly applicable under changed circumstances, did the nobler qualities of such naval magnates as Don John of Austria, Doria, Van Tromp, Jean Bart, the long line of British Admirals and the American Decaturs of 1812 become obsolete with their wooden walls.

Nevertheless, to anybody who can hold the Present at

its worth without being inappreciative of the Past, it may be forgiven, if to such an one the solitary old hulk at Portsmouth, Nelson's *Victory*, seems to float there, not alone as the decaying monument of a fame incorruptible, but also as a poetic reproach, softened by its picturesqueness, to the *Monitors* and yet mightier hulls of the European ironclads. And this not altogether because such craft are unsightly, unavoidably lacking the symmetry and grand lines of the old battle-ships, but equally for other reasons.

There are some, perhaps, who while not altogether inaccessible to that poetic reproach just alluded to, may yet on behalf of the new order, be disposed to parry it; and this to the extent of iconoclasm, if need be. For example, prompted by the sight of the star inserted in the *Victory*'s quarter-deck designating the spot where the Great Sailor fell, these martial utilitarians may suggest considerations implying that Nelson's ornate publication of his person in battle was not only unnecessary, but not military, nay, savored of foolhardiness and vanity. They may add, too, that at Trafalgar it was in effect nothing less than a challenge to death; and death came; and that but for his bravado the victorious Admiral might possibly have survived the battle; and so, instead of having his sagacious dying injunctions overruled by his immediate successor in command, he himself, when the contest was decided, might have brought his shattered fleet to anchor, a proceeding which might have averted the deplorable loss of life by shipwreck in the elemental tempest that followed the martial one.

Well, should we set aside the more disputable point whether for various reasons it was possible to anchor the fleet, then plausibly enough the Benthamites of war may urge the above.

But the *might-have-been* is but boggy ground to build on. And, certainly, in foresight as to the larger issue of an encounter, and anxious preparations for it—buoying the deadly way and mapping it out, as at Copenhagen—few commanders have been so painstakingly circumspect as this same reckless declarer of his person in fight.

Personal prudence even when dictated by quite other than selfish considerations surely is no special virtue in a military man; while an excessive love of glory, impassioning a less burning impulse, the honest sense of duty, is the first. If the name *Wellington* is not so much of a trumpet to the blood as the simpler name *Nelson,* the reason for this may perhaps be inferred from the above. Alfred in his funeral ode on the victor of Waterloo ventures not to call him the greatest soldier of all time, tho' in the same ode he invokes Nelson as "the greatest sailor since the world began."

At Trafalgar Nelson, on the brink of opening the fight, sat down and wrote his last brief will and testament. If under the presentiment of the most magnificent of all victories to be crowned by his own glorious death, a sort of priestly motive led him to dress his person in the jewelled vouchers of his own shining deeds; if thus to have adorned himself for the altar and the sacrifice were indeed vainglory, then affectation and fustian is each more heroic line in the great epics and dramas, since in such lines the poet but embodies in verse those exaltations of sentiment that a nature like Nelson, the opportunity being given, vitalizes into acts.

[5]

Yes, the outbreak at the Nore was put down. But not every grievance was redressed. If the contractors, for example, were no longer permitted to ply some practices peculiar to their tribe everywhere, such as providing shoddy cloth, rations not sound, or false in the measure, not the less impressment, for one thing, went on. By custom sanctioned for centuries, and judicially maintained by a Lord Chancellor as late as Mansfield, that mode of manning the fleet, a mode now fallen into a sort of abeyance but never formally renounced, it was not practicable to give up in those years. Its abrogation would have crippled the indispensable fleet, one wholly under canvas, no steam-power, its innumerable sails and thousands of cannon, everything in short, worked by muscle alone; a fleet the more insatiate in demand for men, because then multiplying its ships of all grades against contingencies present and to come of the convulsed Continent.

Discontent foreran the Two Mutinies, and more or less it lurkingly survived them. Hence it was not unreasonable to apprehend some return of trouble sporadic or general. One instance of such apprehensions: In the same year with this story, Nelson, then Vice Admiral Sir Horatio, being with the fleet off the Spanish coast, was directed by the Admiral in command to shift his pennant from the *Captain* to the *Theseus;* and for this reason: that the latter ship having newly arrived on the station from home where it had taken part in the Great Mutiny, danger was apprehended from the temper of the men; and it was thought that an officer like Nelson was the one, not indeed to terrorize the crew into base subjection, but to win them, by force of his mere presence, back to an allegiance if not as enthusiastic as his own, yet as true. So it was that for a time on more than one quarter-deck anxiety did exist. At sea precautionary vigilance was strained against relapse. At short notice an engagement might come on. When it did, the lieutenants assigned to batteries felt it incumbent on them, in some instances, to stand with drawn swords behind the men working the guns.

[6]

But on board the seventy-four in which Billy now swung his hammock, very little in the manner of the men and nothing obvious in the demeanor of the officers would have suggested to an ordinary observer that the Great Mutiny was a recent event. In their general bearing and conduct the commissioned officers of a war-ship naturally take their tone from the commander, that is if he have that ascendancy of character that ought to be his.

Captain the Honorable Edward Fairfax Vere, to give his full title, was a bachelor of forty or thereabouts, a sailor of distinction even in a time prolific of renowned seamen. Though allied to the higher nobility, his advancement had not been altogether owing to influences connected with that circumstance. He had seen much service, been in various engagements, always acquitting himself as an officer mindful of the welfare of his men, but never tolerating an infraction of discipline; thoroughly versed in the science of his profession, and intrepid to the verge of temerity, though never injudiciously so. For his gallantry in the West Indian waters as flag-lieutenant under Rodney in that Admiral's crowning victory over De Grasse, he was made a post-captain.

Ashore in the garb of a civilian, scarce anyone would have taken him for a sailor, more especially that he never garnished unprofessional talk with nautical terms, and grave in his bearing, evinced little appreciation of mere humor. It was not out of keeping with these traits that on a passage when nothing demanded his paramount action, he was the most undemonstrative of men. Any landsman observing this gentleman, not conspicuous by his stature and wearing no pronounced insignia, emerging from his cabin to the open deck, and noting the silent deference of the officers retiring to leeward, might have taken him for the King's guest, a civilian aboard the King's-ship, some highly honorable discreet envoy on his way to an important post. But in fact this unobtrusiveness of demeanor may have proceeded from a certain unaffected modesty of manhood sometimes accompanying a resolute nature, a modesty evinced at all times not calling for pronounced action, and which shown in any rank of life suggests a virtue aristocratic in kind.

As with some others engaged in various departments of the world's more heroic activities, Captain Vere though practical enough upon occasion would at times betray a certain dreaminess of mood. Standing alone on the weather-side of the quarter deck, one hand holding by the rigging, he would absently gaze off at the blank sea. At the presentation to him then of some minor matter interrupting the current of his thoughts he would show more or less irascibility; but instantly he would control it.

In the navy he was popularly known by the appellation —Starry Vere. How such a designation happened to fall upon one who, whatever his sturdy qualities, was without any brilliant ones was in this wise: A favorite kinsman, Lord Denton, a free-hearted fellow, had been the first to meet and congratulate him upon his return to England from his West Indian cruise; and but the day previous turning over a copy of Andrew Marvell's poems, had lighted, not for the first time however, upon the lines entitled *Appleton House,* the name of one of the seats of their common ancestor, a hero in the German wars of the seventeenth century, in which poem occur the lines,

> "This 'tis to have been from the first
> In a domestic heaven nursed,
> Under the discipline severe
> Of Fairfax and the starry Vere."

And so, upon embracing his cousin fresh from Rodney's great victory wherein he had played so gallant a part, brimming over with just family pride in the sailor of their house, he exuberantly exclaimed, "Give ye joy, Ed; give ye joy, my starry Vere!" This got currency, and the novel prefix serving in familiar parlance readily to distinguish the *Bellipotent*'s Captain from another Vere his senior, a distant relative, an officer of like rank in the navy, it remained permanently attached to the surname.

[7]

In view of the part that the commander of the *Bellipotent* plays in scenes shortly to follow, it may be well to fill out that sketch of his outlined in the previous chapter.

Aside from his qualities as a sea-officer, Captain Vere was an exceptional character. Unlike no few of England's renowned sailors, long and arduous service with signal devotion to it, had not resulted in absorbing and *salting* the entire man. He had a marked leaning toward everything intellectual. He loved books, never going to sea without a newly replenished library, compact but of the best. The isolated leisure, in some cases so wearisome, falling at intervals to commanders even during a war-cruise, never was tedious to Captain Vere. With nothing of that literary taste which less heeds the thing conveyed than the vehicle, his bias was towards those books to which every serious mind of superior order occupying any active post of authority in the world, naturally inclines: books treating of actual men and events no matter of what era—history, biography and unconventional writers, who, free from cant and convention, like Montaigne, honestly and in the spirit of common sense philosophize upon realities.

In this line of reading he found confirmation of his own more reasoned thoughts—confirmation which he had vainly sought in social converse, so that as touching most fundamental topics, there had got to be established in him some positive convictions, which he forefelt would abide in him essentially unmodified so long as his intelligent part remained unimpaired. In view of the troubled period in which his lot was cast this was well for him. His settled convictions were as a dyke against those invading waters of novel opinion, social, political and otherwise, which carried away as in a torrent no few minds in those days, minds by nature not inferior to his own. While other members of that aristocracy to which by birth he belonged were incensed at the innovators mainly because their theories were inimical to the privileged classes, not alone Captain Vere disinterestedly opposed them because they seemed to him incapable of embodiment in lasting institutions, but at war with the peace of the world and the true welfare of mankind.

With minds less stored than his and less earnest, some officers of his rank, with whom at times he would necessarily consort, found him lacking in the companionable quality, a dry and bookish gentleman as they deemed. Upon any chance withdrawal from their company one would be apt to say to another, something like this: "Vere is a noble fellow, Starry Vere. Spite the gazettes, Sir Horatio," meaning him with the Lord title, "is at bottom scarce a better seaman or fighter. But between you and me now, don't you think there is a queer streak of the pedantic running thro' him? Yes, like the King's yarn in a coil of navy-rope?"

Some apparent ground there was for this sort of confidential criticism; since not only did the Captain's discourse never fall into the jocosely familiar, but in illustrating of any point touching the stirring personages and events of the time he would be as apt to cite some historic character or incident of antiquity as that he would cite from the moderns. He seemed unmindful of the circumstance that to his bluff company such remote allusions, however pertinent they might really be, were altogether alien to men whose reading was mainly confined to the journals. But considerateness in such matters is not easy to natures constituted like Captain Vere's. Their honesty prescribes to them directness, sometimes far-reaching like that of a migratory fowl that in its flight never heeds when it crosses a frontier.

[8]

The lieutenants and other commissioned gentlemen forming Captain Vere's staff it is not necessary here to particularize, nor needs it to make any mention of any of the warrant-officers. But among the petty-officers was one who having much to do with the story, may as well be forthwith introduced. His portrait I essay, but shall never hit it. This was John Claggart, the Master-at-arms. But that sea-title may to landsmen seem somewhat equivocal. Originally doubtless that petty-officer's function was the instruction of the men in the use of arms, sword or cutlas. But very long ago, owing to the advance in gunnery making hand-to-hand encounters less frequent and giving to nitre and sulphur the preeminence over steel, that function ceased; the master-at-arms of a great war-ship becoming a sort of Chief of Police, charged among other matters with the duty of preserving order on the populous lower gun-decks.

Claggart was a man about five and thirty, somewhat spare and tall, yet of no ill figure upon the whole. His hand was too small and shapely to have been accustomed to hard toil. The face was a notable one; the features all except the chin cleanly cut as those on a Greek medallion; yet the chin, beardless as Tecumseh's, had something of strange protuberant heaviness in its make that recalled the prints of the Rev. Dr. Titus Oates, the historic deponent with the clerical drawl in the time of Charles II and the fraud of the alleged Popish Plot. It served Claggart in his office that his eye could cast a tutoring glance. His brow was of the sort phrenologically associated with more than average intellect; silken jet curls partly clustering over it, making a foil to the pallor below, a pallor tinged with a faint shade of amber akin to the hue of time-tinted marbles of old. This complexion, singularly contrasting with the red or deeply bronzed visages of the sailors, and in part the result of his official seclusion from the sunlight, tho' it was not exactly displeasing, nevertheless seemed to hint of something defective or abnormal in the constitution and blood. But his general aspect and manner were so suggestive of an education and career incongruous with his naval function that when not actively engaged in it he looked like a man of high quality, social and moral, who for reasons of his own was keeping incog. Nothing was known of his former life. It might be that he was an Englishman; and yet there lurked a bit of accent in his speech suggesting that possibly he was not such by birth, but through naturalization in early childhood. Among certain grizzled sea-gossips of the gun-decks and forecastle went a rumor perdue that the master-at-arms was a *chevalier* who had volunteered into the King's navy by way of compounding for some mysterious swindle whereof he had been arraigned at the King's Bench. The fact that nobody could substantiate this report was, of course, nothing against its secret currency. Such a rumor once started on the gun-decks in reference to almost anyone below the rank of a commissioned officer would, during the period assigned to this narrative, have seemed not altogether wanting in credibility to the tarry old wiseacres of a man-of-war crew. And indeed a man of Claggart's accomplishments, without prior nautical experience, entering the navy at mature life, as he did, and necessarily allotted at the start to the lowest grade in it; a man too who never made allusion to his previous life ashore; these were circumstances which in the dearth of exact knowledge as to his true antecedents opened to the invidious a vague field for unfavorable surmise.

But the sailors' dog-watch gossip concerning him derived a vague plausibility from the fact that now for some period the British Navy could so little afford to be squeamish in the matter of keeping up the muster-rolls, that not only were press-gangs notoriously abroad both afloat and ashore, but there was little or no secret about another matter, namely that the London police were at liberty to capture any able-bodied suspect, any questionable fellow at large and summarily ship him to dockyard or fleet. Furthermore, even among voluntary enlistments there were instances where the motive thereto partook neither of patriotic impulse nor yet of a random desire to experience a bit of sea-life and martial adventure. Insolvent debtors of minor grade, together with the promiscuous lame ducks of morality found in the Navy a convenient and secure refuge. Secure, because once enlisted aboard a King's-Ship, they were as much in sanctuary, as the transgressor of the Middle Ages harboring himself under the shadow of the altar. Such sanctioned irregularities, which for obvious reasons the Government would hardly think to parade at the time, and which consequently, and as affecting the least influential class of mankind, have all but dropped into oblivion, lend color to something for the truth whereof I do not vouch, and hence have some scruple in stating; something I remember having seen in print though the book I can not recall; but the same thing was personally communicated to me now more than forty years ago by an old pensioner in a cocked hat with whom I had a most interesting talk on the terrace at Greenwich, a Baltimore negro, a Trafalgar man. It was to this effect: In the case of a warship short of hands whose speedy sailing was imperative, the deficient quota in lack of any other way of making it good, would be eked out by draughts culled direct from the jails. For reasons previously suggested it would not perhaps be easy at the present day directly to prove or disprove the allegation. But allowed as a verity, how significant would it be of England's straits at the time, confronted by those wars which like a flight of harpies rose shrieking from the din and dust of the fallen Bastille. That era appears measurably clear to us who look back at it, and but read of it. But to the grandfathers of us graybeards, the more thoughtful of them, the genius of it presented an aspect like that of Camoen's Spirit of the Cape, an eclipsing menace mysterious and prodigious. Not America was exempt from apprehension. At the height of Napoleon's unexampled conquests, there were Americans who had fought at Bunker Hill who looked forward to the possibility that the Atlantic might prove no barrier against the ultimate schemes of this French upstart from the revolutionary chaos who seemed in act of fulfilling judgement prefigured in the Apocalypse.

But the less credence was to be given to the gun-deck talk touching Claggart, seeing that no man holding his office in a man-of-war can ever hope to be popular with the crew. Besides, in derogatory comments upon anyone against whom they have a grudge, or for any reason or no reason mislike, sailors are much like landsmen; they are apt to exaggerate or romance it.

About as much was really known to the *Bellipotent*'s tars of the master-at-arms' career before entering the service as an astronomer knows about a comet's travels prior to its first observable appearance in the sky. The verdict of the sea quidnuncs has been cited only by way of showing what sort of moral impression the man made upon rude uncultivated natures whose conceptions of human wickedness were necessarily of the narrowest, limited to ideas of vulgar rascality,—a thief among the swinging hammocks during a night-watch, or the man-brokers and landsharks of the seaports.

It was no gossip, however, but fact, that though, as before hinted, Claggart upon his entrance into the navy was, as a novice, assigned to the least honorable section

of a man-of-war's crew, embracing the drudgery, he did
not long remain there.

The superior capacity he immediately evinced, his constitutional sobriety, ingratiating deference to superiors,
together with a peculiar ferreting genius manifested on a
singular occasion, all this capped by a certain austere patriotism abruptly advanced him to the position of master-
at-arms.

Of this maritime Chief of Police the ship's-corporals, so
called, were the immediate subordinates, and compliant
ones; and this, as is to be noted in some business departments ashore, almost to a degree inconsistent with entire
moral volition. His place put various converging wires of
underground influence under the Chief's control, capable
when astutely worked thro' his understrappers, of operating to the mysterious discomfort, if nothing worse, of
any of the sea-commonalty.

[9]

Life in the fore-top well agreed with Billy Budd. There,
when not actually engaged on the yards yet higher aloft,
the topmen, who as such had been picked out for youth
and activity, constituted an aerial club lounging at ease
against the smaller stun'sails rolled up into cushions, spinning yarns like the lazy gods, and frequently amused with
what was going on in the busy world of the decks below.
No wonder then that a young fellow of Billy's disposition
was well content in such society. Giving no cause of offence
to anybody, he was always alert at a call. So in the merchant service it had been with him. But now such a punc-
tiliousness in duty was shown that his topmates would
sometimes good-naturedly laugh at him for it. This heightened alacrity had its cause, namely, the impression made
upon him by the first formal gangway-punishment he had
ever witnessed, which befell the day following his impressment. It had been incurred by a little fellow, young, a
novice, an after-guardsman absent from his assigned post
when the ship was being put about; a dereliction resulting
in a rather serious hitch to that manœuvre, one demanding
instantaneous promptitude in letting go and making fast.
When Billy saw the culprit's naked back under the scourge
gridironed with red welts, and worse; when he marked
the dire expression on the liberated man's face as with

his woolen shirt flung over him by the executioner he
rushed forward from the spot to bury himself in the crowd,
Billy was horrified. He resolved that never through remiss-
ness would he make himself liable to such a visitation or
do or omit aught that might merit even verbal reproof.
What then was his surprise and concern when ultimately
he found himself getting into petty trouble occasionally
about such matters as the stowage of his bag or something amiss in his hammock, matters under the police oversight of the ship's-corporals of the lower decks, and which
brought down on him a vague threat from one of them.

So heedful in all things as he was, how could this be?
He could not understand it, and it more than vexed him.
When he spoke to his young topmates about it they were
either lightly incredulous or found something comical in
his unconcealed anxiety. "Is it your bag, Billy?" said one.
"Well, sew yourself up in it, bully boy, and then you'll be
sure to know if anybody meddles with it."

Now there was a veteran aboard who because his years
began to disqualify him for more active work had been recently assigned duty as main-mast-man in his watch, looking to the gear belayed at the rail roundabout that great
spar near the deck. At off-times the foretopman had picked
up some acquaintance with him, and now in his trouble
it occurred to him that he might be the sort of person to
go to for wise counsel. He was an old Dansker long
anglicized in the service, of few words, many wrinkles and
some honorable scars. His wizened face, time-tinted and
weather-stained to the complexion of an antique parchment,
was here and there peppered blue by the chance explosion
of a gun-cartridge in action. He was an *Agamemnon*-man;
some two years prior to the time of this story having served
under Nelson, when but Sir Horatio, in that ship immortal
in naval memory, and which, dismantled, and in part
broken up to her bare ribs, is seen a grand skeleton in Hay-
don's etching. As one of a boarding-party from the
Agamemnon he had received a cut slantwise along one
temple and cheek, leaving a long pale scar like a streak of
dawn's light falling athwart the dark visage. It was on
account of that scar and the affair in which it was known
that he had received it, as well as from his blue-peppered
complexion, that the Dansker went among the *Bellipotent*'s crew by the name of "Board-her-in-the-smoke."

Now the first time that his small weazel-eyes happened to light on Billy Budd, a certain grim internal merriment set all his ancient wrinkles into antic play. Was it that his eccentric unsentimental old sapience, primitive in its kind, saw or thought it saw something which, in contrast with the war-ship's environment, looked oddly incongruous in the handsome sailor? But after slyly studying him at intervals, the old Merlin's equivocal merriment was modified; for now when the twain would meet, it would start in his face a quizzing sort of look, but it would be but momentary and sometimes replaced by an expression of speculative query as to what might eventually befall a nature like that, dropped into a world not without some man-traps and against whose subtleties simple courage, lacking experience and address and without any touch of defensive ugliness, is of little avail; and where such innocence as man is capable of does yet in a moral emergency not always sharpen the faculties or enlighten the will.

However it was, the Dansker in his ascetic way rather took to Billy. Nor was this only because of a certain philosophic interest in such a character. There was another cause. While the old man's eccentricities, sometimes bordering on the ursine, repelled the juniors, Billy, undeterred thereby, revering him as a salt hero, would make advances, never passing the old *Agamemnon*-man without a salutation marked by that respect which is seldom lost on the aged however crabbed at times or whatever their station in life.

There was a vein of dry humor, or what not, in the mast-man; and, whether in freak of patriarchal irony touching Billy's youth and athletic frame, or for some other and more recondite reason, from the first in addressing him he always substituted Baby for Billy. The Dansker in fact being the originator of the name by which the foretopman eventually became known aboard ship.

Well then, in his mysterious little difficulty, going in quest of the wrinkled one, Billy found him off duty in a dogwatch ruminating by himself, seated on a shot-box of the upper gun-deck, now and then surveying with a somewhat cynical regard certain of the more swaggering promenaders there. Billy recounted his trouble, again wondering how it all happened. The salt seer attentively listened, accompanying the foretopman's recital with queer twitchings of his wrinkles and problematical little sparkles of his small ferret eyes. Making an end of his story, the foretopman asked, "And now, Dansker, do tell me what you think of it."

The old man, shoving up the front of his tarpaulin and deliberately rubbing the long slant scar at the point where it entered the thin hair, laconically said, "Baby Budd, *Jemmy Legs*" (meaning the master-at-arms) "is down on you."

"*Jemmy Legs!*" ejaculated Billy, his welkin eyes expanding; "what for? Why he calls me *the sweet and pleasant young fellow*, they tell me."

"Does he so?" grinned the grizzled one; then said, "Ay, Baby Lad, a sweet voice has *Jemmy Legs*."

"No, not always. But to me he has. I seldom pass him but there comes a pleasant word."

"And that's because he's down upon you, Baby Budd."

Such reiteration along with the manner of it, incomprehensible to a novice, disturbed Billy almost as much as the mystery for which he had sought explanation. Something less unpleasingly oracular he tried to extract; but the old sea-Chiron, thinking perhaps that for the nonce he had sufficiently instructed his young Achilles, pursed his lips, gathered all his wrinkles together and would commit himself to nothing further.

Years, and those experiences which befall certain shrewder men subordinated life-long to the will of superiors, all this had developed in the Dansker the pithy guarded cynicism that was his leading characteristic.

[*10*]

The next day an incident served to confirm Billy Budd in his incredulity as to the Dansker's strange summing up of the case submitted. The ship at noon, going large before the wind, was rolling on her course, and he below at dinner and engaged in some sportful talk with the members of his mess, chanced in a sudden lurch to spill the entire contents of his soup-pan upon the new scrubbed deck. Claggart, the Master-at-arms, official rattan in hand, happened to be passing along the battery in a bay of which the mess was lodged, and the greasy liquid streamed just across his path. Stepping over it, he was proceeding on his way without comment, since the matter was nothing to take notice of

under the circumstances, when he happened to observe
who it was that had done the spilling. His countenance
changed. Pausing, he was about to ejaculate something
hasty at the sailor, but checked himself, and pointing
down to the streaming soup, playfully tapped him from
behind with his rattan, saying in a low musical voice
peculiar to him at times "Handsomely done, my lad! And
handsome is as handsome did it too!" And with that passed
on. Not noted by Billy, as not coming within his view,
was the involuntary smile, or rather grimace, that accompanied Claggart's equivocal words. Aridly it drew
down the thin corners of his shapely mouth. But everybody
taking his remark as meant for humorous, and at which
therefore as coming from a superior they were bound
to laugh, "with counterfeited glee" acted accordingly; and
Billy tickled, it may be, by the allusion to his being the
handsome sailor, merrily joined in; then addressing his
messmates exclaimed "There now, who says that Jemmy
Legs is down on me!" "And who said he was, Beauty?"
demanded one Donald with some surprise. Whereat the
foretopman looked a little foolish, recalling that it was
only one person, Board-her-in-the-smoke, who had suggested what to him was the smoky idea that this master-
at-arms was in any peculiar way hostile to him. Meantime
that functionary, resuming his path, must have momentarily
worn some expression less guarded than that of the bitter
smile, and usurping the face from the heart, some distorting expression perhaps; for a drummer-boy heedlessly
frolicking along from the opposite direction, and chancing
to come into light collision with his person, was strangely
disconcerted by his aspect. Nor was the impression less-
ened when the official, impulsively giving him a sharp cut
with the rattan, vehemently exclaimed, "Look where you
go!"

[11]

What was the matter with the master-at-arms? And, be
the matter what it might, how could it have direct relation
to Billy Budd with whom, prior to the affair of the spilled
soup, he had never come into any special contact official
or otherwise? What indeed could the trouble have to do
with one so little inclined to give offence as the merchant-
ship's *peacemaker*, even him who in Claggart's own phrase

was "the sweet and pleasant young fellow"? Yes, why should *Jemmy Legs,* to borrow the Dansker's expression, be *down* on the Handsome Sailor? But, at heart and not for nothing, as the late chance encounter may indicate to the discerning, down on him, secretly down on him, he assuredly was.

Now to invent something touching the more private career of Claggart, something involving Billy Budd, of which something the latter should be wholly ignorant, some romantic incident implying that Claggart's knowledge of the young blue-jacket began at some period anterior to catching sight of him on board the seventy-four—all this, not so difficult to do, might avail in a way more or less interesting to account for whatever of enigma may appear to lurk in the case. But in fact there was nothing of the sort. And yet the cause, necessarily to be assumed as the sole one assignable, is in its very realism as much charged with that prime element of Radcliffian romance, *the mysterious,* as any that the ingenuity of the author of the *Mysteries of Udolpho* could advise. For what can more partake of the mysterious than an antipathy spontaneous and profound, such as is evoked in certain exceptional mortals by the mere aspect of some other mortal, however harmless he may be, if not called forth by this very harmlessness itself?

Now there can exist no irritating juxtaposition of dissimilar personalities comparable to that which is possible aboard a great war-ship fully manned and at sea. There, every day among all ranks almost every man comes into more or less of contact with almost every other man. Wholly there to avoid even the sight of an aggravating object one must needs give it Jonah's toss or jump overboard himself. Imagine how all this might eventually operate on some peculiar human creature the direct reverse of a saint?

But for the adequate comprehending of Claggart by a normal nature, these hints are insufficient. To pass from a normal nature to him one must cross "the deadly space between." And this is best done by indirection.

Long ago an honest scholar my senior, said to me in reference to one who like himself is now no more, a man so unimpeachably respectable that against him nothing was ever openly said tho' among the few something was whispered, "Yes, X—— is a nut not to be cracked by the tap of a lady's fan. You are aware that I am the adherent of no organized religion much less of any philosophy built into a system. Well, for all that, I think that to try and get into X——, enter his labyrinth and get out again, without a clue derived from some source other than what is known as *knowledge of the world*—that were hardly possible, at least for me."

"Why," said I, "X——, however singular a study to some, is yet human, and knowledge of the world assuredly implies the knowledge of human nature, and in most of its varieties."

"Yes, but a superficial knowledge of it, serving ordinary purposes. But for anything deeper, I am not certain whether to know the world and to know human nature be not two distinct branches of knowledge, which while they may coexist in the same heart, yet either may exist with little or nothing of the other. Nay, in an average man of the world, his constant rubbing with it blunts that fine spiritual insight indispensable to the understanding of the essential in certain exceptional characters, whether evil ones or good. In a matter of some importance I have seen a girl wind an old lawyer about her little finger. Nor was it the dotage of senile love. Nothing of the sort. But he knew law better than he knew the girl's heart. Coke and Blackstone hardly shed so much light into obscure spiritual places as the Hebrew prophets. And who were they? Mostly recluses."

At the time my inexperience was such that I did not quite see the drift of all this. It may be that I see it now. And, indeed, if that lexicon which is based on Holy Writ were any longer popular, one might with less difficulty define and denominate certain phenomenal men. As it is, one must turn to some authority not liable to the charge of being tinctured with the Biblical element.

In a list of definitions included in the authentic translation of Plato, a list attributed to him, occurs this: "Natural Depravity: a depravity according to nature." A definition which tho' savoring of Calvinism, by no means involves Calvin's dogmas as to total mankind. Evidently its intent makes it applicable but to individuals. Not many are the examples of this depravity which the gallows and jail supply. At any rate for notable instances, since these have no vulgar alloy of the brute in them, but invariably are dominated by intellectuality, one must go elsewhere. Civilization, especially if of the austerer sort, is auspicious to it. It folds itself in the mantle of respectability. It has its certain negative virtues serving as silent auxiliaries. It never allows wine to get within its guard. It is not going too far to say that it is without vices or small sins. There is a phenomenal pride in it that excludes them from anything mercenary or avaricious. In short the depravity here meant partakes nothing of the sordid or sensual. It is serious, but free from acerbity. Though no flatterer of mankind it never speaks ill of it.

But the thing which in eminent instances signalizes so exceptional a nature is this: though the man's even temper and discreet bearing would seem to intimate a mind peculiarly subject to the law of reason, not the less in his heart he would seem to riot in complete exemption from that law, having apparently little to'do with reason further than to employ it as an ambidexter implement for effecting the irrational. That is to say: Toward the accomplishment of an aim which in wantonness of malignity would seem to partake of the insane, he will direct a cool judgement sagacious and sound.

These men are true madmen, and of the most dangerous sort, for their lunacy is not continuous but occasional, evoked by some special object; it is probably secretive, which is as much to say it is self-contained, so that when moreover, most active, it is to the average mind not distinguishable from sanity, and for the reason above suggested that whatever its aims may be, and the aim is never declared—the method and the outward proceeding are always perfectly rational.

Now something such an one was Claggart, in whom was the mania of an evil nature, not engendered by vicious training or corrupting books or licentious living, but born with him and innate, in short "a depravity according to nature."

[12]

[Lawyers, Experts, Clergy
An Episode

By the way, can it be the phenomenon, disowned or at least concealed, that in some criminal cases puzzles the

courts? For this cause have our juries at times not only to
endure the prolonged contentions of lawyers with their
fees, but also the yet more perplexing strife of the medical
experts with theirs?—But why leave it to them? why not
subpoena as well the clerical proficients? Their vocation
bringing them into peculiar contact with so many human
beings, and sometimes in their least guarded hour, in inter-
views very much more confidential than those of physician
and patient; this would seem to qualify them to know something about those intricacies involved in the question of
moral responsibility; whether in a given case, say, the
crime proceeded from mania in the brain or rabies of the
heart. As to any differences among themselves these clerical proficients might develop on the stand, these could
hardly be greater than the direct contradictions exchanged
between the remunerated medical experts.

Dark sayings are these, some will say. But why? Is it because they somewhat savor of Holy Writ in its phrase
"mysteries of iniquity"? If they do, such savor was far
from being intended, for little will it commend these
pages to many a reader of to-day.

The point of the present story turning on the hidden
nature of the master-at-arms has necessitated this chapter.
With an added hint or two in connection with the incident
at the mess, the resumed narrative must be left to vindicate, as it may, its own credibility.]*

[*13*]
Pale ire, envy and despair

That Claggart's figure was not amiss, and his face, save
the chin, well moulded, has already been said. Of these
favorable points he seemed not insensible, for he was not
only neat but careful in his dress. But the form of Billy
Budd was heroic; and if his face was without the intellectual look of the pallid Claggart's, not the less was it lit,
like his, from within, though from a different source. The
bonfire in his heart made luminous the rose-tan in his
cheek.

In view of the marked contrast between the persons of
the twain, it is more than probable that when the master-
at-arms in the scene last given applied to the sailor the

* Melville may have intended to delete this section.

proverb *Handsome is as handsome does;* he there let escape an ironic inkling, not caught by the young sailors who heard it, as to what it was that had first moved him against Billy, namely, his significant personal beauty.

Now envy and antipathy, passions irreconcilable in reason, nevertheless in fact may spring conjoined like Chang and Eng in one birth. Is Envy then such a monster? Well, though many an arraigned mortal has in hopes of mitigated penalty pleaded guilty to horrible actions, did ever anybody seriously confess to envy? Something there is in it universally felt to be more shameful than even felonious crime. And not only does everybody disown it, but the better sort are inclined to incredulity when it is in earnest imputed to an intelligent man. But since its lodgement is in the heart not the brain, no degree of intellect supplies a guarantee against it. But Claggart's was no vulgar form of the passion. Nor, as directed toward Billy Budd did it partake of that streak of apprehensive jealousy that marred Saul's visage perturbedly brooding on the comely young David. Claggart's envy struck deeper. If askance he eyed the good looks, cherry health and frank enjoyment of young life in Billy Budd, it was because these went along with a nature that, as Claggart magnetically felt, had in its simplicity never willed malice or experienced the reactionary bite of that serpent. To him, the spirit lodged within Billy, and looking out from his welkin eyes as from windows, that ineffability it was which made the dimple in his dyed cheek, suppled his joints, and dancing in his yellow curls made him preeminently the Handsome Sailor. One person excepted, the master-at-arms was perhaps the only man in the ship intellectually capable of adequately appreciating the moral phenomenon presented in Billy Budd. And the insight but intensified his passion, which assuming various secret forms within him, at times assumed that of cynic disdain—disdain of innocence. To be nothing more than innocent! Yet in an æsthetic way he saw the charm of it, the courageous free-and-easy temper of it, and fain would have shared it, but he despaired of it.

With no power to annul the elemental evil in him, tho' readily enough he could hide it; apprehending the good, but powerless to be it; a nature like Claggart's surcharged with energy as such natures almost invariably are, what recourse is left to it but to recoil upon itself and like the scorpion for which the Creator alone is responsible, act out to the end the part allotted it.

[14]

Passion, and passion in its profoundest, is not a thing demanding a palatial stage whereon to play its part. Down among the groundlings, among the beggars and rakers of the garbage, profound passion is enacted. And the circumstances that provoke it, however trivial or mean, are no measure of its power. In the present instance the stage is a scrubbed gun-deck, and one of the external provocations a man-of-war's-man's spilled soup.

Now when the Master-at-arms noticed whence came that greasy fluid streaming before his feet, he must have taken it—to some extent wilfully, perhaps—not for the mere accident it assuredly was, but for the sly escape of a spontaneous feeling on Billy's part more or less answering to the antipathy on his own. In effect a foolish demonstration he must have thought, and very harmless, like the futile kick of a heifer, which yet were the heifer a shod stallion, would not be so harmless. Even so was it that into the gall of Claggart's envy he infused the vitriol of his contempt. But the incident confirmed to him certain tell-tale reports purveyed to his ear by *Squeak,* one of his more cunning Corporals, a grizzled little man, so nicknamed by the sailors on account of his squeaky voice, and sharp visage ferreting about the dark corners of the lower decks after interlopers, satirically suggesting to them the idea of a rat in a cellar.

From his Chief's employing him as an implicit tool in laying little traps for the worriment of the Foretopman— for it was from the Master-at-arms that the petty persecutions heretofore adverted to had proceeded—the corporal having naturally enough concluded that his master could have no love for the sailor, made it his business, faithful understrapper that he was, to foment the ill blood by perverting to his Chief certain innocent frolics of the good natured Foretopman, besides inventing for his mouth sundry contumelious epithets he claimed to have overheard him let fall. The Master-at-arms never suspected the veracity of these reports, more especially as to the epithets, for he well knew how secretly unpopular may become a master-at-arms, at least a master-at-arms of those days zealous in his function, and how the blue-jackets shoot at him in private their raillery and wit; the nickname by which he goes among them (*Jemmy Legs*) implying under the form of merriment their cherished disrespect and dislike.

But in view of the greediness of hate for patrolmen, it hardly needed a purveyor to feed Claggart's passion. An uncommon prudence is habitual with the subtler depravity, for it has everything to hide. And in case of an injury but suspected, its secretiveness voluntarily cuts it off from enlightenment or disillusion; and, not unreluctantly, action is taken upon surmise as upon certainty. And the retaliation is apt to be in monstrous disproportion to the supposed offence; for when in anybody was revenge in its exactions aught else but an inordinate usurer? But how with Claggart's conscience? For though consciences are unlike as foreheads, every intelligence, not excluding the Scriptural devils who "believe and tremble," has one. But Claggart's conscience being but the lawyer to his will, made ogres of trifles, probably arguing that the motive imputed to Billy in spilling the soup just when he did, together with the epithets alleged, these, if nothing more, made a strong case against him; nay, justified animosity into a sort of retributive righteousness. The Pharisee is the Guy Fawkes prowling in the hid chambers underlying the Claggarts. And they can really form no conception of an unreciprocated malice. Probably, the master-at-arms' clandestine persecution of Billy was started to try the temper of the man; but it had not developed any quality in him that enmity could make official use of or even pervert into plausible self-justification; so that the occurrence at the mess, petty if it were, was a welcome one to that peculiar conscience assigned to be the private mentor of Claggart. And, for the rest, not improbably it put him upon new experiments.

[15]

Not many days after the last incident narrated, something befell Billy Budd that more gravelled him than aught that had previously occurred.

It was a warm night for the latitude; and the Foretopman, whose watch at the time was properly below, was dozing on the uppermost deck whither he had ascended

from his hot hammock, one of hundreds suspended so
closely wedged together over a lower gun-deck that there
was little or no swing to them. He lay as in the shadow of
a hill-side, stretched under the lee of the booms, a piled
ridge of spare spars amidships between foremast and mainmast and among which the ship's largest boat, the launch,
was stowed. Alongside of three other slumberers from below, he lay near that end of the booms which approaches
the foremast; his station aloft on duty as a foretopman being just over the deck-station of the forecastlemen, enti-
tling him according to usage to make himself more or less
at home in that neighborhood.

Presently he was stirred into semi-consciousness by
somebody, who must have previously sounded the sleep of
the others, touching his shoulder, and then as the Foretopman raised his head, breathing into his ear in a quick
whisper, "Slip into the lee forechains, Billy; there is something in the wind. Don't speak. Quick, I will meet you
there;" and disappeared.

Now Billy like sundry other essentially good-natured
ones had some of the weaknesses inseparable from essential good nature; and among these was a reluctance, almost an incapacity of plumply saying *no* to an abrupt
proposition not obviously absurd, on the face of it, nor
obviously unfriendly, nor iniquitous. And being of warm
blood he had not the phlegm tacitly to negative any proposition by unresponsive inaction. Like his sense of fear, his
apprehension as to aught outside of the honest and natural
was seldom very quick. Besides, upon the present occasion, the drowse from his sleep still hung upon him.

However it was, he mechanically rose, and sleepily wondering what could be in the wind, betook himself to the
designated place, a narrow platform, one of six, outside of
the high bulwarks and screened by the great dead-eyes
and multiple columned lanyards of the shrouds and back-
stays; and, in a great war-ship of that time, of dimensions
commensurate with the hull's magnitude; a tarry balcony
in short overhanging the sea, and so secluded that one
mariner of the *Bellipotent,* a non-conformist old tar of a
serious turn, made it even in daytime his private oratory.

In this retired nook the stranger soon joined Billy Budd.
There was no moon as yet; a haze obscured the star-light.
He could not distinctly see the stranger's face. Yet from

something in the outline and carriage, Billy took him to be, and correctly, for one of the afterguard.

"Hist! Billy," said the man in the same quick cautionary whisper as before; "You were impressed, weren't you? Well, so was I;" and he paused, as to mark the effect. But Billy not knowing exactly what to make of this said nothing. Then the other: "We are not the only impressed ones, Billy. There's a gang of us.—Couldn't you—help—at a pinch?"

"What do you mean?" demanded Billy, here thoroughly shaking off his drowse.

"Hist, hist!" the hurried whisper now growing husky, "see here;" and the man held up two small objects faintly twinkling in the nightlight; "see, they are yours, Billy, if you'll only—"

But Billy broke in, and in his resentful eagerness to deliver himself his vocal infirmity somewhat intruded: "D-D-Damme, I don't know what you are d-d-driving at, or what you mean, but you had better g-g-go where you belong!" For the moment the fellow, as confounded, did not stir; and Billy springing to his feet, said, "If you d-don't start I'll t-t-toss you back over the r-rail!" There was no mistaking this and the mysterious emissary decamped disappearing in the direction of the mainmast in the shadow of the booms.

"Hallo, what's the matter?" here came growling from a forecastleman awakened from his deck-doze by Billy's raised voice. And as the foretopman reappeared and was recognized by him; "Ah, *Beauty,* is it you? Well, something must have been the matter for you st-st-stuttered."

"O," rejoined Billy, now mastering the impediment; "I found an afterguardsman in our part of the ship here and I bid him be off where he belongs."

"And is that all you did about it, foretopman?" gruffly demanded another, an irascible old fellow of brick-colored visage and hair, and who was known to his associate forecastlemen as *Red Pepper;* "Such sneaks I should like to marry to the gunner's daughter!" by that expression meaning that he would like to subject them to disciplinary castigation over a gun.

However, Billy's rendering of the matter satisfactorily accounted to these inquirers for the brief commotion, since of all the sections of a ship's company, the forecastlemen,

veterans for the most part and bigoted in their sea-preju-
dices, are the most jealous in resenting territorial encroach-
ments, especially on the part of any of the afterguard, of
whom they have but a sorry opinion, chiefly landsmen,
never going aloft except to reef or furl the mainsail, and in
no wise competent to handle a marlinspike or turn in a
dead-eye, say.

[*16*]

This incident sorely puzzled Billy Budd. It was an entirely new experience; the first time in his life that he had
ever been personally approached in underhand intriguing
fashion. Prior to this encounter he had known nothing of
the afterguardsman, the two men being stationed wide
apart, one forward and aloft during his watch, the other on
deck and aft.

What could it mean? And could they really be guineas,
those two glittering objects the interloper had held up to
his eyes? Where could the fellow get guineas? Why even
spare buttons are not so plentiful at sea. The more he
turned the matter over, the more he was non-plussed, and
made uneasy and discomforted. In his disgustful recoil
from an overture which tho' he but ill comprehended he
instinctively knew must involve evil of some sort, Billy
Budd was like a young horse fresh from the pasture suddenly inhaling a vile whiff from some chemical factory,
and by repeated snortings tries to get it out of his nostrils
and lungs. This frame of mind barred all desire of holding
further parley with the fellow, even were it but for the
purpose of gaining some enlightenment as to his design in
approaching him. And yet he was not without natural
curiosity to see how such a visitor in the dark would look
in broad day.

He espied him the following afternoon in his first dog-
watch below, one of the smokers on that forward part of
the upper gun deck allotted to the pipe. He recognized
him by his general cut and build, more than by his round
freckled face and glassy eyes of pale blue, veiled with
lashes all but white. And yet Billy was a bit uncertain
whether indeed it were he—yonder chap about his own
age chatting and laughing in free-hearted way, leaning
against a gun; a genial young fellow enough to look at,
and something of a rattle-brain, to all appearance. Rather

chubby too for a sailor, even an afterguardsman. In short the last man in the world, one would think, to be over-burthened with thoughts, especially those perilous thoughts that must needs belong to a conspirator in any serious project, or even to the underling of such a conspirator.

Altho' Billy was not aware of it, the fellow, with a side-long watchful glance had perceived Billy first, and then noting that Billy was looking at him, thereupon nodded a familiar sort of friendly recognition as to an old acquaint-ance, without interrupting the talk he was engaged in with the group of smokers. A day or two afterwards, chancing in the evening promenade on a gun deck, to pass Billy, he offered a flying word of good-fellowship as it were, which by its unexpectedness, and equivocalness under the cir-cumstances so embarrassed Billy that he knew not how to respond to it, and let it go unnoticed.

Billy was now left more at a loss than before. The in-effectual speculation into which he was led was so dis-turbingly alien to him that he did his best to smother it. It never entered his mind that here was a matter which from its extreme questionableness, it was his duty as a loyal blue-jacket to report in the proper quarter. And, probably, had such a step been suggested to him, he would have been deterred from taking it by the thought, one of novice-magnanimity, that it would savor overmuch of the dirty work of a tell-tale. He kept the thing to himself. Yet upon one occasion, he could not forbear a little disburth-ening himself to the old Dansker, tempted thereto perhaps by the influence of a balmy night when the ship lay be-calmed; the twain, silent for the most part, sitting to-gether on deck, their heads propped against the bulwarks. But it was only a partial and anonymous account that Billy gave, the unfounded scruples above referred to preventing full disclosure to anybody. Upon hearing Billy's version, the sage Dansker seemed to divine more than he was told; and after a little meditation during which his wrinkles were pursed as into a point, quite effacing for the time that quizzing expression his face sometimes wore,—"Didn't I say so, Baby Budd?"

"Say what?" demanded Billy.

"Why, *Jemmy Legs* is *down* on you."

"And what," rejoined Billy in amazement, "has *Jemmy Legs* to do with that cracked afterguardsman?"

"Ho, it was an afterguardsman then. A cat's-paw, a cat's-paw!" And with that exclamation, which, whether it had reference to a light puff of air just then coming over the calm sea, or subtler relation to the afterguardsman, there is no telling, the old Merlin gave a twisting wrench with his black teeth at his plug of tobacco, vouchsafing no reply to Billy's impetuous question, tho' now repeated, for it was his wont to relapse into grim silence when interrogated in skeptical sort as to any of his sententious oracles, not always very clear ones, rather partaking of that obscurity which invests most Delphic deliverances from any quarter.

Long experience had very likely brought this old man to that bitter prudence which never interferes in aught and never gives advice.

[*17*]

Yes, despite the Dansker's pithy insistence as to the master-at-arms being at the bottom of these strange experiences of Billy on board the *Bellipotent,* the young sailor was ready to ascribe them to almost anybody but the man who, to use Billy's own expression, "always had a pleasant word for him." This is to be wondered at. Yet not so much to be wondered at. In certain matters, some sailors even in mature life remain unsophisticated enough. But a young seafarer of the disposition of our athletic Foretopman, is much of a child-man. And yet a child's utter innocence is but its blank ignorance, and the innocence more or less wanes as intelligence waxes. But in Billy Budd intelligence, such as it was, had advanced, while yet his simple mindedness remained for the most part unaffected. Experience is a teacher indeed; yet did Billy's years make his experience small. Besides, he had none of that intuitive knowledge of the bad which in natures not good or incompletely so foreruns experience, and therefore may pertain, as in some instances it too clearly does pertain, even to youth.

And what could Billy know of man except of man as a mere sailor? And the old-fashioned sailor, the veritable man-before-the-mast, the sailor from boyhood up, he, tho' indeed of the same species as a landsman, is in some respects singularly distinct from him. The sailor is frankness, the landsman is finesse. Life is not a game with the sailor, demanding the long head; no intricate game of chess where few moves are made in straightforwardness, and ends are attained by indirection; an oblique, tedious, barren game hardly worth that poor candle burnt out in playing it.

Yes, as a class, sailors are in character a juvenile race. Even their deviations are marked by juvenility. And this more especially holding true with the sailors of Billy's time. Then, too, certain things which apply to all sailors, do more pointedly operate here and there, upon the junior one. Every sailor, too, is accustomed to obey orders without debating them; his life afloat is externally ruled for him; he is not brought into that promiscuous commerce with mankind where unobstructed free agency on equal terms—equal superficially, at least—soon teaches one that unless upon occasion he exercise a distrust keen in proportion to the fairness of the appearance, some foul turn may be served him. A ruled undemonstrative distrustfulness is so habitual, not with business-men so much, as with men who know their kind in less shallow relations than business, namely, certain men-of-the-world, that they come at last to employ it all but unconsciously; and some of them would very likely feel real surprise at being charged with it as one of their general characteristics.

[*18*]

But after the little matter at the mess Billy Budd no more found himself in strange trouble at times about his hammock or his clothesbag or what not. While, as to that smile that occasionally sunned him, and the pleasant passing word, these were if not more frequent, yet if anything more pronounced than before.

But for all that, there were certain other demonstrations now. When Claggart's unobserved glance happened to light on belted Billy rolling along the upper gun-deck in the leisure of the second dog-watch, exchanging passing broadsides of fun with other young promenaders in the crowd; that glance would follow the cheerful sea-Hyperion with a settled meditative and melancholy expression, his eyes strangely suffused with incipient feverish tears. Then would Claggart look like the man of sorrows. Yes, and sometimes the melancholy expression would have in it a touch of soft yearning, as if Claggart could even have loved Billy but for fate and ban. But this was an evanescence, and quickly repented of, as it were, by an immitigable look, pinching and shrivelling the visage into the momentary semblance of a wrinkled walnut. But sometimes catching sight in advance of the foretopman coming in his direction, he would, upon their nearing, step aside a little to let him pass, dwelling upon Billy for the moment with the glittering dental satire of a Guise. But upon any abrupt unforeseen encounter a red light would forth from his eye like a spark from an anvil in a dusk smithy. That quick fierce light was a strange one, darted from orbs which in repose were of a color nearest approaching a deeper violet, the softest of shades.

Tho' some of these caprices of the pit could not but be observed by their object, yet were they beyond the construing of such a nature. And the *thews* of Billy were hardly compatible with that sort of sensitive spiritual organisation which in some cases instinctively conveys to ignorant innocence an admonition of the proximity of the malign. He thought the Master-at-arms acted in a manner rather queer at times. That was all. But the occasional frank air and pleasant word went for what they purported to be, the young sailor never having heard as yet of the "too fair-spoken man."

Had the foretopman been conscious of having done or said anything to provoke the ill will of the official, it would have been different with him, and his sight might have been purged if not sharpened. As it was, innocence was his blinder.

So was it with him in yet another matter. Two minor officers—the Armorer and Captain of the Hold—with whom he had never exchanged a word, his position in the ship not bringing him into contact with them; these men now for the first began to cast upon Billy when they chanced to encounter him, that peculiar glance which evidences that the man from whom it comes has been some way tampered with and to the prejudice of him upon whom the glance lights. Never did it occur to Billy as a thing to be noted or a thing suspicious, tho' he well knew the fact, that the Armorer and Captain of the Hold, with the ship's-yeoman, apothecary, and others of that grade, were by naval usage, mess-mates of the master-at-arms, men with ears convenient to his confidential tongue.

But the general popularity that our *Handsome Sailor's* manly forwardness upon occasion, and irresistible good nature, indicating no mental superiority tending to excite an invidious feeling; this good will on the part of most of his shipmates made him the less to concern himself about such mute aspects toward him as those whereto allusion has just been made, aspects he could not fathom as to infer their whole import.

As to the afterguardsman, tho' Billy for reasons already given necessarily saw little of him, yet when the two did happen to meet, invariably came the fellow's off-hand cheerful recognition, sometimes accompanied by a passing pleasant word or two. Whatever that equivocal young person's original design may really have been, or the design of which he might have been the deputy, certain it was from his manner upon these occasions, that he had wholly dropped it.

It was as if his precocity of crookedness (and every vulgar villain is precocious) had for once deceived him, and the man he had sought to entrap as a simpleton had, through his very simplicity ignorantly baffled him.

But shrewd ones may opine that it was hardly possible for Billy to refrain from going up to the afterguardsman and bluntly demanding to know his purpose in the initial interview, so abruptly closed in the fore-chains. Shrewd ones may also think it but natural in Billy to set about sounding some of the other impressed men of the ship in order to discover what basis, if any, there was for the emissary's obscure suggestions as to plotting disaffection aboard. Yes, the shrewd may so think. But something more, or rather, something else than mere shrewdness is perhaps needful for the due understanding of such a character as Billy Budd's.

As to Claggart, the monomania in the man—if that indeed it were—as involuntarily disclosed by starts in the manifestations detailed, yet in general covered over by his self-contained and rational demeanor; this, like a subterranean fire was eating its way deeper and deeper in him. Something decisive must come of it.

[19]

After the mysterious interview in the fore-chains, the one so abruptly ended there by Billy, nothing especially germane to the story occurred until the events now about to be narrated.

Elsewhere it has been said that in the lack of frigates (of course better sailers than line-of-battle ships) in the English squadron up the Straits at that period, the *Bellipotent* was occasionally employed not only as an available substitute for a scout, but at times on detached service of more important kind. This was not alone because of her sailing qualities, not common in a ship of her rate, but quite as much, probably, that the character of her commander, it was thought, specially adapted him for any duty where under unforeseen difficulties a prompt initiative might have to be taken in some matter demanding knowledge and ability in addition to those qualities implied in good seamanship. It was on an expedition of the latter sort, a somewhat distant one, and when the *Bellipotent* was almost at her furthest remove from the fleet, that in the latter part of an afternoon-watch she unexpectedly came in sight of a ship of the enemy. It proved to be a frigate. The latter perceiving thro' the glass that the weight of men and metal would be heavily against her, invoking her light heels, crowded sail to get away. After a chase urged almost against hope and lasting until about the middle of the first dog-watch, she signally succeeded in effecting her escape.

Not long after the pursuit had been given up, and ere the excitement incident thereto had altogether waned away, the Master-at-Arms, ascending from his cavernous sphere, made his appearance cap in hand by the mainmast, respectfully waiting the notice of Captain Vere then solitary walking the weather-side of the quarter-deck, doubtless somewhat chafed at the failure of the pursuit. The spot where Claggart stood was the place allotted to men of lesser grades seeking some more particular interview either with the officer-of-the-deck or the Captain himself. But from the latter it was not often that a sailor or petty-officer of those days would seek a hearing; only some exceptional cause, would, according to established custom, have warranted that.

Presently, just as the Commander absorbed in his reflections was on the point of turning aft in his promenade, he became sensible of Claggart's presence, and saw the doffed cap held in deferential expectancy. Here be it said that

Captain Vere's personal knowledge of this petty-officer had only begun at the time of the ship's last sailing from home, Claggart then for the first, in transfer from a ship detained for repairs, supplying on board the *Bellipotent* the place of a previous master-at-arms disabled and ashore.

No sooner did the Commander observe who it was that now deferentially stood awaiting his notice, than a peculiar expression came over him. It was not unlike that which uncontrollably will flit across the countenance of one at unawares encountering a person who, though known to him indeed, has hardly been long enough known for thorough knowledge, but something in whose aspect nevertheless now for the first provokes a vaguely repellent distaste. But coming to a stand, and resuming much of his wonted official manner, save that a sort of impatience lurked in the intonation of the opening word, he said, "Well? what is it, Master-at-Arms?"

With the air of a subordinate grieved at the necessity of being a messenger of ill tidings, and while conscientiously determined to be frank, yet equally resolved upon shunning overstatement, Claggart at this invitation or rather summons to disburthen, spoke up. What he said, conveyed in the language of no uneducated man, was to the effect following, if not altogether in these words, namely, that during the chase and preparations for the possible encounter he had seen enough to convince him that at least one sailor aboard was a dangerous character in a ship mustering some who not only had taken a guilty part in the late serious troubles, but others also who, like the man in question, had entered His Majesty's service under another form than enlistment.

At this point Captain Vere with some impatience, interrupted him: "Be direct, man; say impressed men."

Claggart made a gesture of subservience, and proceeded.

Quite lately he (Claggart) had begun to suspect that on the gun-decks some sort of movement prompted by the sailor in question was covertly going on, but he had not thought himself warranted in reporting the suspicion so long as it remained indistinct. But from what he had that afternoon observed in the man referred to, the suspicion of something clandestine going on had advanced to a point less removed from certainty. He deeply felt, he added, the serious responsibility assumed in making a report involving such possible consequences to the individual mainly concerned, besides tending to augment those natural anxieties which every naval commander must feel in view of extraordinary outbreaks so recent as those which, he sorrowfully said it, it needed not to name.

Now at the first broaching of the matter Captain Vere, taken by surprise, could not wholly dissemble his disquietude. But as Claggart went on, the former's aspect changed into restiveness under something in the witness' manner in giving his testimony. However, he refrained from interrupting him. And Claggart, continuing, concluded with this:

"God forbid, your honor, that the *Bellipotent*'s should be the experience of the—"

"Never mind that!" here peremptorily broke in the superior, his face altering with anger, instinctively divining the ship that the other was about to name, one in which the Nore Mutiny had assumed a singularly tragical character that for a time jeopardized the life of its commander. Under the circumstances he was indignant at the purposed allusion. When the commissioned officers themselves were on all occasions very heedful how they referred to the recent events, for a petty-officer unnecessarily to allude to them in the presence of his Captain, this struck him as a most immodest presumption. Besides, to his quick sense of self-respect, it even looked under the circumstances something like an attempt to alarm him. Nor at first was he without some surprise that one who so far as he had hitherto come under his notice had shown considerable tact in his function should in this particular evince such lack of it.

But these thoughts and kindred dubious ones flitting across his mind were suddenly replaced by an intuitional surmise which, though as yet obscure in form, served practically to affect his reception of the ill tidings. Certain it is, that long versed in everything pertaining to the complicated gun-deck life, which like every other form of life, has its secret mines and dubious side, the side popularly disclaimed, Captain Vere did not permit himself to be unduly disturbed by the general tenor of his subordinate's report. Furthermore, if in view of recent events prompt action should be taken at the first palpable sign of recurring insubordination, for all that, not judicious would it be, he thought, to keep the idea of lingering disaffection alive by undue forwardness in crediting an informer, even if his own subordinate, and charged among other things with police surveillance of the crew. This feeling would not perhaps have so prevailed with him were it not that upon a prior occasion the patriotic zeal officially evinced by Claggart had somewhat irritated him as appearing rather supersensible and strained. Furthermore, something even in the official's self-possessed and somewhat ostentatious manner in making his specifications strangely reminded him of a bandsman, a perjurous witness in a capital case before a court-martial ashore of which when a lieutenant he, Captain Vere, had been a member.

Now the peremptory check given to Claggart in the matter of the arrested allusion was quickly followed up by this: "You say that there is at least one dangerous man aboard. Name him."

"William Budd. A foretopman, your honor—"

"William Budd," repeated Captain Vere with unfeigned astonishment; "and mean you the man that Lieutenant Ratcliffe took from the merchantman not very long ago—the young fellow who seems to be so popular with the men— Billy, the Handsome Sailor, as they call him?"

"The same, your honor; but for all his youth and good looks, a deep one. Not for nothing does he insinuate himself into the good will of his shipmates, since at the least all hands will at a pinch say a good word for him at all hazards. Did Lieutenant Ratcliffe happen to tell your honor of that adroit fling of Budd's jumping up the cutter's bow under the merchantman's stern when he was being taken off? It is even masqued by that sort of good humored air that at heart he resents his impressment. You have but noted his fair cheek. A man-trap may be under his ruddy-tipped daisies."

Now the *Handsome Sailor,* as a signal figure among the crew, had naturally enough attracted the Captain's attention from the first. Tho' in general not very demonstrative to his officers, he had congratulated Lieutenant Ratcliffe upon his good fortune in lighting on such a fine specimen of the genus homo, who in the nude might have posed for a statue of young Adam before the Fall.

As to Billy's adieu to the ship *Rights-of-Man,* which the boarding lieutenant had indeed reported to him but in a deferential way more as a good story than aught else, Captain Vere, tho' mistakenly understanding it as a satiric sally, had but thought so much the better of the impressed man for it; as a military sailor, admiring the spirit that could take an arbitrary enlistment so merrily and sensibly. The foretopman's conduct, too, so far as it had fallen under the Captain's notice, had confirmed the first happy augury, while the new recruit's qualities as a *sailor-man* seemed to be such that he had thought of recommending him to the executive officer for promotion to a place that would more frequently bring him under his own observation, namely, the captaincy of the mizzen-top, replacing there in the starboard watch a man not so young whom partly for that reason he deemed less fitted for the post. Be it parenthesized here that since the mizzen-top-men having not to handle such breadths of heavy canvas as the lower sails on the main-mast and fore-mast, a young man if of the right stuff not only seems best adapted to duty there, but in fact is generally selected for the captaincy of that top, and the company under him are light hands and often but striplings. In sum, Captain Vere had from the beginning deemed Billy Budd to be what in the naval parlance of the time was called a *"King's bargain,"* that is to say, for His Britannic Majesty's navy a capital investment at small outlay or none at all.

After a brief pause during which the reminiscences above mentioned passed vividly through his mind and he weighed the import of Claggart's last suggestion conveyed in the phrase "man-trap under the daisies," and the more he weighed it the less reliance he felt in the informer's good faith. Suddenly he turned upon him and in a low voice: "Do you come to me, master-at-arms, with so foggy a tale? As to Budd, cite me an act or spoken word of his confirmatory of what you in general charge against him. Stay," drawing nearer to him, "heed what you speak. Just now, and in a case like this, there is a yard-arm-end for the false-witness."

"Ah, your honor!" sighed Claggart mildly shaking his shapely head as in sad deprecation of such unmerited severity of tone. Then, bridling—erecting himself as in virtuous self-assertion, he circumstantially alleged certain words and acts, which collectively, if credited, led to presumptions mortally inculpating Budd. And for some of these averments, he added, substantiating proof was not far.

With gray eyes impatient and distrustful essaying to fathom to the bottom Claggart's calm violet ones, Captain Vere again heard him out; then for the moment stood ruminating. The mood he evinced, Claggart—himself for the time liberated from the other's scrutiny—steadily regarded with a look difficult to render,—a look curious of the operation of his tactics, a look such as might have been that of the spokesman of the envious children of Jacob deceptively imposing upon the troubled patriarch the blood-dyed coat of young Joseph.

Though something exceptional in the moral quality of Captain Vere made him, in earnest encounter with a fellow-man, a veritable touch-stone of that man's essential nature, yet now as to Claggart and what was really going on in him, his feeling partook less of intuitional conviction than of strong suspicion clogged by strange dubieties. The perplexity he evinced proceeded less from aught touching the man informed against—as Claggart doubtless opined—than from considerations how best to act in regard to the informer. At first indeed he was naturally for summoning that substantiation of his allegations which Claggart said was at hand. But such a proceeding would result in the matter at once getting abroad, which in the present stage of it, he thought, might undesirably affect the ship's company. If Claggart was a false witness,—that closed the affair. And therefore before trying the accusation, he would first practically test the accuser; and he thought this could be done in a quiet undemonstrative way.

The measure he determined upon involved a shifting of the scene, a transfer to a place less exposed to observation than the broad quarter-deck. For although the few gun-room officers there at the time had, in due observance of naval etiquette, withdrawn to leeward the moment Captain Vere had begun his promenade on the deck's weather-side; and tho' during the colloquy with Claggart they of course ventured not to diminish the distance; and though throughout the interview Captain Vere's voice was far from high, and Claggart's silvery and low; and the wind in the cordage and the wash of the sea helped the more to put them beyond earshot; nevertheless, the interview's continuance al-

ready had attracted observation from some topmen aloft
and other sailors in the waist or further forward.

Having determined upon his measures, Captain Vere
forthwith took action. Abruptly turning to Claggart he
asked, "Master-at-arms, is it now Budd's watch aloft?"

"No, your honor." Whereupon, "Mr. Wilkes!" summoning the nearest midshipman, "tell Albert to come to me."
Albert was the Captain's hammock-boy, a sort of sea-valet
in whose discretion and fidelity his master had much confidence. The lad appeared. "You know Budd the foretopman?"

"I do, Sir."

"Go find him. It is his watch off. Manage to tell him
out of earshot that he is wanted aft. Contrive it that he
speaks to nobody. Keep him in talk yourself. And not till
you get well aft here, not till then let him know that the
place where he is wanted is my cabin. You understand.
Go.—Master-at-Arms, show yourself on the decks below,
and when you think it time for Albert to be coming with
his man, stand by quietly to follow the sailor in."

[20]

Now when the foretopman found himself closeted there,
as it were, in the cabin with the Captain and Claggart, he
was surprised enough. But it was a surprise unaccompanied
by apprehension or distrust. To an immature nature essentially honest and humane, forewarning intimations of
subtler danger from one's kind come tardily if at all. The
only thing that took shape in the young sailor's mind was
this: Yes, the Captain, I have always thought, looks kindly
upon me. Wonder if he's going to make me his coxswain. I
should like that. And maybe now he is going to ask the
master-at-arms about me.

"Shut the door there, sentry," said the commander;
"stand without, and let nobody come in.—Now, master-
at-arms, tell this man to his face what you told of him to
me;" and stood prepared to scrutinize the mutually confronting visages.

With the measured step and calm collected air of an
asylum-physician approaching in the public hall some patient beginning to show indications of a coming paroxysm,
Claggart deliberately advanced within short range of Billy,

and mesmerically looking him in the eye, briefly recapitulated the accusation.

Not at first did Billy take it in. When he did, the rose-tan of his cheek looked struck as by white leprosy. He stood like one impaled and gagged. Meanwhile the accuser's eyes removing not as yet from the blue dilated ones, underwent a phenomenal change, their wonted rich violet color blurring into a muddy purple. Those lights of human intelligence losing human expression, gelidly protruding like the alien eyes of certain uncatalogued creatures of the deep. The first mesmeric glance was one of serpent fascination; the last was as the hungry lurch of the torpedo-fish.

"Speak, man!" said Captain Vere to the transfixed one struck by his aspect even more than by Claggart's, "Speak! defend yourself." Which appeal caused but a strange dumb gesturing and gurgling in Billy; amazement at such an accusation so suddenly sprung on inexperienced nonage; this, and, it may be horror of the accuser, serving to bring out his lurking defect and in this instance for the time intensifying it into a convulsed tongue-tie; while the intent head and entire form straining forward in an agony of ineffectual eagerness to obey the injunction to speak and defend himself, gave an expression to the face like that of a condemned Vestal priestess in the moment of being buried alive, and in the first struggle against suffocation.

Though at the time Captain Vere was quite ignorant of Billy's liability to vocal impediment, he now immediately divined it, since vividly Billy's aspect recalled to him that of a bright young schoolmate of his whom he had once seen struck by much the same startling impotence in the act of eagerly rising in the class to be foremost in response to a testing question put to it by the master. Going close up to the young sailor, and laying a soothing hand on his shoulder, he said, "There is no hurry, my boy. Take your time, take your time." Contrary to the effect intended, these words so fatherly in tone, doubtless touching Billy's heart to the quick, prompted yet more violent efforts at utterance—efforts soon ending for the time in confirming the paralysis, and bringing to his face an expression which was as a crucifixion to behold. The next instant, quick as the flame from a discharged cannon at night, his right arm shot out, and Claggart dropped to the deck. Whether intentionally or but owing to the young athlete's superior height, the blow had taken effect full upon the forehead, so shapely and intellectual-looking a feature in the master-at-arms; so that the body fell over lengthwise, like a heavy plank tilted from erectness. A gasp or two, and he lay motionless.

"Fated boy," breathed Captain Vere in tone so low as to be almost a whisper, "what have you done! But here, help me."

The twain raised the felled one from the loins up into a sitting position. The spare form flexibly acquiesced, but inertly. It was like handling a dead snake. They lowered it back. Regaining erectness Captain Vere with one hand covering his face stood to all appearance as impassive as the object at his feet. Was he absorbed in taking in all the bearings of the event and what was best not only now at once to be done, but also in the sequel? Slowly he uncovered his face; and the effect was as if the moon emerging from eclipse should reappear with quite another aspect than that which had gone into hiding. The father in him, manifested towards Billy thus far in the scene, was replaced by the military disciplinarian. In his official tone he bade the foretopman retire to a state-room aft (pointing it out), and there remain till thence summoned. This order Billy in silence mechanically obeyed. Then going to the cabin-door where it opened on the quarter-deck, Captain Vere said to the sentry without, "Tell somebody to send Albert here." When the lad appeared his master so contrived it that he should not catch sight of the prone one. "Albert," he said to him, "tell the Surgeon I wish to see him. You need not come back till called." When the Surgeon entered—a self-poised character of that grave sense and experience that hardly anything could take him aback, —Captain Vere advanced to meet him, thus unconsciously intercepting his view of Claggart, and interrupting the other's wonted ceremonious salutation, said, "Nay, tell me how it is with yonder man," directing his attention to the prostrate one.

The Surgeon looked, and for all his self-command, somewhat started at the abrupt revelation. On Claggart's always pallid complexion, thick black blood was now oozing from nostril and ear. To the gazer's professional eye it was unmistakably no living man that he saw.

"Is it so then?" said Captain Vere intently watching him. "I thought it. But verify it." Whereupon the customary test confirmed the Surgeon's first glance, who now looking up in unfeigned concern, cast a look of intense inquisitiveness upon his superior. But Captain Vere, with one hand to his brow, was standing motionless. Suddenly, catching the Surgeon's arm convulsively, he exclaimed, pointing down to the body—"It is the divine judgment on Ananias! Look!"

Disturbed by the excited manner he had never before observed in the *Bellipotent*'s Captain, and as yet wholly ignorant of the affair, the prudent Surgeon nevertheless held his peace, only again looking an earnest interrogation as to what it was that had resulted in such a tragedy.

But Captain Vere was now again motionless standing absorbed in thought. But again starting, he vehemently exclaimed—"Struck dead by an angel of God! Yet the angel must hang!"

At these passionate interjections, mere incoherences to the listener as yet unapprised of the antecedents, the Surgeon was profoundly discomposed. But now as recollecting himself, Captain Vere in less harsh tone briefly related the circumstances leading up to the event.

"But come; we must despatch," he added. "Help me to remove him (meaning the body) to yonder compartment," designating one opposite that where the foretopman remained immured. Anew disturbed by a request that as implying a desire for secrecy, seemed unaccountably strange to him, there was nothing for the subordinate to do but comply.

"Go now," said Captain Vere with something of his wonted manner—"Go now. I shall presently call a drumhead court. Tell the lieutenants what has happened, and tell Mr. Mordant," meaning the captain of marines, "and charge them to keep the matter to themselves."

[21]

Full of disquietude and misgiving the Surgeon left the cabin. Was Captain Vere suddenly affected in his mind, or was it but a transient excitement, brought about by so strange and extraordinary a happening? As to the drumhead court, it struck the Surgeon as impolitic, if nothing more. The thing to do, he thought, was to place Billy Budd in confinement and in a way dictated by usage, and post-

pone further action in so extraordinary a case, to such
time as they should rejoin the squadron, and then refer it
to the Admiral. He recalled the unwonted agitation of Captain Vere and his excited exclamations so at variance with
his normal manner. Was he unhinged? But assuming that
he is, it is not so susceptible of proof. What then can he do?
No more trying situation is conceivable than that of an
officer subordinate under a Captain whom he suspects to
be, not mad indeed, but yet not quite unaffected in his intellect. To argue his order to him would be insolence. To
resist him would be mutiny.

In obedience to Captain Vere he communicated what
had happened to the lieutenants & captain of marines; saying nothing as to the Captain's state. They fully shared his
own surprise and concern. Like him too they seemed to
think that such a matter should be referred to the Admiral.

[22]

Who in the rainbow can draw the line where the violet
tint ends and the orange tint begins? Distinctly we see the
difference of the colors, but where exactly does the one first
blendingly enter into the other? So with sanity and insanity.
In pronounced cases there is no question about them. But
in some supposed cases, in various degrees supposedly less
pronounced, to draw the exact line of demarkation few will
undertake tho' for a fee some professional experts will.
There is nothing namable but that some men will undertake
to do it for pay.

Whether Captain Vere, as the Surgeon professionally and
privately surmised, was really the sudden victim of any
degree of aberration, one must determine for himself by
such light as this narrative may afford.

That the unhappy event which has been narrated could
not have happened at a worse juncture was but too true.
For it was close on the heel of the suppressed insurrections,
an aftertime very critical to naval authority, demanding
from every English sea-commander two qualities not
readily interfusable—prudence and rigor. Moreover there
was something crucial in the case.

In the jugglery of circumstances preceding and attending the event on board the *Bellipotent,* and in the light of
that martial code whereby it was formally to be judged, innocence and guilt personified in Claggart and Budd in

effect changed places. In a legal view the apparent victim of the tragedy was he who had sought to victimize a man blameless; and the indisputable deed of the latter, navally regarded, constituted the most heinous of military crimes. Yet more. The essential right and wrong involved in the matter, the clearer that might be, so much the worse for the responsibility of a loyal sea-commander inasmuch as he was not authorized to determine the matter on that primitive basis.

Small wonder then that the *Bellipotent's* Captain, though in general a man of rapid decision, felt that circumspectness not less than promptitude was necessary. Until he could decide upon his course, and in each detail; and not only so, but until the concluding measure was upon the point of being enacted, he deemed it advisable, in view of all the circumstances to guard as much as possible against publicity. Here he may or may not have erred. Certain it is however that subsequently in the confidential talk of more than one or two gun-rooms and cabins he was not a little criticized by some officers, a fact imputed by his friends, and vehemently by his cousin Jack Denton, to professional jealousy of *Starry Vere*. Some imaginative ground for invidious comment there was. The maintenance of secrecy in the matter, the confining all knowledge of it for a time to the place where the homicide occurred, the quarter-deck cabin; in these particulars lurked some resemblance to the policy adopted in those tragedies of the palace which have occurred more than once in the capital founded by Peter the Barbarian.

The case indeed was such that fain would the *Bellipotent's* Captain have deferred taking any action whatever respecting it further than to keep the foretopman a close prisoner till the ship rejoined the squadron and then submitting the matter to the judgement of his Admiral. But a true military officer is in one particular like a true monk. Not with more of self-abnegation will the latter keep his vows of monastic obedience than the former his vows of allegiance to martial duty.

[The year 1797, the year of this narrative, belongs to a period which, as every thinker now feels, involved a crisis for Christendom not exceeded in its undetermined momentousness at the time by any other era whereof there is record. The opening proposition made by the Spirit of that

Age involved rectification of the Old World's hereditary wrongs. In France, to some extent, this was bloodily effected. But what then? Straightway the Revolution itself became a wrongdoer, one more oppressive than the kings. Under Napoleon it enthroned upstart kings, and initiated that prolonged agony of continual war whose final throe was Waterloo. During those years not the wisest could have foreseen that the outcome of all would be what to some thinkers apparently it has since turned out to be—a political advance along nearly the whole line for Europeans.

Now, as elsewhere hinted, it was something caught from the Revolutionary Spirit that at Spithead emboldened the man-of-war's men to rise against real abuses, long-standing ones, and afterwards at the Nore to make inordinate and aggressive demands—successful resistance to which was confirmed only when the ringleaders were hung for an admonitory spectacle to the anchored fleet. Yet in a way analogous to the operation of the Revolution at large—the Great Mutiny, though by Englishmen naturally deemed monstrous at the time, doubtless gave the first latent prompting to most important reforms in the British navy.]*

Feeling that unless quick action was taken on it, the deed of the foretopman, so soon as it should be known on the gun-decks would tend to awaken any slumbering embers of the Nore among the crew, a sense of the urgency of the case overruled in Captain Vere every other consideration. But though a conscientious disciplinarian he was no lover of authority for mere authority's sake. Very far was he from embracing opportunities for monopolizing to himself the perils of moral responsibility, none at least that could properly be referred to an official superior or shared with him by his official equals or even subordinates. So thinking he was glad it would not be at variance with usage to turn the matter over to a summary court of his own officers, reserving to himself as the one on whom the ultimate accountability would rest, the right of maintaining a supervision of it, or formally or informally interposing at need. Accordingly a drum-head court was summarily convened, he electing the individuals composing it, the First

---

* There is a possibility that Melville may have intended to delete these two paragraphs, which appeared at this point in the manuscript before Mrs. Melville disarranged it; her suggestion that her husband intended this section as a preface was followed in all editions previous to Hayford and Sealts (1962).

Lieutenant, the Captain of marines, and the Sailing Master.

In associating an officer of marines with the sea-lieutenants in a case having to do with a sailor the Commander perhaps deviated from general custom. He was prompted thereto by the circumstance that he took that soldier to be a judicious person, thoughtful, and not altogether incapable of grappling with a difficult case unprecedented in his prior experience. Yet even as to him he was not without some latent misgiving, for withal he was an extremely good-natured man, an enjoyer of his dinner, a sound sleeper, and inclined to obesity. A man who though he would always maintain his manhood in battle might not prove altogether reliable in a moral dilemma involving aught of the tragic. As to the First Lieutenant and the Sailing Master, Captain Vere could not but be aware that though honest natures, of approved gallantry upon occasion, their intelligence was mostly confined to the matter of active seamanship and the fighting demands of their profession. The court was held in the same cabin where the unfortunate affair had taken place. This cabin, the Commander's, embraced the entire area under the poop-deck. Aft, and on either side, was a small state-room; the one room temporarily a jail & the other a dead-house, and a yet smaller compartment leaving a space between, expanding forward into a goodly oblong of length coinciding with the ship's beam. A skylight of moderate dimension was overhead and at each end of the oblong space were two sashed port-hole windows easily convertible back into embrasures for short carronades.

All being quickly in readiness, Billy Budd was arraigned, Captain Vere necessarily appearing as the sole witness in the case, and as such, temporarily sinking his rank, though singularly maintaining it in a matter apparently trivial, namely, that he testified from the ship's weather-side, with that object having caused the court to sit on the lee-side. Concisely he narrated all that had led up to the catastrophe, omitting nothing in Claggart's accusation and deposing as to the manner in which the prisoner had received it. At this testimony the three officers glanced with no little surprise at Billy Budd, the last man they would have suspected either of the mutinous design alleged by Claggart or the undeniable deed he himself had done.

The First Lieutenant, taking judicial primacy and turning toward the prisoner, said, "Captain Vere has spoken. Is it or is it not as Captain Vere says?" In response came syllables not so much impeded in the utterance as might have been anticipated. They were these: "Captain Vere tells the truth. It is just as Captain Vere says, but it is not as the Master-at-Arms said. I have eaten the King's bread and I am true to the King."

"I believe you, my man," said the witness, his voice indicating a suppressed emotion not otherwise betrayed.

"God will bless you for that, Your Honor!" not without stammering said Billy, and all but broke down. But immediately was recalled to self-control by another question, to which with the same emotional difficulty of utterance he said, "No, there was no malice between us. I never bore malice against the Master-at-arms. I am sorry that he is dead. I did not mean to kill him. Could I have used my tongue I would not have struck him. But he foully lied to my face and in presence of my Captain, and I had to say something, and I could only say it with a blow, God help me!"

In the impulsive above-board manner of the frank one, the court saw confirmed all that was implied in words that just previously had perplexed them, coming as they did from the testifier to the tragedy and promptly following Billy's impassioned disclaimer of mutinous intent—Captain Vere's words, "I believe you, my man."

Next it was asked of him whether he knew of or suspected aught savoring of incipient trouble (meaning mutiny, tho' the explicit term was avoided) going on in any section of the ship's company.

The reply lingered. This was naturally imputed by the court to the same vocal embarrassment which had retarded or obstructed previous answers. But in main it was otherwise here; the question immediately recalling to Billy's mind the interview with the afterguardsman in the forechains. But an innate repugnance to playing a part at all approaching that of an informer against one's own shipmates—the same erring sense of uninstructed honor which had stood in the way of his reporting the matter at the time though as a loyal man-of-war-man it was incumbent on him, and failure so to do if charged against him and proven, would have subjected him to the heaviest of penalties; this, with the blind feeling now his, that nothing really was being hatched, prevailed with him. When the answer came it was a negative.

"One question more," said the officer of marines now first speaking and with a troubled earnestness. "You tell us that what the Master-at-arms said against you was a lie. Now why should he have so lied, so maliciously lied, since you declare there was no malice between you?"

At that question unintentionally touching on a spiritual sphere wholly obscure to Billy's thoughts, he was nonplussed, evincing a confusion indeed that some observers, such as can readily be imagined, would have construed into involuntary evidence of hidden guilt. Nevertheless he strove some way to answer, but all at once relinquished the vain endeavor, at the same time turning an appealing glance towards Captain Vere as deeming him his best helper and friend. Captain Vere who had been seated for a time rose to his feet, addressing the interrogator. "The question you put to him comes naturally enough. But how can he rightly answer it? or anybody else? unless indeed it be he who lies within there," designating the compartment where lay the corpse. "But the prone one there will not rise to our summons. In effect, tho', as it seems to me, the point you make is hardly material. Quite aside from any conceivable motive actuating the Master-at-arms, and irrespective of the provocation to the blow, a martial court must needs in the present case confine its attention to the blow's consequence, which consequence justly is to be deemed not otherwise than as the striker's deed."

This utterance, the full significance of which it was not at all likely that Billy took in, nevertheless caused him to turn a wistful interrogative look toward the speaker, a look in its dumb expressiveness not unlike that which a dog of generous breed might turn upon his master seeking in his face some elucidation of a previous gesture ambiguous to the canine intelligence. Nor was the same utterance without marked effect upon the three officers, more especially the soldier. Couched in it seemed to them a meaning unanticipated, involving a prejudgement on the speaker's part. It served to augment a mental disturbance previously evident enough.

The soldier once more spoke; in a tone of suggestive dubiety addressing at once his associates and Captain Vere: "Nobody is present—none of the ship's company,

I mean, who might shed lateral light, if any is to be had, upon what remains mysterious in this matter."

"That is thoughtfully put," said Captain Vere; "I see your drift. Ay, there is a mystery; but, to use a Scriptural phrase, it is 'a mystery of iniquity,' a matter for psychologic theologians to discuss. But what has a military court to do with it? Not to add that for us any possible investigation of it is cut off by the lasting tongue-tie of—him—in yonder," again designating the mortuary state-room. "The prisoner's deed,—with that alone we have to do."

To this, and particularly the closing reiteration, the marine soldier knowing not how aptly to reply, sadly abstained from saying aught. The First Lieutenant who at the outset had not unnaturally assumed primacy in the court, now overrulingly instructed by a glance from Captain Vere, a glance more effective than words, resumed that primacy. Turning to the prisoner, "Budd," he said, and scarce in equable tones, "Budd, if you have aught further to say for yourself, say it now."

Upon this the young sailor turned another quick glance towards Captain Vere; then, as taking a hint from that aspect, a hint confirming his own instinct that silence was now best, replied to the Lieutenant, "I have said all, Sir."

The marine—the same who had been the sentinel without the cabin-door at the time that the foretopman followed by the master-at-arms, entered it—he, standing by the sailor throughout these judicial proceedings, was now directed to take him back to the after compartment originally assigned to the prisoner and his custodian. As the twain disappeared from view, the three officers as partially liberated from some inward constraint associated with Billy's mere presence, simultaneously stirred in their seats. They exchanged looks of troubled indecision, yet feeling that decide they must and without long delay. As for Captain Vere, he for the time stood unconsciously with his back towards them, apparently in one of his absent fits, gazing out from a sashed port-hole to windward upon the monotonous blank of the twilight sea. But the court's silence continuing, broken only at moments by brief consultations in low earnest tones, this seemed to arm him and energize him. Turning, he to-and-fro paced the cabin athwart; in the returning ascent to windward, climbing the slant deck in the ship's lee roll; without knowing it symbolizing thus in his action a mind resolute to surmount difficulties even if against primitive instincts strong as the wind and the sea. Presently he came to a stand before the three. After scanning their faces he stood less as mustering his thoughts for expression, than as one inly deliberating how best to put them to well-meaning men not intellectually mature, men with whom it was necessary to demonstrate certain principles that were axioms to himself. Similar impatience as to talking is perhaps one reason that deters some minds from addressing any popular assemblies.

When speak he did, something both in the substance of what he said and his manner of saying it, showed the influence of unshared studies modifying and tempering the practical training of an active career. This, along with his phraseology now and then was suggestive of the grounds whereon rested that imputation of a certain pedantry socially alleged against him by certain naval men of wholly practical cast, captains who nevertheless would frankly concede that His Majesty's navy mustered no more efficient officers of their grade than *Starry Vere.*

What he said was to this effect: "Hitherto I have been but the witness, little more; and I should hardly think now to take another tone, that of your coadjutor, for the time, did I not perceive in you,—at the crisis too—a troubled hesitancy, proceeding, I doubt not from the clash of military duty with moral scruple—scruple vitalized by compassion. For the compassion, how can I otherwise than share it? But, mindful of paramount obligations I strive against scruples that may tend to enervate decision. Not, gentlemen, that I hide from myself that the case is an exceptional one. Speculatively regarded, it well might be referred to a jury of casuists. But for us here acting not as casuists or moralists, it is a case practical, and under martial law practically to be dealt with.

"But your scruples: do they move as in a dusk? Challenge them. Make them advance and declare themselves. Come now: do they import something like this: If, mindless of palliating circumstances, we are bound to regard the death of the Master-at-arms as the prisoner's deed, then does that deed constitute a capital crime whereof the penalty is a mortal one? But in natural justice is nothing but the prisoner's overt act to be considered? How can we adjudge to summary and shameful death a fellow-creature innocent before God, and whom we feel to be so?—Does that state it aright? You sign sad assent. Well, I too feel that, the full force of that. It is Nature. But do these buttons that we wear attest that our allegiance is to Nature? No, to the King. Though the ocean, which is inviolate Nature primeval, tho' this be the element where we move and have our being as sailors, yet as the King's officers lies our duty in a sphere correspondingly natural? So little is that true, that in receiving our commissions we in the most important regards ceased to be natural free-agents. When war is declared are we the commissioned fighters previously consulted? We fight at command. If our judgements approve the war, that is but coincidence. So in other particulars. So now. For suppose condemnation to follow these present proceedings. Would it be so much we ourselves that would condemn as it would be martial law operating through us? For that law and the rigour of it, we are not responsible. Our vowed responsibility is in this: That however pitilessly that law may operate, we nevertheless adhere to it and administer it.

"But the exceptional in the matter moves the hearts within you. Even so too is mine moved. But let not warm hearts betray heads that should be cool. Ashore in a criminal case will an upright judge allow himself off the bench to be waylaid by some tender kinswoman of the accused seeking to touch him with her tearful plea? Well the heart here denotes the feminine in man is as that piteous woman, and hard tho' it be, she must here be ruled out."

He paused, earnestly studying them for a moment; then resumed.

"But something in your aspect seems to urge that it is not solely the heart that moves in you, but also the conscience, the private conscience. But tell me whether or not, occupying the position we do, private conscience should not yield to that imperial one formulated in the code under which alone we officially proceed?"

Here the three men moved in their seats, less convinced than agitated by the course of an argument troubling but the more the spontaneous conflict within.

Perceiving which, the speaker paused for a moment; then abruptly changing his tone, went on.

"To steady us a bit, let us recur to the facts.—In war-time at sea a man-of-war's-man strikes his superior in grade, and the blow kills. Apart from its effect the blow itself is, according to the Articles of War, a capital crime. Furthermore—"

"Ay, Sir," emotionally broke in the officer of marines, "in one sense it was. But surely Budd purposed neither mutiny nor homicide."

"Surely not, my good man. And before a court less arbitrary and more merciful than a martial one, that plea would largely extenuate. At the Last Assizes it shall acquit. But how here? We proceed under the law of the Mutiny Act. In feature no child can resemble his father more than that Act resembles in spirit the thing from which it derives— War. In His Majesty's service—in this ship indeed—there are Englishmen forced to fight for the King against their will. Against their conscience, for aught we know. Tho' as their fellow-creatures some of us may appreciate their position, yet as navy officers, what reck we of it? Still less recks the enemy. Our impressed men he would fain cut down in the same swath with our volunteers. As regards the enemy's naval conscripts, some of whom may even share our own abhorrence of the regicidal French Directory, it is the same on our side. War looks but to the frontage, the appearance. And the Mutiny Act, War's child, takes after the father. Budd's intent or non-intent is nothing to the purpose.

"But while, put to it by those anxieties in you which I can not but respect, I only repeat myself—while thus strangely we prolong proceedings that should be summary —the enemy may be sighted and an engagement result. We must do; and one of two things must we do—condemn or let go."

"Can we not convict and yet mitigate the penalty?" asked the junior Lieutenant here speaking, and falteringly, for the first.

"Lieutenant, were that clearly lawful for us under the circumstances consider the consequences of such clemency. The people" (meaning the ship's company) "have nativesense; most of them are familiar with our naval usage and tradition; and how would they take it? Even could you explain to them—which our official position forbids—they, long moulded by arbitrary discipline have not that kind of intelligent responsiveness that might qualify them to com-

prehend and discriminate. No, to the people the foretopman's deed however it be worded in the announcement
will be plain homicide committed in a flagrant act of
mutiny. What penalty for that should follow, they know.
But it does not follow. *Why?* they will ruminate. You
know what sailors are. Will they not revert to the recent
outbreak at the Nore? Ay. They know the well-founded
alarm—the panic it struck throughout England. Your
clement sentence they would account pusillanimous. They
would think that we flinch, that we are afraid of them—
afraid of practising a lawful rigor singularly demanded at
this juncture lest it should provoke new troubles. What
shame to us such a conjecture on their part, and how
deadly to discipline. You see then, whither prompted by
duty and the law I steadfastly drive. But I beseech you,
my friends, do not take me amiss. I feel as you do for this
unfortunate boy. But did he know our hearts, I take him
to be of that generous nature that he would feel even for
us on whom in this military necessity so heavy a com-
pulsion is laid."

With that, crossing the deck he resumed his place by
the sashed port-hole, tacitly leaving the three to come to a
decision. On the cabin's opposite side the troubled court
sat silent. Loyal lieges, plain and practical, though at
bottom they dissented from some points Captain Vere had
put to them, they were without the faculty, hardly had the
inclination, to gainsay one whom they felt to be an earnest
man, one too not less their superior in mind than in naval
rank. But it is not improbable that even such of his words
as were not without influence over them, less came home to
them than his closing appeal to their instinct as sea-officers
in the forethought he threw out as to the practical consequences to discipline, considering the unconfirmed tone
of the fleet at the time, should a man-of-war's-man's
violent killing at sea of a superior in grade be allowed to
pass for aught else than a capital crime demanding prompt
infliction of the penalty.

Not unlikely they were brought to something more or
less akin to that harassed frame of mind which in the
year 1842 actuated the commander of the U.S. brig-of-war
Somers to resolve, under the so-called Articles of War,
Articles modelled upon the English Mutiny Act, to resolve
upon the execution at sea of a midshipman and two petty-

officers as mutineers designing the seizure of the brig.
Which resolution was carried out though in a time of
peace and within not many days sail of home. An act
vindicated by a naval court of inquiry subsequently convened ashore. History, and here cited without comment.
True, the circumstances on board the *Somers* were different from those on board the *Bellipotent*. But the
urgency felt, well-warranted or otherwise, was much the
same.

Says a writer whom few know, "Forty years after a battle
it is easy for a non-combatant to reason about how it
ought to have been fought. It is another thing personally
and under fire to direct the fighting while involved in the
obscuring smoke of it. Much so with respect to other
emergencies involving considerations both practical and
moral, and when it is imperative promptly to act. The
greater the fog the more it imperils the steamer, and
speed is put on tho' at the hazard of running somebody
down. Little ween the snug card-players in the cabin of the
responsibilities of the sleepless man on the bridge."

In brief, Billy Budd was formally convicted and sen-
tenced to be hung at the yard-arm in the early morning-
watch, it being now night. Otherwise, as is customary in
such cases, the sentence would forthwith have been carried
out. In war-time on the field or in the fleet, a mortal
punishment decreed by a drum-head court—on the field
sometimes decreed by but a nod from the General—
follows without delay on the heel of conviction without
appeal.

[23]

It was Captain Vere himself who of his own motion
communicated the finding of the court to the prisoner; for
that purpose going to the compartment where he was in
custody and bidding the marine there to withdraw for the
time.

Beyond the communication of the sentence what took
place at this interview was never known. But in view of
the character of the twain briefly closeted in that state-
room, each radically sharing in the rarer qualities of our
nature—so rare indeed as to be all but incredible to average minds however much cultivated—some conjectures
may be ventured.

It would have been in consonance with the spirit of Captain Vere should he on this occasion have concealed nothing from the condemned one—should he indeed have frankly disclosed to him the part he himself had played in bringing about the decision, at the same time revealing his actuating motives. On Billy's side it is not improbable that such a confession would have been received in much the same spirit that prompted it. Not without a sort of joy indeed he might have appreciated the brave opinion of him implied in his Captain's making such a confidant of him. Nor, as to the sentence itself could he have been insensible that it was imparted to him as to one not afraid to die. Even more may have been. Captain Vere in the end may have developed the passion sometimes latent under an exterior stoical or indifferent. He was old enough to have been Billy's father. The austere devotee of military duty, letting himself melt back into what remains primeval in our formalized humanity, may in the end have caught Billy to his heart even as Abraham may have caught young Isaac on the brink of resolutely offering him up in obedience to the exacting behest. But there is no telling the sacrament, seldom if in any case revealed to the gadding world, wherever under circumstances at all akin to those here attempted to be set forth, two of great Nature's nobler order embrace. There is privacy at the time, inviolable to the survivor, and holy oblivion, the sequel to each diviner magnanimity, providentially covers all at last.

The first to encounter Captain Vere in act of leaving the compartment was the senior Lieutenant. The face he beheld, for the moment one expressive of the agony of the strong, was to that officer, tho' a man of fifty, a startling revelation. That the condemned one suffered less than he who mainly had effected the condemnation was apparently indicated by the former's exclamation in the scene soon perforce to be touched upon.

[24]

Of a series of incidents within a brief term rapidly following each other, the adequate narration may take up a term less brief, especially if explanation or comment here and there seem requisite to the better understanding of such incidents. Between the entrance into the cabin of him who never left it alive, and him who when he did leave it left it as one condemned to die; between this and the closeted interview just given less than an hour and a half had elapsed. It was an interval long enough however to awaken speculations among no few of the ship's company as to what it was that could be detaining in the cabin the master-at-arms and the sailor; for a rumor that both of them had been seen to enter it and neither of them had been seen to emerge, this rumor had got abroad upon the gun-decks and in the tops; the people of a great warship being in one respect like villagers taking microscopic note of every outward movement or non-movement going on. When therefore in weather not at all tempestuous all hands were called in the second dog-watch, a summons under such circumstances not usual in those hours, the crew were not wholly unprepared for some announcement extraordinary, one having connection too with the continued absence of the two men from their wonted haunts.

There was a moderate sea at the time; and the moon, newly risen and near to being at its full, silvered the white spar-deck wherever not blotted by the clear-cut shadows horizontally thrown of fixtures and moving men. On either side of the quarter-deck, the marine guard under arms was drawn up; and Captain Vere standing in his place surrounded by all the ward-room officers, addressed his men. In so doing his manner showed neither more nor less than that properly pertaining to his supreme position aboard his own ship. In clear terms and concise he told them what had taken place in the cabin; that the master-at-arms was dead; that he who had killed him had been already tried by a summary court and condemned to death; and that the execution would take place in the early morning watch. The word *mutiny* was not named in what he said. He refrained too from making the occasion an opportunity for any preachment as to the maintenance of discipline, thinking perhaps that under existing circumstances in the navy the consequence of violating discipline should be made to speak for itself.

Their captain's announcement was listened to by the throng of standing sailors in a dumbness like that of a seated congregation of believers in hell listening to the clergyman's announcement of his Calvinistic text.

At the close, however, a confused murmur went up. It began to wax. All but instantly, then, at a sign, it was pierced and suppressed by shrill whistles of the Boatswain and his Mates piping down one watch.

To be prepared for burial Claggart's body was delivered to certain petty-officers of his mess. And here, not to clog the sequel with lateral matters, it may be added that at a suitable hour, the Master-at-arms was committed to the sea with every funeral honor properly belonging to his naval grade.

In this proceeding as in every public one growing out of the tragedy, strict adherence to usage was observed. Nor in any point could it have been at all deviated from, either with respect to Claggart or Billy Budd, without begetting undesirable speculations in the ship's company, sailors, and more particularly men-of-war's-men, being of all men the greatest sticklers for usage.

For similar cause, all communication between Captain Vere and the condemned one ended with the closeted interview already given, the latter being now surrendered to the ordinary routine preliminary to the end. This transfer under guard from the Captain's quarters was effected without unusual precautions—at least no visible ones.

If possible, not to let the men so much as surmise that their officers anticipate aught amiss from them is the tacit rule in a military ship. And the more that some sort of trouble should really be apprehended the more do the officers keep that apprehension to themselves; tho' not the less unostentatious vigilance may be augmented.

In the present instance the sentry placed over the prisoner had strict orders to let no one have communication with him but the Chaplain. And certain unobtrusive measures were taken absolutely to insure this point.

[25]

In a seventy-four of the old order the deck known as the upper gun-deck was the one covered over by the spar-deck which last though not without its armament was for the most part exposed to the weather. In general it was at all hours free from hammocks; those of the crew swinging on the lower gun-deck, and berth-deck, the latter being not only a dormitory but also the place for the stowing of the sailors' bags, and on both sides lined with the large chests or movable pantries of the many messes of the men.

On the starboard side of the *Bellipotent*'s upper gun-deck, behold Billy Budd under sentry, lying prone in irons, in one of the bays formed by the regular spacing of the guns comprising the batteries on either side. All these pieces were of the heavier calibre of that period. Mounted on lumbering wooden carriages they were hampered with cumbersome harness of breeching and strong side-tackles for running them out. Guns and carriages, together with the long rammers and shorter lintstocks lodged in loops overhead—all these, as customary, were painted black; and the heavy hempen breechings, tarred to the same tint, wore the like livery of the undertakers. In contrast with the funereal hue of these surroundings the prone sailor's exterior apparel, white *jumper* and white duck trousers, each more or less soiled, dimly glimmered in the obscure light of the bay like a patch of discolored snow in early April lingering at some upland cave's black mouth. In effect he is already in his shroud or the garments that shall serve him in lieu of one. Over him, but scarce illuminating him, two battle-lanterns swing from two massive beams of the deck above. Fed with the oil supplied by the war-contractors (whose gains, honest or otherwise, are in every land an anticipated portion of the harvest of death), with flickering splashes or dirty yellow light they pollute the pale moonshine all but ineffectually struggling in obstructed flecks thro' the open ports from which the tompioned cannon protrude. Other lanterns at intervals serve but to bring out somewhat the obscurer bays which, like small confessionals or side-chapels in a cathedral, branch from the long dim-vistaed broad aisle between the two batteries of that covered tier.

Such was the deck where now lay the Handsome Sailor. Through the rose-tan of his complexion, no pallor could have shown. It would have taken days of sequestration from the winds and the sun to have brought about the effacement of that. But the skeleton in the cheekbone at the point of its angle was just beginning delicately to be defined under the warm-tinted skin. In fervid hearts self-contained, some brief experiences devour our human tissue as secret fire in a ship's hold consumes cotton in the bale.

But now lying between the two guns, as nipped in the vice of fate, Billy's agony, mainly proceeding from a generous young heart's virgin experience of the diabolical incarnate and effective in some men—the tension of that agony was over now. It survived not the something healing in the closeted interiew with Captain Vere. Without movement, he lay as in a trance. That adolescent expression previously noted as his, taking on something akin to the look of a slumbering child in the cradle when the warm hearth-glow of the still chamber at night plays on the dimples that at whiles mysteriously form in the cheek, silently coming and going there. For now and then in the gyved one's trance a serene happy light born of some wandering reminiscence or dream would diffuse itself over his face, and then wane away only anew to return.

The Chaplain coming to see him and finding him thus, and perceiving no sign that he was conscious of his presence, attentively regarded him for a space, then slipping aside, withdrew for the time, peradventure feeling that even he the minister of Christ, tho' receiving his stipend from Mars, had no consolation to proffer which could result in a peace transcending that which he beheld. But in the small hours he came again. And the prisoner, now awake to his surroundings, noticed his approach, and civilly, all but cheerfully, welcomed him. But it was to little purpose that in the interview following the good man sought to bring Billy Budd to some godly understanding that he must die, and at dawn. True, Billy himself freely referred to his death as a thing close at hand; but it was something in the way that children will refer to death in general, who yet among their other sports will play a funeral with hearse and mourners.

Not that like children Billy was incapable of conceiving what death really is. No, but he was wholly without irrational fear of it, a fear more prevalent in highly civilized communities than those so-called barbarous ones which in all respects stand nearer to unadulterate Nature. And, as elsewhere said, a barbarian Billy radically was; as much so, for all the costume, as his countrymen the British captives, living trophies, made to march in the Roman triumph of Germanicus. Quite as much so as those later barbarians, young men probably, and picked specimens among the earlier British converts to Christianity, at least nominally such and taken to Rome (as today converts from lesser isles of the sea may be taken to London) of whom the Pope of that time, admiring the strangeness of their personal beauty so unlike the Italian stamp, their clear ruddy complexion

and curled flaxen locks, exclaimed, "Angles" (meaning
English the modern derivative) "Angles do you call them?
And is it because they look so like angels?" Had it been
later in time one would think that the Pope had in mind
Fra Angelico's seraphs some of whom, plucking apples
in gardens of the Hesperides have the faint rose-bud complexion of the more beautiful English girls.

If in vain the good Chaplain sought to impress the
young barbarian with ideas of death akin to those conveyed
in the skull, dial, and cross-bones on old tombstones;
equally futile to all appearance were his efforts to bring
home to him the thought of salvation and a Saviour. Billy
listened, but less out of awe or reverence perhaps than
from a certain natural politeness; doubtless at bottom regarding all that in much the same way that most mariners
of his class take any discourse abstract or out of the common tone of the work-a-day world. And this sailor-way of
taking clerical discourse is not wholly unlike the way in
which the pioneer of Christianity full of transcendent
miracles was received long ago on tropic isles by any superior *savage* so called—a Tahitian say of Captain Cook's
time or shortly after that time. Out of natural courtesy he
received, but did not appropriate. It was like a gift placed in
the palm of an out-reached hand upon which the fingers do
not close.

But the *Bellipotent*'s Chaplain was a discreet man possessing the good sense of a good heart. So he insisted not
in his vocation here. At the instance of Captain Vere, a
lieutenant had apprised him of pretty much everything as
to Billy; and since he felt that innocence was even a better
thing than religion wherewith to go to Judgement, he re-
luctantly withdrew; but in his emotion not without first
performing an act strange enough in an Englishman, and
under the circumstances yet more so in any regular priest.
Stooping over, he kissed on the fair cheek his fellow-man,
a felon in martial law, one who though on the confines of
death he felt he could never convert to a dogma; nor for
all that did he fear for his future.

Marvel not that having been made acquainted with the
young sailor's essential innocence (an irruption of heretic
thought hard to suppress) the worthy man lifted not a
finger to avert the doom of such a martyr to martial discipline. So to do would not only have been as idle as

invoking the desert, but would also have been an audacious
transgression of the bounds of his function, one as exactly
prescribed to him by military law as that of the boatswain
or any other naval officer. Bluntly put, a chaplain is the
minister of the Prince of Peace serving in the host of
the God of War—Mars. As such, he is as incongruous as
a musket would be on the altar at Christmas. Why then is
he there? Because he indirectly subserves the purpose
attested by the cannon; because too he lends the sanction
of the religion of the meek to that which practically is the
abrogation of everything but brute Force.

[26]

The night, so luminous on the spar-deck, but otherwise
on the cavernous ones below, levels so like the tiered gal-
leries in a coal-mine—the luminous night passed away.
But, like the prophet in the chariot disappearing in heaven
and dropping his mantle to Elisha, the withdrawing night
transferred its pale robe to the breaking day. A meek shy
light appeared in the East, where stretched a diaphanous
fleece of white furrowed vapor. That light slowly waxed.
Suddenly *eight bells* was struck aft, responded to by one
louder metallic stroke from forward. It was four o'clock
in the morning. Instantly the silver whistles were heard
summoning all hands to witness punishment. Up through
the great hatchways rimmed with racks of heavy shot, the
watch below came pouring, overspreading with the watch
already on deck the space between the mainmast and fore-
mast including that occupied by the capacious *launch* and
the black booms tiered on either side of it, boat and booms
making a summit of observation for the powder-boys and
younger tars. A different group comprising one watch of
topmen leaned over the rail of that sea-balcony, no small
one in a seventy-four, looking down on the crowd below.
Man or boy, none spake but in whisper, and few spake at
all. Captain Vere—as before, the central figure among the
assembled commissioned officers—stood nigh the break of
the poop-deck facing forward. Just below him on the quarter-deck the marines in full equipment were drawn up much
as at the scene of the promulgated sentence.

At sea in the old time, the execution by halter of a military sailor was generally from the fore-yard. In the present
instance, for special reasons the main-yard was assigned.

Under an arm of that yard the prisoner was presently
brought up, the Chaplain attending him. It was noted at
the time and remarked upon afterwards, that in this final
scene the good man evinced little or nothing of the per-
functory. Brief speech indeed he had with the condemned
one, but the genuine Gospel was less on his tongue than
in his aspect and manner towards him. The final preparations personal to the latter being speedily brought to an
end by two boatswain's-mates, the consummation impended.
Billy stood facing aft. At the penultimate moment, his
words, his only ones, words wholly unobstructed in the utterance were these—"God bless Captain Vere!" Syllables
so unanticipated coming from one with the ignominious
hemp about his neck—a conventional felon's benediction
directed aft towards the quarters of honor; syllables too
delivered in the clear melody of a singing-bird on the point
of launching from the twig, had a phenomenal effect, not
unenhanced by the rare personal beauty of the young sailor
spiritualized now thro' late experiences so poignantly profound.

Without volition as it were, as if indeed the ship's populace were but the vehicles of some vocal current electric,
with one voice from alow and aloft came a resonant sympathetic echo—"God bless Captain Vere!" And yet at that
instant Billy alone must have been in their hearts, even
as he was in their eyes.

At the pronounced words and the spontaneous echo that
voluminously rebounded them, Captain Vere, either thro'
stoic self-control or a sort of momentary paralysis induced
by emotional shock, stood erectly rigid as a musket in the
ship-armorer's rack.

The hull deliberately recovering from the periodic roll
to leeward was just regaining an even keel, when the last
signal, a preconcerted dumb one, was given. At the same
moment it chanced that the vapory fleece hanging low in
the East, was shot thro' with a soft glory as of the fleece
of the Lamb of God seen in mystical vision, and simultaneously therewith, watched by the wedged mass of up-
turned faces, Billy ascended; and, ascending, took the full
rose of the dawn.

In the pinioned figure, arrived at the yard-end, to the
wonder of all no motion was apparent, none save that

created by the ship's motion, in moderate weather so majestic in a great ship ponderously cannoned.

[27]

A digression

When some days afterward in reference to the singularity just mentioned, the Purser, a rather ruddy rotund person more accurate as an accountant than profound as a philosopher, said at mess to the Surgeon, "What testimony to the force lodged in will-power," the latter—saturnine spare and tall, one in whom a discreet causticity went along with a manner less genial than polite, replied, "Your pardon, Mr. Purser. In a hanging scientifically conducted —and under special orders I myself directed how Budd's was to be effected—any movement following the completed suspension and originating in the body suspended, such movement indicates mechanical spasm in the muscular system. Hence the absence of that is no more attributable to will-power as you call it than to horse-power—begging your pardon."

"But this muscular spasm you speak of, is not that in a degree more or less invariable in these cases?"

"Assuredly so, Mr. Purser."

"How then, my good sir, do you account for its absence in this instance?"

"Mr. Purser, it is clear that your sense of the singularity in this matter equals not mine. You account for it by what you call will-power, a term not yet included in the lexicon of science. For me I do not, with my present knowledge pretend to account for it at all. Even should we assume the hypothesis that at the first touch of the halyards the action of Budd's heart, intensified by extraordinary emotion at its climax, abruptly stopt—much like a watch when in carelessly winding it up you strain at the finish, thus snapping the chain—even under that hypothesis, how account for the phenomenon that followed?"

"You admit then that the absence of spasmodic movement was phenomenal."

"It was phenomenal, Mr. Purser, in the sense that it was an appearance the cause of which is not immediately to be assigned."

"But tell me, my dear Sir," pertinaciously continued the other, "was the man's death effected by the halter, or was it a species of euthanasia?"

"*Euthanasia,* Mr. Purser, is something like your *will-power:* I doubt its authenticity as a scientific term—begging your pardon again. It is at once imaginative and metaphysical,—in short, Greek. But," abruptly changing his tone, "there is a case in the sick-bay that I do not care to leave to my assistants. Beg your pardon, but excuse me." And rising from the mess he formally withdrew.

[28]

The silence at the moment of execution and for a moment or two continuing thereafter, a silence but emphasized by the regular wash of the sea against the hull or the flutter of a sail caused by the helmsman's eyes being tempted astray, this emphasized silence was gradually disturbed by a sound not easily to be verbally rendered. Whoever has heard the freshet-wave of a torrent suddenly swelled by pouring showers in tropical mountains, showers not shared by the plain; whoever has heard the first muffled murmur of its sloping advance through precipitous woods, may form some conception of the sound now heard. The seeming remoteness of its source was because of its murmurous indistinctness since it came from close-by, even from the men massed on the ship's open deck. Being inarticulate, it was dubious in significance further than it seemed to indicate some capricious revulsion of thought or feeling such as mobs ashore are liable to, in the present instance possibly implying a sullen revocation on the men's part of their involuntary echoing of Billy's benediction. But ere the murmur had time to wax into clamor it was met by a strategic command, the more telling that it came with abrupt unexpectedness.

"Pipe down the starboard watch, Boatswain, and see that they go."

Shrill as the shriek of the sea-hawk the whistles of the Boatswain and his Mates pierced that ominous low sound, dissipating it; and yielding to the mechanism of discipline, the throng was thinned by one half. For the remainder most of them were set to temporary employments connected with trimming the yards and so forth, business readily to be got up to serve occasion by any officer-of-the-deck.

Now each proceeding that follows a mortal sentence pronounced at sea by a drum-head court is characterised by promptitude not perceptibly merging into hurry, tho' bordering that. The hammock, the one which had been Billy's bed when alive, having already been ballasted with shot and otherwise prepared to serve for his canvas coffin, the last offices of the sea-undertakers, the Sail-Maker's Mates, were now speedily completed. When everything was in readiness a second call for all hands made necessary by the strategic movement before mentioned was sounded and now to witness burial.

The details of this closing formality it needs not to give. But when the tilted plank let slide its freight into the sea, a second strange human murmur was heard, blended now with another inarticulate sound proceeding from certain larger sea-fowl, whose attention having been attracted by the peculiar commotion in the water resulting from the heavy sloped dive of the shotted hammock into the sea, flew screaming to the spot. So near the hull did they come, that the stridor or bony creak of their gaunt double-jointed pinions was audible. As the ship under light airs passed on, leaving the burial-spot astern, they still kept circling it low down with the moving shadow of their outstretched wings and the croaked requiem of their cries.

Upon sailors as superstitious as those of the age preceding ours, men-of-war's-men too who had just beheld the prodigy of repose in the form suspended in air and now foundering in the deeps; to such mariners the action of the sea-fowl, tho' dictated by mere animal greed for prey, was big with no prosaic significance. An uncertain movement began among them, in which some encroachment was made. It was tolerated but for a moment. For suddenly the drum beat to quarters, which familiar sound happening at least twice every day, had upon the present occasion a signal peremptoriness in it. True martial discipline long continued superinduces in average man a sort of impulse of docility whose operation at the official sound of command much resembles in its promptitude the effect of an instinct.

The drum-beat dissolved the multitude, distributing most of them along the batteries of the two covered gun-decks. There, as wont, the guns' crews stood by their respective cannon erect and silent. In due course the First Officer, sword under arm and standing in his place on the quarter-deck, formally received the successive reports of the sworded Lieutenants commanding the sections of batteries below; the last of which reports being made, the summed report he delivered with the customary salute to the Commander. All this occupied time, which in the present case, was the object of beating to quarters at an hour prior to the customary one. That such variance from usage was authorized by an officer like Captain Vere, a martinet as some deemed him, was evidence of the necessity for unusual action implied in what he deemed to be temporarily the mood of his men. "With mankind," he would say, "forms, measured forms are everything; and that is the import couched in the story of Orpheus with his lyre spell-binding the wild denizens of the wood." And this he once applied to the disruption of forms going on across the Channel and the consequences thereof.

At this unwonted muster at quarters, all proceeded as at the regular hour. The band on the quarter-deck played a sacred air. After which the Chaplain went thro' the customary morning service. That done, the drum beat the retreat, and toned by music and religious rites subserving the discipline & purpose of war, the men in their wonted orderly manner, dispersed to the places allotted them when not at the guns.

And now it was full day. The fleece of low-hanging vapor had vanished, licked up by the sun that late had so glorified it. And the circumambient air in the clearness of its serenity was like smooth white marble in the polished block not yet removed from the marble-dealer's yard.

[29]

The symmetry of form attainable in pure fiction can not so readily be achieved in a narration essentially having less to do with fable than with fact. Truth uncompromisingly told will always have its ragged edges; hence the conclusion of such a narration is apt to be less finished than an architectural finial.

How it fared with the Handsome Sailor during the year of the Great Mutiny has been faithfully given. But tho' properly the story ends with his life, something in way of sequel will not be amiss. Three brief chapters will suffice.

In the general re-christening under the Directory of the craft originally forming the navy of the French monarchy, the *St. Louis* line-of-battle ship was named the *Athéiste*. Such a name, like some other substituted ones in the Revolutionary fleet, while proclaiming the infidel audacity of the ruling power was yet, tho' not so intended to be, the aptest name, if one consider it, ever given to a war-ship; far more so indeed than the *Devastation*, the *Erebus* (the *Hell*) and similar names bestowed upon fighting-ships.

On the return-passage to the English fleet from the detached cruise during which occurred the events already recorded, the *Bellipotent* fell in with the *Athéiste*. An engagement ensued; during which Captain Vere, in the act of putting his ship alongside the enemy with a view of throwing his boarders across her bulwarks, was hit by a musket-ball from a port-hole of the enemy's main cabin. More than disabled he dropped to the deck and was carried below to the same cock-pit where some of his men already lay. The senior Lieutenant took command. Under him the enemy was finally captured and though much crippled was by rare good fortune successfully taken into Gibraltar, an English port not very distant from the scene of the fight. There, Captain Vere with the rest of the wounded was put ashore. He lingered for some days, but the end came. Unhappily he was cut off too early for the Nile and Trafalgar. The spirit that spite its philosophic austerity may yet have indulged in the most secret of all passions, ambition, never attained to the fulness of fame.

Not long before death, while lying under the influence of that magical drug which soothing the physical frame mysteriously operates on the subtler element in man, he was heard to murmur words inexplicable to his attendant —"Billy Budd, Billy Budd." That these were not the accents of remorse, would seem clear from what the attendant said to the *Bellipotent*'s senior officer of marines who, as the most reluctant to condemn of the members of the drum-head court, too well knew, tho' here he kept the knowledge to himself, who Billy Budd was.

[*30*]

Some few weeks after the execution, among other matters under the head of *News from the Mediterranean*, there appeared in a naval chronicle of the time, an authorized weekly publication, an account of the affair. It was doubtless for the most part written in good faith, tho' the medium, partly rumor, through which the facts must have reached the writer, served to deflect and in part falsify them. The account was as follows:—

"On the tenth of the last month a deplorable occurrence took place on board H.M.S. *Bellipotent*. John Claggart, the ship's master-at-arms, discovering that some sort of plot was incipient among an inferior section of the ship's company, and that the ring-leader was one William Budd; he, Claggart, in the act of arraigning the man before the Captain was vindictively stabbed to the heart by the suddenly drawn sheath-knife of Budd.

"The deed and the implement employed, sufficiently suggest that tho' mustered into the service under an English name, the assassin was no Englishman, but one of those aliens adopting English cognomens whom the present extraordinary necessities of the Service have caused to be admitted into it in considerable numbers.

"The enormity of the crime and the extreme depravity of the criminal, appear the greater in view of the character of the victim, a middle-aged man respectable and discreet, belonging to that minor official grade, the petty-officers, upon whom, as none know better than the commissioned gentlemen, the efficiency of His Majesty's navy so largely depends. His function was a responsible one; at once onerous & thankless and his fidelity in it the greater because of his strong patriotic impulse. In this instance as in so many other instances in these days, the character of this unfortunate man signally refutes, if refutation were needed, that peevish saying attributed to the late Dr. Johnson, that patriotism is the last refuge of a scoundrel.

"The criminal paid the penalty of his crime. The promptitude of the punishment has proved salutary. Nothing amiss is now apprehended aboard H.M.S. *Bellipotent*."

The above, appearing in a publication now long ago superannuated and forgotten, is all that hitherto has stood in human record to attest what manner of men respectively were John Claggart and Billy Budd.

[*31*]

Everything is for a term remarkable in navies. Any tangible object associated with some striking incident of the service is converted into a monument. The spar from which the Foretopman was suspended, was for some few years kept trace of by the blue-jackets. Their knowledge followed it from ship to dock-yard and again from dock-yard to ship, still pursuing it even when at last reduced to a mere dock-yard boom. To them a chip of it was as a piece of the Cross. Ignorant tho' they were of the secret facts of the tragedy, and not thinking but that the penalty was somehow unavoidably inflicted from the naval point of view, for all that they instinctively felt that Billy was a sort of man as incapable of mutiny as of wilful murder. They recalled the fresh young image of the Handsome Sailor, that face never deformed by a sneer or subtler vile freak of the heart within. Their impression of him was doubtless deepened by the fact that he was gone, and in a measure mysteriously gone. At the time, on the gun-decks of the *Bellipotent,* the general estimate of his nature and its unconscious simplicity eventually found rude utterance from another foretopman, one of his own watch, gifted, as some sailors are, with an artless poetic temperament; the tarry hands made some lines which after circulating among the shipboard crew for a while, finally got rudely printed at Portsmouth as a ballad. The title given to it was the sailor's.

Billy in the Darbies

Good of the Chaplain to enter Lone Bay
And down on his marrow-bones here and pray
For the likes just o' me, Billy Budd.—But look:
Through the port comes the moon-shine astray!
It tips the guard's cutlas and silvers this nook;
But 'twill die in the dawning of Billy's last day.
A jewel-block they'll make of me tomorrow,
Pendant pearl from the yard-arm-end
Like the ear-drop I gave to Bristol Molly—
O, 'tis me, not the sentence they'll suspend.
Ay, Ay, all is up; and I must up too
Early in the morning, aloft from alow.
On an empty stomach, now, never it would do.

They'll give me a nibble—bit o' biscuit ere I go.
Sure, a messmate will reach me the last parting cup;
But, turning heads away from the hoist and the belay,
Heavens knows who will have the running of me up!
No pipe to those halyards.—But aren't it all sham?
A blur's in my eyes; it is dreaming that I am.
A hatchet to my hawser? all adrift to go?
The drum roll to grog, and Billy never know?
But Donald he has promised to stand by the plank;
So I'll shake a friendly hand ere I sink.
But—no! It is dead then I'll be, come to think.—
I remember Taff the Welshman when he sank.
And his cheek it was like the budding pink.
But me they'll lash me in hammock, drop me deep.
Fathoms down, fathoms down, how I'll dream fast asleep.
I feel it stealing now. Sentry, are you there?
Just ease this darbies at the wrist, and roll me over fair,
I am sleepy, and the oozy weeds about me twist.

END OF BOOK

w. 1888–1891
p. 1924

WALT WHITMAN

(1819–1892)

"There is no object so foul that intense light will not make beautiful," Emerson wrote. The American Transcendentalists generally meant by such light the light of intuitive Reason, which sees all things symbolically. Bathed in this light, everything in existence is viewed in a process of relationships which lead life out of death, as old forms decay into and fertilize new ones. All forms in nature, therefore, are pictures of their organic function and are so united to one another through the same life-creating process that any one object can mean the entire universe. The Transcendentalists concluded that the meaning of a universe dedicated to the constant creation of relation and life must be cosmic love. To look at the most common of objects in the right light is to look at God. And no one looked at objects with as much light and as much love as Whitman. When he looked at stiff leaves or ant pits or the "mossy scabs of the worm fence," he knew "that a kelson of the creation is love."

In love, all things are equal. Therefore Whitman felt that cosmic democracy was best approached in human affairs through the political democracy of America. Social democracy was best presaged within political democracy by the fiercely individualistic American worker, close to natural process and proud of his vocation. America thus became for Whitman the symbol of nature itself, as the American became the New Man, liberated by democracy to emerge as the highest form of universal pervasive love. To sing one's self as a free man, as the New Adam, was nothing less than to sing one's self

467

as a part of the eternal, infinite, universal process of love. Whitman's nationalism is the ultimate denial of nationalistic separateness: it is a paean to human oneness. "One's self I sing—a simple, separate Person;/Yet utter the word Democratic, the word *En-masse*."

When Whitman celebrated the vitality of the universe— the advance of opposite equals out of the dimness, always knitting, breeding, into an identity of process—he found the materials for embodying his vision, naturally enough, in human sex. But most of his contemporary readers did not subject the objects of sex to a light so intense that they were rendered beautiful. In the little notice that was taken of the first edition of *Leaves of Grass* (1855), there was much shock and outrage. Whitman knew he was ahead of his time and accepted the fact. He was even willing to give up his profession, so certain was he of the fulfillment of his prophetic function as American poet of "the Body and the Soul."

He was a skilled journalist even though he had but five years of schooling behind him in his Long Island boyhood. By 1846 he became the editor of the influential Brooklyn *Eagle*. In 1848, however, the paper's owners decided for business reasons to accommodate the southern Democrats' insistence on extending slavery into the lands acquired by the Mexican War; rather than prostitute his growing poetic sense of America, he quit. After a short extension of his journalistic career, editing the New Orleans *Crescent* and then the Brooklyn *Freeman*, he left newspaper work to become a part-time carpenter so as to devote himself more fully to the poem growing within him—*Leaves of Grass*. Everything of his experience was to go into his central vision as it expanded into separate titles and into various revised editions: his work as an army nurse in the Civil War; the death of President Lincoln; his work in Washington in the Attorney General's division; the attacks made upon him as a civil servant because of his "shocking" and "irresponsible" diction and subject matter. And as the poem grew, so too did his reputation across the Atlantic.

Whitman was not widely recognized in his own country until after his death. But in his last years, living alone in a little house in Camden, New Jersey, he had a gratifying international reputation that helped make up for the neglect at home. In England, France, and Germany, he was increasingly hailed as one of the great makers of a new literature. When on his deathbed he signed the last (1892) edition of *Leaves of Grass*, he was scrawling his name on "A scented gift and remembrancer, designedly dropt,/Bearing the owner's name someway in the corners, that we may see and remark, and say *Whose?*" There is no question about *whose*. Few writers have so unmistakably identified themselves in their times, their nations, their selves as has Walt Whitman.

Editions of the works of Walt Whitman are *Complete Poems and Prose of Walt Whitman, 1855–1888* (1888–1889); *The Complete Prose Works of Walt Whitman* (1892); H. L. Traubel, R. M. Bucke, and T. B. Harned, eds., *The Complete Writings of Walt Whitman*, 10 vols. (1902); and E. Holloway, ed., *Leaves of Grass* (1924, 1954), the standard edition, taken from the edition of 1902. There is no complete collected edition of the works of Whitman, although one is under way. Whitman's published works include *Franklin Evans* (1842); *Leaves of Grass* (1855): hitherto unavailable, this was reissued in 1959, edited by M. Cowley, as *Walt Whitman's Leaves of Grass: The First (1855) Edition; Leaves of Grass* (1856): omits the 1855 Preface, adds poems 14 to 33; *Leaves of Grass* (1860–1861): adds 122 poems to second edition plus "Calamus" and "Children of Adam"; *Leaves of Grass* (1867): adds the following Annexes: *Drum Taps* (1865), *Sequel to Drum Taps* (1865–1866), and *Songs Before Parting; Democratic Vistas* (1871); *Passage to India* (1871); *After All, Not to Create Only* (1871); *Leaves of Grass* (1871): reissued in 1872, this edition adds *Passage to India* and 13 new poems; *As a Strong Bird on Pinions Free* (1872); *Memoranda During the War* (1875–1876); *Leaves of Grass* (1876), the "Author's Edition": the 1871 edition plus *Two Rivulets* (1876), including *Democratic Vistas, Centennial Songs,* and *Passage to India; Leaves of Grass* (1881): the final arrangement of the poems exclusive of those that were later added, this (seventh) edition was reprinted in 1882 and 1888; *Specimen Days and Collect* (1882–1883); *November Boughs* (1888); *Leaves of Grass* (1889), with *Sands at Seventy* (incorporating *November Boughs*) and *A Backward Glance O'er Travel'd Roads; Good-bye My Fancy* (1891); *Autobiographia* (1892); *Leaves of Grass* (1891–1892), the "deathbed" (ninth) edition, adding pp. 381–411 to the edition of 1881, and including *Good-bye My Fancy*; R. M. Bucke, ed., *Calamus: Letters Written during the Years 1868–1880* (1897); R. M. Bucke, ed., *The Wound Dresser* (1898, 1949); R. M. Bucke, ed., *Notes and Fragments* (1899); T. B. Harned, ed., *Letters Written by Walt Whitman to His Mother from 1866 to 1872* (1902); W. S. Kennedy, ed., *Walt Whitman's Diary in Canada* (1904); H. L. Traubel, ed., *An American Primer* (1904); *Lafayette in Brooklyn* (1905); *Criticism: An Essay* (1913); T. B. Harned, ed., *The Letters of Anne Gilchrist and Walt Whitman* (1918); C. Rodgers and J. Black, eds., *The*

Gathering of the Forces, 2 vols. (1920); E. Holloway, ed., *The Uncollected Poetry and Prose of Walt Whitman*, 2 vols. (1921); E. Holloway, ed., *Pictures* (1927); T. O. Mabbott, ed., *The Half-Breed and Other Stories* (1927); C. J. Furness, ed., *Walt Whitman's Workshop* (1928); J. Catel, ed., *The Eighteenth Presidency!* (1928); T. O. Mabbott and R. G. Silver, eds., *A Child's Reminiscence* (1930); E. Holloway and V. Schwartz, eds., *I Sit and Look Out* (1932); C. I. Glicksberg, ed., *Walt Whitman and the Civil War* (1933); E. Holloway and R. Adimari, eds., *New York Dissected* (1936); K. Molinoff, ed., *An Unpublished Whitman Manuscript* (1941); C. Gohdes and R. G. Silver, eds., *Faint Clews and Indirections* (1949); F. B. Freedman, ed., *Walt Whitman Looks at the Schools* (1950); J. Rubin and C. Brown, eds., *Walt Whitman of the New York Aurora: Editor at Twenty-two* (1950); H. Frenz, ed., *Whitman and Rolleston, A Correspondence* (1951); and E. F. Grier, ed., *The Eighteenth Presidency!* (1956).

THE VIKING PORTABLE WHITMAN, edited by Mark Van Doren, contains full selections from *Leaves of Grass*, including the Preface to the 1855 edition, selections from *Specimen Days*, and *A Backward Glance O'er Travel'd Roads*, and *Democratic Vistas* complete.

Studies of the man and his work are to be found in R. L. Stevenson, "The Gospel According to Walt Whitman," *New Quarterly*, X (1879); R. M. Bucke, *Walt Whitman* (1883); E. C. Stedman, *Poets of America* (1883); J. A. Symonds, *Walt Whitman: A Study* (1893); J. Burroughs, *Whitman: A Study* (1896); H. B. Binns, *A Life of Walt Whitman* (1905); B. Perry, *Walt Whitman: His Life and Works* (1906); S. Bradley, ed., H. L. Traubel, *With Walt Whitman in Camden*, I (1906), II and III (1908–1914), IV (1953); F. B. Gummere, *Democracy and Poetry* (1911); B. De Selincourt, *Walt Whitman, A Critical Study* (1914); S. P. Sherman, *Americans* (1922); N. Foerster, *Nature in American Literature* (1923); E. Holloway, *Whitman: An Interpretation in Narrative* (1926); A. Lowell, "Walt Whiman and the New Poetry," *Yale Review*, XVI (1927); N. Foerster, *American Criticism* (1928); H. S. Canby, *Classic Americans* (1931); F. Schyberg, *Walt Whitman* (1933), trans. E. A. Allen (1951); H. Blodgett, *Walt Whitman in England* (1934); G. W. Allen, *American Prosody* (1935); N. Arvin, *Whitman* (1938); S. Bradley, "The Fundamental Metrical Principle in Whitman's Poetry," *American Literature*, X (1938); E. Shephard, *Walt Whitman's Pose* (1938); F. O. Matthiessen, *American Renaissance* (1941); *Index to Early American Periodical Literature, 1728–1870: Part 3, Walt Whitman* (1941); G. W. Allen, *Twenty-five Years of Walt Whitman Bibliography, 1918–1942* (1943); H. S. Canby, *Walt Whitman, An American* (1943); G. W. Allen, *Walt Whitman Handbook* (1946); N. Resnick, *Walt Whitman and the Authorship of The Good Gray Poet* (1948); E. H. Eby, *Concordance of Walt Whitman's Leaves of Grass and Selected Prose Writings* (1949–1954); R. W. B. Lewis, "The Danger of Innocence: Adam as Hero in American Literature," *Yale Review*,

XXXIX (1950); C. B. Willard, *Whitman's American Fame* (1950); J. Beaver, *Walt Whitman, Poet of Science* (1951); R. D. Faner, *Walt Whitman and Opera* (1951); A. Marks, "Whitman's Triadic Imagery," *American Literature*, XXIII (1951); F. Schyberg, *Walt Whitman* (1951); R. Jarrell, *Poetry and the Age* (1953); E. Shephard, "An Inquiry into Whitman's Method of Turning Prose into Poetry," *Modern Language Quarterly*, XIV (1953); R. Asselineau, *L'Evolution de Walt Whitman* (1954); R. P. Adams, "Whitman: A Brief Revaluation," *Tulane Studies in English*, V (1955); E. Allen and G. W. Allen, "Walt Whitman Bibliography 1944–1954," *Walt Whitman Foundation Bulletin*, April (1955); G. W. Allen, *The Solitary Singer* (1955); G. W. Allen, ed., *Walt Whitman Abroad* (1955); G. W. Allen, M. Van Doren, D. Daiches, *Walt Whitman: Man, Poet, Philosopher* (1955); R. Chase, *Walt Whitman Reconsidered* (1955); P. Miller, "The Shaping of the American Character," *New England Quarterly*, XXVIII (1955); M. Hindus, ed., *Leaves of Grass One Hundred Years After* (1955); W. Thorpe, "Walt Whitman," in F. Stovall, ed., *Eight American Authors: A Review of Research and Criticism* (1956); E. H. and R. S. Miller, *Walt Whitman's Correspondence: A Checklist* (1957); J. E. Miller, Jr., *A Critical Guide to Leaves of Grass* (1957); E. Sandeen, "Ego in Eden," in H. C. Gardiner, ed., *American Classics Reconsidered* (1958); K. Shapiro,"The First White Aboriginal," *Walt Whitman Review*, V (1959); R. Asselineau, *The Evolution of Walt Whitman: The Creation of a Personality* (1960); "Special Symposium Issue—Whitman: 1960," *Walt Whitman Review*, VI (1960); E. Holloway, *Free and Lonesome Heart: The Secret of Walt Whitman* (1960); L. Marx, ed., *The Americanness of Walt Whitman* (1960); W. Randal, "Walt Whitman and American Myths," *South Atlantic Quarterly*, LIX (1960); G. W. Allen, *Walt Whitman* (1961); G. W. Allen, *Walt Whitman as Man, Poet, and Legend. With a Checklist of Whitman Publications, 1945–60* (1961); R. Chase, *Walt Whitman* (1961); J. M. Cox, "Walt Whitman, Mark Twain, and the Civil War," *Sewanee Review*, LXIX (1961); C. R. Metzger, *Thoreau and Whitman: A Study of Their Esthetics* (1961); R. H. Pearce, "Whitman Justified: The Poet In 1860," *Minnesota Review*, I (1961); C. F. Strauch, ed., "Symposium on Walt Whitman," *Emerson Society Quarterly*, No. 22 (1961); R. Asselineau, *The Evolution of Walt Whitman: The Creation of a Book* (1962); J. C. Broderick, ed., *Whitman the Poet: Materials for Study* (1962); W. Coyle, ed., *The Poet and the President: Whitman's Lincoln Poems* (1962); R. W. B. Lewis, ed., *The Presence of Walt Whitman: Selected Papers from the English Institute* (1962); J. E. Miller, Jr., *Walt Whitman* (1962); R. H. Pearce, ed., *Whitman: A Collection of Critical Essays* (1962); L. Spitzer, *Essays on English and American Literature* (1962); F. Stovall, ed., *Specimen Days* (1963); V. K. Chari, *Whitman in the Light of Vedantic Mysticism, An Interpretation* (1964); R. W. B. Lewis, "The Aspiring Clown," *Learners and Discerners: A Newer Criticism*, R. Scholes, ed. (1964); A. L. McLeod, ed., *Walt Whitman in Australia and*

New Zealand: A Record of His Reception (1964); E. H. Miller, ed., *The Correspondence of Walt Whitman* (*1842–1885*), 3 vols. (1961–1964); C. N. Stavrou, *Whitman and Nietzsche: A Comparative Study of Their Thought* (1964); E. Fussell, *Frontier: American Literature and the American West* (1965); J. T. F. Tanner, "The Superman in *Leaves of Grass*," *Walt Whitman Review*, XI (1965); and H. J. Waskow, *Whitman: Explorations in Form* (1966).

FROM

Song of Myself

1

I celebrate myself, and sing myself,
And what I assume you shall assume,
For every atom belonging to me, as good belongs to you.

I loafe and invite my Soul;
I lean and loafe at my ease, observing a spear of summer
    grass.

My tongue, every atom of my blood, form'd from this soil,
    this air,
Born here of parents born here from parents the same,
    and their parents the same,
I, now thirty-seven years old in perfect health begin,
Hoping to cease not till death.

Creeds and schools in abeyance,   10
Retiring back a while sufficed at what they are, but never
    forgotten,
I harbor for good or bad, I permit to speak at every hazard,
Nature without check with original energy.

2

Houses and rooms are full of perfumes—the shelves are
    crowded with perfumes,

I breathe the fragrance myself, and know it and like it;
The distillation would intoxicate me also, but I shall not
   let it.

The atmosphere is not a perfume, it has no taste of the
   distillation, it is odorless;
It is for my mouth forever—I am in love with it;
I will go to the bank by the wood, and become undisguised
   and naked;
I am mad for it to be in contact with me.   20
The smoke of my own breath,
Echoes, ripples, buzz'd whispers, love-root, silk-thread,
   crotch and vine,
My respiration and inspiration, the beating of my heart,
   the passing of blood and air through my lungs,
The sniff of green leaves and dry leaves, and of the shore,
   and dark color'd sea-rocks, and of hay in the barn,
The sound of the belch'd words of my voice, words loos'd
   to the eddies of the wind,
A few light kisses, a few embraces, a reaching around of
   arms,
The play of shine and shade on the trees as the supple
   boughs wag,
The delight alone, or in the rush of the streets, or along
   the fields and hill-sides,
The feeling of health, the full-noon trill, the song of me
   rising from bed and meeting the sun.

Have you reckon'd a thousand acres much? have you
   reckon'd the earth much?   30
Have you practis'd so long to learn to read?
Have you felt so proud to get at the meaning of poems?

Stop this day and night with me, and you shall possess the
   origin of all poems;
You shall possess the good of the earth and sun—(there
   are millions of suns left;)
You shall no longer take things at second or third hand,
   nor look through the eyes of the dead, nor feed on
   the spectres in books;
You shall not look through my eyes either, nor take things
   from me:
You shall listen to all sides, and filter them from yourself.

3

I have heard what the talkers were talking, the talk of
the beginning and the end;
But I do not talk of the beginning or the end.

There was never any more inception than there is now,
Nor any more youth or age than there is now,   41
And will never be any more perfection than there is now,
Nor any more heaven or hell than there is now.

Urge and urge and urge,
Always the procreant urge of the world.

Out of the dimness opposite equals advance—always substance and increase, always sex,
Always a knit of identity, always distinction, always a
breed of life.

To elaborate is no avail—learn'd and unlearn'd feel that
it is so.

Sure as the most certain sure, plumb in the uprights,
well entretied, braced in the beams,
Stout as a horse, affectionate, haughty, electrical,   50
I and this mystery, here we stand.

Clear and sweet is my Soul, and clear and sweet is all
that is not my Soul.
Lack one lacks both, and the unseen is proved by the
seen,
Till that becomes unseen, and receives proof in its turn.

Showing the best and dividing it from the worst age
vexes age;
Knowing the perfect fitness and equanimity of things,
while they discuss I am silent, and go bathe and
admire myself.

Welcome is every organ and attribute of me, and of any
man hearty and clean;
Not an inch, nor a particle of an inch, is vile, and none
shall be less familiar than the rest.

I am satisfied—I see, dance, laugh, sing:

As the hugging and loving bed-fellow sleeps at my side
    through the night, and withdraws at the peep of the
    day, with stealthy tread,   60
Leaving me baskets cover'd with white towels, swelling
    the house with their plenty,
Shall I postpone my acceptation and realization, and
    scream at my eyes,
That they turn from gazing after and down the road,
And forthwith cipher and show me to a cent,
Exactly the value of one, and exactly the value of two,
    and which is ahead?

4

Trippers and askers surround me,
People I meet, the effect upon me of my early life, or
    the ward and city I live in, or the nation,
The latest dates, discoveries, inventions, societies, au-
    thors old and new,
My dinner, dress, associates, looks, compliments, dues,
The real or fancied indifference of some man or woman
    I love,   70
The sickness of one of my folks, or of myself, or ill-doing,
    or loss or lack of money, or depressions or exalta-
    tions,
Battles, the horrors of fratricidal war, the fever of doubt-
    ful news, the fitful events;
These come to me days and nights, and go from me
    again,
But they are not the Me myself.

Apart from the pulling and hauling stands what I am,
Stands amused, complacent, compassionating, idle, uni-
    tary,
Looks down, is erect, or bends an arm on an impalpable
    certain rest,
Looking with side-curved head, curious what will come
    next,
Both in and out of the game, and watching and wonder-
    ing at it.

Backward I see in my own days where I sweated through
    fog with linguists and contenders;   80
I have no mockings or arguments—I witness and wait.

5

I believe in you, my soul, the other I am must not abase
    itself to you,
And you must not be abased to the other.

Loafe with me on the grass, loose the stop from your
    throat,
Not words, not music or rhyme I want, not custom or
    lecture, not even the best;
Only the lull I like, the hum of your valved voice.

I mind how once we lay such a transparent summer
    morning,
How you settled your head athwart my hips, and gently
    turn'd over upon me,
And parted the shirt from my bosom-bone, and plunged
    your tongue to my bare-stript heart,
And reach'd till you felt my beard, and reach'd till you
    held my feet.   90

Swiftly arose and spread around me the peace and
    knowledge that pass all the argument of the earth;
And I know that the hand of God is the promise of my
    own,
And I know that the spirit of God is the brother of my
    own;
And that all the men ever born are also my brothers, and
    the women my sisters and lovers,
And that a kelson of the creation is love,
And limitless are leaves, stiff or drooping in the fields,
And brown ants in the little wells beneath them,
And mossy scabs of the worm fence, and heap'd stones,
    elder, mullein and poke-weed.

6

A child said, *What is the grass?* fetching it to me with
    full hands;
How could I answer the child? I do not know what it is,
    any more than he.   100

I guess it must be the flag of my disposition, out of hopeful green stuff woven.

Or I guess it is the handkerchief of the Lord,
A scented gift and remembrancer, designedly dropt,
Bearing the owner's name someway in the corners, that
we may see and remark, and say, *Whose?*

Or I guess the grass is itself a child, the produced babe
of the vegetation.

Or I guess it is a uniform hieroglyphic,
And it means, Sprouting alike in broad zones and nar-
row zones,
Growing among black folks as among white,
Kanuck, Tuckahoe, Congressman, Cuff, I give them the
same, I receive them the same.

And now it seems to me the beautiful uncut hair of
graves.   110

Tenderly will I use you, curling grass,
It may be you transpire from the breasts of young men,
It may be if I had known them I would have loved them,
It may be you are from old people, or from offspring taken
soon out of their mothers' laps,
And here you are the mothers' laps.

This grass is very dark to be from the white heads of old
mothers,
Darker than the colorless beards of old men,
Dark to come from under the faint red roofs of mouths.

O I perceive after all so many uttering tongues!
And I perceive they do not come from the roofs of
mouths for nothing.   120

I wish I could translate the hints about the dead young
men and women,
And the hints about old men and mothers, and the offspring taken soon out of their laps.

What do you think has become of the young and old
    men?
And what do you think has become of the women and
    children?

They are alive and well somewhere;
The smallest sprout shows there is really no death;
And if ever there was, it led forward life, and does not
    wait at the end to arrest it,
And ceas'd the moment life appear'd.

All goes onward and outward—nothing collapses,
And to die is different from what any one supposed, and
    luckier.   130

7

Has any one supposed it lucky to be born?
I hasten to inform him or her, it is just as lucky to die,
    and I know it.

I pass death with the dying, and birth with the new-
    wash'd babe, and am not contain'd between my hat
    and boots;
And peruse manifold objects, no two alike, and every one
    good;
The earth good, and the stars good, and their adjuncts
    all good.

I am not an earth, nor an adjunct of an earth,
I am the mate and companion of people, all just as im-
    mortal and fathomless as myself,
(They do not know how immortal, but I know.)

Every kind for itself and its own, for me mine, male
    and female;
For me those that have been boys, and that love women;
For me the man that is proud, and feels how it stings to
    be slighted;   141
For me the sweet-heart and the old maid, for me mothers,
    and the mothers of mothers;
For me lips that have smiled, eyes that have shed tears;
For me children, and the begetters of children.

Undrape! you are not guilty to me, nor stale, nor discarded;
I see through the broadcloth and gingham, whether or
no,
And am around, tenacious, acquisitive, tireless, and cannot be shaken away.

8

The little one sleeps in its cradle;
I lift the gauze and look a long time, and silently brush
away flies with my hand.

The youngster and the red-faced girl turn aside up the
bushy hill;   150
I peeringly view them from the top.

The suicide sprawls on the bloody floor of the bed-room;
I witness the corpse with its dabbled hair, I note where
the pistol has fallen.

The blab of the pave, tires of carts, sluff of boot-soles,
talk of the promenaders,
The heavy omnibus, the driver with his interrogating
thumb, the clank of the shod horses on the granite
floor,
The snow-sleighs, the clinking, shouted jokes, pelts of
snow-balls,
The hurrahs for popular favorites, the fury of rous'd
mobs,
The flap of the curtain'd litter, a sick man inside, borne
to the hospital,
The meeting of enemies, the sudden oath, the blows and
fall,
The excited crowd, the policeman with his star, quickly
working his passage to the centre of the crowd,   160
The impassive stones that receive and return so many
echoes,
What groans of over-fed or half-starv'd who fall sun-
struck, or in fits,
What exclamations of women taken suddenly, who hurry
home and give birth to babes,

What living and buried speech is always vibrating here,
    what howls restrain'd by decorum;
Arrests of criminals, slights, adulterous offers made, ac-
    ceptances, rejections with convex lips,
I mind them or the show or resonance of them—I come,
    and I depart.

9

The big doors of the country barn stand open and ready,
The dried grass of the harvest-time loads the slow-drawn
    wagon,
The clear light plays on the brown gray and green inter-
    tinged,
The armfuls are pack'd to the sagging mow.   170

I am there, I help, I came stretch'd atop of the load;
I felt its soft jolts, one leg reclined on the other;
I jump from the cross-beams, and seize the clover and
    timothy,
And roll head over heels, and tangle my hair full of
    wisps.

10

Alone, far in the wilds and mountains, I hunt,
Wandering, amazed at my own lightness and glee,
In the late afternoon choosing a safe spot to pass the
    night,
Kindling a fire and broiling the fresh-kill'd game,
Falling asleep on the gather'd leaves, with my dog and
    gun by my side.

The Yankee clipper is under her sky-sails, she cuts the
    sparkle and scud;   180
My eyes settle the land, I bend at her prow, or shout
    joyously from the deck.

The boatmen and clam-diggers arose early and stopt for
    me;
I tuck'd my trowser-ends in my boots, and went and had
    a good time:
You should have been with us that day round the chowder-
    kettle.

I saw the marriage of the trapper in the open air in the
    far west, the bride was a red girl;
Her father and his friends sat near, cross-legged and
    dumbly smoking—they had moccasins to their feet,
    and large thick blankets hanging from their shoul-
    ders;
On a bank lounged the trapper, he was drest mostly in
    skins, his luxuriant beard and curls protected his
    neck, he held his bride by the hand;
She had long eyelashes, her head was bare, her coarse
    straight locks descended upon her voluptuous limbs
    and reach'd to her feet.

The runaway slave came to my house and stopt outside;
I heard his motions crackling the twigs of the woodpile;
Through the swung half-door of the kitchen I saw him
    limpsy and weak,   191
And went where he sat on a log, and led him in and
    assured him,
And brought water, and fill'd a tub for his sweated body
    and bruis'd feet,
And gave him a room that enter'd from my own, and
    gave him some coarse clean clothes,
And remember perfectly well his revolving eyes and his
    awkwardness,
And remember putting plasters on the galls of his neck
    and ankles;
He staid with me a week before he was recuperated and
    pass'd north;
I had him sit next me at table—my fire-lock lean'd in
    the corner.

11

Twenty-eight young men bathe by the shore,
Twenty-eight young men, and all so friendly;   200
Twenty-eight years of womanly life, and all so lonesome.

She owns the fine house by the rise of the bank;
She hides, handsome and richly drest, aft the blinds of
    the window.

Which of the young men does she like the best?
Ah, the homeliest of them is beautiful to her.

Where are you off to, lady? for I see you;
You splash in the water there, yet stay stock still in your
    room.

Dancing and laughing along the beach came the twenty-
    ninth bather;
The rest did not see her, but she saw them and loved
    them.

The beards of the young men glisten'd with wet, it ran
    from their long hair: 210
Little streams pass'd all over their bodies.

An unseen hand also pass'd over their bodies,
It descended tremblingly from their temples and ribs.

The young men float on their backs, their white bellies
    bulge to the sun, they do not ask who seizes fast to
    them;
They do not know who puffs and declines with pendant
    and bending arch;
They do not think whom they souse with spray.

12

The butcher-boy puts off his killing clothes, or sharpens
    his knife at the stall in the market;
I loiter, enjoying his repartee and his shuffle and break-
    down.

Blacksmiths with grimed and hairy chests environ the
    anvil;
Each has his main-sledge, they are all out, there is a
    great heat in the fire.   220

From the cinder-strew'd threshold I follow their move-
    ments,
The lithe sheer of their waists plays even with their mas-
    sive arms;
Over-hand the hammers swing, over-hand so slow, over-
    hand so sure:
They do not hasten, each man hits in his place.

13

The Negro holds firmly the reins of his four horses, the
block swags underneath on its tied-over chain,
The Negro that drives the dray of the stone-yard, steady
and tall he stands, pois'd on one leg on the string-
piece,
His blue shirt exposes his ample neck and breast, and
loosens over his hip-band,
His glance is calm and commanding, he tosses the slouch
of his hat away from his forehead;
The sun falls on his crispy hair and moustache, falls on
the black of his polish'd and perfect limbs.

I behold the picturesque giant, and love him, and I do
not stop there,   230
I go with the team also.

In me the caresser of life wherever moving, backward
as well as forward sluing;
To niches aside and junior bending, not a person or object
missing,
Absorbing all to myself and for this song.

Oxen that rattle the yoke and chain, or halt in the leafy
shade, what is that you express in your eyes?
It seems to me more than all the print I have read in my
life.

My tread scares the wood-drake and wood-duck, on my
distant and day-long ramble;
They rise together, they slowly circle around.

I believe in those wing'd purposes,
And acknowledge red, yellow, white, playing within me,
And consider green and violet, and the tufted crown,
intentional,   241
And do not call the tortoise unworthy because she is not
something else,
And the jay in the woods never studied the gamut, yet
trills pretty well to me,
And the look of the bay mare shames silliness out of me.

14

The wild gander leads his flock through the cool night,
Ya-honk! he says, and sounds it down to me like an invi-
   tation;
The pert may suppose it meaningless, but I listen close,
Find its purpose and place up there toward the wintry sky.

The sharp-hoof'd moose of the north, the cat on the
   house-sill, the chickadee, the prairie-dog,
The litter of the grunting sow as they tug at her teats,
The brood of the turkey-hen, and she with her half-
   spread wings,   251
I see in them and myself the same old law.

The press of my foot to the earth springs a hundred
   affections,
They scorn the best I can do to relate them.

I am enamour'd of growing out-doors,
Of men that live among cattle, or taste of the ocean or
   woods,
Of the builders and steerers of ships, and the wielders of
   axes and mauls, and the drivers of horses;
I can eat and sleep with them week in and week out.

What is commonest, cheapest, nearest, easiest, is Me;
Me going in for my chances, spending for vast returns,
Adorning myself to bestow myself on the first that will
   take me,   261
Not asking the sky to come down to my good will,
Scattering it freely forever.

15

The pure contralto sings in the organ loft,
The carpenter dresses his plank, the tongue of his fore-
   plane whistles its wild ascending lisp,
The married and unmarried children ride home to their
   Thanksgiving dinner,
The pilot seizes the king-pin—he heaves down with a
   strong arm,

The mate stands braced in the whale-boat—lance and
    harpoon are ready,
The duck-shooter walks by silent and cautious stretches,
The deacons are ordain'd with cross'd hands at the altar,
The spinning-girl retreats and advances to the hum of
    the big wheel,   271
The farmer stops by the bars, as he walks on a First-day
    loafe, and looks at the oats and rye,
The lunatic is carried at last to the asylum, a confirm'd
    case,
(He will never sleep any more as he did in the cot in his
    mother's bed-room;)
The jour printer with gray head and gaunt jaws works at
    his case,
He turns his quid of tobacco, while his eyes blurr with
    the manuscript;
The malform'd limbs are tied to the surgeon's table,
What is removed drops horribly in a pail;
The quadroon girl is sold at the auction-stand, the drunkard
    nods by the bar-room stove;
The machinist rolls up his sleeves, the policeman travels
    his beat, the gate-keeper marks who pass;   280
The young fellow drives the express-wagon—(I love him,
    though I do not know him;)
The half-breed straps on his light boots to compete in
    the race;
The western turkey-shooting draws old and young—some
    lean on their rifles, some sit on logs,
Out from the crowd steps the marksman, takes his posi-
    tion, levels his piece;
The groups of newly-come immigrants cover the wharf
    or levee;
As the woolly-pates hoe in the sugar-field, the overseer
    views them from his saddle;
The bugle calls in the ball-room, the gentlemen run for
    their partners, the dancers bow to each other;
The youth lies awake in the cedar-roof'd garret, and
    harks to the musical rain;
The Wolverine sets traps on the creek that helps fill the
    Huron;
The squaw, wrapt in her yellow-hemm'd cloth, is offer-
    ing moccasins and bead-bags for sale;   290

The connoisseur peers along the exhibition-gallery with
half-shut eyes bent sideways;

As the deck-hands make fast the steamboat, the plank is
thrown for the shore-going passengers;

The young sister holds out the skein, while the elder
sister winds it off in a ball, and stops now and then
for the knots;

The one-year wife is recovering and happy, having a
week ago borne her first child;

The clean-hair'd Yankee girl works with her sewing-ma-
chine, or in the factory or mill;

The paving-man leans on his two-handed rammer, the
reporter's lead flies swiftly over the note-book, the
sign-painter is lettering with red and gold;

The canal boy trots on the tow-path, the book-keeper
counts at his desk, the shoemaker waxes his thread;

The conductor beats time for the band, and all the per-
formers follow him;

The child is baptized, the convert is making his first
professions;

The regatta is spread on the bay, the race is begun,
(how the white sails sparkle!)   300

The drover watching his drove sings out to them that
would stray;

The pedler sweats with his pack on his back, (the pur-
chaser higgling about the odd cent;)

The bride unrumples her white dress, the minute-hand
of the clock moves slowly;

The opium-eater reclines with rigid head and just-open'd
lips;

The prostitute draggles her shawl, her bonnet bobs on
her tipsy and pimpled neck;

The crowd laugh at her blackguard oaths, the men jeer
and wink to each other;

(Miserable! I do not laugh at your oaths, nor jeer you;)

The President, holding a cabinet council, is surrounded
by the Great Secretaries;

On the piazza walk three matrons stately and friendly
with twined arms;

The crew of the fish-smack pack repeated layers of hali-
but in the hold;   310

The Missourian crosses the plains, toting his wares and his
cattle;

As the fare-collector goes through the train, he gives
  notice by the jingling of loose change;
The floor-men are laying the floor, the tinners are tin-
  ning the roof, the masons are calling for mortar;
In single file, each shouldering his hod, pass onward the
  laborers;
Seasons pursuing each other, the indescribable crowd is
  gather'd—it is the fourth of Seventh-month—(what
  salutes of cannon and small arms!)
Seasons pursuing each other, the plougher ploughs, the
  mower mows, and the winter-grain falls in the
  ground;
Off on the lakes the pike-fisher watches and waits by the
  hole in the frozen surface;
The stumps stand thick round the clearing, the squatter
  strikes deep with his axe;
Flatboatmen make fast towards dusk near the cotton-
  wood or pecan-trees;
Coon-seekers go through the regions of the Red river, or
  through those drain'd by the Tennessee, or through
  those of the Arkansaw;   320
Torches shine in the dark that hangs on the Chattahoo-
  chee or Altamahaw;
Patriarchs sit at supper with sons and grandsons and
  great-grandsons around them;
In walls of adobie, in canvas tents, rest hunters and
  trappers after their day's sport;
The city sleeps and the country sleeps;
The living sleep for their time, the dead sleep for their
  time;
The old husband sleeps by his wife, and the young hus-
  band sleeps by his wife;
And these one and all tend inward to me, and I tend
  outward to them,
And such as it is to be of these, more or less, I am.
And of these one and all I weave the song of myself.

16

I am of old and young, of the foolish as much as the
  wise,   330
Regardless of others, ever regardful of others,

Maternal as well as paternal, a child as well as a man,
Stuff'd with the stuff that is coarse, and stuff'd with the
stuff that is fine,
One of the Nation of many nations, the smallest the same,
and the largest the same;
A southerner soon as a northerner, a planter nonchalant
and hospitable, down by the Oconee I live;
A Yankee bound by my own way, ready for trade, my
joints the limberest joints on earth, and the sternest
joints on earth;
A Kentuckian walking the vale of the Elkhorn in my
deer-skin leggings, a Louisianian or Georgian;
A boatman over lakes or bays, or along coasts, a Hoo-
sier, Badger, Buckeye;
At home on Kanadian snow-shoes, or up in the bush, or
with fishermen off Newfoundland,
At home in the fleet of ice-boats, sailing with the rest and
tacking, 340
At home on the hills of Vermont, or in the woods of
Maine, or the Texan ranch;
Comrade of Californians, comrade of free north-west-
erners, (loving their big proportions,)
Comrade of raftsmen and coalmen, comrade of all who
shake hands and welcome to drink and meat;
A learner with the simplest, a teacher of the thought-
fullest;
A novice beginning, yet experient of myriads of seasons;
Of every hue and caste am I, of every rank and religion;
A farmer, mechanic, artist, gentleman, sailor, quaker;
A prisoner, fancy-man, rowdy, lawyer, physician, priest.

I resist anything better than my own diversity;
Breathe the air, but leave plenty after me, 350
And am not stuck up, and am in my place.

(The moth and the fish-eggs are in their place;
The bright suns I see, and the dark suns I cannot see,
are in their place;

The palpable is in its place, and the impalpable is in its
place.)

17

These are the thoughts of all men in all ages and lands—
    they are not original with me;
If they are not yours as much as mine, they are nothing,
    or next to nothing;
If they are not the riddle, and the untying of the riddle,
    they are nothing;
If they are not just as close as they are distant, they are
    nothing.

This is the grass that grows wherever the land is, and
    the water is;
This is the common air that bathes the globe.   360

18

With music strong I come, with my cornets and my
    drums,
I play not marches for accepted victors only, I play marches
    for conquer'd and slain persons.

Have you heard that it was good to gain the day?
I also say it is good to fall—battles are lost in the same
    spirit in which they are won.

I beat and pound for the dead;
I blow through my embouchures my loudest and gayest
    for them.

Vivas to those who have fail'd!
And to those whose war-vessels sank in the sea!
And to those themselves who sank in the sea!
And to all generals that lost engagements! and all over-
    come heroes!   370
And the numberless unknown heroes, equal to the great-
    est heroes known!

19

This is the meal equally set, this is the meat for natural
    hunger,

It is for the wicked just the same as the righteous, I
    make appointments with all,
I will not have a single person slighted or left away;
The kept-woman, sponger, thief, are hereby invited;
The heavy-lipp'd slave is invited, the venerealee is invited;
There shall be no difference between them and the rest.

This is the press of a bashful hand, this is the float and
    odor of hair;
This is the touch of my lips to yours, this is the murmur
    of yearning;
This is the far-off depth and height reflecting my own
    face;   380
This is the thoughtful merge of myself, and the outlet
    again.

Do you guess I have some intricate purpose?
Well, I have—for the Fourth-month showers have, and
    the mica on the side of a rock has.

Do you take it I would astonish?
Does the daylight astonish? does the early redstart,
    twittering through the woods?
Do I astonish more than they?

This hour I tell things in confidence;
I might not tell everybody, but I will tell you.

20

Who goes there? hankering, gross, mystical, nude;
How is it I extract strength from the beef I eat?   390

What is a man, anyhow? What am I? What are you?

All I mark as my own, you shall offset it with your own,
Else it were time lost listening to me.

I do not snivel that snivel the world over,
That months are vacuums, and the ground but wallow
    and filth.

Whimpering and truckling fold with powders for invalids
  —conformity goes to the fourth-remov'd;
I wear my hat as I please indoors or out.

Why should I pray? why should I venerate and be
  ceremonious?

Having pried through the strata, analyzed to a hair,
  counsell'd with doctors, and calculated close,
I find no sweeter fat than sticks to my own bones.   400

In all people I see myself—none more, and not one a
  barley-corn less,
And the good or bad I say of myself, I say of them.

And I know I am solid and sound,
To me the converging objects of the universe perpetually flow,
All are written to me, and I must get what the writing
  means.

I know I am deathless,
I know this orbit of mine cannot be swept by the carpenter's compass,
I know I shall not pass like a child's carlacue cut with a
  burnt stick at night.

I know I am august,
I do not trouble my spirit to vindicate itself or be under-
  stood,   410
I see that the elementary laws never apologize;
(I reckon I behave no prouder than the level I plant my
  house by, after all.)

I exist as I am, that is enough;
If no other in the world be aware, I sit content;
And if each and all be aware, I sit content.

One world is aware, and by far the largest to me, and
  that is myself;
And whether I come to my own to-day, or in ten thousand or ten million years,

I can cheerfully take it now, or with equal cheerfulness
    I can wait.

My foothold is tenon'd and mortis'd in granite;
I laugh at what you call dissolution,   420
And I know the amplitude of time.

21

I am the poet of the Body and I am the poet of the Soul.
The pleasures of heaven are with me, and the pains of
    hell are with me,
The first I graft and increase upon myself, the latter I
    translate into a new tongue.

I am the poet of the woman the same as the man,
And I say it is as great to be a woman as to be a man,
And I say there is nothing greater than the mother of
    men.

I chant the chant of dilation or pride,
We have had ducking and deprecating about enough,
I show that size is only development.   430

Have you outstript the rest? Are you the President?
It is a trifle—they will more than arrive there, every one,
    and still pass on.

I am he that walks with the tender and growing night,
I call to the earth and sea, half-held by the night.

Press close, bare-bosom'd night! Press close, magnetic,
    nourishing night!
Night of south winds! night of the large few stars!
Still, nodding night! mad, naked, summer night.

Smile, O voluptuous, cool-breath'd earth!
Earth of the slumbering and liquid trees!
Earth of departed sunset! earth of the mountains, misty-
    topt!   440
Earth of the vitreous pour of the full moon, just tinged
    with blue!

Earth of shine and dark, mottling the tide of the river!
Earth of the limpid gray of clouds, brighter and clearer
   for my sake!
Far-swooping elbow'd earth! rich, apple-blossom'd earth!
Smile, for your lover comes!

Prodigal, you have given me love! Therefore I to you
   give love!
O unspeakable, passionate love!

22

You sea! I resign myself to you also—I guess what you
   mean;
I behold from the beach your crooked inviting fingers,
I believe you refuse to go back without feeling of me;
We must have a turn together, I undress, hurry me
   out of sight of the land,   451
Cushion me soft, rock me in billowy drowse,
Dash me with amorous wet—I can repay you.

Sea of stretch'd ground-swells!
Sea breathing broad and convulsive breaths!
Sea of the brine of life and of unshovell'd yet always-ready
   graves!
Howler and scooper of storms! capricious and dainty
   sea!
I am integral with you—I too am of one phase, and of
   all phases.

Partaker of influx and efflux I—extoller of hate and con-
   ciliation,
Extoller of amies, and those that sleep in each other's
   arms.   460

I am he attesting sympathy;
(Shall I make my list of things in the house, and skip the
   house that supports them?)

I am not the poet of goodness only, I do not decline to
   be the poet of wickedness also.

What blurt is this about virtue and about vice?
Evil propels me, and reform of evil propels me—I stand
    indifferent,
My gait is no fault-finder's or rejector's gait,
I moisten the roots of all that has grown.

Did you fear some scrofula out of the unflagging preg-
    nancy?
Did you guess the celestial laws are yet to be work'd
    over and rectified?

I find one side a balance, and the antipodal side a bal-
    ance;   470
Soft doctrine as steady help as stable doctrine,
Thoughts and deeds of the present, our rouse and early
    start.

This minute that comes to me over the past decillions,
There is no better than it and now.

What behaved well in the past, or behaves well to-day,
    is not such a wonder;
The wonder is always and always how there can be a
    mean man or an infidel.

23

Endless unfolding of words of ages!
And mine a word of the modern, the word En-Masse.

A word of the faith that never balks,
Here or henceforward, it is all the same to me—I accept
    Time absolutely.   480

It alone is without flaw—it rounds and completes all,
That mystic, baffling wonder alone completes all.

I accept Reality, and dare not question it,
Materialism first and last imbuing.

Hurrah for positive science! long live exact demonstra-
    tion!

Fetch stonecrop, mixt with cedar and branches of lilac;
This is the lexicographer, this the chemist, this made
 a grammar of the old cartouches;
These mariners put the ship through dangerous unknown
 seas,
This is the geologist, this works with the scalpel, and
 this is a mathematician.

Gentlemen! to you the first honors always!   490
Your facts are useful, and yet they are not my dwelling,
I but enter by them to an area of my dwelling.

Less the reminders of properties told my words,
And more the reminders they of life untold, and of freedom and extrication,
And make short account of neuters and geldings, and
 favor men and women fully equipt,
And beat the gong of revolt, and stop with fugitives, and
 them that plot and conspire.

24

Walt Whitman, a kosmos, of Manhattan the son,
Turbulent, fleshly, sensual, eating, drinking and breeding;
No sentimentalist, no stander above men and women,
 or apart from them;
No more modest than immodest.   500

Unscrew the locks from the doors!
Unscrew the doors themselves from their jambs!

Whoever degrades another degrades me,
And whatever is done or said returns at last to me.

Through me the afflatus surging and surging, through
 me the current and index.

I speak the pass-word primeval, I give the sign of democracy;
By God! I will accept nothing which all cannot have
 their counterpart of on the same terms.

Through me many long dumb voices,
Voices of the interminable generations of slaves,
Voices of the diseas'd and despairing, and of thieves and
    dwarfs,   510
Voices of cycles of preparation and accretion,
And of the threads that connect the stars, and of wombs,
    and of the father-stuff,
And of the rights of them the others are down upon,
Of the deform'd, trivial, flat, foolish, despised,
Fog in the air, beetles rolling balls of dung.

Through me forbidden voices,
Voice of sexes and lusts, voices veil'd, and I remove the
    veil,
Voices indecent, by me clarified and transfigur'd.

I do not press my fingers across my mouth,
I keep as delicate around the bowels as around the head
    and heart;   520
Copulation is no more rank to me than death is.

I believe in the flesh and the appetites,
Seeing, hearing, feeling, are miracles, and each part and
    tag of me is a miracle.

Divine am I inside and out, and I make holy whatever I
    touch or am touch'd from;
The scent of these arm-pits, aroma finer than prayer;
This head more than churches, bibles, and all the creeds.

If I worship one thing more than another, it shall be the
    spread of my own body, or any part of it.
Translucent mould of me, it shall be you!
Shaded ledges and rests, it shall be you!
Firm masculine colter, it shall be you.   530
Whatever goes to the tilth of me, it shall be you!
You my rich blood! your milky stream, pale strippings
    of my life.
Breast that presses against other breasts, it shall be you!
My brain, it shall be your occult convolutions.
Root of wash'd sweet flag! timorous pond-snipe! nest of
    guarded duplicate eggs! it shall be you!
Mix'd tussled hay of head, beard, brawn, it shall be you!

Trickling sap of maple! fibre of manly wheat! it shall be
    you!
Suns so generous, it shall be you!
Vapors lighting and shading my face, it shall be you!
You sweaty brooks and dews, it shall be you!   540
Winds whose soft-tickling genitals rub against me, it
    shall be you!
Broad, muscular fields! branches of live oak! loving
    lounger in my winding paths! it shall be you!
Hands I have taken, face I have kiss'd, mortal I have
    ever touch'd, it shall be you.

I dote on myself—there is that lot of me, and all so lus-
    cious;
Each moment, and whatever happens, thrills me with
    joy.
I cannot tell how my ankles bend, nor whence the cause
    of my faintest wish;
Nor the cause of the friendship I emit, nor the cause of
    the friendship I take again.

That I walk up my stoop, I pause to consider if it really
    be;
A morning-glory at my window satisfies me more than
    the metaphysics of books.

To behold the day-break!   550
The little light fades the immense and diaphanous shad-
    ows,
The air tastes good to my palate.

Hefts of the moving world, at innocent gambols silently
    rising, freshly exuding,
Scooting obliquely high and low.

Something I cannot see puts upward libidinous prongs,
Seas of bright juice suffuse heaven.

The earth by the sky staid with, the daily close of their
    junction,
The heav'd challenge from the east that moment over
    my head,
The mocking taunt, See then whether you shall be
    master!

25

Dazzling and tremendous, how quick the sun-rise would
    kill me,   560
If I could not now and always send sun-rise out of me.

We also ascend, dazzling and tremendous as the sun,
We found our own, O my Soul, in the calm and cool of
    the daybreak.

My voice goes after what my eyes cannot reach;
With the twirl of my tongue I encompass worlds, and
    volumes of worlds.

Speech is the twin of my vision—it is unequal to meas-
    ure itself;
It provokes me forever, it says sarcastically,
Walt, you contain enough—why don't you let it out then?

Come now, I will not be tantalized—you conceive too
    much of articulation,
Do you not know, O speech, how the buds beneath you
    are folded?   570
Waiting in gloom, protected by frost,
The dirt receding before my prophetical screams,
I underlying causes, to balance them at last,
My knowledge my live parts, it keeping tally with the
    meaning of all things,
Happiness (which whoever hears me let him or her set
    out in search of this day.)

My final merit I refuse you—I refuse putting from me
    what I really am;
Encompass worlds, but never try to encompass me,
I crowd your sleekest and best by simply looking toward
    you.

Writing and talk do not prove me,
I carry the plenum of proof, and everything else, in my
    face;   580
With the hush of my lips I wholly confound the skeptic.

26

I think I will do nothing now but listen,
To accrue what I hear into this song, to let sounds contribute toward it.

I hear bravuras of birds, bustle of growing wheat, gossip
of flames, clack of sticks cooking my meals,
I hear the sound I love, the sound of the human voice,
I hear all sounds running together, combined, fused or
following,
Sounds of the city, and sounds out of the city, sounds
of the day and night,
Talkative young ones to those that like them, the loud
laugh of work-people at their meals,
The angry base of disjointed friendship, the faint tones
of the sick,
The judge with hands tight to the desk, his pallid lips
pronouncing a death-sentence,   590
The heave'e'yo of stevedores unlading ships by the wharves,
the refrain of the anchor-lifters,
The ring of alarm-bells, the cry of fire, the whirr of
swift-streaking engines and hose-carts, with premoni-
tory tinkles, and color'd lights,
The steam-whistle, the solid roll of the train of approaching cars,
The slow-march play'd at the head of the association,
marching two and two,
(They go to guard some corpse, the flag-tops are draped
with black muslin.)

I hear the violoncello ('tis the young man's heart's com-
plaint;)
I hear the key'd cornet—it glides quickly in through my
ears;
It shakes mad-sweet pangs through my belly and breast.

I hear the chorus, it is a grand opera;
Ah, this indeed is music—this suits me.   600

A tenor large and fresh as the creation fills me,
The orbic flex of his mouth is pouring and filling me full.

I hear the train'd soprano—(what work with hers is this?)
The orchestra whirls me wider than Uranus flies.
It wrenches such ardors from me I did not know I pos-
    sess'd them;
It sails me, I dab with bare feet, they are lick'd by the
    indolent waves;
I am cut by bitter and angry hail—I lose my breath,
Steep'd amid honey'd morphine, my windpipe throttled
    in fakes of death,
At length let up again to feel the puzzle of puzzles,
And that we call Being.   610

27

To be, in any form—what is that?
(Round and round we go, all of us, and ever come back
    thither;)
If nothing lay more develop'd, the quahaug in its callous
    shell were enough.

Mine is no callous shell;
I have instant conductors all over me, whether I pass or
    stop;
They seize every object and lead it harmlessly through
    me.

I merely stir, press, feel with my fingers, and am happy;
To touch my person to some one else's is about as much as
    I can stand.

28

Is this then a touch? quivering me to a new identity,
Flames and ether making a rush for my veins,   620
Treacherous tip of me reaching and crowding to help
    them,
My flesh and blood playing out lightning to strike what
    is hardly different from myself;
On all sides prurient provokers stiffening my limbs,
Straining the udder of my heart for its withheld drip,
Behaving licentious toward me, taking no denial,
Depriving me of my best, as for a purpose,
Unbuttoning my clothes, holding me by the bare waist,

Deluding my confusion with the calm of the sunlight and
    pasture-fields,
Immodestly sliding the fellow-senses away,
They bribed to swap off with touch, and go and graze at
    the edges of me;   630
No consideration, no regard for my draining strength or
    my anger,
Fetching the rest of the herd around to enjoy them a
    while,
Then all uniting to stand on a headland and worry me.
The sentries desert every other part of me,
They have left me helpless to a red marauder,
They all come to the headland, to witness and assist against
    me.

I am given up by traitors,
I talk wildly, I have lost my wits, I and nobody else am
    the greatest traitor,
I went myself first to the headland, my own hands car-
    ried me there.

You villain touch! what are you doing? my breath is
    tight in its throat;   640
Unclench your floodgates! you are too much for me.

29

Blind, loving, wrestling touch! sheath'd, hooded, sharp-
    tooth'd touch!
Did it make you ache so, leaving me?

Parting, track'd by arriving, perpetual payment of per-
    petual loan;
Rich, showering rain, and recompense richer afterward.

Sprouts take and accumulate, stand by the curb prolific
    and vital,
Landscapes projected masculine, full-sized and golden.

30

All truths wait in all things,
They neither hasten their own delivery, nor resist it,

They do not need the obstetric forceps of the surgeon; 650
The insignificant is as big to me as any;
(What is less or more than a touch?)

Logic and sermons never convince,
The damp of the night drives deeper into my soul.

(Only what proves itself to every man and woman is so,
Only what nobody denies is so.)

A minute and a drop of me settle my brain;
I believe the soggy clods shall become lovers and lamps,
And a compend of compends is the meat of a man or
    woman,
And a summit and flower there is the feeling they have
    for each other, 660
And they are to branch boundlessly out of that lesson
    until it becomes omnific,
And until every one shall delight us, and we them.

31

I believe a leaf of grass is no less than the journey-work
    of the stars,
And the pismire is equally perfect, and a grain of sand,
    and the egg of the wren,
And the tree-toad is the chef-d'œuvre for the highest,
And the running blackberry would adorn the parlors of
    heaven,
And the narrowest hinge in my hand puts to scorn all
    machinery,
And the cow crunching with depress'd head surpasses any
    statue,
And a mouse is miracle enough to stagger sextillions of
    infidels.

I find I incorporate gneiss, coal, long-threaded moss, fruits,
    grains, esculent roots, 670
And am stucco'd with quadrupeds and birds all over,
And have distanced what is behind me for good reasons,
And call anything close again, when I desire it.

In vain the speeding or shyness,

In vain the plutonic rocks send their old heat against my
approach,
In vain the mastodon retreats beneath its own powder'd
bones,
In vain objects stand leagues off, and assume manifold
shapes,
In vain the ocean settling in hollows, and the great mon-
sters lying low,
In vain the buzzard houses herself with the sky,
In vain the snake slides through the creepers and logs,   680
In vain the elk takes to the inner passes of the woods,
In vain the razor-bill'd auk sails far north to Labrador;
I follow quickly, I ascend to the nest in the fissure of the
cliff.

32

I think I could turn and live with animals, they are so
placid and self-contain'd,
I stand and look at them long and long.

They do not sweat and whine about their condition;
They do not lie awake in the dark and weep for their
sins;
They do not make me sick discussing their duty to God;
Not one is dissatisfied, not one is demented with the mania
of owning things;
Not one kneels to another, nor to his kind that lived thou-
sands of years ago;   690
Not one is respectable or unhappy over the whole earth.

So they show their relations to me, and I accept them;
They bring me tokens of myself—they evince them plainly
in their possession.

I wonder where they get those tokens:
Did I pass that way huge times ago, and negligently drop
them?

Myself moving forward then and now and forever,
Gathering and showing more always and with velocity,
Infinite and omnigenous, and the like of these among them;

Not too exclusive toward the reachers of my remem-
brancers,
Picking out here one that I love, and now go with him
on brotherly terms.   700

A gigantic beauty of a stallion, fresh and responsive to
my caresses,
Head high in the forehead, wide between the ears,
Limbs glossy and supple, tail dusting the ground,
Eyes full of sparkling wickedness, ears finely cut, flexibly
moving.

His nostrils dilate as my heels embrace him;
His well-built limbs tremble with pleasure, as we race
around and return.
I but use you a minute, then I resign you, stallion;
Why do I need your paces, when I myself out-gallop them?
Even as I stand or sit passing faster than you.

33

Space and time! now I see it is true, what I guessed at,   710
What I guess'd when I loaf'd on the grass,
What I guess'd while I lay alone in my bed,
And again as I walk'd the beach under the paling stars of
the morning.

My ties and ballasts leave me, my elbows rest in the
sea-gaps;
I skirt sierras, my palms cover continents,
I am afoot with my vision.

By the city's quadrangular houses—in log huts, camping
with lumbermen;
Along the ruts of the turnpike, along the dry gulch and
rivulet bed;
Weeding my onion-patch, or hoeing rows of carrots and
parsnips, crossing savannas, trailing in forests;
Prospecting, gold-digging, girdling the trees of a new
purchase;   720
Scorch'd ankle-deep by the hot sand—hauling my boat
down the shallow river,

Where the panther walks to and fro on a limb overhead,
    where the buck turns furiously at the hunter,
Where the rattlesnake suns his flabby length on a rock,
    where the otter is feeding on fish,
Where the alligator in his tough pimples sleeps by the
    bayou,
Where the black bear is searching for roots or honey,
    where the beaver pats the mud with his paddle-
    shaped tail;
Over the growing sugar, over the yellow-flower'd cotton
    plant, over the rice in its low moist field,
Over the sharp-peak'd farm house, with its scallop'd scum
    and slender shoots from the gutters,
Over the western persimmon, over the long-leav'd corn,
    over the delicate blue-flower flax;
Over the white and brown buckwheat, a hummer and
    buzzer there with the rest,
Over the dusky green of the rye as it ripples and shades
    in the breeze;   730
Scaling mountains, pulling myself cautiously up, holding
    on by low scragged limbs;
Walking the path worn in the grass, and beat through the
    leaves of the brush;
Where the quail is whistling betwixt the woods and the
    wheat-lot;
Where the bat flies in the Seventh-month eve, where the
    great gold-bug drops through the dark;
Where the brook puts out of the roots of the old tree and
    flows to the meadow;
Where cattle stand and shake away flies with the tremulous
    shuddering of their hides;
Where the cheese-cloth hangs in the kitchen, where andirons
    straddle the hearth-slab, where cobwebs fall in festoons
    from the rafters;
Where trip-hammers crash, where the press is twirling
    its cylinders;
Wherever the human heart beats with terrible throes
    under its ribs;
Where the pear-shaped balloon is floating afloat, (floating
    in it myself, and looking composedly down;)   740
Where the life-car is drawn on the slip-noose, where the
    heat hatches pale-green eggs in the dented sand;

Where the she-whale swims with her calf, and never for-
  sakes it;
Where the steam-ship trails hind-ways its long pennant of
  smoke;
Where the fin of the shark cuts like a black chip out of
  the water;
Where the half-burn'd brig is riding on unknown currents,
Where shells grow to her slimy deck, where the dead are
  corrupting below;
Where the dense-starr'd flag is borne at the head of the
  regiments;
Approaching Manhattan, up by the long-stretching island;
Under Niagara, the cataract falling like a veil over my
  countenance;
Upon a door-step, upon the horse-block of hard wood
  outside;   750
Upon the race-course, or enjoying picnics or jigs, or a
  good game of base-ball;
At he-festivals, with blackguard jibes, ironical license,
  bull-dances, drinking, laughter;
At the cider-mill, tasting the sweets of the brown mash,
  sucking the juice through a straw;
At apple-peelings, wanting kisses for all the red fruit I
  find;
At musters, beach-parties, friendly bees, huskings, house-
  raisings:
Where the mocking-bird sounds his delicious gurgles,
  cackles, screams, weeps;
Where the hay-rick stands in the barn-yard, where the
  dry-stalks are scattered, where the brood-cow waits
  in the hovel;
Where the bull advances to do his masculine work,
  where the stud to the mare, where the cock is
  treading the hen;
Where the heifers browse, where geese nip their food
  with short jerks;
Where sun-down shadows lengthen over the limitless
  and lonesome prairie;   760
Where herds of buffalo make a crawling spread of the
  square miles far and near;
Where the humming-bird shimmers, where the neck of
  the long-lived swan is curving and winding;
Where the laughing-gull scoots by the shore, where she
  laughs her near-human laugh;

Where bee-hives range on a gray bench in the garden, half hid by the high weeds;

Where band-neck'd partridges roost in a ring on the ground with their heads out;

Where burial coaches enter the arch'd gates of a cemetery;

Where winter wolves bark amid wastes of snow and icicled trees;

Where the yellow-crown'd heron comes to the edge of the marsh at night and feeds upon small crabs;

Where the splash of swimmers and divers cools the warm noon;

Where the katy-did works her chromatic reed on the walnut-tree over the well;   770

Through patches of citrons and cucumbers with silver-wired leaves;

Through the salt-lick, or orange glade, or under conical firs;

Through the gymnasium, through the curtain'd saloon, through the office or public hall;

Pleas'd with the native, and pleas'd with the foreign, pleas'd with the new and old;

Pleas'd with the homely women, as well as the handsome;

Pleas'd with the quakeress as she puts off her bonnet and talks melodiously;

Pleas'd with the tune of the choir of the white-wash'd church;

Pleas'd with the earnest words of the sweating Methodist preacher, impress'd seriously at the camp-meeting:

Looking in the shop-windows of Broadway the whole forenoon, flatting the flesh of my nose on the thick plate-glass;

Wandering the same afternoon with my face turn'd up to the clouds, or down a lane or along the beach,   780

My right and left arms round the sides of two friends, and I in the middle:

Coming home with the silent and dark-cheek'd bush-boy—(behind me he rides at the drape of the day;)

Far from the settlements, studying the print of animals' feet, or the moccasin print;

By the cot in the hospital, reaching lemonade to a feverish patient;

Nigh the coffin'd corpse when all is still, examining with a candle:

Voyaging to every port to dicker and adventure;

Hurrying with the modern crowd, as eager and fickle as
    any;
Hot toward one I hate, ready in my madness to knife him;
Solitary at midnight in my back yard, my thoughts gone
    from me a long while;
Walking the old hills of Judea, with the beautiful gentle
    God by my side;   790
Speeding through space, speeding through heaven and the
    stars;
Speeding amid the seven satellites, and the broad ring, and
    the diameter of eighty thousand miles;
Speeding with tail'd meteors, throwing fire-balls like the
    rest;
Carrying the crescent child that carries its own full mother
    in its belly;
Storming, enjoying, planning, loving, cautioning,
Backing and filling, appearing and disappearing,
I tread day and night such roads.

I visit the orchards of spheres, and look at the product,
And look at quintillions ripen'd, and look at quintillions
    green.

I fly those flights of a fluid and swallowing soul;   800
My course runs below the soundings of plummets.

I help myself to material and immaterial,
No guard can shut me off, no law prevent me.

I anchor my ship for a little while only,
My messengers continually cruise away, or bring their
    returns to me.

I go hunting polar furs and the seal, leaping chasms with
    a pike-pointed staff, clinging to topples of brittle and
    blue.

I ascend to the foretruck,
I take my place late at night in the crow's-nest,
We sail the arctic sea, it is plenty light enough;
Through the clear atmosphere I stretch around on the
    wonderful beauty,   810

The enormous masses of ice pass me, and I pass them
——the scenery is plain in all directions;
The white-topt mountains show in the distance, I fling
out my fancies toward them;
We are approaching some great battle-field in which
we are soon to be engaged;
We pass the colossal outposts of the encampment, we pass
with still feet and caution;
Or we are entering by the suburbs some vast and ruin'd
city,
The blocks and fallen architecture more than all the living
cities of the globe.

I am a free companion, I bivouac by invading watch-
fires.
I turn the bridegroom out of bed, and stay with the bride
myself,
I tighten her all night to my thighs and lips.

My voice is the wife's voice, the screech by the rail of
the stairs;   820
They fetch my man's body up dripping and drown'd.

I understand the large hearts of heroes,
The courage of present times and all times;
How the skipper saw the crowded and rudderless wreck
of the steam-ship, and Death chasing it up and down
the storm;
How he knuckled tight, and gave not back one inch, and
was faithful of days and faithful of nights,
And chalk'd in large letters, on a board, *Be of good cheer,
we will not desert you:*
How he follow'd with them, and tack'd with them, and
would not give it up;
How he saved the drifting company at last:
How the lank loose-gown'd women look'd when boated
from the side of their prepared graves;
How the silent old-faced infants, and the lifted sick, and
the sharp-lipp'd unshaved men: 830
All this I swallow, it tastes good, I like it well, it becomes
mine;
I am the man, I suffer'd, I was there.

The disdain and calmness of olden martyrs;
The mother, condemn'd for a witch, burnt with dry wood,
    her children gazing on;
The hounded slave that flags in the race, leans by the
    fence, blowing, cover'd with sweat;
The twinges that sting like needles his legs and neck, the
    murderous buckshot and the bullets;
All these I feel or am.

I am the hounded slave, I wince at the bite of the dogs,
Hell and despair are upon me, crack and again crack the
    marksmen,
I clutch the rails of the fence, my gore dribs, thinn'd
    with the ooze of my skin,   840
I fall on the weeds and stones;
The riders spur their unwilling horses, haul close,
Taunt my dizzy ears, and beat me violently over the head
    with whip-stocks.

Agonies are one of my changes of garments;
I do not ask the wounded person how he feels—I my-
    self become the wounded person;
My hurts turn livid upon me as I lean on a cane and
    observe.

I am the mash'd fireman with breast-bone broken,
Tumbling walls buried me in their debris,
Heat and smoke I inspired, I heard the yelling shouts of
    my comrades;
I heard the distant click of their picks and shovels;   850
They have clear'd the beams away, they tenderly lift me
    forth.

I lie in the night air in my red shirt, the pervading hush
    is for my sake;
Painless after all I lie, exhausted but not so unhappy;
White and beautiful are the faces around me, the heads
    are bared of their fire-caps,
The kneeling crowd faces with the light of the torches.

Distant and dead resuscitate,
They show as the dial or move as the hands of me—I am
    the clock myself.

I am an old artillerist, I tell of my fort's bombardment,
I am there again.

Again the long roll of the drummers, 860
Again the attacking cannon, mortars,
Again, to my listening ears, the cannon responsive.

I take part—I see and hear the whole,
The cries, curses, roar, the plaudits for well-aim'd shots,
The ambulanza slowly passing, trailing its red drip;
Workmen searching after damages, making indispensable
    repairs;
The fall of grenades through the rent roof, the fan-shaped
    explosion;
The whizz of limbs, heads, stone, wood, iron, high in the
    air.

Again gurgles the mouth of my dying general, he fu-
    riously waves with his hand;
He gasps through the clot, *Mind not me—mind—the en-
    trenchments.*   870

34

Now I tell what I knew in Texas in my early youth;
(I tell not the fall of Alamo,
Not one escaped to tell the fall of Alamo,
The hundred and fifty are dumb yet at Alamo;)
'Tis the tale of the murder in cold blood of four hundred
    and twelve young men.

Retreating, they had form'd in a hollow square, with
    their baggage for breastworks;
Nine hundred lives out of the surrounding enemy's, nine
    times their number, was the price they took in ad-
    vance;
Their colonel was wounded and their ammunition gone;
They treated for an honorable capitulation, receiv'd writ-
    ing and seal, gave up their arms, and march'd back
    prisoners of war.

They were the glory of the race of rangers,   880
Matchless with horse, rifle, song, supper, courtship,

Large, turbulent, generous, handsome, proud, and affec-
tionate,
Bearded, sunburnt, drest in the free costume of hunters,
Not a single one over thirty years of age.

The second First-day morning they were brought out in
squads, and massacred—it was beautiful early summer;
The work commenced about five o'clock, and was over by
eight.

None obey'd the command to kneel;
Some made a mad and helpless rush, some stood stark and
straight;
A few fell at once, shot in the temple or heart, the living
and dead lay together;
The maim'd and mangled dug in the dirt, the newcomers
saw them there;   890
Some, half-kill'd, attempted to crawl away;
These were despatch'd with bayonets, or batter'd with the
blunts of muskets;
A youth not seventeen years old seiz'd his assassin till two
more came to release him;
The three were all torn, and cover'd with the boy's blood.

At eleven o'clock began the burning of the bodies:
That is the tale of the murder of the four hundred and
twelve young men.

35

Would you hear of an old-time sea-fight?
Would you learn who won by the light of the moon and
stars?
List to the yarn as my grandmother's father, the sailor,
told it to me.

Our foe was no skulk in his ship, I tell you, (said he;)
His was the surly English pluck, and there is no tougher
or truer, and never was, and never will be;   901
Along the lower'd eve he came, horribly raking us.

We closed with him, the yards entangled, the cannon touch'd;
My captain lash'd fast with his own hands.

We had receiv'd some eighteen pounds shot under the water;
On our lower-gun-deck two large pieces had burst at the first fire, killing all around, and blowing up overhead.

Fighting at sun-down, fighting at dark;
Ten o'clock at night, the full moon well up, our leaks on the gain, and five feet of water reported;
The master-at-arms loosing the prisoners confined in the afterhold, to give them a chance for themselves.

The transit to and from the magazine is now stopt by the sentinels,   910
They see so many strange faces, they do not know whom to trust.

Our frigate takes fire;
The other asks if we demand quarter?
If our colors are struck, and the fighting done?

Now I laugh content, for I hear the voice of my little captain,
We have not struck, he composedly cries, *we have just begun our part of the fighting.*

Only three guns are in use;
One is directed by the captain himself against the enemy's mainmast,
Two well served with grape and canister silence his musketry and clear his decks.

The tops alone second the fire of this little battery, especially the main-top;   920
They hold out bravely during the whole of the action.

Not a moment's cease;
The leaks gain fast on the pumps, the fire eats toward the powder-magazine.

One of the pumps has been shot away, it is generally
    thought we are sinking.

Serene stands the little captain,
He is not hurried, his voice is neither high nor low,
His eyes give more light to us than our battle-lanterns.

Toward twelve, there in the beams of the moon they sur-
    render to us.

36

Stretch'd and still lies the midnight;   929
Two great hulls motionless on the breast of the darkness;
Our vessel riddled and slowly sinking—preparations to
    pass to the one we have conquer'd;
The captain on the quarter-deck coldly giving his orders
    through a countenance white as a sheet;
Near by the corpse of the child that serv'd in the cabin,
The dead face of an old salt with long white hair and
    carefully curl'd whiskers,
The flames, spite of all that can be done, flickering aloft
    and below,
The husky voices of the two or three officers yet fit for
    duty,
Formless stacks of bodies, and bodies by themselves, dabs
    of flesh upon the masts and spars,
Cut of cordage, dangle of rigging, slight shock of the
    soothe of waves,
Black and impassive guns, litter of powder-parcels, strong
    scent,
A few large stars overhead, silent and mournful shining,
Delicate sniffs of sea-breeze, smells of sedgy grass and
    fields by the shore, death-messages given in charge
    to survivors,   941
The hiss of the surgeon's knife, the gnawing teeth of his
    saw,
Wheeze, cluck, swash of falling blood, short wild scream,
    and long, dull, tapering groan;
These so, these irretrievable.

37

You laggards there on guard!   look to your arms!
In at the conquer'd doors they crowd! I am possess'd!

Embody all presence outlaw'd or suffering;
See myself in prison shaped like another man,
And feel the dull unintermitted pain.

950

For me the keepers of convicts shoulder their carbines and
     keep watch;
It is I let out in the morning, and barr'd at night.

Not a mutineer walks handcuff'd to jail, but I am hand-
     cuff'd to him and walk by his side;
(I am less the jolly one there, and more the silent one,
     with sweat on my twitching lips.)

Not a youngster is taken for larceny, but I go up too, and
     am tried and sentenced.

Not a cholera patient lies at the last gasp, but I also lie
     at the last gasp;
My face is ash-color'd, my sinews gnarl, away from me
     people retreat.

Askers embody themselves in me, and I am embodied in
     them;
I project my hat, sit shame-faced, and beg.

38

Enough! enough! enough!   960
Somehow I have been stunn'd. Stand back!
Give me a little time beyond my cuff'd head, slumbers,
     dreams, gaping,
I discover myself on the verge of a usual mistake.

That I could forget the mockers and insults!
That I could forget the trickling tears, and the blows of
     the bludgeons and hammers!
That I could look with a separate look on my own cruci-
     fixion and bloody crowning.

I remember now;
I resume the overstaid fraction;
The grave of rock multiplies what has been confided to
     it, or to any graves;
Corpses rise, gashes heal, fastenings roll from me.   970

I troop forth replenish'd with supreme power, one of an
    average unending procession,
Inland and sea-coast we go, and pass all boundary lines;
Our swift ordinances on their way over the whole earth;
The blossoms we wear in our hats the growth of thousands
    of years.

Eleves, I salute you! come forward!
Continue your annotations, continue your questionings.

39

The friendly and flowing savage, who is he?
Is he waiting for civilization, or past it and mastering it?

Is he some South-westerner rais'd out-doors? is he Kana-
    dian?
Is he from the Mississippi country? Iowa, Oregon, Cali-
    fornia?   980
The mountains? prairie-life, bush-life? or from the sea?

Wherever he goes, men and women accept and desire him;
They desire he should like them, touch them, speak to
    them, stay with them.

Behavior lawless as snow-flakes, words simple as grass,
    uncomb'd head, laughter, and naïveté,
Slow-stepping feet, common features, common modes and
    emanations;
They descend in new forms from the tips of his fingers;
They are wafted with the odor of his body or breath, they
    fly out of the glance of his eyes.

40

Flaunt of the sunshine, I need not your bask,—lie over!
You light surfaces only—I force surfaces and depths also.

Earth! you seem to look for something at my hands;   990
Say, old Top-knot! what do you want?

Man or woman! I might tell how I like you, but cannot;
And might tell what it is in me, and what it is in you, but
    cannot,

And might tell that pining I have, that pulse of my nights
and days.

Behold! I do not give lectures, or a little charity,
When I give I give myself.

You there, impotent, loose in the knees,
Open your scarf'd chops till I blow grit within you;
Spread your palms, and lift the flaps of your pockets;
I am not to be denied, I compel, I have stores plenty and
to spare;   1000
And anything I have I bestow.

I do not ask who you are—that is not important to me,
You can do nothing and be nothing but what I will in-
fold you.

To cotton-field drudge or cleaner of privies I lean;
On his right cheek I put the family kiss,
And in my soul I swear, I never will deny him.

On women fit for conception I start bigger and nimbler
babes;
(This day I am jetting the stuff of far more arrogant
republics.)

To any one dying, thither I speed, and twist the knob of
the door;
Turn the bed-clothes toward the foot of the bed;   1010
Let the physician and the priest go home.

I seize the descending man, and raise him with resistless
will,
O despairer, here is my neck;
By God! you shall not go down! hang your whole weight
upon me.

I dilate you with tremendous breath, I buoy you up;
Every room of the house do I fill with an arm'd force,
Lovers of me, bafflers of graves.

Sleep—I and they keep guard all night;
Not doubt, not decease shall dare to lay finger upon you;

I have embraced you, and henceforth possess you to my-
    self,   1020
And when you rise in the morning you will find what I
    tell you is so.

41

I am he bringing help for the sick as they pant on their
    backs,
And for strong upright men I bring yet more needed help.

I heard what was said of the universe,
Heard it and heard it of several thousand years:
It is middling well as far as it goes,—but is that all?

Magnifying and applying come I,
Outbidding at the start the old cautious hucksters,
Taking myself the exact dimensions of Jehovah,
Lithographing Kronos, Zeus his son, and Hercules his
    grandson;   1030
Buying drafts of Osiris, Isis, Belus, Brahma, Buddha,
In my portfolio placing Manito loose, Allah on a leaf, the
    crucifix engraved,
With Odin, and the hideous-faced Mexitli, and every idol
    and image;
Taking them all for what they are worth, and not a cent
    more;
Admitting they were alive and did the work of their days;
(They bore mites, as for unfledg'd birds, who have now
    to rise and fly and sing for themselves;)
Accepting the rough deific sketches to fill out better in
    myself, bestowing them freely on each man and
    woman I see;
Discovering as much or more in a framer framing a
    house,
Putting higher claims for him there with his roll'd-up
    sleeves, driving the mallet and chisel;
Not objecting to special revelations, considering a curl
    of smoke, or a hair on the back of my hand, just as
    curious as any revelation;   1040
Lads ahold of fire-engines and hook-and-ladder ropes no
    less to me than the gods of the antique wars;

Minding their voices peal through the crash of destruction,
Their brawny limbs passing safe over charr'd laths,
their white foreheads whole and unhurt out of the
flames;
By the mechanic's wife with her babe at her nipple in-
terceding for every person born,
Three scythes at harvest whizzing in a row from three
lusty angels with shirts bagg'd out at their waists,
The snag-tooth'd hostler with red hair redeeming sins past
and to come,
Selling all he possesses, traveling on foot to fee lawyers
for his brother, and sit by him while he is tried for
forgery;
What was strewn in the amplest strewing the square rod
about me, and not filling the square rod then,
The bull and the bug never worship'd half enough,
Dung and dirt more admirable than was dream'd,   1050
The supernatural of no account—myself waiting my
time to be one of the supremes,
The day getting ready for me when I shall do as much
good as the best, and be as prodigious;
By my life-lumps! becoming already a creator;
Putting myself here and now to the ambush'd womb of
the shadows.

42

A call in the midst of the crowd;
My own voice, orotund, sweeping, and final.

Come my children,
Come my boys and girls, my women, household, and in-
timates,
Now the performer launches his nerve, he has pass'd
his prelude on the reeds within.

Easily written, loose-finger'd chords—I feel the thrum of
your climax and close.   1060

My head slues round on my neck;
Music rolls, but not from the organ;
Folks are around me, but they are no household of mine.

Ever the hard, unsunk ground,
Ever the eaters and drinkers, ever the upward and down-
    ward sun—ever the air and the ceaseless tides,
Ever myself and my neighbors, refreshing, wicked, real,
Ever the old inexplicable query, ever that thorn'd thumb,
    that breath of itches and thirsts,
Ever the vexer's *hoot! hoot!* till we find where the sly one
    hides and bring him forth;
Ever love, ever the sobbing liquid of life,
Ever the bandage under the chin, ever the trestles of
    death.   1070

Here and there with dimes on the eyes walking,
To feed the greed of the belly, the brains liberally spoon-
    ing,
Tickets buying, taking, selling, but in to the feast never
    once going;
Many sweating, ploughing, thrashing, and then the chaff for
    payment receiving,
A few idly owning, and they the wheat continually claim-
    ing.

This is the city, and I am one of the citizens;
Whatever interests the rest interests me, politics, wars,
    markets, newspapers, schools,
The mayor and councils, banks, tariffs, steamships, fac-
    tories, stocks, stores, real estate, and personal estate.

The little plentiful mannikins skipping around in collars
    and tail'd coats,
I am aware who they are—(they are positively not worms
    or fleas,)   1080
I acknowledge the duplicates of myself, the weakest and
    shallowest is deathless with me,
What I do and say, the same waits for them,
Every thought that flounders in me, the same flounders
    in them.

I know perfectly well my own egotism,
Know my omnivorous lines, and must not write any less,
And would fetch you whoever you are flush with myself.

Not words of routine this song of mine,
But abruptly to question, to leap beyond yet nearer bring:
This printed and bound book—but the printer, and the
    printing-office boy?
The well-taken photographs—but your wife or friend close
    and solid in your arms?   1090
The black ship, mail'd with iron, her mighty guns in her
    turrets—but the pluck of the captain and engineers?
In the houses, the dishes and fare and furniture—but the
    host and hostess, and the look out of their eyes?
The sky up there—yet here, or next door, or across the
    way?
The saints and sages in history—but you yourself?
Sermons, creeds, theology—but the fathomless human
    brain,
And what is reason? and what is love? and what is life?

43

I do not despise you, priests, all time, the world over,
My faith is the greatest of faiths, and the least of faiths,
Enclosing worship ancient and modern, and all between
    ancient and modern,
Believing I shall come again upon the earth after five
    thousand years,   1100
Waiting responses from oracles, honoring the gods, salut-
    ing the sun,
Making a fetish of the first rock or stump, powwowing
    with sticks in the circle of obis,
Helping the lama or brahmin as he trims the lamps of
    the idols,
Dancing yet through the streets in a phallic procession—
    rapt and austere in the woods, a gymnosophist,
Drinking mead from the skull-cup—to Shastas and Vedas
    admirant, minding the Koran,
Walking the teokallis, spotted with gore from the stone
    and knife, beating the serpent-skin drum,
Accepting the Gospels, accepting him that was crucified,
    knowing assuredly that he is divine,
To the mass kneeling, or the puritan's prayer rising, or
    sitting patiently in a pew,
Ranting and frothing in my insane crisis, or waiting dead-
    like till my spirit arouses me,

Looking forth on pavement and land, or outside of pavement and land, 1110

Belonging to the winders of the circuit of circuits.

One of that centripetal and centrifugal gang, I turn and talk like a man leaving charges before a journey.

Down-hearted doubters, dull and excluded,
Frivolous, sullen, moping, angry, affected, dishearten'd, atheistical;
I know every one of you, I know the sea of torment, doubt, despair and unbelief.

How the flukes splash!
How they contort rapid as lightning, with spasms, and spouts of blood!

Be at peace, bloody flukes of doubters and sullen mopers;
I take my place among you as much as among any;
The past is the push of you, me, all, precisely the same, 1120
And what is yet untried, and afterward is for you, me, all, precisely the same.

I do not know what is untried and afterward,
But I know it will in its turn prove sufficient, and cannot fail.

Each who passes is consider'd, each who stops is consider'd, not a single one can it fail.

It cannot fail the young man who died and was buried,
Nor the young woman who died and was put by his side,
Nor the little child that peep'd in at the door, and then drew back, and was never seen again,
Nor the old man who has lived without purpose, and feels it with bitterness worse than gall,
Nor him in the poor house tubercled by rum and the bad disorder,
Nor the numberless slaughter'd and wreck'd—nor the brutish koboo call'd the ordure of humanity, 1130
Nor the sacs merely floating with open mouths for food to slip in,

Nor anything in the earth, or down in the oldest graves
of the earth,
Nor anything in the myriads of spheres, nor the myriads
of myriads that inhabit them,
Nor the present, nor the least wisp that is known.

44

It is time to explain myself—let us stand up.

What is known I strip away;
I launch all men and women forward with me into the
Unknown.

The clock indicates the moment—but what does eternity
indicate?

We have thus far exhausted trillions of winters and summers,
There are trillions ahead, and trillions ahead of them.   1140

Births have brought us richness and variety,
And other births will bring us richness and variety.

I do not call one greater and one smaller;
That which fills its period and place is equal to any.

Were mankind murderous or jealous upon you, my brother,
my sister?
I am sorry for you—they are not murderous or jealous
upon me,
All has been gentle with me, I keep no account with
lamentation,
(What have I to do with lamentation?)

I am an acme of things accomplish'd, and I an encloser
of things to be.

My feet strike an apex of the apices of the stairs,   1150
On every step bunches of ages, and larger bunches be-
tween the steps;
All below duly travel'd, and still I mount and mount.

Rise after rise bow the phantoms behind me,
Afar down I see the huge first Nothing—I know I was
    even there;
I waited unseen and always, and slept through the lethargic
    mist,
And took my time, and took no hurt from the fetid carbon.

Long I was hugg'd close—long and long.

Immense have been the preparations for me,
Faithful and friendly the arms that have help'd me.

Cycles ferried my cradle, rowing and rowing like cheer-
    ful boatmen,   1160
For room to me stars kept aside in their own rings,
They sent influences to look after what was to hold me.

Before I was born out of my mother, generations guided
    me;
My embryo has never been torpid, nothing could over-
    lay it.

For it the nebula cohered to an orb,
The long slow strata piled to rest it on,
Vast vegetables gave it sustenance,
Monstrous sauroids transported it in their mouths, and
    deposited it with care.

All forces have been steadily employ'd to complete and
    delight me;
Now on this spot I stand with my robust soul.   1170

45

O span of youth! ever-push'd elasticity!
O manhood, balanced, florid, and full.

My lovers suffocate me!
Crowding my lips, thick in the pores of my skin,
Jostling me through streets and public halls, coming naked
    to me at night,
Crying by day *Ahoy!* from the rocks of the river, swing-
    ing and chirping over my head,

Calling my name from flower-beds, vines, tangled under-
    brush,
Lighting on every moment of my life,
Bussing my body with soft balsamic busses,
Noiselessly passing handfuls out of their hearts, and giving
    them to be mine.   1180

Old age superbly rising! O welcome, ineffable grace of
    dying days!
Every condition promulges not only itself—it promulges
    what grows after and out of itself,
And the dark hush promulges as much as any.

I open my scuttle at night and see the far-sprinkled systems,
And all I see, multiplied as high as I can cipher, edge
    but the rim of the farther systems.

Wider and wider they spread, expanding, always expanding,
Outward and outward, and forever outward.

My sun has his sun, and round him obediently wheels,
He joins with his partners, a group of superior circuit,
And greater sets follow, making specks of the greatest in-
    side them.   1190

There is no stoppage, and never can be stoppage,
If I, you, and the worlds, and all beneath or upon their
    surfaces, were this moment reduced back to a pallid
    float, it would not avail in the long run;
We should surely bring up again where we now stand,
And as surely go as much farther—and then farther and
    farther.

A few quadrillions of eras, a few octillions of cubic leagues,
    do not hazard the span, or make it impatient;
They are but parts, anything is but a part.

See ever so far, there is limitless space outside of that,
Count ever so much, there is limitless time around that.

My rendezvous is appointed, it is certain,
The Lord will be there, and wait till I come on perfect
    terms,   1200

The great Camerado, the lover true for whom I pine, will
be there.

46

I know I have the best of time and space, and was never
measured, and never will be measured.

I tramp a perpetual journey—(come listen all!)
My signs are a rain-proof coat, good shoes, and a staff cut
from the woods;
No friend of mine takes his ease in my chair,
I have no chair, no church, no philosophy,
I lead no man to a dinner-table, library, or exchange,
But each man and each woman of you I lead upon a knoll,
My left hand hooking you round the waist,
My right hand pointing to landscapes of continents and the
public road.   1210

Not I, not any one else can travel that road for you,
You must travel it for yourself.

It is not far, it is within reach;
Perhaps you have been on it since you were born, and did
not know;
Perhaps it is everywhere on water and on land.

Shoulder your duds, dear son, and I will mine, and let
us hasten forth,
Wonderful cities and free nations we shall fetch as we
go.
If you tire, give me both burdens, and rest the chuff of
your hand on my hip,
And in due time you shall repay the same service to me,
For after we start, we never lie by again.   1220

This day before dawn I ascended a hill, and look'd at the
crowded heaven,
And I said to my spirit, *When we become the enfolders
of those orbs, and the pleasure and knowledge of
everything in them, shall we be fill'd and satisfied
then?*
And my spirit said, *No, we but level that lift to pass and
continue beyond.*

You are also asking me questions and I hear you,
I answer that I cannot answer, you must find out for yourself.

Sit a while dear son,
Here are biscuits to eat and here is milk to drink,
But as soon as you sleep and renew yourself in sweet
clothes, I kiss you with a good-bye kiss, and open the
gate for your egress hence.

Long enough have you dream'd contemptible dreams,
Now I wash the gum from your eyes,   1230
You must habit yourself to the dazzle of the light and of
every moment of your life.

Long have you timidly waded holding a plank by the
shore,
Now I will you to be a bold swimmer,
To jump off in the midst of the sea, rise again, nod to
me, shout, and laughingly dash with your hair.

47

I am the teacher of athletes,
He that by me spreads a wider breast than my own, proves
the width of my own,
He most honors my style who learns under it to destroy
the teacher.

The boy I love, the same becomes a man, not through
derived power, but in his own right,
Wicked, rather than virtuous out of conformity or fear,
Fond of his sweetheart, relishing well his steak,   1240
Unrequited love, or a slight, cutting him worse than sharp
steel cuts,
First-rate to ride, to fight, to hit the bull's eye, to sail a
skiff, to sing a song or play on the banjo,
Preferring scars and the beard and faces pitted with small-
pox over all latherers,
And those well tann'd to those that keep out of the sun.

I teach straying from me, yet who can stray from me?
I follow you, whoever you are, from the present hour,
My words itch at your ears till you understand them.

I do not say these things for a dollar or to fill up the time
    while I wait for a boat,
(It is you talking just as much as myself—I act as the
    tongue of you,
Tied in your mouth, in mine it begins to be loosen'd.)   1250

I swear I will never again mention love or death inside a
    house,
And I swear I will never translate myself at all, only to
    him or her who privately stays with me in the open
    air.

If you would understand me, go to the heights or water-
    shore,
The nearest gnat is an explanation, and a drop or motion
    of waves a key,
The maul, the oar, the hand-saw, second my words.

No shutter'd room or school can commune with me,
But roughs and little children better than they.

The young mechanic is closest to me, he knows me well,
The woodman that takes his axe and jug with him shall
    take me with him all day,
The farm-boy ploughing in the field feels good at the
    sound of my voice,   1260
In vessels that sail, my words sail—I go with fishermen
    and seamen, and love them.

The soldier camp'd or upon the march is mine,
On the night ere the pending battle, many seek me, and
    I do not fail them,
On the solemn night (it may be their last,) those that
    know me seek me.

My face rubs to the hunter's face when he lies down alone
    in his blanket,
The driver thinking of me does not mind the jolt of his
    wagon,
The young mother and old mother comprehend me,
The girl and the wife rest the needle a moment, and forget
    where they are,
They and all would resume what I have told them.

48

1270

I have said that the soul is not more than the body,
And I have said that the body is not more than the soul,
And nothing, not God, is greater to one than one's self is,
And whoever walks a furlong without sympathy, walks to
    his own funeral, drest in his shroud,
And I or you pocketless of a dime may purchase the pick
    of the earth,
And to glance with an eye, or show a bean in its pod,
    confounds the learning of all times,
And there is no trade or employment but the young man
    following it may become a hero,
And there is no object so soft but it makes a hub for the
    wheel'd universe,
And I say to any man or woman, Let your soul stand
    cool and composed before a million universes.

And I say to mankind, Be not curious about God,
For I who am curious about each am not curious about
    God,
(No array of terms can say how much I am at peace about
    God and about death.)   1280

I hear and behold God in every object, yet understand
    God not in the least,
Nor do I understand who there can be more wonderful
    than myself.

Why should I wish to see God better than this day?
I see something of God each hour of the twenty-four, and
    each moment then,
In the faces of men and women I see God, and in my own
    face in the glass,
I find letters from God dropt in the street—and every one
    is sign'd by God's name,
And I leave them where they are, for I know that where-
    soe'er I go,
Others will punctually come for ever and ever.

49

And as to you, Death, and you bitter hug of mortality,
    it is idle to try to alarm me.   1290

To his work without flinching the accoucheur comes,
I see the elder-hand, pressing, receiving, supporting,

I recline by the sills of the exquisite flexible doors,
And mark the outlet, and mark the relief and escape.

And as to you, Corpse, I think you are good manure, but
that does not offend me;
I smell the white roses sweet-scented and growing,
I reach to the leafy lips, I reach to the polish'd breasts
of melons.

And as to you, Life, I reckon you are the leavings of many
deaths,
(No doubt I have died myself ten thousand times before.)

I hear you whispering there, O stars of heaven,   1300
O suns! O grass of graves! O perpetual transfers and pro-
motions!
If you do not say anything, how can I say anything?

Of the turbid pool that lies in the autumn forest,
Of the moon that descends the steeps of the soughing
twilight,
Toss, sparkles of day and dusk—toss on the black stems
that decay in the muck,
Toss to the moaning gibberish of the dry limbs.

I ascend from the moon, I ascend from the night,
I perceive that the ghastly glimmer is noonday sun-beams
reflected,
And debouch to the steady and central from the offspring great or small.

50

There is that in me—I do not know what it is—but I
know it is in me.   1310

Wrench'd and sweaty—calm and cool then my body
becomes
I sleep—I sleep long.

I do not know it—it is without name—it is a word unsaid;
It is not in any dictionary, utterance, symbol.

Something it swings on more than the earth I swing on,
To it the creation is the friend whose embracing awakes
me.

Perhaps I might tell more. Outlines! I plead for my brothers
and sisters.

Do you see, O my brothers and sisters?
It is not chaos or death—it is form, union, plan—it is
eternal life—it is Happiness.

51

The past and present wilt—I have fill'd them, emptied
them,   1320
And proceed to fill my next fold of the future.

Listener up there! what have you to confide to me?
Look in my face while I snuff the sidle of evening,
(Talk honestly—no one else hears you, and I stay only a
minute longer.)

Do I contradict myself?
Very well then I contradict myself;
(I am large, I contain multitudes.)

I concentrate toward them that are nigh, I wait on the
door-slab.

Who has done his day's work? who will soonest be through
with his supper?
Who wishes to walk with me?   1330

Will you speak before I am gone? will you prove already
too late?

52

The spotted hawk swoops by and accuses me, he complains
of my gab and my loitering.

I too am not a bit tamed, I too am untranslatable,
I sound my barbaric yawp over the roofs of the world.

The last scud of day holds back for me,
It flings my likeness after the rest and true as any on the
    shadow'd wilds,
It coaxes me to the vapor and the dusk.

I depart as air, I shake my white locks at the runaway
    sun,
I effuse my flesh in eddies, and drift it in lacy jags.

I bequeathe myself to the dirt to grow from the grass
    I love,   1340
If you want me again, look for me under your boot-
    soles.

You will hardly know who I am, or what I mean,
But I shall be good health to you nevertheless,
And filter and fibre your blood.

Failing to fetch me at first keep encouraged,
Missing me one place search another;
I stop somewhere waiting for you.
                                        1855, 1881–1882

Crossing Brooklyn Ferry

1

Flood-tide below me! I see you face to face!
Clouds of the west! sun there half an hour high! I see
    you also face to face.

Crowds of men and women attired in the usual costumes,
    how curious you are to me!
On the ferry-boats, the hundreds and hundreds that cross,
    returning home, are more curious to me than you
    suppose,
And you that shall cross from shore to shore years hence
    are more to me, and more in my meditations, than you
    might suppose.

2

The impalpable sustenance of me from all things, at all
    hours of the day,
The simple, compact, well-join'd scheme, myself disin-
    tegrated, every one disintegrated, yet part of the
    scheme,
The similitudes of the past, and those of the future,
The glories strung like beads on my smallest sights and
    hearings, on the walk in the street and the passage
    over the river,
The current rushing so swiftly, and swimming with me
    far away,   10
The others that are to follow me, the ties between me
    and them,
The certainty of others, the life, love, sight, hearing of
    others.

Others will enter the gates of the ferry, and cross from
    shore to shore,
Others will watch the run of the flood-tide,
Others will see the shipping of Manhattan north and
    west, and the heights of Brooklyn to the south and
    east,
Others will see the islands large and small;
Fifty years hence, others will see them as they cross, the
    sun half an hour high,
A hundred years hence, or ever so many hundred years
    hence, others will see them,
Will enjoy the sunset, the pouring in of the flood-tide,
    the falling back to the sea of the ebb-tide.

3

It avails not, neither time or place—distance avails not,
I am with you, you men and women of a generation, or
    ever so many generations hence,   21
Just as you feel when you look on the river and sky, so
    I felt,
Just as any of you is one of a living crowd, I was one of
    a crowd,
Just as you are refresh'd by the gladness of the river and
    the bright flow, I was refresh'd,

Just as you stand and lean on the rail, yet hurry with
 the swift current, I stood yet was hurried;
Just as you look on the numberless masts of ships, and
 the thick-stem'd pipes of steamboats, I look'd.

I too many and many a time cross'd the river, of old,
Watched the Twelfth-month sea-gulls, saw them high
 in the air, floating with motionless wings, oscillating
 their bodies,
Saw the glistening yellow lit up parts of their bodies,
 and left the rest in strong shadow,
Saw the slow-wheeling circles and the gradual edging to-
 ward the south.   30
Saw the reflection of the summer sky in the water,
Had my eyes dazzled by the shimmering track of beams,
Look'd at the fine centrifugal spokes of light around the
 shape of my head in the sun-lit water,
Look'd on the haze on the hills southward and south-
 westward,
Look'd on the vapor as it flew in fleeces tinged with
 violet,
Look'd toward the lower bay to notice the vessels arriv-
 ing,
Saw their approach, saw aboard those that were near
 me,
Saw the white sails of schooners and sloops—saw the
 ships at anchor,
The sailors at work in the rigging, or out astride the
 spars,
The round masts, the swinging motion of the hulls, the
 slender serpentine pennants,   40
The large and small steamers in motion, the pilots in
 their pilot-houses,
The white wake left by the passage, the quick tremulous
 whirl of the wheels,
The flags of all nations, the falling of them at sun-set,
The scallop-edged waves in the twilight, the ladled cups,
 the frolicsome crests and glistening,
The stretch afar growing dimmer and dimmer, the gray
 walls of the granite store-houses by the docks,
On the river the shadowy group, the big steam-tug closely
 flank'd on each side by the barges—the hay-boat,
 the belated lighter,

On the neighboring shore, the fires from the foundry
chimneys burning high and glaringly into the
night,
Casting their flicker of black, contrasted with wild red
and yellow light, over the tops of houses, and down
into the clefts of streets.

4

These, and all else, were to me the same as they are to
you;
I loved well those cities;   50
The men and women I saw were all near to me;
Others the same—others who look back on me, because
I look'd forward to them;
(The time will come, though I stop here to-day and to-
night.)

5

What is it then between us?
What is the count of the scores of hundreds of years
between us?

Whatever it is, it avails not—distance avails not, and place
avails not.
I too lived—Brooklyn, of ample hills, was mine;
I too walk'd the streets of Manhattan Island, and bathed
in the waters around it,
I too felt the curious abrupt questionings stir within
me,
In the day, among crowds of people, sometimes they
came upon me,   60
In my walks home late at night, or as I lay in my bed,
they came upon me.
I too had been struck from the float forever held in so-
lution;
I too had receiv'd identity by my body;
That I was I knew was of my body, and what I should
be, I knew I should be of my body.

6

It is not upon you alone the dark patches fall,
The dark threw patches down upon me also;
The best I had done seem'd to me blank and suspicious,
My great thoughts as I supposed them were they not in
    reality meagre?
Nor is it you alone who know what it is to be evil;
I am he who knew what it was to be evil;   70
I too knitted the old knot of contrariety,
Blabb'd, blush'd, resented, lied, stole, grudg'd,
Had guile, anger, lust, hot wishes I dared not speak,
Was wayward, vain, greedy, shallow, sly, cowardly, malig-
    nant,
The wolf, the snake, the hog, not wanting in me,
The cheating look, the frivolous word, the adulterous
    wish, not wanting,
Refusals, hates, postponements, meanness, laziness, none
    of these wanting,
Was one with the rest, the days and haps of the rest,
Was call'd by my nighest name by clear loud voices of
    young men as they saw me approaching or passing,
Felt their arms on my neck as I stood, or the negligent
    leaning of their flesh against me as I sat,   80
Saw many I loved in the street, or ferry-boat, or public
    assembly, yet never told them a word,
Lived the same life with the rest, the same old laughing,
    gnawing, sleeping,
Play'd the part that still looks back on the actor or
    actress,
The same old role, the role that is what we make it, as
    great as we like,
Or as small as we like, or both great and small.

7

Closer yet I approach you;
What thought you have of me, I had as much of you—
    I laid in my stores in advance;
I consider'd long and seriously of you before you were
    born.

Who was to know what should come home to me?
Who knows but I am enjoying this?   90

Who knows but I am as good as looking at you now, for
all you cannot see me?

8

Ah what can ever be more stately and admirable to me than
my mast-hemm'd Manhattan?
River and sun-set and scallop-edg'd waves of flood-tide?
The sea-gulls oscillating their bodies, the hay-boat in
the twilight, and the belated lighter?
What Gods can exceed these that clasp me by the hand,
and with voices I love call me promptly and loudly
by my nighest names as I approach?
What is more subtle than this which ties me to the woman
or man that looks in my face?
Which fuses me into you now, and pours my meaning
into you?

We understand, then, do we not?
What I promis'd without mentioning it, have you not
accepted?
What the study could not teach—what the preaching
could not accomplish, is accomplish'd, is it not?   100

9

Flow on, river! flow with the flood-tide, and ebb with
the ebb-tide!
Frolic on, crested and scallop-edg'd waves!
Gorgeous clouds of the sun-set! drench with your splendor me, or the men and women generations after
me!
Cross from shore to shore, countless crowds of passengers!
Stand up, tall masts of Mannahatta!—stand up, beautiful hills of Brooklyn!
Throb, baffled and curious brain! throw out questions
and answers!
Suspend here and everywhere, eternal float of solution!
Gaze, loving and thirsting eyes, in the house, or street,
or public assembly!
Sound out, voices of young men! loudly and musically
call me by my nighest name!

Live, old life! play the part that looks back on the actor
or actress! 110
Play the old role, the role that is great or small, according as one makes it!
Consider, you who peruse me, whether I may not in unknown ways be looking upon you;
Be firm, rail over the river, to support those who lean
idly, yet haste with the hasting current;
Fly on, sea-birds! fly sideways, or wheel in large circles
high in the air;
Receive the summer sky, you water! and faithfully hold
it, till all downcast eyes have time to take it from
you;
Diverge, fine spokes of light, from the shape of my head,
or any one's head, in the sun-lit water!
Come on, ships from the lower bay! pass up or down,
white-sail'd schooners, sloops, lighters!
Flaunt away, flags of all nations! be duly lower'd at sunset;
Burn high your fires, foundry chimneys! cast black shadows at nightfall! cast red and yellow light over the
tops of the houses!
Appearances, now or henceforth, indicate what you
are; 120
You necessary film, continue to envelop the soul;
About my body for me, and your body for you, be hung
our divinest aromas;
Thrive, cities! bring your freight, bring your shows, ample and sufficient rivers;
Expand, being than which none else is perhaps more
spiritual;
Keep your places, objects than which none else is more
lasting.

You have waited, you always wait, you dumb, beautiful
ministers,
We receive you with free sense at last, and are insatiate
henceforward;
Not you any more shall be able to foil us, or withhold
yourselves from us,
We use you, and do not cast you aside—we plant you
permanently within us,

We fathom you not—we love you—there is perfection
    in you also,   130
You furnish your parts toward eternity,
Great or small, you furnish your parts toward the soul.
           1856, 1881–1882

Out of the Cradle Endlessly Rocking

1

Out of the cradle endlessly rocking,
Out of the mocking-bird's throat, the musical shuttle,
Out of the Ninth-month midnight,
Over the sterile sands, and the fields beyond, where the
    child, leaving his bed, wander'd alone, bareheaded,
    barefoot,
Down from the shower'd halo,
Up from the mystic play of shadows, twining and twist-
    ing as if they were alive,
Out from the patches of briers and blackberries,
From the memories of the bird that chanted to me,
From your memories, sad brother—from the fitful ris-
    ings and fallings I heard,
From under that yellow half-moon, late-risen, and swollen
    as if with tears,   10
From those beginning notes of yearning and love, there
    in the mist,
From the thousand responses of my heart, never to
    cease,
From the myriad thence-arous'd words,
From the word stronger and more delicious than any,
From such, as now they start, the scene revisiting,
As a flock, twittering, rising, or overhead passing,
Borne hither, ere all eludes me, hurriedly,
A man, yet by these tears a little boy again,
Throwing myself on the sand, confronting the waves,
I, chanter of pains and joys, uniter of here and here-
    after,   20
Taking all hints to use them—but swiftly leaping beyond
    them,
A reminiscence sing.

Once, Paumanok,
When the lilac-scent was in the air, and Fifth-month grass
     was growing,
Up this sea-shore, in some briers,
Two guests from Alabama—two together,
And their nest, and four light-green eggs, spotted with
     brown,
And every day the he-bird, to and fro, near at hand,
And every day the she-bird, crouch'd on her nest, silent,
     with bright eyes,
And every day I, a curious boy, never too close, never
     disturbing them,   30
Cautiously peering, absorbing, translating.

Shine! shine! shine!
Pour down your warmth, great Sun!
While we bask—we two together.

Two together!
Winds blow south, or winds blow north,
Day come white, or night come black,
Home, or rivers and mountains from home,
Singing all time, minding no time,
While we two keep together.   40

Till of a sudden,
May-be kill'd, unknown to her mate,
One forenoon the she-bird crouch'd not on the nest,
Nor return'd that afternoon, nor the next,
Nor ever appear'd again.

And thenceforward, all summer, in the sound of the sea,
And at night under the full of the moon in calmer
     weather,
Over the hoarse surging of the sea,
Or flitting from brier to brier by day,
I saw, I heard at intervals, the remaining one, the he-
     bird,   50
The solitary guest from Alabama.

Blow! blow! blow!
Blow up, sea-winds, along Paumanok's shore!
I wait and I wait, till you blow my mate to me.

Yes, when the stars glisten'd,
All night long, on the prong of a moss-scallop'd stake,
Down, almost amid the slapping waves,
Sat the lone singer wonderful causing tears.

He call'd on his mate,
He pour'd forth the meanings which I, of all men, know.

Yes, my brother, I know;   61
The rest might not—but I have treasur'd every note;
For more than once dimly down to the beach gliding,
Silent, avoiding the moonbeams, blending myself with
    the shadows,
Recalling now the obscure shapes, the echoes, the sounds
    and sights after their sorts,
The white arms out in the breakers tirelessly tossing,
I, with bare feet, a child, the wind wafting my hair,
Listen'd long and long.

Listen'd, to keep, to sing—now translating the notes,
Following you, my brother.   70

Soothe! soothe! soothe!
Close on its wave soothes the wave behind,
And again another behind, embracing and lapping, every
    one close,
But my love soothes not me, not me.

Low hangs the moon, it rose late;
O it is lagging—O I think it is heavy with love, with
    love.

O madly the sea pushes upon the land,
With love, with love.

O night! do I not see my love fluttering out there among
    the breakers?
What is that little black thing I see there in the white?

Loud! loud! loud!   81
Loud I call to you, my love!
High and clear I shoot my voice over the waves;

Surely you must know who is here, is here;
You must know who I am, my love.

Low-hanging moon!
What is that dusky spot in your brown yellow?
O it is the shape, the shape of my mate!
O moon, do not keep her from me any longer.

Land! land! O land! 90
Whichever way I turn, O I think you could give me my
*   mate back again, if you only would;*
For I am almost sure I see her dimly whichever way I
*   look.*

O rising stars!
Perhaps the one I want so much will rise, will rise with
*   some of you.*

O throat! O trembling throat!
Sound clearer through the atmosphere!
Pierce the woods, the earth;
Somewhere listening to catch you, must be the one I
*   want.*

Shake out carols!
Solitary here—the night's carols! 100
Carols of lonesome love! death's carols!
Carols under that lagging, yellow, waning moon!
O, under that moon, where she droops almost down into
*   the sea!*
O reckless, despairing carols.

But soft! sink low!
Soft! let me just murmur;
And do you wait a moment, you husky-noised sea;
For somewhere I believe I heard my mate responding to
*   me,*
So faint—I must be still, be still to listen;
But not altogether still, for then she might not come im-
*   mediately to me.* 110

Hither, my love!
Here I am! Here!

With this just-sustain'd note I announce myself to you,
This gentle call is for you my love, for you.

Do not be decoy'd elsewhere,
That is the whistle of the wind—it is not my voice;
That is the fluttering, the fluttering of the spray;
Those are the shadows of leaves.

O darkness! O in vain!
O I am very sick and sorrowful.   120

O brown halo in the sky near the moon, drooping upon
*   the sea!*
O troubled reflection in the sea!
O throat! O throbbing heart!
And I singing uselessly, uselessly all the night.

Yet I murmur, murmur on!
O murmurs—you yourselves make me continue to sing,
*   I know not why.*

O past! O happy life! O songs of joy!
In the air, in the woods, over fields;
Loved! loved! loved! loved! loved!
But my love no more, no more with me!   130
We two together no more.

The aria sinking,
All else continuing, the stars shining,
The winds blowing, the notes of the bird continuous echo-
    ing,
With angry moans the fierce old mother incessantly moan-
    ing,
On the sands of Paumanok's shore, gray and rustling;
The yellow half-moon enlarged, sagging down, drooping,
    the face of the sea almost touching;
The boy ecstatic, with his bare feet the waves, with his
    hair the atmosphere dallying,
The love in the heart long pent, now loose, now at last
    tumultuously bursting,
The aria's meaning, the ears, the soul, swiftly deposit-
    ing,   140
The strange tears down the cheeks coursing,
The colloquy there, the trio, each uttering,

The undertone, the savage old mother, incessantly crying,
To the boy's soul's questions sullenly timing, some drown'd
    secret hissing,
To the outsetting bard.

Demon or bird! (said the boy's soul,)
Is it indeed toward your mate you sing? or is it really to
    me?
For I, that was a child, my tongue's use sleeping, now I
    have heard you,
Now in a moment I know what I am for—I awake,
And already a thousand singers, a thousand songs, clearer,
    louder and more sorrowful than yours,   150
A thousand warbling echoes have started to life within
    me, never to die.

O you singer solitary, singing by yourself, projecting me;
O solitary me, listening, never more shall I cease perpet-
    uating you,
Never more shall I escape, never more the reverbera-
    tions,
Never more the cries of unsatisfied love be absent from
    me,
Never again leave me to be the peaceful child I was be-
    fore what there, in the night,
By the sea, under the yellow and sagging moon,
The messenger there arous'd, the fire, the sweet hell within,
The unknown want, the destiny of me.

O give me the clew! (it lurks in the night here some-
    where;)   160
O if I am to have so much, let me have more!

A word then, (for I will conquer it,)
The word final, superior to all,
Subtle, sent up—what is it?—I listen;
Are you whispering it, and have been all the time, you
    sea-waves?
Is that it from your liquid rims and wet sands?

Whereto answering, the sea,
Delaying not, hurrying not,

Whisper'd me through the night, and very plainly be-
fore daybreak,
Lisp'd to me the low and delicious word death; 170
And again death—ever death, death, death,
Hissing melodious, neither like the bird, nor like my
arous'd child's heart,
But edging near, as privately for me, rustling at my feet,
Creeping thence steadily up to my ears, and laving me
softly all over,
Death, death, death, death, death.

Which I do not forget,
But fuse the song of my dusky demon and brother,
That he sang to me in the moonlight on Paumanok's
gray beach,
With the thousand responsive songs at random,
My own songs, awaked from that hour; 180
And with them the key, the word up from the waves,
The word of the sweetest song, and all songs,
That strong and delicious word which, creeping to my
feet,
(Or like some old crone rocking the cradle, swathed in sweet
garments, bending aside,)
The sea whisper'd me.

1859, 1881–1882

Facing West from California's Shores

Facing west, from California's shores,
Inquiring, tireless, seeking what is yet unfound,
I, a child, very old, over waves, towards the house of
maternity, the land of migrations, look afar,
Look off the shores of my Western Sea—the circle al-
most circled;
For, starting westward from Hindustan, from the vales
of Kashmere,
From Asia, from the north, from the God, the sage, and
the hero,
From the south—from the flowery peninsulas, and the
spice islands;
Long having wander'd since, round the earth having
wander'd,

Now I face home again, very pleas'd and joyous;
(But where is what I started for, so long ago?   10
And why is it yet unfound?)

                                        1860

When Lilacs Last in the Door-yard Bloom'd

1

When lilacs last in the door-yard bloom'd,
And the great star early droop'd in the western sky in
     the night,
I mourn'd, and yet shall mourn with ever-returning spring.

Ever-returning spring! trinity sure to me you bring;
Lilac blooming perennial, and drooping star in the west,
And thought of him I love.

2

O powerful western fallen star!
O shades of night—O moody, tearful night!
O great star disappear'd—O the black murk that hides
     the star!
O cruel hands that hold me powerless—O helpless soul
     of me!   10
O harsh surrounding cloud that will not free my soul!

3

In the door-yard fronting an old farm-house, near the
     whitewash'd palings,
Stands the lilac bush, tall-growing, with heart-shaped leaves
     of rich green,
With many a pointed blossom, rising delicate, with the
     perfume strong I love,
With every leaf a miracle—and from this bush in the
     door-yard,
With delicate-color'd blossoms, and heart-shaped leaves
     of rich green,
A sprig with its flower I break.

4

In the swamp, in secluded recesses,
A shy and hidden bird is warbling a song.

Solitary, the thrush,   20
The hermit, withdrawn to himself, avoiding the settle-
    ments,
Sings by himself a song.

Song of the bleeding throat!
Death's outlet song of life—(for well, dear brother, I
    know
If thou wast not gifted to sing, thou would'st surely die.)

5

Over the breast of the spring, the land, amid cities,
Amid lanes, and through old woods, where lately the
      violets peep'd from the ground, spotting the gray
      debris;
Amid the grass in the fields each side of the lanes, passing
    the endless grass;
Passing the yellow-spear'd wheat, every grain from its
    shroud in the dark-brown fields uprisen,
Passing the apple-tree blows of white and pink in the
    orchards,   30
Carrying a corpse to where it shall rest in the grave,
Night and day journeys a coffin.

6

Coffin that passes through lanes and streets,
Through day and night, with the great cloud darkening
    the land,
With the pomp of the inloop'd flags, with the cities
    draped in black,
With the show of the States themselves, as of crape-
    veil'd women, standing,
With processions long and winding, and the flambeaus
    of the night,
With the countless torches lit, with the silent sea of faces,
    and the unbared heads,

With the waiting depot, the arriving coffin, and the sombre
    faces,
With dirges through the night, with the thousand voices
    rising strong and solemn;   40
With all the mournful voices of the dirges, pour'd around
    the coffin,
The dim-lit churches and the shuddering organs—where
    amid these you journey,
With the tolling, tolling bells' perpetual clang;
Here, coffin that slowly passes,
I give you my sprig of lilac.

7

(Nor for you, for one alone,
Blossoms and branches green to coffins all I bring:
For fresh as the morning, thus would I carol a song for
    you, O sane and sacred death.

All over bouquets of roses,
O death, I cover you over with roses and early lilies;
But mostly and now the lilac that blooms the first,   51
Copious I break, I break the sprigs from the bushes;
With loaded arms I come, pouring for you,
For you, and the coffins all of you, O death.)

8

O western orb, sailing the heaven!
Now I know what you must have meant, as a month since
    I walk'd,
As I walk'd in silence the transparent shadowy night,
As I saw you had something to tell, as you bent to me
    night after night,
As you droop'd from the sky low down, as if to my side,
    (while the other stars all look'd on;)
As we wander'd together the solemn night, (for some-
    thing, I know not what, kept me from sleep;)   60
As the night advanced, and I saw on the rim of the west
    how full you were of woe;
As I stood on the rising ground in the breeze in the cool
    transparent night,
As I watch'd where you pass'd and was lost in the nether-
    ward black of the night,

As my soul in its trouble dissatisfied sank, as where you,
    sad orb,
Concluded, dropt in the night, and was gone.

9

Sing on, there in the swamp,
O singer bashful and tender! I hear your notes, I hear your
    call;
I hear, I come presently, I understand you;
But a moment I linger, for the lustrous star has detain'd
    me,   69
The star, my departing comrade, holds and detains me.

10

O how shall I warble myself for the dead one there I
    loved?
And how shall I deck my song for the large sweet soul
    that has gone?
And what shall my perfume be, for the grave of him I
    love?

Sea-winds, blown from east and west,
Blown from the eastern sea, and blown from the western
    sea, till there on the prairies meeting,
These, and with these, and the breath of my chant,
I perfume the grave of him I love.

11

O what shall I hang on the chamber walls?
And what shall the pictures be that I hang on the walls,
To adorn the burial-house of him I love?   80

Pictures of growing spring, and farms, and homes,
With the Fourth-month eve at sundown, and the gray
    smoke lucid and bright,
With floods of the yellow gold of the gorgeous, indolent,
    sinking, sun, burning, expanding the air,
With the fresh sweet herbage under foot, and the pale
    green leaves of the trees prolific,
In the distance the flowing glaze, the breast of the river,
    with a wind-dapple here and there;

With ranging hills on the banks, with many a line against
  the sky, and shadows;
And the city at hand, with dwellings so dense, and stacks
  of chimneys,
And all the scenes of life, and the workshops, and the
  workmen homeward returning.

12

Lo, body and soul—this land,
My own Manhattan with spires, and the sparkling and
  hurrying tides, and the ships,   90
The varied and ample land—the South and the North in
  the light—Ohio's shores, and flashing Missouri,
And ever the far-spreading prairies cover'd with grass and
  corn.

Lo, the most excellent sun, so calm and haughty,
The violet and purple morn, with just-felt breezes,
The gentle soft-born measureless light,
The miracle spreading bathing all, the fulfill'd noon;
The coming eve delicious, the welcome night, and the stars,
Over my cities shining all, enveloping man and land.

13

Sing on, sing on, you gray-brown bird,
Sing from the swamps, the recesses, pour your chant from
  the bushes,   100
Limitless out of the dusk, out of the cedars and pines.
Sing on, dearest brother—warble your reedy song;
Loud human song, with voice of uttermost woe.

O liquid, and free, and tender!
O wild and loose to my soul! O wondrous singer!
You only I hear—yet the star holds me, (but will soon
  depart,)
Yet the lilac with mastering odor holds me.

14

Now while I sat in the day, and look'd forth,
In the close of the day, with its light, and the fields of
  spring, and the farmers preparing their crops,

In the large unconscious scenery of my land, with its
    lakes and forests,   110
In the heavenly aerial beauty, (after the perturb'd winds,
    and the storms;)
Under the arching heavens of the afternoon swift pass-
    ing, and the voices of children and women,
The many-moving sea-tides,—and I saw the ships how
    they sail'd,
And the summer approaching with richness, and the fields
    all busy with labor,
And the infinite separate houses, how they all went on,
    each with its meals and minutia of daily usages;
And the streets, how their throbbings throbb'd, and the
    cities pent—lo, then and there,
Falling upon them all, and among them all, enveloping
    me with the rest,
Appear'd the cloud, appear'd the long black trail,
And I knew death, its thought, and the sacred knowl-
    edge of death.

Then with the knowledge of death as walking one side
    of me,   120
And the thought of death close-walking the other side
    of me,
And I in the middle, as with companions, and as holding
    the hands of companions,
I fled forth to the hiding receiving night that talks not,
Down to the shores of the water, the path by the swamp
    in the dimness,
To the solemn shadowy cedars, and ghostly pines so
    still.

And the singer so shy to the rest receiv'd me;
The gray-brown bird I know receiv'd us comrades three,
And he sang what seem'd the carol of death, and a verse
    for him I love.

From deep secluded recesses,
From the fragrant cedars, and the ghostly pines so still,
Came the carol of the bird.   131

And the charm of the carol rapt me,
As I held, as if by their hands, my comrades in the
    night,

And the voice of my spirit tallied the song of the bird.

Come, lovely and soothing death,
Undulate round the world, serenely arriving, arriving,
In the day, in the night, to all, to each,
Sooner or later, delicate Death.

Prais'd be the fathomless universe,
For life and joy, and for objects and knowledge curious;
And for love, sweet love—but praise! praise! praise! 141
For the sure-enwinding arms of cool-enfolding death.

Dark mother, always gliding near, with soft feet,
Have none chanted for thee a chant of fullest welcome?
Then I chant it for thee—I glorify thee above all;
I bring thee a song that when thou must indeed come,
*   come unfalteringly.*

Approach, strong deliveress!
When it is so, when thou hast taken them, I joyously
*   sing the dead,*
Lost in the loving, floating ocean of thee,
Laved in the flood of thy bliss, O death. 150
From me to thee glad serenades,
Dances for thee I propose, saluting thee, adornments and
*   feastings for thee;*
And the sights of the open landscape, and the high-spread
*   sky, are fitting,*
And life and the fields, and the huge and thoughtful
*   night.*

The night, in silence, under many a star;
The ocean shore, and the husky whispering wave, whose
*   voice I know;*
And the soul turning to thee, O vast and well-veil'd
*   death,*
And the body gratefully nestling close to thee.

Over the tree-tops I float thee a song!
Over the rising and sinking waves, over the myriad fields,
*   and the prairies wide;* 160
Over the dense-pack'd cities all, and the teeming wharves
*   and ways,*
I float this carol with joy, with joy to thee, O death!

15

To the tally of my soul,
Loud and strong kept up the gray-brown bird,
With pure deliberate notes, spreading, filling the night.

Loud in the pines and cedars dim,
Clear in the freshness moist, and the swamp-perfume;
And I with my comrades there in the night.

While my sight that was bound in my eyes unclosed,
As to long panoramas of visions.   170

I saw askant the armies,
And I saw, as in noiseless dreams, hundreds of battle-
    flags,
Borne through the smoke of the battles, and pierc'd with
    missiles, I saw them,
And carried hither and yon through the smoke, and torn
    and bloody;
And at last but a few shreds left on the staffs, (and all
    in silence,)
And the staffs all splinter'd and broken.

I saw battle-corpses, myriads of them,
And the white skeletons of young men—I saw them;
I saw the debris and debris of all the slain soldiers of
    the war;
But I saw they were not as was thought;   180
They themselves were fully at rest, they suffer'd not;
The living remain'd and suffer'd, the mother suffer'd,
And the wife and the child, and the musing comrade
    suffer'd,
And the armies that remain'd suffer'd.

16

Passing the visions, passing the night,
Passing, unloosing the hold of my comrades' hands,
Passing the song of the hermit bird, and the tallying song
    of my soul,
Victorious song, death's outlet song, yet varying, ever-
    altering song,
As low and wailing, yet clear the notes, rising and fall-
    ing, flooding the night,

Sadly sinking and fainting, as warning and warning, and
    yet again bursting with joy,   190
Covering the earth, and filling the spread of the heaven,
As that powerful psalm in the night I heard from re-
    cesses,
Passing, I leave thee, lilac with heart-shaped leaves,
I leave thee there in the door-yard, blooming, returning
    with spring.

I cease from my song for thee,
From my gaze on thee in the west, fronting the west,
    communing with thee,
O comrade lustrous, with silver face in the night.

Yet each to keep and all, retrievements out of the night,
The song, the wondrous chant of the gray-brown bird,
And the tallying chant, the echo arous'd in my soul,   200
With the lustrous and drooping star, with the counte-
    nance full of woe,
With the holders holding my hand, nearing the call of
    the bird,
Comrades mine, and I in the midst, and their memory
    ever I keep, for the dead I loved so well;
For the sweetest, wisest soul of all my days and lands
    —and this for his dear sake;
Lilac and star and bird twined with the chant of my soul,
There in the fragrant pines, and the cedars dusk and
    dim.

                            1865, 1881

Passage to India

1

Singing my days,
Singing the great achievements of the present,
Singing the strong, light works of engineers,
Our modern wonders, (the antique ponderous Seven
    outvied,)
In the Old World, the east, the Suez canal,
The New by its mighty railroad spann'd,
The seas inlaid with eloquent, gentle wires,

Yet first to sound, and ever sound, the cry with thee O soul,
The Past! the Past! the Past!

The Past! the dark, unfathom'd retrospect!   10
The teeming gulf! the sleepers and the shadows!
The past! the infinite greatness of the past!
For what is the present, after all, but a growth out of
   the past?
(As a projectile, form'd, impell'd, passing a certain line,
   still keeps on,
So the present, utterly form'd, impell'd by the past.)

2

Passage O soul to India!
Eclaircise the myths Asiatic, the primitive fables.

Not you alone, proud truths of the world,
Nor you alone, ye facts of modern science,
But myths and fables of eld—Asia's, Africa's fables,   20
The far-darting beams of the spirit, the unloos'd dreams,
The deep diving bibles and legends,
The daring plots of the poets, the elder religions;
O you temples fairer than lilies, pour'd over by the rising
   sun!
O you fables spurning the known, eluding the hold of
   the known, mounting to heaven!
You lofty and dazzling towers, pinnacled, red as roses,
   burnish'd with gold!
Towers of fables immortal, fashion'd from mortal dreams!
You too I welcome, and fully, the same as the rest!
You too with joy I sing.

Passage to India!   30
Lo, soul! seest thou not God's purpose from the first?
The earth to be spann'd, connected by net-work,
The races, neighbors, to marry and be given in mar-
   riage,
The oceans to be cross'd, the distant brought near,
The lands to be welded together.

A worship new, I sing,
You captains, voyagers, explorers, yours,

You engineers! you architects, machinists, yours!
You, not for trade or transportation only,
But in God's name, and for thy sake, O soul.   40

3

Passage to India!
Lo, soul, for thee, of tableaus twain,
I see, in one, the Suez canal initiated, open'd,
I see the procession of steamships, the Empress Eugenie's
    leading the van;
I mark from on deck the strange landscape, the pure
    sky, the level sand in the distance;
I pass swiftly the picturesque groups, the workmen
    gather'd,
The gigantic dredging machines.

In one again, different, (yet thine, all thine, O soul, the
    same,)
I see over my own continent the Pacific Railroad, sur-
    mounting every barrier;
I see continual trains of cars winding along the Platte,
    carrying freight and passengers;   50
I hear the locomotives rushing and roaring, and the
    shrill steam-whistle,
I hear the echoes reverberate through the grandest scen-
    ery in the world;
I cross the Laramie plains, I note the rocks in grotesque
    shapes, the buttes;
I see the plentiful larkspur and wild onions, the barren,
    colorless, sage-deserts;
I see in glimpses afar, or towering immediately above
    me, the great mountains—I see the Wind River
    and the Wahsatch mountains;
I see the Monument mountain and the Eagle's Nest—I
    pass the Promontory—I ascend the Nevadas;
I scan the noble Elk mountain, and wind around its
    base;
I see the Humboldt range—I thread the valley and
    cross the river,
I see the clear waters of Lake Tahoe—I see forests of
    majestic pines,

Or, crossing the great desert, the alkaline plains, I be-
    hold enchanting mirages of waters and meadows;
Marking through these, and after all, in duplicate slender
    lines,   61
Bridging the three or four thousand miles of land travel,
Tying the Eastern to the Western sea,
The road between Europe and Asia.

(Ah Genoese, thy dream! thy dream!
Centuries after thou art laid in thy grave,
The shore thou foundest verifies thy dream!)

4

Passage to India!
Struggles of many a captain, tales of many a sailor dead,
Over my mood, stealing and spreading they come,   70
Like clouds and cloudlets in the unreach'd sky.

Along all history, down the slopes,
As a rivulet running, sinking now, and now again to the
    surface rising,
A ceaseless thought, a varied train—lo, soul, to thee, thy
    sight, they rise,
The plans, the voyages again, the expeditions:
Again Vasco da Gama sails forth;
Again the knowledge gain'd, the mariner's compass,
Lands found, and nations born, thou born, America,
For purpose vast, man's long probation fill'd,
Thou, rondure of the world, at last accomplish'd.   80

5

O, vast Rondure, swimming in space,
Cover'd all over with visible power and beauty,
Alternate light and day, and teeming spiritual darkness;
Unspeakable high processions of sun and moon and count-
    less stars above;
Below, the manifold grass and waters, animals, moun-
    tains, trees;
With inscrutable purpose, some hidden, prophetic inten-
    tion;

Now first it seems, my thought begins to span thee.

Down from the gardens of Asia, descending, radiating,
Adam and Eve appear, then their myriad progeny after
    them,
Wandering, yearning, curious, with restless explorations,
With questionings, baffled, formless, feverish, with never-
    happy hearts,   91
With that sad, incessant refrain, *Wherefore, unsatisfied
    Soul?* and *Whither, O mocking life?*

Ah, who shall soothe these feverish children?
Who justify these restless explorations?
Who speak the secret of impassive earth?
Who bind it to us? What is this separate Nature, so un-
    natural?
What is this Earth, to our affections? (unloving earth,
    without a throb to answer ours,
Cold earth, the place of graves.)

Yet, soul, be sure the first intent remains, and shall be
    carried out;
Perhaps even now the time has arrived.   100

After the seas are all cross'd, (as they seem already
    cross'd,)
After the great captains and engineers have accomplish'd
    their work,
After the noble inventors, after the scientists, the chem-
    ist, the geologist, ethnologist,
Finally shall come the poet, worthy that name,
The true son of God shall come, singing his songs.

Then, not your deeds only, O voyagers, O scientists and
    inventors, shall be justified,
All these hearts, as of fretted children, shall be sooth'd,
All affection shall be fully responded to, the secret shall
    be told;
All these separations and gaps shall be taken up, and
    hook'd and link'd together;
The whole earth, this cold, impressive, voiceless earth,
    shall be completely justified;   110

Trinitas divine shall be gloriously accomplish'd and com-
    pacted by the true son of God, the poet,
(He shall indeed pass the straits and conquer the moun-
    tains,
He shall double the Cape of Good Hope to some pur-
    pose;)
Nature and Man shall be disjoin'd and diffused no more,
The true son of God shall absolutely fuse them.

6

Year at whose open'd, wide-flung door I sing!
Year of the purpose accomplish'd!
Year of the marriage of continents, climates and oceans!
(No mere Doge of Venice now, wedding the Adriatic;)
I see, O year, in you the vast terraqueous globe, given
    and giving all,   120
Europe to Asia, Africa join'd, and they to the New
    World;
The lands, geographies, dancing before you, holding a
    festival garland,
As brides and bridegrooms hand in hand.

Passage to India!
Cooling airs from Caucasus far, soothing cradle of man,
The river Euphrates flowing, the past lit up again.

Lo, soul, the retrospect, brought forward;
The old, most populous, wealthiest of earth's lands,
The streams of the Indus and the Ganges, and their
    many affluents;
(I, my shores of America walking to-day, behold, resuming
    all,)   130
The tale of Alexander, on his warlike marches, suddenly
    dying,
On one side China, and on the other side Persia and
    Arabia,
To the south the great seas, and the Bay of Bengal;
The flowing literatures, tremendous epics, religions,
    castes,
Old occult Brahma, interminably far back, the tender and
    junior Buddha,
Central and southern empires, and all their belongings,
    possessors,

The wars of Tamerlane, the reign of Aurungzebe,
The traders, rulers, explorers, Moslems, Venetians, By-
zantium, the Arabs, Portuguese,
The first traveler, famous yet, Marco Polo, Batouta the
Moor,
Doubts to be solv'd, the map incognita, blanks to be
fill'd,   140
The foot of man unstay'd, the hands never at rest,
Thyself, O soul, that will not brook a challenge.

The medieval navigators rise before me,
The world of 1492, with its awaken'd enterprise;
Something swelling in humanity now like the sap of the
earth in spring,
The sunset splendor of chivalry declining.

And who art thou, sad shade?
Gigantic, visionary, thyself a visionary,
With majestic limbs, and pious, beaming eyes,
Spreading around, with every look of thine, a golden
world,   150
Enhuing it with gorgeous hues.

As the chief histrion,
Down to the footlights walks, in some great scena,
Dominating the rest, I see the Admiral himself,
(History's type of courage, action, faith;)
Behold him sail from Palos, leading his little fleet;
His voyage behold, his return, his great fame,
His misfortunes, calumniators, behold him a prisoner,
chain'd,
Behold his dejection, poverty, death.

(Curious, in time, I stand, noting the efforts of heroes;   160
Is the deferment long? bitter the slander, poverty,
death?
Lies the seed unreck'd for centuries in the ground? Lo!
to God's due occasion,
Uprising in the night, it sprouts, blooms,
And fills the earth with use and beauty.)

7

Passage indeed O soul to primal thought,
Not lands and seas alone, thy own clear freshness,
The young maturity of brood and bloom,
To realms of budding bibles.

O soul, repressless, I with thee, and thou with me,
Thy circumnavigation of the world begin;   170
Of man, the voyage of his mind's return,
To reason's early paradise,
Back, back to wisdom's birth, to innocent intuitions,
Again with fair creation.

8

O we can wait no longer,
We too take ship, O soul,
Joyous, we too launch out on trackless seas,
Fearless, for unknown shores, on waves of ecstasy to sail,
Amid the wafting winds, (thou pressing me to thee, I
    thee to me, O soul,)
Caroling free, singing our song of God,   180
Chanting our chant of pleasant exploration.

With laugh, and many a kiss,
(Let others deprecate—let others weep for sin, remorse,
    humiliation;)
O soul, thou pleasest me, I thee.

Ah, more than any priest, O soul, we too believe in God,
But with the mystery of God we dare not dally.

O soul, thou pleasest me, I thee;
Sailing these seas, or on the hills, or waking in the
    night,
Thoughts, silent thoughts, of Time, and Space, and Death,
    like waters flowing,
Bear me, indeed, as through the regions infinite,   190
Whose air I breathe, whose ripples hear, lave me all
    over;
Bathe me, O God, in thee, mounting to thee,
I and my soul to range in range of thee.

O Thou transcendant,
Nameless, the fibre and the breath,
Light of the light, shedding forth universes, thou centre
of them,
Thou mightier centre of the true, the good, the loving,
Thou moral, spiritual fountain—affection's source—thou
reservoir,
(O pensive soul of me—O thirst unsatisfied—waitest not
there?
Waitest not haply for us, somewhere there, the Comrade
perfect?)   200
Thou pulse! thou motive of the stars, suns, systems,
That, circling, move in order, safe, harmonious,
Athwart the shapeless vastness of space!
How should I think, how breathe a single breath, how
speak, if, out of myself,
I could not launch, to those, superior universes?

Swiftly I shrivel at the thought of God,
At Nature and its wonders, Time and Space and Death,
But that I, turning, call to thee, O soul, thou actual Me,
And lo! thou gently masterest the orbs,
Thou matest Time, smilest content at Death,   210
And fillest, swellest full, the vastness of Space.

Greater than stars or suns,
Bounding, O soul, thou journeyest forth;
—What love, than thine and ours could wider amplify?
What aspirations, wishes, outvie thine and ours, O soul?
What dreams of the ideal? what plans of purity, perfection,
strength?
What cheerful willingness, for others' sake, to give up
all?
For others' sake to suffer all?

Reckoning ahead, O soul, when thou, the time achiev'd,
The seas all cross'd, weather'd the capes, the voyage
done,   220
Surrounded, copest, frontest God, yieldest, the aim attain'd,
As, fill'd with friendship, love complete, the Elder Brother
found,
The Younger melts in fondness in his arms.

9

Passage to more than India!
Are thy wings plumed indeed for such far flights?
O soul, voyagest thou indeed on voyages like those?
Disportest thou on waters such as those?
Soundest below the Sanscrit and the Vedas?
Then have thy bent unleash'd.

Passage to you, your shores, ye aged fierce enigmas!   230
Passage to you, to mastership of you, ye strangling prob-
    lems!
You, strew'd with the wrecks of skeletons, that, living,
    never reach'd you.

Passage to more than India!
O secret of the earth and sky!
Of you, O waters of the sea! O winding creeks and rivers!
Of you, O woods and fields! of you strong mountains of
    my land!
Of you, O prairies! of you, gray rocks!
O morning red! O clouds! O rain and snows!
O day and night, passage to you!

O sun and moon, and all you stars! Sirius and Jupiter!   240
Passage to you!

Passage, immediate passage! the blood burns in my veins!
Away, O soul! hoist instantly the anchor!
Cut the hawsers—haul out—shake out every sail!
Have we not stood here like trees in the ground long
    enough?
Have we not grovell'd here long enough, eating and drink-
    ing like mere brutes?
Have we not darken'd and dazed ourselves with books
    long enough?

Sail forth! steer for the deep waters only!
Reckless, O soul, exploring, I with thee, and thou with me,
For we are bound where mariner has not yet dared to go,
And we will risk the ship, ourselves and all.   251

O my brave soul!
O farther, farther sail!
O daring joy, but safe! are they not all the seas of God?
O farther, farther, farther sail!

1871

HENRY WADSWORTH LONGFELLOW

(1807–1882)

Longfellow was born into the family of a Portland, Maine, lawyer whose career was to include a trusteeship in Bowdoin College, a judgeship, and membership in Congress. The father's extensive library exerted an early influence on the boy, who practiced imitations of the prose style of Washington Irving, published his first poem ("The Battle of Lovell's Pond") in the Portland *Gazette* at the age of thirteen, and soon came to yearn for pre-eminence in contemporary American literature.

He went to Bowdoin College, where Nathaniel Hawthorne was also a student. Upon his graduation in 1825 he was offered a professorship in modern languages if he would first study abroad. Consequently, from 1826 to 1829, he traveled and studied in Spain, France, England, Germany, and Italy and returned to Maine to assume his teaching duties at Bowdoin. His marriage to Mary Potter in 1831 helped to ease some of Longfellow's growing discontent with Bowdoin, as did the serialization of his European impressions in the *New England Magazine* in 1831 and 1832. The serial appeared in book form as *Outre-Mer* in 1835.

When George Ticknor prepared to resign the Smith Chair in Modern Languages, Harvard looked about for a replacement, and in 1834 beckoned to Bowdoin's Longfellow. He responded gladly, voyaging again to Europe in 1835 to prepare himself for his new classes—but his happiness was destroyed by the death of his wife in Rotterdam. Nevertheless, Longfellow remained at Heidelberg for further study and, while traveling in Switzerland, met and fell in love with Frances Appleton, the attractive daughter of an enormously wealthy industrialist from Lowell, Massachusetts. In melodramatic nineteenth-century style, he fought her evasions for seven years, finally winning her hand in 1843.

Longfellow began his Harvard years in 1836, and by 1839, with the publication of *Voices of the Night* as well as *Hyperion*, he was nationally established as a poet. His father-in-law bought the Craigie House and hired servants for the young couple, and they settled down to a happy life of gentility, affluence, and ease; Longfellow was not dependent on the Harvard salary for his manuscript paper. In 1854 he resigned his chair (which was next filled by James Russell Lowell) in order to be a full-time poet. He had already published *Ballads and Other Poems* (1841), *Poems on Slavery* (1842), *The Belfry of Bruges* (1846), *Evangeline* (1847), *The Seaside and the Fireside* (1849), and *The Golden Legend* (1851). He followed his resignation with the *Song of Hiawatha* (1855) and *The Courtship of Miles Standish* (1858). When his second wife died in 1861, a great part of Longfellow's life came to an end; but he continued to write, finding in his work an anodyne to the pain of bereavement. *Tales of a Wayside Inn* appeared in 1863; the translation of Dante's *Divine Comedy* occupied him from 1865 to 1869; *Christus: A Mystery* was published in 1872 (it incorporated *The Divine Tragedy* of 1871 as Part I, *The Golden Legend* as Part II, and *The New England Tragedies* of 1861 as Part III); *Ultima Thule* in 1880, and Part II of *Ultima Thule* (*In the Harbor*) in 1882, the year of his death.

In his day, Longfellow was the most widely known, best-loved, and most successful poet in America. His reputation was inflated by many factors: he acquainted self-conscious Americans hungry for an identification with "culture" with the legends of Europe, at the same time providing them with native legends in which they could take nationalistic pride. His moral obviousness and Victorian gentility pleased a sentimental and optimistic age that equated poetry with regular cadence, easy rhyme, "pretty" subjects, and moral uplift. The iconoclastic 1920's and the hard-bitten 1930's, however, rejected his work as the maudlin effusions of an era whose gods were dead and whose sentiments were false. Today he occupies a middle ground as a minor poet whose really good work still merits reading by an audience of more than schoolchildren.

Some of the titles included in Longfellow's bibliography, besides those mentioned above, are *The Spanish Student: A Play in Three Acts* (1843); *Poems* (1845); *Kavanagh* (1849); *Noël* (1864); *Household Poems* (1865); *Flower-de-Luce* (1867); *The Alarm-Bell of Atri* (1871); *The Masque of Pandora and Other Poems* (1875); *Kéramos and Other Poems* (1878); and *From My Arm-Chair* (1879).

Editions and accounts of the man and his work are to be found in D. G. Dexter, *The Life and Works of Henry Wadsworth Longfellow* (1882); *The Complete Poetical and Prose Works of Henry Wadsworth Longfellow*, 11 vols. (1886); S. Longfellow, ed., *The Works of Henry Wadsworth Longfellow*, 14 vols. (1886–1891); G. R. Carpenter, *Henry Wadsworth Longfellow* (1901); T. W. Higginson, *Henry Wadsworth Longfellow* (1902); P. E. More, *Shelburne Essays*, Fifth Series (1907); C. E. Norton, *Henry Wadsworth Longfellow* (1907); L. S. Livingston, *A Bibliography of . . . the Writings of Henry Wadsworth Longfellow* (1908); W. P. Trent, *Longfellow and Others Essays* (1908); H. S. Gorman, *A Victorian American* (1926); J. T. Hatfield, *New Light on Longfellow* (1933); G. W. Allen, *American Prosody* (1935); V. W. Brooks, *The Flowering of New England* (1936); L. Thompson, *Young Longfellow* (1938); C. L. Johnson, *Professor Longfellow of Harvard* (1944); A. Hilen, *Longfellow and Scandinavia* (1947); R. Von Abele, "A Note on Longfellow's Poetic," *American Literature*, XXIV (1952); J. M. Cox, "Longfellow and His Cross of Snow," *PMLA*, LXXV (1960); R. S. Ward, "Longfellow and Melville: The Ship and the Whale," *Emerson Society Quarterly*, No. 22 (1961); N. Arvin, "Early Longfellow," *Massachusetts Review*, II (1962); N. Arvin, *Longfellow: His Life and Work* (1963); M. Bewley, "The Poetry of Longfellow," *Hudson Review*, XVI (1963); L. E. Hart, "The Beginnings of Longfellow's Fame," *New England Quarterly*, XXXVI (1963); E. H. Moyne, *Hiawatha and Kalevala: A Study of the Relationship Between Longfellow's "Indian Edda" and the Finnish Epic* (1963); E. L. Hirsh, *Henry Wadsworth Longfellow* (1964); and C. B. Williams, *Henry Wadsworth Longfellow* (1964); E. Wagenknecht, *Henry Wadsworth Longfellow* (1966); and A Hilen, ed., *The Letters of Henry Wadsworth Longfellow* (1966).

A Psalm of Life

What the Heart of the Young Man Said to the Psalmist

Tell me not, in mournful numbers,
  Life is but an empty dream!—
For the soul is dead that slumbers,
  And things are not what they seem.

Life is real! Life is earnest!
  And the grave is not its goal;
Dust thou art, to dust returnest,
  Was not spoken of the soul.

Not enjoyment, and not sorrow,
  Is our destined end or way;   10
But to act, that each to-morrow
  Find us farther than to-day.

Art is long, and Time is fleeting,
  And our hearts, though stout and brave,
Still, like muffled drums, are beating
  Funeral marches to the grave.

In the world's broad field of battle,
  In the bivouac of Life,
Be not like dumb, driven cattle!
  Be a hero in the strife!   20

Trust no Future, howe'er pleasant!
  Let the dead Past bury its dead!
Act,—act in the living Present!
  Heart within, and God o'erhead!

Lives of great men all remind us
  We can make our lives sublime,
And, departing, leave behind us
  Footprints on the sands of time;

Footprints, that perhaps another,
  Sailing o'er life's solemn main,   30
A forlorn and shipwrecked brother,
  Seeing, shall take heart again.

Let us, then, be up and doing,
  With a heart for any fate;
Still achieving, still pursuing,
  Learn to labor and to wait.

1838

Hymn to the Night

'Ασπασίη, τρίλλιστος [*Welcome, thrice prayed for*]

I heard the trailing garments of the Night
  Sweep through her marble halls!
I saw her sable skirts all fringed with light
  From the celestial walls!

I felt her presence, by its spell of might,
  Stoop o'er me from above;
The calm, majestic presence of the Night,
  As of the one I love.

I heard the sounds of sorrow and delight,
  The manifold, soft chimes,   10
That fill the haunted chambers of the Night,
  Like some old poet's rhymes.

From the cool cisterns of the midnight air
  My spirit drank repose;
The fountain of perpetual peace flows there,—
  From those deep cisterns flows.

O holy Night! from thee I learn to bear
  What man has borne before!
Thou layest thy finger on the lips of Care,
  And they complain no more.   20

Peace! Peace! Orestes-like I breathe this prayer!
  Descend with broad-winged flight,
The welcome, the thrice-prayed-for, the most fair,
  The best-beloved Night!

                1839

The Arsenal at Springfield

This is the Arsenal. From floor to ceiling,
  Like a huge organ, rise the burnished arms;
But from their silent pipes no anthem pealing
  Startles the villages with strange alarms.

Ah! what a sound will rise, how wild and dreary,
  When the death-angel touches those swift keys!
What loud lament and dismal Miserere
  Will mingle with their awful symphonies!

I hear even now the infinite fierce chorus,
  The cries of agony, the endless groan,   10
Which, through the ages that have gone before us,
  In long reverberations reach our own.

On helm and harness rings the Saxon hammer,
  Through Cimbric forest roars the Norseman's song,
And loud, amid the universal clamor,
  O'er distant deserts sounds the Tartar gong.

I hear the Florentine, who from his palace
  Wheels out his battle-bell with dreadful din,
And Aztec priests upon their teocallis
  Beat the wild war-drum made of serpent's skin;   20

The tumult of each sacked and burning village;
  The shout that every prayer for mercy drowns;
The soldiers' revels in the midst of pillage;
  The wail of famine in beleaguered towns;

The bursting shell, the gateway wrenched asunder,
  The rattling musketry, the clashing blade;
And ever and anon, in tones of thunder,
  The diapason of the cannonade.

Is it, O man, with such discordant noises,
  With such accursed instruments as these,   30
Thou drownest Nature's sweet and kindly voices,
  And jarrest the celestial harmonies?

Were half the power, that fills the world with terror,
  Were half the wealth, bestowed on camps and courts,
Given to redeem the human mind from error,
  There were no need of arsenals or forts:

The warrior's name would be a name abhorrèd!
  And every nation, that should lift again
Its hand against a brother, on its forehead
  Would wear forevermore the curse of Cain!   40

Down the dark future, through long generations,
   The echoing sounds grow fainter and then cease;
And like a bell, with solemn, sweet vibrations,
   I hear once more the voice of Christ say, "Peace!"

Peace! and no longer from its brazen portals
   The blast of War's great organ shakes the skies!
But beautiful as songs of the immortals,
   The holy melodies of love arise.   1844

Seaweed

When descends on the Atlantic
   The gigantic
Storm-wind of the equinox,
Landward in his wrath he scourges
   The toiling surges,
Laden with seaweed from the rocks:

From Bermuda's reefs; from edges
   Of sunken ledges,
In some far-off, bright Azore;
From Bahama, and the dashing,   10
   Silver-flashing
Surges of San Salvador;

From the tumbling surf, that buries
   The Orkneyan skerries,
Answering the hoarse Hebrides;
And from wrecks of ships, and drifting
   Spars, uplifting
On the desolate, rainy seas;—

Ever drifting, drifting, drifting
   On the shifting   20
Currents of the restless main;
Till in sheltered coves, and reaches
   Of sandy beaches,
All have found repose again.

So when storms of wild emotion
   Strike the ocean
Of the poet's soul, erelong

From each cave and rocky fastness,
    In its vastness,
Floats some fragment of a song: 30

From the far-off isles enchanted,
    Heaven has planted
With the golden fruit of Truth;
From the flashing surf, whose vision
    Gleans Elysian
In the tropic clime of Youth;

From the strong Will, and the Endeavor
    That forever
Wrestle with the tides of Fate;
From the wreck of Hopes far-scattered,   40
    Tempest-shattered,
Floating waste and desolate;—

Ever drifting, drifting, drifting
    On the shifting
Currents of the restless heart;
Till at length in books recorded,
    They, like hoarded
Household words, no more depart.

                                            1845

Mezzo Cammin [Mid-way on the road of life]

Half of my life is gone, and I have let
    The years slip from me and have not fulfilled
    The aspiration of my youth, to build
    Some tower of song with lofty parapet.
Not indolence, nor pleasure, nor the fret
    Of restless passions that would not be stilled,
    But sorrow, and a care that almost killed,
    Kept me from what I may accomplish yet;
Though, half-way up the hill, I see the Past
    Lying beneath me with its sounds and sights,—   10
    A city in the twilight dim and vast,
With smoking roofs, soft bells, and gleaming lights,—
    And hear above me on the autumnal blast
    The cataract of Death far thundering from the heights.

                                            w. 1842
                                            p. 1846

The Evening Star

Lo! in the painted oriel of the West,
  Whose panes the sunken sun incarnadines,
  Like a fair lady at her casement, shines
The evening star, the star of love and rest!
And then anon she doth herself divest
  Of all her radiant garments, and reclines
  Behind the sombre screen of yonder pines,
  With slumber and soft dreams of love oppressed.
O my beloved, my sweet Hesperus!
  My morning and my evening star of love!   10
  My best and gentlest lady! even thus,
As that fair planet in the sky above,
  Dost thou retire unto thy rest at night,
  And from thy darkened window fades the light.   1846

The Jewish Cemetery at Newport

How strange it seems! These Hebrews in their graves,
  Close by the street of this fair seaport town,
Silent beside the never-silent waves,
  At rest in all this moving up and down!

The trees are white with dust, that o'er their sleep
  Wave their broad curtains in the southwind's breath,
While underneath these leafy tents they keep
  The long, mysterious Exodus of Death.

And these sepulchral stones, so old and brown,
  That pave with level flags their burial-place,   10
Seem like the tablets of the Law, thrown down
  And broken by Moses at the mountain's base.

The very names recorded here are strange,
  Of foreign accent, and of different climes;
Alvares and Rivera interchange
  With Abraham and Jacob of old times.

"Blessed be God! for he created Death!"
  The mourners said, "and Death is rest and peace;"
Then added, in the certainty of faith,
  "And giveth Life that nevermore shall cease."   20

Closed are the portals of their Synagogue,
  No Psalms of David now the silence break,
No Rabbi reads the ancient Decalogue
  In the grand dialect the Prophets spake.

Gone are the living, but the dead remain,
  And not neglected; for a hand unseen,
Scattering its bounty, like a summer rain,
  Still keeps their graves and their remembrance green.

How came they here? What burst of Christian hate,
  What persecution, merciless and blind,   30
Drove o'er the sea—that desert desolate—
  These Ishmaels and Hagars of mankind?

They lived in narrow streets and lanes obscure,
  Ghetto and Judenstrass, in mirk and mire;
Taught in the school of patience to endure
  The life of anguish and the death of fire.

All their lives long, with the unleavened bread
  And bitter herbs of exile and its fears,
The wasting famine of the heart they fed,
  And slaked its thirst with marah of their tears.   40

Anathema maranatha! was the cry
  That rang from town to town, from street to street;
At every gate the accursed Mordecai
  Was mocked and jeered, and spurned by Christian feet.

Pride and humiliation hand in hand
  Walked with them through the world where'er they went;
Trampled and beaten were they as the sand,
  And yet unshaken as the continent.

For in the background figures vague and vast
  Of patriarchs and of prophets rose sublime,   50
And all the great traditions of the Past
  They saw reflected in the coming time.

And thus forever with reverted look
  The mystic volume of the world they read,
Spelling it backward, like a Hebrew book,
  Till life became a Legend of the Dead.

But ah! what once has been shall be no more!
   The groaning earth in travail and in pain
Brings forth its races, but does not restore,
   And the dead nations never rise again.   60

w. 1852
p. 1854

My Lost Youth

Often I think of the beautiful town
   That is seated by the sea;
Often in thought go up and down
The pleasant streets of that dear old town,
   And my youth comes back to me.
      And a verse of a Lapland song
      Is haunting my memory still:
      "A boy's will is the wind's will,
And the thoughts of youth are long, long thoughts."

I can see the shadowy lines of its trees,   10
   And catch, in sudden gleams,
The sheen of the far-surrounding seas,
And islands that were the Hesperides
   Of all my boyish dreams.
      And the burden of that old song,
      It murmurs and whispers still:
      "A boy's will is the wind's will,
And the thoughts of youth are long, long thoughts."

I remember the black wharves and the slips,
   And the sea-tides tossing free;   20
And Spanish sailors with bearded lips,
And the beauty and mystery of the ships,
   And the magic of the sea.
      And the voice of that wayward song
      Is singing and saying still:
      "A boy's will is the wind's will,
And the thoughts of youth are long, long thoughts."

I remember the bulwarks by the shore,
   And the fort upon the hill;
The sunrise gun, with its hollow roar,   30
The drum-beat repeated o'er and o'er,
   And the bugle wild and shrill.
      And the music of that old song

Throbs in my memory still:
"A boy's will is the wind's will,
And the thoughts of youth are long, long thoughts."

I remember the sea-fight far away,
  How it thundered o'er the tide!
And the dead captains, as they lay
In their graves, o'erlooking the tranquil bay   40
  Where they in battle died.
    And the sound of that mournful song
    Goes through me with a thrill:
    "A boy's will is the wind's will,
And the thoughts of youth are long, long thoughts."

I can see the breezy dome of groves,
  The shadows of Deering's Woods;
And the friendships old and the early loves
Come back with a Sabbath sound, as of doves
  In quiet neighborhoods.   50
    And the verse of that sweet old song,
    It flutters and murmurs still:
    "A boy's will is the wind's will,
And the thoughts of youth are long, long thoughts."

I remember the gleams and glooms that dart
  Across the school-boy's brain;
The song and the silence in the heart,
That in part are prophecies, and in part
  Are longings wild and vain.
    And the voice of that fitful song   60
    Sings on, and is never still:
    "A boy's will is the wind's will,
And the thoughts of youth are long, long thoughts."

There are things of which I may not speak;
  There are dreams that cannot die;
There are thoughts that make the strong heart weak,
And bring a pallor into the cheek,
  And a mist before the eye.
    And the words of that fatal song
    Come over me like a chill: 70
    "A boy's will is the wind's will,
And the thoughts of youth are long, long thoughts."

Strange to me now are the forms I meet
  When I visit the dear old town;
But the native air is pure and sweet,
And the trees that o'ershadow each well-known street,
    As they balance up and down,
      Are singing the beautiful song,
      Are sighing and whispering still:
        "A boy's will is the wind's will,   80
And the thoughts of youth are long, long thoughts."

And Deering's Woods are fresh and fair,
  And with joy that is almost pain
My heart goes back to wander there,
And among the dreams of the days that were,
    I find my lost youth again.
      And the strange and beautiful song,
      The groves are repeating it still:
        "A boy's will is the wind's will,
And the thoughts of youth are long, long thoughts."   90
                            1855

Divina Commedia

I

Oft have I seen at some cathedral door
  A laborer, pausing in the dust and heat,
  Lay down his burden, and with reverent feet
  Enter, and cross himself, and on the floor
Kneel to repeat his paternoster o'er;
  Far off the noises of the world retreat;
  The loud vociferations of the street
  Become an undistinguishable roar.
So, as I enter here from day to day,
  And leave my burden at this minster gate,   10
  Kneeling in prayer, and not ashamed to pray,
The tumult of the time disconsolate
  To inarticulate murmurs dies away,
  While the eternal ages watch and wait.

                            1865

II

How strange the sculptures that adorn these towers!
  This crowd of statues, in whose folded sleeves
  Birds build their nests; while canopied with leaves
  Parvis and portal bloom like trellised bowers,
And the vast minster seems a cross of flowers!
  But fiends and dragons on the gargoyled eaves
  Watch the dead Christ between the living thieves,
  And, underneath, the traitor Judas lowers!
Ah! from what agonies of heart and brain,
  What exultations trampling on despair,   10
  What tenderness, what tears, what hate of wrong,
What passionate outcry of a soul in pain,
  Uprose this poem of the earth and air,
  This medieval miracle of song!   1865

III

I enter, and I see thee in the gloom
  Of the long aisles, O poet saturnine!
  And strive to make my steps keep pace with thine.
  The air is filled with some unknown perfume;
The congregation of the dead make room
  For thee to pass; the votive tapers shine;
  Like rooks that haunt Ravenna's groves of pine
  The hovering echoes fly from tomb to tomb.
From the confessionals I hear arise
  Rehearsals of forgotten tragedies,   10
  And lamentations from the crypts below;
And then a voice celestial that begins
  With the pathetic words, "Although your sins
  As scarlet be," and end with "as the snow."   1866

IV

With snow-white veil and garments as of flame,
  She stands before thee, who so long ago
  Filled thy young heart with passion and the woe
  From which thy song and all its splendors came;
And while with stern rebuke she speaks thy name,
  The ice about thy heart melts as the snow
  On mountain heights, and in swift overflow

Comes gushing from thy lips in sobs of shame.
Thou makest full confession; and a gleam,
  As of the dawn on some dark forest cast,   10
  Seems on thy lifted forehead to increase;
Lethe and Eunoë—the remembered dream
  And the forgotten sorrow—bring at last
  That perfect pardon which is perfect peace.

                  1866

V

I lift mine eyes, and all the windows blaze
  With forms of Saints and holy men who died,
  Here martyred and hereafter glorified;
  And the great Rose upon its leaves displays
Christ's Triumph, and the angelic roundelays,
  With splendor upon splendor multiplied;
  And Beatrice again at Dante's side
  No more rebukes, but smiles her words of praise.
And then the organ sounds, and unseen choirs
  Sing the old Latin hymns of peace and love   10
  And benedictions of the Holy Ghost;
And the melodious bells among the spires
  O'er all the housetops and through heaven above
  Proclaim the elevation of the Host!

                  1867

VI

O star of morning and of liberty!
  O bringer of the light, whose splendor shines
  Above the darkness of the Apennines,
  Forerunner of the day that is to be!
The voices of the city and the sea,
  The voices of the mountains and the pines,
  Repeat thy song, till the familiar lines
  Are footpaths for the thought of Italy!
Thy flame is blown abroad from all the heights,
  Through all the nations, and a sound is heard,   10
  As of a mighty wind, and men devout,
Strangers of Rome, and the new proselytes,
  In their own language hear the wondrous word,
  And many are amazed and many doubt.

                  1867

Hawthorne

How beautiful it was, that one bright day
    In the long week of rain!
Though all its splendor could not chase away
    The omnipresent pain.

The lovely town was white with apple-blooms,
    And the great elms o'erhead
Dark shadows wove on their aerial looms
    Shot through with golden thread.

Across the meadows, by the gray old manse,
    The historic river flowed:
I was as one who wanders in a trance,
    Unconscious of his road.

The faces of familiar friends seemed strange;
    Their voices I could hear,
And yet the words they uttered seemed to change
    Their meaning to my ear.

For the one face I looked for was not there,
    The one low voice was mute;
Only an unseen presence filled the air,
    And baffled my pursuit.   20

Now I look back, and meadow, manse, and stream
    Dimly my thought defines;
I only see—a dream within a dream—
    The hill-top hearsed with pines.

I only hear above his place of rest
    Their tender undertone,
The infinite longings of a troubled breast,
    The voice so like his own.

There in seclusion and remote from men
    The wizard hand lies cold,   30
Which at its topmost speed let fall the pen,
    And left the tale half told.

Ah! who shall lift that wand of magic power,
  And the lost clew regain?
The unfinished window in Aladdin's tower
  Unfinished must remain!   1867

Chaucer

An old man in a lodge within a park;
The chamber walls depicted all around
With portraitures of huntsman, hawk, and hound,
And the hurt deer. He listeneth to the lark,
Whose song comes with the sunshine through the dark
Of painted glass in leaden lattice bound;
He listened and he laugheth at the sound,
Then writeth in a book like any clerk.
He is the poet of the dawn, who wrote
The Canterbury Tales, and his old age   10
Made beautiful with song; and as I read
I hear the crowing cock, I hear the note
Of lark and linnet, and from every page
Rise odors of ploughed field or flowery mead.   w. 1873
                                               p. 1875

Milton

I pace the sounding sea-beach and behold
  How the voluminous billows roll and run,
  Upheaving and subsiding, while the sun
  Shines through their sheeted emerald far unrolled
And the ninth wave, slow gathering fold by fold
  All its loose-flowing garments into one,
  Plunges upon the shore, and floods the dun
  Pale reach of sands, and changes them to gold.
So in majestic cadence rise and fall
  The mighty undulations of thy song,   10
  O sightless Bard, England's Mæonides!
And ever and anon, high over all
  Uplifted, a ninth wave superb and strong,
  Floods all the soul with its melodious seas.

                                         w. 1873
                                       p. 1875

Venice

White swan of cities, slumbering in thy nest
  So wonderfully built among the reeds
  Of the lagoon, that fences thee and feeds,
  As sayeth thy old historian and thy guest!
White water-lily, cradled and caressed
  By ocean streams, and from the silt and weeds
  Lifting thy golden filaments and seeds,
  Thy sun-illumined spires, thy crown and crest!
White phantom city, whose untrodden streets
  Are rivers, and whose pavements are the shifting   10
  Shadows of palaces and strips of sky;
I wait to see thee vanish like the fleets
  Seen in mirage, or towers of cloud uplifting
  In air their unsubstantial masonry.

                           1875

The Tide Rises, the Tide Falls

The tide rises, the tide falls,
The twilight darkens, the curlew calls;
Along the sea-sands damp and brown
The traveller hastens toward the town,
  And the tide rises, the tide falls.

Darkness settles on roofs and walls,
But the sea, the sea in the darkness calls;
The little waves, with their soft, white hands,
Efface the footprints in the sands,
  And the tide rises, the tide falls.   10

The morning breaks; the steeds in their stalls
Stamp and neigh, as the hostler calls;
The day returns, but nevermore
Returns the traveller to the shore,
  And the tide rises, the tide falls.

                           1880

The Cross of Snow

In the long, sleepless watches of the night,
    A gentle face—the face of one long dead—
    Looks at me from the wall, where round its head
    The night-lamp casts a halo of pale light.
Here in this room she died; and soul more white
    Never through martyrdom of fire was led
    To its repose; nor can in books be read
    The legend of a life more benedight.
There is a mountain in the distant West
    That, sun-defying, in its deep ravines   10
    Displays a cross of snow upon its side.
Such is the cross I wear upon my breast
    These eighteen years, through all the changing scenes
    And seasons, changeless since the day she died.

                     w. 1879
                     p. 1886

Dedication from Michael Angelo: a Fragment

Nothing that is shall perish utterly,
    But perish only to revive again
    In other forms, as clouds restore in rain
    The exhalations of the land and sea.
Men build their houses from the masonry
    Of ruined tombs; the passion and the pain
    Of hearts, that long have ceased to beat, remain
    To throb in hearts that are, or are to be.
So from old chronicles, where sleep in dust
    Names that once filled the world with trumpet tones,   10
    I build this verse; and flowers of song have thrust
Their roots among the loose disjointed stones,
    Which to this end I fashion as I must.
    Quickened are they that touch the Prophet's bones.

                     1883

JOHN GREENLEAF WHITTIER

(1807–1892)

Born on a seacoast farm near Haverhill, Massachusetts, Whittier was reared by his Quaker family which, though poor, tried to give him whatever meager education it could. Influenced by religious readings, the poetry of Robert Burns, and the simple, humanitarian piety of his Quaker background, Whittier became interested in abolitionism and in poetry devoted to the circumstances of common life. He published some of his early poetry in William Lloyd Garrison's Newburyport *Free Press* and, warmed by Garrison's friendship, became more militant in his abolitionist sympathies. After a year at Haverhill Academy in 1827, Whittier embarked upon a career of journalism and politics. At the age of twenty-one he became the editor of a Boston paper, *The American Manufacturer*, and his poems began to appear with some regularity in newspapers and periodicals.

After one year in Boston, however, Whittier had to return home when his father became too ill to work the farm. After his father's death in 1830 he moved to Hartford, Connecticut, to become the editor of the *New England Weekly Review*. One year later his first book, *Legends of New England*, appeared. Ill health dogged him in his various enterprises, forcing his resignation from the *New England Weekly Review* in 1831 and later from the Philadelphia antislavery newspaper, *The Pennsylvania Freeman*, which he edited from 1838 to 1840. Yet all the while he continued to produce the abolitionist writing which, with the publication of *Justice and Expediency* in 1833, brought him national fame as a crusader of the times.

His public reception was mixed: in 1835 Massachusetts elected him to its legislature in Boston, and New Hampshire mobbed him in Concord. The following year he edited the *Essex Gazette* and moved to Amesbury, the quiet country place that was to be his home for the rest of his life. After editing the Lowell *Middlesex Standard* from 1844 to 1845, he published *Voices of Freedom* (1846), a collection of his antislavery writings that consolidated his political reputation and made him corresponding editor of the renowned *National Era* of Washington, D. C. His lifelong desire to emulate Burns as the poet of the common people kept him at his writing desk celebrating what he himself knew so well: the beauties of the country, the life of the farm folk, the conditions of the working man. *Songs of Labor* appeared in 1850, *The Chapel of the Hermits and Other Poems* in 1853, and *The Panorama and Other Poems* in 1856. In 1857 he became associated with Lowell and Holmes in founding the *Atlantic Monthly*, an association that, because of Lowell's astute editorial suggestions, was to help Whittier achieve a fuller and more mature control of his medium. The conclusion of the Civil War ended his career as an agitator, and the publication of *Snow-Bound* in 1866 established him nationally as the poet of the people and as a leading literary figure of his age.

Although Whittier will occupy no more than a minor niche in our literary pantheon, some of his poetry—particularly *Snow-Bound*—still deserves reading as a commemoration of an American panorama and an era that has irreclaimably faded from view. Indeed, it is more than nostalgia or tradition that demands the preservation of a part of Whittier's poetry, for those few works that transcend his general sentimentality are minor masterpieces of the simple familiar style.

Included among his works, besides those mentioned above, are *Poems* (1838); *Ballads and Other Poems* (1844); *Poems* (1849); *The Sycamores* (1857); *Home Ballads* (1860); *The Tent on the Beach* (1867); *Among the Hills* (1869); *The Pennsylvania Pilgrim* (1872); *Hazel-Blossoms* (1875); *At Sundown* (1890); and *The Demon Lady* (1894).

Editions and accounts of the man and his work are to be found in H. E. Scudder and J. G. Whittier, eds., *The Writings of John Greenleaf Whittier*, 7 vols. (1888–1889), which in the issue of 1894 becomes the standard edition; M. B. Claflin, *Personal Recollections of John G. Whittier* (1893); A. A. Fields, *Whittier* (1893); S. T. Pickard, *The Life and Letters of John Greenleaf Whittier*, 2 vols. (1894); H. E. Scudder, ed., *The Complete Poetical Works of John Greenleaf Whittier* (1894);

S. T. Pickard, _Whittier as a Politician_ (1900); T. W. Higginson, _John Greenleaf Whittier_ (1902); G. R. Carpenter, _John Greenleaf Whittier_ (1903); C. J. Hawkins, _The Mind of Whittier_ (1904); F. M. Pray, _A Study of Whittier's Apprenticeship as a Poet_ (1930); A. Mordell, _Quaker Militant_ (1933); W. Bennett, _Whittier: Bard of Freedom_ (1941); J. A. Pollard, _John Greenleaf Whittier, Friend of Man_ (1949); E. H. Cady and H. H. Clark, eds., _Whittier on Writers and Writing_ (1950); G. Arms, _The Fields Were Green_ (1953); D. Hall, "Whittier," _Texas Quarterly_, III (1960); L. Leary, _John Greenleaf Whittier_ (1961); W. T. Scott, _Exiles and Fabrications_ (1961); J. B. Pickard, _John Greenleaf Whittier_ (1961); and P. Miller, "John Greenleaf Whittier: The Conscience in Poetry," _Harvard Review_, II (1964).

Massachusetts to Virginia

The blast from Freedom's Northern hills, upon its Southern
  way,
Bears greeting to Virginia from Massachusetts Bay:
No word of haughty challenging, nor battle bugle's peal,
Nor steady tread of marching files, nor clang of horsemen's
  steel,

No trains of deep-mouthed cannon along our highways go;
Around our silent arsenals untrodden lies the snow;
And to the land-breeze of our ports, upon their errands far,
A thousand sails of commerce swell, but none are spread
  for war.

We hear thy threats, Virginia! thy stormy words and high
Swell harshly on the Southern winds which melt along our
  sky;   10
Yet not one brown, hard hand foregoes its honest labor
  here,
No hewer of our mountain oaks suspends his axe in fear.

Wild are the waves which lash the reefs along St. George's
  bank;
Cold on the shores of Labrador the fog lies white and dank;
Through storm, and wave, and blinding mist, stout are the
  hearts which man
The fishing-smacks of Marblehead, the seaboats of Cape
  Ann.

The cold north light and wintry sun glare on their icy forms,
Bent grimly o'er their straining lines or wrestling with the
  storms;

Free as the winds they drive before, rough as the waves
    they roam,
They laugh to scorn the slaver's threat against their rocky
    home.   20

What means the Old Dominion? Hath she forgot the day
When o'er her conquered valleys swept the Briton's steel
    array?
How, side by side with sons of hers, the Massachusetts men
Encountered Tarleton's charge of fire, and stout Cornwallis,
    then?

Forgets she how the Bay State, in answer to the call
Of her old House of Burgesses, spoke out from Faneuil
    Hall?
When, echoing back her Henry's cry, came pulsing on each
    breath
Of Northern winds the thrilling sounds of "Liberty or
    Death!"

What asks the Old Dominion? If now her sons have proved
False to their fathers' memory, false to the faith they
    loved;   30
If she can scoff at Freedom, and its great charter spurn,
Must we of Massachusetts from truth and duty turn?

We hunt your bondmen, flying from Slavery's hateful hell;
Our voices, at your bidding, take up the bloodhound's yell;
We gather, at your summons, above our fathers' graves,
From Freedom's holy altar-horns to tear your wretched
    slaves!

Thank God! not yet so vilely can Massachusetts bow;
The spirit of her early time is with her even now;
Dream not because her Pilgrim blood moves slow and calm
    and cool,
She thus can stoop her chainless neck, a sister's slave and
    tool!   40

All that a sister State should do, all that a free State may,
Heart, hand, and purse we proffer, as in our early day;

But that one dark loathsome burden ye must stagger with
    alone,
And reap the bitter harvest which ye yourselves have sown!

Hold, while ye may, your struggling slaves, and burden
    God's free air
With woman's shriek beneath the lash, and manhood's wild
    despair;
Cling closer to the "cleaving curse" that writes upon your
    plains
The blasting of Almighty wrath against a land of chains.

Still shame your gallant ancestry, the cavaliers of old,
By watching round the shambles where human flesh is
    sold;   50
Gloat o'er the new-born child, and counts his market value,
    when
The maddened mother's cry of woe shall pierce the slaver's
    den!

Lower than plummet soundeth, sink the Virginia name;
Plant, if ye will, your fathers' graves with rankest weeds
    of shame;
Be, if ye will, the scandal of God's fair universe;
We wash our hands forever of your sin and shame and
    curse.

A voice from lips whereon the coal from Freedom's shrine
    hath been,
Thrilled, as but yesterday, the hearts of Berkshire's moun-
    tain men:
The echoes of that solemn voice are sadly lingering still
In all our sunny valleys, on every windswept hill.   60

And when the prowling man-thief came hunting for his
    prey
Beneath the very shadow of Bunker's shaft of gray,
How, through the free lips of the son, the father's warning
    spoke;
How, from its bonds of trade and sect, the Pilgrim city
    broke!

A hundred thousand right arms were lifted up on high,
A hundred thousand voices sent back their loud reply;
Through the thronged towns of Essex the startling summons
    rang,
And up from bench and loom and wheel her young
    mechanics sprang!

The voice of free, broad Middlesex, of thousands as of one,
The shaft of Bunker calling to that of Lexington;   70
From Norfolk's ancient villages, from Plymouth's rocky
    bound
To where Nantucket feels the arms of ocean close her
    round;

From rich and rural Worcester, where through the calm
    repose.
Of cultured vales and fringing woods the gentle Nashua
    flows,
To where Wachuset's wintry blasts the mountain larches
    stir,
Swelled up to Heaven the thrilling cry of "God save
    Latimer!"

And sandy Barnstable rose up, wet with the salt sea spray;
And Bristol sent her answering shout down Narragansett
    Bay!
Along the broad Connecticut old Hampden felt the thrill,
And the cheer of Hampshire's woodmen swept down from
    Holyoke Hill.   80

The voice of Massachusetts! Of her free sons and daughters,
Deep calling unto deep aloud, the sound of many waters!
Against the burden of that voice what tyrant power shall
    stand?
No fetters in the Bay State! No slave upon her land!

Look to it well, Virginians! In calmness we have borne,
In answer to our faith and trust, your insult and your scorn;
You've spurned our kindest counsels; you've hunted for
    our lives;
And shaken round our hearths and homes your manacles
    and gyves!

We wage no war, we lift no arm, we fling no torch within
The fire-damps of the quaking mine beneath your soil of
    sin;   90
We leave ye with your bondmen, to wrestle, while ye can,
With the strong upward tendencies and godlike soul of man!

But for us and for our children, the vow which we have
    given
For freedom and humanity is registered in heaven;
No slave-hunt in our borders,—no pirate on our strand!
No fetters in the Bay State,—no slave upon our land!

                                            1843

Skipper Ireson's Ride

Of all the rides since the birth of time,
Told in story or sung in rhyme,—
On Apuleius's Golden Ass,
Or one-eyed Calender's horse of brass,
Witch astride of a human back,
Islam's prophet on Al-Borák,—
The strangest ride that ever was sped
Was Ireson's, out from Marblehead!
    Old Floyd Ireson, for his hard heart,
      Tarred and feathered and carried in a cart   10
        By the women of Marblehead!

Body of turkey, head of owl,
Wings a-droop like a rained-on fowl,
Feathered and ruffled in every part,
Skipper Ireson stood in the cart.
Scores of women, old and young,
Strong of muscle, and glib of tongue,
Pushed and pulled up the rocky lane,
Shouting and singing the shrill refrain:
    "Here's Flud Oirson, fur his horrd horrt,   20
      Torr'd an' futherr'd an' corr'd in a corrt
        By the women o' Morble'ead!"

Wrinkled scolds with hands on hips,
Girls in bloom of cheek and lips,
Wild-eyed, free-limbed, such as chase

Bacchus round some antique vase,
Brief of skirt, with ankles bare,
Loose of kerchief and loose of hair,
With conch-shells blowing and fish-horns' twang,
Over and over the Maenads sang: 30
   "Here's Flud Oirson, fur his horrd horrt,
   Torr'd an' futherr'd an' corr'd in a corrt
     By the women o' Morble'ead!"

Small pity for him!—He sailed away
From a leaking ship in Chaleur Bay,—
Sailed away from a sinking wreck,
With his own town's-people on her deck!
"Lay by! lay by!" they called to him.
Back he answered, "Sink or swim!
Brag of your catch of fish again!"   40
And off he sailed through the fog and rain!
   Old Floyd Ireson, for his hard heart,
   Tarred and feathered and carried in a cart
     By the women of Marblehead!

Fathoms deep in dark Chaleur
That wreck shall lie forevermore.
Mother and sister, wife and maid,
Looked from the rocks of Marblehead
Over the moaning and rainy sea,—
Looked for the coming that might not be!   50
What did the winds and the sea-birds say
Of the cruel captain who sailed away—?
   Old Floyd Ireson, for his hard heart,
   Tarred and feathered and carried in a cart
     By the women of Marblehead!

Through the street, on either side,
Up flew windows, doors swung wide;
Sharp-tongued spinsters, old wives gray,
Treble lent the fish-horn's bray.
Sea-worn grandsires, cripple-bound,   60
Hulks of old sailors run aground,
Shook head, and fist, and hat, and cane,
And cracked with curses the hoarse refrain:
   "Here's Flud Oirson, fur his horrd horrt,
   Torr'd an' futherr'd an' corr'd in a corrt
     By the women o' Morble'ead!"

Sweetly along the Salem road
Bloom of orchard and lilac showed.
Little the wicked skipper knew
Of the fields so green and the sky so blue.   70
Riding there in his sorry trim,
Like an Indian idol glum and grim,
Scarcely he seemed the sound to hear
Of voices shouting, far and near:
   "Here's Flud Oirson, fur his horrd horrt,
   Torr'd an' futherr'd corr'd in a corrt
     By the women o' Morble'ead!"

"Hear me, neighbors!" at last he cried,—
"What to me is this noisy ride?
What is the shame that clothes the skin   80
To the nameless horror that lives within?
Waking or sleeping, I see a wreck,
And hear a cry from a reeling deck!
Hate me and curse me,—I only dread
The hand of God and the face of the dead!"
   Said old Floyd Ireson, for his hard heart,
   Tarred and feathered and carried in a cart
     By the women of Marblehead!

Then the wife of the skipper lost at sea
Said, "God has touched him! why should we!"   90
Said an old wife mourning her only son,
"Cut the rogue's tether and let him run!"
So with soft relentings and rude excuse,
Half scorn, half pity, they cut him loose,
And gave him a cloak to hide him in,
And left him alone with his shame and sin.
   Poor Floyd Ireson, for his hard heart,
   Tarred and feathered and carried in a cart
     By the women of Marblehead!   1857

Snow-Bound

A Winter Idyl

*As the Spirits of Darkness be stronger in the dark, so
Good Spirits, which be Angels of Light, are augmented
not only by the Divine light of the Sun, but also by our*

*common VVood Fire: and as the Celestial Fire drives
away dark spirits, so also this our Fire of VVood doth the
same.*—COR. AGRIPPA, Occult Philosophy, *Book. I. ch. v.*

> *Announced by all the trumpets of the sky,*
> *Arrives the snow, and, driving o'er the fields,*
> *Seems nowhere to alight: the whited air*
> *Hides hills and woods, the river and the heaven,*
> *And veils the farm-house at the garden's end.*
> *The sled and traveller stopped, the courier's feet*
> *Delayed, all friends shut out, the housemates sit*
> *Around the radiant fireplace, enclosed*
> *In a tumultuous privacy of storm.*
> —EMERSON, "The Snow-Storm"

The sun that brief December day
Rose cheerless over hills of gray,
And, darkly circled, gave at noon
A sadder light than waning moon.
Slow tracing down the thickening sky
Its mute and ominous prophecy,
A portent seeming less than threat,
It sank from sight before it set.
A chill no coat, however stout,
Of homespun stuff could quite shut out,   10
A hard, dull bitterness of cold,
That checked, mid-vein, the circling race
Of life-blood in the sharpened face,
The coming of the snow-storm told.
The wind blew east; we heard the roar
Of Ocean on his wintry shore,
And felt the strong pulse throbbing there
Beat with low rhythm our inland air.

Meanwhile we did our nightly chores,—
Brought in the wood from out of doors,   20
Littered the stalls, and from the mows
Raked down the herd's-grass for the cows:
Heard the horse whinnying for his corn;
And, sharply clashing horn on horn,
Impatient down the stanchion rows
The cattle shake their walnut bows;
While, peering from his early perch
Upon the scaffold's pole of birch,

The cock his crested helmet bent
And down his querulous challenge sent.   30

Unwarmed by any sunset light
The gray day darkened into night,
A night made hoary with the swarm
And whirl-dance of the blinding storm,
As zigzag, wavering to and fro,
Crossed and recrossed the wingèd snow:
And ere the early bedtime came
The white drift piled the window-frame,
And through the glass the clothes-line posts
Looked in like tall and sheeted ghosts.   40

So all night long the storm roared on:
The morning broke without a sun;
In tiny spherule traced with lines
Of Nature's geometric signs,
In starry flake, and pellicle,
All day the hoary meteor fell;
And, when the second morning shone,
We looked upon a world unknown,
On nothing we could call our own.
Around the glistening wonder bent   50
The blue walls of the firmament,
No cloud above, no earth below,—
A universe of sky and snow!
The old familiar sights of ours
Took marvellous shapes; strange domes and towers
Rose up where sty or corn-crib stood,
Or garden-wall, or belt of wood;
A smooth white mound the brush-pile showed,
A fenceless drift what once was road;
The bridle-post an old man sat   60
With loose-flung coat and high cocked hat;
The well-curb had a Chinese roof;
And even the long sweep, high aloof,
In its slant splendor, seemed to tell
Of Pisa's leaning miracle.

A prompt, decisive man, no breath
Our father wasted: "Boys, a path!"
Well pleased (for when did farmer boy

Count such a summons less than joy?)
Our buskins on our feet we drew;   70
With mittened hands, and caps drawn low,
To guard our necks and ears from snow,
We cut the solid whiteness through.
And, where the drift was deepest, made
A tunnel walled and overlaid
With dazzling crystal: we had read
Of rare Aladdin's wondrous cave,
And to our own his name we gave,
With many a wish the luck were ours
To test his lamp's supernal powers.   80
We reached the barn with merry din,
And roused the prisoned brutes within.
The old horse thrust his long head out,
And grave with wonder gazed about;
The cock his lusty greeting said,
And forth his speckled harem led;
The oxen lashed their tails, and hooked,
And mild reproach of hunger looked;
The hornèd patriarch of the sheep,
Like Egypt's Amun roused from sleep,   90
Shook his sage head with gesture mute,
And emphasized with stamp of foot.

All day the gusty north-wind bore
The loosening drift its breath before;
Low circling round its southern zone,
The sun through dazzling snow-mist shone.
No church-bell lent its Christian tone
To the savage air, no social smoke
Curled over woods of snow-hung oak.
A solitude made more intense   100
By dreary-voicèd elements,
The shrieking of the mindless wind,
The moaning tree-boughs swaying blind,
And on the glass the unmeaning beat
Of ghostly finger-tips of sleet.
Beyond the circle of our hearth
No welcome sound of toil or mirth
Unbound the spell, and testified
Of human life and thought outside.
We minded that the sharpest ear   110

The buried brooklet could not hear,
The music of whose liquid lip
Had been to us companionship,
And, in our lonely life, had grown
To have an almost human tone.

As night drew on, and, from the crest
Of wooded knolls that ridged the west,
The sun, a snow-blown traveller, sank
From sight beneath the smothering bank,
We piled, with care, our nightly stack   120
Of wood against the chimney-back,—
The oaken log, green, huge, and thick,
And on its top the stout back-stick;
The knotty forestick laid apart,
And filled between with curious art
The ragged brush; then, hovering near,
We watched the first red blaze appear,
Heard the sharp crackle, caught the gleam
On whitewashed wall and sagging beam,
Until the old, rude-furnished room   130
Burst, flower-like, into rosy bloom;
While radiant with a mimic flame
Outside the sparkling drift became,
And through the bare-boughed lilac-tree
Our own warm hearth seemed blazing free.
The crane and pendant trammels showed,
The Turks' heads on the andirons glowed:
While childish fancy, prompt to tell
The meaning of the miracle,
Whispered the old rhyme: *"Under the tree,*   140
When fire outdoors burns merrily,
There the witches are making tea."
The moon above the eastern wood
Shone at its full; the hill-range stood
Transfigured in the silver flood,
Its blown snows flashing cold and keen,
Dead white, save where some sharp ravine
Took shadow, or the sombre green
Of hemlocks turned to pitchy black
Against the whiteness at their back.   150
For such a world and such a night
Most fitting that unwarming light,

Which only seemed where'er it fell
To make the coldness visible.

Shut in from all the world without,
We sat the clean-winged hearth about,
Content to let the north-wind roar
In baffled rage at pane and door,
While the red logs before us beat
The frost-line back with tropic heat;   160
And ever, when a louder blast
Shook beam and rafter as it passed,
The merrier up its roaring draught
The great throat of the chimney laughed;
The house-dog on his paws outspread
Laid to the fire his drowsy head,
The cat's dark silhouette on the wall
A couchant tiger's seemed to fall;
And, for the winter fireside meet,
Between the andirons' straddling feet,   170
The mug of cider simmered slow,
The apples sputtered in a row,
And, close at hand, the basket stood
With nuts from brown October's wood.

What matter how the night behaved?
What matter how the north-wind raved?
Blow high, blow low, not all its snow
Could quench our hearth-fire's ruddy glow.
O Time and Change!—with hair as gray
As was my sire's that winter day,   180
How strange it seems, with so much gone
Of life and love, to still live on!
Ah, brother! only I and thou
Are left of all that circle now,—
The dear home faces whereupon
That fitful firelight paled and shone.
Henceforward, listen as we will,
The voices of that hearth are still;
Look where we may, the wide earth o'er
Those lighted faces smile no more.   190
We tread the paths their feet have worn,
    We sit beneath their orchard trees,
    We hear, like them, the hum of bees

And rustle of the bladed corn;
We turn the pages that they read,
    Their written words we linger o'er,
But in the sun they cast no shade,
No voice is heard, no sign is made,
    No step is on the conscious floor!
Yet Love will dream, and Faith will trust   200
(Since He who knows our need is just)
That somehow, somewhere, meet we must.
Alas for him who never sees
The stars shine through his cypress-trees!
Who, hopeless, lays his dead away,
Nor looks to see the breaking day
Across the mournful marbles play!
Who hath not learned, in hours of faith,
    The truth to flesh and sense unknown,
That Life is ever lord of Death,   210
    And Love can never lose its own!

We sped the time with stories old,
Wrought puzzles out, and riddles told,
Or stammered from our school-book lore
"The Chief of Gambia's golden shore."
How often since, when all the land
Was clay in Slavery's shaping hand,
As if a far-blown trumpet stirred
The languorous sin-sick air, I heard:
"Does not the voice of reason cry,   220
    Claim the first right which Nature gave,
From the red scourge of bondage fly,
    Nor deign to live a burdened slave!"
Our father rode again his ride
On Memphremagog's wooded side;
Sat down again to moose and samp
In trapper's hut and Indian camp;
Lived o'er the old idyllic ease
Beneath St. Francois' hemlock-trees;
Again for him the moonlight shone   230
On Norman cap and bodiced zone;
Again he heard the violin play
Which led the village dance away,
And mingled in its merry whirl
The grandam and the laughing girl.

Or, nearer home, our steps he led
Where Salisbury's level marshes spread
   Mile-wide as flies the laden bee;
Where merry mowers, hale and strong,
Swept, scythe on scythe, their swaths along   240
   The low green prairies of the sea.
We shared the fishing off Boar's Head,
   And round the rocky Isles of Shoals
   The hake-broil on the drift-wood coals;
The chowder on the sand-beach made,
Dipped by the hungry, steaming hot,
With spoons of clam-shell from the pot.
We heard the tales of witchcraft old,
And dream and sign and marvel told
To sleepy listeners as they lay   250
Stretched idly on the salted hay,
Adrift along the winding shores,
When favoring breezes deigned to blow
The square sail of the gundelow
And idle lay the useless oars.

Our mother, while she turned her wheel
Or run the new-knit stocking-heel,
Told how the Indian hordes came down
At midnight on Cocheco town,
And how her own great-uncle bore   260
His cruel scalp-mark to fourscore.
Recalling, in her fitting phrase,
   So rich and picturesque and free
   (The common unrhymed poetry
Of simple life and country ways),
The story of her early days,—
She made us welcome to her home;
Old hearths grew wide to give us room;
We stole with her a frightened look
At the gray wizard's conjuring-book,   270
The fame whereof went far and wide
Through all the simple country-side;
We heard the hawks at twilight play,
The boat-horn on Piscataqua,
The loon's weird laughter far away;
We fished her little trout-brook, knew
What flowers in wood and meadow grew,

What sunny hillsides autumn-brown
She climbed to shake the ripe nuts down,
Saw where in sheltered cove and bay   280
The ducks' black squadron anchored lay,
And heard the wild-geese calling loud
Beneath the gray November cloud.

Then, haply, with a look more grave,
And soberer tone, some tale she gave
From painful Sewel's ancient tome,
Beloved in every Quaker home,
Of faith fire-winged by martyrdom,
Or Chalkley's Journal, old and quaint,—
Gentlest of skippers, rare sea-saint!—   290
Who, when the dreary calms prevailed,
And water-butt and bread-cask failed,
And cruel, hungry eyes pursued
His portly presence mad for food,
With dark hints muttered under breath
Of casting lots for life or death,
Offered, if Heaven withheld supplies,
To be himself the sacrifice.
Then, suddenly, as if to save
The good man from his living grave,   300
A ripple on the water grew,
A school of porpoise flashed in view.
"Take, eat," he said, "and be content;
These fishes in my stead are sent
By Him who gave the tangled ram
To spare the child of Abraham."

Our uncle, innocent of books,
Was rich in lore of fields and brooks,
The ancient teachers never dumb
Of Nature's unhoused lyceum.   310
In moons and tides and weather wise,
He read the clouds as prophecies,
And foul or fair could well divine,
By many an occult hint and sign,
Holding the cunning-warded keys
To all the woodcraft mysteries;
Himself to Nature's heart so near
That all her voices in his ear

Of beast or bird had meanings clear,
Like Apollonius of old,   320
Who knew the tales the sparrows told,
Or Hermes, who interpreted
What the sage cranes of Nilus said;
A simple, guileless, childlike man,
Content to live where life began;
Strong only on his native grounds,
The little world of sights and sounds
Whose girdle was the parish bounds,
Whereof his fondly partial pride
The common features magnified,   330
As Surrey hills to mountains grew
In White of Selborne's loving view,—
He told how teal and loon he shot,
And how the eagle's eggs he got,
The feats on pond and river done,
The prodigies of rod and gun;
Till, warming with the tales he told,
Forgotten was the outside cold,
The bitter wind unheeded blew,
From ripening corn the pigeons flew,   340
The partridge drummed i' the wood, the mink
Went fishing down the river-brink;
In fields with bean or clover gay,
The woodchuck, like a hermit gray,
  Peered from the doorway of his cell;
The muskrat plied the mason's trade,
And tier by tier his mud-walls laid;
And from the shagbark overhead
  The grizzled squirrel dropped his shell.

Next, the dear aunt, whose smile of cheer   350
And voice in dreams I see and hear—
The sweetest woman ever Fate
Perverse denied a household mate,
Who, lonely, homeless, not the less
Found peace in love's unselfishness,
And welcome whereso'er she went,
A calm and gracious element,
Whose presence seemed the sweet income
And womanly atmosphere of home—
Called up her girlhood memories,   360

The huskings and the apple-bees,
The sleigh-rides and the summer sails,
Weaving through all the poor details
And homespun warp of circumstance
A golden woof-thread of romance.
For well she kept her genial mood
And simple faith of maidenhood;
Before her still a cloud-land lay,
The mirage loomed across her way;
The morning dew, that dries so soon   370
With others, glistened at her noon;
Through years of toil and soil and care,
From glossy tress to thin gray hair,
All unprofaned she held apart
The virgin fancies of the heart.
Be shame to him of woman born
Who hath for such but thought of scorn.

There, too, our elder sister plied
Her evening task the stand beside;
A full, rich nature, free to trust,   380
Truthful and almost sternly just,
Impulsive, earnest, prompt to act,
And make her generous thought a fact,
Keeping with many a light disguise
The secret of self-sacrifice.
O heart sore-tried! thou hast the best,
That Heaven itself could give thee,—rest,
Rest from all bitter thoughts and things!
    How many a poor one's blessing went
    With thee beneath the low green tent   390
Whose curtain never outward swings!

As one who held herself a part
Of all she saw, and let her heart
    Against the household bosom lean,
Upon the motley-braided mat
Our youngest and our dearest sat,
Lifting her large, sweet, asking eyes,
    Now bathed in the unfading green
And holy peace of Paradise.
Oh, looking from some heavenly hill,   400
    Or from the shade of saintly palms,

Or silver reach of river calms,
Do those large eyes behold me still?
With me one little year ago:—
The chill weight of the winter snow
    For months upon her grave has lain;
And now, when summer south-winds blow
    And brier and harebell bloom again,
I tread the pleasant paths we trod,
I see the violet-sprinkled sod   410
Whereon she leaned, too frail and weak
The hillside flowers she loved to seek,
Yet following me where'er I went
With dark eyes full of love's content.
The birds are glad; the brier-rose fills
The air with sweetness; all the hills
Stretch green to June's unclouded sky;
But still I wait with ear and eye
For something gone which should be nigh,
A loss in all familiar things,   420
In flower that blooms, and bird that sings.
And yet, dear heart! remembering thee,
    Am I not richer than of old?
Safe in thy immortality,
    What change can reach the wealth I hold?
    What chance can mar the pearl and gold
Thy love hath left in trust with me?
And while in life's late afternoon,
    Where cool and long the shadows grow,
I walk to meet the night that soon   430
    Shall shape and shadow overflow,
I cannot feel that thou art far,
Since near at need the angels are;
And when the sunset gates unbar,
    Shall I not see thee waiting stand,
And, white against the evening star,
    The welcome of thy beckoning hand?

Brisk wielder of the birch and rule,
The master of the district school
Held at the fire his favored place,   440
Its warm glow lit a laughing face
Fresh-hued and fair, where scarce appeared
The uncertain prophecy of beard.

He teased the mitten-blinded cat,
Played cross-pins on my uncle's hat,
Sang songs, and told us what befalls
In classic Dartmouth's college halls.
Born the wild Northern hills among,
From whence his yeoman father wrung   450
By patient toil subsistence scant,
Not competence and yet not want,
He early gained the power to pay
His cheerful, self-reliant way;
Could doff at ease his scholar's gown
To peddle wares from town to town;
Or through the long vacation's reach
In lonely lowland districts teach,
Where all the droll experience found
At stranger hearths in boarding round,
The moonlit skater's keen delight,   460
The sleigh-drive through the frosty night,
The rustic-party, with its rough
Accompaniment of blind-man's-bluff,
And whirling-plate, and forfeits paid,
His winter task a pastime made.
Happy the snow-locked homes wherein
He tuned his merry violin,
Or played the athlete in the barn,
Or held the good dame's winding-yarn,
Or mirth-provoking versions told   470
Of classic legends rare and old,
Wherein the scenes of Greece and Rome
Had all the commonplace of home,
And little seemed at best the odds
'Twixt Yankee pedlers and old gods;
Where Pindus-born Arachthus took
The guise of any grist-mill brook,
And dread Olympus at his will
Became a huckleberry hill.

A careless boy that night he seemed;   480
    But at his desk he had the look
And air of one who wisely schemed,
    And hostage from the future took
    In trainèd thought and lore of book.
Large-brained, clear-eyed, of such as he

Shall Freedom's young apostles be,
Who, following in War's bloody trail,
Shall every lingering wrong assail:
All chains from limb and spirit strike,
Uplift the black and white alike;
Scatter before their swift advance
The darkness and the ignorance,
The pride, the lust, the squalid sloth,
Which nurtured Treason's monstrous growth,
Made murder pastime, and the hell
Of prison-torture possible;
The cruel lie of caste refute,
Old forms remould, and substitute
For Slavery's lash the freeman's will,
For blind routine, wise-handed skill;   500
A school-house plant on every hill,
Stretching in radiate nerve-lines thence
The quick wires of intelligence;
Till North and South together brought
Shall own the same electric thought,
In peace a common flag salute,
And, side by side in labor's free
And unresentful rivalry,
Harvest the fields wherein they fought.

Another guest that winter night   510
Flashed back from lustrous eyes the light.
Unmarked by time, and yet not young,
The honeyed music of her tongue
And words of meekness scarcely told
A nature passionate and bold,
Strong, self-concentred, spurning guide,
Its milder features dwarfed beside
Her unbent will's majestic pride,
She sat among us, at the best,
A not unfeared, half-welcome guest,   520
Rebuking with her cultured phrase
Our homeliness of words and ways.
A certain pard-like, treacherous grace
Swayed the lithe limbs and dropped the lash,
Lent the white teeth their dazzling flash;
And under low brows, black with night,
Rayed out at times a dangerous light;

The sharp heat-lightnings of her face
Presaging ill to him whom Fate
Condemned to share her love or hate.   530
A woman tropical, intense
In thought and act, in soul and sense,
She blended in a like degree
The vixen and the devotee,
Revealing with each freak or feint
    The temper of Petruchio's Kate,
The raptures of Siena's saint.
Her tapering hand and rounded wrist
Had facile power to form a fist;
The warm, dark languish of her eyes   540
Was never safe from wrath's surprise.
Brows saintly calm and lips devout
Knew every change of scowl and pout;
And the sweet voice had notes more high
And shrill for social battle-cry.

Since then what old cathedral town
Has missed her pilgrim staff and gown,
What convent-gate has held its lock
Against the challenge of her knock!
Through Smyrna's plague-hushed thoroughfares,   550
Up sea-set Malta's rocky stairs,
Gray olive slopes of hills that hem
    Thy tombs and shrines, Jerusalem,
Or startling on her desert throne
The crazy Queen of Lebanon
With claims fantastic as her own,
Her tireless feet have held their way;
And still, unrestful, bowed, and gray,
She watches under Eastern skies,
    With hope each day renewed and fresh,   560
    The Lord's quick coming in the flesh,
Whereof she dreams and prophesies!

Where'er her troubled path may be,
    The Lord's sweet pity with her go!
The outward wayward life we see,
    The hidden springs we may not know.
Nor is it given us to discern
    What threads the fatal sisters spun,

Through what ancestral years has run
The sorrow with the woman born,   570
What forged her cruel chain of moods,
What set her feet in solitudes,
    And held the love within her mute,
What mingled madness in the blood,
    A life-long discord and annoy,
    Waters of tears with oil of joy,
And hid within the folded bud
Perversities of flower and fruit.
It is not ours to separate
    The tangled skein of will and fate,   580
To show what metes and bounds should stand
Upon the soul's debatable land,
And between choice and Providence
Divide the circle of events;
But He who knows our frame is just,
Merciful and compassionate,
And full of sweet assurances
And hope for all the language is,
That He remembereth we are dust!

At last the great logs, crumbling low,   590
Sent out a dull and duller glow,
The bull's eye watch that hung in view,
Ticking its weary circuit through,
Pointed with mutely warning sign
Its black hand to the hour of nine.
That sign the pleasant circle broke:
My uncle ceased his pipe to smoke,
Knocked from its bowl the refuse gray,
And laid it tenderly away;
Then roused himself to safely cover   600
The dull red brands with ashes over.
And while, with care, our mother laid
The work aside, her steps she stayed
One moment, seeking to express
Her grateful sense of happiness
For food and shelter, warmth and health,
And love's contentment more than wealth,
With simple wishes (not the weak,
Vain prayers which no fulfilment seek,
But such as warm the generous heart,   610

O'er-prompt to do with Heaven its part)
That none might lack, that bitter night,
For bread and clothing, warmth and light.

Within our beds awhile we heard
The wind that round the gables roared,
With now and then a ruder shock,
Which made our very bedsteads rock.
We heard the loosened clapboards tost,
The board-nails snapping in the frost;
And on us, through the unplastered wall,   620
Felt the light sifted snow-flakes fall.
But sleep stole on, as sleep will do
When hearts are light and life is new;
Faint and more faint the murmurs grew,
Till in the summer-land of dreams
They softened to the sound of streams,
Low stir of leaves, and dip of oars,
And lapsing waves on quiet shores.

Next morn we wakened with the shout
Of merry voices high and clear;   630
And saw the teamsters drawing near
To break the drifted highways out.
Down the long hillside treading slow
We saw the half-buried oxen go,
Shaking the snow from heads uptost,
Their straining nostrils white with frost.
Before our door the straggling train
Drew up, an added team to gain.
The elders threshed their hands a-cold,
    Passed, with the cider-mug, their jokes   640
    From lip to lip; the younger folks
Down the loose snow-banks, wrestling, rolled,
Then toiled again the cavalcade
    O'er windy hill, through clogged ravine,
    And woodland paths that wound between
Low drooping pine-boughs winter-weighed.
From every barn a team afoot,
At every house a new recruit,
Where, drawn by Nature's subtlest law,
Haply the watchful young men saw   650
Sweet doorway pictures of the curls

And curious eyes of merry girls,
Lifting their hands in mock defence
Against the snow-ball's compliments,
And reading in each missive tost
The charm with Eden never lost.

We heard once more the sleigh-bells' sound;
   And, following where the teamsters led,
The wise old Doctor went his round,
Just pausing at our door to say,   *660*
In the brief autocratic way
Of one who, prompt at Duty's call,
Was free to urge her claim on all,
   That some poor neighbor sick abed
At night our mother's aid would need.
For, one in generous thought and deed,
   What mattered in the sufferer's sight
   The Quaker matron's inward light,
The Doctor's mail of Calvin's creed?
All hearts confess the saints elect   *670*
   Who, twain in faith, in love agree,
And melt not in an acid sect
   The Christian pearl of charity!

So days went on: a week had passed
Since the great world was heard from last.
The Almanac we studied o'er,
Read and reread our little store
Of books and pamphlets, scarce a score;
One harmless novel, mostly hid
From younger eyes, a book forbid,   *680*
And poetry (or good or bad,
A single book was all we had),
Where Ellwood's meek, drab-skirted Muse,
   A stranger to the heathen Nine,
   Sang, with a somewhat nasal whine,
The wars of David and the Jews.
At last the floundering carrier bore
The village paper to our door.
Lo! broadening outward as we read,
To warmer zones the horizon spread;   *690*
In panoramic length unrolled
We saw the marvels that it told.

Before us passed the painted Creeks,
   And daft McGregor on his raids
   In Costa Rica's everglades.
And up Taygetos winding slow
Rode Ypsilanti's Mainote Greeks,
A Turk's head at each saddle-bow!
Welcome to us its week-old news,
Its corner for the rustic Muse,   700
   Its monthly gauge of snow and rain,
Its record, mingling in a breath
The wedding bell and dirge of death:
Jest, anecdote, and love-lorn tale,
The latest culprit sent to jail;
Its hue and cry of stolen and lost,
Its vendue sales and goods at cost,
   And traffic calling loud for gain.
We felt the stir of hall and street,
The pulse of life that round us beat;   710
The chill embargo of the snow
Was melted in the genial glow;
Wide swung again our ice-locked door,
And all the world was ours once more!

Clasp, Angel of the backward look
   And folded wings of ashen gray
   And voice of echoes far away,
The brazen covers of thy book;
The weird palimpsest old and vast,
Wherein thou hid'st the spectral past;   720
Where, closely mingling, pale and glow
The characters of joy and woe;
The monographs of outlived years,
Or smile-illumed or dim with tears,
   Green hills of life that slope to death,
And haunts of home, whose vistaed trees
Shade off to mournful cypresses
   With the white amaranths underneath.
Even while I look, I can but heed
   The restless sands' incessant fall,   730
Importunate hours that hours succeed,
Each clamorous with its own sharp need,
   And duty keeping pace with all.
Shut down and clasp the heavy lids;

I hear again the voice that bids
The dreamer leave his dream midway
For larger hopes and graver fears;
Life greatens in these later years,
The century's aloe flowers to-day!
Yet, haply, in some lull of life,   740
Some Truce of God, which breaks its strife,
The worldling's eyes shall gather dew,
   Dreaming in throngful city ways
Of winter joys his boyhood knew;
And dear and early friends—the few
Who yet remain—shall pause to view
   These Flemish pictures of old days;
Sit with me by the homestead hearth,
And stretch the hands of memory forth
   To warm them at the wood-fire's blaze!   750
And thanks untraced to lips unknown
Shall greet me like the odors blown
From unseen meadows newly mown,
Or lilies floating in some pond,
Wood-fringed, the wayside gaze beyond;
The traveller owns the grateful sense
Of sweetness near, he knows not whence,
And, pausing, takes with forehead bare
The benediction of the air.

1866

OLIVER WENDELL HOLMES

(1809–1894)

A descendant of Anne Bradstreet, Oliver Wendell Holmes was the Beacon Hill Yankee *par excellence*, at home both in the genteel circles of Boston and in the polite society of Europe. He was born in Cambridge, Massachusetts, and had the education that was *de rigueur* for a young Brahmin. He attended Phillips Academy at Andover and then went to Harvard in the class of 1829, whose reunions he commemorated annually in poetry. After a year of law he traveled in Europe, studied medicine in Paris (1833–1835), and returned to Harvard in 1836 to receive his M. D. He was so assured of his station in the world that Europe never turned his head, as it did with many less culturally secure Americans: "The Boston State House," he once commented, "is the hub of the solar system."

Yet Holmes ridiculed the very snobbery with which he identified himself. A conservative aristocrat of democratic temperament, he was a spry and peppery little man whose urbane wit, broad, keen sense of humor, and scientific exactitude placed him in two worlds at once. On the one hand, he allied himself with the brisk rationalism of eighteenth-century style and attitudes rather than with contemporary romanticism, which he never fully understood; for literary models he turned to Campbell, Mackenzie, Pope, Sterne, and the Roman of the Enlightenment, Horace. On the other hand, he renounced the Calvinism of his home and schooling in order to champion a modern view of human responsibility. He took from his medical training a deterministic attitude toward sin, feeling that it was not something to be denounced from the pulpit, but something to be understood and treated by the geneticist and physician. His "medicated" novels—*Elsie Venner* (1861), *The Guardian Angel* (1867), and *A Mortal Antipathy* (1885)—are polemical defenses of this view. Though unsuccessful as novels, they are interesting as gropings toward modern psychological exploration.

After his return from Paris, Holmes set up general practice, which he disliked, in Boston. He abandoned private practice to become a brilliant professor of anatomy, first at Dartmouth College from 1838 to 1840, and then in 1847 at Harvard, where he remained for thirty-five years. From 1847 to 1853 he was Dean of the Harvard School of Medicine.

Although part of his fame rests upon his medical pioneering —he was held in great repute as a teacher and clinician and for his many medical publications, including *Homeopathy and Its Kindred Delusions* (1842) and the famous essay on "The Contagiousness of Puerperal Fever" (1843)—he is more widely remembered for his poetry and familiar essays. He attained national fame in 1830 with his "Old Ironsides," an irate patriotic defense of *The Constitution* that put a stop to the projected scrapping of that historic warship. In 1831–1832 he published two "Autocrat" essays in the *New England Magazine*, and after his return from Europe he published *Poems* (1836), *Urania* (1846), and *Poems* (1849). He named the *Atlantic Monthly* on its founding in 1857, and twenty-six years after the first publication of the "Autocrat" papers, he resumed them for the *Atlantic Monthly* with the *Autocrat of the Breakfast-Table* (collected in book form in 1859), which opened with the words, "I was just going to say when I was interrupted. . . ." As an active member of the Saturday Club, a group recruited from the *Atlantic Monthly* people for good talk and good companionship, he collected his *Monthly* contributions in *The Professor at the Breakfast-Table* (1859), *The Poet at the Breakfast-Table* (1872), and *Over the Tea-Cups* (1890). He also wrote biography, producing studies of John Lothrop Motley (1878), Ralph Waldo Emerson (1885), and Henry Jacob Bigelow (1891).

As a poet he wrote gracious and amusing verse. Although some of it is still good fun to read, it is mostly *vers de société* and *vers d'occasion* of an ephemeral quality that marks him as a minor literary figure. At a time when Boston and the nation were undergoing the strenuous social changes that a writer like Whitman understood and celebrated, Holmes believed that culture could be preserved by the philanthropic establishment of

museums and music societies. The strength of his Brahmin identity, which gave him an ordered world, also limited his participation in the major literature that sounded the broad movements of national development.

In addition to the titles mentioned above, some of his works
are *Songs in Many Keys* (1862); *Soundings from the Atlantic*
(1864); *Humorous Poems* (1865); *Songs and Poems of the
Class of Eighteen Hundred and Twenty-nine: Third Edition*
(1868); *Mechanism in Thought and Morals* (1871); *Songs of
Many Seasons, 1862–1874* (1875); *Poetical Works* (1877);
The Iron Gate and Other Poems (1880); and *Medical Essays
1842–1882* (1883).

Editions and accounts of the man and his works are to be
found in W. S. Kennedy, *Oliver Wendell Holmes* (1883); E. E.
Brown, *Life of Oliver Wendell Holmes* (1884); *The Writings of
Oliver Wendell Holmes,* 13 vols. (1891); *The Works of Oliver
Wendell Holmes,* 13 vols. (1892); H. E. Scudder, ed., *The
Complete Poetical Works of Oliver Wendell Holmes* (1895);
J. E. A. Smith, *The Poet among the Hills* (1895); J. T. Morse,
Jr., *The Life and Letters of Oliver Wendell Holmes* (1896);
W. L. Schroeder, *Oliver Wendell Holmes* (1909); A. H. Strong,
American Poets and Their Theology (1916); E. E. Emerson,
The Early Years of the Saturday Club (1918); M. A. DeW.
Howe, *Holmes of the Breakfast-Table* (1937); C. P. Obendorf,
The Psychiatric Novels of Oliver Wendell Holmes (1943); E. M.
Tilton, *Amiable Autocrat* (1947); A. C. Kern, "Dr. Oliver
Wendell Holmes Today," *University of Kansas City Review,*
XIV (1948); G. E. Hamilton, *Oliver Wendell Holmes* (1949);
E. M. Tilton and T. F. Currier, *Bibliography of Oliver Wendell
Holmes* (1953); L. Dexter, "A Vanished America in Stereo,"
American Heritage, XII (1961); M. R. Small, *Oliver Wendell
Holmes* (1962); K. P. Wentersdorf, "The Underground Work-
shop of Oliver Wendell Holmes," *American Literature,* XXXV
(1963); and E. M. Tilton, "Holmes and His Critic Motley,"
American Literature, XXXVI (1965).

My Aunt

My aunt! my dear unmarried aunt!
  Long years have o'er her flown;
Yet still she strains the aching clasp
  That binds her virgin zone;
I know it hurts her,—though she looks
  As cheerful as she can;
Her waist is ampler than her life,
  For life is but a span.

My aunt! my poor deluded aunt!
   Her hair is almost gray;   10
Why will she train that winter curl
   In such a spring-like way?
How can she lay her glasses down,
   And say she reads as well,
When, through a double convex lens,
   She just makes out to spell?

Her father—grandpapa! forgive
   This erring lip its smiles—
Vowed she should make the finest girl
   Within a hundred miles;   20
He sent her to a stylish school;
   'Twas in her thirteenth June;
And with her, as the rules required,
   "Two towels and a spoon."

They braced my aunt against a board,
   To make her straight and tall;
They laced her up, they starved her down,
   To make her light and small;
They pinched her feet, they singed her hair,
   They screwed it up with pins;—
O never mortal suffered more
   In penance for her sins.

So, when my precious aunt was done,
   My grandsire brought her back;
(By daylight, lest some rabid youth
   Might follow on the track;)
"Ah!" said my grandsire, as he shook
   Some powder in his pan,
"What could this lovely creature do
   Against a desperate man!"   40

Alas! nor chariot, nor barouche,
   Nor bandit cavalcade,
Tore from the trembling father's arms
   His all-accomplished maid.
For her how happy had it been!
   And Heaven had spared to me

To see one sad, ungathered rose
  On my ancestral tree.

1831

The Last Leaf

I saw him once before,
As he passed by the door,
   And again
The pavement stones resound
As he totters o'er the ground
   With his cane.

They say that in his prime,
Ere the pruning-knife of Time
   Cut him down,
Not a better man was found   10
By the Crier on his round
   Through the town.

But now he walks the streets,
And he looks at all he meets
   Sad and wan,
And he shakes his feeble head,
That it seems as if he said,
   "They are gone."

The mossy marbles rest
On the lips that he has prest   20
   In their bloom,
And the names he loved to hear
Have been carved for many a year
   On the tomb.

My grandmamma has said—
Poor old lady, she is dead
   Long ago—
That he had a Roman nose,
And his cheek was like a rose
   In the snow.   30

But now his nose is thin,
And it rests upon his chin
   Like a staff,
And a crook is in his back,
And a melancholy crack
   In his laugh.

I know it is a sin
For me to sit and grin
   At him here;
But the old three-cornered hat,   40
And the breeches, and all that,
   Are so queer!

And if I should live to be
The last leaf upon the tree
   In the spring,
Let them smile, as I do now,
At the old forsaken bough
   Where I cling.

                            1831

The Chambered Nautilus

This is the ship of pearl, which, poets feign,
   Sails the unshadowed main,—
     The venturous bark that flings
On the sweet summer wind its purpled wings
In gulfs enchanted, where the Siren sings,
   And coral reefs lie bare,
Where the cold sea-maids rise to sun their streaming hair.

Its webs of living gauze no more unfurl;
   Wrecked is the ship of pearl!
     And every chambered cell,   10
Where its dim dreaming life was wont to dwell,
As the frail tenant shaped his growing shell,
   Before thee lies revealed,—
Its irised ceiling rent, its sunless crypt unsealed!

Year after year beheld the silent toil
  That spread his lustrous coil;
  Still, as the spiral grew,
He left the past year's dwelling for the new,
Stole with soft step its shining archway through,
  Built up its idle door,   20
Stretched in his last-found home, and knew the old no more.

Thanks for the heavenly message brought by thee,
  Child of the wandering sea,
  Cast from her lap, forlorn!
From thy dead lips a clearer note is born
Than ever Triton blew from wreathèd horn!
  While on mine ear it rings,
Through the deep caves of thought I hear a voice that
    sings:—

Build thee more stately mansions, O my soul,
  As the swift seasons roll!   30
  Leave thy low-vaulted past!
Let each new temple, nobler than the last,
Shut thee from heaven with a dome more vast,
  Till thou at length art free,
Leaving thine outgrown shell by life's unresting sea!

                                                          1858

The Deacon's Masterpiece

or, The Wonderful "One-Hoss Shay": A Logical Story

Have you heard of the wonderful one-hoss shay,
That was built in such a logical way
It ran a hundred years to a day,
And then, of a sudden, it—ah, but stay,
I'll tell you what happened without delay,
Scaring the parson into fits,
Frightening people out of their wits,—
Have you ever heard of that, I say?

Seventeen hundred and fifty-five.
Georgius Secundus was then alive,—   10

Snuffy old drone from the German hive.
That was the year when Lisbon-town
Saw the earth open and gulp her down,
And Braddock's army was done so brown,
Left without a scalp to its crown.
It was on the terrible Earthquake-day
That the Deacon finished the one-hoss shay.

Now in building of chaises, I tell you what,
There is always *somewhere* a weakest spot,—
In hub, tire, felloe, in spring or thill,   20
In panel, or crossbar, or floor, or sill,
In screw, bolt, thoroughbrace,—lurking still,
Find it somewhere you must and will,—
Above or below, or within or without,—
And that's the reason, beyond a doubt,
That a chaise *breaks down,* but doesn't *wear out.*
But the Deacon swore (as Deacons do,
With an "I dew vum," or an "I tell *yeou*")
He would build one shay to beat the taown
'N' the keountry 'n' all the kentry raoun';   30
It should be so built that it *couldn'* break daown;
"Fur," said the Deacon, " 't's mighty plain
Thut the weakes' place mus' stan' the strain;
'N' the way t' fix it, uz I maintain,
　Is only jest
T' make that place uz strong uz the rest."

So the Deacon inquired of the village folk
Where he could find the strongest oak,
That couldn't be split nor bent nor broke,—
That was for spokes and floors and sills;   40
He sent for lancewood to make the thills;
The crossbars were ash, from the straightest trees,
The panels of white-wood, that cuts like cheese,
But lasts like iron for things like these;
The hubs of logs from the "Settler's ellum,"—
Last of its timber,—they couldn't sell 'em,

Never an axe had seen their chips,
And the wedges flew from between their lips,
Their blunt ends frizzled like celery-tips;
Step and prop-iron, bolt and screw,   50

Spring, tire, axle, and linchpin too,
Steel of the finest, bright and blue;
Thoroughbrace bison-skin, thick and wide;
Boot, top, dasher, from tough old hide
Found in the pit when the tanner died.
That was the way he "put her through."
"There!" said the Deacon, "naow she'll dew!"

Do! I tell you, I rather guess
She was a wonder, and nothing less!
Colts grew horses, beards turned gray,   60
Deacon and deaconess dropped away,
Children and grandchildren—where were they?
But there stood the stout old one-hoss shay
As fresh as on Lisbon-earthquake-day!

EIGHTEEN HUNDRED;—it came and found
The Deacon's masterpiece strong and sound.
Eighteen hundred increased by ten;—
"Hahnsum kerridge" they called it then.
Eighteen hundred and twenty came;—
Running as usual; much the same.   70
Thirty and forty at last arrive,
And then come fifty, and FIFTY-FIVE.

Little of all we value here
Wakes on the morn of its hundredth year
Without both feeling and looking queer.
In fact, there's nothing that keeps its youth,
So far as I know, but a tree and truth.
(This is a moral that runs at large;
Take it.—You're welcome.—No extra charge.)

FIRST OF NOVEMBER,—the Earthquake-day,—   80
There are traces of age in the one-hoss shay,
A general flavor of mild decay,
But nothing local, as one may say.
There couldn't be,—for the Deacon's art
Had made it so like in every part
That there wasn't a chance for one to start.
For the wheels were just as strong as the thills,
And the floor was just as strong as the sills,
And the panels just as strong as the floor,

And the whipple-tree neither less nor more, 90
And the back crossbar as strong as the fore,
And spring and axle and hub *encore.*
And yet, *as a whole,* it is past a doubt
In another hour it will be *worn out!*

First of November, 'Fifty-five!
This morning the parson takes a drive.
Now, small boys, get out of the way!
Here comes the wonderful one-hoss shay,
Drawn by a rat-tailed, ewe-necked bay.
"Huddup!" said the parson.—Off went they. 100
The parson was working his Sunday's text,—
Had got to *fifthly,* and stopped perplexed
At what the—Moses—was coming next.
All at once the horse stood still,
Close by the meet'n'-house on the hill.
First a shiver, and then a thrill,
Then something decidedly like a spill,—
And the parson was sitting upon a rock,
At half past nine by the meet'n'-house clock—
Just the hour of the Earthquake shock! 110
What do you think the parson found,
When he got up and stared around?
The poor old chaise in a heap or mound,
As if it had been to the mill and ground!
You see, of course, if you're not a dunce,
How it went to pieces all at once,—
All at once, and nothing first,—
Just as bubbles do when they burst.

End of the wonderful one-hoss shay.
Logic is logic. That's all I say. 120

1858

Dorothy Q.

A Family Portrait

Grandmother's mother: her age, I guess,
Thirteen summers, or something less;
Girlish bust, but womanly air;

Smooth, square forehead with up-rolled hair,
Lips that lover has never kissed;
Taper fingers and slender wrist;
Hanging sleeves of stiff brocade;
So they painted the little maid.

On her hand a parrot green
Sits unmoving and broods serene.   10
Hold up the canvas full in view—
Look! there's a rent the light shines through,
Dark with a century's fringe of dust—
That was a Red-Coat's rapier-thrust!
Such is the tale the lady old,
Dorothy's daughter's daughter, told.

Who the painter was none may tell—
One whose best was not over well;
Hard and dry, it must be confessed,
Flat as a rose that has long been pressed;   20
Yet in her cheek the hues are bright,
Dainty colors of red and white,
And in her slender shape are seen
Hint and promise of stately mien.

Look not on her with eyes of scorn—
Dorothy Q. was a lady born!
Ay! since the galloping Normans came,
England's annals have known her name;
And still to the three-hilled rebel town
Dear is that ancient name's renown,   30
For many a civic wreath they won,
The youthful sire and the gray-haired son.

O Damsel Dorothy! Dorothy Q.!
Strange is the gift that I owe to you;
Such a gift as never a king
Save to daughter or son might bring,—
All my tenure of heart and hand,
All my title to house and land;
Mother and sister and child and wife
And joy and sorrow and death and life!   40

What if a hundred years ago
Those close-shut lips had answered No,

When forth the tremulous question came
That cost the maiden her Norman name,
And under the folds that look so still
The bodice swelled with the bosom's thrill?
Should I be I, or would it be
One tenth another, to nine tenths me?

Soft is the breath of a maiden's Yes:
Not the light gossamer stirs with less; 50
But never a cable that holds so fast
Through all the battles of wave and blast,
And never an echo of speech or song
That lives in the babbling air so long!
There were tones in the voice that whispered then
You may hear to-day in a hundred men.

O lady and lover, how faint and far
Your images hover—and here we are,
Solid and stirring in flesh and bone—
Edward's and Dorothy's—all their own— 60
A goodly record for Time to show
Of a syllable spoken so long ago!—
Shall I bless you, Dorothy, or forgive
For the tender whisper that bade me live?

It shall be a blessing, my little maid!
I will heal the stab of the Red-Coat's blade,
And freshen the gold of the tarnished frame,
And gild with a rhyme your household name;
So you shall smile on us brave and bright
As first you greeted the morning's light, 70
And live untroubled by woes and fears
Through a second youth of a hundred years.

1875

FROM

The Autocrat of the Breakfast-Table

I

I was just going to say, when I was interrupted, that one
of the many ways of classifying minds is under the heads

of arithmetical and algebraical intellects. All economical and practical wisdom is an extension or variation of the following arithmetical formula: $2 + 2 = 4$. Every philosophical proposition has the more general character of the expression $a + b = c$. We are mere operatives, empirics, and egotists, until we learn to think in letters instead of figures.

They all stared. There is a divinity student lately come among us to whom I commonly address remarks like the above, allowing him to take a certain share in the conversation, so far as assent or pertinent questions are involved. He abused his liberty on this occasion by presuming to say that Leibnitz had the same observation.—No, sir, I replied, he has not. But he said a mighty good thing about mathematics, that sounds something like it, and you found it, *not in the original,* but quoted by Dr. Thomas Reid. I will tell the company what he did say, one of these days.

—— If I belong to a Society of Mutual Admiration?— I blush to say that I do not at this present moment. I once did, however. It was the first association to which I ever heard the term applied; a body of scientific young men in a great foreign city who admired their teacher, and to some extent each other. Many of them deserved it; they have become famous since. It amuses me to hear the talk of one of those beings described by Thackeray—

'Letters four do form his name'—

about a social development which belongs to the very noblest stage of civilization. All generous companies of artists, authors, philanthropists, men of science, are, or ought to be, Societies of Mutual Admiration. A man of genius, or any kind of superiority, is not debarred from admiring the same quality in another, nor the other from returning his admiration. They may even associate together and continue to think highly of each other. And so of a dozen such men, if any one place is fortunate enough to hold so many. The being referred to above assumes several false premises. First, that men of talent necessarily hate each other. Secondly, that intimate knowledge or habitual association destroys our admiration of persons whom we esteemed highly at a distance. Thirdly, that a circle of clever fellows, who meet together to dine and have a good time, have signed a constitutional compact to glorify themselves and to put down him and the fraction of the human race not belonging to their number. Fourthly, that it is an outrage that he is not asked to join them.

Here the company laughed a good deal, and the old gentleman who sits opposite said, 'That's it! that's it!'

I continued, for I was in the talking vein. As to clever people's hating each other, I think *a little* extra talent does sometimes make people jealous. They become irritated by perpetual attempts and failures, and it hurts their tempers and dispositions. Unpretending mediocrity is good, and genius is glorious; but a weak flavor of genius in an essentially common person is detestable. It spoils the grand neutrality of a commonplace character, as the rinsings of an unwashed wine-glass spoil a draught of fair water. No wonder the poor fellow we spoke of, who always belongs to this class of slightly flavored mediocrities, is puzzled and vexed by the strange sight of a dozen men of capacity working and playing together in harmony. He and his fellows are always fighting. With them familiarity naturally breeds contempt. If they ever praise each other's bad drawings, or broken-winded novels, or spavined verses, nobody ever supposed it was from admiration; it was simply a contract between themselves and a publisher or dealer.

If the Mutuals have really nothing among them worth admiring, that alters the question. But if they are men with noble powers and qualities, let me tell you, that, next to youthful love and family affections, there is no human sentiment better than that which unites the Societies of Mutual Admiration. And what would literature or art be without such associations? Who can tell what we owe to the Mutual Admiration Society of which Shakespeare, and Ben Jonson, and Beaumont and Fletcher were members? Or to that of which Addison and Steele formed the centre, and which gave us the Spectator? Or to that where Johnson, and Goldsmith, and Burke, and Reynolds, and Beauclerk, and Boswell, most admiring among all admirers, met together? Was there any great harm in the fact that the Irvings and Paulding wrote in company? or any unpardonable cabal in the literary union of Verplanck and Bryant and Sands, and as many more as they chose to associate with them?

The poor creature does not know what he is talking about, when he abuses this noblest of institutions. Let him inspect its mysteries through the knot-hole he has secured, but not use that orifice as a medium for his popgun. Such a society is the crown of a literary metropolis; if a town has not material for it, and spirit and good feeling enough to organize it, it is a mere caravansary, fit for a man of genius to lodge in, but not to live in. Foolish people hate and dread and envy such an association of men of varied powers and influence, because it is lofty, serene, impregnable, and, by the necessity of the case, exclusive. Wise ones are prouder of the title M.S.M.A. than of all their other honors put together.

——— All generous minds have a horror of what are commonly called 'facts.' They are the brute beasts of the intellectual domain. Who does not know fellows that always have an ill-conditioned fact or two which they lead after them into decent company like so many bull-dogs, ready to let them slip at every ingenious suggestion, or convenient generalization, or pleasant fancy? I allow no 'facts' at this table. What! Because bread is good and wholesome and necessary and nourishing, shall you thrust a crumb into my windpipe while I am talking? Do not these muscles of mine represent a hundred loaves of bread? and is not my thought the abstract of ten thousand of these crumbs of truth with which you would choke off my speech?

(The above remark must be conditioned and qualified for the vulgar mind. The reader will of course understand the precise amount of seasoning which must be added to it before he adopts it as one of the axioms of his life. The speaker disclaims all responsibility for its abuse in incompetent hands.)

This business of conversation is a very serious matter. There are men whom it weakens one to talk with an hour more than a day's fasting would do. Mark this which I am going to say, for it is as good as a working professional man's advice, and costs you nothing: It is better to lose a pint of blood from your veins than to have a nerve tapped. Nobody measures your nervous force as it runs away, nor bandages your brain and marrow after the operation.

There are men of *esprit* who are excessively exhausting to some people. They are the talkers who have what may be called *jerky* minds. Their thoughts do not run in the natural order of sequence. They say bright things on all possible subjects, but their zigzags rack you to death. After a jolting half-hour with one of these jerky companions, talking with a dull friend affords great relief. It is like taking the cat in your lap after holding a squirrel.

What a comfort a dull but kindly person is, to be sure, at times! A ground-glass shade over a gas-lamp does not bring more solace to our dazzled eyes than such a one to our minds.

'Do not dull people bore you?' said one of the lady-boarders,—the same who sent me her autograph-book last week with a request for a few original stanzas, not remembering that 'The Pactolian' pays me five dollars a line for every thing I write in its columns.

'Madam,' said I (she and the century were in their teens together), 'all men are bores, except when we want them. There never was but one man whom I would trust with my latch-key.'

'Who might that favored person be?'

'Zimmermann.'

—— The men of genius that I fancy most have erectile heads like the cobra-di-capello. You remember what they tell of William Pinkney, the great pleader; how in his eloquent paroxysms the veins of his neck would swell and his face flush and his eyes glitter, until he seemed on the verge of apoplexy. The hydraulic arrangements for supplying the brain with blood are only second in importance to its own organization. The bulbous-headed fellows who steam well when they are at work are the men that draw big audiences and give us marrowy books and pictures. It is a good sign to have one's feet grow cold when he is writing. A great writer and speaker once told me that he often wrote with his feet in hot water; but for this, *all* his blood would have run into his head, as the mercury sometimes withdraws into the ball of a thermometer.

—— You don't suppose that my remarks made at this table are like so many postage-stamps, do you,—each to be only once uttered? If you do, you are mistaken. He must be a poor creature who does not often repeat himself. Imagine the author of the excellent piece of advice, 'Know thyself,' never alluding to that sentiment again during the course of a protracted existence! Why, the truths a man carries about with him are his tools; and do you think a carpenter is bound to use the same plane but once to smooth a knotty board with, or to hang up his hammer after it has driven its first nail? I shall never repeat a conversation, but an idea often. I shall use the same types when I like, but not commonly the same stereotypes. A thought is often original, though you have uttered it a hundred times. It has come to you over a new route, by a new and express train of associations.

Sometimes, but rarely, one may be caught making the same speech twice over, and yet be held blameless. Thus, a certain lecturer, after performing in an inland city, where dwells a *littératrice* of note, was invited to meet her and others over the social teacup. She pleasantly referred to his many wanderings in his new occupation. 'Yes,' he replied, 'I am like the Huma, the bird that never lights, being always in the cars, as he is always on the wing.'—Years elapsed. The lecturer visited the same place once more for the same purpose. Another social cup after the lecture, and a second meeting with the distinguished lady. 'You are constantly going from place to place,' she said. 'Yes,' he answered, 'I am like the Huma,'—and finished the sentence as before.

What horrors, when it flashed over him that he had made this fine speech, word for word, twice over! Yet it was not true, as the lady might perhaps have fairly inferred, that he had embellished his conversation with the Huma daily during that whole interval of years. On the contrary, he had never once thought of the odious fowl until the recurrence of precisely the same circumstances brought up precisely the same idea. He ought to have been proud of the accuracy of his mental adjustments. Given certain factors, and a sound brain should always evolve the same fixed product with the certainty of Babbage's calculating machine.

—— What a satire, by the way, is that machine on the mere mathematician! A Frankenstein-monster, a thing without brains and without heart, too stupid to make a blunder; which turns out results like a corn-sheller, and never grows any wiser or better, though it grind a thousand bushels of them!

I have an immense respect for a man of talents *plus* 'the mathematics.' But the calculating power alone should seem to be the least human of qualities, and to have the smallest amount of reason in it; since a machine can be made to do the work of three or four calculators, and better than any one of them. Sometimes I have been troubled that I had not a deeper intuitive apprehension of the relations of numbers. But the triumph of the cyphering hand-organ has consoled me. I always fancy I can hear the wheels clicking in a calculator's brain. The power of dealing with numbers is a kind of 'detached lever' arrangement, which may be put into a mighty poor watch. I suppose it is about as common as the power of moving the ears voluntarily, which is a moderately rare endowment.

—— Little localized powers, and little narrow streaks of specialized knowledge, are things men are very apt to be conceited about. Nature is very wise; but for this encouraging principle how many small talents and little accomplishments would be neglected! Talk about conceit as much as you like, it is to human character what salt is to the ocean; it keeps it sweet, and renders it endurable. Say rather it is like the natural unguent of the sea-fowl's plumage, which enables him to shed the rain that falls on him and the wave in which he dips. When one has had *all* his conceit taken out of him, when he has lost *all* his illusions, his feathers will soon soak through, and he will fly no more.

'So you admire conceited people, do you?' said the young lady who has come to the city to be finished off for —the duties of life.

I am afraid you do not study logic at your school, my dear. It does not follow that I wish to be pickled in brine because I like a salt-water plunge at Nahant. I say that conceit is just as natural a thing to human minds as a centre is to a circle. But little-minded people's thoughts move in such small circles that five minutes' conversation gives you an arc long enough to determine their whole curve. An arc in the movement of a large intellect does not sensibly differ from a straight line. Even if it have the third vowel as its centre, it does not soon betray it. The highest thought, that is, is the most seemingly impersonal; it does not obviously imply any individual centre.

Audacious self-esteem, with good ground for it, is always imposing. What resplendent beauty that must have been which could have authorized Phryne to 'peel' in the way she did! What fine speeches are those two: *'Non omnis moriar'* [I shall not die altogether], and 'I have taken all knowledge to be my province'! Even in common people, conceit has the virtue of making them cheerful; the man who thinks his wife, his baby, his house, his horse, his dog, and himself severally unequalled, is almost sure to be a good-humored person, though liable to be tedious at times.

—— What are the great faults of conversation? Want of ideas, want of words, want of manners, are the principal ones, I suppose you think. I don't doubt it, but I will tell you what I have found spoil more good talks than anything else;—long arguments on special points between people who differ on the fundamental principles upon which these points depend. No men can have satisfactory relations with each other until they have agreed on certain *ultimata* of belief not to be disturbed in ordinary conversation, and unless they have sense enough to trace the secondary questions depending upon these ultimate beliefs to their source. In short, just as a written constitution is essential to the best social order, so a code of finalities is a necessary condition of profitable talk between two persons. Talking is like playing on the harp; there is as much in laying the hand on the strings to stop their vibrations as in twanging them to bring out their music.

—— Do you mean to say the punquestion is not clearly settled in your minds? Let me lay down the law upon the subject. Life and language are alike sacred. Homicide and *verbicide*—that is, violent treatment of a word with fatal results to its legitimate meaning, which is its life—are alike forbidden. Manslaughter, which is the meaning of the one, is the same as man's laughter, which is the end of the other. A pun is *primâ facie* an insult to the person you are talking with. It implies utter indifference to, or sublime contempt for his remarks, no matter how serious. I speak of total depravity, and one says all that is written on the subject is deep raving. I have committed my self-respect by talking with such a person. I should like to commit him, but cannot, because he is a nuisance. Or I speak of geological convulsions, and he asks me what was the cosine of Noah's ark; also, whether the Deluge was not a deal huger than any modern inundation.

A pun does not commonly justify a blow in return. But if a blow were given for such cause, and death ensued, the jury would be judges both of the facts and of the pun, and might, if the latter were of an aggravated character, return a verdict of justifiable homicide. Thus, in a case lately decided before Miller, J., Doe presented Roe a subscription paper, and urged the claims of suffering humanity. Roe replied by asking, When charity was like a top? It was in evidence that Doe preserved a dignified silence. Roe then said, 'When it begins to hum.' Doe then—and not till then —struck Roe, and his head happening to hit a bound volume of the *Monthly Rag-bag* and *Stolen Miscellany,* intense mortification ensued, with a fatal result. The chief laid down his notions of the law to his brother justices, who unanimously replied, 'Jest so.' The chief rejoined, that no man should jest so without being punished for it, and charged for the prisoner, who was acquitted, and the pun ordered to be burned by the sheriff. The bound volume was forfeited as a deodand, but not claimed.

People that make puns are like wanton boys that put coppers on the railroad tracks. They amuse themselves and other children, but their little trick may upset a freight train of conversation for the sake of a battered witticism.

I will thank you, B.F., to bring down two books, of which I will mark the places on this slip of paper. (While he is gone, I may say that this boy, our landlady's youngest, is called BENJAMIN FRANKLIN, after the celebrated philosopher of that name. A highly merited compliment.)

I wish to refer to two eminent authorities. Now be so good as to listen. The great moralist says: 'To trifle with the vocabulary which is the vehicle of social intercourse is to tamper with the currency of human intelligence. He who would violate the sanctities of his mother tongue would invade the recesses of the paternal till without remorse, and repeat the banquet of Saturn without an indigestion.'

And, once more, listen to the historian. 'The Puritans hated puns. The Bishops were notoriously addicted to them. The Lords Temporal carried them to the verge of license. Majesty itself must have its Royal quibble. "Ye be burly, my Lord of Burleigh," said Queen Elizabeth, "but ye shall make less stir in our realm than my Lord of Leicester." The gravest wisdom and the highest breeding lent their sanction to the practice. Lord Bacon playfully declared himself a descendant of 'Og, the King of Bashan. Sir Philip Sidney, with his last breath, reproached the soldier who brought him water, for wasting a casqueful upon a dying man. A courtier, who saw *Othello* performed at the Globe Theatre, remarked, that the blackamoor was a brute, and not a man. "Thou hast reason," replied a great Lord, "according to Plato his saying; for this be a two-legged animal *with* feathers." The fatal habit became universal. The language was corrupted. The infection spread to the national conscience. Political double-dealings naturally grew out of verbal double meanings. The teeth of the new dragon were sown by the Cadmus who introduced the alphabet of equivocation. What was levity in the time of the Tudors grew to regicide and revolution in the age of the Stuarts.'

Who was that boarder that just whispered something about the Macaulay-flowers of literature?—There was a dead silence.—I said calmly, I shall henceforth consider any interruption by a pun as a hint to change my boarding-house. Do not plead my example. If *I* have used any such, it has been only as a Spartan father would show up a drunken helot. We have done with them.

——— If a logical mind ever found out anything with its logic?—I should say that its most frequent work was to build a *pons asinorum* [bridge of the asses] over chasms which shrewd people can bestride without such a structure. You can hire logic, in the shape of a lawyer, to prove anything that you want to prove. You can buy treatises to show that Napoleon never lived, and that no battle of Bunker-hill was ever fought. The great minds are those with a wide span, which couple truth related to, but far removed from, each other.

Logicians carry the surveyor's chain over the track of which these are the true explorers. I value a man mainly for his primary relations with truth, as I understand truth,—not for any secondary artifice in handling his ideas. Some of the sharpest men in argument are notoriously unsound in judgment. I should not trust the counsel of a clever debater, any more than that of a good chess-player. Either may of course advise wisely, but not necessarily because he wrangles or plays well.

The old gentleman who sits opposite got his hand up, as a pointer lifts his forefoot, at the expression, 'his relations with truth, as I understand truth,' and when I had done, sniffed audibly, and said I talked like a transcendentalist. For his part, common sense was good enough for him.

Precisely so, my dear sir, I replied; common sense, *as*

you understand it. We all have to assume a standard of judgment in our own minds, either of things or persons. A man who is willing to take another's opinion has to exercise his judgment in the choice of whom to follow, which is often as nice a matter as to judge of things for one's self. On the whole, I had rather judge men's minds by comparing their thoughts with my own, than judge of thoughts by knowing who utter them. I must do one or the other. It does not follow, of course, that I may not recognize another man's thoughts as broader and deeper than my own; but that does not necessarily change my opinion, otherwise this would be at the mercy of every superior mind that held a different one. How many of our most cherished beliefs are like those drinking-glasses of the ancient pattern, that serve us well so long as we keep them in our hand, but spill all if we attempt to set them down! I have sometimes compared conversation to the Italian game of *mora,* in which one player lifts his hand with so many fingers extended, and the other gives the number if he can. I show my thought, another his; if they agree, well; if they differ, we find the largest common factor, if we can, but at any rate avoid disputing about remainders and fractions, which is to real talk what tuning an instrument is to playing on it.

—— What if, instead of talking this morning, I should read you a copy of verses, with critical remarks by the author? Any of the company can retire that like.

Album Verses

When Eve had led her lord away,
    And Cain had killed his brother,
The stars and flowers, the poets say,
    Agreed with one another

To cheat the cunning tempter's art,
    And teach the race its duty,
By keeping on its wicked heart
    Their eyes of light and beauty.

A million sleepless lids, they say,
    Will be at least a warning;
And so the flowers would watch by day,
    The stars from eve to morning.

On hill and prairie, field and lawn,
  Their dewy eyes upturning,
The flowers still watch from reddening dawn
  Till western skies are burning.

Alas! each hour of daylight tells
  A tale of shame so crushing,
That some turn white as sea-bleached shells,
  And some are always blushing.

But when the patient stars look down
  On all their light discovers,
The traitor's smile, the murderer's frown,
  The lips of lying lovers,

They try to shut their saddening eyes,
  And in the vain endeavor
We see them twinkling in the skies,
  And so they wink for ever.

What do *you* think of these verses, my friends?—Is that
piece an impromptu? said my landlady's daughter. (Æt.
19+. Tender-eyed blonde. Long ringlets. Cameo pin. Gold
pencil-case on a chain. Locket. Bracelet. Album. Autograph-book. Accordion. Reads Byron, Tupper, and Syl-
vanus Cobb, junior, while her mother makes the puddings.
Says, 'Yes?' when you tell her anything.)—*Oui et non, ma
petite,*—Yes and no, my child. Five of the seven verses
were written off-hand; the other two took a week,—that is,
were hanging round the desk in a ragged, forlorn, unrhymed condition as long as that. All poets will tell you
just such stories. *C'est le* DERNIER *pas qui coûte* [It's the
last step that counts]. Don't you know how hard it is for
some people to get out of a room after their visit is really
over? They want to be off, and you want to have them off,
but they don't know how to manage it. One would think
they had been built in your parlor or study, and were waiting to be launched. I have contrived a sort of ceremonial
inclined plane for such visitors, which being lubricated with
certain smooth phrases, I backed them down, metaphori-
cally speaking, stern-foremost, into their 'native element,'
the great ocean of outdoors. Well, now, there are poems as
hard to get rid of as these rural visitors. They come in
glibly, use up all the serviceable rhymes, *day, ray, beauty,*

duty, skies, eyes, other, brother, mountain, fountain, and the like; and so they go on until you think it is time for the wind-up, and the wind-up won't come on any terms. So they lie about until you get sick of the sight of them, and end by thrusting some cold scrap of a final couplet upon them, and turning them out of doors. I suspected a good many 'impromptus' could tell just such a story as the above.

—Here turning to our landlady, I used an illustration which pleased the company much at the time, and has since been highly commended. 'Madam,' I said, 'you can pour three gills and three quarters of honey from that pint jug, if it is full, in less than one minute; but, madam, you could not empty that last quarter of a gill, though you were turned into a marble Hebe, and held the vessel upside down for a thousand years.'

One gets tired to death of the old, old rhymes, such as you see in that copy of verses,—which I don't mean to abuse, or to praise either. I always feel as if I were a cobbler, putting new top-leathers to an old pair of boot-soles and bodies, when I am fitting sentiments to these venerable jingles.

> . . . . . youth
> . . . . . morning
> . . . . . truth
> . . . . . warning.

Nine tenths of the 'Juvenile Poems' written spring out of the above musical and suggestive coincidences.

'Yes?' said our landlady's daughter.

I did not address the following remark to her, and I trust, from her limited range of reading, she will never see it; I said it softly to my next neighbor.

When a young female wears a flat circular side-curl, gummed on each temple,—when she walks with a male, not arm in arm, but his arm against the back of hers,—and when she says 'Yes?' with the note of interrogation, you are generally safe in asking her what wages she gets, and who the 'feller' was you saw her with.

'What were you whispering?' said the daughter of the house, moistening her lips, as she spoke, in a very engaging manner.

'I was only laying down a principle of social diagnosis.'
'Yes?'

—— It is curious to see how the same wants and tastes find the same implements and modes of expression in all times and places. The young ladies of Otaheite, as you may see in *Cook's Voyages,* had a sort of crinoline arrangement fully equal in radius to the largest spread of our own lady-baskets. When I fling a Bay-State shawl over my shoulders, I am only taking a lesson from the climate that the Indian had learned before me. A *blanket*-shawl we call it, and not a plaid; and we wear it like the aborigines, and not like the Highlanders.

—— We are the Romans of the modern world,—the great assimilating people. Conflicts and conquests are of course necessary accidents with us, as with our prototypes. And so we come to their style of weapon. Our army sword is the short, stiff, pointed *gladius* of the Romans; and the American bowie-knife is the same tool, modified to meet the daily wants of civil society. I announce at this table an axiom not to be found in Montesquieu or the journals of Congress:—

The race that shortens its weapons lengthens its boundaries.

Corollary. It was the Polish *lance* that left Poland at last with nothing of her own to bound.

'Dropped from her nerveless grasp the *shattered spear*!'

What business had Sarmatia to be fighting for liberty with a fifteen-foot pole between her and the breasts of her enemies? If she had but clutched the old Roman and young American weapon, and come to close quarters, there might have been a chance for her; but it would have spoiled the best passage in 'The Pleasures of Hope.'

—— Self-made men?—Well, yes. Of course everybody likes and respects self-made men. It is a great deal better to be made in that way than not to be made at all. Are any of you younger people old enough to remember that Irishman's house on the marsh at Cambridgeport, which house he built from drain to chimney-top with his own hands? It took him a good many years to build it, and one could see that it was a little out of plumb, and a little wavy in outline, and a little queer and uncertain in general aspect. A regular hand could certainly have built a better house; but it was a very good house for a 'self-made' carpenter's house, and people praised it, and said how remarkably well the Irishman had succeeded. They never thought of praising the fine blocks of houses a little farther on.

Your self-made man, whittled into shape with his own jack-knife, deserves more credit, if that is all, than the regular engine-turned article, shaped by the most approved pattern, and French polished by society and travel. But as to saying that one is every way the equal of the other, that is another matter. The right of strict social discrimination of all things and persons, according to their merits, native or acquired, is one of the most precious republican privileges. I take the liberty to exercise it, when I say, that *other things being equal,* in most relations of life I prefer a man of family.

What do I mean by a man of family?—Oh, I'll give you a general idea of what I mean. Let us give him a first-rate fit out; it costs us nothing.

Four or five generations of gentlemen and gentlewomen; among them a member of his Majesty's Council for the Province, a Governor or so, one or two Doctors of Divinity, a member of Congress, not later than the time of long boots with tassels.

Family portraits. The member of the Council, by Smibert. The great merchant-uncle, by Copley, full length, sitting in his arm-chair, in a velvet cap and flowered robe, with a globe by him, to show the range of his commercial transactions, and letters with large red seals lying round, one directed conspicuously to *The Honorable,* etc., etc. Great-grandmother, by the same artist; brown satin, lace very fine, hands superlative; grand old lady, stiffish, but imposing. Her mother, artist unknown; flat, angular, hanging sleeves; parrot on fist. A pair of Stuarts, viz., 1. A superb full-blown, mediæval gentleman, with a fiery dash of Tory blood in his veins, tempered down with that of a fine old rebel grandmother, and warmed up with the best of old India Madeira; his face is one flame of ruddy sunshine; his ruffled shirt rushes out of his bosom with an impetuous generosity, as if it would drag his heart after it; and his smile is good for twenty thousand dollars to the Hospital, besides ample bequests to all relatives and dependents. 2. Lady of the same; remarkable cap; high waist, as in time of Empire; bust *à la Josephine*; wisps of curls, like celery-tips, at sides of forehead; complexion clear and warm, like rose-cordial. As for the miniatures by Malbone, we don't count them in the gallery.

Books, too, with the names of old college-students in them,—family names;—you will find them at the head of their respective classes in the days when students took rank on the catalogue from their parents' condition. Elzevirs, with the Latinized appellations of youthful progenitors, and *Hic liber est meus* on the title-page. A set of Hogarth's original plates. Pope, original edition, 15 volumes, London, 1717. Barrow on the lower shelves, in folio. Tillotson on the upper, in a little dark platoon of octo-decimos.

Some family silver; a string of wedding and funeral rings; the arms of the family curiously blazoned; the same in worsted, by a maiden aunt.

If the man of family has an old place to keep these things in, furnished with claw-footed chairs and black mahogany tables, and tall bevel-edged mirrors, and stately upright cabinets, his outfit is complete.

No, my friends, I go (always, other things being equal) for the man who inherits family traditions and the cumulative humanities of at least four or five generations. Above all things, as a child, he should have tumbled about in the library. All men are afraid of books, who have not handled them from infancy. Do you suppose our dear *didascalos* [teacher, i.e., J. R. Lowell] over there ever read *Poli Synopsis,* or consulted *Castelli Lexicon,* while he was growing up to their stature? Not he; but virtue passed through the hem of their parchment and leather garments whenever he touched them, as the precious drugs sweated through the bat's handle in the Arabian story. I tell you he is at home wherever he smells the invigorating fragrance of Russia leather. No self-made man feels so. One may, it is true, have all the antecedents I have spoken of, and yet be a boor or a shabby fellow. One may have none of them, and yet be fit for councils and courts. Then let them change places. Our social arrangement has this great beauty, that its strata shift up and down as they change specific gravity, without being clogged by layers of prescription. But I still insist on my democratic liberty of choice, and I go for the man with the gallery of family portraits against the one with the twenty-five-cent daguerreotype, unless I find out that the last is the better of the two.

—— I should have felt more nervous about the late comet if I had thought the world was ripe. But it is very green yet, if I am not mistaken; and besides, there is a great deal of coal to use up, which I cannot bring myself to think was made for nothing. If certain things, which seem to me essential to a millennium, had come to pass, I should have been frightened; but they haven't. Perhaps you would like to hear my

Latter-Day Warnings

When legislators keep the law,
    When banks dispense with bolts and locks,
When berries, whortle- rasp- and straw-
    Grow bigger *downwards* through the box,—

When he that selleth house or land
    Shows leak in roof or flaw in right,—
When haberdashers choose the stand
    Whose window hath the broadest light,—

When preachers tell us all they think,
    And party leaders all they mean,—
When what we pay for, that we drink,
    From real grape and coffee-bean,—

When lawyers take what they would give,
    And doctors give what they would take,—
When city fathers eat to live,
    Save when they fast for conscience' sake,—

When one that hath a horse on sale
    Shall bring his merit to the proof,
Without a lie for every nail
    That holds the iron on the hoof,—

When in the usual place for rips
    Our gloves are stitched with special care,
And guarded well the whalebone tips
    Where first umbrellas need repair,—

When Cuba's weeds have quite forgot
    The power of suction to resist,

And claret-bottles harbor not
  Such dimples as would hold your fist,—

When publishers no longer steal,
  And pay for what they stole before,—
When the first locomotive's wheel
  Rolls through the Hoosac tunnel's bore;—

Till then let Cumming blaze away,
  And Miller's saints blow up the globes;
But when you see that blessed day,
  Then order your ascension robe!

The company seemed to like the verses, and I promised
them to read others occasionally, if they had a mind to hear
them. Of course they would not expect it every morning.
Neither must the reader suppose that all these things I have
reported were said at any one breakfast-time. I have not
taken the trouble to date them, as Raspail, *père,* used to
date every proof he sent to the printer; but they were scattered over several breakfasts; and I have said a good many
more things since, which I shall very possibly print some
time or other, if I am urged to do it by judicious friends.

I finish off with reading some verses of my friend the
Professor, of whom you may perhaps hear more by and by.
The Professor read them, he told me, at a farewell meeting,
where the youngest of our great Historians met a few of his
many friends at their invitation.

Yes, we knew we must lose him,—though friendship may
    claim
To blend her green leaves with the laurels of fame;
Though fondly, at parting, we call him our own,
'Tis the whisper of love when the bugle has blown.

As the rider who rests with the spur on his heel,—
As the guardsman who sleeps in his corselet of steel,—
As the archer who stands with his shaft on the string,
He stoops from his toil to the garland we bring.

What pictures yet slumber unborn in his loom
Till their warriors shall breathe and their beauties shall
    bloom,
While the tapestry lengthens the life-glowing dyes
That caught from our sunsets the stain of their skies!

In the alcoves, of death, in the charnels of time,
Where flit the gaunt spectres of passion and crime,
There are triumphs untold, there are martyrs unsung,
There are heroes yet silent to speak with his tongue!

Let us hear the proud story which time has bequeathed
From lips that are warm with the freedom they breathed!
Let him summon its tyrants, and tell us their doom,
Though he sweep the black past like Van Tromp with his
    broom!

The dream flashes by, for the west-winds awake
On pampas, on prairie, o'er mountain and lake,
To bathe the swift bark; like a sea-girdled shrine,
With incense they stole from the rose and the pine.

So fill a bright cup with the sunlight that gushed
When the dead summer's jewels were trampled and
    crushed:
THE TRUE KNIGHT OF LEARNING,—the world holds him
    dear,—
Love bless him, Joy crown him, God speed his career!

                         1857

JAMES RUSSELL LOWELL

(1819–1891)

A Cambridge figure like Holmes and the descendant of an illustrious family which included the founder of Lowell, Massachusetts, James Russell Lowell was born in Cambridge in the
family home of "Elmwood." He attended Harvard—of course
—and was graduated with the class of 1838, which chose him
as its class poet. The Ode he wrote was not delivered at commencement, because its author had been rusticated for disciplinary reasons. In 1840 Lowell took his degree from the Harvard
Law School, and he persisted unhappily for more than a year
in the pretense that he was a practicing attorney. He had begun
contributing poems to various periodicals, and in 1841 he published a collection of poems, *A Year's Life*. This volume, together with *Poems* (1844), revealed the influence of his fiancée,
Maria White, whose "transcendental" and abolitionist persuasions strengthened Lowell's own early romantic and antislavery
leanings.

In 1843 he founded his own magazine, the *Pioneer*, which
was an immediate failure. The year after his marriage in 1844,
he published some literary essays, *Conversations of Some of the
Old Poets*. Established as a writer, he worked for the antislavery
Pennsylvania Freeman in 1846, then returned to "Elmwood,"
his home for the rest of his life. He published *Poems, Second
Series* in 1847, and continued his political writings as corresponding editor of the *National Anti-Slavery Standard* from
1848 to 1851. But it was the year 1848 that proved to be most
important for him, for in that year he published much of his
best work: *The Fable for Critics*, the *First Series* of *The Biglow*

Papers in acidly humorous opposition to the Mexican War, *The Vision of Sir Launfal*, and many of his antislavery essays.

By 1853, three of his four children and his wife had died, and unable to reignite his poetic fires, he turned to prose. As a sequel to his lecture on the English poets at the Lowell Institute in 1855, he was appointed to succeed Longfellow as the Smith Professor of Modern Languages at Harvard. After a preparatory sojourn in Europe, he returned to Cambridge to assume his teaching duties in 1856. The following year he remarried and became editor of the *Atlantic Monthly*, which he helped to found.

As his earlier liberalism waned in the 1850's, he moved toward political and literary attitudes that emphasized moral stewardship and classical restraint. Writings such as *Among My Books* (1870) and *My Study Window* (1871) made him a "founder" of a line of American critical thought that extends through the "New Humanists" such as Irving Babbitt, Paul Elmer More, and Stuart Pratt Sherman to some of the "New Critics" inspired by the "classicism" of T. E. Hulme. In the 1860's and 1870's, though his major work was devoted to prose, particularly criticism, he did publish many Civil War poems, the "Harvard Commemoration Ode" (1865), *The Biglow Papers, Second Series* (1867), *Under the Willows* (1869), and the labored *The Cathedral* (1870). With Charles Eliot Norton he became co-editor of the influential *North American Review* in 1864 and held the editorship until 1872, the year he retired from Harvard. His European journeys from 1872 on were rendered memorable by honorary degrees from Cambridge and Oxford and by his appointments as Minister to Spain from 1877 to 1880 and as Ambassador to Great Britain from 1880 to 1885. After 1885, when his second wife died, he took only brief trips away from "Elmwood," where he died in 1891.

Despite his wide reputation as a poet during his lifetime (made wider by his fame as a scholar, a critic, and a diplomat), Lowell enjoys relatively minor standing as a poet today. He may prove to be significant more for his critical attitudes than for his poetry or the critical essays themselves.

Included among his works, in addition to those mentioned above, are *Fireside Travels* (1864); *Three Memorial Poems* (1877); *Democracy and Other Addresses* (1887); *The English Poets* (1888); *Political Essays* (1888); and *Heartsease and Rue* (1888).

Editions and accounts of the man and his work are to be

found in W. C. Wilkinson, *A Free Lance in the Field of Life and Letters* (1874); B. Taylor, *Critical Essays and Literary Notes* (1880); *The Writings of James Russell Lowell,* 10 vols. (1890); G. W. Curtis, *James Russell Lowell* (1892); H. James, *Essays in London and Elsewhere* (1893); F. H. Underwood, *The Poet and the Man* (1893); W. D. Howells, *Literary Friends and Acquaintance* (1900); E. E. Hale, *James Russell Lowell and His Friends* (1901); C. E. Norton, ed., *The Complete Writings of James Russell Lowell,* 16 vols. (1904) which includes both a biography—H. E. Scudder, *James Russell Lowell,* 2 vols. (1901)—and the edition by C. E. Norton of the *Letters of James Russell Lowell,* 3 vols. (1904); F. Greenslet, *James Russell Lowell* (1905); G. W. Cooke, *A Bibliography of James Russell Lowell* (1906); W. R. Hudson, *Lowell and His Poetry* (1914); L. S. Livingston, *A Bibliography of . . . James Russell Lowell* (1914); J. J. Reilly, *James Russell Lowell as a Critic* (1915); M. A. DeW. Howe, ed., *New Letters of James Russell Lowell* (1932); R. C. Beatty, *James Russell Lowell* (1942); T. M. Smith, ed., *The Uncollected Poetry of James Russell Lowell* (1950); L. Howard, *Victorian Knight Errant* (1952); M. A. DeW. Howe and G. W. Cottrell, Jr., eds., *The Scholar Friends* (1952); P. Graham, ed., "Some Lowell Letters," *Texas Studies in Language and Literature,* III (1962); R. Cary, "Lowell to Cabot," *Colby Library Quarterly* (1963); L. H. Klibbe, *James Russell Lowell's Residence in Spain* (1964); and G. R. Hudson, ed., *Browning to His American Friends: Letters between the Brownings, the Storys and James Russell Lowell* (1965).

FROM

The Biglow Papers, Second Series

The Courtin'

God makes sech nights, all white an' still
   Fur'z you can look or listen,
Moonshine an' snow on field an' hill,
   All silence an' all glisten.

Zekle crep' up quite unbeknown
   An' peeked in thru' the winder,
An' there sot Huldy all alone,
   'ith no one nigh to hender.

A fireplace filled the room's one side
   With half a cord o' wood in—   10
There warn't no stoves (tell comfort died)
   To bake ye to a puddin'.

The wa'nut logs shot sparkles out
  Towards the pootiest, bless her,
An' leetle flames danced all about
  The chiny on the dresser.
Agin the chimbley crook-necks hung,
  An' in amongst 'em rusted
The ole queen's-arm thet gran'ther Young
  Fetched back f'om Concord busted.   20

The very room, coz she was in,
  Seemed warm f'om floor to ceilin',
An' she looked full ez rosy agin
  Ez the apples she was peelin'.

'Twas kin' o' kingdom-come to look
  On such a blessed cretur,
A dogrose blushin' to a brook
  Ain't modester nor sweeter.

He was six foot o' man, A 1,
  Clear grit an' human natur'.   30
None couldn't quicker pitch a ton
  Nor dror a furrer straighter.

He'd sparked it with full twenty gals,
  Hed squired 'em, danced 'em, druv 'em,
Fust this one, an' then thet, by spells—
  All is, he couldn't love 'em.

But long o' her his veins 'ould run
  All crinkly like curled maple,
The side she breshed felt full o' sun
  Ez a south slope in Ap'il.   40

She thought no v'ice hed sech a swing
  Ez hisn in the choir;
My! when he made Ole Hundred ring,
  She *knowed* the Lord was nigher.

An' she'd blush scarlit, right in prayer,
  When her new meetin'-bunnet
Felt somehow thru' its crown a pair
  O' blue eyes sot upun it.

Thet night, I tell ye, she looked *some!*
  She seemed to 've gut a new soul,   50
For she felt sartin-sure he'd come,
  Down to her very shoe-sole.

She heered a foot, an' knowed it tu,
    A-raspin' on the scraper,—
All ways to once her feelin's flew
    Like sparks in burnt-up paper.

He kin' o' l'itered on the mat,
    Some doubtfle o' the sekle,
His heart kep' goin' pity-pat,
    But hern went pity Zekle.   60

An' yit she gin her cheer a jerk
    Ez though she wished him furder,
An' on her apples kep' to work,
    Parin' away like murder.

"You want to see my Pa, I s'pose?"
    "Wal . . . no . . . I come dasignin' "—
"To see my Ma? She's sprinklin' clo'es
    Agin to-morrer's i'nin'."

To say why gals acts so or so,
    Or don't, 'ould be persumin';   70
Mebby to mean *yes* an' say *no*
    Comes nateral to women.

He stood a spell on one foot fust,
    Then stood a spell on t'other,
An' on which one he felt the wust
    He couldn't ha' told ye nuther.

Says he, "I'd better call agin!"
    Says she, "Think likely, Mister":
Thet last word pricked him like a pin,
    An' . . . Wal, he up an' kist her.   80

When Ma bimeby upon 'em slips,
    Huldy sot pale ez ashes,
All kin' o' smily roun' the lips
    An' teary roun' the lashes.

For she was jes' the quiet kind
    Whose naturs never vary,
Like streams that keep a summer mind
    Snowhid in Jenooary.

The blood clost roun' her heart felt glued
    Too tight for all expressin',   90

Tell mother see how metters stood,
    An' gin 'em both her blessin'.

Then her red come back like the tide
    Down to the Bay o' Fundy,
An' all I know is they was cried
    In meetin' come nex' Sunday.

1867

FROM

A Fable for Critics

[Emerson]

"There comes Emerson first, whose rich words, every
    one,
Are like gold nails in temples to hang trophies on,
Whose prose is grand verse, while his verse, the Lord
    knows,
Is some of it pr— No, 't is not even prose;
I'm speaking of metres; some poems have welled
From those rare depths of soul that have ne'er been ex-
    celled;
They're not epics, but that doesn't matter a pin,
In creating, the only hard thing's to begin;
A grass-blade's no easier to make than an oak;
If you've once found the way, you've achieved the grand
    stroke;
In the worst of his poems are mines of rich matter,
But thrown in a heap with a crash and a clatter;
Now it is not one thing nor another alone
Makes a poem, but rather the general tone,
The something pervading, uniting the whole,
The before unconceived, unconceivable soul,
So that just in removing this trifle or that, you
Take away, as it were, a chief limb of the statue;
Roots, wood, bark, and leaves singly perfect may be,
But, clapt hodge-podge together, they don't make a
    tree.   20

"But, to come back to Emerson (whom, by the way,
I believe we left waiting),—his is, we may say,
A Greek head on right Yankee shoulders, whose range
Has Olympus for one pole, for t'other the Exchange;
He seems, to my thinking (although I'm afraid
The comparison must, long ere this, have been made),
A Plotinus-Montaigne, where the Egyptian's gold mist
And the Gascon's shrewd wit cheek-by-jowl coexist;
All admire, and yet scarcely six converts he's got
To I don't (nor they either) exactly know what;   30
For though he builds glorious temples, 'tis odd
He leaves never a doorway to get in a god.
'T is refreshing to old-fashioned people like me
To meet such a primitive Pagan as he,
In whose mind all creation is duly respected
As parts of himself—just a little projected;
And who's willing to worship the stars and the sun,
A convert to—nothing but Emerson.
So perfect a balance there is in his head,
That he talks of things sometimes as if they were dead;   40
Life, nature, love, God, and affairs of that sort,
He looks at as merely ideas; in short,
As if they were fossils stuck round in a cabinet,
Of such vast extent that our earth's a mere dab in it;
Composed just as he is inclined to conjecture her,
Namely, one part pure earth, ninety-nine parts pure lec-
    turer;
You are filled with delight at his clear demonstration,
Each figure, word, gesture, just fits the occasion,
With the quiet precision of science he'll sort 'em,
But you can't help suspecting the whole a *post mortem.*   50

    "There are persons, mole-blind to the soul's make and
        style,
Who insist on a likeness 'twixt him and Carlyle;
To compare him with Plato would be vastly fairer,
Carlyle's the more burly, but E. is the rarer;
He sees fewer objects, but clearlier, truelier,
If C.'s as original, E.'s more peculiar;
That he's more of a man you might say of the one,
Of the other he's more of an Emerson;
C.'s the Titan, as shaggy of mind as of limb,—
E. the clear-eyed Olympian, rapid and slim;   60

The one's two thirds Norseman, the other half Greek,
Where the one's most abounding, the other's to seek;
C.'s generals require to be seen in the mass,—[generals:
                                          generalizations]
E.'s specialties gain if enlarged by the glass;
C. gives nature and God his own fits of the blues,
And rims common-sense things with mystical hues,—
E. sits in a mystery calm and intense,
And looks coolly around him with sharp common-sense;
C. shows you how every-day matters unite
With the dim transdiurnal recesses of night,—   70
While E., in a plain, preternatural way,
Makes mysteries matters of mere every day;
C. draws all his characters quite *a la* Fuseli,—
Not sketching their bundles of muscles and thews illy,
He paints with a brush so untamed and profuse,
They seem nothing but bundles of muscles and thews;
E. is rather like Flaxman, lines strait and severe,
And a colorless outline, but full, round, and clear;—
To the men he thinks worthy he frankly accords
The design of a white marble statue in words.   80
C. labors to get at the centre, and then
Take a reckoning from there of his actions and men;
E. calmly assumes the said centre as granted,
And, given himself, has whatever is wanted.

"He has imitators in scores, who omit
No part of the man but his wisdom and wit,—
Who go carefully o'er the sky-blue of his brain,
And when he has skimmed it once, skim it again;
If at all they resemble him, you may be sure it is
Because their shoals mirror his mists and obscurities,   90
As a mud-puddle seems deep as heaven for a minute,
While a cloud that floats o'er is reflected within it.

·   ·   ·

[Bryant]

"There is Bryant, as quiet, as cool, and as dignified,
As a smooth, silent iceberg, that never is ignified,
Save when by reflection 'tis kindled o' nights

With a semblance of flame by the chill Northern Lights.
He may rank (Griswold says so) first bard of your nation
(There's no doubt that he stands in supreme ice-olation),
Your topmost Parnassus he may set his heel on,
But no warm applauses come, peal following peal on,— 100
He's too smooth and too polished to hang any zeal on:
Unqualified merits, I'll grant, if you choose, he has 'em.
But he lacks the one merit of kindling enthusiasm;
If he stir you at all, it is just, on my soul,
Like being stirred up with the very North Pole.

"He is very nice reading in summer, but *inter*
Nos, we don't want *extra* freezing in winter,
Take him up in the depth of July, my advice is,
When you feel an Egyptian devotion to ices.
But, deduct all you can, there's enough that's right good in
     him,   110
He has a true soul for field, river, and wood in him;
And his heart, in the midst of brick walls, or where'er it is,
Glows, softens, and thrills with the tenderest charities—
To you mortals that delve in this trade-ridden planet?
No, to old Berkshire's hills, with their limestone and gran-
     ite.
If you're one who *in loco* (add *foco* here) *desipis,*
You will get of his outermost heart (as I guess) a piece;
But you'd get deeper down if you came as a precipice,
And would break the last seal of its inwardest fountain,
If you only could palm yourself off for a mountain.   120
Mr. Quivis, or somebody quite as discerning,
Some scholar who's hourly expecting his learning,
Calls B. the American Wordsworth; but Wordsworth
May be rated at more than your whole tuneful herd's
     worth.
No, don't be absurd, he's an excellent Bryant;
But, my friends, you'll endanger the life of your client,
By attempting to stretch him up into a giant:
If you choose to compare him, I think there are two per-
sons fit for a parallel—Thompson and Cowper;*

---

* [At this point Lowell added the following footnote:]
      To demonstrate quickly and easily how per-
      versely absurd 'tis to sound his Cowper
      As people in general call him named super
      I remark that he rhymes it himself with horse-trooper.

I don't mean exactly—there's something of each,   130
There's T.'s love of nature, C.'s penchant to preach;
Just mix up their minds so that C.'s spice of craziness
Shall balance and neutralize T.'s turn for laziness,
And it gives you a brain cool, quite frictionless, quiet,
Whose internal police nips the buds of all riot,—
A brain like a permanent straight-jacket put on
The heart that strives vainly to burst off a button,—
A brain which, without being slow or mechanic,
Does more than a larger less drilled, more volcanic;
He's a Cowper condensed, with no craziness bitten,   140
And the advantage that Wordsworth before him had
    written.

"But, my dear little bardlings, don't prick up your ears
Nor suppose I would rank you and Bryant as peers;
If I call him an iceberg, I don't mean to say
There is nothing in that which is grand in its way;
He is almost the one of your poets that knows
How much grace, strength, and dignity lie in Repose;
If he sometimes fall short, he is too wise to mar
His thought's modest fulness by going too far;
'T would be well if your authors should all make a trial 150
Of what virtue there is in severe self-denial,
And measure their writings by Hesiod's staff,
Which teaches that all has less value than half.

[Whittier]

"There is Whittier, whose swelling and vehement heart
Strains the strait-breasted drab of the Quaker apart,
And reveals the live Man, still supreme and erect,
Underneath the bemummying wrappers of sect;
There was ne'er a man born who had more of the swing
Of the true lyric bard and all that kind of thing;
And his failures arise (though he seem not to know it) 160
from the very same cause that has made him a poet,—
A fervor of mind which knows no separation
'Twixt simple excitement and pure inspiration,
As my Pythoness erst sometimes erred from not knowing
If 'twere I or mere wind through her tripod was blowing;
Let his mind once get head in its favorite direction

And the torrent of verse bursts the dams of reflection,
While, borne with the rush of the metre along,
The poet may chance to go right or go wrong,
Content with the whirl and delirium of song;   170
Then his grammar's not always correct, nor his rhymes,
And he's prone to repeat his own lyrics sometimes,
Not his best, though, for those are struck off at whiteheats
When the heart in his breast like a trip-hammer beats,
And can ne'er be repeated again any more
Than they could have been carefully plotted before:
Like old what's-his-name there at the battle of Hastings
(Who, however, gave more than mere rhythmical bastings),
Our Quaker leads off metaphorical fights
For reform and whatever they call human rights,   180
Both singing and striking in front of the war,
And hitting his foes with the mallet of Thor;
Anne haec, one exclaims, on beholding his knocks,
Vestis filii tui, O leather-clad Fox?
          [Anne . . . tui: Is this indeed thy son's robe?]
Can that be thy son, in the battle's mid din,
Preaching brotherly love and then driving it in
To the brain of the tough old Goliath of sin,
With the smoothest of pebbles from Castaly's spring
Impressed on his hard moral sense with a sling?

"All honor and praise to the right-hearted bard   190
Who was true to The Voice when such service was hard,
Who himself was so free he dared sing for the slave
When to look but a protest in silence was brave;
All honor and praise to the women and men
Who spoke out for the dumb and the down-trodden then!
It needs not to name them, already for each
I see History preparing the statue and niche;
They were harsh, but shall *you* be so shocked at hard words
Who have beaten your pruning-hooks up into swords,
Whose rewards and hurrahs men are surer to gain   200
By the reaping of men and of women than grain?
Why should *you* stand aghast at their fierce wordy war, if
You scalp one another for Bank or for Tariff?
Your calling them cut-throats and knaves all day long
Doesn't prove that the use of hard language is wrong;
While the World's heart beats quicker to think of such men
As signed Tyranny's doom with a bloody steel-pen,

While on Fourth-of-Julys beardless orators fright one
With hints at Harmodius and Aristogeiton,
You need not look shy at your sisters and brothers   210
Who stab with sharp words for the freedom of others;—
No, a wreath, twine a wreath for the loyal and true
Who, for sake of the many, dared stand with the few,
Not of blood-spattered laurel for enemies braved,
But of broad, peaceful oak-leaves for citizens saved!

.   .   .

[*Hawthorne*]

"There is Hawthorne, with genius so shrinking and rare
That you hardly at first see the strength that is there;
A frame so robust, with a nature so sweet,
So earnest, so graceful, so lithe and so fleet,
Is worth a descent from Olympus to meet;   220
'Tis as if a rough oak that for ages had stood,
With his gnarled bony branches like ribs of the wood,
Should bloom, after cycles of struggle and scathe,
With a single anemone trembly and rathe;
His strength is so tender, his wildness so meek,
That a suitable parallel sets one to seek,—
He's a John Bunyan Fouqué, a Puritan Tieck;
When Nature was shaping him, clay was not granted
For making so full-sized a man as she wanted,
So, to fill out her model, a little she spared   230
From some finer-grained stuff for a woman prepared,
And she could not have hit a more excellent plan
For making him fully and perfectly man.
The success of her scheme gave her so much delight,
That she tried it again, shortly after, in Dwight;
Only, while she was kneading and shaping the clay,
She sang to her work in her sweet childish way,
And found, when she'd put the last touch to his soul,
That the music had somehow got mixed with the whole.

.   .   .

[Poe]

"There comes Poe, with his raven, like Barnaby
      Rudge,   240

Three-fifths of him genius and two-fifths sheer fudge,
Who talks like a book of iambs and pentameters,
In a way to make people of common sense damn metres,
Who has written some things quite the best of their kind,
But the heart somehow seems all squeezed out by the mind,
Who— But hey-day! What's this? Messieurs Mathews and
    Poe,
You mustn't fling mud-balls at Longfellow so,
Does it make a man worse that his character's such
As to make his friends love him (as you think) too much?
Why, there is not a bard at this moment alive   250
More willing than he that his fellows should thrive;
While you are abusing him thus, even now
He would help either one of you out of a slough;
You may say that he's smooth and all that till you're hoarse,
But remember that elegance also is force;
After polishing granite as much as you will,
The heart keeps its tough old persistency still;
Deduct all you can, *that* still keeps you at bay;
Why, he'll live till men weary of Collins and Gray.
I'm not over-fond of Greek metres in English,   260
To me rhyme's a gain, so it be not too jinglish,
And your modern hexameter verses are no more
Like Greek ones than sleek Mr. Pope is like Homer;
As the roar of the sea to the coo of a pigeon is,
So, compared to your moderns, sounds old Melesigenes;
                           [Melesigenes: Homer]
I may be too partial, the reason, perhaps, o't is
That I've heard the old blind man recite his own rhapsodies,
And my ear with that music impregnate may be,
Like the poor exiled shell with the soul of the sea,
Or as one can't bear Strauss when his nature is cloven   270
To its deeps within deeps by the stroke of Beethoven;
But, set that aside, and 'tis truth that I speak,
Had Theocritus written in English, not Greek,
I believe that his exquisite sense would scarce change a line
In that rare, tender, virgin-like pastoral Evangeline.
That's not ancient nor modern, its place is apart
Where time has no sway, in the realm of pure Art,
'Tis a shrine of retreat from Earth's hubbub and strife
As quiet and chaste as the author's own life.

* * *

[*Irving*]

"What! Irving? thrice welcome, warm heart and fine
    brain,   280
You bring back the happiest spirit from Spain,
And the gravest sweet humor, that ever was there
Since Cervantes met death in his gentle despair;
Nay, don't be embarrassed, nor look so beseeching,
I sha'n't run directly against my own preaching,
And having just laughed at their Raphaels and Dantes,
Go to setting you up beside matchless Cervantes;
But allow me to speak what I honestly feel,—
To a true poet-heart add the fun of Dick Steele,
Throw in all of Addison *minus* the chill,   290
With the whole of that partnership's honest good-will,
Mix well, and while stirring, hum o'er, as a spell,
The fine *old* English Gentleman, simmer it well,
Sweeten just to your own private liking, then strain,
That only the finest and clearest remain,
Let it stand out of doors till a soul it receives
From the warm lazy sun loitering down through green
    leaves,
And you'll find a choice nature, not wholly deserving
A name either English or Yankee,—just Irving.

· · ·

[*Holmes*]

"There's Holmes, who is matchless among you for
    wit;   300
A Leyden-jar always full-charged, from which flit
The electrical tingles of hit after hit;
In long poems 'tis painful sometimes, and invites
A thought of the way the new Telegraph writes,
Which pricks down its little sharp sentences spitefully
As if you got more than you'd title to rightfully,
And you find yourself hoping its wild father Lightning
Would flame in for a second and give you a fright'ning.
He has perfect sway of what *I* call a sham metre,
But many admire it, the English pentameter,   310
And Campbell, I think, wrote most commonly worse,

With less nerve, swing, and fire in the same kind of verse,
Nor e'er achieved aught in't so worthy of praise
As the tribute of Holmes to the grand *Marseillaise*.
You went crazy last year over Bulwer's New Timon;—
Why, if B., to the day of his dying, should rhyme on,
Heaping verses on verses and tomes upon tomes,
He could ne'er reach the best point and vigor of Holmes.
His are just the fine hands, too, to weave you a lyric
Full of fancy, fun, feeling, or spiced with satiric   320
In a measure so kindly, you doubt if the toes
That are trodden upon are your own or your foes'.

[Lowell]

"There is Lowell, who's striving Parnassus to climb
With a whole bale of *isms* tied together with rhyme,
He might get on alone, spite of brambles and boulders,
But he can't with that bundle he has on his shoulders,
The top of the hill he will ne'er come nigh reaching
Till he learns the distinction 'twixt singing and preaching;
His lyre has some chords that would ring pretty well,
But he'd rather by half make a drum of the shell,   330
And rattle away till he's old as Methusalem,
At the head of a march to the last new Jerusalem."

                                                   1848

The Darkened Mind

The fire is burning clear and blithely,
Pleasantly whistles the winter wind;
We are about thee, thy friends and kindred,
On us all flickers the firelight kind;
There thou sittest in thy wonted corner
Lone and awful in thy darkened mind.

There thou sittest; now and then thou moanest;
Thou dost talk with what we cannot see,
Lookest at us with an eye so doubtful,
It doth put us very far from thee;   10
There thou sittest; we would fain be nigh thee,
But we know that it can never be.

We can touch thee, still we are no nearer;
Gather round thee, still thou art alone;
The wide chasm of reason is between us;
Thou confutest kindness with a moan;
We can speak to thee, and thou canst answer,
Like two prisoners through a wall of stone.

Hardest heart would call it very awful
When thou look'st at us and seest—oh, what?   20
If we move away, thou sittest gazing
With those vague eyes at the selfsame spot,
And thou mutterest, thy hands thou wringest,
Seeing something—us thou seest not.

Strange it is that, in this open brightness,
Thou shouldst sit in such a narrow cell;
Strange it is that thou shouldst be so lonesome
Where those are who love thee all so well;
Not so much of thee is left among us
As the hum outliving the hushed bell.   30

1868

Auspex [Soothsayer]

My heart, I cannot still it,
Nest that had song-birds in it;
And when the last shall go,
The dreary days, to fill it,
Instead of lark or linnet,
Shall whirl dead leaves and snow.

Had they been swallows only,
Without the passion stronger
That skyward longs and sings—
Woe's me, I shall be lonely   10
When I can feel no longer
The impatience of their wings!

A moment, sweet delusion,
Like birds the brown leaves hover;

But it will not be long
Before their wild confusion
Fall wavering down to cover
The poet and his song.

1878

The Recall

Come back before the birds are flown,
Before the leaves desert the tree,
And, through the lonely alleys blown,
Whisper their vain regrets to me
Who drive before a blast more rude,
The plaything of my gusty mood,
In vain pursuing and pursued!

Nay, come although the boughs be bare,
Though snowflakes fledge the summer's nest,
And in some far Ausonian air [Ausonian: Italian]   10
The thrush, your minstrel, warm his breast.
Come, sunshine's treasurer, and bring
To doubting flowers their faith in spring,
To birds and me the need to sing!

1888

Verses

Intended to Go with a Posset Dish to My
Dear Little Goddaughter, 1882

In good old times, which means, you know,
The time men wasted long ago,
And we must blame our brains or mood
If that we squander seems less good,
In those blest days when wish was act
And fancy dreamed itself to fact,
Godfathers used to fill with guineas
The cups they gave their pickaninnies,
Performing functions at the chrism
Not mentioned in the Catechism.   10
No millioner, poor I fill up
With wishes my more modest cup,

Though had I Amalthea's horn
It should be hers the newly born.
Nay, shudder not! I should bestow it
So brimming full she couldn't blow it.
Wishes aren't horses: true, but still
There are worse roadsters than goodwill.
And so I wish my darling health,
And just to round my couplet, wealth,   20
With faith enough to bridge the chasm
'Twixt Genesis and Protoplasm,
And bear her o'er life's current vext
From this world to a better next,
Where the full glow of God puts out
Poor reason's farthing candle, Doubt.
I've wished her healthy, wealthy, wise,
What more can godfather devise?
But since there's room for countless wishes
In these old-fashioned posset dishes,   30
I'll wish her from my plenteous store
Of these commodities two more,
Her father's wit, veined through and through
With tenderness that Watts (but whew!
Celia's aflame, I mean no stricture
On his Sir Josh-surpassing picture)—
I wish her next, and 't is the soul
Of all I've dropt into the bowl,
Her mother's beauty—nay, but two
So fair at once would never do.   40
Then let her but the half possess,
Troy was besieged ten years for less.
Now if there's any truth in Darwin,
And we from what was, all we are win,
I simply wish the child to be
A sample of Heredity,
Enjoying to the full extent
Life's best, the Unearned Increment
Which Fate her Godfather to flout
Gave *him* in legacies of gout.   50
Thus, then, the cup is duly filled;
Walk steady, dear, lest all be spilled.

1895

INDEX OF AUTHORS, TITLES, AND
FIRST LINES OF POEMS

☆ ☆

Ah, broken is the golden bowl!—the spirit flown forever, 95
American Democrat, The, 65
"American Scholar, The," 267
An old man in a lodge within a park, 581
"Annabel Lee," 111
Announced by all the trumpets of the sky, 217
"Arsenal at Springfield, The," 569
At midnight, in the month of June, 96
"Auspex," 657
Autocrat of the Breakfast-Table, The, 623

Bartleby, 351
"Bells, The," 108
Biglow Papers, Second Series, The, 644
Billy Budd, Sailor, 387
"Brahma," 228
BRYANT, WILLIAM CULLEN, 68
Bulkeley, Hunt, Willard, Hosmer, Meriam, Flint, 224
Burly, dozing humble-bee, 210
By a route obscure and lonely, 99
By the rude bridge that arched the flood, 207

"Cask of Amontillado, The," 165
"Chambered Nautilus, The," 617
"Chaucer," 581
"City in the Sea, The," 93
Come back before the birds are flown, 658
"Compensation," 218
"Concord Hymn," 207
COOPER, JAMES FENIMORE, 49
"Courtin', The," 644
"Cross of Snow, The," 583
"Crossing Brooklyn Ferry," 532

"Darkened Mind, The," 656
Daughters of Time, the hypocritic Days, 227
"Days," 227
"Deacon's Masterpiece, The," 618
Dedication from *Michael Angelo: A Fragment,* 583
"Divina Commedia," 577
"Dorothy Q.," 621
"Dream Within a Dream, A," 90
"Dream-Land," 99
"Dreams," 86

"Each and All," 209

660

"Eldorado," 112
EMERSON, RALPH WALDO, 204
"Evening Star, The," 573
"Experience," 309

"Fable," 219
Fable for Critics, A, 647
"Facing West from California's Shores," 545
"Fall of the House of Usher, The," 128
Flood-tide below me! I see you face to face, 532
"Forest Hymn, A," 76

Gaily bedight, 112
"Give All to Love," 223
Gleanings in Europe: England, 55
God makes sech nights, all white an' still, 644
"Grace," 219
Grandmother's mother: her age, I guess, 621

Half of my life is gone, and I have let, 572
"Hamatreya," 224
Have you heard of the wonderful one-hoss shay, 618
"Hawthorne," 580
HAWTHORNE, NATHANIEL, 344
Hear the sledges with the bells, 108
Helen, thy beauty is to me, 91
HOLMES, OLIVER WENDELL, 612
How beautiful it was, that one bright day, 580
How much, preventing God! how much I owe, 219
How strange it seems! These Hebrews in their graves, 573
"Humble-Bee, The," 210
"Hymn to the Night," 569

I celebrate myself, and sing myself, 472
I heard the trailing garments of the Night, 569
I like a church; I like a cowl, 212
I pace the sounding sea-beach and behold, 581
I saw him once before, 616
If the red slayer think he slays, 228
In good old times, which means, you know, 658
In Heaven a spirit doth dwell, 92
In May, when sea-winds pierced our solitudes, 208
In the long, sleepless watches of the night, 583
"Inscription for the Entrance to a Wood," 72
IRVING, WASHINGTON, 1
"Israfel," 92
It fell in the ancient periods, 226
It is time to be old, 228
It was many and many a year ago, 111

"Jewish Cemetery at Newport, The," 573
Journals (Emerson), 331

"Last Leaf, The," 616
"Legend of Sleepy Hollow, The," 19

"Lenore," 95
"Ligeia," 113
Little thinks, in the field, yon red-cloaked clown, 209
Lo! Death has reared himself a throne, 93
Lo! in the painted oriel of the West, 573
LONGFELLOW, HENRY WADSWORTH, 565
LOWELL, JAMES RUSSELL, 642

"Massachusetts to Virginia," 586
"Milton," 581
MELVILLE, HERMAN, 347
"Merops," 219
"Mezzo Cammin," 572
"My Aunt," 614
My aunt! my dear unmarried aunt, 614
My heart, I cannot still it, 657
"My Lost Youth," 575

Nature, 229
'Neath blue-bell or streamer, 88
Nothing that is shall perish utterly, 583
Notions of the Americans, 52

"Ode: Inscribed to W. H. Channing," 220
Of all the rides since the birth of time, 590
Oft have I seen at some cathedral door, 577
Often I think of the beautiful town, 575
Oh! that my life were a lasting dream, 86
Once upon a midnight dreary, while I pondered, weak and
        weary, 100
"Out of the Cradle Endlessly Rocking," 539

"Passage to India," 554
"Philosophy of Composition, The," 178
POE, EDGAR ALLAN, 83
"Poetic Principle, The," 190
"Prairies, The," 79
"Problem, The," 212
"Psalm of Life, A," 567
"Purloined Letter, The," 147

"Recall, The," 658
"Raven, The," 100
"Rhodora, The," 208
"Rip Van Winkle," 3
"Romance," 87
Romance, who loves to nod and sing, 87

Science! true daughter of Old Time thou art, 88
"Seaweed," 571
"Self-Reliance," 285
Singing my days, 554
"Skipper Ireson's Ride," 590
"Sleeper, The," 96
Snow-Bound, 592

"Snow-Storm, The," 217
"Song from *Al Aaraaf*," 88
"Song of Myself," 472
"Sonnet—Silence," 98
"Sonnet—To Science," 88
Stranger, if thou hast learned a truth which needs, 72

Take this kiss upon the brow, 90
Tell me not, in mournful numbers, 567
"Terminus," 228
"Thanatopsis," 70
The blast from Freedom's Northern hills, upon its Southern
       way, 586
The fire is burning clear and blithely, 656
The groves were God's first temples. Ere man learned, 76
The mountain and the squirrel, 219
The skies they were ashen and sober, 105
The sun that brief December day, 593
The wings of Time are black and white, 218
There are some qualities—some incorporate things, 98
There comes Emerson first, whose rich words, every one, 647
These are the gardens of the Desert, these, 79
This is the Arsenal. From floor to ceiling, 569
This is the ship of pearl, which, poets feign, 617
THOREAU, HENRY DAVID, 342
Thou blossom bright with autumn dew, 79
Thou wast that all to me, love, 97
Though loath to grieve, 220
"Tide Rises, the Tide Falls, The," 582
"To a Waterfowl," 74
"To Helen," 91
To him who in the love of Nature holds, 70
"To One in Paradise," 97
"To the Fringed Gentian," 79
"*Twice-Told Tales,* by Nathaniel Hawthorne: A Review," 171

"Ulalume," 105
"Uriel," 226

"Venice," 582
"Verses," 658

What care I, so they stand the same, 219
When beechen buds begin to swell, 75
When descends on the Atlantic, 571
"When Lilacs Last in the Door-Yard Bloom'd," 546
When the pine tosses its cones, 213
White swan of cities, slumbering in thy nest, 582
Whither, 'midst falling dew, 74
WHITMAN, WALT, 467
WHITTIER, JOHN GREENLEAF, 584
"Woodnotes, I," 213

"Yellow Violet, The," 75

CONTENTS OF OTHER VOLUMES
IN THIS SERIES

☆

Colonial and Federal · To 1800

General Introduction and Preface by the Editors

JOHN SMITH
Selection from *A Description of New England*.

WILLIAM BRADFORD
Selections from *Of Plymouth Plantation*.

THOMAS MORTON
Selections from *New English Canaan*.

EDWARD JOHNSON
Selections from *The Wonder-Working Providence of Sion's Savior in New England*.

JOHN WINTHROP
Selections from *Journal*.

NATHANIEL WARD
Selection from *The Simple Cobbler of Aggawam*. Poem: "On Mrs. Bradstreet's *Tenth Muse*."

SAMUEL SEWALL
Selections from *The Diary, The Selling of Joseph*, and *Phaenomena quaedam Apocalyptica*.

COTTON MATHER
Selections from *The Wonders of the Invisible World, Magnalia Christi Americana*, and *Manuductio ad Ministerium*.

ROBERT CALEF
Selections from *More Wonders of the Invisible World*.

JONATHAN EDWARDS
Selections from *God Glorified in Man's Dependence, Freedom of the Will*, and *The Nature of True Virtue*. "Sarah Pierrepont," "Narrative of Surprising Conversions," "Personal Narrative," and "Sinners in the Hands of an Angry God."

THE BAY PSALM BOOK
Selection from "The Preface" and "Psalm 23."

ANNE BRADSTREET
Ten poems, including "The Author to Her Book," "Before the Birth of One of Her Children," and "Upon the Burning of Our House."

MICHAEL WIGGLESWORTH
Selections from *The Day of Doom*.

EDWARD TAYLOR
Selections from *Preparatory Meditations before My Approach to the Lord's Supper, God's Determinations Touching His Elect*, and miscellaneous poems.

ROGER WILLIAMS
Selections from *The Bloody Tenent of Persecution*. Two poems.

WILLIAM BYRD II
Selections from *The Secret Diary* and *The History of the Dividing Line*.

JOHN WOOLMAN
Selections from *The Journal*.

ST. JEAN DE CREVECOEUR
Selections from *Letters from an American Farmer*.

BENJAMIN FRANKLIN
Selections from *The Autobiography*. "A Witch Trial at Mount Holly," "The Way to Wealth," "An Edict by the King of Prussia," "The Ephemera," and "Information for Those Who Would Remove to America," Letters to Peter Collinson, Sir Joseph Banks, and Ezra Stiles.

THOMAS PAINE
Selections from *The Crisis* and *The Age of Reason*.

THOMAS JEFFERSON
Selections from *Notes on the State of Virginia*. "The Declaration of Independence" and "First Inaugural Address." Letters to James Madison, Benjamin Rush, John Adams, Benjamin Waterhouse, and James Monroe.

ALEXANDER HAMILTON
Selections from *The Federalist*.

JAMES MADISON
Selection from *The Federalist*.

JOHN TRUMBULL
Selections from *The Progress of Dulness* and *M'Fingal*.

TIMOTHY DWIGHT
Selection from *Greenfield Hill*. "Columbia, Columbia, to Glory Arise."

JOEL BARLOW
Selection from *Advice to the Privileged Orders*. "The Hasty Pudding."

ROYALL TYLER
The Contrast.

PHILIP FRENEAU
Selections from *The House of Night*. Seventeen other poems, including "The Power of Fancy," "To the Memory of the Brave Americans," and "Stanzas to an Alien."

☆ ☆ ☆

Nation and Region · 1860–1900

General Introduction by the Editors

Prefatory Essay by Howard Mumford Jones

WALT WHITMAN
A comprehensive bibliography.

HENRY TIMROD
"Ethnogenesis," "Charleston," and "Ode."

SIDNEY LANIER
Selection from "The New South." Six poems, including "The Symphony" and "The Marshes of Glynn."

EMILY DICKINSON
One hundred and twelve poems, including "After Great Pain a Formal Feeling Comes," "I Dreaded

That First Robin So," and "I Never Saw a Moor."

CHARLES FARRAR BROWNE
Selections from *Artemus Ward: His Book; Artemus Ward: His Travels;* and *Artemus Ward in London and Other Papers.*

GEORGE WASHINGTON CABLE
"Belles Demoiselles Plantation."

JOEL CHANDLER HARRIS
Selection from *Nights with Uncle Remus.* "Free Joe and the Rest of the World."

BRET HARTE
"Muck-A-Muck" from *Condensed Novels.* "The Luck of Roaring Camp" and the poem "The Society upon the Stanislaus."

SARAH ORNE JEWETT
"Miss Tempy's Watchers."

MARY E. WILKINS FREEMAN
"The Revolt of 'Mother'."

MARK TWAIN
A comprehensive bibliography.

WILLIAM DEAN HOWELLS
Selections from *Criticism and Fiction.* "A Romance of Real Life" and "Editha."

HENRY JAMES
"Daisy Miller," "The Art of Fiction," and "The Jolly Corner."

AMBROSE BIERCE
Selections from *Fantastic Fables* and *The Cynic's Word Book.* "An Occurrence at Owl Creek Bridge."

JACK LONDON
"The White Silence."

HAMLIN GARLAND
Selections from *Crumbling Idols.* "Under the Lion's Paw."

STEPHEN CRANE
Maggie: A Girl of the Streets, "The Open Boat," and "The Blue Hotel." Ten poems, including "War Is Kind," "A Little Ink More or Less," and "A Slant of Sun."

FRANK NORRIS
"A Plea for Romantic Fiction" and "A Deal in Wheat."

WILLIAM VAUGHN MOODY
Four poems, including "An Ode in Time of Hesitation," "The Menagerie," and "Ode to a Soldier Fallen in the Philippines."

TRUMBULL STICKNEY
Four poems, including "In Ampezzo" and "At Sainte-Marguerite."

WILLIAM JAMES
Selection from *Pragmatism.*

HENRY ADAMS
Selection from *The Education of Henry Adams.*

EDITH WHARTON
"The Other Two."

The Twentieth Century

General Introduction by the Editors

Prefatory Essay by Malcolm Cowley

THEODORE DREISER
"The Second Choice."

WILLA CATHER
"Neighbor Rosicky."

SHERWOOD ANDERSON
"I Want to Know Why."

F. SCOTT FITZGERALD
"Winter Dreams."

ERNEST HEMINGWAY
A comprehensive bibliography.

SINCLAIR LEWIS
Nobel Prize Address: "The American Fear of Literature."

JOHN DOS PASSOS
Selections from the novels of the U.S.A. trilogy: *42nd Parallel; 1919; The Big Money.*

THOMAS WOLFE
Selections from *Of Time and the River* and *You Can't Go Home Again.*

JOHN STEINBECK
"The Leader of the People."

JAMES T. FARRELL
"A Jazz-Age Clerk."

KATHERINE ANNE PORTER
"Flowering Judas."

EUDORA WELTY
"Keela, the Outcast Indian Maiden."

WILLIAM FAULKNER
A comprehensive bibliography.

EUGENE O'NEILL
The Hairy Ape.

EUGENE JOLAS
"Manifesto. The Revolution of the Word."

IRVING BABBITT
"The Critic and American Life."

H. L. MENCKEN
Selection from *Prejudices: Third Series.*

SOUTHERN AGRARIANS
Selections from *I'll Take My Stand.*

EDMUND WILSON
"The Historical Interpretation of Literature."

NORMAN MAILER
"The White Negro."

EDWIN ARLINGTON ROBINSON
Twenty-nine poems, including "Flammonde" and "The Man Against the Sky."

AMY LOWELL
"Patterns" and "Lilacs."

EDNA ST. VINCENT MILLAY
Four poems, including "I Know I Am But Summer to Your Heart" and "Justice Denied in Massachusetts."

VACHEL LINDSAY
"General William Booth Enters into Heaven," "Abraham Lincoln Walks at Midnight," and "The Santa-Fé Trail."

CARL SANDBURG
Selection from *The People, Yes.* Six other poems, including "Chicago" and "To a Contemporary Bunkshooter."

ROBERT FROST
Twenty poems, including "The Death of the Hired Man," "Birches," and "Stopping by Woods on a Snowy Evening."

STEPHEN VINCENT BENET
Selection from *John Brown's Body.* "American Names."

EZRA POUND
Selections from *Hugh Selwyn Mauberley.* "A Virginal," "In a Station of the Metro," and "The River-Merchant's Wife: A Letter."

T. S. ELIOT
The Waste Land. Selection from *Four Quartets.* Four other poems, including "The Love Song of J. Alfred Prufrock" and "Gerontion." Essay: "Tradition and the Individual Talent."

WALLACE STEVENS
Eleven poems, including "Sunday Morning" and "A

Postcard from the Volcano."

ROBINSON JEFFERS
Five poems, including "Roan Stallion" and "Boats in a Fog."

JOHN CROWE RANSOM
Four poems, including "Antique Harvesters" and "The Equilibrists."

WILLIAM CARLOS WILLIAMS
Seven poems, including "Tract," "Queen-Ann's-Lace," and "The Yachts."

E. E. CUMMINGS
Eight poems, including "Buffalo Bill's defunct." "I sing of Olaf," and "anyone lived in a pretty how town."

HART CRANE
Selections from *The Bridge*. "Voyages: II."

MARIANNE MOORE
"Poetry," "The Fish," and "A Grave."

ARCHIBALD MACLEISH
"You, Andrew Marvell," "American Letter," and "Speech to Those Who Say Comrade."

ALLEN TATE
"Death of Little Boys" and "Ode to the Confederate Dead."

ROBERT PENN WARREN
"The Last Metaphor,"

"Bearded Oaks," and "Revelation."

KENNETH FEARING
"Dirge."

RICHARD EBERHART
"The Groundhog" and "The Fury of Aerial Bombardment."

THEODORE ROETHKE
"Dolor" and "The Waking."

ELIZABETH BISHOP
"The Man-Moth."

DELMORE SCHWARTZ
"Starlight Like Intuition Pierced the Twelve" and "The True-Blue American."

KARL SHAPIRO
"Troop Train" and "The Conscientious Objector."

RANDALL JARRELL
"Losses" and "Nestus Gurley."

ROBERT LOWELL
"Mr. Edwards and the Spider," "After the Surprising Conversions," and "Skunk Hour."

RICHARD WILBUR
"Juggler" and "Advice to a Prophet."

ALLEN GINSBERG
"A Supermarket in California."

SYLVIA PLATH
"Daddy."

JAMES SCULLY
"Crew Practice."